SOFT BRIDES FOR THE BEAST OF BLOOD

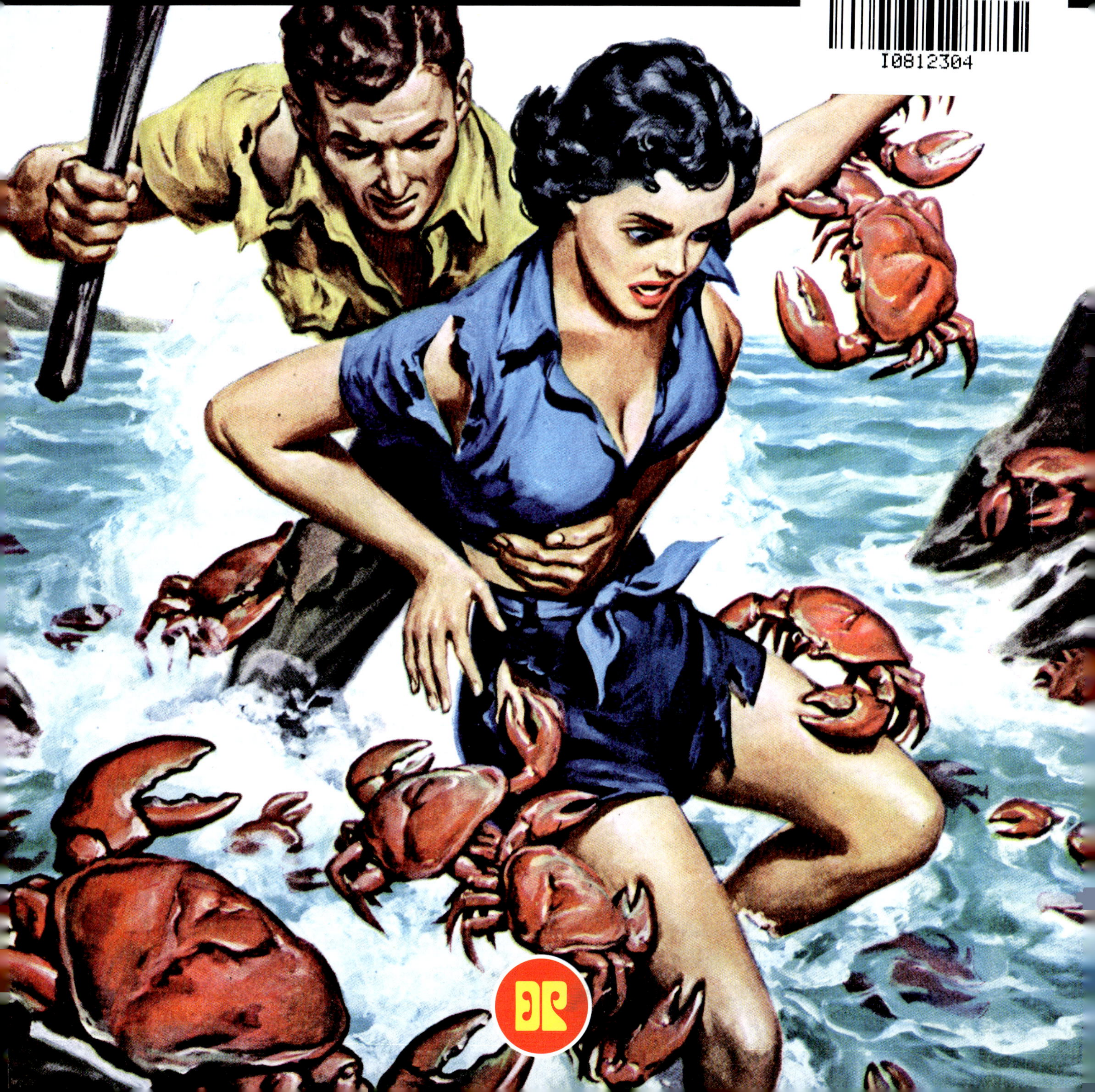

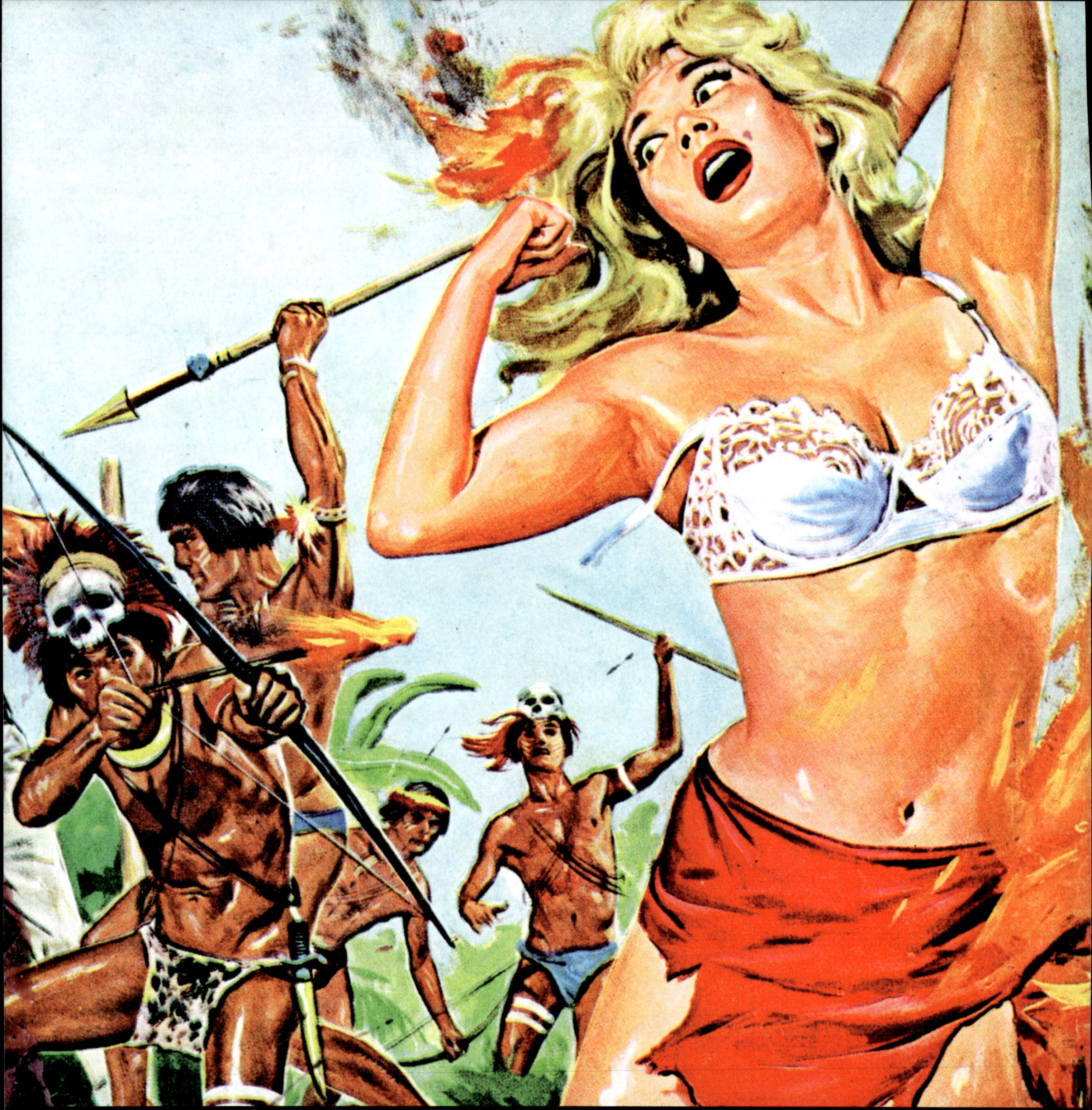

SOFT BRIDES FOR THE BEAST OF BLOOD

FICTION, FEATURES AND ART FROM CLASSIC MEN'S ADVENTURE MAGAZINES

PULP MAYHEM, VOLUME THREE

Edited by Pep Pentangeli
Design by Broken Fang Cryptography
Published 2015 by Deicide Press
ISBN 978-1-84068-668-5

FOREWORD 005

FEATURES

FICTION

COLOR ILLUSTRATIONS 201

FRONT ILLUSTRATIONS

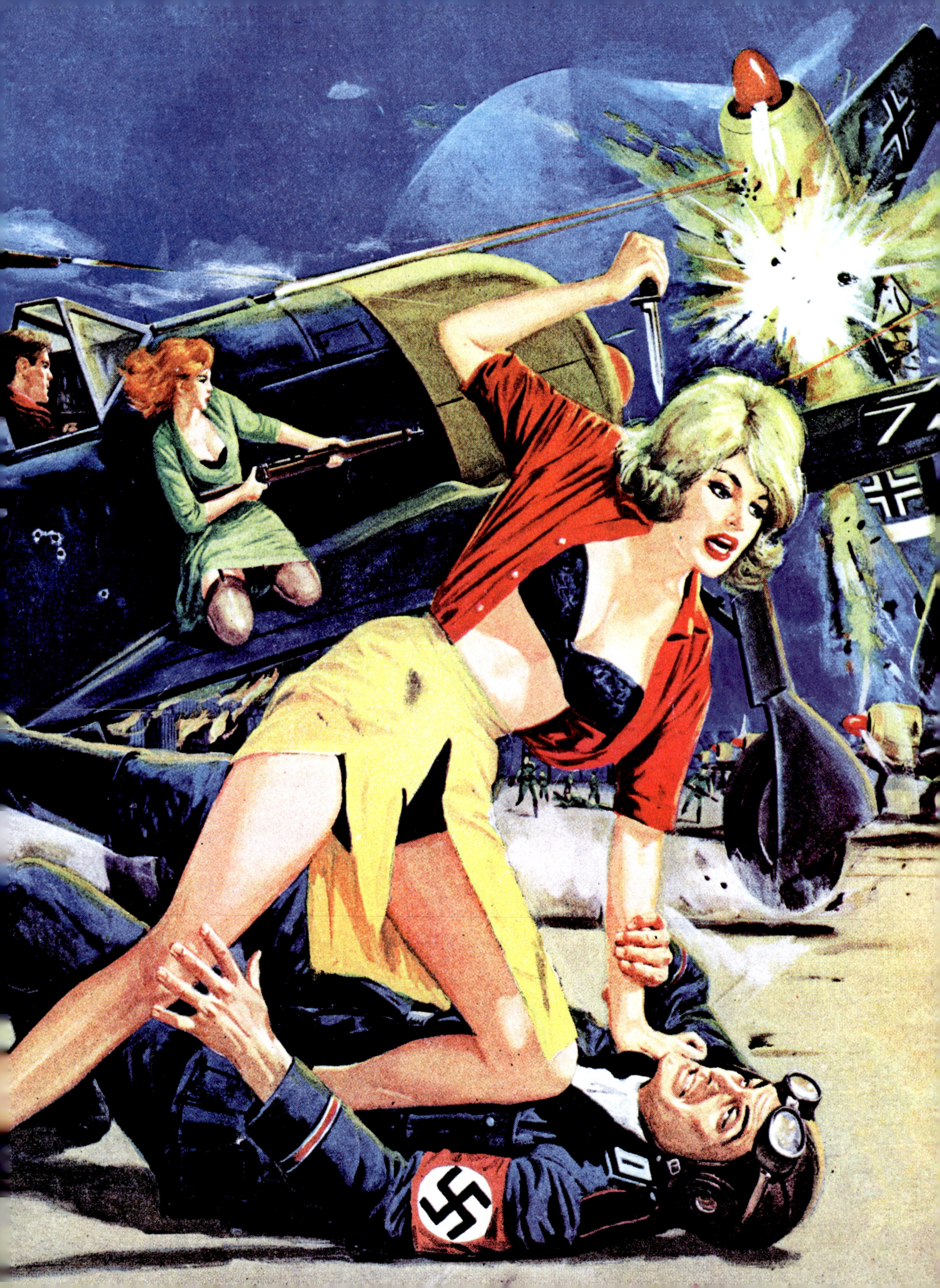

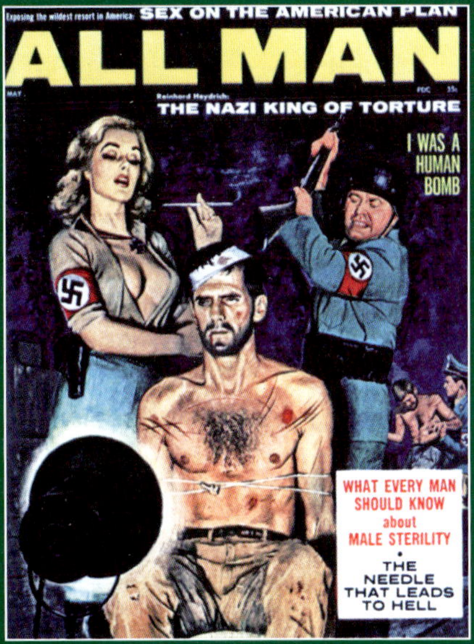

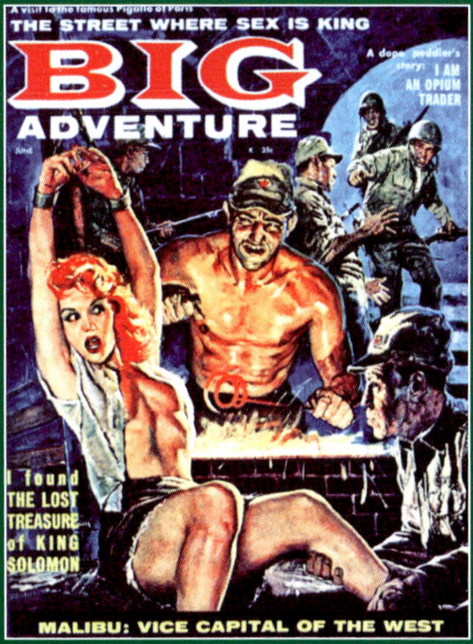

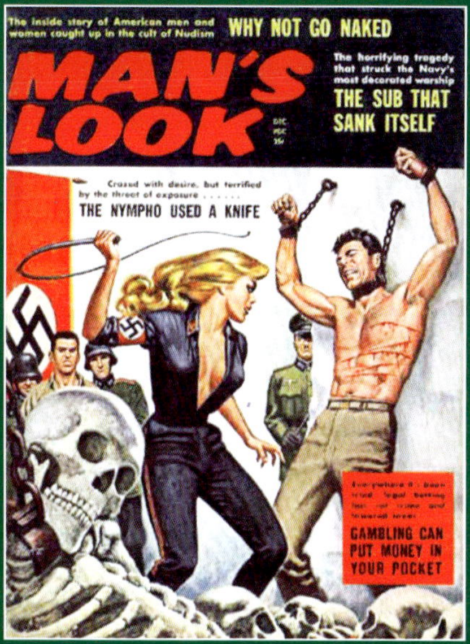

Men's adventure magazines were a form of pulp publishing which flourished in 1950s and 1960s America, pandering to the cruelty and lust of young men with luridly illustrated stories of war, sleaze and savagery.[1] Some of them, such as **Battle Cry**, arose in direct response to the inauguration of the Comics Code in 1954, as a way of circumventing censorship by presenting material in a new, "adults-only" format.

As with pulp magazines from earlier decades, scantily-dressed women-in-peril were a favourite subject for men's adventure cover designs; but in the late 50s and early 60s, magazines such as **Man's Story** and **Men Today** saw sales rocket when they mixed this staple imagery with new, fetishistic and taboo elements of extreme bondage, torture and, in particular, the sinister sign of the swastika.

Some of the more risqué adventure magazines pursued this type of material to its permissible extremes during the ensuing decade. Publications such as **Man's Daring**, **World Of Men**, **Man's Book** and **Wildcat Adventures** revelled in lurid tales and supposedly true accounts of mayhem, and became known as "sweat mags". Typical examples of their cover art include a female prisoner about to be raped by Nazi-trained mandrills, two half-naked young women tied up by Nazis and about to be eaten alive by rats, a tightly-bound girl being threatened by a Nazi with a flame-thrower, and a she-Nazi hunting female concentration camp victims with chained wolves.

SOFT BRIDES FOR THE BEAST OF BLOOD is a new anthology which collects some prime examples of text and artwork from a range of men's adventure magazines published during the key years of the genre. The book is divided into two sections: FEATURES includes a selection of semi-factual confessions and case histories on such sensationalistic subjects as Nazi doctors, tortures of the Spanish Inquisition, cannibal serial killers, vice, juvenile delinquency and other aberrations; and FICTION assembles a wild collection of garishly illustrated short pulp fiction, with categories including war, white slavery, Nazi horror, jungle curses, Red menace, torture, sadism and erotic carnage. The book also features numerous examples of interior art from classic men's adventure magazines, and includes a total of 35 features and stories, with more than 50 full-size illustrations, including 16 pages in full colour.

The prime years of the men's adventure magazine unleashed a deluge of exposed flesh, bloody mayhem and sexual delinquency beneath the all-pervasive sign of the swastika, representing a unique cultural phenomenon in US publishing and art. The texts and artworks presented in this anthology stand as testament to this phenomenon, and also as a reminder to the lurid but innocent fun which people once enjoyed, before the invention of "political correctness" by repressive, soulless and sexless religio-fascist vermin bent on pulling popular culture – and life – back into the dark ages of censorship.

1. A comprehensive history of men's adventure magazines has already been provided by two outstanding publications: **It's A Man's World** (Feral House, 2003) and **Men's Adventure Magazines** (Taschen, 2008). A website dedicated to the subject, **www.menspulpmags.com**, is also highly recommended.

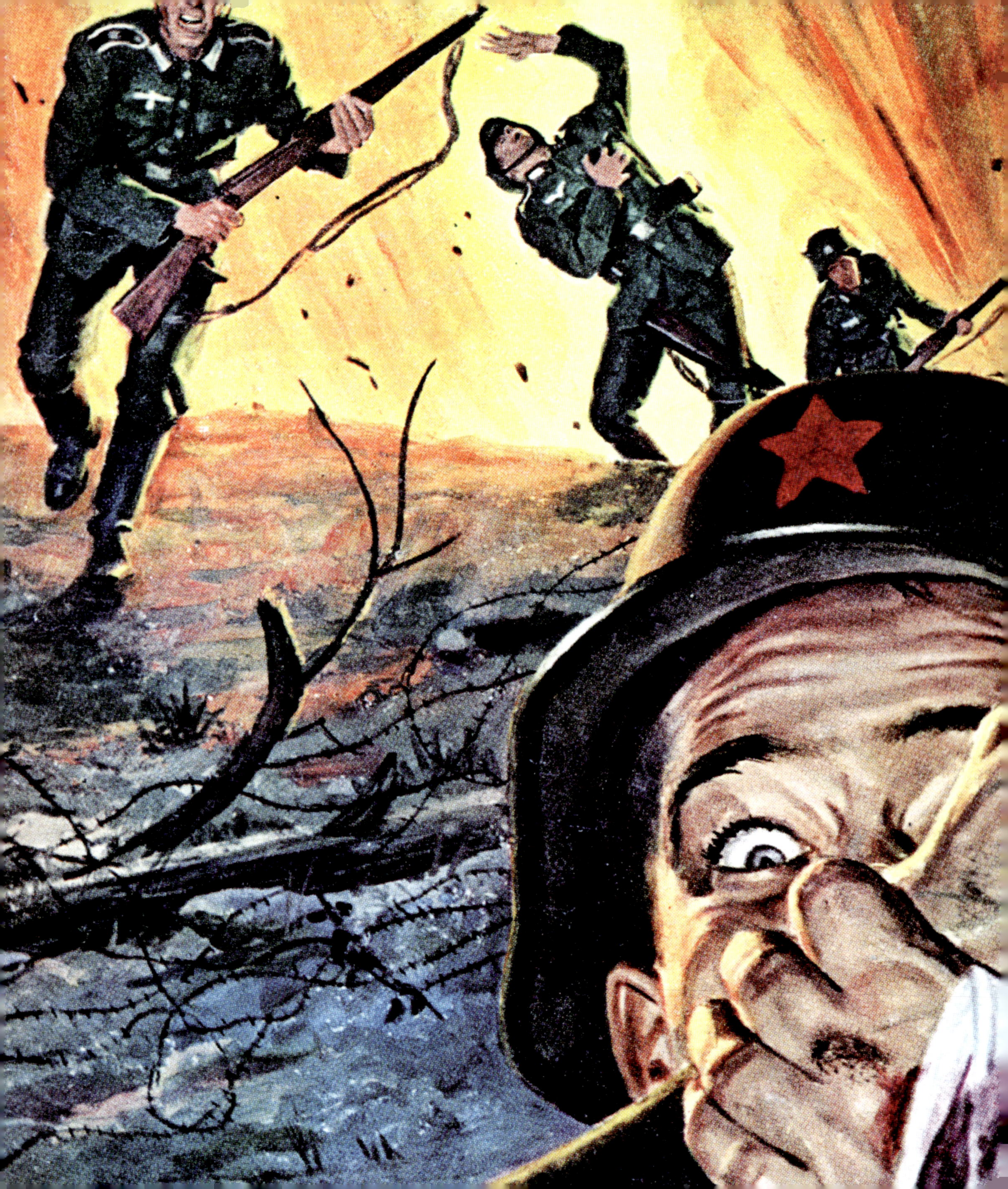

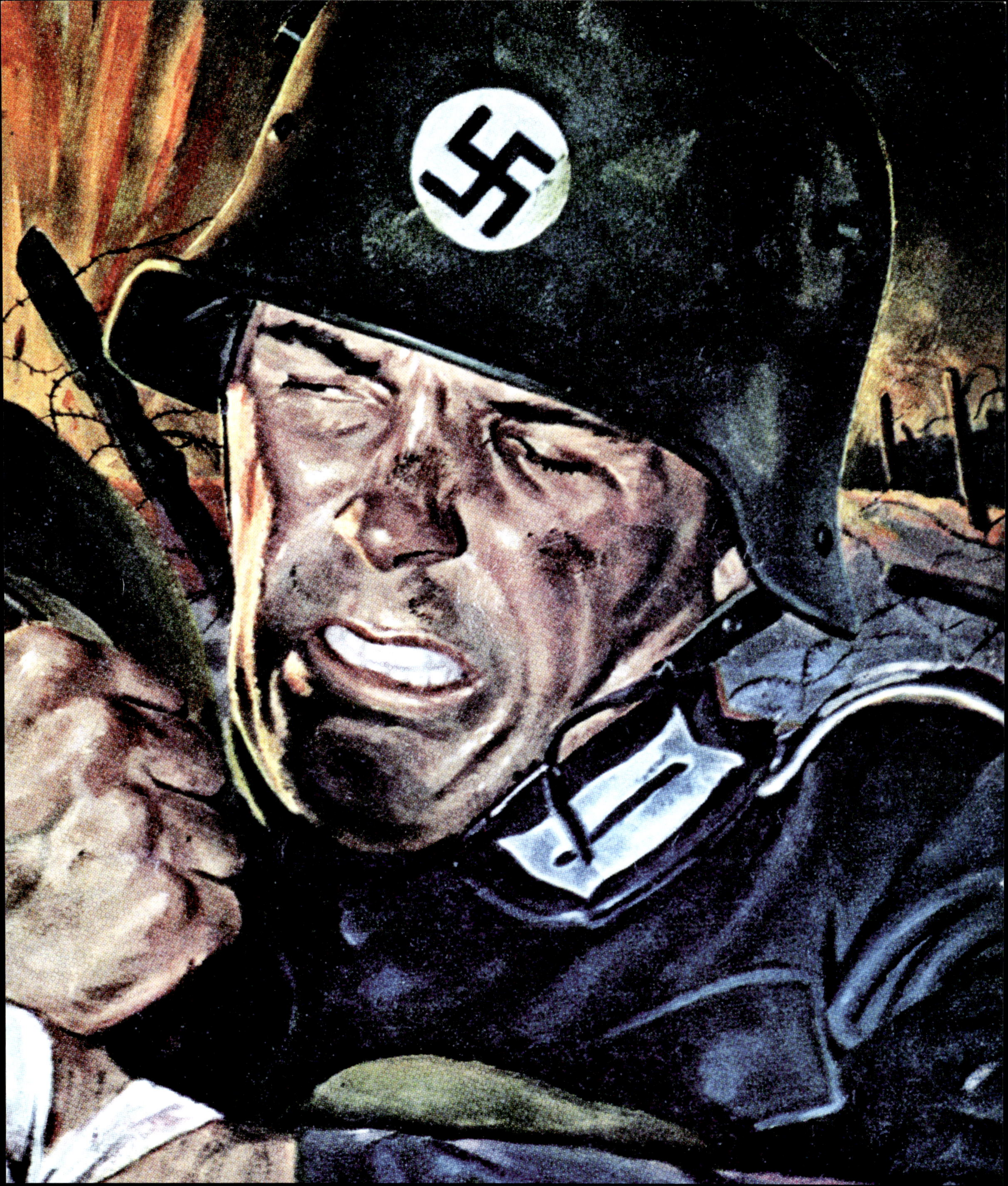

FEATURES AND FICTION

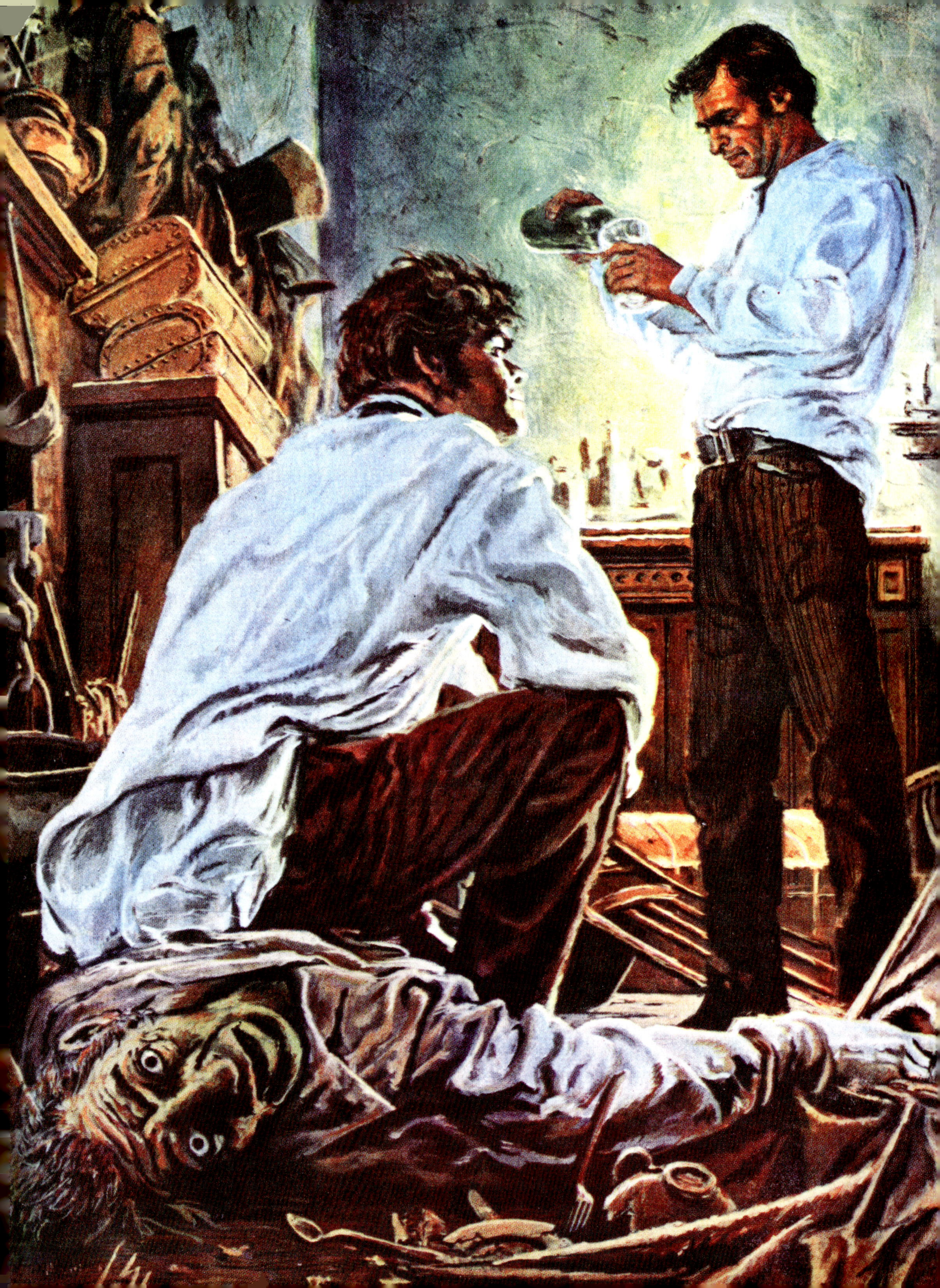

THE FABULOUS GHOULS

Burke and Hare – the pair of depraved wretches behind a grisly market in human corpse-flesh!

IT TOOK SIXTEEN MURDERS to do it, but took sixteen murders to do it, but Burke and Hare finally won permanent fame as benefactors of medical science. They killed sixteen men, women and children before the law managed to halt their good works.

William Burke's skeleton, with the hangman's rope still around the neck, is now on exhibit in a glass case at Scotland's University of Edinburgh. It was that University's school of medicine which Burke so richly endowed with needed corpses. William Hare, who turned Crown's evidence at Burke's trial, was let off free, though his hands were no less bloody. He disappeared one dark night, pursued by an angry mob. Some said he turned up later on the streets of London as a blind beggar, but there is no real evidence to support this claim. Blindness would have been too good for him.

In our time, cadavers for use in medical research are easier to get than they were in Scotland in the 1820s. Medical schools are not so short of dissectables today. But in Burke and Hare's day there were laws against the practice of cutting up dead people to examine their insides.

Medical students turned to grave-robbing, and a whole society of cadaver thieves grew up in the city. These ambitious body snatchers became known as The Resurrectionists of Edinburgh. The bodies were sold to the school of medicine.

In those days, families of the deceased built heavy-barred iron cages over the graves to keep robbers out. Or they would stand armed guard nightly over the remains of their loved ones.

So the Resurrectionist business was a risky one, and the men of the profession were often as foolhardy as they were depraved.

It took two enterprising scoundrels like Burke and Hare to realize that one needn't run the risk of getting a carcass full of buckshot if one dealt in fresh corpses that had never been laid in the ground. So that's how this murderous pair got into the grisly business of corpse manufacture and distribution.

The two men were quite different in many respects. Hare was a muscular lout, not too bright. He was loud and quarrelsome. He showed no sign of remorse over his deeds.

Burke, on the other hand, the more intelligent of the pair, was deeply troubled by his conscience. He needed a lighted candle and a bottle of whiskey by his bed to get through each night. He was a small. wiry man, about five feet five. He was generally liked in his neighborhood and could be counted on for a lively Irish jig when the whiskey was flowing free. He and his colleague, Hare, were constantly on the booze, and it's hardly likely they were sober a day during the nine months their corpse factory was in operation.

Hare was the landlord of an Edinburgh flophouse in which Burke lived for a time. Hare had come into the hotel business by sharing the bed of the former owner's widow. Though she was described as Hare's wife in later accounts, there is no record that they were ever married. She was a skinny rumpot, anyway, and it is doubtful she could have gotten any man to take her to a church.

Burke was living with a Helen McDougal, although he had a wife and several children back in Ireland. McDougal had a couple of kids by Burke's predecessor. She was not married to the father of her children, either, although she took his name, McDougal.

B. & H. Limited's first parcel of merchandise was, in one important respect, unlike the sixteen that followed. The first one died of natural causes in Hare's house. He was an old pensioner who owed Hare some back rent. Hare, not one to he done out of a halfpenny, pulled the corpse out of its coffin and filled the long box with tanners' bark. The bark was given a Christian burial, but the body was sold to Dr. Robert Knox, a lecturer in anatomy at Surgeon's Square. He paid about £8 for it.

Knox was a famous surgeon of the day, and a very popular lecturer. His classes were always crowded. One of the reasons, no doubt, was that he was able to provide enough cadavers for every one of his students. In fact, he boldly advertised this advantage in his handbills.

Knox was actually a one-eyed ghoul, who in his past had once been a man. He had a distinguished military record, and was known as a good shot and horseman. He was also a gifted teacher and anatomist. Yet he was utterly lacking in heart and conscience.

Not once did he ask Burke and Hare how they got their bodies. Being a doctor, he couldn't have examined the sixteen corpses without suspecting that their owners had died by violence. Yet he never alerted the police. On the contrary, he assured Burke and Hare that he would he glad to see them whenever they had another body to dispose of.

It was this warm welcome, no questions asked, that decided Burke and Rare on their career; Knox's gold, they knew, could make theirs a brighter, finer, wetter life. There was only one drawback: people did not die quickly enough for Burke and Hare. They knew they would have to devise some plan to hurry nature.

The first murder differed in technique a little from the following fifteen. but it is enough to say that the cause of death was shortage of breath. The victim, an ailing lodger of Hare's, couldn't catch his breath; strong hands, it seems, were holding a pillow over his face. He was sold to Dr. Knox for £10.

Most of the other "subjects", as Knox called them, died because Hare and Burke simply held them down and suffocated them. The refinement of the pillow had been dropped. Only the hands were used to stop up the breathing passages.

Most of the victims were lured to Hare's place, made drunk, and then dispatched quietly. Few put up much resistance in their drunken stupor. Those that managed to scream attracted no attention; passers-by were used to the screams of the drunken wretches who lived in that unsavory neighborhood.

SOME OF the victims were more interesting as people, and others were interesting because of the circumstances of their deaths.

An old woman with her twelve-year-old grandson came to Hare's in the summer of 1828 seeking lodging. The woman was given a drink and fell asleep in her bed. Burke and Hare suffocated her and then the boy. They stuffed the two bodies into a herring barrel and carried it to Dr. Knox's quarters.

One case that excited much public interest at the time of Burke's trial was that of the beauteous Mary Paterson. Mary, though a prostitute, was as delicately feminine and perfectly formed as any of her sisters. She was a bold orphan girl who had to make her way in the world; although only in her teens, she traded on the only talent she had.

She and a sister practitioner, Janet Brown, were drinking at a grog shop early one day when they saw Burke ogling them. He was very much on the rum that morning. By this time Burke was well established in his trade, and was always on the lookout for fresh merchandise to fill the ever-growing demand of Dr. Knox and his students.

He bought them three rounds of drinks. Then he invited both girls to come to his quarters, which he said were close by.

He bought each of the girls a bottle of whiskey and they went with him to breakfast. They had a few more belts from the bottles and sat down to eat. Whatever they ate was washed down with whiskey.

Mary had drunk such a good breakfast, in fact, that she passed out. Burke tried to put the Brown girl in the same murderable condition, but she had a hollow leg.

As Burke was trying to get Brown to take a few more drinks. Mrs. McDougal showed up in a fit of rage. The virtuous McDougal indicated that she expected finer things of a man like Burke, and didn't dream she'd find him with a couple of streetwalkers.

He ended her angry harangue by slugging her above one eye with a heavy glass. Blood gushed from the gash and she ran out the door. Burke hustled Janet out the same door and made her promise she would come back later. He promised to take care of her friend.

Hare had arrived by then and the two men did take care of Mary. When she was dead they stripped her body and packed it into a tea chest and decided to deliver her quickly to Dr. Knox.

Dr. Knox's assistant opened the chest and saw the still warm, white body of Mary. He had met her once, and he recognized her. He asked Burke where he got the corpse. Burke said he had bought it from some old woman who was related to the deceased.

Dr. Knox came in to examine the finely proportioned figure of the late Mary Paterson. He even brought in a painter to look her over.

One of Dr. Knox's students, writing afterward, said: "The body of the girl Paterson would not fail to attract attention by its voluptuous form and beauty; students crowded around the table on which she lay, and artists came to study a model worthy of Phidias and the best Greek art."

Dr. Knox kept Mary in a keg of whiskey for three months before he finally got around to dissecting her.

Janet Brown, who had luckily escaped the same fate as Mary, inquired about her later, but got no satisfactory answer. She didn't pursue the matter with the police, for, in her profession, she never found contact with the law profitable.

Burke and Hare must have thought they had an easy "shot" – their term for victim – when they decided to kill James Wilson. Wilson was known around town as Daft Jamie. He was a big hulk of a youth, about eighteen years old, with the mind of a small child. He would be easily persuaded to come to their lair. Jamie was a gentle person. He would not even defend himself against the five- and six-year-olds who tormented him as he roamed about the streets.

Burke met Daft Jamie in the Grassmarket. The youth was looking for his mother. Burke told the poor fellow that he knew where to find her. He got Jamie to Hare's place and persuaded him to take some liquor. Jamie fell asleep on the floor after a few snorts. Burke jumped on him and started to strangle him. Jamie awoke and wasn't having any of that.

He had started to break Burke in two when Hare stepped into the fight. Hare tripped Jamie from behind, a characteristic maneuver, and the two murderers jumped atop the frightened moron. Although Jamie struggled mightily and must have inflicted some injuries on his assailants, he soon kicked his last.

The murderers stripped Jamie's corpse and gave the clothes to Burke's brother's children, an unusual act of charity. Then they put Jamie in an old tea chest and carried him off to Dr. Knox. Although Jamie was well-known around town, and although some of the students recognized him, Dr. Knox said they must be mistaken in their identifications. No one called in the law and Jamie was quickly dissected, making identification by the police impossible.

IT WAS a little old Irish woman, Mrs. Docherty, who brought the whole grisly business to an end. Mrs. Docherty was enticed into the corpse factory by Burke, who met her at a pub. She had been looking for her son.

Affable Burke, always on the lookout for a shot, convinced her that she was a distant relative of his from Ireland. They both had come from the same country and his mother's name was the same as hers, he said. He invited her to stay with him and then promised to help find the son.

It was Halloween, and a party was going on in Burke's room. It was a rip-roaring fracas, with whiskey, fights and fun. After most of the other guests had gone, Burke and Hare were left alone with Mrs. Docherty, who had drunk her fill, and was feeling no pain – yet. They knocked her down and suffocated her, then stuffed her body under the bed.

The killing and the sale of the body might have gone on in the same routine way as the others, had not a roomer of Hare's been searching the next day for a stocking her child had left when her family occupied the room. She looked under the bed.

Burke and Hare were both out at the time, running down more to drink. The woman, a Mrs. Gray, reported finding time body under the bed to her husband and then to the police.

By the time the police swung into action, the body of Mrs. Docherty was already in Dr. Knox's cellar and Burke and Hare had been paid half their fee. The assistant who took in the body told them they would get the remainder of the money after Dr. Knox had a chance to view the corpse. The police impounded the body and arrested Hare and his wife, and Burke and Mrs. McDougal, and carted them off to jail. An autopsy confirmed the suspicions of the authorities on the manner in which the old woman had met her death.

Since the other corpses had been disposed of in the dissecting rooms at Surgeon's Square, it was difficult to prove murder. The only body that could be shown was Mrs. Docherty's, so the prosecution was hard-pressed.

The prosecutor wanted to make sure that at least one of the fiends would swing, so he promised immunity to Hare and his wife if they would testify against Burke and Mrs. McDougal. The Hares agreed, and the trial began on the day before Christmas in 1828.

All of England and Scotland was interested in the trial. Even Sir Walter Scott wrote of the developments and attended the hanging. Robert Louis Stevenson used the case later for the basis of at least one of his mystery yarns.

The courtroom and yard were jammed. The panels of prosecuting and defense attorneys were loaded with the most famous lawyers of the day. The trial itself is still reviewed by law students because of the important elements of law that became part of it.

For instance, the immunity of Hare from prosecution for crimes in which he was as guilty as Burke, simply because he turned state's evidence, is an extremely important legal point. He went free despite the public clamor for his death and the legal pressure that was brought to bear to send him to the scaffold.

Dr. Knox, though listed as a witness, was never called upon to testify. The doctor and his assistants certainly encouraged the murderers in their deeds. It seems improbable that Knox did not know his "subjects" were murdered. Yet no indictment was prepared against him and he did not appear on the stand.

The trial lasted for twenty-four hours without a break. Burke did not testify. The two Hares were the star witnesses for the prosecution as well as the chief attraction for the spectators. Hare sat in the witness stand and ticked off the murders as coolly as if he were discussing the price of cheese. Mrs. Hare held a squalling infant in her arms as she gave her testimony concerning the barbarisms committed under her roof. Hare laid most of the blame on Burke and Mrs. McDougal, but Burke, in his confessions after conviction, evened the record as far as the Hares were concerned.

Burke was convicted and sentenced to die; McDougal was acquitted and freed. She had been a knowing accomplice during the entire time the corpse factory was in operation. Burke was calm at the sentence and remained steady during the period of confinement. His strangest request was for the remainder of the fee that Dr. Knox owed him for Mrs. Docherty's cadaver. Burke wanted the money for new clothes to die in.

It was pouring rain on Burke's execution day. His step to the gallows was firm at first, then later he leaned a bit on the arm of his guard. There were 25,000 shouting people in the square to see the show. Some cried, "Burke him, Burke him!" He gave the word to the language. In the dictionary it is defined as follows: "To murder by suffocation, or with few marks of violence."

Burke died well for the wretch that he was. After he was cut down, the crowd surged forward and demolished the gallows for souvenirs.

The body was taken to a medical lecture classroom and a Dr. Monro dissected it, giving a two-hour lecture on it as he did. Because only a few medical students could be accommodated in the classroom, riots broke out near the building as thousands pressed in to try to get a view of the murderer's corpse. So great was the demand that provision was made for the public to see Burke's body. More than 30,000 saw it during the two days it was on display.

The body was then further dissected and put into barrels for future lectures. The skeleton, as noted before, was enclosed in a glass case. So Burke, who had sent seventeen bodies to Surgeon's Square, himself made number eighteen – a fitting end for Scotland's most famous murderer.

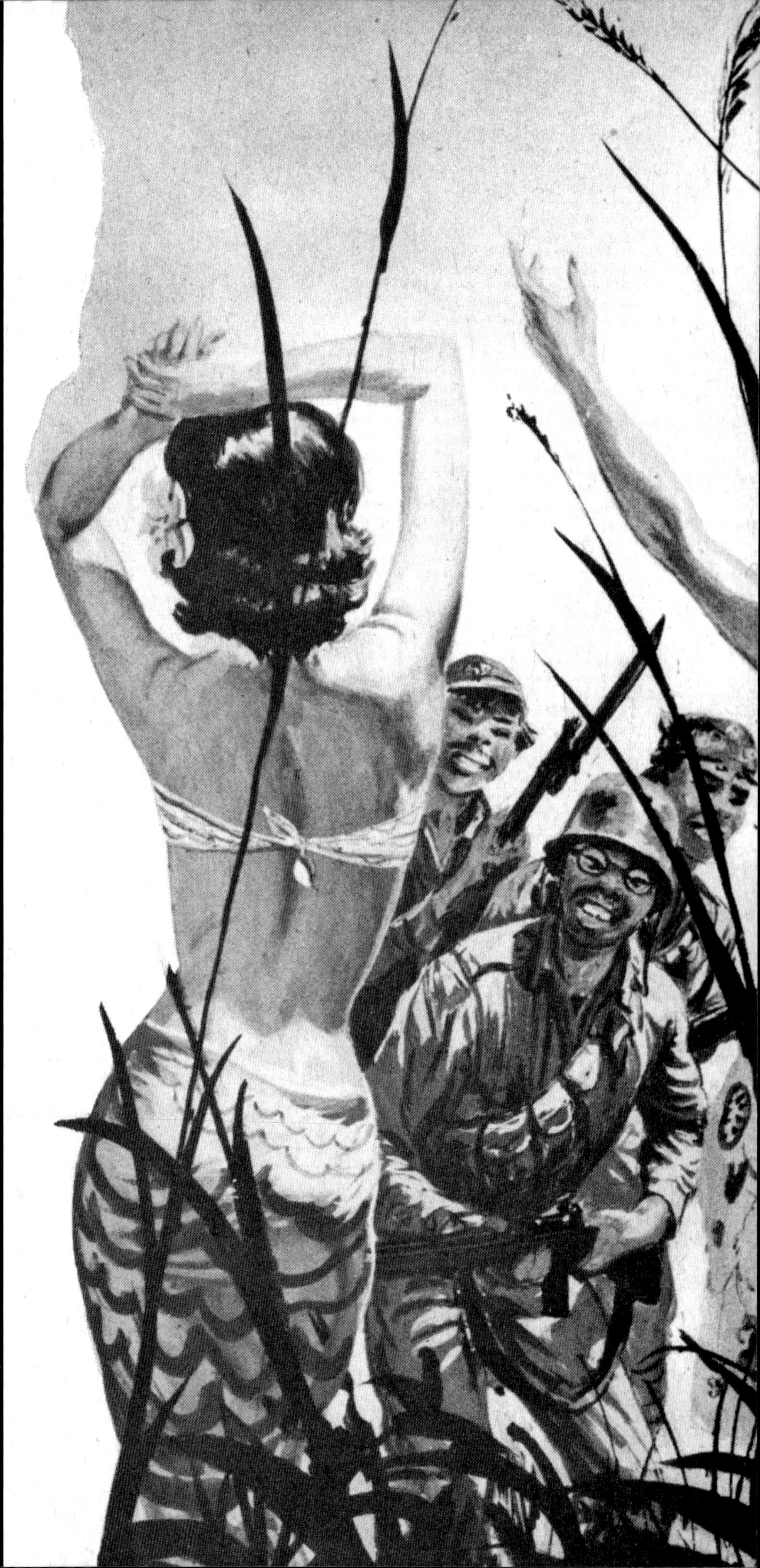

"MASK OF A HERO";
detail from interior art,
MAN'S ILLUSTRATED,
February 1960.
Art uncredited; attributed to
Norman Saunders (1959).

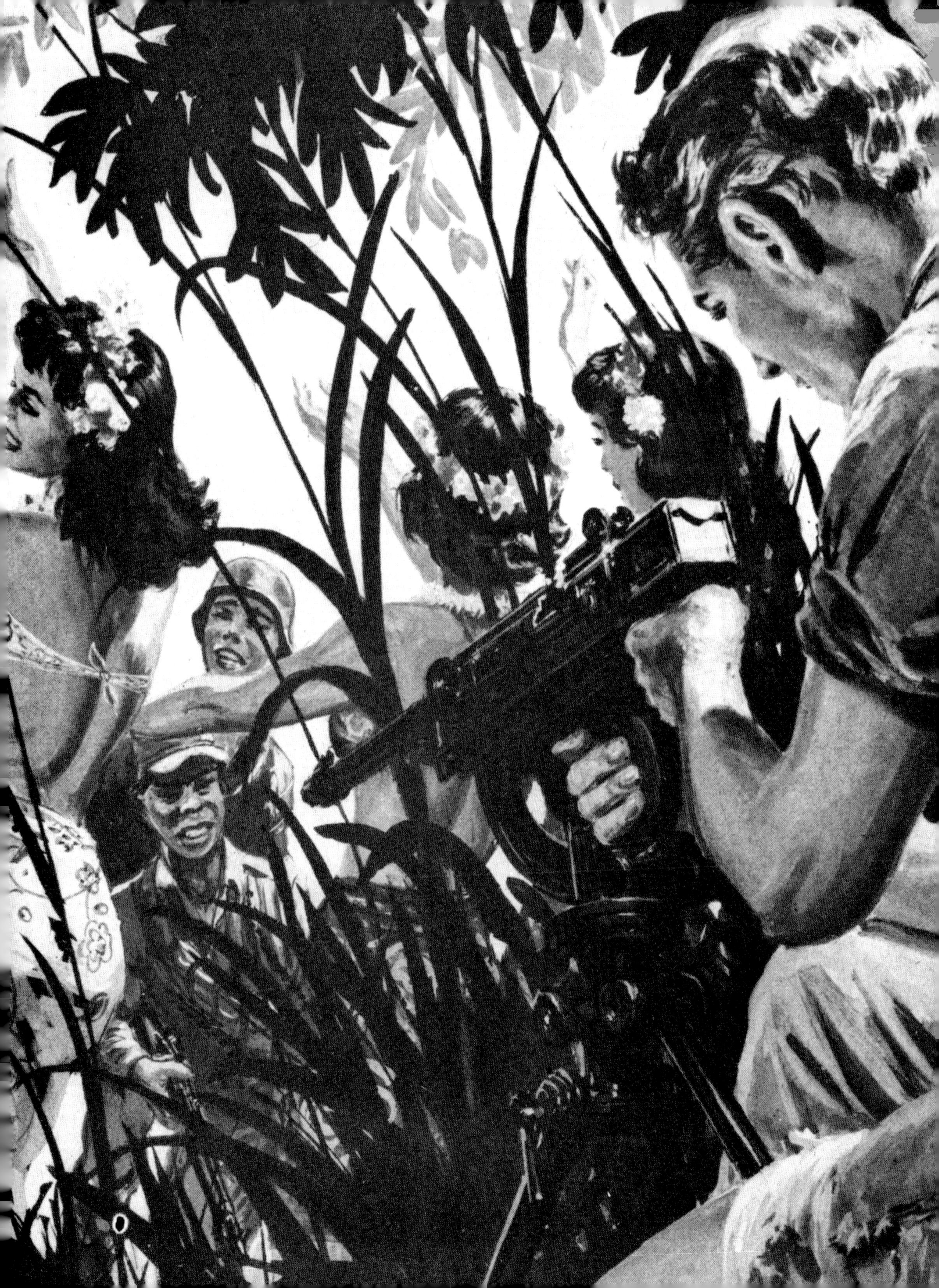

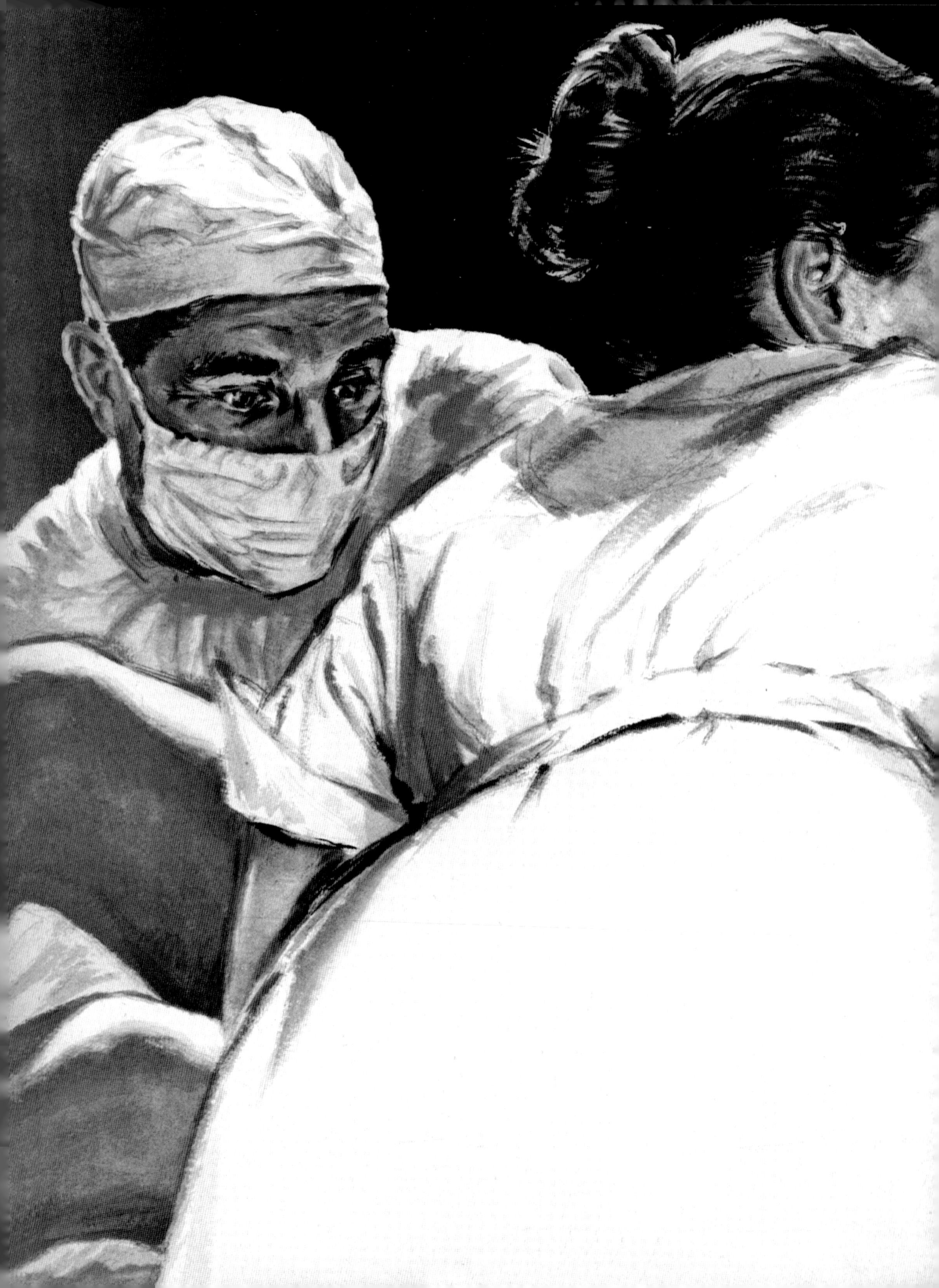

DEMON DOCTOR OF RAVENSBRUCK

Mad surgeon Percival Treite made Nazi concentration camp Ravensbruck into a special Hell for women.

THE YOUNG SURGEON LOOKED every inch a well-bred Englishman. His handsome face had that fine-boned, aristocratic quality so often found in the sons of England's landed gentry. His lithe, muscular figure was that of a man in his 30's who had ridden to the hounds and shot grouse on the moors.

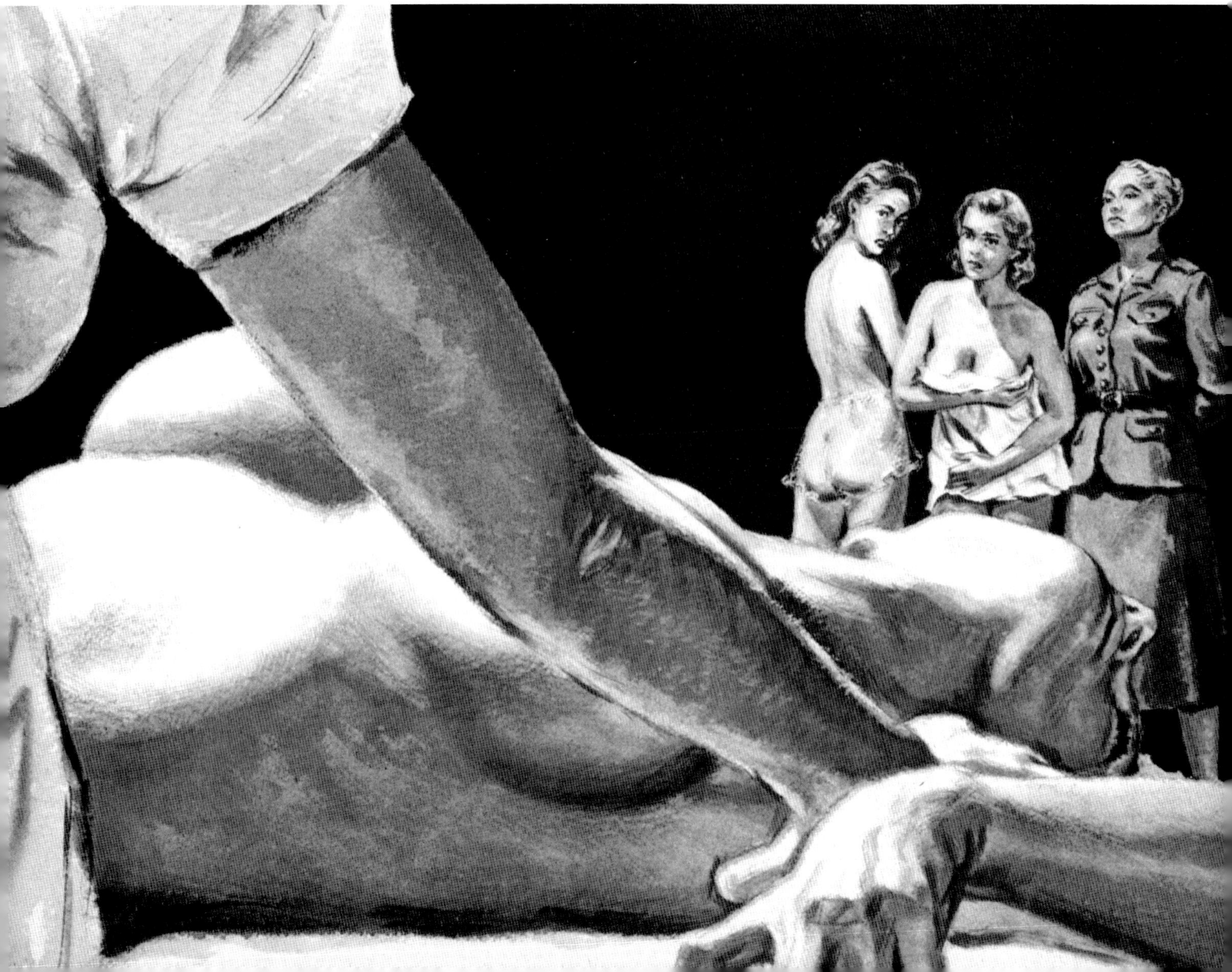

He busied himself at the cabinet filled with gleaming surgical implements and hypodermic syrings. Then he turned to a comely nurse, one Elizabeth Marshall, who was seated behind a small desk piled high with medical records.

"Pick out the 12 worst mental patients, Elizabeth," he drawled casually. "We'll finish them off tonight. Be sure you make out the usual 'died from natural causes' death certificates this afternoon and sign my name to them."

"Don't you want to check the certificates?"

"You know how I detest paperwork," Dr. Percival Treite said, pretending to shudder. "It's a terrible bore for me – and I'm certian that you'll make them out exactly right."

Returning to the cabinet, he took out three or four large syringes and some hypodermic needles, and laid them on a little table.

"I'll drop around at 10 tonight and give the ones you've selected their injections," Dr. Treite declared. "Then they can be cremated first thing tomorrow morning."

He shut the cabinet door, yawned and walked over to the window next to Nurse Marshall's desk. He stood there for several seconds staring absently at the small flower garden outside.

He grew moody and philosophical – as he always did on the days that he made the decisions to kill some of his patients.

"Why can't human beings be like flowers – and just live and die quietly and unobtrusively?" he mused aloud. "Why do they insist on becoming so troublesome that we have to put them out of the way?"

Nurse Marshall made no reply to this ghastly soliloquy. She merely gazed up at Treite, her round face glowing, reflecting the hot, unrequited passion that gripped her whenever she was near Percival Treite. She wanted to reach out and touch the hard, lean man who was her idol, her demi-god who could do no wrong and to whom she was inexorably bound by the scores of murders they had committed together.

Treite moved away from the window. Nurse Marshall's brown eyes followed him hungrily.

"I think I'll take a quick look around the wards," he announced. "After that, I'll be in my quarters." He paused thoughtfully.

"Oh, one more thing," he added. "Perhaps you'd better have our 'subjects' for tonight moved to an unused building. I'd rather not have the other patients hear them screaming after the injections begin to take effect..."

After Dr. Treite left the room, Nurse Marshall reached into a drawer and took out a pad of death certificate blanks. Then, she started thumbing through the card records of the hospital's mental patients. Every now and then, she removed a card from the file and laid it to one side...

WITHOUT DOUBT, Percival Treite, M.D., would have become a mass murderer even if there had been no Second World War. Savage sadism and homicidal mania were deeply embedded in his malevolent personality. The coincidental accident of World War II only made it possible for him to sate his monstrous bloodlust more easily – and on a scale that beggars description.

Strictly speaking, this cultured, brilliant – but utterly depraved – son of a stodgy and respectable English father cannot be classed as a common criminal. Because he served the Nazis and committed his murders and abominations at the Ravensbruck concentration camp for women prisoners, he must technically be classified as a "war" criminal.

This circumstance in no way alters the fact that Treite was a kill-crazy monster, the very embodiment of the blood-mad, maniacal surgeon often found in factual case-histories dealing with psychopaths, and even more often in horror fiction.

But there is nothing fictional about Percival Treite.

Nor do the bare facts of his outrages need any embellishment to make the most imaginative horror tales invented by Poe pale into feeble insignificance.

There is no accurate and complete tally to establish the exact number of victims who were murdered by Dr. Percival Treite.

Evidence that he had directly and personally killed over 500 women was amassed for use in his 1946-47 trial. These were only the slayings that could be readily and definitely proved against him!

There were many hundreds more.

Murder alone was not enough for Treite, however. Killing, even wholesale slaughter, did not suffice to calm the terrible forces that raged within him and drove him to wallow in human gore.

He derived hellish satisfaction from wielding his surgeon's instruments on women – hacking, cutting, maiming and disfiguring them. He took particular delight in performing such operations as sterilizations and hysterectomies without employing anaesthetics.

Cruelty was his passion, human suffering his ecstasy, the stench of death perfume to his delicately-molded nostrils.

L'Enfer des Femmes – "Women's Hell". This was the name that French women who were confined there gave to the Ravensbruck concentration camp. It was precisely that for them – and for the women of all nationalities who were imprisoned there and died there.

Ravensbruck was established by the Nazis shortly after World War II began in 1939. Located in the Mecklenburg swamps a little more than 50 miles north of Berlin, the Ravensbruck "main camp" was exclusively for women.

Some 125,000 women and girls of all ages and of all European nationalities were sent there between 1939 and 1945. At least 50,000 of them died or were killed there. Another 40,000 were shipped from Ravensbruck to death factories for final "liquidation." When the war finally ended, less than 35,000 women remained alive in *L'Enfer des Femmes*.

Against such a background of carnage, the 500 – or even 1,000 – murders committed by Ravensbruck camp doctor Percival Treite might seem only a relatively minor, fragmentary part of an overwhelming horror. At first glance, Treite himself might appear to be only a single – and hardly singular – figure in a vast, charnel panorama.

But there is much that sets Percival Treite apart, and makes his moral guilt greater than that of other butchers at Ravensbruck. There are many factors that cause his figure to loom particularly large, sinister and terrifying.

Treite did not kill and torture and mutilate because he was blindly following orders from his Nazi superiors. He did these things because he wanted to do them – because he enjoyed doing them.

Yet, he knew the difference between right and wrong – the classic test by which humanity judges sanity. Conscience-stricken, Treite would at times perform difficult, delicate operations to save the lives of some poor wretches and, perhaps, even use his considerable influence to save them from the gas chambers or crematories. While such unpredictable ambivalence proves irrationality and points to schizophrenia, it also makes his crimes all the more terrible.

Treite was highly-educated, cultured and refined – a man who had enjoyed every opportunity and advantage in life.

He was, in short, a gentleman.

Treite's father was a well-to-do Englishman of excellent family, who married a German woman.

Since Treite wanted to be a doctor from an early age, and German medical schools were the best in the world in the era between the two World Wars, Percival was sent off to be educated in Germany.

Percival was still attending pre-medical school when he determined that he would not only be a doctor, but a surgeon and, even more specifically, a gynecologist. He became almost obsessed with the idea of gynecological surgery.

Withal, he demonstrated a natural aptitude for surgery in medical school.

"This student may well become a brilliant – even a great – surgeon," one of Treite's professors wrote about him. "He has an outstanding talent..."

Treite graduated with honors and continued to show great promise as an intern. He continued to specialize in gynecology. When older surgeons suggested that he obtain some experience in other forms of surgery, he angrily rejected their advice.

When he started on his career, he performed operations on his women patients at any and every opportunity. According to many reliable reports, he conducted a lucrative practice on the side as an abortionist.

Although he was, from a legal standpoint, a British subject, Treite was strongly influenced by his German mother and, at her instigation, renounced all claim to British citizenship and became a German citizen.

Treite was not a fanatical Nazi at any time – and no Nazi at all until World War II began. Being a physical as well as a moral coward, he feared being called into the Wehrmacht and being sent off to combat as a frontline surgeon. To prevent this from happening, he enrolled in the Nazi Party and volunteered for the SS, Hitler's "political army" which, Percival Treite reasoned, would remain well behind the firing line.

There isn't much information available about his activities during the early years of the war. Some say that he was assigned to a prisoner of war camp where – because he spoke fluent and unaccented English – he interrogated British prisoners.

Other versions have him performing assembly-line sterilization operations on Polish and Russian women in 1941 and 1942. Yet others hold that he served as a staff-surgeon in a "Hitler Jugend" camp run by the SS. for teenage boys and girls – but this last seems highly unlikely, for such camps were established to breed children, not to bring about abortions or to sterilize women.

Whatever the truth, it is hardly important or relevant, save as it might help to round out Treite's character – but even that is well and clearly established by the story of his career at Ravensbruck.

DR. PERCIVAL Treite – by then an *SS-Hauptsturmführer*, or Captain – was assigned to the Ravensbruck concentration camp in 1943. The senior medical officer there was Dr. Gerd Schidlausky – a far different type than Treite.

Schidlausky was a Nazi fanatic of the worst and vilest type. He was a third- or fourth-rate doctor – a coarse, totally worthless quack who had gotten his medical degree, after failing his medical courses, as a "gift" from the Nazi Party for his early loyalty to Hitler.

"You can take over the hospital for the prisoners – such as it is," the brute-faced Schidlausky told Treite. "I seldom go there myself. I can't understand why Berlin doesn't allow us to liquidate all these women, instead of only a few hundred at a time..."

Treite found the hospital to be a hideous sinkhole. There were some huts, and in them were tiered wire-netting bunks. There were not enough of these to go around, and often two or three disease-raddled, emaciated women lay in a single bunk. Sometimes, a woman died and remained where she lay for a day or more.

And this was the hospital – not the camp proper, where conditions were infinitely worse!

Dr. Treite was introduced to Nurse Elizabeth Marshall, the *Oberschwester*, or head matron. Nurse Marshall was another devout Nazi. She, too, had some English forebears, but they were rather distant ones. She fell madly in love with the dapper, good-looking surgeon at first sight.

Treite sensed this, and he was clever enough to realize that the woman's infatuation could be used to advantage.

From the very first day, Elizabeth Marshall was Treite's slave – and even though their relationship remained, strangely enough, platonic to the very end, she was his partner in his most diabolic atrocities.

At first, Treite appeared to be shocked by what he found in the *revier* ("sick bay"). He did cause some improvements to be made – but only because conditions as he found them offended his personal sense of cleanliness.

By his orders, healthy – and the term is purely relative – camp inmates were detailed to the hospital. They emptied the latrine buckets and cleaned away the worst of the filth.

But Dr. Treite soon lost interest in such matters.

"Send someone out to find a few women," he'd say to Elizabeth Marshall. "We'll spend the day operating..."

Under Hitler's *Rassenschande* – "Race Shame" – and other directives, concentration camp doctors were authorized to perform abortions on all women inmates. The "Race Shame" order allowed the individual doctor to decide if the woman had been gotten pregnant by a man from a "race" other than her own. This was a serious crime according to the Nazi "laws."

The order applied not only to, say, Jews and Gentiles or Germans and Poles. It applied with equal force, say, to a Danish woman and a Dutch male.

Nurse Marshall would bustle off, screeching orders to the SS. guards – both male and female – who were assigned to the hospital. These would comb through prison "blocks" until they'd gathered together a few dozen women in various stages of pregnancy and herded them to the hospital.

Treite would inspect the wretched, half-starved women after they were packed into an empty hut. Whether they were married or single, girls in their teens or 20's or mature women made no difference.

"Obviously, they're all guilty of *Rassenschande*," he'd rasp to Nurse Marshall, who hovered near him. "Get their names, make the appropriate notations on their records and get them ready for surgery."

The operations continued all day – until Dr. Treite was temporarily sated. Then he would retire to his quarters and sleep – while the women on whom he'd operated were flung into already overcrowded wards. There many died and many others, realizing what had been done to them, contrived to commit suicide.

"You know, I've never had much experience in general surgery," Treite confided to Elizabeth Marshall one day. "I intend to remedy that lack."

Within the next two weeks the butcher performed nearly 150 operations of one kind and another. Nurse Marshall's "agents" scoured the prisoners' barracks seeking women who suffered from operable ailments – not because anyone wanted to cure them or help them, but because Dr. Treite needed "practice"!

He'd never performed a goiter operation in his life. Six or seven men were found with goiters. Only two lived through their operations. The others died on the operating table while Dr. Treite experimented and "perfected his technique".

THESE DEATHS were not even counted when the charges were finally drawn up against Percival Treite. No, the case against Treite was not built on deaths caused by his bungling. It was built on cold-blooded, premeditated murders he committed.

Among these were his injection-killings of mental patients, which began in early November, 1943 – because his leisure reading was interrupted.

Dr. Treite had many English books, and he liked to read them. He was sitting in his office one afternoon reading Shakespeare's *Hamlet*, according to Nurse Marshall's testimony at his trial.

For some reason or another, a woman confined to the pig-sty mental ward was being brought to the dispensary at about that time. She broke loose from her guards and ran shrieking past Dr. Treite's window.

"Elizabeth!" he shouted, slamming his book shut in sudden fury.

"Yes, Doctor?"

"Send in a stenographer."

There were several stenographer-typists assigned to the hospital, for the Nazis demanded that voluminous records and reports be kept and made on all matters, including deaths, executions, and liquidations.

A flaxen-haired stenographer entered. Treite dictated a letter to higher authority – through his immediate superior – requesting blanket permission to liquidate all mental patients. Dr. Schidlausky endorsed his approval on the letter and sent it forward. When no answer from Berlin was received within a week, he took matters into his own hands.

"We'll have a periodic house-cleaning," he told Nurse Marshall. "From time to time, we'll cut out the 10 or 12 worst ones among the madwomen and rid ourselves of them."

Elizabeth Marshall prepared the drugs and filled the syringes. Treite sometimes chose the victims himself. Sometimes he let Marshall do the picking, and he administered the hypodermics.

The death certificate always read the same way: "Died of natural causes." Occasionally, he signed them personally, but most often he allowed Elizabeth Marshall to relieve him of this onerous task. The certificates were duly forwarded in batches to the proper SS offices in Berlin. No questions were ever asked. Only the slips of paper were needed to satisfy Nazi bureaucratic protocol.

As for the dead women? They were cremated in the mortuary ovens that operated day and night at Ravensbruck.

"I want all young and attractive Polish women sent to the hospital as soon as they arrive," was his next order to Nurse Marshall. All Poles had been officially classified as belonging to an "inferior race" by Hitlerian edict. This gave concentration camp staffs *carte blanche* to deal with all Poles as they deemed fit.

The madness had seized Percival Treite once more. Polish girls between the ages of 14 and 25 who arrived in prisoner "transports" at Ravensbruck were taken directly to the hospital. Treite performed sterilization operations on them all – without anesthetics!

One witness later said that she had accidentally entered a room near the primitive operating "theater" after Treite had performed five such operations in a row one morning. She said that he was still wearing his blood-drenched surgical gown and staring wildly at himself in a mirror that hung on the wall.

Not long after this grisly incident, Treite was struck by remorse. This lasted three, perhaps four days. During that short period, he ministered carefully – even tenderly – to several score women. He ordered the most ill be given extra rations and that bedding be thoroughly deloused.

The urge to atone for his sins was soon replaced by the much more powerful urge to sin again.

With the same insane illogic that characterized so many processes and procedures in Hitlerian Germany, women who managed to be admitted to the *revier* were seldom sent to the gas chambers or otherwise executed "officially." The theory seemed to be that they would probably die in the hospital anyway.

Prisoners who were to be liquidated were chosen at periodic roll-call formations from among the inmates of the camp in general. If a woman happened to recover from what illness she had and returned to her "block" or barracks, she once again became subject to "selection", and "eligible" for liquidation!

The methods for choosing the women who were to be gassed or shot was fairly simple. Members of the camp staff picked out those who appeared too old or too weak to work.

"I think I'd like to make the selections," Percival Treite announced on a bitter-cold day in mid-winter.

When the roll-call was held, it was Treite who strode up and down along the ranks of shivering, terror-stricken women. He poked and punched those who appeared weak. If they staggered or fell, he told the SS guards to drag them away to the area where those who were to be liquidated were being assembled.

Among the prisoners at that time were several dozen Englishwomen. Some were internees – civilians who happened to be caught in Germany when the war began. Others were women and girls who had been parachuted into occupied countries on intelligence or sabotage missions and had been captured by the Nazis or by collaborationists.

Treite found two such girls in one group lined up before a barracks. He stopped and began talking to them in the English he spoke perfectly – and which, in fact, was really his native tongue.

"Where are your homes?" he asked the girls. Startled, they both replied at once.

"Manchester – London."

Dr. Treite appeared to know both cities well. He began chatting about them. He wondered how Piccadilly Circus looked now that London had been so heavily bombed. He wondered if Manchester was still as gloomy and smog-ridden as always.

"I'd like to go back to London some day," he grinned.

"So would I!" the girl whose home was there breathed fervently.

Treite's manner changed instantly. Instead of the pleasant, almost charming English-squire type that he had been playing for several minutes, he became ugly, vicious.

"I'll see London – *you* never will!" he snarled. Then he turned and barked to the SS guards.

"These two – take them!" he ordered in German.

The girls, although they had been prisoners for only a short time and were in comparatively excellent health, were dragged away.

DR. TREITE enjoyed visiting the grisly necropolis that was the crematorium. He liked to stand amidst the piled-high corpses and watch the SS men detailed from punishment battalions thrust the bodies into the ovens.

He also enjoyed watching the notorious Corporal Schultz carry out his daily quota of 50 executions by *Genickschuss* – shooting his victims through the back of the neck at the base of the skull.

"Would you like to try, Herr Doktor? the moronic Schultz asked him on one occasion, offering Treite his pistol.

"No, thanks," Treite replied, laughing. "I have better ways."

Hundreds of mentally sick women died at Ravensbruck because one madwoman had run past his window screaming. Hundreds more were consigned to gas chambers because Dr. Treite suddenly decided that he didn't want "tuberculars" in the camp.

"I can tell when a person has tuberculosis just by looking at him," he boasted.

He ordered that several thousand women strip naked, line up, and parade past him. "Just by looking" he selected 250 one time, 175 another, and 310 a third, declaring them to be "tuberculars."

Nurse Marshall had three stenographers typing up the "T.B. certificates" – on which Dr. Treite rubber-stamped his signature – and the women were sent to the gas chambers!

Shortly after the invasion of Europe by Allied Forces in June, 1944, Percival Treite had another unexpected attack of conscience. He had medicines distributed and ordered that bandages be changed more often. Was he worried about his own future? If so, he did not worry very long.

By July, he had reverted to form. Mental patients continued to enter the hospital – women who had suffered breakdowns or had gone mad in the hell that was Ravensbruck. Treite and Marshall kept the mental "ward" thinned out – with lethal injections.

Several hundred gypsy women had been rounded up by SS troops throughout Europe and sent to Ravensbruck. Hitler – recovering from the injuries he suffered in the July, 1944, assassination attempt – had ordered that all gypsy women be sterilized, regardless of age.

Treite flung himself into this new task with maniacal pleasure. He performed his operations as he always had – without anesthetics. The youngest girl to pass through his surgery was only seven. The oldest woman – according to records introduced at his trial – was 72!

The procedures were always the same. The "patients" were strapped or tied to the operating table. Dr. Treite did his ghastly work despite the shrieks and screams.

Naturally, as many as half of all those on whom he operated died, either on the table or within a few hours afterwards.

When not "professionally engaged," Percival Treite relaxed the way a "gentleman" should.

His quarters were pleasantly – even luxuriously – furnished. The walls were hung with English hunting prints. He, himself, hunted often, particularly for the ducks and geese which abound in the Mecklenburg swamps.

He listened to good music on his phonograph. He was a perfect guest – and a perfect host. He made frequent trips to Berlin, where he had many friends.

There weren't many doctors left in Berlin. Most had been called into one branch of service or another. Dr. Treite willingly examined and treated his friends when he was off-duty or on leave – and never charged them for his services.

The visits to Berlin grew less frequent as 1944 drew to a close. German armies retreating on the Eastern Front were sending fresh hordes of prisoners back to Germany. They were sweeping the areas from which they retreated clean. All civilians were shipped off to concentration camps to bolster the Reich's labor force, to be held as hostages – or merely to be exterminated.

The new influx of women kept Dr. Treite very busy.

Nurse Marshall had to requisition fresh supplies of lethal drugs often from the central medical warehouse in Berlin. In January, 1945, records showed that she sent in eight different orders – enough for over 9,000 fatal doses.

By no means were all of these administered by Dr. Treite. He had several nurses of Marshall's caliber and other assistants to "put the inmates to sleep." Nonetheless, the killings were carried out under his supervision and at his order.

Once again, such killings were not "charged against him" when he was brought to justice. He was accused only of those murders which he personally, and with his own hands, had committed with clear intent to kill.

ADOLF HITLER'S "1,000 Year" Reich was crumbling fast in early 1945.

The Russians were closing in from the East, the British and Americans from the West.

"What will happen, Doctor?" Elizabeth Marshall asked him fearfully in March. "Can we still hope to win?"

"No." Treite shook his head.

"What will happen to us – to you, me and the others who worked here at Ravensbruck ?"

"Nothing – nothing at all," Percival Treite replied confidently. "When it's all over, we'll all just disappear – go to various parts of Germany, perhaps change our names, and wait for the Allies to forget about the war." He began to laugh.

"What – what is so funny, Doctor Treite ?" Nurse Marshall asked.

"I was just thinking that I won't even have to hide. I'll go right to the British, tell them some lies and offer to help them."

Percival Treite played an important role in the final mass blood-letting at Ravensbruck. Just before the war ended, orders were issued to kill as many prisoners as possible – and as quickly as possible.

It was the last ghastly act. More than 5,000 women were butchered in those final days – and Treite did his share of the slaughter.

Rumors were spreading across Germany. They reached Ravensbruck. Il appeared that the British were arresting – and even tracking down – camp staff members and charging them with "war crimes."

Percival Treite tried to get away. He thought that if he could avoid arrest for a few months, the Allies' desire for vengeance would dissipate itself and that it would be safe to re-emerge.

Treite quite honestly believed that would be all there was to it. He even made plans to go into private practice – and went so far as to correspond with people in several German cities asking about "opportunities" for a gynecologist in their areas!

Group-Captain Anthony Somerhough, of the Royal Air Force, was the officer in charge of the war-crimes investigations centering on Ravensbruck. A brilliant attorney and prosecutor, Somerhough had a large corps of trained investigators on his staff. These men – and women – fanned out across beaten Germany.

These crack agents and operatives took mountains of testimony from women who had survived the Ravensbruck horrors. They ferreted out and seized records and documents. And they tracked down the killers and the torturers – Percival Treite among them.

Painstakingly, the cases were built up. Nothing that could not be proven beyond any doubt was included in the charges. Every offense and crime was investigated – and then investigated again.

The Ravensbruck trials began on December 6, 1946. Among the 16 defendants seated in the prisoners' dock were Dr. Percival Treite and Nurse Elizabeth Marshall.

An endless parade of witnesses appeared and gave testimony. Still broken in health, the outrages of Ravensbruck horribly fresh in their minds, the women spoke out .

"Dr. Treite ordered me strapped to the operating table. Then he began to cut..."

"I personally saw Treite give fatal injections to ten women. I even remember their names..."

"He killed twenty-five women in a single morning with poison..."

"I was present when he murdered eleven children..."

Witnesses' testimony was bolstered, supported, authenticated by documentary evidence.

When the last court session ended and the judges retired to consider their verdict. Percival Treite was ashen, pale and trembling.

On the day that the verdicts were to be issued and sentences passed, he had to be carried into the courtroom.

When he heard the judgment "guilty!", and the sentence – "to be hanged by the neck until dead" – he collapsed completely, begging for mercy.

Nurse Elizabeth Marshall received the same sentence.

She accepted the judgment without a word. She did not even glance at Percival Treite as she was led from the courtroom. Ironically, his partner in terrible crimes –but nonetheless a woman – turned on him at the end.

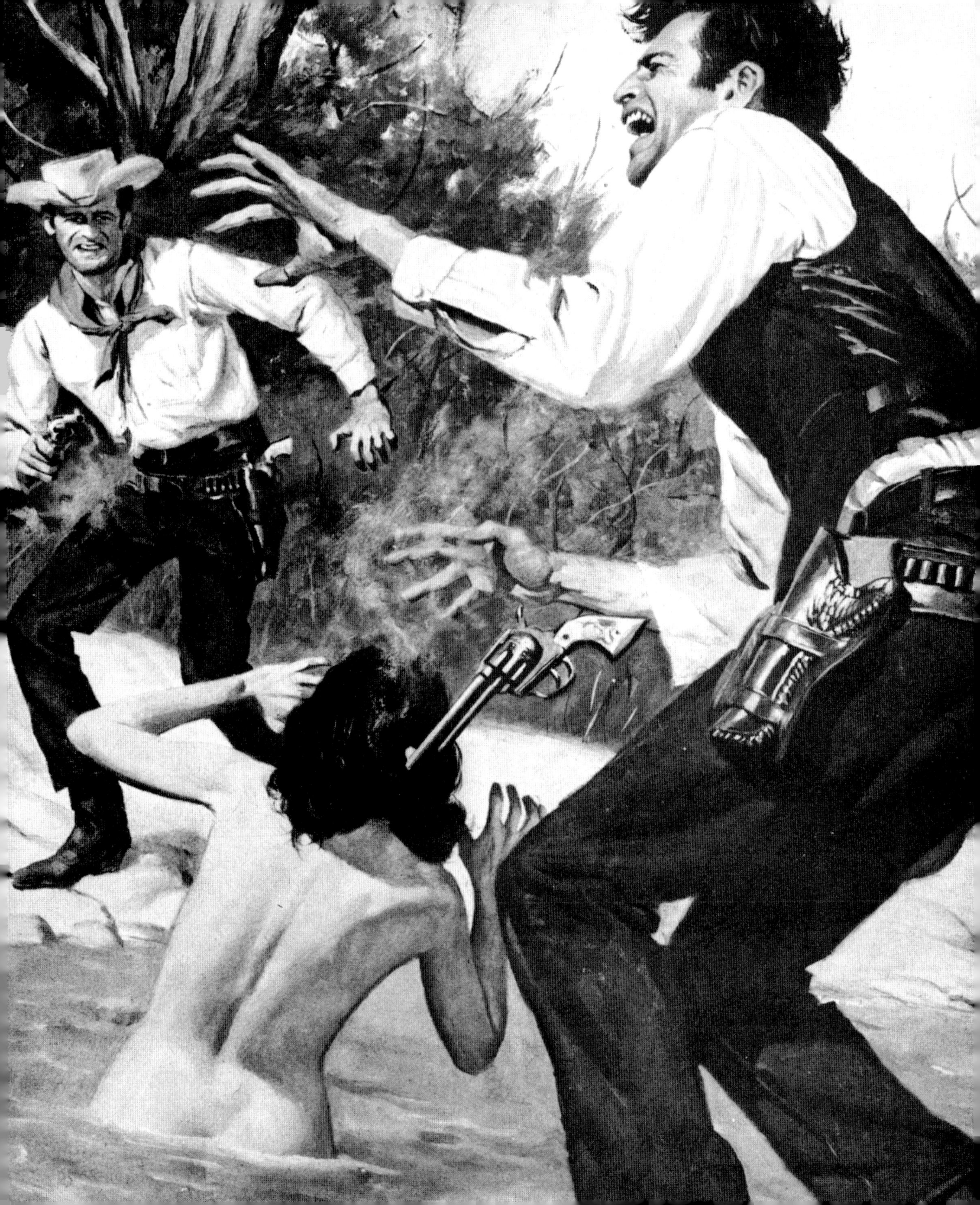

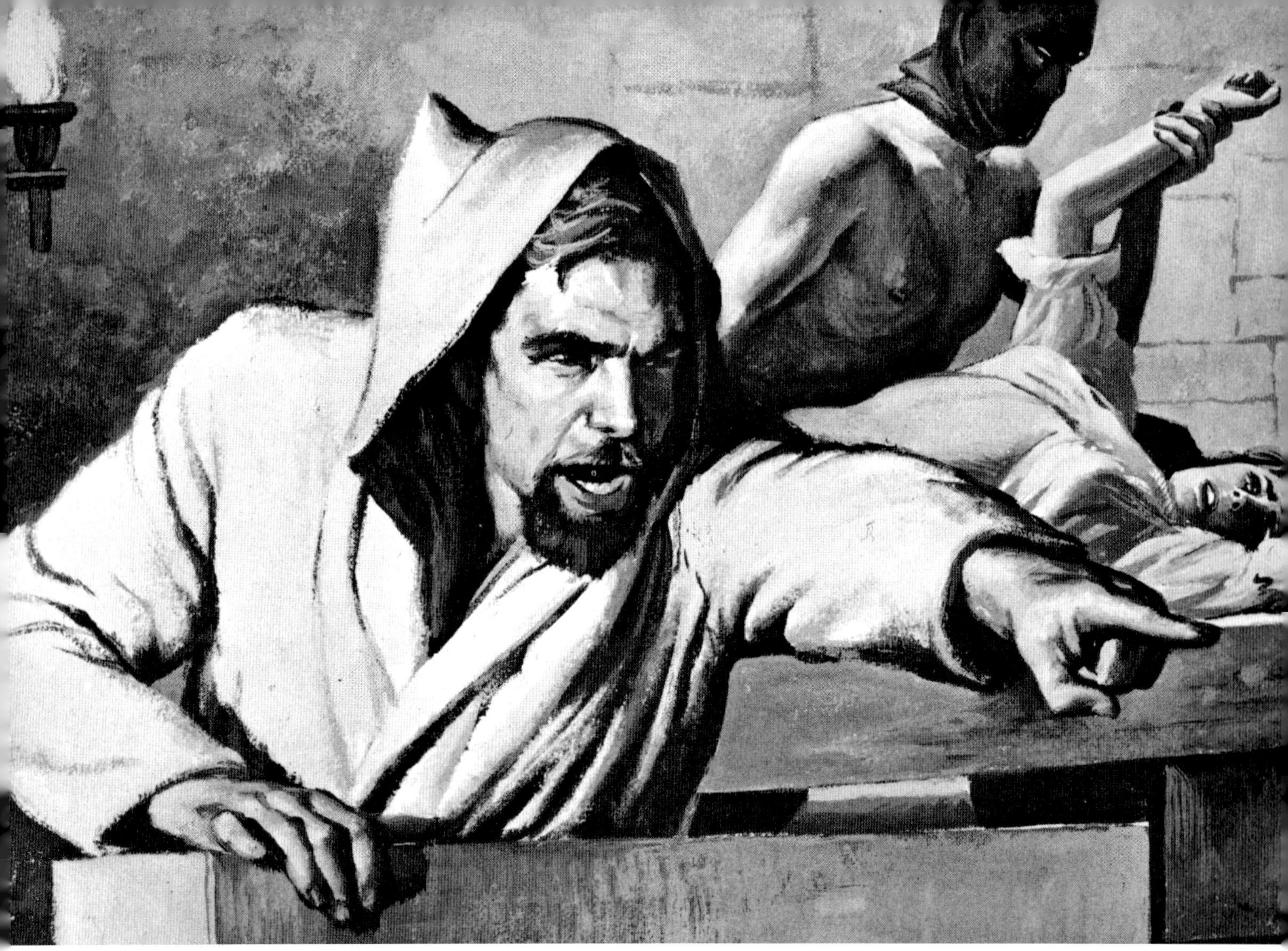

5,000 BEAUTIES FOR THE DEVIL'S RACK

No maiden was safe from the blood and pain orgies of history's most insane butcher.

THE HEAVY IRON DOOR swings open, creaking on rusty hinges. Daylight darts into the dank darkness, and touches the girl. She is young, her long, dark hair like a mantle over her bare shoulders. The light reveals her kneeling on the cold, wet stone floor. She is shivering. Her dress is in tatters, showing patches of her white flesh. The intrusion of light sends the rats scurrying into the separate corner of the dungeon.

But light means hope. The girl stops moaning, and

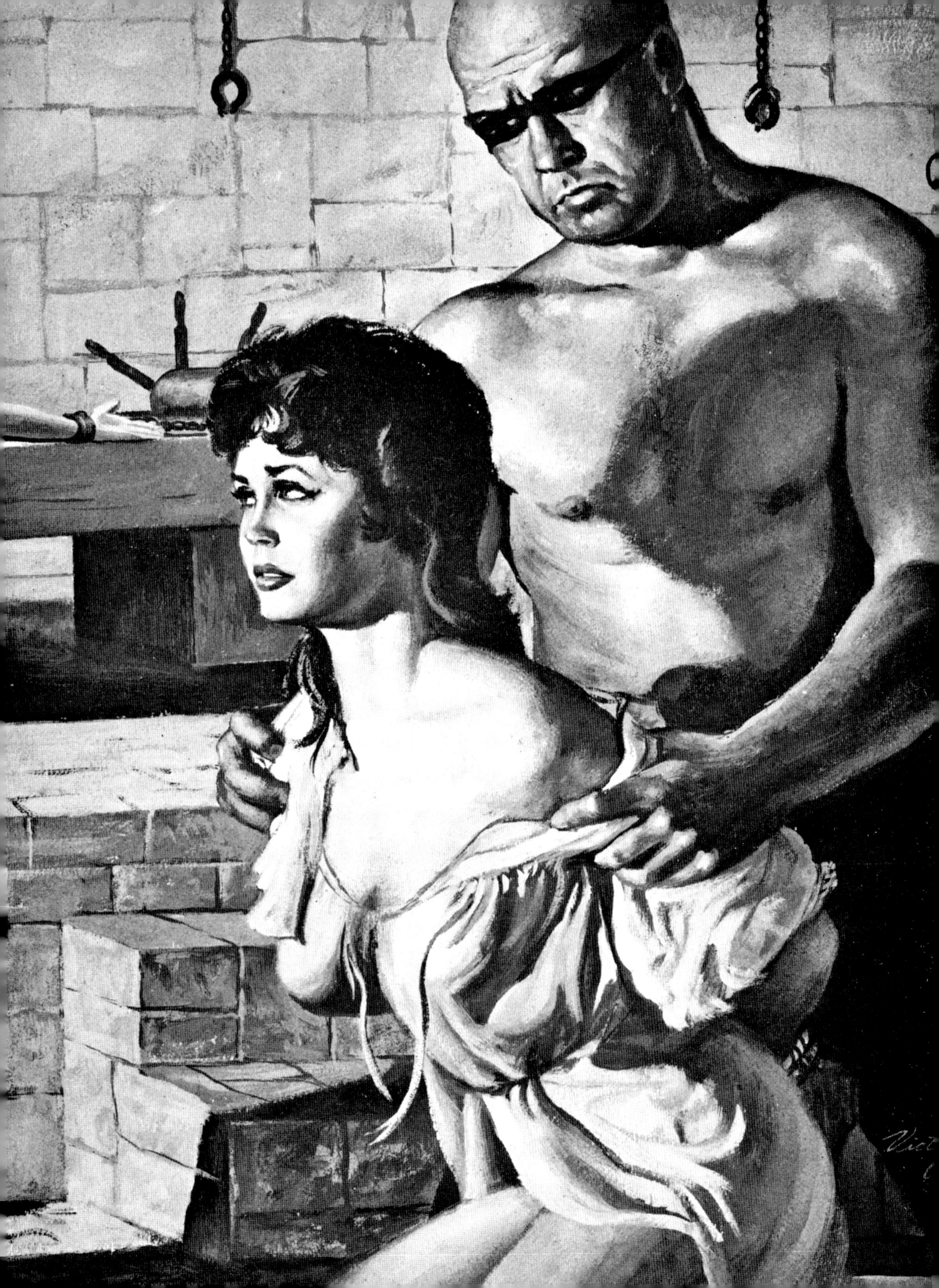

stares upward at the brightness. She has been praying, praying for hours or days. Has the Saviour heard her? Has He sent a messenger of hope in this year of our Lord 1481?

The iron door clangs shut, and daylight escapes, leaving darkness. But not quite. Above her, at the head of the steep, block-stone stairway, she sees the wavering yellow light of torches.

The light begins to descend the stairway. She sees a dark procession – four figures, shapeless under the black hoods and black robes. Three stop half way down, and another figure continues down the steps, bearing a candle, towards her.

The girl knows he is a friar of importance. His hood is black like the others, but his robe is snowy white, a sign of his high office.

As he approaches, she turns toward him on her knees. Her hands are clutched to her half bare breast. Silent words of prayer tremble on her lips. Hope, hope is all she has left.

The white robe is before her. She could reach out and touch it now. Her eyes travel fearfully, hopefully to see the hooded face, and then they shut tight to block out the sight. She begins to wail, her cries echoing through the empty dungeon. All hope is gone now. Only a wish remains – the wish for death.

The girl has seen the face before. It is cold, expressionless, with tight thin lips and blazing eyes. It is the face of Torquemada.

Torquemada. The very sound of the name makes her blood run cold. At a distance, she has seen him a dozen times, surrounded by an escort of black-hooded Dominicans, driving barefooted heretics to the stake and death by fire. Torquemada, the Grand Inquisitor of 15th century Spain.

"Silence," he orders. Her breath catches in her throat.

"Remove your garment," he demands, "that you may be stripped clean in the eyes of the Lord."

She obeys, conscious of the fiery weight of his eyes on her body. She is weak, too weak to resist, too desperate to care.

She feels his hand on her head.

"You have but to confess, my child, confess your heresy. Confess and repent, and you will find salvation."

His long, tapering fingers pull her dark tresses away from her bosom. She is totally nude now before the Grand Inquisitor, and her shame is greater even than her fear.

He stares long and hard at her, his eyes devouring her flesh. She sees his hands tremble, his breathing become labored.

She will let him, she promises herself. She will let this holy man of the cloth smash his churchly vows on her body. She will soil him as he violates her.

"Confess, my child," he murmurs, a Latin prayer emerging from his lips.

And something within her rebels.

She bolts, runs shrieking to a dark corner of the dungeon, pitches herself on the cold stone floor and prays sobbingly.

Torquemada snaps his fingers briskly. A moment later the girl is lifted by two of the black Dominicans.

"Not the rack for this heretic," Torquemada's voice rings out. "The hoist."

The hoist. She has heard people in the village speak of it as worse than the rack. At least it is not to be the dreaded water torture. Small consolation.

The torture chamber is a bare stone room, its walls thick to shield the screams of its victims. The girl is held by two of the black monks while two others pinion her wrists behind her back. She hears a weird squealing sound as a rope is lowered from a pulley in the ceiling. One end of the rope is looped around her bound wrists. She is allowed to stand for a moment. Then two of the monks begin to pull at the other end of the rope.

Slowly, the girl is hoisted from the ground. Now only her bare toes touch the floor. She is screaming. For almost all of her weight is on her arms, all but tugging them out of their sockets.

Her gleaming, nude body seems strangely elongated now. And the Friars stare at her ripe, uplifted breasts.

Torquemada places his hand in the small of her back and swings her tortured body towards him.

"You will confess, child," he says coldly. "But not before torture purifies your soul of sin."

He nods at the monks, watches as the girl's body is pulled high into the air, turns away as the monks tug at the rope, and the body jerks in the air like a human puppet. Torquemada pulls his hood closer about his ears.

"They are strong, these peasant wenches," he remarks. "They weary me. She will confess when her arms are dislocated. Return her, then, to the dungeon, and prepare her for the fire."

THE TIME is 1481. The place is Seville, Spain, during the reign of Ferdinand and Isabella. And shrewd, calculating Queen Isabella who was to finance Columbus' voyage of discovery of the New World 11 years later, has an earlier protégé – Frey Tomas de Torquemada, a sadistic genius of evil, torture and sadism in the name of holiness and financial profit.

Before the year 1481 is over, Torquemada will have burned at the stake over 8,000 victims, and he will have tortured tens of thousands of others. By the time he has retired some 15 years later, he will have achieved a record of brutality and viciousness unequaled in the annals of bloody history. He will have sent tens of thousands of innocent people to death in flames, sent hundreds of thousands fleeing the borders of Spain, confiscated vast fortunes in property and divided it with money-hungry Isabella, and created a reputation which persists to this day as the world's most fanatic murderer.

Born in 1420, Torquemada joined the order of Saint Dominic, and followed the rule of poverty with fanatic zeal. He never used linen on his bed nor ate meat. He was cold, austere, uncommunicative, self-abnegating – on the surface an excellent, holy Dominican monk.

His fine record as a religious zealot soon came to the attention of Isabella. They were, in a way, brother and sister under the skin: both were cool, calculating, power-hungry. Torquemada became the personal confessor to Isabella.

Yet, somewhere deep inside this perfect man of the cloth lurked the heart and soul of a mad beast. When, in 1480, Isabella received permission from the Pope to establish an Inquisition in Spain to repress heretics, she named Torquemada the Inquisitor in Seville.

Isabella, in reality, cared little about the threat of heretics, except as they constituted an economic problem to her and the young Kingdom of Spain which was struggling for financial stability.

What Isabelle wanted was to confiscate the property

of the wealthier people of her kingdom – be they Jews, Moors, or converted Christians. The red herring of heresy became her device to grab wealth.

For his part, Torquemada was a power-mad fanatic. Whether he deluded himself that his bloody purges were for the good of the Church, or whether he directed the rites of torture and murder for his own worldly gain, is a moot point. Whatever his original motivation, Torquemada soon showed himself to be a maniacal demon who spilled blood as though it were cheap wine.

Looking back at his ruthless bloodlettings through the eyes of modern psychiatrists, it seems safe to say that murder, torture and sadism were Torquemada's way of expressing a twisted sexual urge.

Who else but a sex maniac would order all of his victims – men, women and children – stripped naked before he would permit them to confess and abjure?

Who else but a maniac would insist on tortures as vicious and sadistic as smearing the feet with fat and toasting them with flames; tearing people limb from limb on the rack; using the hoist to pull their arms out of their sockets; or submitting them to the unimaginable anguish of the water torture?

And, with the often strange logic of a psychotic, Torquemada carefully drew up a code of accusation and of torture. Torquemada's "book" on how to spot heretics, blasphemers, sorcerers, infidels, and devil-worshippers stands as a masterpiece of a sick but ingenious brain.

The way a man turned in his sleep, for example, was a sign of whether he was a heretic, according to Torquemada. And the mere fact of being accused of heresy was tantamount to guilt.

Certainly, Torquemada gave his victims trials – of a sort. The trial was held in secret. The judges were also the accusers. The victims had the right to a lawyer but the lawyer was a cleric hired and payed by the Suprema, the Supreme Council of the Inquisition. The accused had no right to confront his accusers. The witnesses were all prosecution witnesses. Moreover, they could not retract derogatory testimony. If they tried that, they themselves would be accused, tortured and burned, and their original testimony would still stand against the victim.

Witnesses themselves did not have to be of sound mind or even mental maturity. In a number of cases, young children, no more than ten years old, were held to be duly qualified witnesses for the prosecution.

The startling truth about this whole elaborate facade of court procedure was this: never was there any case of acquittal, pure and simple. Once you were accused, you either confessed and underwent punishment; or you didn't confess, were found guilty, and died in flames.

Practically no one in all of Spain was safe from the Inquisition. Some Bishops of the church were accused. And, probably the grisliest fact of all – hundreds of dead bodies were exhumed and burned as heretics. Even the grave was no escape from the sadism of Torquemada.

This blood-thirsty fanatic set up an intricate espionage network to unearth alleged heretics. Mothers accused their own children, and children their own parents.

INQUISITIONS IN more moderate form had gone on in most of the countries of Europe for centuries in the name of protecting the church from heresy, and saving souls for the Lord.

But the mad genius of Torquemada appalled even the most devout officials of the Church. It wasn't long before the Pope condemned the cruelties of Torquemada's mass murders. But, supported by Isabella, the mad priest went on feeding his flames with human fuel.

Being burned alive was, in effect, a blessing compared with the infamous water torture – Torquemada's favorite device, and one he used especially on handsome women.

He received a deep sexual thrill from the sight of a voluptuous, naked woman, strapped to a ladder-like device by leather thongs. He himself, on occasion, would insert a rod under the thongs and twist it like a tourniquet until the thongs cut through the skin and flesh of the victim, drenching her in blood.

And this was as nothing compared with the water torture which followed. The woman's mouth was pried open and held that way by a wedge-like device. Her nostrils were plugged up. A long strip of linen was placed in the mouth of the victim, and water was poured on it in a continuous stream. The ladder was tilted so that the victim's head was below her feet.

Water dripped through the cloth into her throat. She had the choice of holding her breath or inhaling water – suffocating or confessing.

Historians have long speculated whether Torquemada spared some of the more attractive women from these tortures for the pleasure of his own bed. But the consensus seems to be that this genius of evil held strictly true to his vow of chastity and never had a woman – or was physically incapable of having one.

Whatever the truth, Torquemada took his sex through ordering, witnessing and participating in sadistic torture. Most likely he was a voyeur, a man of strong sexual emotions whose guilt feelings at the temptation of breaking the vow of chastity led him to avenge himself on the whole human race by breaking their bodies, smashing their souls, and rationalizing the whole mad performance in the name of churchly duty.

Ironically, this fiend thrived on perversion. He did not relinquish his role as Grand Inquisitor until 1496, when he was 76 years old.

Gradually, the madness of the Inquisition faded. But to his final day, Torquemada attended every public ceremony at which alleged heretics were sentenced to death by flames.

He marched in every *auto-da-fe* (fire procession), looked on wild-eyed as the victims were chained to the stake, murmured incoherently beside the naked women as they were prepared for the fire.

And, some say, long after the flames had died, long after ashes and bones were all that remained of the victims, Torquemada would poke through the cold remains as if there, somehow, were still a chance of seeing naked female flesh.

Torquemada – one of the most blood-curdling madmen of all time, a man whose lust could not be contained despite all the trappings of the church. Torquemada – his name resounds of the very devil he purported to fight – a man remembered solely because he symbolizes and warns us of the depravity to which a human being can sink.

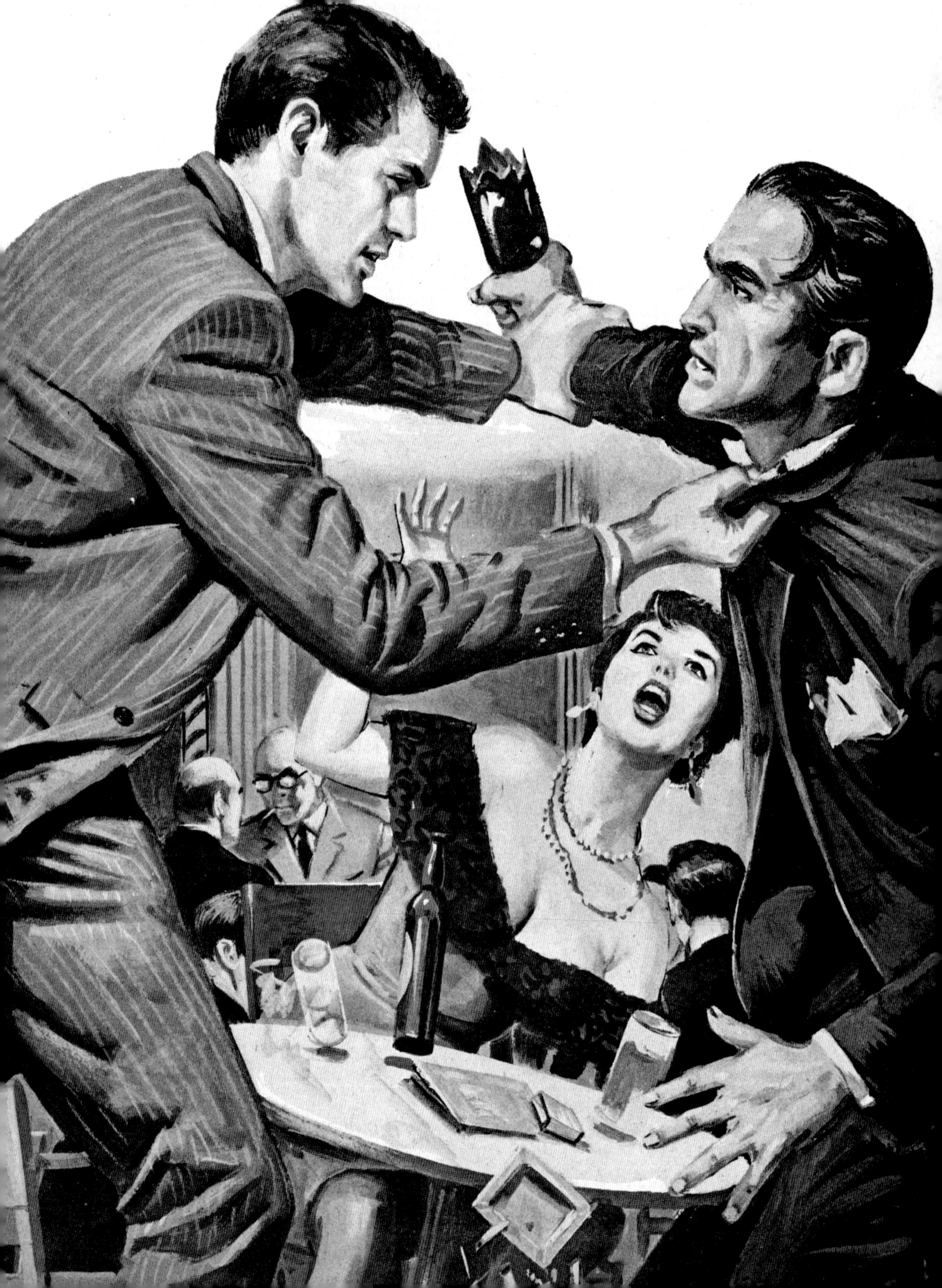

THE DOLL WHO MADE THE BEER BARONS DANCE HER POLKA

Look the wrong way at Francie and you'd get your face carved by a broken bottle. She was the mob's darling – until the smirking "Mad Dog" decided she was for him.

THE MAD DOG WIPED a thin film of sweat from his fuzz-covered upper lip. In all of his twenty-two years, he had never seen anything like it. He kicked the Dutchman under the table and pointed towards the statuesque blonde who caressed the floor mike.

"That's mine, Dutch," he grunted in appreciation. "Man, what I'm going to do to her."

Ramona, I hear the missionary bells.

The sultry, husky tones of the girl's voice filtered over the pungent layers of blue cigar smoke. Its clear tones competing with the sounds of raucous laughter which erupted from a bunch of drunks at the next table. The Dutchman's cold eyes swept the group of noise-makers. "Shut the bastards up, Vince," Dutch Schultz ordered.

Coll grinned happily. This was he wanted even more than the blonde. A mean snarl curled his lip as he reached for the beer bottle and snapped it in two on the table top. With lightning speed he crossed the narrow aisle. Suddenly a woman's shriek of sheer horror drowned out the girl's song. There was a muffled gasp, then a low moan of pain. Vincent "Mad Dog" Coll had struck.

His victim sat hunched over the table, hands covering his mangled face. Bright scarlet oozed through the writhing fingers. A woman laughed hysterically as the hands fell away, revealing two gaping holes where the eyes had been. Slowly the man slipped from his chair, thudded to the floor and rolled over, his mutilated face staring sightlessly at the ceiling.

Coll's snicker turned into a maniacal laugh. He stared wildly around the room, licking his lips and watching Owney Madden's boys begin to close in on him. Somebody yelled "Lights!" and Mickey's Place was plunged into stygian blackness.

The Dutchman heard the cries and curses of struggling men. He skittered away from the main area of action. In the confusion he made for the rear exit. Whatever else Dutch Schultz may have been, he never looked for a fight when the odds came anywhere near being even.

He forced his sweating body through the narrow doorway. Immediately he smelled the sweet fragrance of exotic perfume. His hand reached out and touched soft, yielding flesh.

The girl screamed low in her throat. "Come on, Doll," Schultz reassured. "We're cutting out."

Before Francie Richards knew what was happening to her, she found herself being dragged into a huge Buick limousine. She huddled against the cool leather cushions, her tortured lungs straining for breath.

"That Coll," Schultz snickered. "Don't know what the hell I keep him around for."

Francie regarded the tall, thin figure who sat with his arm around her shoulder, patting her naked flesh. Right about then she wished she were back on Walton Avenue. She cursed whatever demons had possessed her to try to embark on a career as an entertainer. She'd tried to shut her eyes to the primitive orgies that went on nightly in Mickey's Place. Yet her whole being had been filled with disgust at what she'd been exposed to.

Up until tonight, it hadn't been so bad. The gangsters had come and gone, but they hadn't forced their attentions on her. There was something about Francie Richards' statuesque beauty which kept even the hoods from trying to muscle in on her against her will.

Francie had managed to delude herself that she was advancing her career. She'd learned to look the other way when the drunken battles had broken out among the liquored-up sluts from downtown. She could even stand the sight of two ape-like goons squaring off on the postage stamp dance floor. But the sight of a man having his face smashed in with the broken ends of a beer bottle was too much. She wept silently with the Dutchman.

Thus began one of the strangest relationships of New York's prohibition wars.

FRANCIE RICHARDS represented something different to the swaggering, camel hair-coated hoodlums who overran the city's streets. For some unexplained reason, the Dutchman decided to treat her differently from all the other dames he met and manhandled. Perhaps it was her goddess-like physical qualities or the low voice which throbbed so eloquently or the fact that even the Dutchman had never dreamed of being in the company of anything but rolled stocking flappers who'd do anything for anybody for the right price.

However, those who were at Mickey's Place that night and knew the inside workings of the mob report that the Dutchman drove Francie home. When she resisted his first pass, he backed off immediately. She allowed him to peck her lightly on the cheek and Dutch Schultz went no further.

Francie Richards probably became the first girl who didn't have to worry about the romantic intentions of her benefactor. He had other ideas for her. Things were coming to a climax in his district. Schultz wanted to expand. Already raking in close to a million dollars a year through his control of Bronx nightclubs and New Jersey breweries, Schultz was interested in branching out. He rankled at the idea that Lepke had sewed up the labor extortion rackets and Luciano had things pretty much his own way in narcotics and prostitution. It annoyed him to be thought of as about as important as a roach by the big men of the mob.

He needed a meeting ground with them – something of a no-man's land where the crime board of directors could come to negotiate without fear or favor.

With this in mind, Dutch contacted Francie and set her up in a plush Riverdale house. There the decor was beyond reproach, the food left nothing to be desired, and Francie's lilting voice hung over the whispered conniving of the various mob negotiations.

For all of her associations with the strong-arm yeggs, Francie never dropped the pose of being a fine lady. She would tolerate no loud or brutish behavior – and the gangsters respected her for it.

The Riverdale house became a symbol. Here the representatives of various underworld units could come without fear of being burned down on the spot. The sanctuary extended no further than the front door. While the Dutchman paid the freight, other mobsters were free to come and go as they pleased.

Schultz and Francie reached something of an understanding. She knew what he was, but didn't dwell on it. In return, the Dutchman let it be known that he would tolerate no hanky-panky with his hostess.

As time went on, the upstairs rooms of the house were used for the most secretive meetings of the mobs. Here came Owney Madden to try to work out a no-raiding agreement on Connecticut speakeasies. Here arrived Chicken Head Gurino and Buggsy Goldstein to receive their instructions of murder. Here sat soft-spoken Lepke as he plotted the murder of a recalcitrant labor leader,

Only Mad Dog Coll fought the self-imposed discipline of the mob. Those who knew him well said Coll had only one love in life. That was to cause as much pain among as many people as he could.

Coll – like his former boss – couldn't stand to be thought of as small-time. Being a hired torpedo would never be enough for him. He saw no reason why he couldn't personally take over the heavy Mack Bulldogs which rolled into the city groaning under their canvas topped weight of beer casks.

The punk even had the effrontery to grab off some of the Dutchman's trucks and repaint them.

On finding this out, the Dutchman called Coll to the Riverdale retreat. As Francie's singing lulled the guests below, Dutch turned on his former lieutenant.

"You lousy bastard creep," Dutch growled in his death-like voice. "Just three months ago I go to the well for 25 Gs to spring you on the Sheffield job. Can you imagine that. A guy on my payroll pulling a stupid stunt like becoming a heist artist and I spring him out of the goodness of my heart?"

Coll sat before his former boss, a mean sneer playing over his face. "So what?" he growled.

"So this, punk. I catch you messing around any more of my Macks and you've got a date at Andy's yard." (Dutch was referring to the junk yard where a number of his victims had been burned to crisps in the old wrecks which had become their coffins.)

The Dutchman warmed to his subject. For over a half an hour he lashed out at Coll, his invective cutting like a knife.

Finally the Dutchman waved imperiously, a signal that the interview was over. Coll slammed out of the room, his face burning. He'd get the hotshot bastard.

But Coll's hate was bigger than for Schultz alone. He wanted Madden and his associate "Big Frenchy" DeMange as well as the Dutchman. He'd declared war on the entire organization. Like a rabid dog he'd been cut loose from the pack. Now he was a total loner. It was kill or be killed. And in his mad brain there was no better way to declare war than to go after Francie, who'd become the focal point of the mob's more civilized approach.

ON CHRISTMAS Eve, Vinnie Coll caught up with Francie. Somehow he obtained entry to her private apartment in the Bronx and lay there waiting for her. When the girl arrived home towards dawn of Christmas Day, she found the maniacal killer standing in the middle of the floor, his .45 cocked and raised to a level between her firm, jutting breasts.

"Wh... what are you doing here?" Francie managed to whisper.

"I've got a Christmas present for the Dutchman," Coll sneered in his high-pitched voice.

Francie had learned how to keep her emotions under iron control. "Vinnie, if it's business between you two, I have nothing to do with it. Owney and all the other guys know that."

"I said you're going to be my Christmas present to the bastards," Coll repeated. His eyes held Francie's. She searched them desperately, hoping for some signs of mercy.

But there was no mercy in the cheap hood who had gunned down May Smith in cold blood only months before. There was no humanity in a guy who would blast a five-year-old child to death because he had gotten in the way of Coll's attempt at a vengeance killing.

Francie whimpered in fright as Coll stepped forward. The barrel of his .45 twisted cruelly in the soft flesh of her stomach.

"I've always wanted you," the Mad Dog snarled. "Now I'm going to take you – my way. I'm going to show the Dutch bastard he can't tell me what broads to touch and which ones to leave alone."

"No, Vinnie!" Francie pleaded. "I never did anything to you. Don't take it out on me. I'm just a singer. I don't know about hijacking or beer shipments. I don't know about anything."

"You know about being a broad, don't you?" Coll giggled. "You know about being a snotty broad who won't look at a guy. You won't be so high and mighty when I get done with you."

In a nightmare of pain, Francie felt the gunman stripping the clothes from her back. His attack was savage and depraved. When he'd vented his lust on her, Coll hurled her naked body into a filthy snowbank on Walton Avenue.

For weeks Francie hovered between life and death in a hospital room. Picked teams of headquarters detectives questioned her about the atrocious assault. Whether out of fear or the unwritten law of the underworld, Francie's lips remained tightly sealed under the heavy bandages which swathed her face.

But while she lay still and weak, the wheels were grinding. Coll had gone too far. He'd hurt the girl the mob had sworn to protect.

The Dutchman called a meeting in the Riverdale house. The most unlikely assortment of hoods gathered in the private room. Many had battled each other for years in the war to control the beer and whiskey trade. Their torpedoes had gunned down more than a hundred lesser lights in the blood-bath.

The air was charged with hate and mutual distrust until the Dutchman stood up and pounded the table. "Vinnie," he said in his quiet voice, "must go.

There was the sound of shuffling feet as the hoods inched closer to the table. By the time the meeting broke up a kitty of $25,000 had been underwritten to pay off three top bleeders.

On February 9th, Mad Dog Coll slid into a telephone booth in a drug store at 23rd Street and Eighth Avenue. As he slipped a nickel into the coin slot and dialed a number, the booth door slammed open. Vincent Coll stared down the barrel of a Thompson submachine-gun. He shrank back against the wall, seeking to hide his thin body from the fusillade of slugs. Coll's scream was cut off at its height. He died no braver than his victims.

Six months later Francie Richards walked out of the hospital on a cane. Her beauty had been permanently destroyed, despite the desperate efforts of the best plastic surgeons money could buy.

By now the mob was too immersed in its own troubles to waste time on the troubles of a mere slip of a girl. Francie disappeared into the big city, never to be heard from again. Her scars reflected the end of an era gone mad with blood lust.

I WAS A CALL-GIRL'S BOYFRIEND

Every girl in the den of iniquity was for sale – but what he wanted, money couldn't buy!

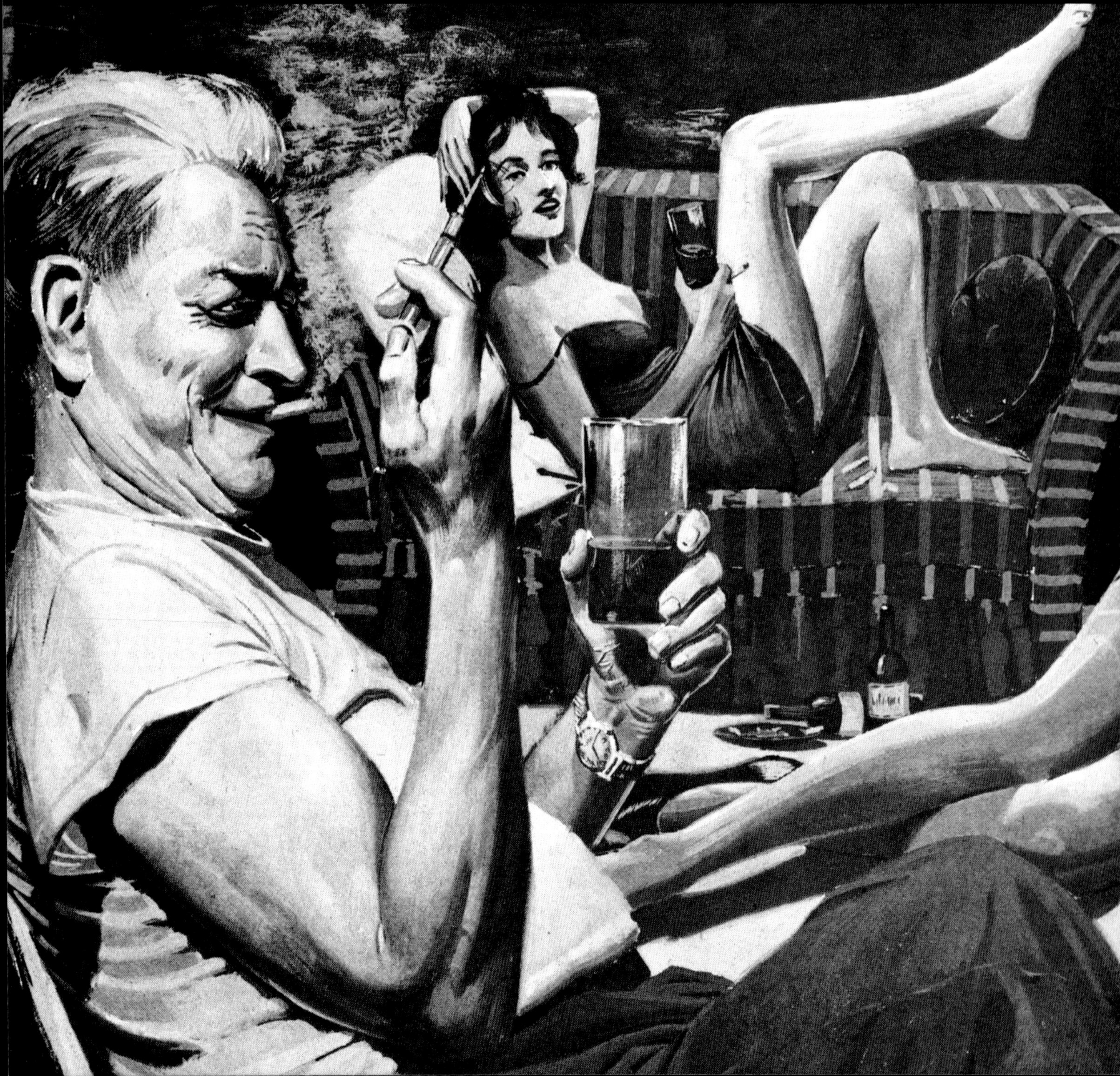

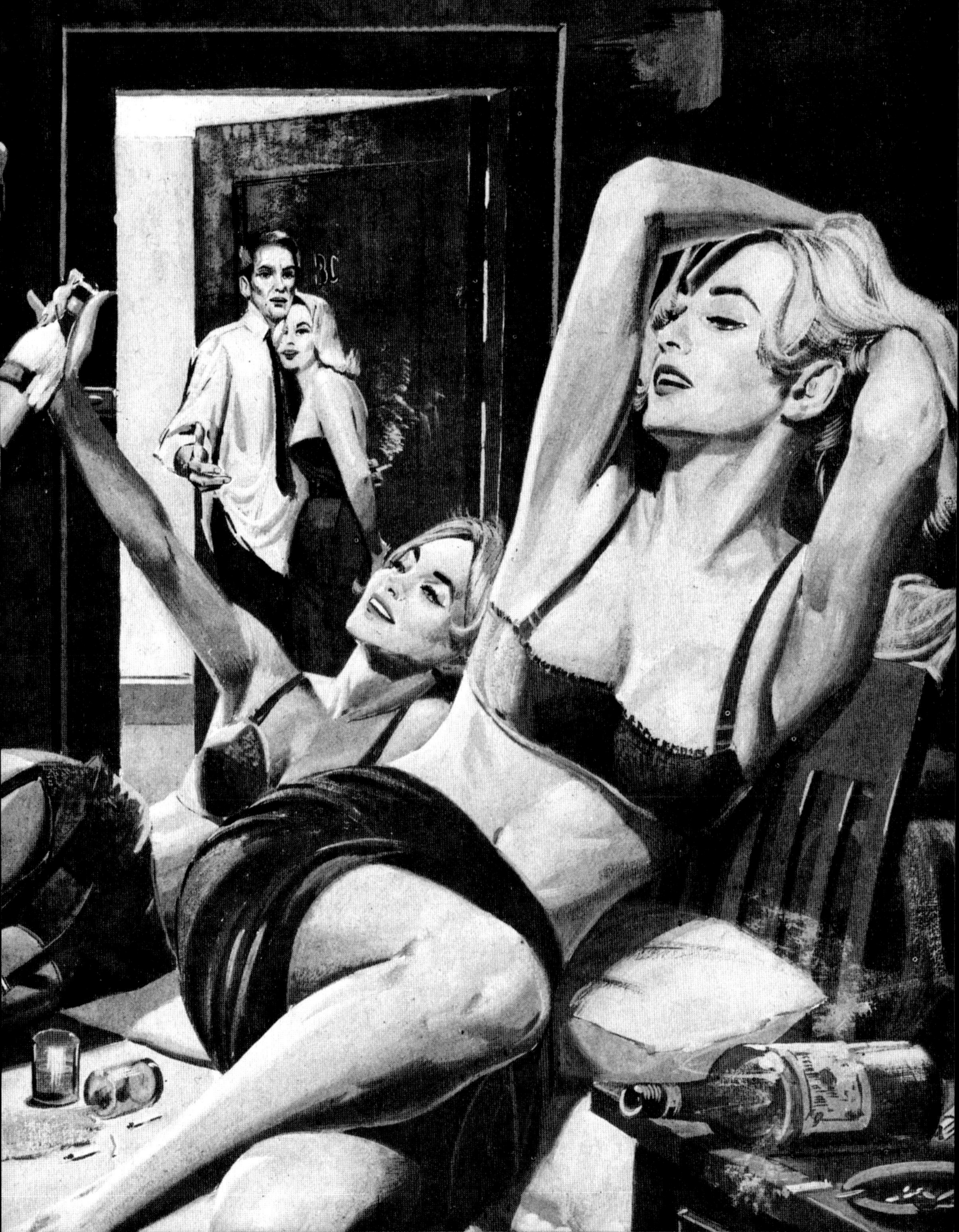

THIS MAY BE THE last thing I ever write if "they" find out where I've holed up. I've had to change my name, and my facial appearance, and taken on jobs as a migrant fruit-picker to earn a few bucks while keeping constantly on the move. After finishing my investigation for the organization that hired me, I couldn't risk staying in New York – or in the east, for that matter.

During my crime-busting career, I've explored many stinking hellholes in the world: Phenix City, Hong Kong, Singapore, Marseille, Marrakesh; but right in the heart of New York City is a strip of sidewalk more rotten and corrupt than any of them. This street is a concrete island of the damned. Once, its fashionable brownstones housed the elite, its curbs lined with limousines and elms. Today, it's an alley of decadence, with the smell of cheap gin, filthy language, garbage and tension stinging the air.

Pimps and streetwalkers loiter on the streets; drunks and coked-up heaps of humanity sprawl in doorways. Behind shuttered windows and drawn, dirty green shades, every kind of crime against decency is plotted or committed. The paint-peeling, rat-infested flats are nests for packs of muggers who roam dark streets, for drug addicts, for petty thieves and car rustlers, degenerates and sex deviates.

Who are they? Where did they come from? What influence have they on the welfare of the city? Some of them are the scum who floated to this street from many corners of the city. Others came up from the south and the islands in the Caribbean, subsisting on relief. Why didn't law enforcement and health agencies rout them? Because they were indifferent, or regarded the job as hopeless, or were paid off by the bosses who made a buck out of human misery.

My job? Get the names and facts, brutal and shocking as they are, with enough documentation for my organization to submit to the prosecutor to deliver to a Grand Jury.

ON THE humid night of August 14, 1961, I went into action. I allowed myself to be picked up. Her name was Lucy. In the glare of the shattered street light, I could see she was well above the average.

There was no romancing. It was strictly love on a C.O.D. basis. We went into a brownstone building reeking of strange smells, climbed three flights of rickety steps and entered a shabby room. After she inquired whether I wanted a shot to stimulate me, to which I said no, Lucy went into the bathroom while I undressed. She returned a few minutes later, threw off her kimono, and scrambled under the thin blanket.

I've made love to many women in my time and I've been loved in many strange ways, but Lucy was the most unusual. She was never still for a minute, tossing, writhing and caressing me all the time. She seemed happy and free of the fatigue that had weighed her down a short while ago. She was insatiable.

After a while, she dozed off, and it was then that I got the first jolt of my shock-proof career. She had given herself a "joy-pop" – a hypodermic of cocaine in the bathroom. By the collection of needle pricks and holes in her thigh, she was obviously an addict. Something turned in my stomach. I put the five-dollar bill on top of her purse on a chair, dressed and hurriedly left.

When I took the assignment, I'd been warned it called for a guy with strong guts. That first night with Lucy was all I needed to condition myself. I felt she might be my lead to cracking this case. Now that I knew she took "snow," the stale odors packing the hallway were sure to be drugs. The next night, I loaded the microfilm in my camera – which was disguised as a wrist watch – and went out to find Lucy.

It wasn't hard. She greeted me like an old pal. "You look like an okay guy," she said, linking her arm in mine. I'd gladly have broken it, but I hid my contempt and smiled. "How'd you like to see what plays behind the Beaded Curtain?"

This time, we went to a back room on the second floor. She gave three rapid raps followed by two slow ones. The door opened and she prodded me forward. The light was poor and smoke so thick, I couldn't see for a minute. Then I got my first unmistakable whiff of opium. We moved further into the room as my eyes became accustomed to the gloom. It was a bizarre, shocking orgy. Men and women lay on pillows on the floor with a few of the less inhibited making love, completely disregarding the presence of the others who were too busy with their own affairs.

In a corner, several girls and their customers dreamily sucked on the long stems of their opium pipes.

I didn't notice the books lying on the floor until Lucy pulled me down and flipped one open to reveal a cache of reefers. "This is our best-seller. Have one," she said, extending them to me.

I declined with a shake of my head. "I've got something better," I said in a whisper. "Let's go to your room where we can be alone."

I followed her up the stairs, hypnotically watching the lazy movements of her hips, the seams of her stockings on her firm legs vanishing under the hem of her dress. To her surprise, I pulled a wad of absorbent cotton from my pocket and separated it to reveal a hypo.

"Give me your arm," I said. "You never had a kick like this." I plunged the needle into her forearm, watching the syringe of mescaline and sodium pentothal (the "truth drug") vanish into her vein.

We sat down on the bed, waiting for the reaction to set in. It came fast enough. She began to complain of palpitations, then hot and cold feelings. She squirmed restlessly, then began to mutter incoherently. All at once, she began to kiss me wildly, crushing her lips over mine, not stopping until I pushed her aside. She fell back exhausted and began to murmur again. I lay my head on her shoulder to hear her better.

"Menotti... he started me on drugs... runs whole, rotten racket... tried to get away... warned me it wouldn't be lucky... Always been unlucky... now I got lucky... hands across the sea... Big Street, shake hands with sunny Italy."

I didn't get the drift at first, then all of a sudden I got the message, loud and clear. Menotti was tied in with an international syndicate run from a base abroad, and those foul smells permeating the hallways not only came from behind the so-called Beaded Curtain, but somewhere in this house, drugs were imported, cut and packed for distribution throughout this country. The keg of dynamite was right here – and Lucy was the fuse leading me to it!

Her arms snaked out, coiled sinuously around my shoulders. "I need you, lover... need you," she murmured. I pulled her close to me.

"Where is Menotti?" I hissed into her ear.

She kissed me, then whispered, "First floor... back... kiss me, *kiss me again...!*"

In my time, I'd grilled many people, but this was the weirdest. As soon as Lucy fell into a deep, and what seemed like a troubled sleep, I dressed, checked the film in my camera which I'd used a short while ago to "shoot" the orgy in progress, then slipped out. I had to get some real evidence on Menotti. That plan would take time to work out.

SINCE MY first meeting with Lucy, I'd noticed a change in her. She seemed paler, exhausted, more frail and depressed. Her appetite was diminishing to the point that she was starving herself. I sought her out the night of August 21st, not as a paying customer but as a benefactor. Believe me, I wasn't playing the part of the good samaritan. No, that instinct didn't motivate me. I'd have done as much for a stray dog.

I insisted on taking her to a bar and grill and filling her, much against her wishes, with a steak, salad and milk. She objected until I told her she'd lose all her appeal if she became a bag of skin and bones. That cinched it. Every night, for a week, I treated her to a solid meal.

Since the presence of a camera would arouse suspicions, I continued to use the miniature disguised as a wrist watch. This subterfuge gave me protection from prying eyes, enabling me to "shoot" the building used by Menotti as well as the sordid characters who came and left. I used regular micro-film during the day and an infra-red lens at night. After several days passed, I realized I hadn't seen Lucy. After all, I felt obligated for the lead she'd given me.

There was no response to my knock on her door. I tried again. This time, she answered. Her voice was thick and blurry. "Go 'way, whoever you are! Get outa here, you creep!"

And then I heard a hoarse male voice: "C'mon, baby, let's make it a real ball. Light up another one." From under the doorway came the unmistakable whiff of marihuana. I stamped away in disgust and anger.

But I knew I to see Lucy again. I prowled the neighborhood the next night and the night after that, and it was with immense relief that I found her at home one morning around eight.

"Make yourself at home, pal, while I get into something more comfortable," she said with a smile that ended in a scowl.

I don't know what was coming over me. Something kept driving me inexorably to her. She'd become like a whirlpool, sucking me down to the doom that awaited the both of us. But I found it impossible to stay away. The next night, I passed by her stoop just as she was coming out. I fell into step with her as she walked briskly towards Central Park West.

"Sorry, but I have a previous appointment," she said. "I can't tie myself down only with you. I gotta make more than you can give me. Menotti doesn't come cheap. Not once you've become hooked. I'll see you, mister."

"No," I said, grabbing her arm possessively.

She broke away. "Cut it out! Who do you think you are – my boy friend?"

"Don't go," I appealed. "I'll give you some money!"

"Are you kidding?" she sneered. "This is a Park Avenue job. This client sings only in C-notes."

She popped into a cab on the curb and whipped off. I signaled the taxi behind and told the driver to follow. We threaded through the park, then she entered the swank lobby. I watched the elevator indicator stop at the 15th floor. When it came down, I stepped inside and jabbed the button.

There were only two doors in the small, private foyer, and I spotted immediately the one she had used. Over the din of music rose her loud laugh. I went downstairs and paced the sidewalk. *Her boy friend?* she'd said. What kind of a crack was that to make? Out of pity, I'd brought her food and tried to help her. But why? Why? The question plagued me. Why was I worried about her? Why was I trying only to get her off the junk? Why was I trying to convince her to restrict her favors exclusively to me? Then the thought hit me with the impact of a steamroller – was I in love with her? Unknown to me, had I really thought of myself as her boy friend? The sudden sweat on my hands and face betrayed the chill that shot up my spine.

That soft body which had yielded to me, even with its punctures of dozens of hypo injections – I had to protect it. I had to get up there and get Lucy out! The elevator shot me up to the 15th floor. I was about to press the bell when I heard a shrill scream, followed by a swishing sound and a man's brutal laugh, then Lucy's cry again, full of pain and anguish.

"Not with the buckle, please!"

I jammed the bell, pounded the door in a frenzy. Nobody answered. Inside, it suddenly became quiet. I returned to the street to take up my vigil. A brassy, September sun was beginning to rise, sending splays of light among the spires and rooftops when I decided to give up the watch. Menotti! I could deal with him.

IT WAS easy to find his room. The odors became more pungent as I approached. I hadn't formulated any plan in getting my pictures. Everything was so vague, I had to play it by ear. The response to my knock was so fast, it seemed he was waiting for me. The door opened a few inches, and a fat, greasy face, sitting on folded jowls, poked out at me.

"Yeah?"

"Menotti?" He nodded curtly. "I just got in from Frisco," I went on. "I'm in the market for some 'tea.' One of your girls, Lucy, told me to contact you."

"I don't know no Lucy. I don't know what you're talking about," his gravelly voice shot back. He made a sudden effort to slam the door, but I balked it with a thrust of my foot.

"I've got a tall recommendation," I said. "It's a very lucky one, you understand – very lucky."

The key word turned the trick. He swung open the door and jerked his head, motioning me inside. The room was bare except for a table loaded with equipment to dilute the drugs and small paper packets.

While I talked with Menotti, I worked swiftly but

secretly with my camera. "I'll pick out my order and have a couple of my boys come around to pick it up," I said.

"You talk okay, but money talks louder," Menotti said.

"Sure, sure. You'll get the dough before I move anything. I wanted to see what you got and how much I could have. If I get a good deal here, I'll tell Lucy. I'll do all my business with you."

I caught the glint in Menotti's eye. I'd struck home. While I moved along examining the stuff on the shelves, I kept shooting my pictures while Menotti busied himself weighing "tea" on a set of scales.

"You know, I just thought of something," his voice grated behind me. "How come another guy from Frisco was here last week?"

Of all the cities I could've chosen–! I spun around, to look into the ugly barrel of a .32.

"Whatta you – a copper or something? I oughta blast you right now!" His voice was uglier than the gun.

I brought my knee up sharply, pile-driving him in the groin. A cry of pain erupted from his throat. As he dropped the .32, I hammered my fists into his pudgy belly. Something must've ripped in that bloated carcass as a blob of blood burst from his bulbous lips. He sank to the floor like a torpedoed freighter, the ribbon of blood coursing down his chin, beading his expensive white-on-white shirt. His hands groped wildly at his chest.

I wasn't aware that she was framed in the doorway until I heard her voice. "You shouldn't have come here! They'll kill you!" Lucy had arrived during the melee. Quickly, she closed and bolted the door.

"How'd you know I was here?" I asked.

"Too many questions from too nice a guy," she said. She made a move as if to kiss me but suddenly stopped, probably by memories of events that had occurred too recently on Park Avenue. Her hand flew involuntarily to her shoulder. It didn't quite cover the terrible, raw bruise inflicted by a belt buckle.

I seized her wrists and wrenched her towards me. "Lucy, it isn't too late. We can both get away. You'll have a new start, a new life. Nobody'll ever know. Come with me, right now!"

The words had spilled out of me in a frenzy. I realized I'd wanted to say them for a long time. A groan from Menotti brought us up sharply.

"Digitalis... nitroglycerin pills... help... help me..." His flabby hand wormed into his pocket, struggled free with a small tin. But his strength was ebbing; it was as far as he could go. He held out the tin to us, his eyes round with pain and pleading, as his free hand clawed feebly at his chest.

"I owe the rat something for what he did to me," Lucy snapped. Her foot lashed out, kicking the tin from his trembling hand, sending the capsules scattering across the floor. Menotti moaned, gasped and lay still, a lifeless hulk.

Feet pounded down the hallway, paused outside the door. "Hey, boss, you inside?" a voice asked. Lucy motioned me to be quiet. The doorknob turned and held, then we heard a whispered conversation. *Thud!* Brawny shoulders slammed against the door, once, twice. I grabbed Lucy.

"The window! Let's get out of here or we're dead pigeons!" I shouted. I ran to the window, unbolted it and whipped it open. I turned to wave Lucy on, but she calmly stooped and recovered Menotti's .32. She motioned to me to get out on the fire escape as she retreated.

"Go ahead. I'll cover you," she said in a hard voice.

No sooner did I step out than the window slammed down behind me. Lucy had done it to stay behind to protect me and to get her own sweet revenge. I pounded on the glass pane, but she paid no attention. The door splintered and fell in a hundred pieces as five mugs swarmed into the room. Five shots punctuated the oaths that sprang from their throats. As the smoke cleared, five bodies lay sprawling grotesquely in a sea of blood.

Not too far off, I heard the shrill siren of a police car growing louder as it sped towards us. Lucy waved a hand in farewell to me, then moved quickly towards the open doorway. I could not let her get away to resume that horrible life. She needed help desperately if she was to be restored to health in mind and body. No, I daren't let her escape.

I pulled out my pistol, aimed carefully and triggered it. The bullet that smashed through the window, spider-webbing the pane, was a bull's-eye. Lucy clutched her right arm, staggered, and went down. I'd fired a one-inch hollow needle containing a concentrated dose of nicotine I'd made long ago. As soon as the syringe struck her, she was immobilized for 10 minutes, making her capture easy. The last time I saw her, she was staring up at me in shocked disbelief. She didn't know then that I had saved her life... but she must realize it now, wherever she is.

I couldn't afford risking the time to develop my tell-tale evidence. One of Menotti's mugs survived the shooting, and his description of me must have fanned out like a brush fire to the syndicate. I started to run, mailing the undeveloped film to my organization when I hit Pittsburgh, and I've been running ever since, to keep away from the murderous tentacles of the criminal octopus threatening this country. But I'm hoping that one day fairly soon the hellholes of all the "Big Streets" will be exterminated, and I'll be able to come back, back to Lucy, if I can find her – back to claim my rights as her boyfriend.

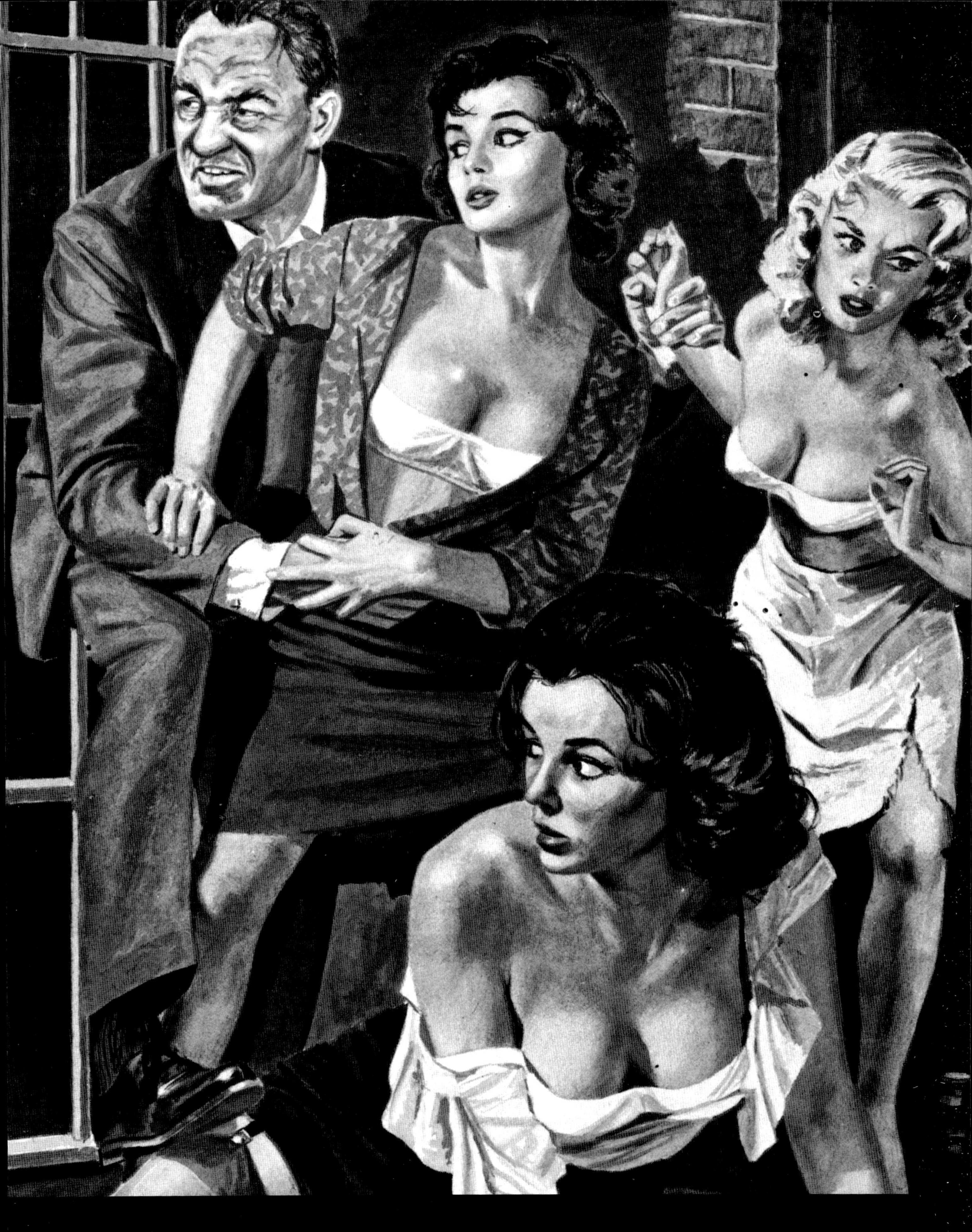

"HARLOW KAISER'S 6-YEAR RAMPAGE OF SEDUCTION"; detail from interior art, **MAN'S DARING**, 08/62.

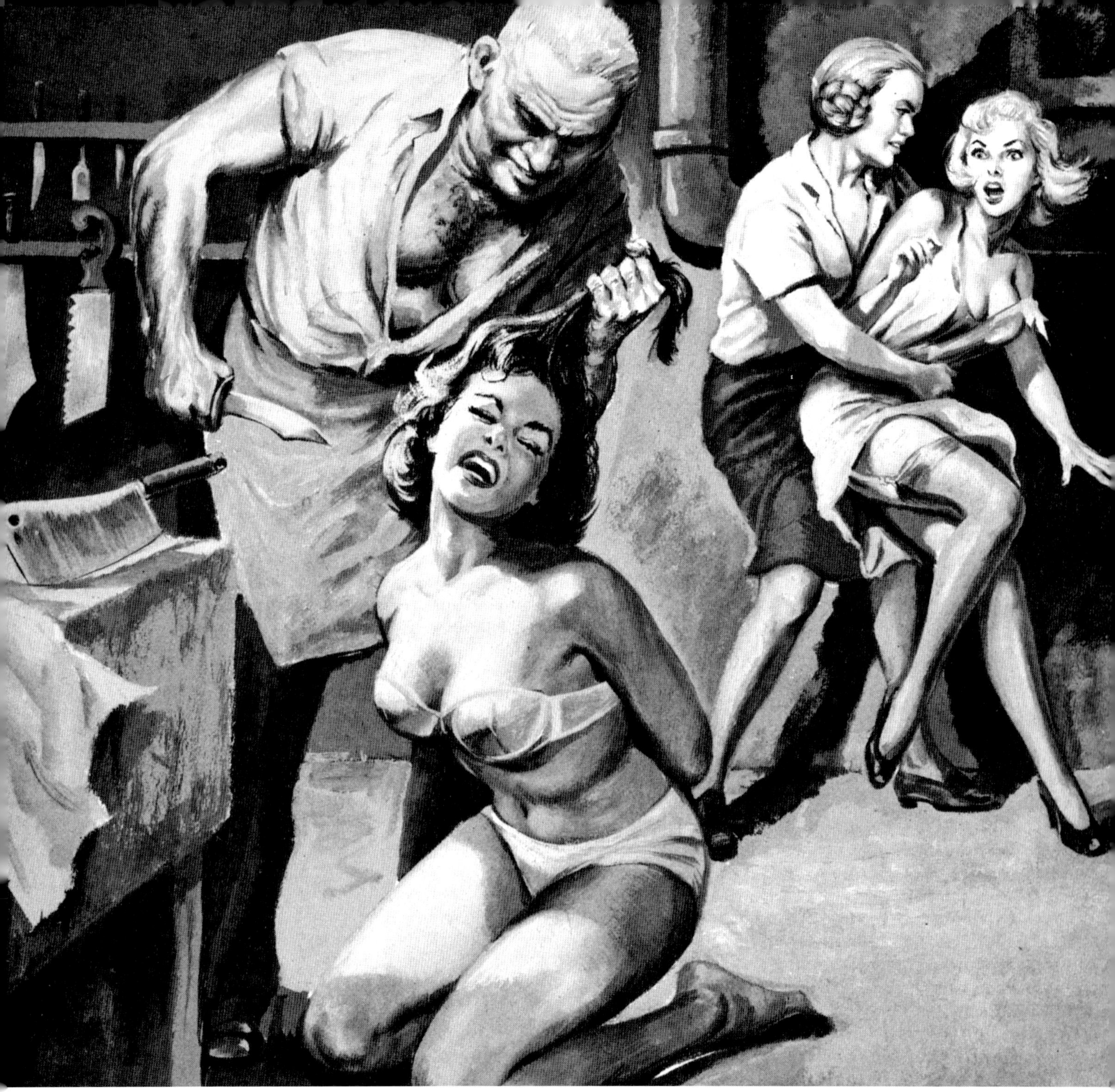

THE CANNIBAL BUTCHER OF HANOVER

The battles raging in the city were nothing compared to the bloody carnage beneath the ground.

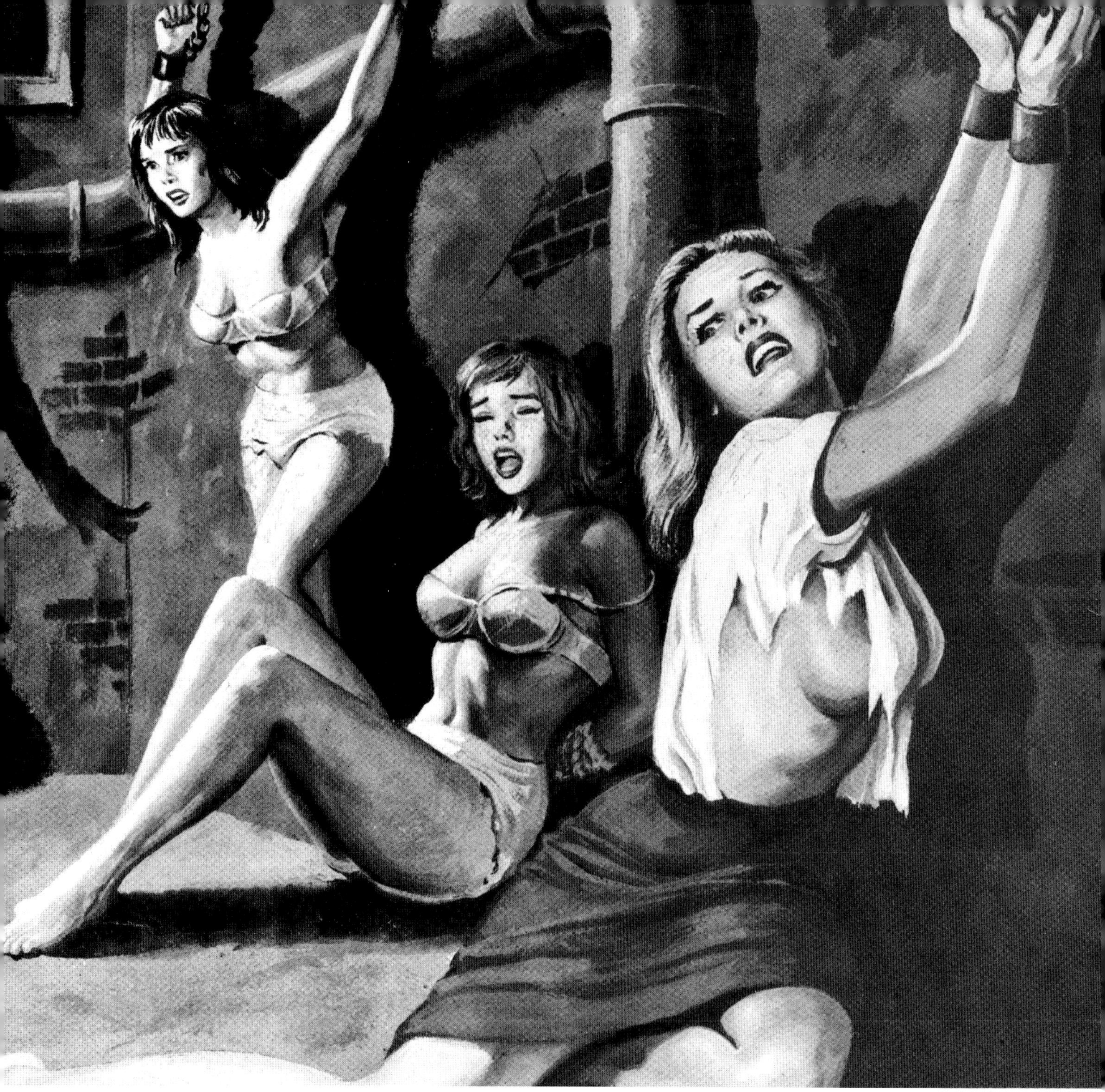

IT IS WITH GOOD – and ghastly – reason that Europeans still persist in calling Hanover, a bustling West German metropolis in Lower Saxony, the "City of Cannibals".

Even today, there are hundreds – or more probably thousands – of men and women among Hanover's half-million residents who have known what it is to gorge themselves on human meat. Countless solid Hanoverian Burghers and their *fraus* can remember a half-decade during which they often wolfed down *sauerbrauten* and *schnitzels* – only to learn later that they had eaten human flesh!

Incredible as it may sound, savage, cold-blooded murders – possibly more than 400 in all – provided the human carcasses from which such loathsome meat for Hanoverian tables was cut!

By any standards, the sensational classic crime cases should have become the most notorious and highly-publicized horror-story of the 20th century. That it didn't is due to the frantic – and effective – measures which were taken to hush up the macabre scandals that erupted when the monster responsible for the mass-slaughters was finally brought to justice.

Neither Hanover's authorities nor its citizens dared allow the full truth to become known. Had they done so, they would have branded themselves publicly and forever as cannibals, as man-eaters in the most literal sense of the term. Investigator's reports were carefully expunged, trial-testimony censored and "directed." The ensuing trial itself was elaborately stage-managed and all records and data pertaining to the monstrous crimes were meticulously blue-pencilled.

Hence, it is necessary to dig deep and far to obtain all the fulsome details in the bizarre, shocking story...

THE GRISLY chronicle begins on a late-summer morning in 1918, when a fat, pasty-faced man wearing a shoddy, ill-cut suit walked into the Hanover *Kriminalpolizei* headquarters.

"My name is Fritz Haarmann," he announced, cringing before the beefy detective seated at the nearest desk. "I've just been released from prison, and I've come to report."

The police had Haarmann's dossier ready. It had been taken from the files two days earlier, when the Nieder Sachsen penitentiary notified Hanover authorities that Haarmann's five-year-sentence was up and that he was being released.

Fritz Haarmann's dismal, unsavory life-history was condensed into a one-page resumé clipped to the dossier-cover. Born in 1879, Fritz developed androgynous tendencies early in life, dressing in his sister's clothes and often playing that he was a girl. At 16, he enlisted in the German Army – but was soon discharged on medical grounds. Returning home, he was constantly in trouble – for thievery and for molesting small children. He spent some time in a mental institution.

"Completely devoid of morals," was one doctor's judgment of Fritz.

At 22, Haarmann again enlisted in the German Army – and again, after two years or so, was dishonorably discharged. He spent the next eleven years at various jobs – and in various jails. In 1913, he was arrested for stealing and embezzling money from the firm for which he worked. He was sentenced to five years in the penitentiary. It was this sentence he had just completed when he reported at the Hanover *Kriminalpolizei* station.

"What do you intend doing now?" the detective demanded.

"Why, look for work, of course," was Haarmann's reply.

"You'll find precious little work," the officer said coldly. "You were better off in prison – where at least you were fed regularly."

Kaiser Wilhelm's German Empire was crumbling. The war was almost over. Germany's people were on the verge of starvation. There were no jobs; even munitions factories were closing down because they lacked raw materials.

"I'll find something," Haarmann said. "I won't starve."

"I wish you luck," the detective grunted drily. "Here's your identification card. Now get out!"

He tossed the card to Haarmann, who grabbed it and made a hasty exit. Three days later, he was back at the *Kriminalpolizei* station – a new man. He'd discovered there was money to be made on the burgeoning black market – and had already pulled off a few successful deals.

"I want to see the *kommandant* of detectives," he announced.

He'd decided to make another deal with police – to obtain protection for his black market activities in return for information. He would, in short, act as a stool-pigeon for the police.

"I know five men who are distributing propaganda tracts attacking the government," he told the detective bureau chief. "I'll give you their names..."

IN THAT chaotic era, German police were more concerned about revolt and civil unrest than they were about crime. Already faced with virtual anarchy, fearing what would happen when the defeated troops returned from the Front, the *polizei* were glad to make deals with informers. Fritz Haarmann became an "official" spy and stoolie for the Hanover *Kriminalpolizei*. In return for his services, the authorities agreed to turn a blind eye on his black market operations.

"I shall start a black-market meat business," he told the police.

"Very well," he was assured. "You won't be bothered – as long as you continue to furnish us with information."

"Don't forget to bring around some meat once in a while," a detective winked to Haarmann. "We can all use some..."

All food was scarce in 1918 Germany – but the scarcest of all was meat in any form. In Hanover, as in other German cities, scores of illicit butcher shops had sprung up. Racketeering "butchers" used backyards and cellars for abattoirs; they slaughtered horses, mules, even domestic animals, selling the flesh for astronomical prices to eager buyers.

Fritz Haarmann had hatched a hellish scheme. Not content with the profits that could be made by slaughtering, say, an ancient drayhorse, he wanted to make large sums – fast. His degenerate, evil brain had devised what he considered a "perfect" method by which he could establish himself in a lucrative business and, at the same time, gratify his lusts.

In early October, he picked up 18-year-old Fredericka Rothe, enticed the girl to his slum-district flat and, after giving her food, cigarettes and liquor, he made love to her. Then, he calmly strangled the girl.

Draining the girl's blood into a bucket, Haarmann disjointed the corpse and neatly boned the remains. He carried the bones out in a gunny-sack and threw them into the river Leine not far from where he lived. Then, Haarmann packaged the human flesh, putting a kilogram or so into each parcel – and sold it as "pork" on the black market!

He'd made a mistake, however. The dead girl had parents – and they instituted a search for their daughter. The trail led to Fritz Haarmann, but the police made only a haphazard investigation. They were, however, forced to arrest him. When they went to Fritz's apartment, they found him alone with a 15-year-old girl. The cops might have closed their eyes, but there were civilian witnesses – and Haarmann was sent to prison for eight months on a morals charge.

When he was released from prison, World War I had been over for seven months. Economic conditions were far worse than they had been before. Haarmann returned to the *Kriminalpolizei* station.

"Does our agreement still hold?" he asked the police.

"Yes, we can use any information you bring us. But be a bit more careful about your sex-life," the detectives said.

Haarmann found new lodgings, blandly informing the landlady that he was a black-market meat dealer.

"I'll have visitors at all hours," he told her. "I'll be

using the rooms as a butcher shop."

The landlady gladly rented the rooms, even lowering the rent on Haarmann's promise that he'd let her have a little meat for her own use every now and then.

The monster selected his next victim with great care. He found a 16-year-old boy near the main railroad station. The youngster was a war orphan, homeless and hungry. Fritz brought him home – and killed him.

Long before dawn, Haarmann was at work with knives, saws and cleavers. Bones, skull, all parts that could be identified as being human were wrapped in gunny sacks and dumped into the River Leine. The flayed flesh was hacked up, wrapped and sold as "fresh pork" on the Hanover black market.

With the money he made, Haarmann went on a spree in the nightclubs of Hanover. The pattern was established. The monster hunted his victims in the hobo jungles and among the penniless youths who hung about the freight yards and railroad stations. He enticed them to his flat, killed them, dismembered their bodies and sold their meat as "pork."

There is no way to determine accurately how many murders he committed in the first period of his ghastly operations. The best estimates place the number of his killings at about one every week or ten days.

THEN, HAARMANN fell in love – as only a criminal mind *can* fall in love. The object of his affections was surly, sneering Hilda Grans, at 16 already a hardened gutter-rat. In the sick frenzy of their epicene eroticism, Haarmann confided in Hilda, telling her the hideous truth about his butcher's trade.

Hilda eagerly volunteered to be the enticer, the finger-woman. She combed the hobo-camps and skid-row areas, searching for likely – and safe – prospects. When Hilda selected a victim, she took the youth – usually an orphan or runaway – to the apartment she now shared with Haarmann.

"My friend will be home soon," Hilda would tell the pitiful dupe. "Help yourself to schnapps and cigarettes."

Haarmann would come home sometime during the night. By then, the victim was usually asleep. The rest was routine murder and butchery.

Not even the officers at the *Kriminalpolizei* ever wondered about the roasts, steaks and cutlets that Haarmann brought or sent them. The explanation is simple. Not one in ten million people in so-called "civilized" countries knows the taste of human meat – which does taste somewhat like pork. In appearance, when raw, it looks no different than animal meat. Then, the timeless taboo against cannibalism is so deeply engrained in most human beings that it creates a mental block against conscious consideration of the subject. No one could possibly imagine that he had been given human flesh, much less had eaten it.

As for the police, they trusted Haarmann. He was a "very useful man – a jewel among informers."

By the beginning of 1922, Fritz Haarmann was well established in Hanover. His business flourished. The great German inflation was continuing unchecked. Prices on most commonplace items were figured in bushel-baskets of marks. Crime and vice were rampant. An entire nation was losing its anchors, its last shreds of morality.

Official records show that 367 males between 13 and 18 were reported to have "disappeared" in Hanover in 1922. No one bothered investigating. No one really cared. It is a moot question how many among these "missing" boys and youths were killed by Fritz Haarmann and Hilda Grans. Certainly, not all of them were butchered by the diabolic pair. But how many were – 50?...100? More?

No one knows. No one will ever know. All that is known is that in 1922, Fritz Haarmann appeared more prosperous than ever before.

There were more disappearances, but by 1923 the police hardly took the trouble to keep count. All Germany was in turmoil. Starving, jobless people wandered aimlessly from city to city seeking work or food. It would have been impossible to check all the reports of disappearances.

It was toward the close of 1923 that the first faint suspicions were voiced about Haarmann. Police received some anonymous tips that their favorite stool-pigeon was engaged in criminal activities far more terrible than mere black-marketing. The cops ignored the tips.

Then, on three occasions in 1923 and early 1924, relatives of youths who had vanished made their own independent investigations. They traced the missing boys and learned that in each instance they had been last seen with either Haarmann or Hilda. The relatives went to the police, who made cursory investigations.

Invariably, they found Haarmann at home and in a blood-splattered butcher's apron. There were always large quantities of meat on shelves and drainboards in the apartment.

"We've come to ask you some questions, Fritz," the cops would begin.

"I'm happy to help in any way I can," Haarmann would pipe.

No. He didn't know the missing boy's whereabouts. Did he ever see him in the past? Oh, possibly – perhaps even probably.

"I sometimes check with these wandering boys for information, and occasionally hire them as delivery boys..."

Haarmann's stories were pat, logical, believable.

Cannibalism? The thought never – NEVER – entered anyone's mind. It couldn't. The mental block was there. The curtain rolled down the moment detectives saw the fresh meat, still oozing blood onto the drainboards. The very sight of the meat, of Haarmann standing near his chopping table, calmly answering questions, was enough to bring the curtain down. The conscious mind would reject any such notion. The casual openness of Fritz Haarmann's actions would cause – would force – rejection.

And so, after each interview with Haarmann, the detectives would grin and even apologize for bothering him. They would start for the door – and stop when Fritz called after them.

"Wait a minute. I'll just cut off a few chops for each of you to take home,,,"

IN THE spring of 1924, Lower Saxony, Saxony and Westphalia experienced an unseasonal and unusual drought. Streams dried up and the water-levels dropped alarmingly in lakes and rivers.

Among the rivers affected was the Leine – which cuts through the center of Hanover. Week after week, the drought continued – and the Leine, a sluggish stream at best, dropped lower and lower. On May 16, 1924, the Leine dropped so far that much of its banks were exposed. Embedded in the ooze not far from the city's center, some children found a human skull. The next day, another skull was found, and, two weeks later, two additional human skulls were discovered.

At first, these discoveries caused no great excitement. Hanover is an ancient city. Authorities reasoned the skulls could have been in the river since Medieval times. Then, in the days that followed, more grisly trophies were recovered – more skulls, and arm and leg bones. These latter had been chopped or sawn through. Laboratory examinations proved the bones and skulls to be those of boys and very young men – and that they had been in the river for only months, a year or two at the most.

Now, at long last, all the pieces to the puzzle that had lain in plain sight before the police for nearly five years began to fit into a pattern. The missing youths, the bones and skulls, the anonymous tips, the strange coincidences that whenever a boy was missing and traced, his trail always led to Fritz Haarmann or Hilda Grans...

But even then, the *Kriminalpolizei* refused to believe the evidence. "Why would Haarmann kill?" they wondered. "What would be his motive?" The reason, the motive, were too revolting for them to permit themselves to see.

But whispers began to make the rounds – and Hanover newspapers began to exert pressure on the police. Haarmann was finally arrested. For the first time, detectives searched his lodgings without his being present. They found large quantities of clothing and personal items that had belonged to youths who had been listed as "missing." Now the police were face-to-face with the greatest of all horrors. Now they, too, knew – but even then they did not dare *admit* that they knew.

The police were not the only ones involved and affected. Ordinary housewives, mothers of families, businessmen, poor men and rich men, restaurant owners. All had patronized the clever Herr Haarmann – who always seemed to have fresh meat to sell.

Even magistrates and civic leaders, wealthy industrialists and members of the City Council...

Hilda Grans was also arrested. She and Haarmann both broke down under questioning. They admitted everything. Horrified, the police withheld the news from the public, but some information leaked. Hysteria bordering on madness swept the city as thousands learned that they had probably gorged themselves on human meat over the years!

There were eighteen suicides in a single 12-hour period; innumerable mental breakdowns occurred. A woman went mad and disembowelled her entire family and herself. Another killed her five children. Another...

The authorities realized that something had to be done – and quickly, before all Hanover was engulfed by horror-and-guilt hysteria. A hurried conference was called.

"All mentions of cannibalism must be eliminated from this case!" the Burgomeister declared. "For the sake of our citizen's sanity, we must minimize the entire affair – but Haarmann must die!"

HAARMANN AND Hilda Grans were brought to trial in November, 1924. In many ways, the trial was a travesty. Only picked German reporters – journalists who were "reliable" – were allowed to cover the trial.

Haarmann was charged with having committed only 26 murders. This was the figure set by the Public Prosecutor because it tallied with the number of victims who could be identified from the clothes and personal effects found in Haarmann's rooms. The prosecution maintained that Haarmann and Hilda had killed only to obtain these effects – that their motive was profit, and no mention was ever made of cannibalism.

Yes. The people of Hanover believed this – because they wanted to believe it. They *had* to believe it – or live forever with their horror and guilt. It was Orwellian double-think – 1984 in 1924. Hanover grasped at the double-think and the double-talk in desperation.

Haarmann was quoted as saying that, while he had committed the murders, he had sold only pork – real pork. The police trotted out a peasant who said that he had supplied Haarmann with the pork.

That's all he was allowed to say – and then he was bundled off. A French reporter traced down the peasant and learned that the man had never owned either land or pigs, that he was a tenant-farmer who had been paid the equivalent of $50 to tell his story – which the police had taught him verbatim!

Haarmann openly – even boastfully – admitted 24 of the 26 murders, and then wanted to admit that he had committed "about 400" others and to talk about his "butcher business" in human meat. Whenever he tried to speak, he was silenced by courtroom attaches.

Both Fritz Haarmann and Hilda Grans were found guilty. Haarmann was sentenced to death by beheading, a Medieval custom that prevailed in Germany until the end of World War II. Hilda Grans was sentenced – unaccountably – to life imprisonment rather than death.

Haarmann, the monster of Hanover, was executed in January, 1925. His fat body had to be pumped full of drugs before he could be dragged, shrieking for mercy, from his cell to the headsman's block.

"I'm not the only guilty one!" he screamed. "There were others who knew I was selling human flesh. There were police who..."

"Kill him – fast!" the warden barked to the headsman.

Haarmann's balding head was shoved down onto the block. The great axe flashed up – then down.

For reasons never explained, Hilda Grans' sentence was later reduced to 25 years in prison. She did not even serve this. After the Nazis came to power in Germany, she was released and eventually became a Nazi guard in a concentration camp.

But Hanover could – and did – close its books on the Haarmann case immediately after the ogre was executed. Hanover's citizens wanted to forget, and pretend that none of it had really happened.

"It was pork," they told themselves.

Even so, it was a long, long time before many Hanoverians could bring themselves to eat meat of any kind again.

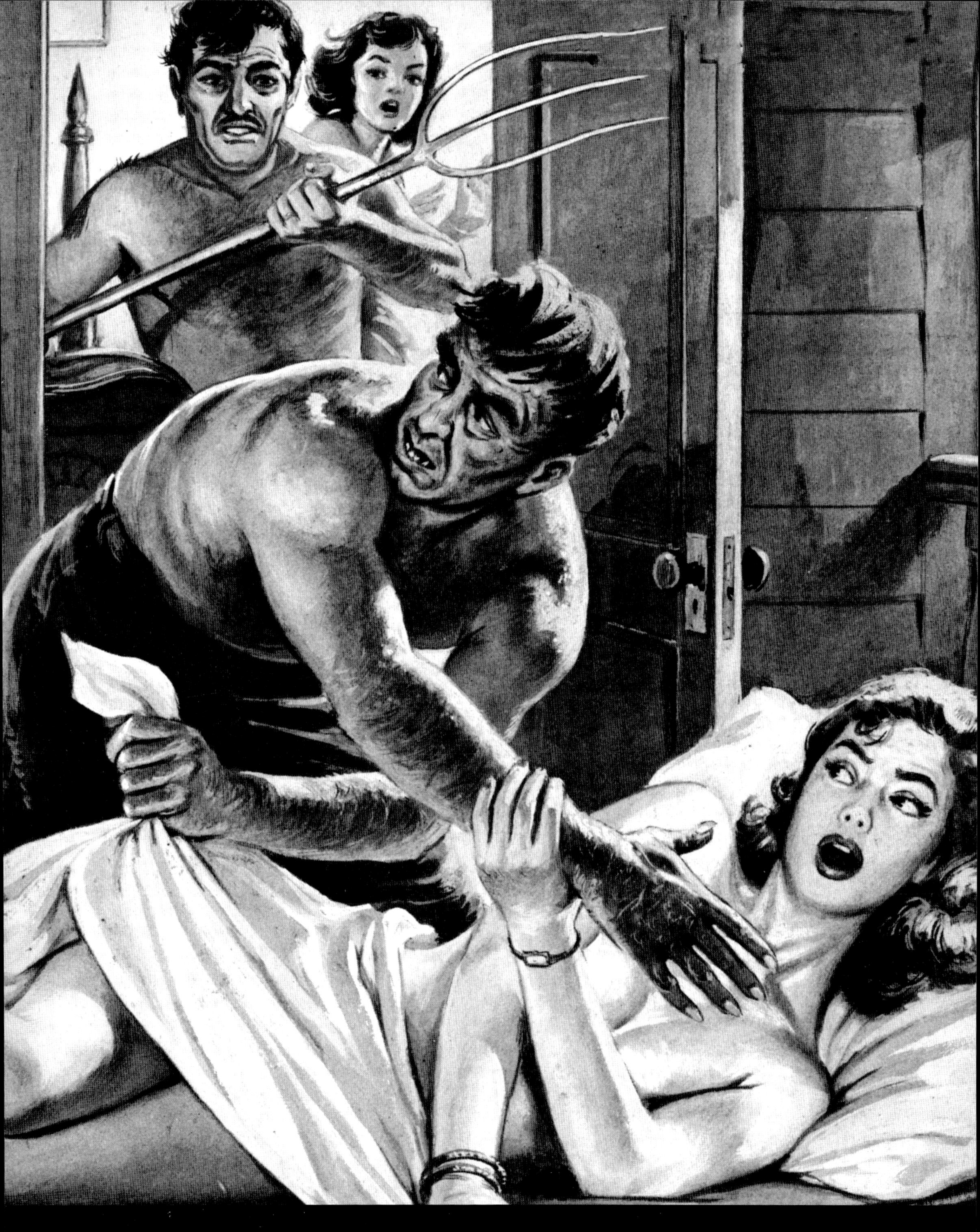

"THE LUST-CRAZED MAN WHO COULDN'T TALK!"; detail from interior art, **MAN'S ACTION**, 11/62.
Art uncredited; attributed to Victor Olson.

COOL BROADS, HOT RODS!

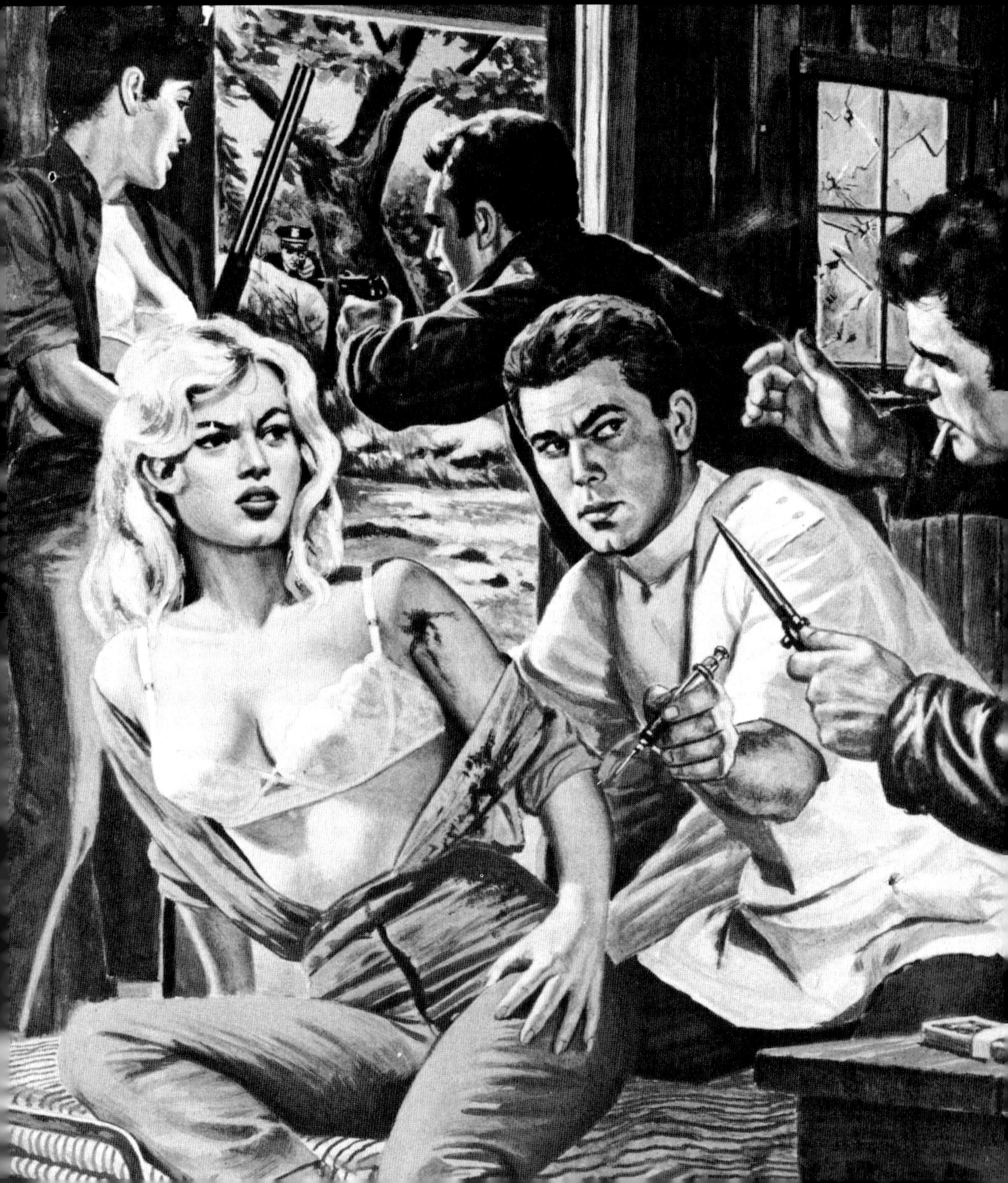

Speed is the stimulant that sends these kick-itchy delinquents into an erotic tailspin!

THE NEWSPAPER HEADLINE READ: *"Two teenagers shot after kidnapping doctor".*

The story that followed was a nightmare of speeding cars, gunfire, dope and raw sex.

"Pursued by the law for committing vehicular homicide, two boys and two girls, all in their teens, broke through a police barricade after causing the hit-run death of a pedestrian. State police, at a roadblock, fired at the fast-moving car and wounded Miss—, 16. Two hours later one of the boys kidnapped Dr.— from his office and drove him to an abandoned shack where he treated the wounded girl. When the police closed in the teenagers fired upon them and the police were forced to shoot back. Tear gas was used and the gang surrendered after both of the boys were slightly wounded. The car was found to contain narcotics, pornographic pictures and a supply of ammunition."

This is an example of what can be the result of the shocking highway "games" now becoming the latest hell-raising fad among daredevil teenage drivers across the country. The police chief of a Midwestern town put it succinctly when he spoke before a speeding control commission recently.

"We used to call teenagers with souped-up cars 'hot-rodders'," he told the listening men. "Well – we've got a new breed on our hands. These latest highway maniacs are more like Hell-rodders!"

Hot-rodding, while never a harmless sport by any means, is a far cry from the frequently suicidal antics of the Hell-rodders. Hot-rod clubs all over the country stress safety and highway courtesy, and members confine their speed trials to specific and designated places, such as unused airstrips or especially-built tracks.

In many areas, community service clubs back the hot-rod clubs, and contests for driving techniques are held with the town's blessing. The mechanically-minded youngsters take great pride in their rebuilt, or "souped-up" automobiles, and their activities are constructive and beneficial.

THE HELL-RODDERS are a far cry from the accepted hot-rodder. In actual fact, they are only a cut or two above the out-and-out juvenile delinquent. They may, or may not, carry a switchblade or a gun – but they drive a car, which can be even more deadly.

They are by no means the children of underprivileged or poverty-ridden families. In fact, in the greater percentage of cases, exactly the opposite is true. Many of the Hell-rodders come from highly affluent homes. Spoiled by over-indulgent parents and not given basic responsibilities, the bored, jaded teenagers turn to speed and violence and sex for their thrills.

Completely undisciplined and out of parental control, they gang up together with other equally spoiled adolescents of their age group. Their ego and confidence boosted by membership in a group, they attempt to outdo each other in daring, death-defying – and sometimes death-dealing – stunts on the highway.

"They endanger or destroy many lives other than their own," points out Dr. Stephen Macdonald, the California psychoanalyst who has specialized in the problems prevalent during the adolescent years. "They are, of course, a deadly menace to innocent drivers or pedestrians. They are also destroying their own morals and values – and those of any other teenager who joins the group. The sexual motivation and orientation of the whole 'Hell-rodder' problem is an explosively dangerous one."

The death-wish syndrome is glaringly apparent in every one of their highway "games." The frequently heard cry of "Chicken," sometimes also called "Swerve," demonstrates this with sickening clarity.

"Chicken' is usually played by two drivers at a time. There are variations. Sometimes only the driver is allowed to be in the car; at others, five or six passengers clamber in to share the "thrill." In another variation, four to six cars are involved – but the details depend on the particular Hell-rodding group's "rules" and customs.

The game itself is as simple as it is dangerous. Two cars are parked facing each other at a pre-set distance. At a signal, they race at top speed straight at each other. The driver who "chickens out" first – that is, who swerves out of the oncoming car's path to avoid a head-on crash – loses the game.

The winner can then be challenged by other drivers in the group. The pointless, deadly dangerous game goes on until all the drivers have had a chance to prove that they are not "chicken."

A cursory glance at newspaper back files will show that hundreds of teenagers have been killed "playing" this "game" during the past several years.

Another favorite automobile "sport" for the Hell-rodders is "Choo-Choo," which immediately involves people who are unaware that they are participating – namely, the drivers and occupants of a train about to pass a level-crossing.

Three teenagers – two boys and a girl – were killed outright early this year when their car failed to clear the level-crossing in time. The only survivor was a 16-year-old girl. It was she was explained the rules and regulations of "Choo-Choo" to the police who questioned her – after she had recovered sufficiently from her injuries to be able to talk to them.

"I don't know what went wrong," she told them. "We'd played the game so many times before. Maybe Jimmy didn't rev enough before slipping in the clutch – I don't know."

She went on to tell the police that she was one of the "founding members" of her group. "Choo-Choo" was by far their favorite driving pastime. She shrugged when asked about "Chicken."

"That's for sissies!" she grimaced. The fact that three of her former friends were dead did not seem to have changed her warped, thrill-seeking outlook on life.

The whole gang had gathered a short distance away from the level-crossing. They waited until the train was in sight. Then "Jimmy," the driver of the death car, started his engine.

"We knew we had to take off the moment the engine got even with the last row of houses," the young survivor went on. "Jimmy did – and I figured this time would be like all the other times. We'd scream down the road and over the rails – just before the train made it. It's the greatest kick in the world. But I guess something went wrong..."

Questioned further, the girl revealed that a "Choo-Choo" game was always followed by a "real wild party" in a deserted warehouse the gang members referred to as their "club room." Her description of the sexual promiscuity and partner-swapping that occurred at every post-game party only served to emphasize once again the ineradicable link between the Hell-rodders' highway habits and their sexual immorality.

The sixteen-year-old survivor was put under psychiatric care after her multiple physical injuries had healed. The psychiatrist attending her has told her parents that it will be months – perhaps years – before their daughter is able to readjust her whole way of thinking along normal patterns.

"To the emotionally immature, speed is a strong sexual stimulant," explains the doctor. "All the teenagers involved in the Hell-rodders' gangs are emotionally insecure, confused youngsters. Many come from broken homes. Not given the proper guidance by their parents, they seek other people to admire. A boy who is a reckless daredevil suddenly becomes a 'brave' person – and thus someone to admire."

Their immaturity prevents them from seeing the difference between genuine courage and futile, useless, "show-off" tactics.

Another Hell-rodder driving "test" is known variously as "Blackout," "Flying Blind" or "Aces." The name changes according to the area of the country – but the Hell-rodders play at it with the same rules, whether they live in Miami, Montana or Maine. All they need is a stretch of highway and a dark night.

The group chooses the road distance and area that is to be covered. The automobiles start up in what is, basically, a night race – but with doused headlights. The souped-up jalopies roar down the highway, completely blacked out. The winner is literally a "winner-take-all." He has his pick of the gang's girls for the post-race sex-party.

"Spinning" – taking a designated curve at increasingly higher speeds – is yet another of their perilous stunts. Seven teenagers – all boys – ranging in age from fifteen to nineteen, were arrested for "Spinning" after one of the five cars involved spun out on the curve, caromed off the embankment and landed, upside down, in the front yard of the local doctor's house. No one was killed – but the driver and the front seat occupant were badly injured.

The incident made headlines in the New England state where it occurred, not only because of the accident itself but because of the boys' attitudes. Defiant and surly, they seemed incapable of understanding why their parents, the police and all other adults around them were so concerned.

"If we kill ourselves – that's our business!" snarled one of them, a seventeen-year-old. "We get our kicks this way – and we like it. Man, there's nothing like speed in this world – but nothing!"

When their attention was called to the obvious – that they were a menace to innocent people on the highway – the boy muttered something about telling the "squares" to "keep out of the way."

FEW OF the girls ever sit behind the wheel. Some of them, in fact, do not even know how to drive, and do not wish to learn. The boys are in complete agreement.

"Speed rigs are for men," was the way a youth from Ohio worded it. "Sure – I dig having a chick along. But she's got other things to do – if she wants to stick around!"

Most of the "other things" he enumerated showed that the Hell-rodders' "chicks" are mainly sexual playthings as far as the boys are concerned.

"A chick can hand me my tools when I work on the plant," the teenager conceded. (An automobile engine is frequently referred to as the "plant" or the "powerpad" by Hell-rodders.) "But she'd better know more about revving in the back seat with me than about handing a screwdriver across the hood!"

The Hell-rodders' jargon is a mixture of beatnik words, coined phrases with a strong influence of mechanical terms and, lately, an added smattering of space-probe words and phrases, such as "Green for Go." They also refer to automobiles' "systems" – the wire or "string" system, the fluid system, and so forth.

Mechanically adept and inventive, the Hell-rodders "soup up," "channel" and "style" their automobiles. That is, they modify the engines so as to produce more power and greater speed, cut down and lower the body, and add new and different items to the automobile to make each one as individual as possible.

Their mechanical aptitude also serves to combine structural or system alteration with driving "test." One of their favorites can only be done after the brakes have been bled and thus rendered useless.

Known as "Trail 2," the Hell-rod test requires that the driver pilot his car through heavy city traffic for the minimum of an hour without brakes. He must then head for a nearby highway and drive a predetermined section of it within a time limit – also without brakes. The time allowed for the second section of "Trail 2" makes it imperative that he exceed the speed limit by a considerable degree.

Whereas "Trail 2" may not sound as violently

dangerous as some of their other automobile antics, the mere fact that many more innocent drivers, passengers and pedestrians are bound to be encountered on the Hell-rodder's route raises the possibility of a traffic tragedy.

Their disdainful attitude to all other people on the road is also a contributing factor. The average person has no way of knowing that the automobile hurtling towards them has no brakes whatsoever, and that the driver expects everyone to "get the hell out of my way."

With or without brakes, sex is always the underlying motivation.

A group of twenty Hell-rodding teenagers were arrested recently on the West Coast. Highway patrolmen pulled them in when the five cars in which they were riding were caught drag-racing on a freeway, shortly after midnight. The officers found that all the passengers were having sexual relations with each other, while under the influence of narcotics. They made little attempt to hide the fact from the police.

"It's kicks, Dad," leered one of the boys. "Speed, junk and sex – like wow!"

Even when they were herded into a magistrate's office some time later, the youngsters' attitudes were those of defiance or disinterest.

Trying to reason with them proved almost hopeless. Attempts to question their immediate, conscious motives drew responses comparable to those of Hell-rodders all over the country.

"My future?" echoed one of the boys, when asked what were his aims and plans, "I just think of today, Mister!"

"I don't need to work," scoffed another. "My old man hands over loot whenever I ask him, so why bother? Work is for slobs who *have* to work."

"The chicks don't have to stay," shrugged a third, when warned he risked ruining his pretty brunette partner's reputation and life. "She and all the others can cut out any time they want. More always turn up."

Conceited as that may sound, it is the unpleasant truth. The combination of speed and dope-stimulated sexuality, plus the "hero symbol" quality of the reckless drivers, proves to be an irresistible attraction for a great many teenage girls. Sexually immature, emotionally unstable and lacking any proper sense of direction or guidance in life, they avidly seek the approval of the highway daredevils.

Whenever a new girl joins a gang, a competition is immediately scheduled. The event may be a night-time drag race, or a timed "Trail 2", or any other of their "games." The winner gets the new girl as his sex-partner after the competition is over.

"The rest of us don't do so bad, either," snickers a Hell-rodder well-known to police in his Midwestern home town. "The other janes are always around, so even if you don't win on the track, you make out like a bandit later at the blowout!"

Barred from any legitimate drag-racing strips or properly organized hot-rod club competitions, Hell-rod gangs frequently get together for inter-gang "game" challenges. The outcome of these gatherings is practically always predictable. Either a vicious brawl breaks out between the two gangs – highly comparable to city JD gang "rumbles" – or a wild sex-marathon takes place after the "games" are over, or several gang members get involved in relatively minor multiple-car wrecks.

That is – if they're lucky.

Those who aren't so lucky are the ones who wind up in reformatories. Or in prison for manslaughter – or on a cold marble slab in the morgue.

Action is needed to stop this growing highway horror before it kills even more people – whether they are the hell-bent Hell-rodders themselves or blameless passers-by. Increased parental concern, proper guidance from civic leaders and a close study of this latest teenage menace would do much to counteract the underlying problems and tensions that are triggering the adolescents' automobile carnage.

If no plan is put into action – and put into action immediately – then more and more lives are going to be taken by the deadly highway "games" and "tests." The Hell-rodders will live up to their name – and turn our thruways, highways and city streets into blood-drenched, corpse-littered hells!

I WAS EATEN DOWN TO THE BONE

Ants were ripping my flesh, crawling over me and into my ears, eyes and mouth as I fought for my very life.

THERE ARE A COUPLE of things about the South Seas that tourist agencies conveniently forget to mention when discussing "that dream trip." One of them is getting drunk and forgetting where you put your body, and the second is white ants. In essence, they amount to the same thing: slow, creeping death. Hideous death, in fact.

Years before I took a sloop around to Tiutira, one of the Cook chain, I'd lived in Mexico and heard of Pancho Villa's exploits with ants and captives. Villa, a sadist from the word go, would stake out his victims, anoint them with honey, and let the ants go to work. In a matter of a few hours, the screaming victim was bones; perhaps a stain of blood, and bones.

Three years ago, at the height of the South Seas tourist season, I brought a sloop down from the Cocos Islands for a spot of Gauguin-type living. My sloop, *Hesperus*, was rigged out for anything in fins. It required only two men, myself and Jim Balch, to operate. Balch, like myself, had put in too many years behind a desk, dreaming. We were both bachelors, and both heeled enough to take a year's leave without feeling the pinch.

On the 21st of January, 1953, we sidled *Hesperus* up to a long, white string-piece at Tiutira, a Polynesian island of no mean beauty, and there dropped our hook. We figured we'd hang around for a month or so, clean up *Hesperus* after her long and uneventful trip down, and, naturally, raise a little

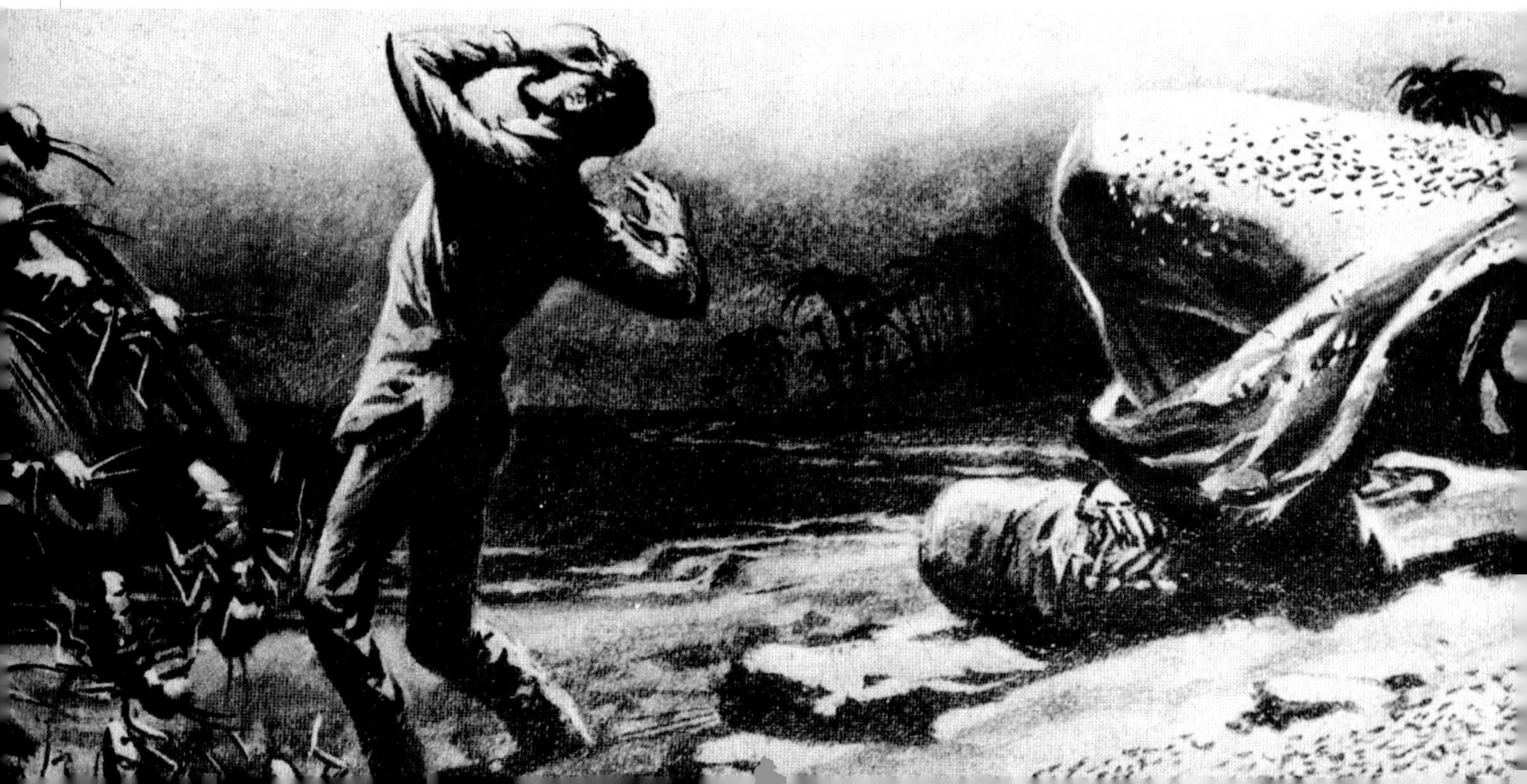

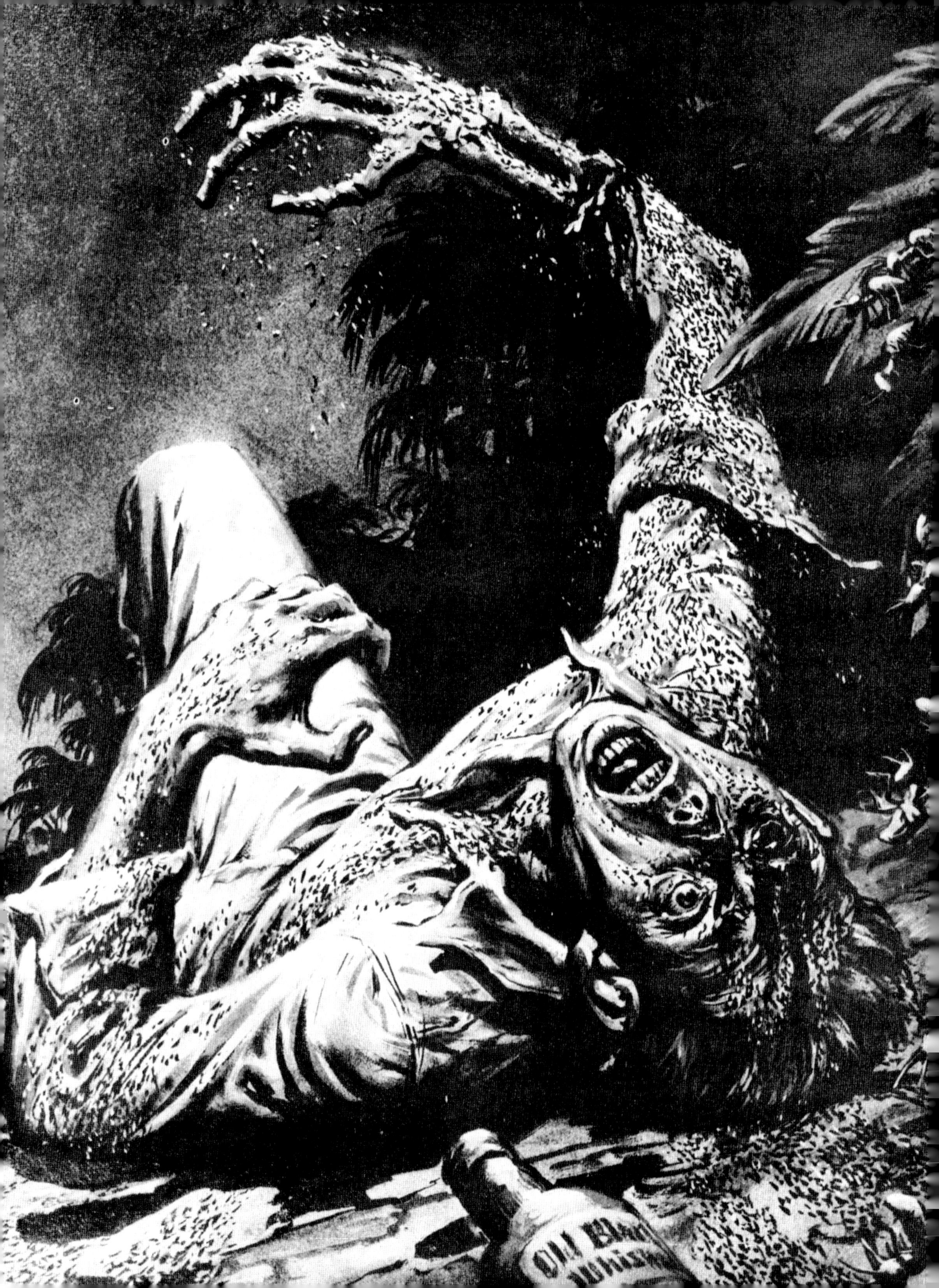

harmless hell on the side.

These things we did in time, living, as it were, like a couple of beachcombers. Or I should say, like a couple of *heeled* beachcombers, because nowadays, the provincial government doesn't tolerate *joie de vivre* on the arm. It was a nice, carefree existence, and it agreed with us. The uninhibited, unrestricted manner of native love was a little shocking to Jim's puritanical background at first, but he steeled himself after a while, and even took to wearing grass skirts.

All this is a matter of background to the episode that turned our island paradise into living hell one quiet afternoon at the end of February. By that time, Balch and I were accepted among the resident French and Polynesians. We violated nobody's confidence, nor tradition, and didn't overdo the grass-skirt and-uke business. In a nutshell, we behaved like a couple of normal guys on a vacation.

That afternoon, we were sitting back in the stern, kicking around the idea of visiting other islands of the chain. For me, staying put was good enough, but Balch was tiring fast of milk and honey. He squinted at me, the way he used to do when unsure of his ground.

"Jim," he drawled, shoving a splinter of wood between his teeth. "There's a string of coral atolls ten miles west of here. On Waiut they're having some sort of native *paavu* tonight. How's for going – and staying? Let's go native all the way. This island civilization's beginning to get me. I'm beginning to feel like I'm slumming on Fifth Ave–"

"Bad as that?"

He shrugged. "Too long in one place, I figure," Balch nodded. "For a while it was great. Now I'd like to see something of the world beyond."

"I like it here," I said. "No complaints. But if you want to shove off for a while–"

"Great!" he beamed. "I knew you'd see it!"

I let him rave. After all, there were two of us involved in this cruise. What one wanted, the other had to go along with. And besides, we were too many years planning this trip to let it sour now. It was about one of a hot, bright afternoon, and the quay was rapidly filling with citified tourists. He had a point, I could see. A man had to shave to be presentable, and that's not what we'd had in mind in the beginning.

"We'll go out on the motor," I nodded. "You take her. It's your island–"

And in less than an hour we were gone. By four, we'd moored the sloop in a quiet, green lagoon inside a reef. The place was a riot of flowers, king palms, and the heavy, sensuous smell of the offbeat paradise. The island, an atoll of a mile in circumference was Waiut, peopled only by natives and a couple of French Jesuits.

We took the dinghy and rowed ashore. I felt like Captain Cook; like this was the first time a Caucasian had stepped ashore in the trades. I had to hand it to Balch. His version of getting away from it all made far more sense than mine.

"Here's a place I can do standing on my ear!" Balch roared. "Let's go find that *paavu*..."

IN AN hour, we were seated in the company of a genial Polynesian, Waiut's chief, a rotund little toothless man named Luani Sam. Sam did most of the talking. The Jesuits weren't present, so Sam really cut loose. Between bites of stuffed, skewered pig, which we ate with the digits, Sam gave us the breakdown on his island.

"Goddam place is like nothing else in this world, believe me!" Luani Sam intoned. "Those snotty French women and their priggish customs don't touch us here, boys, thank God!"

"How do you avoid it?" I asked.

"Oh," he laughed. "I or one of my people do something primitive. Scares them the hell away. The resident has a fit because he thinks he can develop this island, too. But me, I won't let him. Father Jacques," Sam grinned, slyly, "sort of sees it my way. We don't want to spoil all of the South Pacific, so we really put on a show..."

"Like what?" Balch looked up.

Luani Sam shrugged. "Anything, damned near. Paganism, mostly. The boys like acting up with their knives. That old show about drinking the blood of squealing pig always gets 'em!"

He went into a couple of more rituals, and I stopped eating. He roared, slapping his thigh. His yarn about ants got me.

"You see? Well, when we really make it look good – 'authentic', as they say – there's damned few of them bloody French prigs about to louse up our island–"

"Where'd you pick up your lingo?"

"Two navies," Sam beamed. "British and U.S.N.; almost enlisted myself before the war!"

So it went, an orgy of eating and about twenty-five pleasant, nicely crocked ladies and gents, sitting around enjoying a *paavu* on our behalf. There was nothing out of line, not even the dances. Finally, about 10, we excused ourselves and walked back to the lagoon. It was the longest route home I'd ever taken.

Luani Sam's parting gift was a gallon of local brew he called *ani*. It was supposed to raise hair on a bald man's head.

"Tug on that, boys!" Sam said. "If the crickets bother you and you kill the *ani*, you'll sleep pretty good. Whenever they set off one of their bombs, we all drink it heavy. Cuts the glare, you know–"

Jim Balch and I didn't talk much en route to the boat. Both of us were pretty beat after the hectic day. We just walked, and thirsted. We walked to the wrong end of the island, and decided the hell with it. It was too late, and too long back.

Palm fronds make a reasonably comfortable bed at times, and this was one of them. Balch and I scooted around collecting fronds until the soft sand felt like an innerspring. Then we set the jug down between us, reminiscing and drinking. It tasted like pure fire, but the odd part about it was the more we gagged, the more we drank.

"Gosh!" Balch slurped. "This is really the end. I'm roasting inside!"

I tried to give him a coherent answer, but didn't make it. We took another couple of wild tugs apiece and killed the bottle. I was blind, literally, absolutely blind. My head felt like roman candles were being set off by the battery-load. My stomach pounded like a storm surf. I wanted to vomit but couldn't, so I started to crawl off to the lagoon. Salt water, I thought, dimly, would straighten me out.

IT WAS then, about that time that Jim Balch suddenly went *ani* mad, picking up the jug and cracking it against the base of a palm. The bottle cut his right thumb, but he dismissed it and lay down on the frond bed. I collapsed blind drunk at the edge of the lagoon, moaning my guts out.

The things crawling up my pants leg weren't a drunken hallucination! I tried suddenly to move, and was aware just as suddenly of Balch moaning hideously. A jumble of incongruous thoughts raced through my mind as my body quickly became a race of fantastic pain. It was as though thousands of pinpricks of fire were boring through the skin. Instinctively, I swatted my leg but the labor of the movement, combined with the effect of the *ani*, seemed to paralyze my arm. It remained down, in a grotesque position, clutching my leg.

"Balch! For God's sake, Balch! Help me!" I moaned, trying to squeeze my mouth shut as pinpricks of fire began entering my lips.

I could hear his response, as muted, incoherent as my own words, and I felt like I was losing my mind. I heard Jim Balch grunt:

"Ants! Jim! They're eating me!"

I heard him say it, saw his body slowly thrashing on the fronds, unable to crawl away. In the cold glare of the moon, I rolled over on my side, screaming, as thousands of ants, visible now, poured from the bloody sand where his body lay to mine. He was half sitting up, swatting himself in slow motion, shrieking.

His left hand was only bone, white skeletal bone, glistening in the moonlight. The army of ants surged over his features, coating him. I watched, paralyzed myself, unable to pinch away the scourge. I could feel the ants, small, white ants, crawling down my shirt, crawling up my neck and burrowing in my ear. I could feel, and scream, yet I was as helpless as poor Balch.

I kept hearing slobbering, animal sounds rasping from my throat as the fire penetrated deeper and deeper into my flesh. I watched my own right hand vanish before my eyes, become skeletal and twitching, void of blood. The ants moved casually, up and down, from the sand to my bones and back.

I was four yards from the water, yet crawling an inch was literally like ten miles. I couldn't move. I could feel the heavy numbness in my limbs, above which were the roaring pains. *Move!* I kept screaming. Move or die. I lost consciousness slowly, and when I came away from the screaming torpor, my right hand was down to the bone. Jim was sitting there, and just the sight of him made me want to die. The flesh on one side of his face was eaten completely away. I passed out again, and my own shrieks awoke me.

Excruciating agony surged up through the marrow of my bones. I could feel the zillions of bloated crawling things squeezing between my teeth, under my tongue, into my nostrils. I crawled by some God-given superhuman effort, and almost drowned myself in preference to the slower death.

They found Jim crocked up against the tree, his head and hands gone. Beneath the limp clothes, his body had been eaten away. I survived only because of the lagoon. Cannibal ants, they told me weeks later, detest water. They told me about it after they'd given me shock treatment for two amputated hands. For my legs, they did what they could, grafting skin from volunteers. I was flown to Papeete, and later shipped to a hospital in Baltimore. The boat was sold to pay for my hospitalization.

Actually, it didn't happen on the island, but rather on an isolated atoll which was traversable at dead low water. In our drunken stupor, we'd crossed to it and there slept. It was the place of the white ants – and my own, personal grave.

BEAUTIFUL MAN-KILLERS

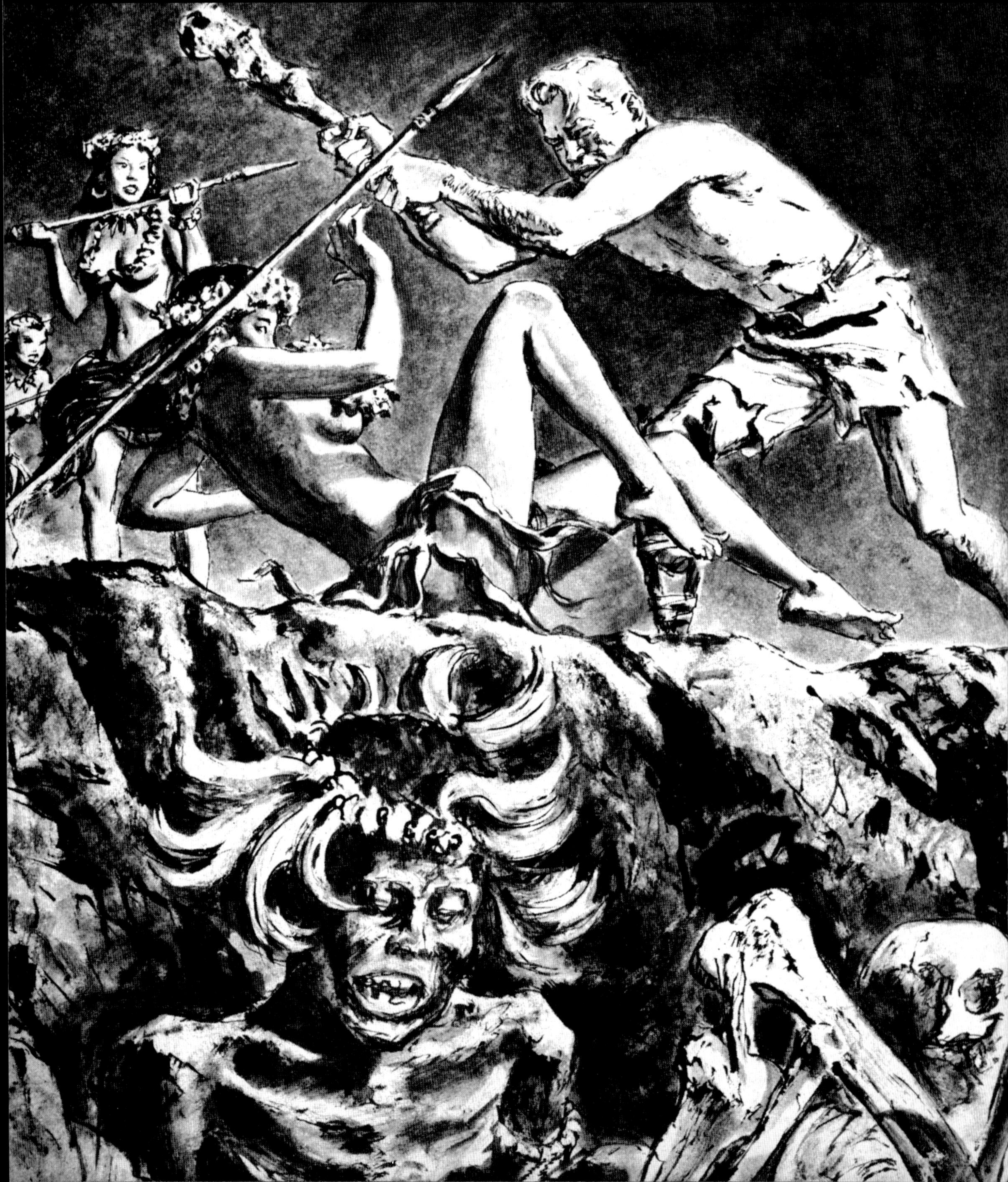

FROM EROMONGA ISLAND

Trapped on the island of the damned, with the mutilated victims of the native she-beasts.

THE *S.S. BONAVENTURE* HAD a dashing and mettlesome ring to it, for the ship's owners had chosen a romantic name for the 5,000-ton, paint-peeling hunk of scrap iron. She was 40 years old and a real crone.

Her name was the only attractive thing about her on this sultry, tropic night as the three of us – Max Gunnison, the second engineer, "Brassnose" Frayne, the bo'sun's mate, and I lay stretched out on the poop deck trying to catch a breath of air.

We were bound for San Diego with the holds jammed with copra, palm oil, and sulphur. Brassnose voiced the dark thoughts that had plagued us for days. His full name was Foster Lukuklu Frayne and he was fair of skin and his hair was bleached white from the elements. His nickname had been bestowed on him because Frayne was the grandson of a long-dead native chieftain on Taui in the Admiralty Islands.

He spoke the Manu dialects after a fashion, but it was hard for us to remember that this Nordic-looking giant had a grand-daddy who probably, several generations back, had eaten seamen like ourselves. He muttered:

"God Almighty, what a tub! We'd be in real trouble if there was an emergency. The Old Man is always tight and we haven't had a fire drill in two years."

I was worried, too. The hose outlets along the upper decks were clogged with dirt and refuse. The pulleys and apparatus of the lifeboats were caked with layers of old paint and rust. It would have taken dynamite to blast the boats loose if we needed them. They were bone-dry and their seams would open fast, once they were in the sea.

Gunnison, a squat Limey with hairy ears, said: "Come off it, mates! Let old Max play you a tune on the music box I bought in Genoa."

He owned a really beautiful accordion, filigreed in silver and with countless doodads and buttons and keys. I sprawled on a wooden grating where the big hawsers were coiled and listened to Max wail to the music, "I Love My Wife so Dearly," which was funny because Max was a confirmed bachelor and would flee in terror if a barmaid so much as winked at him.

Suddenly, Brassnose Frayne sat bolt upright and sniffed the air. "Stow the noise, Max! Do you smell it, men? Smoke!"

The three of use were quickly on our feet. Even as we detected the acrid fumes of burning sulphur, the ship's bell clanged the fire alarm.

It was the moment any sailor dreads. I had double reason to fear it for I am an anthropologist, not a seaman, and had signed on as a crewman merely to visit certain of the Admiralty Islands at no cost to myself in this Depression year of 1932.

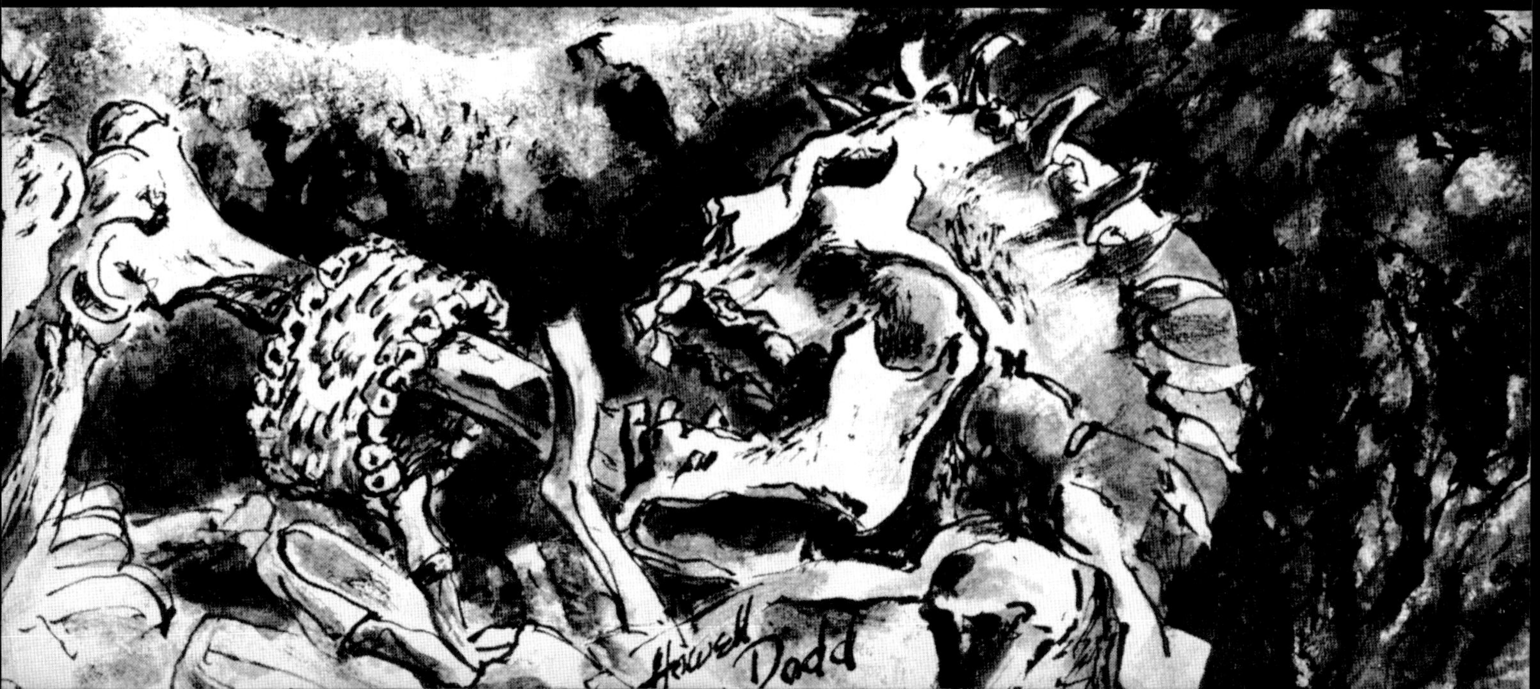

Sulphur, oil, and copra make the kind of tinder any firebug dreams of. I suppose a Lascar sailor had sneaked a cigarette in the hold and touched off the blaze. Now, roaring up in great oily clouds of smoke and flames, the fierce heat quickly drove us to the stern where we huddled like suffocating sheep, not knowing what to do...

The lifeboats were stuck fast. We couldn't budge them. I heard a cry from a stoker as a pillar of flame leaped from a hatch and tongued the man's bare back. He sprinted to the rail and leaped overboard into the shark-infested waters.

One especially bad detonation shook Lifeboat No. 3, which trembled violently in the davits. Brassnose yelled: "Come on, Sommers, Max... *step on it, we got a chance now.* Heave on those ropes; the boat's come unstuck."

We pulled and swore and yanked and wept, scraping our hands until they bled profusely. The *Bonaventure* was quivering and lurching like an old spavined mare. Her stern was down and a sharp list helped us to cut loose the lifeboat which dropped heavily into the water.

Brassnose, Max and I leaped into the sea and swam to the boat. "Let's get away fast," said Brassnose, shaking water from his mop of bleached hair. "That tub is going to explode all at once."

Then the *Bonaventure* seemed to disintegrate with a roar of live steam, geysers of sparks and flames, and a dense cloud of black-and-orange smoke. Dimly, we heard the voices of men in mortal agony but we couldn't go back into that inferno.

Already our leaky lifeboat was filled with five inches of water. "Sommers, you bail while we row," Brassnose commanded.

As best I could determine, we were some 700 miles west of New Guinea, in the Bismarck Archipelago. Three days previously, we had steamed past barren Rennell Island in the distance. Now we peered anxiously for any speck of land in the Pacific, for this interminable bailing would have to stop soon. There were gigantic blisters and rope burns on our hands; our muscles were hot wires of pain.

Brassnose was strangely silent. The big man with the whitened hair murmured something: his words sounded as if they were in the Manu tongue, which I recognized, having studied the dialect in my Anthropology VI class at the University of Chicago.

He then said something which struck a chord in my memory.

"God help us if we're near the island of Eromonga. We'd be in real trouble then. I'd rather keep bailing – or sink."

I was puzzled by the remark, then I recalled the voice of mild Professor Howard Griggs three years ago in a university lecture on primitive societies. He had been speaking of this archipelago:

"Even when the islands were under German mandate before World War I, Europeans gave Eromonga a wide berth. The place is inhabited by several hundred war-like women who are anachronisms in the 20th Century – stone-age amazons who live in an all-female, matriarchal society which is self-sufficient."

I remembered, too, the jesting voice of a classmate, Bobby Pauson: "But how do they reproduce, Dr. Griggs? I'm sure that males have something to do with that process!"

There had been classroom guffaws which quickly subsided as Professor Griggs said dryly: "I see your point, Pauson. Of course, males play a role there, but believe me when I say you wouldn't enjoy yourself one bit on Eromonga. Indeed, you wouldn't live long, for the females either drive the men they've seized from neighboring islands back to their boats after exploiting them for amatory purposes, or they destroy them by revolting but ingenious methods. In fact, one important aspect of their very religion is the annihilation of men."

"I think I know what you mean, Brassnose," I said. "I know something about Eromonga. Let's hope we come to a safer place."

BUT WE didn't. Three hours later, while we were bailing desperately, a dot of land came into view. Foster Lukuklu Frayne made a sign over his heart with his two linked thumbs: I recognized it as an ancient Manu gesture intended to propitiate the Devil.

A half-hour passed; we had drifted closer. In a voice so frightened as to seem not his own, the big bo'sun's mate quavered:

"*Tchalo!* It is Eromonga – look hard, you can see with your naked eye the wooden scaffolding on the cliff."

I squinted at the looming shoreline. There was a wooden tower or derrick there, something like a ski jump; it was perhaps 80 feet high and had been artfully constructed of logs. A fine example of engineering in a primitive society.

"What is the scaffolding for, Brassnose ?"

He made a sound of despair deep in his throat. It was embarrassing to see strapping, blond Brassnose comport himself like a child who talks about bogeymen.

"*Aaa-ee!* It is their *tultul*, the 'jumping platform' of death. It is the last of the three tests of manhood which the women impose, to discover if a male is worthy of survival there. Often, I heard my uncles and cousins speak of it when I was a small boy growing up in Rabaul. They had never seen a *tultul* but they had heard about it from their fathers."

Our lifeboat was filling rapidly, and despite what I had heard of the inhabitants of Eromonga, I was glad to see a long and graceful outrigger manned by three bronzed girls glide out of a lagoon into the open sea and toward our craft.

I expected Brassnose – as a man with a strain of Melanesian in his blood – to speak to them. But he had turned a sickly green and appeared tongue-tied or panicked.

So, I mustered my few words of the Manu dialect and said, "We greet you in peace. In *ngandlu*. My friends and I come from a ship which was destroyed by fire. We are thirsty and hungry; our sore and burned hands and arms need attention."

The girl in the prow of the outrigger turned a smile like a beacon on me. I noted that her full breasts were bare and that she wore a garland of red pandanus fruit in her blue-black hair.

She said, "My name is Songau and these girls are Ponkob and Piwen. You are welcome to Eromonga. My people await you on the shore. You shall have food, water and rest."

Thirty minutes later, the outrigger grated on sand and other girls, waiting on shore, rushed forward to pull it up on the beach and make it fast with vine ropes to a large boulder. I saw a dozen or so other outriggers moored there.

I looked at the *tultul*. All my rosy visions of rest and even pleasure on this island vanished at the sight. There was a mound of bleached human bones and skulls at the base of the big wooden derrick. Some had been there for years; others still had whitened shreds of decayed flesh sticking to them.

There was one object which sickened yet fascinated me. This was also a corpse – a male, judging from the coral arm bands, the tribal scars still discernible on the maggoty face, the painted bone of the warrior caste which still pierced the septum of the rotting nose.

The body may have been two or three weeks dead. I looked with revulsion at the legs. They were shattered. Many small bones protruded crazily from the shreds of flesh. The man must have leaped to his death from the topmost rung of the *tultul*.

As if divining my thoughts, the girl Songau smiled warmly and said in the casual tone an American woman might use in describing her rose garden:

"This is our *tultul*, a jumping platform, *maku*. Later, you shall know it better. Is it not well-made? Our old one blew down in a storm at the time of the *pokeneu* festival fifteen moons ago. It took thirty of our women almost six moons to build this one, which is higher and stronger than the old one. We are very proud of it."

"You have every right to be," I replied gravely in the Manu dialect, but my attention was fixed on Brassnose, the biggest and strongest of us. He looked as if he was going to keel over. I felt a queasiness in my own stomach but it wouldn't do to show these girls that we were afraid. Not so soon, anyway.

I clapped the big man with the bleached hair on his shoulder and said heartily, hoping it would make an impression on the women: "This one is the *maku* Frayne. He speaks your language too, for he is the grandson of a chieftain on Taui who made much magic and was strong and cunning. The *maku* Frayne has inherited this strength from his grandfather."

This was the worst thing I could have said. Brassnose turned a stricken face toward me and said brokenly, "Sommers, you meddling Yank, you're a fool! They despise males who brag of their strength; they destroy such men with their damned tests. You've ruined me, blast you!"

At first, I thought he was out of his head, talking wildly like this. But a glance at Songau and the other women confirmed what Brassnose had blurted out.

The women's faces had hardened after my statement. At a nod from Songau, four lithe and muscular girls darted to Frayne's side and seized him by the arms. The man was an ox, and he put up a creditable struggle; but four Eromonga women are more than a match for the strongest male that ever lived.

Besides, terror had sapped some of Frayne's vitality and will. My last impression as they led him off to a stockade was of his pale face.

In the Manu tongue, "eromonga" means manhood – a quality which the women derisively toasted in weekly feasts at which great quantities of a brew like *kava* were imbibed.

In the hut to which I was assigned – Max had his own quarters – my food was brought to me by a wrinkled crone with bare drooping breasts who seemed to enjoy conversing with me in rudimentary phrases.

Her name was L'Turu and she told me many things. For an anthropologist, loquacious old L'Turu was a mine of information. Though I had a great dread of the island and felt I would never leave it alive, I eagerly wrote down everything she told me about its women. (Her account was later confirmed by the Scobee-Frazier Expedition from the University of Manitoba in 1951.)

From L'Turu, I heard that until about 1850 the people of this island – which was about the size of Guam or smaller – had been of both sexes, and that the normal family life of Melanesian tribes was observed here with minor variations.

But in the middle of the last century an island woman named "Karipo" seized a spear in the heat of an inter-tribal battle and rallied the women after their men had fled. Miraculously, Karipo and her women had succeeded in driving a hundred invaders from the isle of Pamasu back to their war canoes, after considerable loss of life on both sides.

Karipo was something of a politician as well as a militarist. She quickly exploited the exalted position she now occupied, by harassing the disorganized males and even putting many of them to death. Within a decade or less, few men were left and a feminist society had sprung up.

"Karipo was great goddess, told our mothers that men were not necessary except to father children," the crone told me. "All men went away from here. Those who stayed had to pass tests. Few passed." She cackled with mirth, showing the stumps of betel-stained teeth. "Karipo's women then named this place 'Eromonga' – manhood – for only the strongest men could stay here. Come, I show you."

The old woman arose stiffly and led me to a clearing where a small hut stood. In the shade of a palm tree in front of the squalid dwelling I saw four figures in a semi-circle on the ground. They were cleaning and polishing dog teeth, the currency of most Manu tribes.

Then I gave a grunt of surprise. "But these are males, L'Turu!"

Half-men would have been a more accurate designation. One grinning brown fellow swung himself along the earth on simian arms; his legs were just useless shriveled sticks – as if they had been smashed in a great fall.

Another man had but one arm; his other limb ended in a red and lacerated stump as if flesh and bone had been eaten by living things.

It was difficult for me to gaze upon the remaining two men without showing horror. One was blind: he worked with deft hands sorting the dog teeth and cowrie shells. Two great staring holes showed where his eyes had been. Spear points could have gouged those empty sockets.

His companion had barely a trace of face. Spears had furrowed his forehead, cheeks and chin, had severed his ears and his upper lip; the wounds had healed long ago but his features I still see in my troubled sleep.

L'Turu nudged me. "You see, *maku*? We left them life, because they passed the manhood tests. These. few are very brave; we honor and respect them." She handed a fistful of twisted pepper root to the creatures who nodded gratefully and gnawed it with relish.

I had no more time for questioning venerable L'Turu. A signal drum from the village reached our ears, and the 86-year-old woman listened attentively and translated.

"Perhaps you are a lucky man, *maku*. The drum says our leader Songau wants you in her house tonight. That is a great honor, to lie with Songau. Go now, but do not tell her how my tongue has wagged..."

THROUGHOUT THE Melanesian islands, sex and love-play have been exalted to a commanding role in the lives of primitives who have little else – other than hunting and fishing – to keep them busy. On Eromonga, the original 200 females had shrunk drastically in a century, largely because of small wars, epidemics, and lack of men. There were only fifty women there in 1932; there may be none left now.

And so, when an occasional male drifted to the island, or came out of curiosity, or was captured, it was inevitable that he should be utilized to the fullest for the propagation of the species before taking the grim tests I shall describe later.

I was ushered into Songau's large and scrupulously clean house by six women called *taute*, or honor guards. Two girls sat cross-legged on the mat-covered dirt floor, stroking and kneading Songau's arms, legs and stomach. My own dungarees were removed by the *taute* and I was pushed onto a dyed mat as two new girls entered the thatched hut. They, too, began to knead my body in the same business-like manner.

This ceremony, I was told by Songau, who spoke as if enjoying every minute of it, is called the *romiromi*. It both relaxes and stimulates a couple preparatory to a passionate interlude culminating in the love act.

Next, came an odd bit of manipulation called *kea*. The girls pulled and jerked my legs, tugging so hard that I almost shrieked with pain. They did the same to Songau's exquisite, perfumed limbs. But when the girls eased up on me, there was a delightful feeling of lassitude and numbness in my entire being. My brain began to churn with erotic visions; forgotten were the dread *tultul* and the twisted male survivors I had seen briefly.

I only knew that I desperately needed Songau's body.

But she was not ready for me yet. The girl in used fish scales and clam shells as tweezers and carefully plucked her brows, bending over a coconut shell filled with water which served as a crude mirror. She adjusted bamboo combs in her piled hair, and her handmaidens then rubbed her nude form with *lolo* oil and turmeric, which gave off a tantalizing scent.

Was she ready now? I hoped so. I wanted this girl very much – and damn the consequences! But she spoke sharply, "Not just yet, *maku*. You still have to go through the *takani* rite."

"*Takani*" means tread in the Manu lexicon. What was she talking about? As I fretted, two semi-dressed girls entered and lay down behind me, placing their bare feet against my back. They began a slow rotary movement, gentle at first, then picking up speed and pressure until they were pounding my back and neck with their feet and I felt splendidly alive and vital. An osteopath might have been able to explain the effect the treatment had on me; all I know is that my sexual appetite now was whetted to an unbearable degree.

As if she sensed this, Songau said quietly, "Extinguish the oil lanterns and withdraw now. I wish to be alone for the night with this *maku*..."

These, then, were the remarkable preliminaries to my ten-hour session with this girl who was the leader of the dwindling band of women on Eromonga Island. To men of the West, the rites and acts may seem unnecessary, time-consuming, even embarrassing.

But as I write this, I must confess that at times – despite the horrors I subsequently witnessed – I still experience the greatest of longing, and wish again for the exquisite sensations of the *romiromi*, the *kea*, and the *takani*.

SOMEWHERE ON the island a cock crowed. Morning was near.

From a nearby hut where little Max had been ordered to sleep with Piwen, one of Songau's aides. I heard the quavering notes of his accordion and smiled to myself. Poor Max! Always afraid of girls, and now fearful for his own skin, he was trying to charm Piwen with his music, if one could call it that.

Songau stirred in her slumber at the sounds. As she became conscious of his music, the young woman awoke with a start and jumped to her feet. A look of panic and dismay darkened her oval face. Vainly, I tried to explain.

"It's just a music box – we call it an accordion, Songau. It's nothing to fear. Haven't you ever heard music on this island?"

She hadn't. The girl was beyond all reason as she raced unclad from the hut and shouted orders for her lieutenants to light the tribal fires and to bring the *maku* Max before her. I hurriedly dressed and followed her to the clearing.

Songau glared at me accusingly. "The little *maku* is your friend. He brings an evil spirit – a terrible *arata* – in the box-which-speaks. Hear the bad spirit groan and laugh as he holds it in his hands! It must be destroyed quickly or it will destroy us."

I shouted that she was daft, that it was just a harmless accordion, but Songau's eyes were glazed with fear of a magic greater than any commemorated in her tribe's legends. I felt my arms pinioned as three strong girls lashed me to a banyan tree so I could not interfere.

Max Gunnison, dragging his accordion in the dust, was pulled from the hut by six spear-carrying women. Songau snapped an order: their spears punctured the accordion, ripping the fine bellows, slicing off the ivory keys and valves of the $600 instrument. I heard Max shrilly protest this desecration of his treasure. "'Ere, now, you bloody heathens, you can't do that. The box cost me a fortune in Naples, it did–"

Songau herself grabbed up a spear and confronted the little engineer of the *S.S. Bonaventure*. She muttered words I didn't understand, then hurled the spear like a javelin at his throat. The shaft passed through his palate and vertebra. The little music-lover toppled face forward, driving the spear deeper into his body. He lay like a reddened sack on the sandy earth – an impaled insect.

Max twitched once and then lay quite still. I knew he was dead.

Songau chanted an Eromonga victory cry:

"*Ko te maine toso ka horuhoro!*"

("Females have triumphed over another male!")

Then she ceremoniously washed her hands three times from an earthen jar, and said brusquely to me as if I were now a foe instead of her lover:

"Come, we must eat and then you shall see the *maku* Frayne face his first test of manhood. I hope for his sake that he is a man of great courage..."

I was escorted almost a mile along the beach to where some Eromonga women were clustered around a large pit. The hole, I saw, was about four feet in diameter and probably seven feet deep. At Songau's command, I dropped to my knees and peered over the rim.

A briny stench arose from the depths. I dimly saw crawling things: gigantic crabs, spiny and wicked-looking fish of a species unknown to me, coiled and restless eels, some at least five feet long. The pit was alive with creatures of the deep.

My worst fears were realized when I heard a melancholy roll on a gourd drum and saw Brassnose, escorted by three girls – with hands tied behind his back – approaching the pit.

He was mumbling an ancient prayer of the Manu people, recited only in adversity, and seemed not to notice me: "*Ko te muma eaha, ko te mien tiru.*" The man's face was ashen but his body was in superb condition; with luck, he might be able to withstand the torture.

At a signal from Songau, the girls sliced the thongs which bound his hands and he was shoved roughly into the hole. Frayne disappeared from view and I heard him gasp as something in that terrible hole struck at him or bit him.

"He must stay there until the sun goes down," Songau said matter-of-factly. "Then, if he lives, he will be feted as a brave one who passed our first test. Few makers do on Manhood Island."

I said something unprintable to her. She smiled brightly as if I had paid her a compliment; luckily for me, Songau didn't comprehend English curses.

At 7 PM, a semi-conscious human figure was pulled by a crude winch from the slimy pit. Brassnose was alive. His right leg was eaten away; the eels, fish, and massive crustaceans had done their work well.

But with his bare hands he had taken a terrific toll of his watery tormentors. The sandy rim of the pit was littered with their heads and carcasses.

I couldn't look on as two women called *beglus* (doctors) smeared his poor leg stump with coca butter and applied a burning brand to the flesh to seal and heal it. No sound came from Frayne; in extremity, he had the fortitude of his Manu grandfather.

Songau said, "By the next moon, he should be able to take the second test. This one has heart; he may pass it..."

THE DAYS and weeks passed. Brassnose had enviable vitality; he recuperated. By my reckoning it probably was March 27 or 28 now, in the year of our Lord 1932. The crippled man seemed absorbed in his own thoughts and rarely spoke to me.

At high noon that day, Brassnose was escorted to an enclosure marked off by bamboo stakes. My shipmate was given a stout wooden club with which to defend himself. Fitted to his stump was a crude artificial leg he had carved from driftwood.

"Because he has but one leg now, only three girls instead of the customary five shall fight him with spears," Songau decreed.

I said, "That's damned generous of you."

Even now, decades afterward, I can relive the details of that unequal battle in my mind's eye. Poor Brassnose, flailing away with his club, his eyes rolling and spittle falling on his bare chest... He took at least four vicious jabs in his body from the wicked spear-points, one of which just missed his jugular.

But he gave as good as he got. I saw this amazing man knock one girl senseless with his stave, smashing the spear from her numbed hands. He ducked the frenzied lunge of another who managed to gash the calf of his one leg with her weapon.

Again his own club swung in a desperate arc; this time, Frayne smashed a female warrior's forearm and she dropped her spear, howling frightfully. He limped in the arena, half naked and dripping blood, a crippled gladiator who was determined to sell his life high. A torrent of Manu curses flowed from his mouth. The girls understood.

The third woman, irresolute and afraid now, suddenly threw her spear into the sand and walked away while the crowd hooted. I leaped the fence and helped poor Brassnose to a log seat, swabbing his face with spring water and crowing, "You made it, man – you passed the second test! Thank God, Frayne, you're still alive."

He smiled wanly as four girls arrived with a litter to carry him off to his well-guarded hut. "Yes, I'm alive – but for how long, Sommers? You've seen the *tultul*. All you can do now is to pray for me..."

He didn't survive the terrible leap into space.

Brassnose Frayne was one of the bravest men I ever met. Two weeks after the ordeal of the spears, he climbed laboriously, wooden leg and all, to the top of the tower and stood looking down at us. I knew the fear that was in him, but in the end his Manu blood gave him quiet serenity to do what he had to do.

With two legs, if he was very lucky, he just might have survived the fall though he would have been a crippled wreck like the other pathetic survivors I had seen. But with one leg he didn't have a chance.

Brassnose plummeted down to the sand and lay spread-eagled, his two arms and one poor leg fractured in many places. He was haemorrhaging. While I cradled his tortured frame in my arms, he died.

It would he satisfying to write an account of how I, in turn, survived the three tests of Manhood Island. But, at the risk of being anti-climactic, I must admit that I am a great coward. The thought of even one test still unnerves me completely.

Five nights later, having given a somewhat dull-wilted girl thirty cowrie shells for the "loan" of her outrigger, I blindly struck out from Eromonga with a goatskin bag of fresh water, some taro and bread-fruit, and a desperate hope that a ship would save me from the sea. But I was prepared to face any fate rather than stay here and be destroyed.

I spent 16 days in that bobbing craft, quite out of my mind at times, my body encrusted with salt and burned to the consistency of leather by the savage sun.

I must have drifted into the steamer lanes at last, for (so they told me) on April 18 I was plucked from the water – quite out of my head – by the crew of the Greek tanker, *Pallas Athene*. I had lost 41 pounds and was dangerously dehydrated.

After five weeks in an Auckland, New Zealand, hospital, I was discharged and returned to the States as a paying passenger on a sturdier ship than the ill-fated *Bonaventure*. Two months later, luck favored me and I was offered a teaching post at a small Ohio college where I have remained ever since.

Sometimes I wonder if any of that dwindling band of cruel women are left on Eromonga. But I wouldn't go there to find out for all the gold in the world.

NUDE VIRGINS FOR THE SERPENTS OF LUST

Writhing in unendurable agony, the captive beauties shrieked at the thing's hideous caresses.

ICY FEAR FROZE THE young Spanish noblewoman's brain as she peered down into the murky depths of the pit.

Bearer of one of the proudest names of Imperial Castile, Magdelena de Montalban, daughter of the Viceroy of Spain in the Americas, had been on her way to join her illustrious parent in Peru when the galleon in which she was a passenger fell prey to pirates.

"Please!" sobbed the terrified girl, "Have mercy!"

Slowly her throat and stomach muscles constricted, knotting into terrible spasms of fear as she stared at the thing that stirred in those awful depths. She shuddered violently and sweat beaded her lovely naked body as she realized what it was that moved – the loathsome, slimy, flesh-creeping coils of a gigantic serpent.

Held by grotesquely masked Priests of Set, Magdelena stared in frozen horror at those impatiently writhing coils. Handed over to the Quetzalcoatl Indians by her brutal pirate captors, she was about to become a human sacrifice.

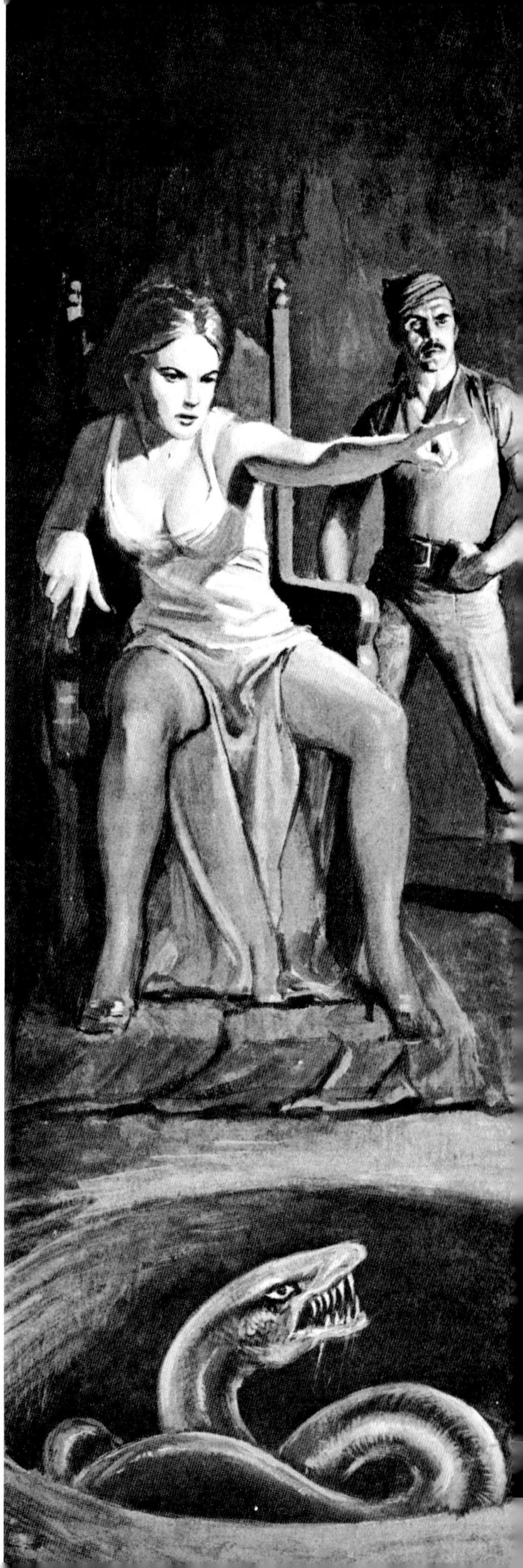

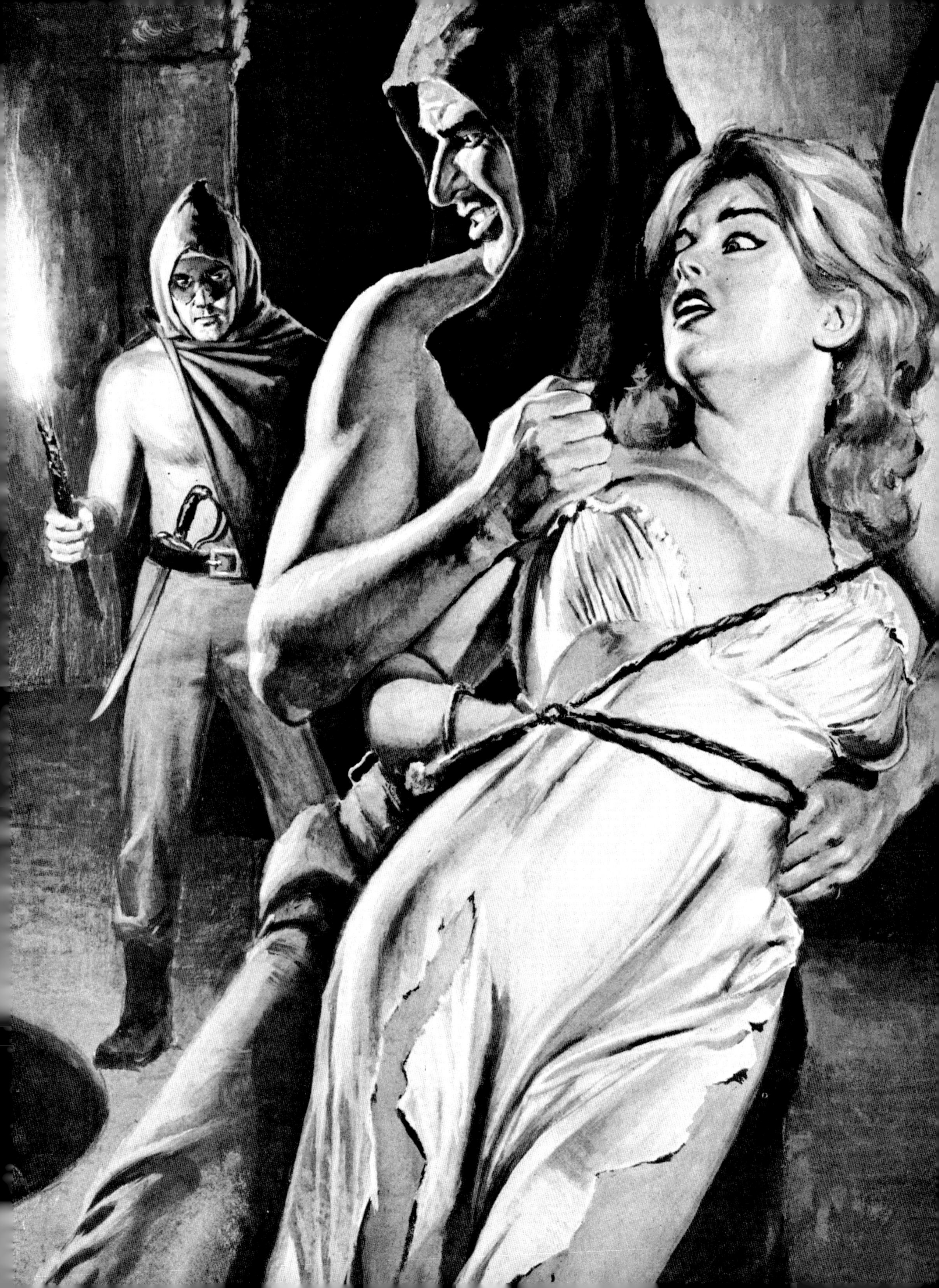

It was then that Magdelena's proud heritage deserted her and she began to scream in abject terror, the shrill notes of her shrieks echoing about the dark stone walls of the red-glowing chamber of sacrifice as the throbbing drums of the outer temple suddenly ceased their hellish beating.

A thousand pairs of eyes, burning with lust and madness, were riveted on the blonde Goddess of Set seated upon her golden throne overlooking the mouth of the pit. The worshippers were waiting for her to pronounce the sacred words that would condemn Magdelena to unspeakable horror.

The goddess's scarlet-painted lips twisted into a cruel smile. She enjoyed torturing this haughty Spanish beauty, took pleasure in making her crawl. She lounged voluptuously against the throne cushions, luxuriating at their silken feel as she watched the writhing coils of darkly glistening horror in the pit below.

Her name was Hortense Cerbalaud, and she was blonde and beautiful and evil. A trick of fate had taken her from her native Normandy as the mistress of one of the bloodiest buccaneers to roam the blue waters of the Pacific. By an even more unlikely circumstance she had come to rule over the fanatical followers of Set, the proud and savage Quetzalcoatls, in their jungle citadel of Iztopolopo.

Suddenly she pointed a richly bejeweled finger at the quivering Magdelena, her ice blue eyes gleaming with sadistic pleasure as she hissed the dreadful words of death:

"Ka nama kaa lajerama!"

Guessing what was about to happen, Magdelena fell upon her knees begging for mercy.

But the priests, ignoring her pleas, dragged her screaming to her feet and tossed her over the edge of the pit.

She closed her eyes and screamed as she plunged headlong toward the writhing horror below.

A sharp shock knocked the breath from her body.

She was lying naked at the bottom of the pit. In the dim light she saw living coils rippling to strike. Then, with a hissing rush, the unspeakable obscenity enfolded her and a huge wedge-shaped head, as big as a wolfhound's, swayed menacingly above her.

She felt stinking fetid breath upon her face, saw slavering jaws widen as a monstrous forked tongue came flicking out between sharp discolored fangs.

The slimy wetness of disgusting scaleless skin slithered over her delicate flesh, hardening and swelling obscenely about her nude body, thickly pulsing with loathsome and repugnant life.

"Kaa lajerama!" howled the masked priests ecstatically as they danced about the mouth of the Sacred Pit. And the worshippers in the temple took up the cry: *"Kaa lajerama!"*

Sprawled on her throne of silk and gold, below the squatting image of a toad-like deity, the blond Goddess of Set thrilled with unnatural rapture as she watched the great snake crushing its lovely victim in its abominable coils.

As the serpent gradually tightened its hold, inhuman shrieks tore from Magdalena's distorted mouth.

She gave one final scream of agony. Then her rib cage caved in and her organs were crushed under the relentless pressure of the heaving, slimy coils.

Meanwhile, in another part of the temple, a bearded buccaneer sat chuckling to himself.

He had good reason to chuckle, for the little wizened High Priest who sat opposite him, nodding his bird-like head approvingly, had paid a small fortune for the Viceroy's ill-fated daughter.

"Bring us more of these pale Spanish beauties," he cackled. "Our coffers are deep and the Great Serpent is ever hungry for the flesh of these pampered virgins of Castile."

THE EVENTS leading up to this monstrous trafficking in virgins to serve as human sacrifices had their beginning in Normandy some years earlier.

In the summer of 1669, a local scandal involving a drunken orgy and the death of a fourteen-year-old girl forced the dissolute young Chevalier Lucien de Tonnay-Charente to flee his chateau near Caen. With him he took a young woman named Hortense Cerbalaud.

Hortense, at twenty-three, was a hellion of dubious background and undisclosed attainments. She was tall with the kind of figure that made men sweat. She had deep-set, cruel blue eyes and her hair was a golden untamable torrent that cascaded wildly about her tawny shoulders. She also had an insatiable taste for blood, and it was undoubtedly she who first turned the renegade Chevalier's thoughts to piracy.

With what remained of his fortune, the Chevalier purchased a fast fighting vessel and recruited a crew of cut-throats from among the seafaring riff-raff that thronged the waterfronts of Brest, St. Marlo and Le Havre.

Like many buccaneers of the period – French, English and Dutch – he chose the New World as his area of operations. There the pirates, the infamous Brotherhood of the Sea, enjoyed the unofficial sanction of their respective countries provided they confined their activities to raiding the gold-laden galleons and rich cities of the Spanish Empire.

For in the 17th century Spain stood astride the Americas like a colossus, and no people anywhere at any time were more hated than the avaricious Dons.

A century or more before, the Conquistadores – monsters such as Pizarro, De Soto and Cortez – had wiped out the flourishing Aztec and Maya civilizations, pitting cannon and armor against the naked bodies of the Indians and butchering tens of thousands. Thousands more were condemned to the living hell of the gold and silver mines, and in a few short years Central and South America became one vast concentration camp.

The Chevalier's rackish craft, *El Murcielago*, ranged up and down the western shores of Spain's crimson empire, a hideous vampire bat emblem flying from her mizen in place of the conventional skull and crossbones, spreading terror in her wake. Faster and more heavily armed than anything the Spaniards could send against her, *El Murcielago* was one of the first buccaneering vessels to operate in the Pacific rather than the Caribbean.

"Don José, what do you make of that vessel?"

Capitan Don Francisco Montez y Belmonte, of the galleon *Santa Maria*, passed his spyglass to his first officer, braced himself against the main weather shrouds, and waited. The *Santa Maria*, a huge vessel for the time and a sluggish sailor in the light air currents then prevailing off the Galapagos, was outward bound from Manila for Peru. In her coffers reposed treasure destined for the King of Spain, and among her passengers was Magdelena de Montalban, daughter of the Viceroy himself.

"She's smartly handled, Capitan. I'd estimate she mounts fifty guns. She flies no flag."

"I don't like her looks at all, Don José," boomed the portly Don Francisco. "Call all hands, load the guns, and order the soldiers into the forts."

"*Si, señor,*" answered the first officer, loosening his rapier in its scarlet scabbard.

But it was already too late. Suddenly the notorious black, white and crimson bat flag of *El Murcielago* unfurled in the gentle breeze, and cutting swiftly through the swell, the dreaded pirate raider raked the unwieldy *Santa Maria* with a murderous broadside.

Half an hour later the great Spanish galleon was a blazing hulk wallowing in a crimson wash, her bloody fire-gutted decks strewn with the butchered bodies of her crew.

Aboard *El Murcielago*, Tonnay-Charente regarded a miserable group of prisoners huddled under the poop.

He turned to his blood-spattered mistress who stood beside him hands on hips, devouring her smooth-muscled body with his hawk-like eyes. His gaze swept upward from the full curve of her thighs, to the swell of her jutting breasts, straining against a garish satin blouse.

"*Ma cherie,*" he began, "there is one fundamental which I regard as essential to a successful buccaneering career – you must be cruel, very cruel. Terror, that is the secret. Now what do you suggest we do with the prisoners?"

Hortense knew exactly what he meant. She smiled. "Give them to me," she hissed.

"They're yours," said the Chevalier. He was intrigued to see what his bloodthirsty paramour would do with the Spaniards who stood before him. He knew it was sure to entertain the crew. Torture was one thing, but when it was supervised by a beautiful and sadistic young woman...

"What's your name, pig?"

Hortense spat the words at a young Spaniard who stood a little aside from the main group of prisoners.

"Don José Ibbara y Frances."

"On your knees."

The Spaniard remained standing.

Black leather snaked through the air and slashed the flesh of his cheek. Hortense was an expert with the whip!

Hastily the Spaniard got down on his knees.

"Now tell me," she purred silkily, coiling the whip in her hand, "who is the young woman over there who resembles you?"

"My sister, Pilar," the young man replied eagerly.

"Ah, so!" Hortense exclaimed so softly that few could have heard her. "Repeat after me: The King of Spain is a fat swine and his soldiers are cowardly dogs."

"Never!" The young Spaniard got angrily to his feet.

Everyone waited for the whiplash they felt was sure to come. But Hortense simply shrugged her slim shoulders and smiled covertly to herself. "We'll see," she commented laconically. "Strip the girl called Pilar."

Two of the pirates, a coal-black mulatto and a deformed Basque, seized the girl and began ripping off her clothes.

As in a dream the petrified young *señorita* felt the garments being torn from her back. Suddenly her black satin chemise was gone, and she was standing in the sunlight before the lust-filled eyes of the pirates clad in nothing but silk stockings, garters and high-heeled shoes.

"Now lash her to the mast."

Brutal and eager hands dragged the now screaming girl over to the mainmast, quickly lashing her wrists above her head in such a manner that she was forced to stand on tip-toe, her smooth white body satiny in the sunlight.

"No... no... no! Spare her!" The girl's brother fell once more imploringly upon his knees.

Hortense ignored him.

With the loping, hip-rolling walk that had served her so well in the ports of her native Normandy, she strode idly over to where the Spanish girl was bound, cracking her vicious whip across the deck.

She looked at the girl contemptuously. She was not her type.

"*Sacre nom*, now we shall see something, I warrant!"

The Chevalier touched his famous Van Dyck beard, then ran a pale hand through his long black hair. A faint diamond-hard brilliance shone in his eyes. Not since the old days in Normandy, in the luxurious cellars of his château near Caen – cellars furnished for a pervert's delight – had he seen his paramour beat a woman to death.

Hortense raised the whip over her shoulder. It trailed behind her on the deck.

The pirates murmured and nudged one another.

Whip upraised, the blonde hellion turned to the young Spaniard, still groveling on the deck.

"Is King Philip a fat swine? Are his soldiers cowardly dogs?"

"*Si, si,*" shrilled the young man.

Hortense's lips curled in contempt and her laugh trilled out across the blue water.

Then she went up on her toes and the great black lash whistled through the air.

A livid red weal scarred the Spanish girl's nude body. She screamed in agony, writhing from side to side, and clawed at the mast with lacquered fingernails.

After ten lashes, the girl sagged unconscious, hanging only by her wrists.

"Cut her down," Hortense ordered, coiling her whip.

The Chevalier looked at her, surprised.

Hortense slowly lifted her arm. "Look!" she cried, pointing aft.

A number of sinister black triangles cut through the creamy wake of the ship.

"Toss her overboard!"

Ignoring the girl's shrieks and her brother's hysterical entreaties, several of the pirates hastened to do Hortense's bidding, grabbing the girl's arms and legs and heaving her naked and bleeding over the side.

She hit the blue water with a crimson splash.

Immediately a black shadow cut the water behind her. It circled the girl twice. Then it went over on its back.

The girl kicked frantically, shrieking with terror as the ominous black shadow loomed under her. The shark was so big that instead of snapping at her soft flesh, it seized her whole between its teeth.

Beating upon the monster's bony and barnacled head with her puny fists, the girl thrashed in bloodstained agony. Slowly the great shark sank deeper, the bleeding white body squirming between its jaws. Then, wild and frenzied, the big fish dived.

Aboard *El Murcielago* a mad cheer rose above the slap of the waves. Intoxicated with bloodlust, drunk with rum, the pirates leered drunkenly at the rest of the prisoners.

Hortense egged them on.

"What are you waiting for," she howled. "Over the side with the men and take the women below."

As the Spanish women were dragged into the hold, their men followed the girl over the side, while the sharks, excited to a mad frenzy by so much blood, lashed the sea to a red-flecked foam.

THAT NIGHT, while the Chevalier and his men disported themselves on deck with their captives, Hortense ordered that the Viceroy's daughter be brought to her cabin.

Flanked by two of Hortense's dusky eunuch bodyguards, Magdelena stared fascinated at the blonde woman, naked like herself, who leered up at her from a cougar skin.

"Leave us," Hortense commanded, and the two eunuchs withdrew.

Then terror-stricken understanding dawned suddenly in Magdelena's mind – comprehension of the twisted light shining out of the fierce blue eyes of this queen of the pirates.

A small mocking smile worked its way over Hortense Cerbalaud's red lips.

Magdelena retreated a step as the pirate girl rose up off the cougar skin. The captive looked for a place to run. Weakness, exhaustion, near-madness were stealing upon her, turning her limbs to jelly.

One of Hortense's eyebrows quirked quizzically. Magdelena saw her shudder from a voluptuous thrill. Outside the cabin was obscene laughter and the shrieks of outraged virgins.

Still Hortense stared at the Spanish girl, taking in every detail of her shimmering-white, exposed body.

If only she'd stop smiling, Magdelena thought. That awful, filthy smile, with the tip of her tongue like a bud between her teeth .

"Do you think I'm beautiful?" Hortense purred, sidling closer.

"Stay... stay away from me."

Magdelena's eye lit on an ivory and silver pistol resting atop a little sandalwood table. She darted after it, but Hortense was a shade faster.

The blonde girl swept the pistol from the table with a stroke of her hand, sent it flying with a clatter into a far corner of the cabin. Then she took a step that effectively blocked Magdelena's passage to that corner. She laughed. The sound had an edge of madness in it.

"This time, *ma petite*," she said sibilantly, "I think you'll have to do what you're told. You're proud but weak, very weak. That's good. Perhaps I can protect you from those men outside."

"You evil filth!" Magdelena screamed.

Hortense's vicious back-hander sent the Spanish girl sprawling. Blood trickled from her split lip.

"All right, you little fool, have it your own way," Hortense snarled. And grabbing Magdelena by her long black hair she dragged her out of the cabin.

On deck an unimaginable orgy was in progress, naked and semi-naked human beings practising cruelties only possible of conception in the lust-crazed minds of beasts.

Shrieking with mad laughter, the blonde pirate queen flung Magdelena naked into the sea of writhing carnality.

"See if you like them any better," she howled.

Then, teeth bared like a tigress, she herself plunged into the midst of the tangle of bodies.

Next morning the pirate chief, the Chevalier de Tonnay-Charente, held a conference in his cabin.

"Tlaloc here," he said, indicating the *mestizo* who had recently become his second in command, "has often spoken of the forbidden city of Iztopolopo, and of the great riches to be found there."

He paused, waiting for this to sink in.

"It seems that the Quetzatcoatls have a legend that a blonde goddess will come from the sea to lead the warriors against their enemies. They are snake worshipers, sacrificing maidens to the Great Serpent of Set in a temple made of solid gold..."

The pirate captain's eyes blazed with avarice.

"But," the Chevalier went on, "no man, no white man that is, has ever set foot in the forbidden city and lived."

"That's true," shouted a red-bearded giant. "All who venture into the forbidden city are cast into the pit of sacrifice."

"My friends," purred the Chevalier, "have you considered what the Priests of Set would give to get their hands on the..." he smiled suggestively, "...virgins in our hold?"

"Another thing, my friends," continued the bearded Tonnay-Charente, "have you ever thought of Hortense in the role of a blonde goddess?"

Slowly the light of understanding dawned in the eyes of the pirates, and for long hours they planned their expedition into the interior of Ecuador, a feat of endurance that was to rank with Morgan's march on Panama.

How Tonnay-Charente and his pirates hacked their way through the dripping Ecuadorian jungle, surviving the swarms of malarial mosquitoes that attacked them; how they finally reached the forbidden city of Iztopolopo, and how Hortense Cerbalaud, the first blonde white woman the Quetzalcoatl Indians had ever seen, became the Goddess of Set, is all set down in history. Thomas Manderling's *History of the Buccaneers* and St. John Mortimer's *Strange Deities* carry detailed and graphic accounts, the latter describing how

Magdelena de Montalban was sold as a human sacrifice to the Indians and how greed for the red gold of Set turned this transaction into a regular trafficking in captive virgins. Finally, in *Six Evil Women* by Hedda Laas, it is told how Hortense eventually betrayed her pirate lover to the Spaniards when he objected to her having a love affair with an Indian maid.

The Spaniards surprised Tonnay-Charente and a few of his men at their point of disembarkation on the Ecuador coast, having had word from Hortense by messenger.

The Chevalier was taken in chains to Lima, where his eyes were burnt out and he was flung into a dungeon in the Spanish fortress of El Moto.

On the 2th of September, 1671, just a little more than two years after he fled his native Normandy, Lucien de Tonnay-Charente was lead out into the public square of Lima, before an almost entirely female crowd, for execution by quartering.

As the muffled drums rolled their dirge of death, and the gnomish executioners attached the chains to his limbs and to the horses that would rip him asunder, the pirate smiled sardonically to himself.

He had never told his treacherous mistress of the codicil to his agreement with the High Priest of Set: that should he fail to provide a sacrifice for the thing in the pit, the blonde goddess herself would be the substitute.

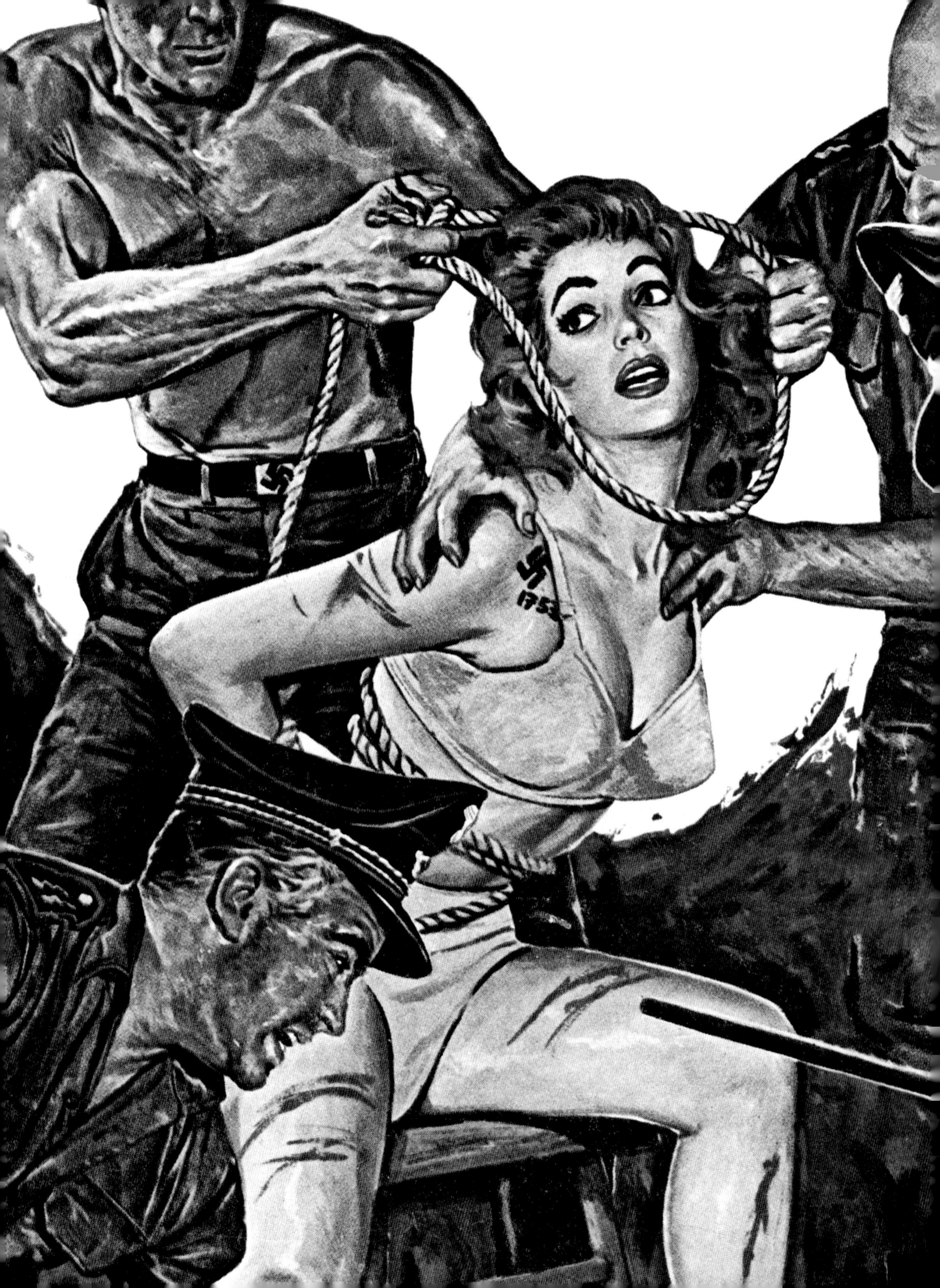

A SOFT WHITE THROAT FOR THE DEVIL'S HANGMAN

Savagely the Das Reich sadist tightened the noose. Simone's body quivered in torment...

HENRIQUE'S FACE WAS FEARFUL to behold. It screwed up into a thing of unbelievable hate. The Kraut saw it and squealed out his fear. He felt the cold steel of the bayonet pressing against his neck.

I watched in sick fascination as the Kraut's fists clawed the ground beneath him. His helmet rolled off on the turf beside him. His mouth worked insanely as he realized there was no hope.

"Not yet," I growled at Henrique. "We'll need him."

The Maquis' mad eyes searched mine for a moment. Then he eased the pressure on our captive.

"Speak!" he ordered in a low voice which held sheer menace.

"A farmhouse. Three kilometers north of Limoge. It is the only one around. You can't miss it." The German's words raced over each other as he lay beneath my booted foot. Then the superman's voice cracked in a crescendo of blubbering sobs.

I grabbed him by the back of the neck and lifted him to a sitting position. He gasped in terror at the sight of his three comrades already frozen in the grotesque positions of violent death.

Now stripped of their uniforms, they looked something less than arrogant members of the Das Reich Division. As a matter of fact they resembled rag dolls more than men.

Our captive covered his eyes with his trembling hands. "*Mein Herr*, I am but a lowly corporal. I merely carry out orders. If I do not, I too will swing from the trees."

Henrique studied the cowering hulk at our feet. "The filthy Boche does not even have the courage to die as a man," he whispered in pure venom. "He has courage only to string helpless women from the trees."

"I never hanged anyone," the Kraut gibbered. "I am a soldier. I would not commit such atrocities."

"You are a pig." Henrique answered. "You are a loathsome pig."

"Let's get on with it," I pleaded. "Every second counts. We may be too late already."

"But *non, mon ami*. The Boche will not allow Simone the privilege of a swift clean death. Even if she had no secrets in her head, they would revel in her torment. She is – how you say – the prize package."

In helpless fury, I knew Henrique was right. Simone would be kept alive to sate the perverted lusts of the Das Reich fiends. Even now she was probably enduring indescribable agony at the hands of the Panzer Division's chief interrogators. The thought made me clench my fist until the blood flowed where my fingernails had ripped the flesh of my palms.

"I am but a lowly non-commissioned officer," our captive began all over again.

"You are a liar. You are SS-Obersturmführer Gruber. We know all about you. Only an Obersturmführer would be allowed to drive a command car."

"We're getting nowhere," I blurted. "Get the swine on his feet. He's going to give us safe conduct into Limoge."

The Nazi's eyes rolled wildly. For the first time since we had ambushed his command car on the little dirt road, he saw some hope for himself.

"I will do what you tell me. I promise," he sputtered.

"You're damned right you will, buddy boy," I grinned. There was no humor in my smile. "Because the first time you step out of line, your square head rolls right out alongside your helmet. Now get the hell up on your feet."

Swiftly, as I guarded the Kraut, Henrique stripped off his own outer clothes and rolled them into a tight ball. Then he donned the camouflaged fatigues of one of the corpses. Jacques was next. Then I followed.

Once we had completed the change of clothing, we dragged the nearly prostrate German to the car. My knife pricked his back, speeding him along. At last he sat trembling beside me as I fiddled with the ignition. I cursed the thought that we would have to drive right smack through the stricken city to get to he farm house. But it was a risk we couldn't avoid.

Gruber seemed to gain some of his composure as we rattled along the road. His back stiffened and a shade of his old arrogance seemed to reassert itself. Henrique leaned over from the back seat and let him feel the steel of his knife again.

"Remember, Boche," he hissed. "One word, one look

of betrayal, and your entire division will be unable to save you."

Gruber's face turned a dirty gray and he swallowed hard. Sweat rolled down his crew-cut blond hair and oozed over his face. He shifted his weight to ease the pressure of the blade in his back. Morosely he gazed out on the scenery.

By now we were passing little clusters of German vehicles which chugged along the road. A tank commander waved at us from his turret.

He held a bottle of French champagne to his mouth and the liquid ran down his chin.

I could have cut the bastard's throat from ear to ear. But I forced myself to grin back at him.

Traffic became heavier as we neared the village. A troop carrier rolled along, kicking up a cloud of dust. Drunken soldiers leaned over the sides, singing and shouting. My blood was suddenly frozen by the terrified scream of a woman.

I nearly drove the command car into a mud ditch as I saw the Krauts pick a young girl up by the heels and swing her head first over the side of the truck.

She had been stripped stark naked, and even from this distance I could see the marks of mutilation all over her once beautiful body. Her head banged against the steel side of the truck with a sickening crunch. She cried out once more as rough hands seized her and dragged her back into the truck. Then her body hurtled through the air, splattering on the road. The tank following in the line of the convoy never even slowed down as its clanking treads mashed the girl's body to pulp.

It had been too much for Henrique. Before I could stop him, the blade had sunk a good nine inches into Gruber's back. The Das Reich Division officer gurgled something in a welter of his own blood, then slumped forward.

We'd bought real trouble now. Here we were – an American pursuit pilot and two Maquis dressed in Kraut uniforms, cruising along with a corpse in the midst of the vaunted Das Reich Panzer Division of the Elite Guard.

Swiftly I swerved the command car to the side of the road. With my boot I shoved Gruber out. His body flopped face down in the ditch.

Luckily the other Krauts on the road were too busy with their bloody lust orgies to give us any attention. They had taken off their wraps and wallowed in the worst type of bestiality.

I gunned the engine and goosed the vehicle through the long lines of equipment. We were in the outskirts of Limoge itself. As we turned towards the main square, I had to bring the car to a screeching stop. In impotent fury we sat and waited while a group of ten or twelve Nazis dragged a young woman from the door of a house.

One of the Krauts held her in his powerful arms while two others brutally stripped her dress from her. The indomitable girl held her head high, looking towards the sky. She seemed unaware that she stood before the lecherous gaze of her captors clad only in the briefest silk panties and bra.

One of the Germans stepped behind her with a short length of rope. Swiftly he seized her wrists and bound them securely behind her back. Then as we watched, unable to accept the fact that this atrocity was taking place right before our eyes, rough hands stripped the last of her clothing from her buxom body.

A Kraut had shinnied up a tree with a long coil of rope. Laughingly he secured it to a stout branch and dropped the other end to a comrade in the street below.

The French girl didn't utter a sound as the noose was dropped over her head. Soon her strangled breathing mingled with her mother's mad grief as she was hefted aloft. Her legs danced wildly in the lowering sun. Her whole body jerked in horrible spasms of agony. The bastards weren't even going to allow her to die swiftly on a broken neck. She would swing from the branch until the last vestiges of breath were choked from her body.

"Let's get out of here!" Henrique growled in my ear. "We can do nothing for the *pauvre enfant*!"

AS I stomped down on the accelerator, it all flashed through my fevered brain. This was Central France. April, 1944. This was the terror of the Nazis being played out to its mad conclusion.

The Das Reich Division had been sent into the Limoge Military District to put an end to all French resistance.

The Kraut High Command reasoned the Allied Invasion would strike at any hour. The Germans could not leave their backs open to the actions of the Maquis, the FFI and Allied Saboteurs who had been dropped in the area.

Yet they could not flush out the underground. No matter how they tried, no matter how many Maquis they tortured and killed, there were always others to take their place.

So a systematic program of reprisals against helpless civilians had been devised. They would pay with agony and death for the activities of their fighting countrymen.

And now, Simone would pay for her gallantry in a way even more horrible than the girl whose body twisted and blackened at the end of the swinging rope.

I hadn't been the first flier to be shot down behind enemy lines as the Eighth Air Force stepped up its runs over occupied Europe in preparation for Overlord. Nor had I been the first who had been spirited under cover of night to Simone Fabray's home to await a secret trip to the sanctuary of an Allied PT boat.

Yet I liked to think that what Simone and I had in the weeks of my enforced presence in her attic was something special.

I'd never forget the first time I had seen Simone, standing blonde and magnificent in the half-light of her fireplace. Only hours ago I'd ditched my Mustang in a haystack and, according to S.O.P., had set fire to it. Then I'd sat down to await capture, knowing that I'd probably sit out the rest of the war in an internment camp.

I hadn't reckoned with the speed and efficiency of the FFI. They had swooped down like so many ghosts and spirited me to Simone's place.

As I stood before her, I was conscious of the filth of my oil-splattered uniform. I ran a hand over the stubble of my jaw, knowing I must make one hell of a sight to this girl who had the face and form of an angel.

"Monsieur looks very attractive and virile that way," Simone had laughed. The sound of her voice was like a brook singing over glistening stones. I found myself grinning back at her, for the moment all thoughts of the war and my predicament driven from my mind by her presence.

"One will want a bath and a change of clothes, *n'est-ce pas*?" she smiled.

"One might," I answered back with a lop-sided grin. "But it has to be fast. You could buy yourself a pack of trouble if the Krauts find me here."

"The Boche," she murmured in derision. "The stupid Boche. What do I care for them?" Yet even as she spoke, involuntarily her eyes darted to the huge wooden front door. "*L'Americain* must go upstairs now."

Henrique, who had brought me to the house, nodded to me to follow my breath-taking hostess. "It will be better if I leave now," he said. "Who can say which neighbor has sworn allegiance to Vichy? Who can say which eye is that of Judas?"

Silently he slid through the door into the terrifying darkness of the night.

"A bath, a change of clothes, an aperitif perhaps, and then we will talk, Monsieur," Simone suggested.

I found my eyes riveted to her magnificent body. Immediately I took in the impudent swell of her breasts as they fought the restraining tightness of her black dress. My gaze flew over the flatness of her stomach, the supple swell of her hips, the plump thighs which were outlined by her skirt. She was the most woman I had ever seen.

It may not have been the fastest bath on record, but it was a close second. I couldn't believe that this could be happening to me. It sounded like one of those "Miss Lace" strips we used to guffaw over back at Bristol.

But as I rubbed myself dry on the towel, I was brought back to the desperateness of my situation by a sudden knock at the door.

Simone stood breathlessly. "Hurry!" she whispered. She was completely unaware that I was jaybird naked. "The Gestapo is searching the area. One must hide in the attic."

With nothing more than a towel wrapped around me, I raced through the hallway and up the attic ladder. The air in the room was stifling and I almost drowned in my own sweat. From below I heard guttural voices barking orders. Simone answered quickly. Boots stamped on the steps. There was the sound of overturned furniture and doors being slammed open and shut. I didn't dare to breathe.

Suddenly the voices were directly beneath me. This was it. In seconds the Krauts would climb the stairs and pull me out. Goose bumps of terror wriggled over my skin. I wasn't afraid for myself. It was the thought of what they'd do to Simone.

Then I heard Simone saying, "A schnapps perhaps. Vintage champagne. But of course, in the wine cellar. Where else?"

The boots receded down the corridor. I whispered a prayer of thanks and ran a trembling hand over my brow. Then I wedged my body deeper behind some dusty crates and waited.

About an hour later, I heard the tap of high heels mounting the ladder. I raised my head. There she stood before me, her luscious body framed in the light from below,

"Pigs," Simone laughed good naturedly. "Stupid pigs. They work with Vichy and they take Vichy's word for everything. Little do they know that every top Maquis is listed with Vichy as a collaborator. It gives us room to move around."

I watched Simone, the light of hatred in her eyes giving the lie to the smile on her lips. She knew well how closely she lived with the threat of exposure, torture and death.

But for the moment we didn't talk about it. I stood up and wrapped the towel more tightly. Simone grinned wantonly at my discomfort.

"But this is France, Monsieur," she breathed impishly. "Here one does not believe in false modesty, especially when tomorrow one may be a corpse lying in a ditch."

"You've got something there," I grinned back. But still I held onto the towel for dear life. Simone disregarded the gesture.

"You must stay up here tonight," she warned. "The Boche always make the rounds after a plane crashes. They wish to parade captured fliers in Berlin to show the populace how wonderfully well the war goes with Goering's Luftwaffe."

I nodded my agreement. Right now being alone in a room – even a dusty attic – with Simone was enough to take my mind off Hitler, Goering and the whole stinking Wehrmacht. I guess she sensed it too. Without a word she was across the room and in my arms.

Her body was soft and vibrant as I embraced her. My hands ran over the contours of her back, tracing the brief hemline of her panties under the tight dress. Our breathing was choked and ragged. Her lips burned mine with their insistent fire. Her fingers toyed with my ear lobe, sending little shivers of delight racing over my nerves.

She moaned low in her throat and her nails clawed my naked shoulder. Our hips ground together in mounting desire.

"*Cheri*, I have but this dress to wear. Be careful how you take it off," she whispered. Her hands guided me to the clasps. Slowly, reverently, I raised her skirt over her head, glorying in the magnificence of her beauty as it shimmered through the transparency of her pink silk panties and bra.

"The floor will not be too uncomfortable, *cheri*," she murmured, her moist lips pressed against my ear.

For a week I considered myself the luckiest guy in all of SHAEF. My adventure was the kind that recruiting posters are made of. Here I was hiding out in the soft arms of the most gorgeous woman I had ever imagined. Lazily I spent my time forgetting the hell of the saturation strafing missions. I was selfish enough to admit that I didn't care whether the war ever ended.

But if I had forgotten the war, nobody else had. I learned that the night Henrique came bustling into Simone's house with the dreaded news.

"The Boche are moving a whole division into Limoge," he sputtered. "They will carry out a campaign of terror against the civilian population. Their plan is diabolical. They must break the French spirit before the Allies land in Europe. They reason this will keep us from giving aid to our friends."

"They do not know the French spirit," Simone cut in.

"And you do not know the Germans for the beasts they are. You have never heard of the Das Reich Panzer Division? They are worse than the guards at Dachau."

Our council of war continued through he night. We decided that we couldn't risk my being placed on the underground railroad to Calais at this time. I would join Henrique's action group and fight from the surrounding hills. Simone would continue her espionage through her contacts with the Nazis. Periodically there would be clandestine meetings at her house to bring us up to date on the Das Reich dispositions.

For the next two weeks the Maquis stepped up their operations. We raced through the countryside putting the torch to ammo dumps, leaving our demolition charges along major roads, blasting away at airdromes.

I'd stolen whatever moments I could with Simone. We'd filter into her house under cover of night, there to be briefed on the latest coordinated operations. For several hours we were all business. Then as the others melted into the darkness, I would remain behind. My comrades understood with a typical continental shrug of their shoulders. They knew what comfort a girl like Simone could bring. They knew too that she had little in common with the farmers of Limoge. Perhaps she longed for a return to the *Comedie Francaise*. Perhaps I reminded her of better days before the Krauts had swaggered across Europe in their spotted fatigues, their truncheons swinging from their belts.

Things were fast moving to a climax. We heard that the Das Reich Division had taken 250 residents of Limoge as hostages against our next action. Much as we hated them, we couldn't bring ourselves to believe that the Germans would carry out reprisals against helpless women and children for the activities of our army. How wrong we were.

After our raid on a bunker on 5 April, we learned that fifteen persons had been strung up from trees in the Haute Vienne.

That night at Simone's house we debated long and loud the advisability of suspending our raids for awhile. Even though I hadn't seen the bodies of women and children swinging in the breeze, I was all for holing up.

"We cannot, *mon ami*," Henrique pointed out. "Every Boche we kill will be one less to infest the invasion coast when the landings come. Even the civilians must assume the risks of total war."

Simone's face was white and set. Yet she knew as well as I did that there was no arguing with Henrique's reasoning. She squared her shoulders and spread a map on the little wooden table. "This is the area for tonight's strike," she commented quietly.

NOW, AS we raced through the village, I realized how much more than the rest of us Simone had known of the dangers involved. As she had lain in my arms later that night, she had told me that she was under constant surveillance.

"The Boche have their ways of finding out things," she had whispered. "Soon they will come. *C'est la guerre*. I only hope that I will be brave like my lover here when they take me away. I will not cry. I will not plead. I will die for France."

I smothered her mouth with my kisses, trying to blot out the hideous words she spoke. Simone was life. She couldn't be defiled by the Nazis.

But the yammering of my command car's engine told me how wrong I'd been. Simone was a human being. She was a woman. She could feel agony. She could bleed and writhe and die. And at this very moment she was being held in the diabolical torture chamber the Das Reich command had built in Limoge. I wondered why I was crazy enough to believe that there still might be hope.

As we careened past the wild troops of the Das Reich Division, I was sickened by the sights. All semblance of discipline had been removed. On every street corner, young girls were being stripped and raped before the very eyes of their sweethearts and parents. Once the Nazi beasts had vented their lust on their victims, the girls were bound band and foot and hanged from the trees. Not content with the murders, the Krauts were belaboring the girls with heavy truncheons adding to the torture of slow strangulation.

Henrique sat immobile beside me. Only the way his hand worked at the Mauser he had lifted from Gruber gave away his true feelings. In his Das Reich uniform, he could have been any "superman" on a courier's mission.

Quickly I outlined my plan to him while we sped onwards. He and Jacques were to remain in the command car outside of the farm house. I would go in and demand that Simone be placed in my custody for further interrogation by the Waffen SS. If anything went wrong, if I weren't back in the command car within a half an hour, Henrique was to let go with a potato masher and blow the farm house to hell.

Ten minutes later we squealed to a stop. Arrogantly I swung down from the car. Nobody questioned my rank. The Das Reich troops were careful to obscure insignia of rank. It was a way of building the terror in the hearts of the captive populace.

Even as the armed guard stepped aside and I walked through the heavy oaken door of the farm house, my guts churned with horror. The sight was more than I could stand.

The bastard in charge had taken a young red-headed girl and strung her to the overhead ceiling by her thumbs. Two other torturers were stripping her. They had already taken her dress away and she swung back and forth at the rope's end, her sweating body nude except for her black silk panties.

The Nazis didn't bother looking at me. They busied themselves attaching heavy lengths of chain to the girl's fettered ankles. The chains were run through a ring in the floor to a winch. One of the bastards began cranking the winch. The girl's body heaved in a paroxysm of torment. I heard a sickening sound such as that made by a cracking chicken bone. The girl's screams tore through the room.

Now a Nazi walked up behind her. His hands slid under the waistband of her panties. The material ripped viciously. His heavy rubber truncheon exploded across her flesh where the cloth had been. The girl's pain crazed eyes rolled back in her head.

"*Ach so*," grunted the leading Kraut. "Now you, can tell us about the Maquis, my love. Where are they located? How many of them are there? What are their names?"

"I know nothing," the girl cried out between her sobs. "Nothing at all."

The Nazi nodded to the man at the winch. The chain clanked ominously. The straining captive's head went up as new agony raced through her tortured thumbs. Suddenly she shuddered violently and her head fell forward on her breast.

For the first time the Kraut became aware of my presence. "They are stubborn," he grunted. "But we break them. Cut this sow down and bring in the other one."

I felt my hand moving towards my side arm. How easy it would be to put a slug through this fiend's head. Yet I couldn't. I'd have to play along with him, bide my time. As we waited for the tortured girl to be cut loose, the Kraut offered me a cigarette. I fought down my revulsion as my hand brushed his.

"You are just in time," he smirked. "We have brought in a really delectable morsel. Not like these peasants. This one looks almost Aryan. But she is a French Resistance sow."

"She may be the one I'm looking for," I said in my best German, hoping that the bastard wouldn't catch wise "There is one who is to be given special treatment."

"There is no treatment you can give which is as effective as mine. I have had experience. I learned at Ravensbruck." The Nazi glowed with pride at mention of the infamous women's concentration camp. "I'll show you how we tore secrets from their cunning lips with the use of nothing more than a rope."

He nodded again and the two noncoms moved out of the room. They returned in a moment dragging Simone between them. I prayed that she would not give rue away by any show of recognition.

I was scared now. The Kraut would not give up his prisoner easily. If I threw my weight around too much, he would suspect something phoney. [here was only one thing to do – if only I could bring myself to do it – I would have to wait until I could show a lack of patience at his torture methods for their failure to wrest the desired information.

Simone's eyes swept the room. Her face was pale, but otherwise she exhibited no other sign of fear.

"Take off your dress," the Nazi ordered. His captive stood rigid. "Off! I said off!" he shouted.

Slowly Simone reached for the hem of her skirt. Her body trembled but she said nothing as she peeled the material up over her head. The perverted gaze of the Nazi was drawn to her beauty now that it stood revealed against the delicate pink of her silk panties and bra.

"She will talk," the chief torturer gloated. "She will beg to talk. They always did at Ravensbruck." Then he turned towards Simone as one of the other captors jammed a rough-hewn chair against the backs of her knees. "Sit down, sow," he ordered.

Simone collapsed into the chair. In a trice the Nazis had seized her arms and bound them securely behind the chair's back. Simone shrank from their perverted touch but refused to cry out, even when her ankles were cruelly tied to the chairs legs. Then a heavy rope was passed around her plump thighs, digging white furrows in her pink flesh. Her waist was tightly bound to the back of the chair.

"You have never seen the garrotte?" the Das Reich officer asked me. "It is magnificent for wresting information."

"This is the prisoner I'm to escort," I cut in.

"In time. You would not deny us our sport?"

"I must be back soon."

"It won't take long. The Gestapo can wait a few minutes."

He talked to me through the side of his mouth as his eyes bugged out watching the other Nazi fashioning a noose out of a heavy coil of rope.

"Who are your friends, sow?" the chief torturer asked.

"I have no friends, *monsieur*," Simone gasped.

In horror I remembered her vow to die bravely. I recoiled in terror as the noose was dropped over her head.

Simone's face blanched. One of the Nazis threw the coil of rope over a ceiling beam. Then two of them grabbed the loose end and pulled on it heavily.

Simone's lithe body strained upwards. Still the heavy ropes which bound her held her to the stout chair. Her face grew red and then purple. I could see the angry blood trying to burst its way through constricted vessels.

"You see how it works?" the chief torturer gloated. "It is slow strangulation. We ease up the pressure just long enough to keep the woman alive. There is no agony to match it."

Simone thrashed against her bonds. Little rivulets of blood ran down her legs and arms where the splintery ropes cut in.

"Who are your friends?" the torturer repeated as he stood over her, tearing away her panties and bra. His nails left vicious streaks on her superb white skin.

"I have no friends," she whispered in choked gasps.

"Again," the torture master ordered. Once more the rope grew taught. Simone gurgled horribly. I was rapidly growing violently ill at the sight.

"You'll have to work with another," stepped in imperiously. "General Kaltenbrunner will not be kept waiting. I have my orders to transport this sow while she is still alive. I would not want to tell the general that you were uncooperative."

The torturer sighed in disappointment. Reluctantly he ordered the stranglers to stop. I moved in and hacked the ropes which held Simone to the chair. Mercifully, she had fainted. I picked her soft body up in my arms and strode towards the door. I was immediately aware of Jacques and Henrique storming past me. The Das Reich men seemed confused. Then the farmhouse was alive with submachine-gun fire. Hurriedly I raced into the road. I placed my precious naked burden on the front seat beside me.

The chatter of small arms fire was all around us. I wrestled with the command car's ignition. The engine coughed to life just as two racing forms emerged from the building carrying a naked woman between them. Other figures staggered after them.

"Hurry!" Henrique shouted as he piled into the back seat.

"The others!" I yelled, "They're following you."

"Not for long," he grinned.

My tires squealed on the road as I executed a tight turn. At that very instant the farm house disintegrated in a blood red flash of fire and smoke. It was then I remembered Henrique's potato masher. It had done its work well.

Insolently we drove slowly through the streets of Limoge. None of the Das Reich fiends so much as batted an eye as they saw three men in German uniforms holding two battered naked women between them. Some of the Krauts even grinned and waved whiskey bottles at us.

That night we moved back into the hills to revamp our sabotage plans. Yet the thought of what our operations would cost the civilians in the villages below put a damper on our spirits. Nobody could have come through the hell hole that was Limoge untouched by the sights and sounds of bestiality.

THE ARMY OF MUTILATED MEN

They were the living dead – and because life had no meaning to them, they ravaged, raped and killed.

IT WAS ABOUT AN hour before sunset. The little town of Clearspring, Kansas, population 303, was just sitting down to supper. the date was April 9, 1866: exactly one year after Lee had surrendered his army at Appomattox.

The three men who were lounging about in front of the general store drew stares of curiosity and pity from the few townspeople who were still abroad at that hour. The tattered remnants of old uniforms proclaimed them to be veterans of

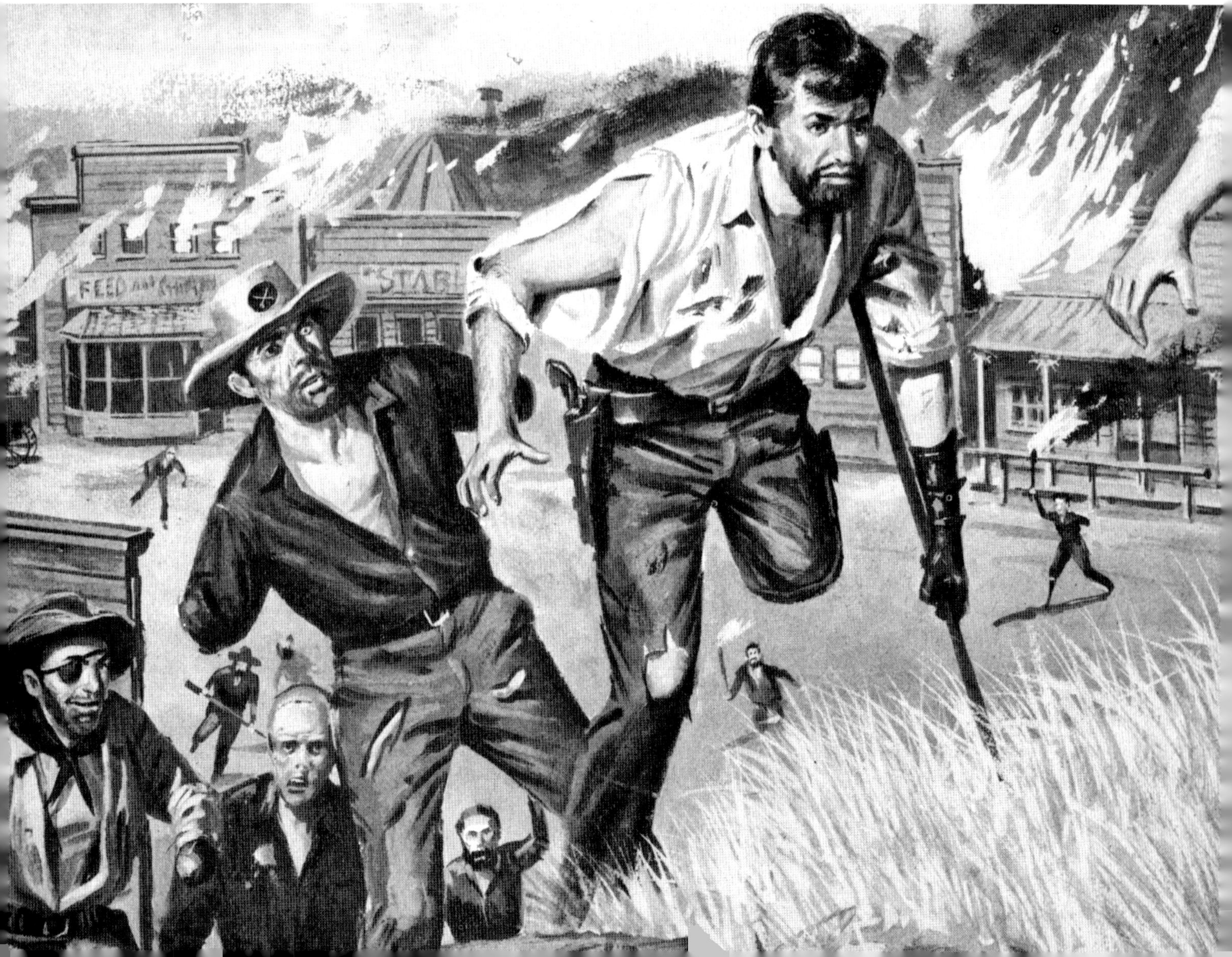

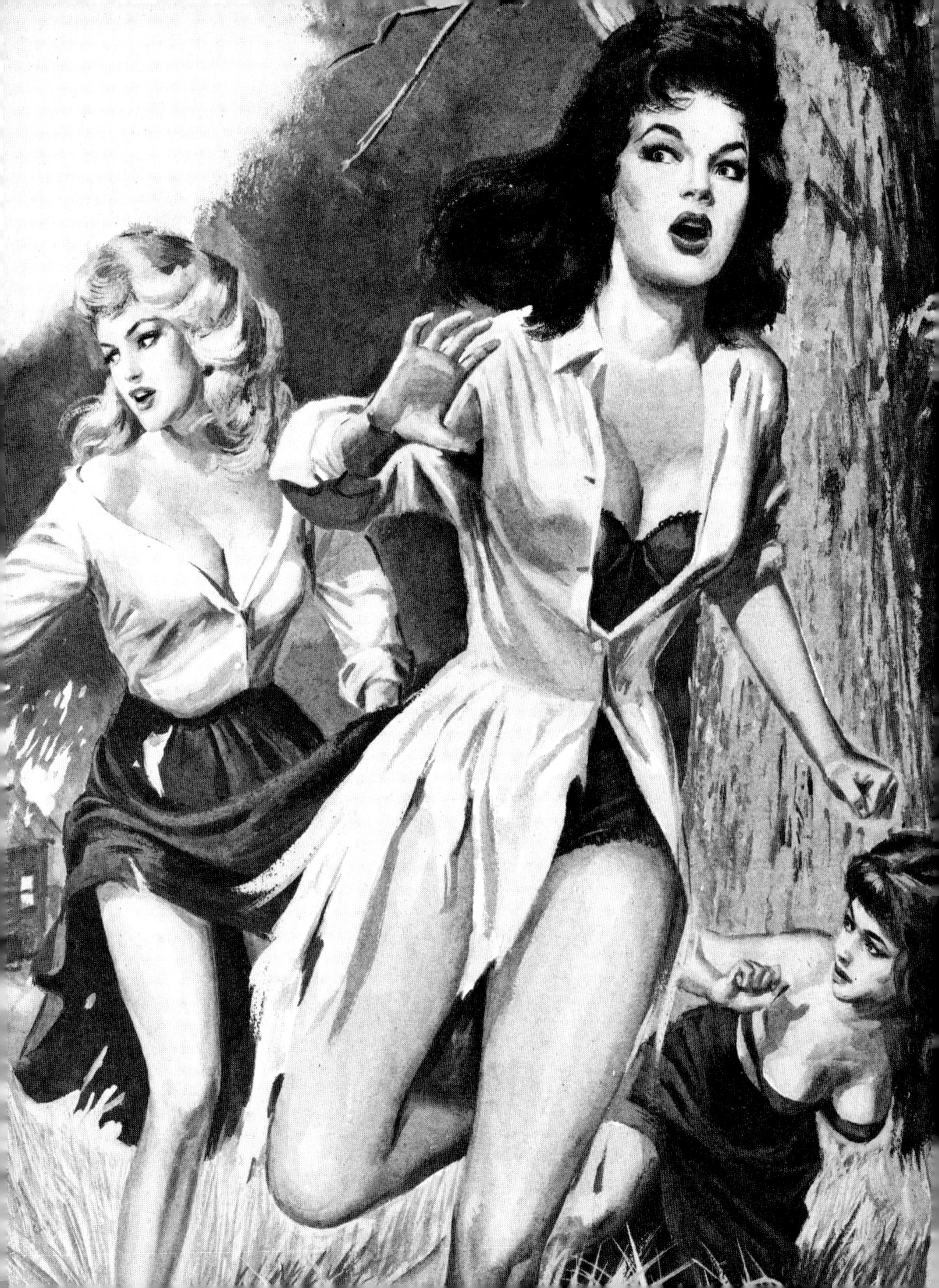

the Civil War, like the thousands of homeless, jobless drifters who had been roaming the country since the previous spring. Two of the men wore Union blue, while the third wore the remains of Confederate gray – an unusual alliance in the bitter aftermath of those post-war days.

But if they had been foes during the war, they were brothers now in their common misery. For all three had been horribly wounded; their scars and disabilities had made it forever impossible for them to live in ordinary society.

The man in gray had suffered a particularly ghastly wound. His nose and his entire lower jaw had been shot away, and his tongue lolled pink and hideous from the inhuman ruins of his face. Almost as gruesome was the blind man sitting on the empty cracker barrel nearby; his face was a mass of burn scars, lumpy and purple. The third man, leaning on his crutch, had lost his left arm and his right leg. Unquenchable bitterness burned in his eyes and tightened his mouth to a thin line.

Every once in a while, the storekeeper would peer anxiously out at them. Their presence was driving away business, but he could not bring himself to ask them to leave. They had come into the town from nowhere, early that morning, and parked themselves first in front of the livery stable and now here. No one had said a word to them. Folks hurried by, their eyes averted, after the first look.

Now the man in gray pointed at the setting sun and said something. The man with the crutch nodded. Balancing himself on his one leg, he leaned his crutch against the cracker barrel, drew an old army pistol from beneath his shirt and fired it in the air.

And suddenly the ridge on the eastern border of the little town was alive. A ragged horde of men came boiling over the skyline, whooping and shouting; waving rifles and rusty sabers, shooting pistols in the air.

The proprietor of the general store came rushing outside. "What's going on?" he shouted.

Deliberately, the man with the missing jaw raised a pistol and shot him through the face.

The men who were swarming by the hundreds down the main street of Clearspring were no ordinary invaders. To the horrified townspeople who were now seeing them at close quarters, they must have seemed a troop of fiends out of Hell. Every one of them had been mutilated in some way. Many of them, in addition, had fearfully damaged faces.

They flowed like a tattered tide down the street, a motley of Union blue and Confederate gray, hopping or crawling if they had missing legs, some with empty sleeves flapping in the wind. Blind men groped among them, grasping the tunics of crippled men with eyes. A man whose mouth was a black hole in a face like raw meat shouted hysterically. A giant of a man swung a cavalry saber that had been strapped to his handless forearm. A wild-eyed hobgoblin, made into a dwarf by some impersonal cannonball, waddled on the leather-wrapped stumps of his legs, waving two pistols.

The town of Clearspring didn't have a chance. Its men were slaughtered in the streets or burned out of their houses if they tried to barricade themselves indoors. Its women were raped again and again, then, if they were lucky, forgotten while they crawled away, whimpering. If they were unlucky, they were clubbed to death or sliced apart by those members of the mob whose disability included the loss of manhood – a disability that had given them a taste for more grisly pleasures than sex.

THE HELLISH scene was described years later by one of the survivors of the massacre, a man named Luke Shaw, who at the time was a boy of sixteen.

"They were breaking into the general store and the saloons, helping themselves to the liquor and anything else that took their fancy. Half of them were drunk by sundown. The street was bright as day, though, because they'd set fire to a lot of houses.

"They never found out I was there, and I was glad, because those crippled men, they were mean. My neighbor, Mr. Cozzens, tried to fight them off with a rifle, but they took it away from him before he had got off more than a shot or two. They did awful things to him. One of them stuck a knife in his eye, and when he screamed, they just laughed. Then the one with the knife, he cut off Mr. Cozzens' ears. When they took down his pants, I couldn't look no more. I didn't want to see them do it. But I heard Mr. Cozzens scream. I never heard a man scream like that before, and I never hope to hear anything like it again. The next time I looked, they were pouring kerosene over him, and they set him on fire. He flopped around like a fish on land, screaming all the while. I was glad when he finally died.

"They stripped Mrs. Cozzens naked. A couple of them held her down, and the rest of them lined up as if they were waiting for a turn at the mess hall. They were laughing and joking, and passing around a jug of whiskey. Sometimes the man who was next would yell to the one ahead of him to hurry up, and the rest of them would laugh and make remarks. All the time, Mrs. Cozzens was sobbing. She kept her eyes closed. I guess she didn't want to see them. They were an awful sight, all right. Men with missing limbs and scarred faces. One of them had a hole where his nose was supposed to be. Another one of them had his cheeks torn away. I guess you could say he had no face at all. One of them was a blind man, and they guided his hands over her body. He kept asking, 'Is she purty, fellows?' They told him what she looked like.

"The line kept growing. More of the men came over when they saw what was going on. They were drunk, and their pockets were bulging with stuff they'd stolen from the houses they'd broken into – silver and trinkets and goods from the store. Mrs. Cozzens wasn't making any more sounds. It was a mercy that she'd fainted. I guess just about every woman and girl in town got the same kind of treatment. Lucy Howard killed herself the next day. Mrs. Cozzens, she went crazy. I hear they put her in a hospital back East.

"The only one that didn't seem to be taking part in the murder and looting was a man in a Union coat with captain's bars and a Confederate hat. You couldn't rightly say what he was, except that he was once an officer. He was mounted on a big white horse, and he wore a cavalry saber at his side. There was a brace of pistols in his belt His right leg was missing above the knee, and his left hand was missing three fingers. His face looked as if it had been taken apart and pasted back together again by someone who hadn't been very good at the job. The bones must have been smashed, and there was a wide purple furrow all down one side.

"He rode up and down the street all night, watching everything, but not taking part. In the morning, he started rousing the men where they'd passed out, leaning over and whacking them with the flat of his sword. He got them mustered up. They obeyed him as if he was the commanding officer. He got them out of town an hour before the Army arrived. Bert Fisher had escaped at the beginning of it all, and had ridden out to fetch the troopers. They looked for them for days, but they never found them. They were hiding out in the hills, I guess."

A horrifying total of fourteen towns in Kansas, Missouri and Oklahoma suffered the same fate as Clearspring. The U.S. Army was powerless. The band of mutilated men would descend on some helpless settlement and strip it bare. They would massacre the men, rape the women, rob and loot. When they were finished, they would fling the remains of the town aside like the carcass of a barbequed chicken. By the time the Army arrived on the scene, the mutilated men were safe in the hills. The soldiers never were able to engage them in battle.

WHERE DID the bizarre horde come from? Who was the man on the white horse who seemed to be its leader? These questions may never be answered. The man on the white horse called himself Sam Moessler, but a thorough search of the records of both the Union and Confederate armies were unable to match him up with any officer or enlisted man of that name.

Stories pieced together years later, however, indicate a sequence something like this. Moessler – whose real identity may never be known – had found himself, at the end of the Civil War, a pitiful remnant of the man he once must have been. He did not want to return to his home, wherever it was, because of his ghastly wounds. Rumour has supplied him with a beautiful fiancée whom he could not bear to face. Whatever the truth of the matter, Moessler became a drifter; a drifter who could not get a job in a land where even able-bodied men were out of work, and whose face was so revolting that it repelled even people with charitable impulses who might have helped him.

He fell in with three or four men like himself, all mutilated in some way by the war. They took to robbing lonely farm houses for food and money. The women they found there, they took by force. No normal woman would have anything to do with them ordinarily, and they took a savage satisfaction in assaulting the wives and daughters of the farmers they robbed.

One by one, other wounded veterans joined them. When their number reached twenty, they had become a widely-known and feared band. Other mutilated men, attracted by their fame, sought out the band and joined them. There was no shortage of maimed and disfigured men in the fall and winter of 1865. All of them were desperate and hungry. All were resentful of the society that had used them for cannon fodder, then flung them away unwanted. None were turned away by Moessler.

The blind were led by the crippled. The crippled were supported by the blind. Those without hands were fed by those without legs. Each man did the job he was able to do. Nobody in Moessler's strange army was repelled by the despoiled faces of his companions.

Hurt themselves, they took pleasure in hurting others. Rejected by women, they had their revenge in brutally ravaging their female victims. Barred from human society, they hit back by looting, burning and killing.

No one was asked whether he was a Yankee or a Johnnie Reb. That was a part of the past that had injured them all. A scarred face or a mutilated body was the only badge of admission.

By the fall of 1866, Moessler's band had grown to almost a thousand men, armed with leftover army weapons, clad in a motley of old uniforms. They had horses, supply wagons, and even a reconditioned cannon. Moessler had had the gleam of a new ambition: to sack a really big city, like Memphis or St. Louis. He wanted to carve out a little empire for himself in the heart of the United States. An empire ruled by mutilated men.

Perhaps this ambition was not as mad as it sounds. There were recruits aplenty for Moessler after the horrors of the Civil War. And the country was so devastated that a relatively small force could paralyze a large area. Moessler believed that all he had to do was avoid the regular Army force that could be brought against him until he was strong enough to defeat it.

But his very growth and strength was the factor that led to his downfall. It's a lot harder to hide a force of a thousand men in the hills than it is to hide a few hundred. And when that thousand is burdened with wagons and supplies, as well as the limping and hobbling men who make up a large part of it, it becomes even harder.

Moessler was first met by a small U.S. Army force in late October, 1866. His mutilated veterans, fired by hatred of the military world that had maimed them, fought the soldiers to a standstill, then withdrew once more to the hills.

But the success of his band was beginning to create alarm in Washington. A larger force was sent against him, and a decisive battle was fought in southwestern Kansas on November 3, 1866. The soldiers, overcome with distaste at the thought of fighting the crippled and disfigured veterans, nevertheless caused a complete rout. More than two hundred of Moessler's men were killed, and most of the rest were captured. Moessler himself was among the prisoners.

He showed no remorse whatsoever at his trial. When the prosecuting attorney cited the horrors he had inflicted upon innocent people, he replied, with a touch of the histrionic: "It was these same loving mothers that, sent us off to battle. It was this, same innocent womanhood, wives and sweethearts, that sent us off to kill our brothers. It was these same men who shot us and burned us and rode us down, who made us what we are. We could have no pity for our murderers."

Moessler and a dozen of his companions were sentenced to be hanged. Most of the rest of the captured band received varying prison sentences, which, with the state of the prisons of the day and their own shattered physical condition, really amounted to a sentence of death.

Moessler was unrelenting to the very end. When they put the black hood over his head, he said: "This is not meant to protect me from the sight of the gallows. It is to protect you from the sight of my face." They stood him on the trap door, and he threw away his crutch, balancing himself on one leg. Those nearest to him heard him say: "The rest of me died at Bull Run and Gettysburg. What is left is glad to follow," And when the executioner put the noose around his neck, he said, "I am not the murderer. You are the murderer."

So ended the career of the man known as Sam Moessler, whose army of mutilated men provided one of the strangest chapters in the history of our country.

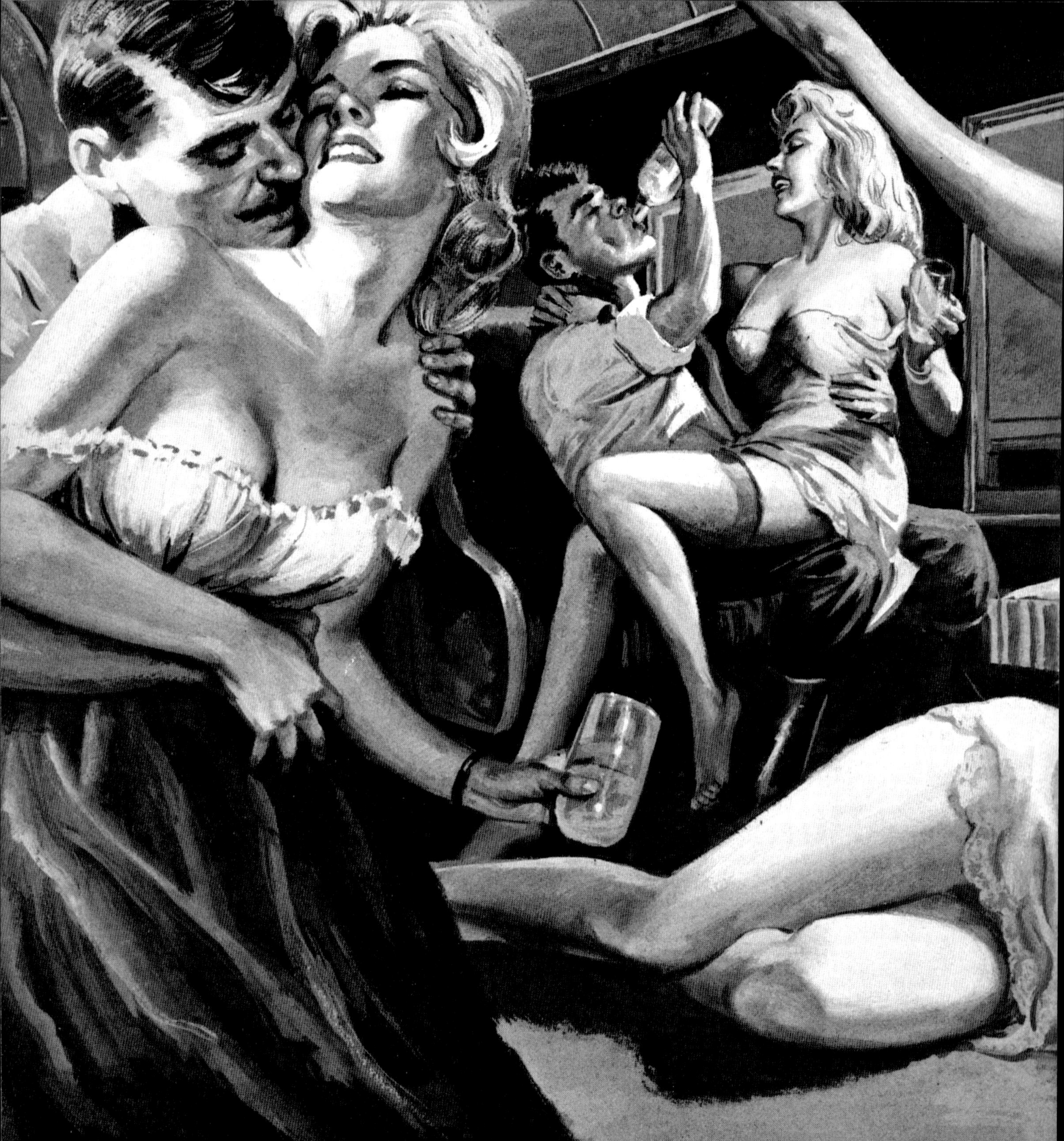

THE JOY TRAIN OF ALBANIA'S

The whistle-stop beauties were just passing playthings for the Commie officers –

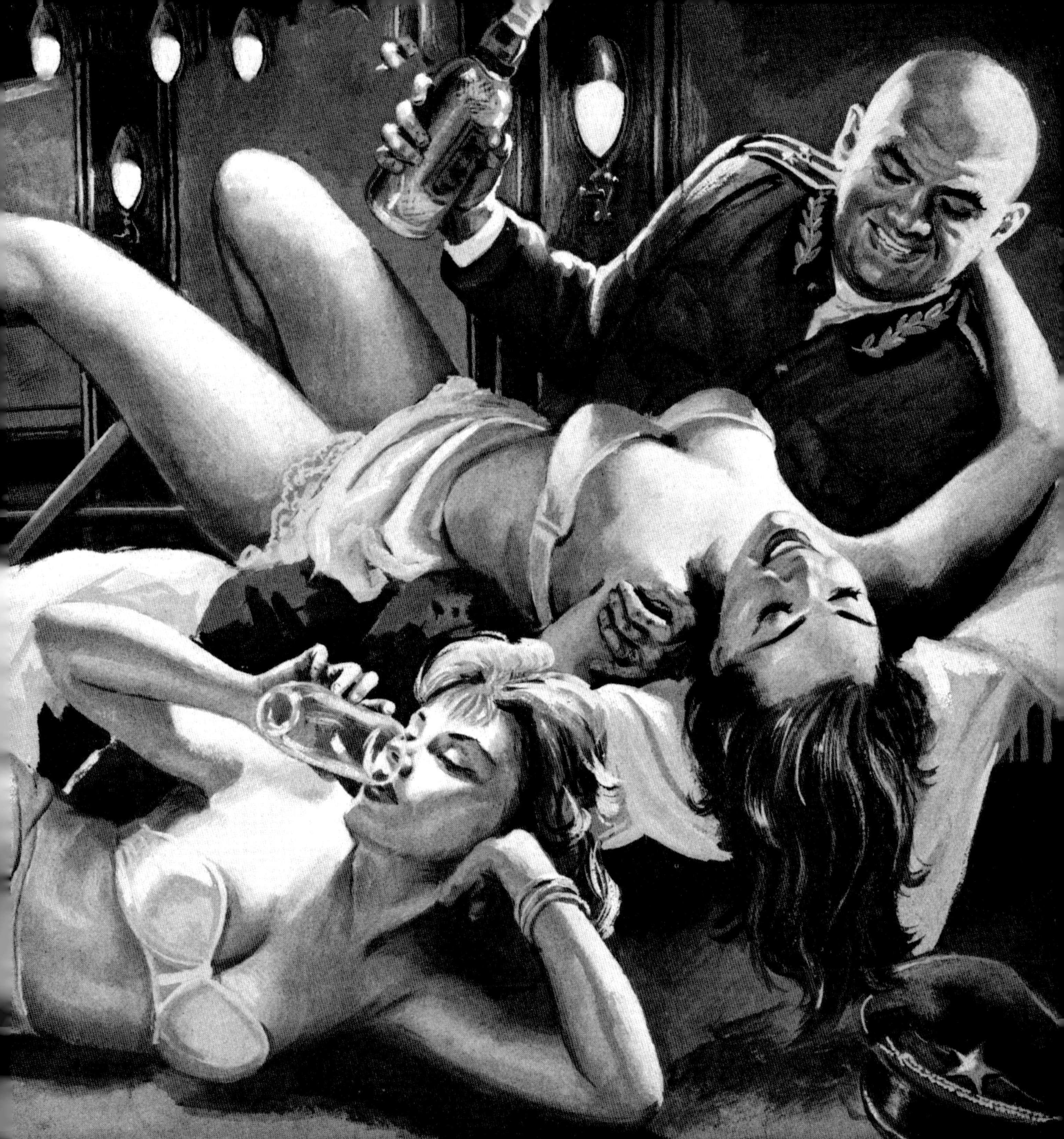

LOVE-STARVED COMMISSARS

but the brand of love-making they dealt out was steeped in hatred and revenge

ON SEPTEMBER 14, 1959 – at 4:30 in the morning – the slumbering Albanian village of Nekropa was rudely awakened by the rumbling of heavy trucks and motorcycles driving over the town's cobblestone streets. Before any of the inhabitants could rush to their windows and peer out, rifle-butts were banging on every door in the village. Even before the terrible din began, Nekropa's fearful townspeople knew why the trucks had come. In Albania, an early-morning knock on the door doesn't mean the milkman...

"Just a minute... just a minute!" called Klemente Proxha. He pushed his curious wife and sleepy-eyed daughter back into the bedroom and locked them in. The banging continued.

"Open this damned door or we'll break it down," shouted an angry voice outside.

Proxha unlatched the door and opened it. He was rudely pushed aside by a tommy gun-toting noncom of the People's Police. The cold-faced sergeant motioned three of his men into the thatched-roof house.

Proxha stood by helplessly as the green-tunicked militiamen searched each room thoroughly. During the search, the non-com consulted an official list. Proxha noticed the official red hammer-and-sickle stamp at the top of the sheet.

"Hmm... let's see..." mumbled the soldier, "Napke... Pimovics... ah, here we are... *Proxha*."

Looking arrogantly down at the stocky peasant, the sergeant said, "You have two daughters, one seventeen and one nineteen. Where are they, comrade?"

"My daughters?" replied the peasant in a surprised tone. "They left last night for Tirane, Comrade Sergeant, and won't be back in Nekropa until the end of the week."

"You lie, comrade," snapped the non-com, grabbing Proxha by the collar of his nightshirt. "This village has been under surveillance now for three days, and your daughters never left here. Now where are they?"

Just then – as if in answer to the sergeant's demand – a muffled sneeze came from the locked bedroom. Releasing Proxha, the sergeant dashed across the room to the locked door.

"Smash it in!" he commanded his men.

"No! No... please, Comrade Sergeant," pleaded the excited peasant, jumping in front of the entrance.

"Get away from that door, you old fool!" shouted the sergeant.

"No!" yelled Proxha defiantly. "You shall never put your filthy hands on my girls. You..."

The middle-aged peasant never finished his statement. At the sergeant's signal, three gun butts crashed down on the man's bare head, smashing in his skull. He crumpled to the floor, dead, in a pool of his own blood.

Kicking the corpse aside, the non-com motioned his men into the bedroom. There they found the terror-stricken women cowering behind the high-posted double bed. Seizing the sobbing mother first, the soldiers threw her out the bedroom door onto the living room floor. At the sight of her murdered husband, the hysterical woman uttered a piercing shriek, and began to cry uncontrollably.

"Just a minute," ordered the sergeant, as his men herded the murdered man's two daughters out of the room. The group halted.

The girls, scantily clad in their nightgowns, blushed deeply under the appraising glances of the soldiers. Gina, the oldest one – a tall, full-breasted brunette – showed a festering hatred for the killers of her father. The other, Andrea – a wide-eyed blonde girl – held her head down in shame and fright. Both girls' ripe, young bodies were bursting out of their negligées.

Shutting the door and bolting it from the inside, the non-com took hold of the brunette around the waist and forced her down on the bed. The others began to snicker and make obscene remarks as the assaulted girl clawed and kicked at her attacker.

Then two of the soldiers grabbed hold of the seventeen-year-old and threw her to the floor. The frightened girl screamed for her mother and sobbed bitterly as the excited men ripped off her nightclothes and took their pleasure.

AFTER PACKING most of Nekropa's young women into the military vehicles, the troops headed for their first stop-off – a group of special wooden compounds just outside Tirane, Albania's capital city.

There, the apprehensive girls were driven into the former Nazi concentration camp with gun butts and bullwhips brandished by People's Police, especially trained for the job. Fierce police dogs were also used. Needless to say, very little resistance was displayed by the captive girls.

After a shower, a thorough medical check-up and a change of clothes, the women were assigned to special cells called "Training Parlours for Proletarian Joy."

Despite their protests, many a strong-willed girl was utterly broken in this process. Each girl was forced to stand under blinding Klieg lights and strip. Unseen eyes would carefully examine every inch of the girl, from head to toe. The wretched prisoner was also made to stand unflinchingly – under the pain of cruel torture – while deft and experienced hands felt here and there for bodily firmness and perfection. Usually these examinations were followed by an even more revolting ordeal. The approved girls were not released until they submitted to two or three of their examiners. Then the ravished women were sent back to their compounds to rest up and prepare for the next day's "activities."

Each day, the girls were subjected to fresh indignities and outrages by their captors who, unknown to most of the women, were grooming them for one of the most fantastic white slavery set-ups ever put into operation.

Gina Proxha well remembers the day she finished her "parlour course," after two and a half gruelling months of unbelievable degradation and beatings. She was now considered "fit for proletarian labor," according to the commissar in charge of the compound, and was expected to make her "fruitful contribution to Communist society."

"What is going to become of us, Gina?" sobbed the brunette's younger sister, back in the barracks.

"Don't worry, Andrea," comforted the elder sister, caressing the girl gently. "Right now, I don't know how we'll manage it, but somehow I'll get us out of this living hell. Just don't give up hope."

That afternoon, the girls were moved by military transport to the northern town of Vernasik, where they were lined up in the rain before three sealed railroad coaches. In spite of the drizzle, Gina noticed that the darkened cars were sleepers.

A local commissar with an umbrella mounted the rear of a transport truck and began to address the sullen women.

"Welcome to your new home," he said, pointing at the coaches. "I hope you will all make yourselves as comfortable as possible in the cars, because you will not be leaving them for a long time to come. As you know, you are the property of the people now, and will therefore be utilized to fulfill the needs of our People's Commissars throughout the country. You will play a major role in building morale, comrades. I envy you."

"Oh, no!" wailed the girls. "We thought you were finished with us back at the barracks. Now we'll be love slaves on that train till we're sent to die like dogs in a labor camp!"

"Quiet! Quiet, all of you..." the man on the track shouted.

"Come on, girls," yelled a wide-hipped redhead, "let's escape from here before it's too late!"

Screaming and slapping at their startled guards, the frantic women surged forward down the dirt road alongside the tracks.

They hadn't dashed ten paces down the road when the rattle of a machine gun stopped them cold. Six girls fell in their tracks, victims of fire from a concealed guard tower.

Their captors were on the girls in seconds with dogs and bullwhips, driving them back up the road and into the railroad coaches. Andrea was unlucky enough to stumble and fall.

"On your feet!" ordered a nearby soldier, brandishing his whip.

"I can't," sobbed the girl. "I've broken my ankle."

"Oh, you can't, eh?" mocked the uniformed man, laying into the prostrate blonde with his whip. Andrea howled with pain as the lash tore her back and shoulders into bloody ribbons. Then the girl collapsed on the soldier's muddy boots.

Gina's eyes blazed with hatred. She picked up her sister's limp body, and, stumbling under the load of dead weight, carried it into the coach assigned her. Once inside, she rushed down the narrow aisle to her berth, pushed back the curtain, and gently laid her sister on the lower bunk. The blonde's hair was now caked with dry blood, and the torn flesh on the unconscious girl's upper body was beginning to curl up and fester.

"Those swine will pay for this," Gina muttered through clenched teeth. "I'll make them pay if it's the last thing I do!"

That evening, Andrea Proxha went into a coma and died. Her body was carted away by two soldiers, and how they disposed of it Gina never found out. She cried bitter tears that night, again swearing to avenge her father's and sister's deaths.

The girls were rudely awakened early in the morning, and told to dress up in their most alluring clothing. This was their first assignment and they would be closely supervised by special agents. Failure to perform their duties satisfactorily, the girls were warned, would result in severe punishment.

Gina felt the car jerk just as she pulled her nylon hose tightly over her shapely thighs. A whistle shrieked and she was thrown off balance. So, she thought, at last this devilish train is on the move. She wondered how long it would be before her chance to escape came along.

Her thoughts were interrupted by the curtain to her berth being suddenly parted. In the aisle stood a squat man in a Commissar's uniform. His weak, well-fed face was twisted into a lewd smile.

"Ah, good morning, my darling," he said, looking the half-clad brunette up and down. "They told me you were attractive, but not this ravishing."

Gina shuddered inside. The commissar's piggish face and stinking breath made her slightly ill. Yet she had enough presence of mind to invite him in. The official removed his tunic and moved close to the girl on the bed.

"You don't have to wear stockings for me, my pet," he said with a sour smile. Pulling Gina closer to him, the aroused man took hold of the girl's hose and tore it off her leg. Laying his fat, well-manicured hand on her exposed thigh, the commissar pulled her down on her back.

"I love you!" he panted, fumbling with her slip. "I want you!"

Gina felt her stomach knot up as the stout man's hands caressed her body.

THE NEXT few weeks proved to be a living hell for the thirty-six residents of the sleepers. The sealed train methodically chugged into the depots between Tirane and the northernmost tip of the country. And, without fail, from ten to a hundred local commissars were always eagerly waiting to board the heavily guarded cars and partake of the lusty pleasures inside.

In time, Gina – along with the others – became calloused and automatically seductive toward the unending legions of love-starved party officials who exploited her body at every whistle stop.

However, during the few hours respite given her each day, she constantly plotted her escape from the rolling bordello. She unselfishly hoped to accomplish two objectives: first, to obtain enough explosives to blow the train sky high, and, second, to make it across the Greek frontier, and tell the whole world how she survived the Red terror in her homeland.

She launched her risky plan one evening by deliberately playing up to the night guard assigned to her berth.

"Why don't you come in out of that drafty aisle and rest awhile, comrade?" she said seductively to the soldier outside.

"Sh-h-h," hissed the man with the tommy gun, "do you want to get me shot?"

"Oh, come on in," coaxed Gina, "I'm not going to tell anyone. Why shouldn't you have a little fun too?"

Looking furtively up and down the aisle, the guard laid his weapon against the wall and climbed into the berth with Gina.

That was his fatal mistake. He was found in the morning on the bed, a nail file thrust deep into his chest. Gina was gone.

It was discovered during a bed check that six other girls had jumped train that night with Gina. The furious authorities surmised that the girls must have jumped off when the train slowed down on a steep grade during the night. An alarm was sent out immediately for the girls' arrest.

Meanwhile, Gina and her desperate friends had hurried to the nearest peasant village, where they received food, clothing and a good night's sleep.

With the eager help of the six other escapees, Gina realized that her plan for destroying the love train could now be put into action.

A few weeks later, seven women dressed in brightly-colored peasant blouses and babushkas over their heads approached the ominously darkened coaches of the sealed love train, which was resting on a rail siding in a small village. The hammer-and-sickle emblem had been freshly painted on the side of the coaches.

Offering a variety of fruits and vegetables to the sullen guards, the women maneuvered close enough to the train to whisper a few unnoticed instructions through the barred windows.

Minutes later, all hell broke loose. Suddenly dumping the food on the ground, the women vendors whipped tommy guns out of their baskets and began blasting away at the guards. In seconds, sixteen Red soldiers pitched headlong into the oil and tar of the railroad bed, cut to ribbons by the girls' deadly fire. The chatter of guns continued until all the train's guards lay dead on the tracks.

The liberated girls cried with joy as they poured out of the coaches. They had turned on their hated masters and beaten eleven commissars black and blue. Some of the Red officials even had their faces battered in and their bones broken by the vengeful women.

"Help! Guards..." a few of the commissars yelled from inside, "don't let those prisoners escape! Stop them."

"Stand back, girls!" yelled Gina. "We'll give those swine something to yell about!" Lighting three sticks of dynamite, she heaved a sputtering stick into each coach, and ran for cover.

The train blew up with a mighty blast which rocked the entire village. When everything settled, masses of bone and bloody flesh lay strewn among the smoking ruins of the train.

Gina, with eleven of her comrades, escaped across the Greek frontier and eventually appeared before the World Court of justice to testify against the inhuman leaders of her country.

She hopes to return to her native village of Nekropa some day, when her homeland is once more the free and happy country she knew as a child.

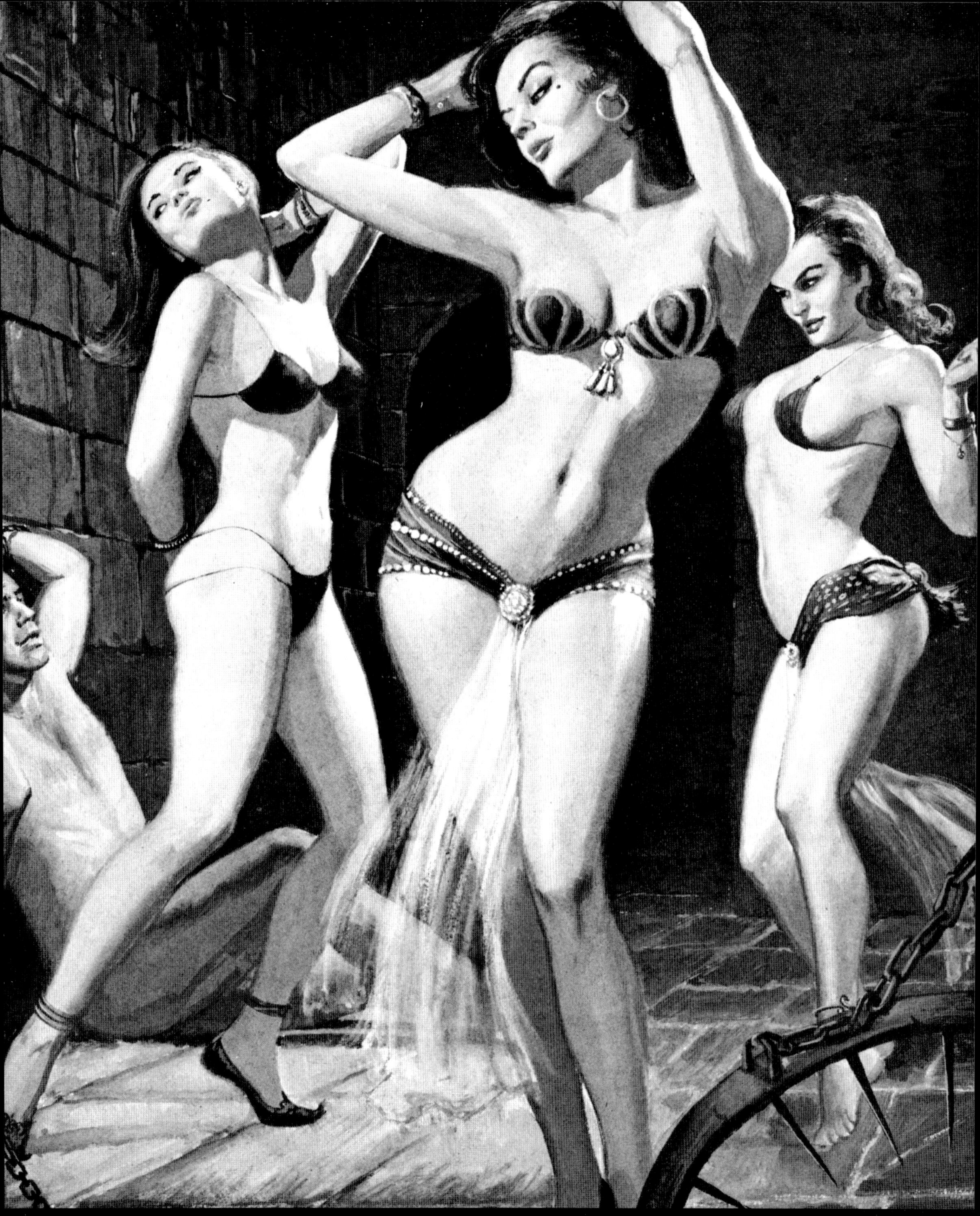

"REVENGE OF THE ALGERIAN REBEL GIRLS"; detail from interior art, **MAN'S TRUE DANGER**, 08/62.
Art uncredited.

THE ORGIASTIC GATES OF HELL

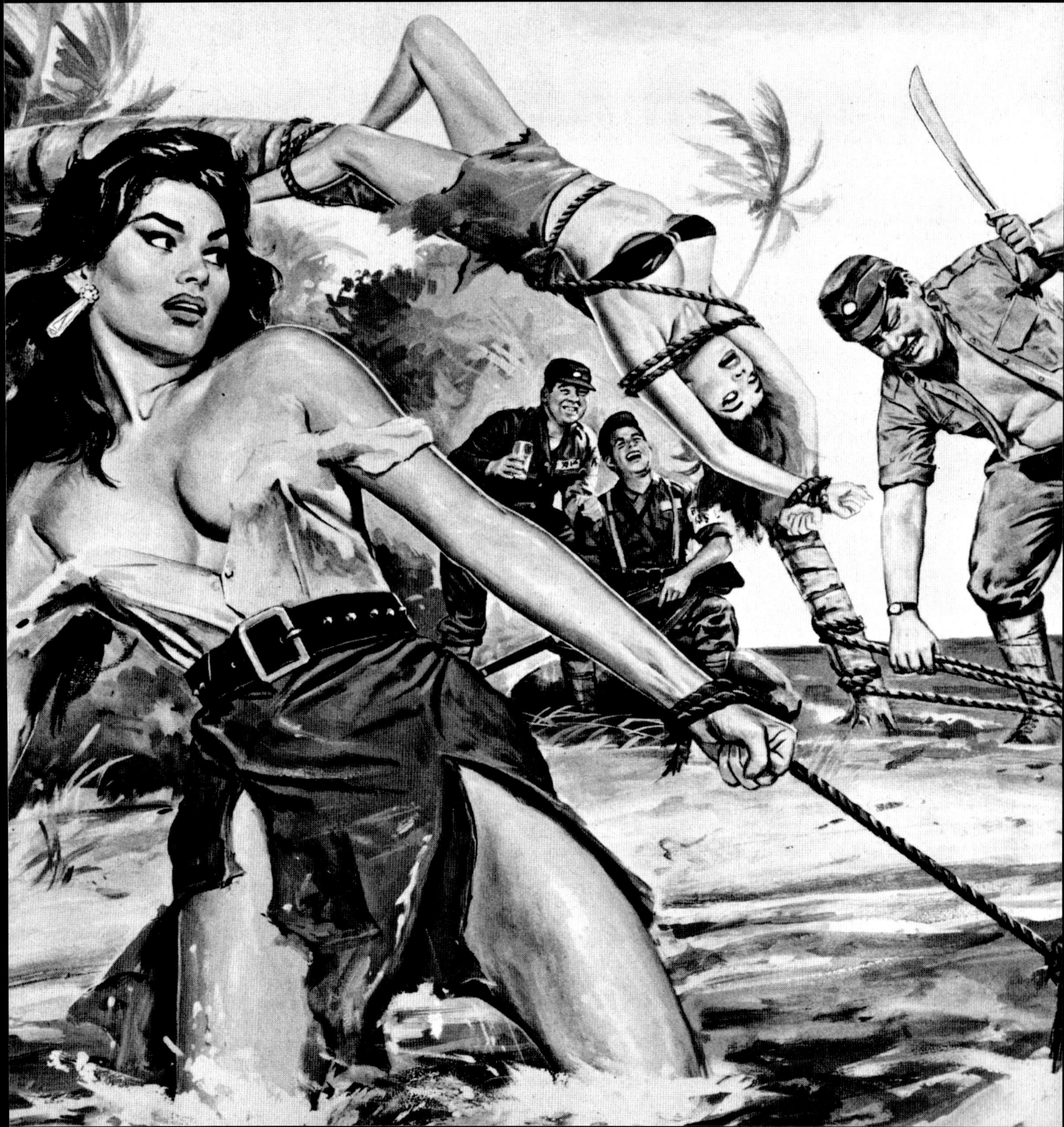

The defeated, lust-mad Japs were hungry for revenge – and two helpless girls were the only ones left on the island they could use to satisfy their mad desires.

I KNEW WITHOUT ASKING that something was wrong that hot summer morning in 1945. The Japs hadn't come for me the way they did every morning. They didn't show up with their toothy grins and the bayonet stickers on the ends of their Mitsui rifles to take me out on my daily inspection of the latex trees we were bleeding on the plantation.

There was a feeling of foreboding, of trouble, hanging in the hot, moist air. Even Fran McKendrick sensed it. Fran was American like myself, a chemist who had been caught when the Japs had over-run the Malay Peninsula and taken Singapore. She, too, had been made a prisoner on the rubber plantation.

She was thoughtful, more silent than usual, when she sat down with me for breakfast that morning. She sat in the sunlight, and her red hair shone like burnished copper against the ivory of her skin. Looking at her I remembered how hungrily the Japs' eyes feasted on her trim body whenever they saw her. And fat Major Ituki, the commanding Jap, who let his hands rest on her every chance he had. I knew quite well what Fran's fate would be if the Japs didn't need her in the laboratory to work on the latex, to improve the quality of the product shipped to Japan for the greater war effort the Emperor was always asking for.

Maya, the Malay girl, beautiful as a bird, with tiny upturned breasts that trembled when she walked, came in to serve us. She was nervous, obviously frightened by something out of the ordinary.

"What's the trouble, Maya?" I asked as she spooned some curried shrimp into my plate.

"Japanese officer and soldier," she said, "make much tears. Much heavy drink *sake*. Much noise."

The Malay natives had heard much wailing from the Jap quarters in the other plantation house, Maya told us. Many of the plantation workers had gone into hiding. She herself was afraid. Last night she had been ordered to prepare the Jap Major's Shinto ceremonial robes. I didn't know what was up with Major Ituki, but whatever it was I didn't like it. It meant no good for us.

And then it began, halfway through our breakfast meal. The Japs had turned up the power on their wireless. We could hear the static crackling on their radio receiver and some crazy Jap announcer jabbering away. The sound came across the clearing and filled the room in which we were taking breakfast. It didn't take much to guess that whatever Major Ituki was hearing was upsetting him.

I looked across at Fran. A look of worry flickered across her face. At that moment I wished she would wear more clothes. I knew the heat was stifling in that laboratory of hers, with all the retorts cooking over gas flames, and that was the reason the redhead wore the flimsiest of halters and briefs in which to work. Although I myself drew pleasure from looking at her near nakedness, I wished then that she didn't present such an inviting picture to the Japanese, that she wasn't so obviously desirable.

Fran flushed warmly under my steady gaze. And at that moment there was a loud slam from across the clearing. The doors of the house the Japs had taken over flew open. Two Jap soldiers came flying out, with Major Ituki right behind them. The fat major kicked them down the stairs and then jabbed a thick finger in the direction of our plantation house. He disappeared inside the house, slamming the door behind him, while his two Jap soldiers picked themselves up, brushed themselves off, and then came across the clearing in our direction.

They were both obviously drunk. Their bayonets fixed on their rifles, they staggered across the clearing towards our house. One leered at us and wiped the back of his hand across his lips.

The other sucked a *sake* bottle dry, and heaved the empty at our house. It barely missed the window and thudded up against the wall.

They kicked the door in and swaggered into the room. One of them knocked our breakfast table over, sending the dishes to the floor with a clatter. One of them wrapped an arm around the frightened Malay girl's waist and started dragging her to the door. I was half out of my chair when the other grabbed Fran McKendrick.

"You, too!" they yelled at me. "You come! Major Ituki want see!"

"What the hell is going on?" I yelled. I swung on the Jap trying to wrestle Fran across the floor. I caught him on the side of the head, knocking him loose. He stood there with a silly look on his face for a second, and then that look turned to a maniacal grin. The little monkey was fast. Before I could get out of the way, he had turned Fran loose, and was lunging at me with his bayoneted rifle. The tip of the bayonet caught me in the cheek as I fell back and laid the flesh open to the bone. Fran moved to help me, and the Jap slapped her across the mouth, dropping her to the floor.

AT THAT moment it was useless to resist any further. We let the two Japs herd us out of the room, down the stairs, and across the clearing to the other house. We didn't know it yet, but we had be gun what we would always remember as the nightmare hours.

Blood was flowing down my face and staining my shirt when one of the Jap soldiers kicked me inside the house they had commandeered. Fran and the Malay girl were herded in, too.

Big, fat Major Ituki was standing there waiting for us, tears streaming down his face. He was listening to the radio blaring Japanese loud enough to drive you insane. When he saw me, and the deep cut on my face, he stopped weeping.

"That is good," he said. "Good to see you suffer, too, on this terrible day when the sun stop in sky and world come to an end." His jelly body convulsed and heaved in a mixture of laughter and tears.

"Stop the nonsense, Major," I said, "and tell me what the hell is going on."

The Jap Major stopped laughing and took a swig from a *sake* bottle. Then he pointed at the radio, bleating its hysterical Japanese and static, and at his ceremonial *samurai* robes and sword. "It is the end," he said brokenly. "We have gotten news on the radio that Japan Emperor have surrender to evil American devil. It is end to dream of world conquest. Japan now disgraced in eyes of world. Defeat. Everybody know – it is shameful."

As the news percolated through my mind, I realized that the long ordeal of forced labor for the Japs was over and we would be free again. We'd able to get off this cursed peninsula when we pleased – or come back again if we wanted to without being afraid of the Japs.

While these thoughts were running through my mind, Major Ituki went right on talking. He was as drunk as an owl, as were his two enlisted assistants, and at first I didn't pay any attention to what he was saying. His voice just droned on and on – his words sounded like they were coming from a long distance. And then the meaning of his words penetrated.

"We are going to have one last party," Major Ituki was saying. "We have a good time before committing *hara-kiri*. We finish off the *sake* we have been so carefully hoarding for a victory celebration. We have good time with Miss McKendrick and Malay girl. We teach them how to be good *geisha* in these last few hours. They dance for me. Give me bath. Make bed-bed with me. They give me pleasure. And then, when I am through, I turn the women over to my men."

Major Ituki's words finally snapped me out of dreamland. Just what he was driving at, what he wanted, finally penetrated my fool brain. And by that time it was too late to try and talk him out of it. He was already moving hungrily, his arms outstretched, towards Fran McKendrick.

Sick with the realization of what was happening, I watched fat Major Ituki corner Fran, working her into a corner from which she could not dodge him or escape. His hands pawed at her body. His fingers hooked into her clothes and started to tear at them.

With a savage oath I flung myself across the room. I leaped for the major's back. But one of the Jap soldiers was even quicker. He swung his rifle like a baseball bat, holding it by the muzzle. The heavy butt end of the rifle caught me across a knee cap. I heard a cracking sound and my leg gave way. I was down on the floor, sliding on my face, hardly even knowing how I got there.

The grinning Jap wasn't through with me yet. He rained blows down on my head, beating me savagely with the butt of his rifle. Only once did he stop, and that was to drain a *sake* bottle, pouring the hot liquid down his throat. And then he beat me savagely on the head with the empty *sake* bottle until it broke and left him with the neck of the bottle in his hand. With a fiendish howl of joy he jabbed the razor-edged glass into my shoulder and ground it in, twisting and turning it to lacerate my flesh. The little Jap was drunkenly overcome with what he had done. He fell back, screaming and laughing, collapsing on a wicker chair.

I groaned with pain. Major Ituki looked back at me with amusement. "We only kept you alive," he said with a smirk, "in order to keep the rubber plantation running with maximum efficiency. Now I will thank you not to interfere. After all, what difference does one or two women more or less make between men of the world?"

I LAY there, trying to gather my strength while the Japs swilled *sake*. Ituki had worked both women into a corner, and had a gross arm around each, his hands pawing at their bodies, stripping and tearing their clothes from them a piece at a time. But it wasn't that easy. Fran and the Malay girl fought him all the way, scratching and clawing at him. This resistance only seemed to excite him all the more. It only intensified his efforts to get his great blubbery hands on their bodies.

Finally, bit by bit, I pulled myself up off the floor. The two Jap enlisted men were so busy with their bottles of *sake*, they were ignoring me for the moment. I lurched forward, towards Major Ituki, pain stabbing at my knee and shoulder. I threw myself on his back, clawing at the rolls of fat on his neck spilling over his collar, tried to get a handhold on them so that I could pull him down on the floor with me and off the girls. Ituki shook me off his huge back like a fly. He twisted around and sent me crashing to the floor. He stood over me for a second, leering down at me with a vicious grin. Then he raised one of his heavy legs as high as he could and smashed the heel of his boot down on my thigh. I screamed with the pain. I tried to squirm away from that stabbing heel, but it did no good. Ituki followed me, and I writhed under the rain of stabbing blows. He jammed his boot into my mid-section, then into my elbow, crushing the bone. Then he put his boot into my groin, and jammed all of his weight down on my sensitive private parts, grinding them with the heel of his boot into limp bags of mucous, blood, and ruptured tissue. I screamed and screamed, and it seemed my own voice would never stop.

And then Major Ituki was off me, moving fast, with the grace of a heavy man. He stepped across the room to a table on which there was an obscene cake, made in the shape of a Shinto shrine. The postal wrappings, and the string that had tied it together, hung over the table from the base of the cake. In that cake there was a ceremonial sword which had been used to slice a piece of the cake. Major Ituki pulled that sword out of the cake and then strode back across the room until he stood over me.

I was paralyzed. I could not move. I heard Fran scream and then I saw the point of that sword coming down for my face. And then it was screwing into my right eye – and

I could no longer see out of that eye for the searing pain as the major neatly cut the eyeball out. The major severed most of the muscles behind the eyeball with the point of his sword and the eye hung down the side of my face. Fat Major Ituki was chuckling hysterically at what was to him an amusing sight when Fran and the Malay girl landed on his back, clawing and screaming, and pulled him away from me.

Momentarily the girls took the major's full attention. He slammed them both up against the wall. They both stood there, blood leaking from their mouths, where he had hit them.

The Major was contrite for a moment. "Why you be not good to me?" he said to Fran. "I only wish to pleasure you. It is great honor for woman in my country when she is pleasured by Army major."

"I'd rather be thrown," Fran said acidly, "through the gates of Hell first."

Major Ituki was thoughtful for a minute. Then he picked up a coil of rope that was on the floor in a corner and motioned to his two enlisted men to lay their *sake* bottles aside and join him. He moved the girls towards the door, and I heard him say, "If it is to be thrown through the gates of Hell you want, then I will do that for you."

And then they were gone, and I was left alone with my agony and pain. I. tore a strip of cloth from my shirt and bound it around my eye socket. Then I dragged myself across the floor until I could reach and grab the *samurai* sword next to the Shinto cake. With that sword in my possession I dragged myself across the floor and then out the door.

I dragged myself across the clearing and on the trail that led down to the sea. I had to get to the women before Major Ituki killed them – for I knew what the Jap was talking about when he said he would give them what they wanted – throwing them through the gates of Hell.

I dragged myself the two hundred yards to the rocks that overlooked the shore, and then I peered over. Now I could see and verify with my one good eye what the Jap, Ituki, had meant. For there before me, literally, were the gates of Hell – two big rocks offshore through which a wicked whirlpool current ran. That whirlpool had occasionally trapped the small boat of an unwary Malay native, and sucked man and boat under, to cast up the body and boat an hour or more later.

ITUKI WAS insane with grief over the Jap loss of the war. It is the only explanation for the fiendish thing he was doing now. He and his men had staked the Malay girl down in the water so that she could not run off. And as for Fran McKendrick, they were planning to throw – to catapult – her through the rocks that were the gates of Hell. They had lashed a palm tree and bent its top almost to the ground, securing it to giant rocks with ropes. And they had tied Fran to the top of that palm tree. When the tensile force of that palm tree was released, it would fling Fran through the air. She would either smash up on the rocks that were the gates of Hell or be sucked under in the whirlpool to her death.

The major was ready to cut the ropes that held the palm tree down when I raised myself from the ground – and running, stumbling, falling, and rising again, I rushed down the slope and charged the last few yards at him, the ceremonial sword held low in both my hands. Major Ituki saw me coming. He changed his swing in midair and directed it at me. He was off balance and missed. But I did not. I swung the *samurai* sword up in an uppercut blow. The razor sharp blade skimmed his groin and cut into the soft flesh of his underbelly. It continued up, opening up his abdominal cavity completely.

He was disembowelled, and his fat intestines spilled out on the ground like a huge, white, writhing worm. The major sat down suddenly, smiling through his tears of pain. And then he thanked me for spilling his guts out on the ground.

"I didn't really have the courage to commit *hara-kiri*, Mr. Hackford," he said. "You made it easy for me." And then he pitched forward.

I cut Fran loose. She looked in horror over my shoulder and I spun around. The two Jap enlisted men were charging up the beach at us, their bayonets fixed. They could cut us into ribbons.

The *sake* leaked from their lips. They sounded their *banzai* scream. And I waited, trying to gauge the distance. When they were within range I slashed desperately at the ropes that held the palm tree down. Suddenly it was free, whipping forward. It came down like a pile-driver on the heads of the two Japs with a cracking sound that could be heard for a half mile. The force actually drove them into the ground, telescoping their bodies into something that was hardly recognizable as human – just a bag of mixed-up flesh and bones and blood in their wet uniforms.

I walked around the bloody mess and into the water, and untied the Malay girl. Together she and Fran helped me back to the plantation where they put me to bed and gave me what medical treatment they could. We waited out a week that way until the first of the Allied troops reached us, and then transported me down the peninsula to the hospital at Singapore. When I came out of the ether and a spell in surgery, both girls were waiting at the foot of my bed for me...

PRISON BREAK MASSACRE FROM CHAWCAGEE HELL HOLE

A violent, bloody and brutal escape by women without names, without futures, and without men.

I STOOD KNEE-DEEP in the filthy water of the swamp, the scum-covered dirty brown now laced with bright red swirls of the matron's blood. The Chawcagee swamp had always been a place of mystery and death. Now it had seen the gruesome beheading of the prison matron – and it would see more at any moment.

Ahead of me, racing toward the land that sloped up to the highway, were the five girls I'd helped break out of the Homerton Women's Penitentiary. And that sight made the headless corpse floating in the slimy water seem like a joke. For leading the girls in their fanatic charge was the gorgeous Jenny, her left hand whirling a butcher knife around her head. And tucked under her right arm, like a halfback carrying a football for a touchdown, was the grisly severed head of the dead matron.

I stood paralyzed with horror, an icy shiver knifing into my bones, a sickly hot sourness churning my stomach. The wild girls, led by the insane blonde, were going to charge the State Troopers up on the highway. If I charged with them, I'd be gunned down; if I tried running back into the swamp, I'd

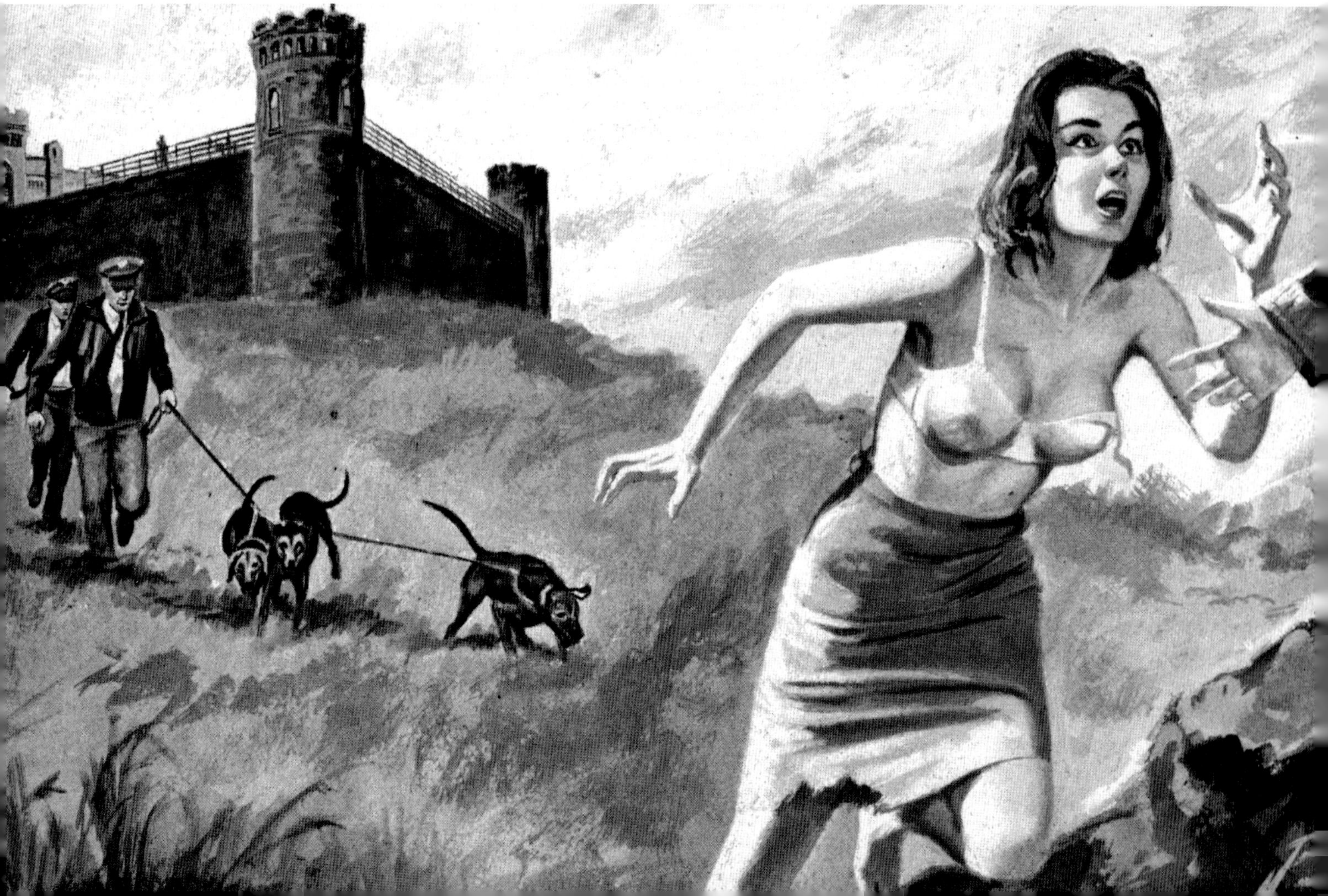

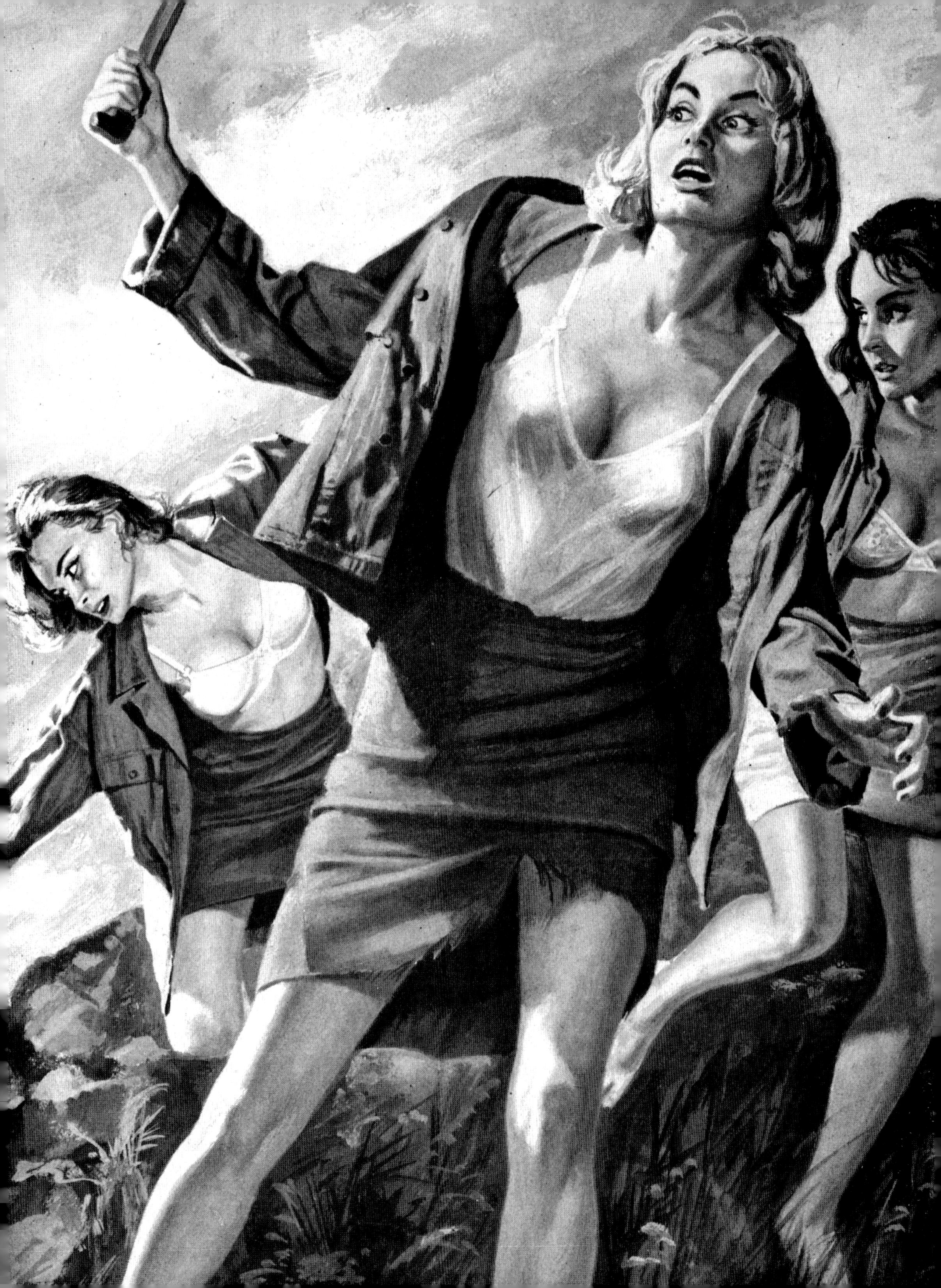

end up shriveling to death from starvation and fever. Either way, the crime I'd committed in the name of Justice was about to cost me my life.

WHEN I got out of the Army's MP Corps in '53, I came back to the States and found a job as a wall guard for the Homerton Women's Penitentiary, about twenty miles north of the treacherous Chawcagee. The prison was a grim, desolate place, but the women imprisoned there were just as bad. They were a hardened bunch who'd done everything from passing phony money to plunging a pair of scissors in their husband's back.

There were two dozen of us changing shifts in the towers, and the only other men there were our captain, and Warden Lockey. Keeping the inmates in line was the job of the matron and her staff of female guards. The matron was perfect for the job. She was a tough number nearing forty, with the build of a tank and the temper of a bull. It didn't take long to learn that she ruled that place with an iron fist, and anyone who got out of line learned to play ball her way, fast.

On March 13, 1960 the old captain retired and I became the new Guard Captain, which meant that I acted as an assistant to Warden Lockey. The job entailed quite a bit of work inside the prison itself, and that's when I first saw the matron in action. I went down to the solitary cell block one morning to check on something. It was a small section of cells that were solid, except for small barred windows in the steel doors.

Coming to one, I heard thumping sounds, like someone beating a carpet. I went to see what it was. Looking in the opening, I saw the broad shoulders of the matron standing over the bent figure of an inmate. The matron's arm was raised, and in her hand she held a foot-long length of rubber hose. As I watched, the arm cut down like a flash, and the hose cracked across the prisoner's neck, leaving a livid red welt. Other parts of her back were raised in the angry red marks.

I could see the outline of the prisoner's face. It had been iron-hard and set, the teeth clenched, eyes shut tight. But this last blow must have been too much, and her face cracked into a mask of agony. She cried out, begging the matron to stop. The man-like shoulders began to shake, and a low, deep laugh rolled around the cell.

It was a rough way to handle prisoners, but then, they weren't Sunday afternoon darlings. Even though I assisted the warden, it was still none of my business how the matron ran things. It wasn't up to me to agree or disagree with her methods, so I kept my mouth shut. The prisoner probably deserved what she got twice over.

The matron had her favorites among the girls, and there were always plenty of whisperings when some new girl caught the matron's eye. She'd start calling the prisoner out of her cell in the evening for special "rehabilitation" talks. These were held in the matron's quarters, and everyone knew what was going on except the warden. In return for her favors, the prisoner would be assigned easy jobs on work detail, would be able to have extra money sent in, and extra visitors. The other girls would get angry, but they knew the score. The first one to squawk would end up in solitary.

For three months things went smoothly, the warden telling me I'd be getting his job when he retired in a couple of years. The matron and I never did hit it off, but we didn't try to do each other's job, so things were peaceful. The girls knew the buttered side of the bread, so they were quiet.

IT ALL came to an end one warm summer morning. It was on June 19th when the detention car drove through the front gate at eight-thirty. It pulled up to the administration wing, and a woman guard got out, followed by a young blonde, handcuffed to her wrist. The trouble started when she walked through the door into the hail. From that moment on, the prison became a powder keg, and the blonde lit the fuse.

The girl was gorgeous. Even in the denim prison outfit, you could see the long, curved legs, the rounded thighs, the full, firm breasts. When she walked, every luscious curve flowed sensuously. The matron, standing there next to me, gasped, but I was too busy staring at the new girl to look at the bulky matron.

We took her into the matron's office to process her and orient her to the prison. I couldn't help running my eyes over the girl's rich body, but when her eyes met mine, she thrust out her breasts and the corners of her mouth turned down into a sneering challenge.

But it wasn't the girl's smile that meant trouble; it was the hungry stare of the matron when she looked over the prisoner, Jenny Deare.

Jenny was tough, and maybe that was why she wouldn't play the matron's game. The matron started by trying to be extra nice to Jenny, but she wanted no part of it. In fact, she had started off the second day there by slapping her cellmate around to show her who was boss. It wasn't the guards or the authority she openly fought, but she automatically established herself among the girls as someone to leave alone.

As June turned to July, the matron seemed more and more disinterested in the other girls, and found more and more reason to watch Jenny. Rumors went about that she'd promised every comfort possible to Jenny, but the young girl refused to become the matron's "pet."

The matron now found reasons to punish and restrict Jenny. Her old methods usually got her what she wanted, but not with Jenny. Soon Jenny got extra work, was sent to solitary. The final punishment was beyond anything the matron had ever tried.

I walked by the matron's rooms one evening. From under the door I saw the light, and I heard sharp cracking sounds from inside. I could hear a woman's voice sobbing, crying out in pain. I ran to the door and opened it. The matron didn't even hear me. Jenny was on her hands and knees, the matron standing over her. In her hand she waved a whip. Her face was ugly with hate, wild with rage.

Jenny's prison jacket was ripped off, and her back was a mass of red, torn skin and flesh. Blood ran down her sides, from the pulpy, shredded skin. It was an ugly sight, beyond any possible reason, without excuse. The matron lashed down again and the whip bit into the girl's back. She screamed, falling to the floor. Quickly the matron fell on her, rolling the girl over. The matron started fumbling with her clothes.

A hot rage poured over me. I'd worked in this prison eight years, and I had always remained silent to the matron's brutal methods. But this was insane, mad brutality.

I raced across the room and grabbed the matron to pull her off the girl. Her fist shot out, smashing into my mouth. I tasted the blood gushing out. She was a bull; her vicious, horrible lust giving her terrific strength. It wasn't a woman I was fighting but a wild animal. I slammed a fist into her face, cracking her head to the floor. She kicked a foot into my groin and I staggered back, a hot flame darting through me. The matron jumped up, started toward me. Then her eyes bulged and she froze still, her jaw sagging as she looked beyond me to the door.

I heard their screams just as I spun around. Piling through the door were four other prisoners, waving butcher knives around their heads, their eyes burning with hate and murder...

With the matron and me as hostages, the girls commandeered one of the prison's pick-up trucks. They led Jenny along – she was glassy-eyed, silent, almost in a coma of shock. Two of the girls held those razor-sharp blades to our necks. One move and the knives would slit our throats.

I don't know how those girls got the knives, or out of their cells. But they hadn't planned on the truck being almost out of gas. We raced down the highway towards the swamp. Just as we got to the edge of it, the motor sputtered to a stop. "Back into the swamp," one of the girls shouted. "They'll never be able to follow us."

We ran down the slope, and plunged into the swamp as the sirens screeched in the distance. Jenny, still in a daze, slipped and crashed into the dirty water. It snapped her out of the trance. She jumped up, a look of hate and death lining her face. She raced over to the girl guarding the matron, yelling an animal sound of rage which drowned out the sirens.

She kept her eyes, like burning coals from Hell, on the matron. Grabbing the other girl's butcher knife, Jenny stalked towards the matron. The matron's face seemed ready to melt into raw fear, her teeth chattered.

It was Jenny's revenge. The matron's whip had plunged her mind into a burning world of madness. Now Jenny's arm waved high, like the matron's had with the whip. But Jenny's hand held the huge knife, the blade gleaming in the moonlight. Then in one swift swing the knife sliced an arc in front of Jenny, snipping clear through the matron's neck like it was butter.

There was a gory splash of red, then the head toppled off into the water.

I was helpless, frozen with revulsion, yet a part of me knew that Jenny deserved revenge, and that the prison had been a torture chamber for the girls in it. But the sight of Jenny scooping that grisly head out of the water cemented me still with horror, disbelief.

THE STATE Troopers had arrived up on the highway. I saw them pouring out of their cars, rifles gleaming. In a moment we'd be cut down by whining bullets. But my legs wouldn't move, my mind was numb.

Jenny whirled and cried out to the others to follow her. She ripped off her clothes frantically, then started running, completely naked, back towards the highway, the head tucked under her arm. The others stripped too, and followed her, screaming wild banshee cries, whipping their knives above their heads.

The sight of the naked girls charging them surprised the Troopers for awhile, but when the girls went tearing into them with those deadly knives, the police quickly forgot they were fighting women. Two of the inmates were seriously wounded, and Jenny was shot as she plunged her knife into a policeman's shoulder.

With the matron and Jenny dead, there are no witnesses to back up my story of what happened in the prison. The officials don't want the true story known about the mad matron's methods – it would anger the public, stir up trouble. So they have charged me with aiding the prison break and, worse, of being an accomplice to the matron's murder, since I hadn't tried to stop it.

How can I hope to make them believe my fantastic story? When I claim the girls acted in self defense, how can I expect them to believe me – when they won't even admit the prison was controlled by a sadistic animal?

I acted only to help Jenny; to stop a barbarous injustice. But by doing so, I have condemned myself in the eyes of the Law. They are going to hang me, and I don't want to die! Won't somebody help me? Please... *please!*

A CRYPT OF AGONY

FOR THE SCREAMING BEAUTIES OF BELGIUM

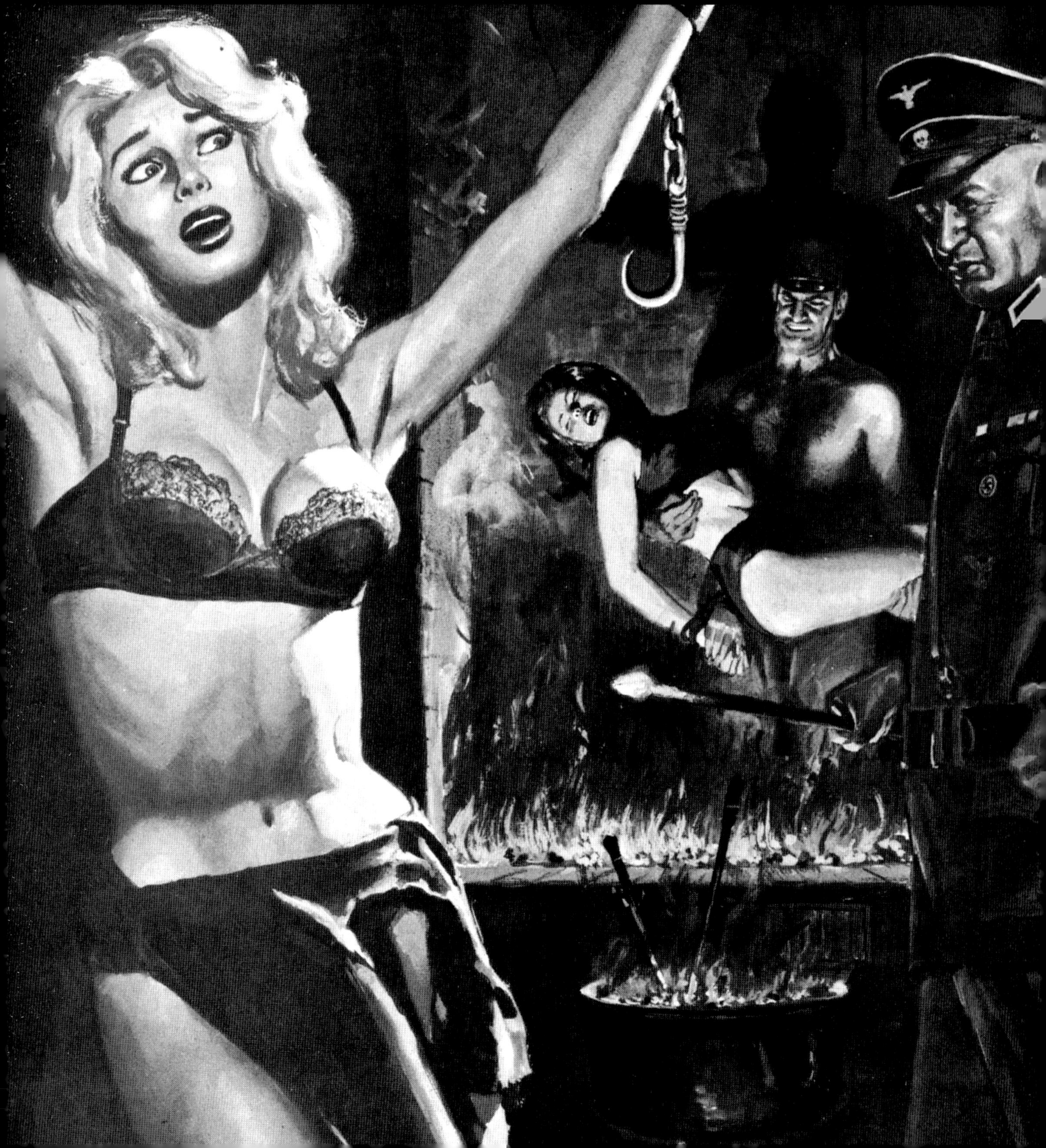

Von Faulkenhausen's eunuch monster kept the house of pain for his own special vengeance against the lovely victims whose beauty inflamed his twisted cravings.

BEATRIX ROELX PEDALED FURIOUSLY along the main Brussels-Louvain Road. The October sun was warm on her firm young flesh. A breeze riffled her flaxen hair. She was happy – almost.

At last she was doing something. At last she could forget Leopold's betrayal of the Allies. At last she and thousands of other Belgians and Frenchmen were fighting back against the hated *Allemain*.

Tonight her voice would carry the news of hope across western Europe. She would be able to tell her countrymen that *Les Angleterres* still controlled the sky. Her clandestine broadcast would recount the smashing of the vaunted Luftwaffe over England's tracer-ravaged skies.

It was almost good to be alive – even if it was the Fall of 1940, and all Europe once again lay under the boot of the hated Hun.

As her bicycle sped over the dusty road, Beatrix thought of Albert Mouscron. A bittersweet smile touched her bright lips, lending animation to her face. How desperately she missed the broad-shouldered young Belgian. How wonderful it would be to feel his arms encircling her once more.

Yet it was good to know that her man had not followed the craven king of the Belgians in complete surrender to Von Faulkenhausen's marauding butchers.

She wondered whether Albert had made it to the Haute Savoy. She wished with all her heart that he had allowed her to accompany him across the border. But his words had had a ring of finality in them.

"The Resistance is not for you, *ma cherie*. As yet one cannot trust his neighbors. War is a man's work. You must stay in Brussels and make sure that you are as lovely as now when I return. That is definite."

She had wriggled against him in the dark of the night, feeling his gentle hand moving over the soft contours of her naked hip.

"Albert, there is no difference," she had pouted. "Man, woman, child, we are all the same. We are all soldiers of Belgium. Sex is of no consequence."

"Sex will always be of consequence," he had teased, crushing her to him until she had to fight for her breath.

"*Bête*," she whispered. But there was no sting in her word. It had murmured through the night like the soft rustling of silk. "*Ma bête brave*."

His lips had closed over hers in the dark. The electric spark of his touch had seared her very soul. She'd responded to him in an ecstasy of abandon. She was in love. They'd parted the next morning with the words which each had wanted to tell each other locked firmly within their hearts. A smile, the gentle touch of the palm of his hand against her smooth cheek, the constriction of her throat, the burning sensation in her eyes as she fought back the tears – and then Albert was gone.

It has been six long weeks, she thought as her trim young legs pushed harder on the pedals of her bicycle. Yet it has been as if he were always at my side.

She could almost see his image now, the strong white teeth, the curling black hair, the look of wild courage in his eye.

And she could see more. She could sense his anger if he should learn that she was the voice of liberty which broadcast over the clandestine radio transmitter which had been set up in the physics laboratory at the University of Louvain.

She remembered his last warning: "War is for men, *ma cherie*. Do not do anything foolish. The Hun is no respecter of women."

Yet wouldn't he be proud of her? Wasn't she carrying out her heritage? Wasn't this the way her parents had fought a quarter of a century ago when the swarms of spiked-helmeted *Allemain* had swarmed over the border at Liège?

To Beatrix, schooled in the stories of the atrocities of Von Kluck's World War I legions, who had violated her country's neutrality in their wild plunge towards France, it was inconceivable that she accept the Germans as her conquerors.

Hadn't she seen the grave markers clearly foretelling the future?

"Shot by the Germans, August 19th, 1914."

Now they called themselves Nazis, and Von Kluck and Ludendorff and Von Hindenburg were dead. But they were still the rampaging hordes which made the word HUN resonate with shrieking terror.

Already Von Faulkenhausen had shown his ruthlessness. Already the mass shootings had begun. The only way to fight terror was with terror.

I am but a woman, she thought as she pedaled towards the campus of Louvain. Yet a woman can be a deadly enemy.

She watched the arrogant SD men wheeling through the streets on their sidecar-attached motorcycles. They roared past her, unconcerned by the fact that they had nearly driven her into the ditch beside the road by their wild driving. One of the cyclists looked back and grinned. His companion in the sidecar, who wore the insignia of an Obersturmführer, shouted something at his driver over the engine's roar. The driver immediately faced forward. His neck turned crimson with humiliation at the tongue-lashing he was receiving.

Beatrix smiled to herself. She managed to right the bicycle and pedaled quickly along the road, attempting to make up for lost time. Her effort caused her skirt to fluff out in the breeze and she felt the cool air touching her naked thighs and playing at the hem of her lace panties.

Albert would be proud of me, she thought as the spires of Louvain loomed up before her. Whatever he might say to the contrary, he would be proud of what I'm doing.

A cloud came over the sun, causing a chill to stir in her body. It dispelled the mood of gaiety which had swept over her. She wondered whether it was merely the threat of a storm or the sudden increase of military traffic on the road. A number of Volkswagen command cars had joined the procession of cyclists. Now a lorry ground past her, its open tail gate swinging noisily, SD soldiers sat rigidly under the canvas top, staring at each other.

Beatrix continued pedaling. She realized the worst thing she could do would be to show any sign of fear concerning the convoy. As far as the *Allemain* were concerned, she was merely a young college girl late for a class.

She swung off the road at a side gate and rode through a tree-lined lane. Because of the lateness of the hour, the campus was quite empty. A few girls walked quickly towards the library – the very same library that the Germans had burned during World War I out of sheer bestiality.

Beatrix's clear blue eyes swept the campus. How different it was now. Last year at this time, it had been alive with young couples strolling arm in arm. Their happy voices had cut through the fall air in a steady hum.

Now there were no men to be seen. Those who were not in German prisoner of war camps, were probably hidden in the Haute Savoy awaiting the chance to strike back. But this did not account for all the youth of Louvain.

Beatrix knew well that some had tasted the ruthlessness of Von Faulkenhausen's SD already. For them love, hate, life were all over.

Beatrix swung her trim leg over the rear wheel of her bicycle and began walking it towards the physics lab. The need to tell her countrymen of England's smashing victory in the Battle of Britain crowded all other thoughts from her mind.

It had fallen as her task because the underground trusted and respected her. It had become her duty because the underground felt she had the best chance of any of carrying the mission off. In her tweed skirt and tight sweater she looked every inch the student. Her comings and goings on the campus would cause the Germans little interest.

Now she leaned the bicycle against a wall. Her plump hips moved against the tweed of her skirt as her heels clicked swiftly up the stone steps. She looked up once to see the sun completely covered by a heavy cloud layer.

AT THAT instant the calm of the campus was broken by the sputtering of a number of coughing engines. The earth seemed to tremble under the roar of advancing motorcycles and the lumbering lorry.

As if in a dream, Beatrix watched the SD men jumping from their vehicles. With practiced precision they sealed off the University's main gate. Their Schmeissers shone dully in the gathering gloom. A Sturmbannführer shouted something at a Standartenjunker in gutteral tones. The Standartenjunker turned with a clicking of heels and repeated the order to the rifle-bearing squads. The men lined up in a tight cordon and moved slowly forward, their bayonets pointing in front of them.

In a moment of panic, Beatrix thought about running. She reasoned the Nazis had found out about the radio broadcasts and were about to conduct an intensive search of the university buildings. The transmitter was sure to be found.

It would mean almost certain death for Professor Lessaines. More important, it would mean an end of hope to the Belgians who huddled by their radios at night risking execution for one word of hope from the outside.

Beatrix shrank against a wall, feeling the rough stones digging into her back. A shrill cry sounded over the campus as a black-uniformed Nazi reached out for a young red-headed girl and grabbed her arm in a bone-crunching grip.

The cordon of Germans moved silently towards the center of the rectangle. As if in a dream, Beatrix felt the cold steel of a bayonet probing the softness of her flesh. Her eyes locked with those of the hard-faced Nazi who held the bayonet. His face carried an unnatural flush and his hands trembled.

"Over there!" he ordered, gesturing in the direction of the quadrangle where a small group of girls were being herded together.

Beatrix hesitated a moment. The point of the bayonet dug deeper. She squared her shoulders and moved towards the group.

For long minutes the Belgian girls were forced to stand at rigid attention. The Nazis scurried through the buildings, dragging others out, shoving them forward.

The terror mounted within Beatrix. She felt her efforts for the resistance had brought peril to her classmates. Their blood would be on her hands.

She looked from one to the other of the girls. Their faces were chalk-white. Some bit their lips. Others hugged themselves as if to cover their young breasts from the insolent gaze of the Nazis. One wept unashamedly. But none of them begged. They managed to keep their heads high.

A pudgy little Standartenführer paced pompously up and down the hastily-formed band of women. His head moved in quick little motions which reminded Beatrix of a pigeon. His pink face was unlined and almost effeminate. But there was no mistaking the lust of the eyes, the sadistic twitch of the lips.

The over-sized riding crop he carried slapped relentlessly against the top of his jack boots with a sharp crack.

At last the Standartenjunker approached him, arm raised stiffly outward in the Nazi salute. He said something in guttural German, and the officer smiled briefly.

The officer turned towards the huddled girls. "I am Standartenführer Klausner," he began in a quiet voice. "I have been assigned to Louvain by General von Faulkenhausen himself." He puffed up his chest in pride, taking on even more of the aspect of a deadly pigeon.

"Last night *franc-tireurs* in the pay of England carried out a cowardly and traitorous attack against the Kessel-Lo railroad depot. Because of their treachery, you are being placed under military arrest to be held as hostages pending their surrender." The quiet voice had gathered force and now the words shrilled out in a high-pitched scream. You will climb into the lorry and be conducted to Gestapo Headquarters. *Achtung*, forward!"

The girls were herded like so many heads of cattle towards the truck. Beatrix was conscious of the hurried press of soft bodies around her. From behind she heard the sickening crunch of a rifle butt against flesh and the agonized cry of a woman.

She saw the naked thighs of girls climbing over the open tail gate and the hot, lustful stares of the SD men watching them. Then she was being dragged upwards by the arms and thrust onto the smelly floorboards.

She was almost suffocated by the weight of those who were hurled over her prone and shuddering body. She huddled there, her face scraping against the bottom of the truck, trying to control the spasms which jerked her arms and legs.

"We will be shot!" a girl cried piteously.

"We will die with dignity," another answered. "We will die as proud Belgians."

The sounds of sobbing were stilled as the truck lumbered through the university gates. "If we must die, let us make the Hun ashamed for what he does." The words were repeated over and over as one after the other took up the pledge. Each knew it would be her only weapon against her depraved captors.

An hour later the girls were herded out of the truck and to the sound of cracking whips conducted into a huge house which stood on a hill overlooking the small town of Louvain.

For what seemed like an eternity they were forced to stand facing the wall, their noses pressed against the evil-smelling plaster, their arms high above their heads. The SD men walked behind them. Now and then a girl would cry out in pain and revulsion as the SD men committed some indecency on their young bodies.

This was typical of Nazi tactics, Let the prisoners gnaw away at the fear which built up in them. It was a crude attempt at psychological procedures prescribed by Gestapo Mueller himself. Let the mounting discomfort of their cramped positions begin to take hold of their brains. Only terror would bring the *franc-tireur* to its knees.

NIGHT CAME and with it damp, clammy cold. From time to time a detail led by a Standartenjunker would come into the room and a girl would be lead out. The others remained waiting – for what, they didn't know.

Beatrix forced her mind to dwell on other things. She thought of Albert and the life they had known. At least he was safe. She wondered whether he had participated on the raid against the Kessel-Lo railroad junction. She could see him, the bandolier of bullets slung carelessly over his strong shoulders, the British sten bucking in his hands, the snarl of defiance curving his lips back from his even teeth.

Her mind whirled to other things. Von Faulkenhausen's orders were well known to the partisans. Any suspect was to be summarily tortured on the off-hand chance that the person might be carrying information which would prove valuable to the SD.

She quickly risked a sideways glance at the girls who still remained lined up against the wall. Did they have secrets which meant death? Or were they to die for no other reason than they were Belgians and, according to the Hun, had no right to live.

Terror clawed at Beatrix, turning her knees to jelly. How many graves would she open up when it came her time for interrogation? How many of her countrymen would die because of her?

She didn't have time to dwell on this thought. A clammy hand gripped the back of her neck. "*You!* Next! This way!"

She was aware of being hustled down a long corridor and out into the night and then into a cellar entrance. As her eyes became accustomed to the place, she gasped in spite of herself. It was as if Hell had opened up to swallow her. The crypt like room was bathed in a sickly red glow which made the walls appear to be bleeding. Heat waves shimmered through the chamber, searing her eyes and throat with their radiation.

But worst of all were the thick chains which hung from the overhead beams waiting to receive their victims. The iron links glowed red in the fire's reflection, as if they had been heated to melting point already.

Klausner, the SD Standartenführer, stood with his back to the fire which sputtered and sparked in a long trough. His hands were folded behind him. His beady eyes stared hypnotically at Beatrix.

"*Ach*, and now we have the most beautiful one of them, eh Gerber?" he simpered. 'It is a shame that she must come to us this way, is it not Gerber? She is so young, so radiant, so fearful of pain. But we have much pain to show her here, don't we Gerber?"

"*Jawohl*," the bigger man said briskly. He had stripped to the waist, and his muscular torso glistened in the firelight as he stirred the coals.

"This one must know much," Klausner smirked. "One as lovely as she must have had many friends among the Belgian men. Her pretty head must be crammed with their secrets. How could any men keep secrets away from such a beautiful woman as she curled beside him on a double bed?'

Klausner's voice was deceptively reasonable. Only his mad eyes betrayed the unnatural desires which burned within him. Klausner too well remembered that day some twenty-six years before, when the Belgian grenade had destroyed his manhood. If he had become a eunuch before Liège, a new generation of Belgian women would suffer for his loss.

His fist shot out and twisted in Beatrix' sweater, drawing her to him until she could see the saliva running down his discolored yellow teeth. His other hand locked in the tawny strands of her silken hair, bending her head back until her body arched against his like a taut bow. His closeness numbed her with terror and disgust.

From another compartment a wild scream filled the night. It sounded almost animal-like, but Beatrix knew it was a woman in mortal agony. Involuntarily Beatrix' back stiffened at the sound. A shiver of horror ran through her loins. She struggled in the madman's grip.

"This one will last long, Gerber," Klausner gloated. "She is quite strong. We will take our time with her. Nothing too quick, mind you, Gerber."

"*Jawohl*," the big brute answered. His eyes held the vacant, glassy expression of a moron. But evidently the Nazis had found a certain talent within him, which was designed to meet needs of the SD. "*Ja*, just like with Obersturmführer Dirlewanger. Gerber made them last long in Poland," he intoned as he strode toward Beatrix.

The terrified girl lashed out at her captors with puny fists and delicate feet. Her efforts drove the Nazis to wild laughter. Quickly Gerber's arms circled her waist and lifted her from her feet. She was carried to a spot under two dangling chains. Her terrified eyes saw the thin manacle dangling over her wrists. The jaws closed, pinching the tender skin of her arms.

She felt Gerber's horny hands prying her ankles apart, forcing them towards the iron rings imbedded in the floor. She felt the thick leg irons bruise her as she hung suspended and spread-eagled before their lusting gaze.

The man called Gerber had the strength of an ox. He reached for the neck of Beatrix's sweater, shredding it down her front. Not to be outdone, Klausner struggled with the hooks of her skirt. The waves of heat beat at her exposed flesh. Beatrix looked down the column of her body and saw that the only garments which covered her were her silk panties and bra. She felt no shame, only rage. She couldn't think of being ashamed before wild animals.

Gerber shuffled off, the muscles of his broad naked back glistening under the skin. Klausner stood before the chained girl, his pudgy hands running up and down her body, savoring the velvet of her skin and the silken promise of her clothing. Never would he fulfill that promise in a normal way. But the war had given him an outlet for his morbid needs.

"I hate you," he whispered. "I hate you for your youth, your beauty, your health. More than anything else in the world, I hate you."

With remarkable clarity Beatrix saw this man. He was not interested in information. His maniacal need to torture would never be appeased by the confessions of his victims. Hanging from her chains, nearly naked and completely at the mercy of the sadist and his idiotic stooge, Beatrix understood. That understanding could save Albert Mouscron's life.

The man called Gerber reappeared, carrying with him a glowing brazier which resembled a blacksmith's. He placed it before Beatrix. Her eyes widened as she saw the irons growing cherry red in the flames. The anticipation of them smoldering against her flesh wracked her with wave on wave of nausea.

The man called Gerber reached for an iron. The coals hissed around its end.

"Wait, you fool!" Klausner screamed. "Let her first see what fire can do. Gestapo Chief Mueller has always advised us to allow a prisoner to watch the interrogation of another. It is part of this business of psychology." Klausner laughed insanely. Gerber regarded him, his brute-like brain understanding that he was supposed to laugh too. His slobbering bellows filled the room.

Seconds later he was back in the crypt, carrying a young dark-haired girl whose arms had been tightly bound behind her. Brutally he stood her on her feet and stripped the dress from her back. Huge tears rolled from her smooth cheeks as she was prepared for torture.

Clad in cobweb-thin panties and bra, she doubled up to hide her charms from the fiends who busily strapped her feet together. Viciously she was smashed to the floor and Gerber produced a heavy metal hook-rod and a length of thick chains. As Gerber held her shoulders pinned against the dank stone floor, Klausner clawed at her bra. The girl shrieked her horror as the heavy chain was fitted around her shoulders and under her arms and attached to the hook. Her back arched. She writhed in Gerber's grip. Klausner moved quickly. He tore her panties down over her milk white thighs, her trim calves. Completely nude and helpless, the girl felt herself being lifted into the air and swung over the huge fire which crackled in the brick oven.

With tremendous effort she raised her legs, holding them as high above the searing flames as her muscles would allow. The gloating Gerber slowly played out the chain so that she was carried lower. The pain of the fire was matched by the strain of her position. Her legs began to quiver and jerk as the screeching muscles protested her position. Despite her struggles, the twin alabaster columns were dragged down by gravity to the oven.

As the soles of her feet began to smolder, she was jerked towards the ceiling. Beatrix realized that the torment of fire could go on for aeons. The sadistic fiends were masters at their art.

At last the girl's body shuddered in one head-to-toe convulsion. Her head fell forward on her naked bosom. The agony still remained etched on her face, although she had lost consciousness.

Gerber and Klausner worked at the chains swinging her away from the fire. Beatrix knew that her own turn had come.

ABANDONING THE girl like a discarded side of beef, the SD maniacs turned their attention to Beatrix. Almost with ceremony, they slowly ripped the last covering from her body. Gerber pulled at the chains which held her arms above her head until her body stretched taut in a column of sheer agony. Sweat stood out on her naked body. Her stretched flesh lay before the iron which Klausner held in his diabolical grasp. While it was still a foot away from her, she became aware of the torture of its glow.

"And now you pay for what the *franc-tireurs* did last night," he hissed over the sputtering iron.

The first pain came with a numbing crash that Beatrix felt down to the tips of her toes. The chains which held her rattled as her muscles contracted. Gerber stood beside her taking in the struggles of his lovely victim. His stinking breath swirled around her, nauseating her.

"She will tell us of all her friends," Klausner gloated. "This one has had many. One with such young beauty knows much."

The stench of her burning flesh filled the room. Klausner noticed the tip of the branding iron losing its redness.

He took it from the spot on her belly and plunged it into the fire once more.

He was standing at the brazier with his back to the door of the crypt when the first bullet tore into his head. Like a broken rag doll he pitched forward, the angry flames licking his evil face, forming a satanic halo around his head.

Stupidly Gerber whirled. His ox-like eyes began to register at the sight of the wild-looking man with the curly hair and the even white teeth who sighted down the length of a Sten gun at him. The gun roared again, its bullets etching their way across Gerber's throat. His dismembered head crashed to the floor with the sound of a rotten melon. Beatrix cried out in disbelief and then mercifully fainted.

Days later she lay in Albert Mouscron's arms as he nursed her back to health. "*Ma bête brave*," she whispered in a weak voice. "But how did you know?"

He told her of the raid on the Kessel-Lo railroad junction and of having received news of the Germans taking hostages for reprisal. Against the warning of his superiors, Mouscron had organized a rescue party for a lightning stab at the Gestapo Headquarters. Once the objective had been carried out, the Resistance group had moved quickly back to Brussels, where it was still relatively simple to hide out in the slum sections from the Nazis.

Several months later, under cover of night, Beatrix was aboard a British torpedo patrol boat which had braved the Western Scheldt to carry out its rendezvous mission. She had begged Mouscron to accompany her. But the patriot had insisted that his work remained on the continent.

In 1945 a detachment of the 101st Airborne Division came upon a grave marked *"Albert Mouscron, Hero of the Resistance"*.

Following her work with the British Office of Executive Services, Beatrix dropped from sight to become one of those who roamed Europe in hope of building a new life in the post-war world.

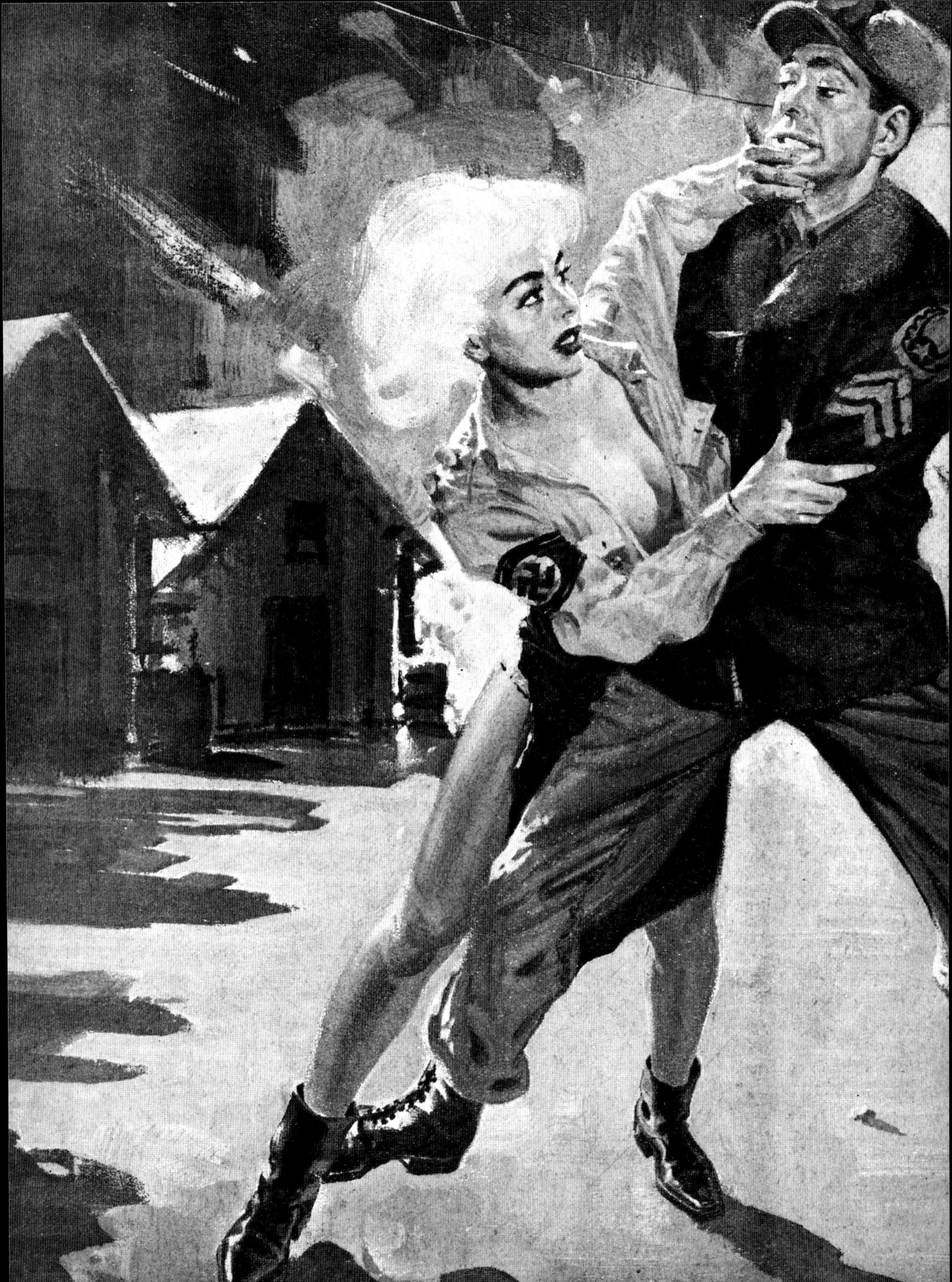

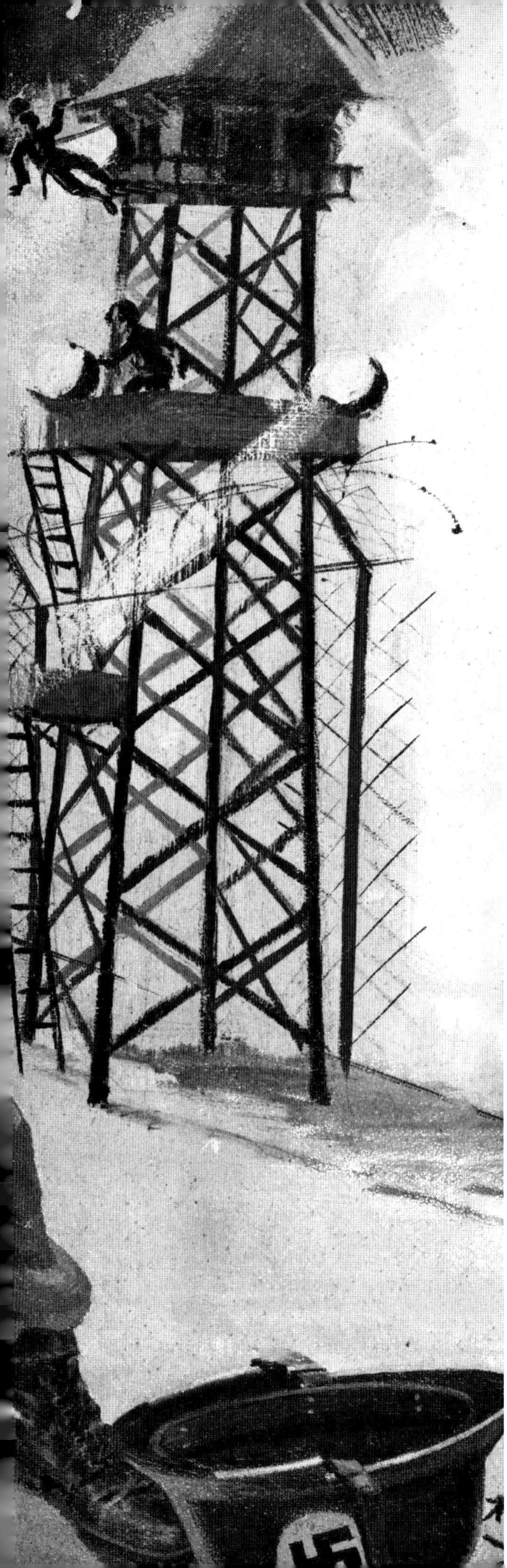

BLAST OUT OF HELL WITH THE SHE-BEAST OF PLOESTI

The whole stalag wanted her dead – but now the SS torture-hellcat had her value.

SS-UNTERSCHARFÜHRER MARTHA ZENT, STALAG 606 at Ploesti, Roumania, stiffened as the .45 bored into her back. The sadistic Nazi SS bitch started to let out a yelp, but the second emphatic jolt choked it.

She snarled, "*Schwein!* They'll kill you before you get fifty feet!"

"Then they kill two of us, baby," I snapped. "This gun goes off when I get mine. Start moving."

B-24's were bombing Ploesti. The blonde cursed and wheeled, her right knee digging into my groin. I didn't drop the gun. First I bit down through my lip to gushing blood, then I slammed her in the mouth with my fist. "Zent! I'll kill you Zent! *Move!*"

The blonde Unterscharführer of Stalag 606 got the message. Stepping gingerly through the bomb-torn fencing, Martha Zent, beauteous assassin of 133 American and British plane guys, reluctantly walked down the burning hill. Behind, sirens wailing, Nazi anti-aircraft gunners plastering flak against sixteen low-flying Fifteenth Air Force 24's, Stalag 606 groaned under the impact of the biggest raid of the war.

"*Schnell!*" I jabbed her. "One of 'em sets down, I want

on it!"

Martha Zent began to sob as blockbusters opened a flaming vent on the west wall of the prison compound. She turned, threw both arms around me and screamed into my neck, "*Bitte!* You made a mistake, Yank," she sobbed, "I just did my job because I had to."

The blonde made it sound good, but not good enough. I wasn't in Stalag 606 but a couple of weeks. Most of the "fun" I'd missed, being a new POW, but not all of it. I'd watched the blonde line up a British crew. Stripped down to her underwear, blonde Martha Zent, Unterscharführer, had paraded before the Limeys in a weird exhibition that ended in sixteen deaths.

First they made love to her, then she killed them. It was May, 1944. The big compound a few miles from the rich Roumanian oil fields was noted for its unspeakable depravity and oversexed guards. All Nazi SS women. There were seventy-five women guards, supported by tough veterans of General Guderian's misspent winter at Moscow.

Zent's boss was SS-Oberscharführer Paul Koch (brother of the notorious Ilse), a hermaphrodite maniac who not only devised the system of making lampshades of human skin, but also, as a matter of policy, executed at least three prisoners a day – one with every meal.

The raids on Ploesti began on August 1, 1943. Low-level bombing raids, they were strictly the work of the Fifteenth Air Force of which I was then a part. Intermittently, for ten months, using the Bengazi strip as a jumping-off point, the B-24's smeared out and hit the Nazis in the deepest recesses of Europe.

I'd bombardier'd twenty-three missions into France, Holland and Roumania when I made my last run over Ploesti, stick-bombing it. I thought my luck would never snap. All around *The Lady Hazard*, my best friends had been splashed out of the skies. Raid after raid, *The Lady Hazard* came through – holed, once with her underpinning half shot away, once with a dead pilot and tail-gunner – but always the gifted mechanics of the Fifteenth put her together again. Then, one morning at the end of April, a flight of ME-109s climbed on her, snapped her string. *I bailed out.*

THE JERRIES machine-gunned every man in the crew but me. In parachuting, I remembered to play dead. Oddly, it worked. Bullets zipped into the shroud-lines and I thrashed like hell, then stopped. The ME pilot got bored.

"Name is Hyde. My serial number..." I told the Major Klein who interrogated me. "I'm a prisoner of war. Under the articles of war that's all you get–"

"Now that's all I get," Klein shrugged. "At Stalag 606, where you're going, Herr Captain, we'll get the rest. Everything comes out into the, er – open at Stalag 606!"

"Name is Hyde... Serial number is–"

Oberscharführer Koch grinned fiendishly.

"So! You believe in the Geneva Conference eh, Captain? Well, a few days here will change your mind."

A few days did, but not the way Koch figured. I bunkered with the toughest lot of men the Lord ever created. British and American, a few Polish fighter pilots mixed in, and a smattering of Free French. Some of them, as myself, were new to the prison camp. Others had already gone through the living hell – and looked it.

Some wore bandages where there had been fingers, or no bandages at all. Once a day we were lined up and addressed by Koch; told that our bombers were being slaughtered and that soon German air supremacy would not only assert itself over Europe, but over America as well. Germany was readying a new guided missile, Koch said. It would reach New York, Chicago, San Francisco, the White House.

"Aw, you're full of crap!" a kid belly-gunner made the mistake of blurting out.

Koch's reaction, one that I came to know quite well in two weeks, was merely an upraised, furled eyebrow and the snap of his fingers.

"Down on your knees, *Schwein!*" A blonde SS girl slammed the boy with a rifle butt. She was a gigantic witch. She hit him a shot with at least 175 pounds behind it. Koch, drawing a thin, silver stiletto from his belt, slowly advanced on the airman.

"For every scream, another cut," the Oberscharführer smiled broadly.

Blood quickly spread down the boy's right cheek, a river of it. Then another river of it on the left cheek. He groaned and fell forward on his face.

"*Ja,*" Koch chuckled, replacing the knife after first wiping the blade on the uniform. "I think he now understands how we do things here."

Four SS girls were standing behind the rapidly-bleeding-to-death airman. They sat him up against a peg driven into the ground behind him. Martha Zent took over then. It was the first time I watched "Queenie," as the British called her, work. She picked four men at random, made them strip and urinate on the dying boy. Two of them balked. Two of the SS assassins, blondes and bosomy, moved behind them with bayonets. They still refused. Zent nodded. The bayonets went in at the belt-line and came out their navels – three deaths for breakfast. Back home the trout were riding to dry flies; at Stalag 606 the black flies were riding to human blood occasioned by Zent and her cohorts.

The SS ladies-in-waiting shot the two others, nevertheless. Zent was already in her dining room preparing for our day. In the evenings when the dross of prison camp weighed heavily on her, Martha Zent felt a compulsion to find love. At any time the notion struck her, she would muster the ranks and choose ten, possibly twenty, of the largest men in camp. These, for the next few hours (under SS supervision), became her lovers. If they satisfied her they lived another day; if not, they died.

Sixteen British airmen who refused to submit were butchered by Zent shortly after, their bodies then being skinned as a favor for her boss, who promptly turned them into lampshades.

Three days after that I was due for questioning. How good were our bombsights? And when were the Americans expected again? The men of my barracks, among them Wing Cdr. Barns Parker, RAF (a Canadian) did me the favor of administering an injection of something – how or where he got it he didn't say, nor did I ask – that brought on violent diarrhea.

The SS favorite drug was Evipan, which put a man to sleep permanently. Mine, a nicotinous base, merely turned me mildly insane. I was still in the infirmary, expected to die, when the Oberscharführer got his questions answered.

AMERICAN B-24's bombed the hell out of Ploesti. They plastered the fields, the capital, the Nazi big-gun positions behind the internment camp. They even bombed the outskirts of the camp and the hospital. The daylight raid brought panic to the super-race, and it was determined, before the last bombs fell, that in reprisal all prisoners would be shot. The news spread very fast.

The slaughter was about to take place in the barracks at Stalag 606. Koch, his SS girls, his SS troops had lined up nearly 700 of us. He stood there screaming his curses at the 24's as they streaked in low, skip-bombing. The last thing he said before a load of eggs exploded at the west wall was, "They are inhuman! They have no mercy – shoot them down!"

Koch meant the planes. His SS troops, confused and terrified by the deafening roar rolling over them, turned their weapons on the men. Another element on the German 20's slammed out a lucky shot at a wingman. The big bomber ditched its load over the German gun position, then panned around and bellied into the Nazi headquarters. There it blew up. My eardrum burst from concussion.

"Fools! Shoot the planes!" Koch screamed over a loudspeaker. "*The planes!*"

A few of us played possum then. It had saved me once and I damned sure tried it again. I crawled to a few yards of the flaming plane and lay there. The guards raced to man machine-guns at the damaged gate, and the anti-aircraft battery was reoccupied.

I didn't know the guy whose .45 I found. His hat and his gun fit, though. So did his shrapnel – it fit in both legs and burned. Blood sloshed in my shoes as I snaked along the smoking rubble toward the gate. More bombs then and a plane circling low, wiggling its wings. Over the brow of the hill was a landing strip, made of the sweat and blood of our men for German convenience. The plane circled, motors throbbing as the anti-aircraft gunners suddenly got the range.

Ahead, dead ahead suddenly was the SS maniac Zent. I didn't kill her. I used her as a convenience for getting out of hell, but then when one of our eggs stitched a close one, Zent went to pieces. Sobbing, clawing me, her head buried in my chest, passionate Zent shrieked the craziest tale of all. Koch had made her do everything. Everything was Koch's idea. Wouldn't I please let her go! She crushed her full blonde body against mine, pleading and kissing at the same time.

"Sure," I said. 'Sure, I'll let you go, Zent."

The hill was swarming with Nazis. Ahead of the Nazis were maybe thirty escapees out of the entire 700. I said to Zent, "Quiet, baby. We're gonna be nice and quiet when the Oberscharführer passes now, aren't we?"

The blonde twisted away and laughed.

Zent stood up waving to the Kommandant. I drew a bead on the dapper Nazi closing in. At fifty feet I put two bullets in his face. Then I spun Martha Zent around. Below the plane was landed, door open, five crew members firing at the Nazis who were chasing the escapees.

"Zent. 'Bye Zent." I pulled the trigger till the gun clicked empty. Then I ran down the rest of the hill. I don't remember getting aboard; don't remember the shrapnel. I floated off in a roaring haze and next saw the light of day as we landed at Bengazi. I was out of my squadron only two weeks – two of the longest weeks I'll ever live. The place was Ploesti, big refinery, crazy Nazis and a compound. Stalag 606.

HIDEOUS SECRETS OF HITLER'S MAD DOCTOR OF AGONY

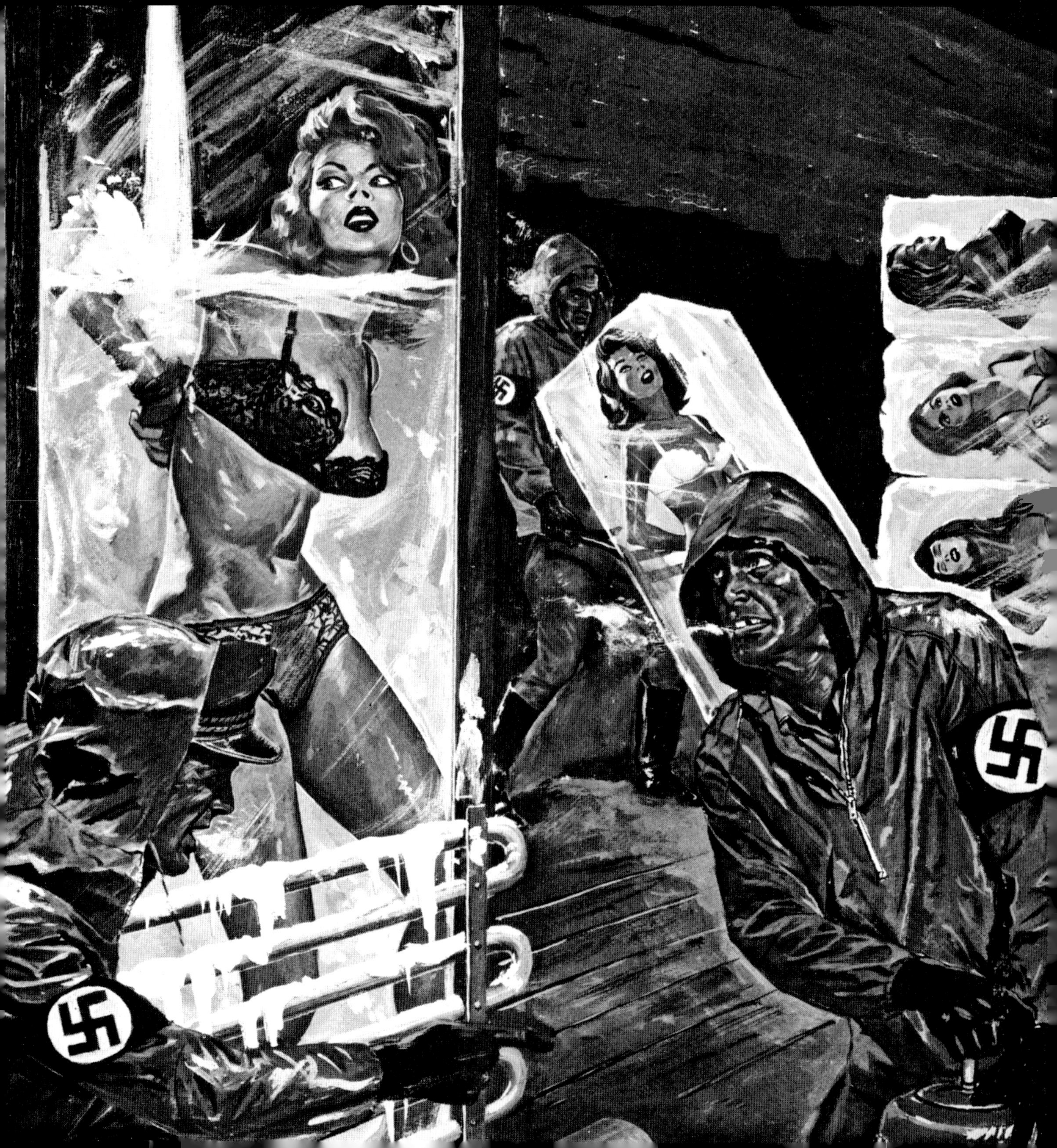

Odette had spurned the advances of the Führer's chief medical scientist. Now, in the icy confines of a clandestine Nazi laboratory, she would discover the true horror of his human experiments.

ODETTE MICHAUD KNELT BESIDE the writhing man. She saw the bloody foam flecking his lips. Her medical training told her that a splintered rib had punctured the soft tissue of his lungs. Death was only moments away.

She cradled his head against her soft young breasts, easing his rigors as much as possible. She felt the violent muscle spasms convulsing his body.

The man's pain dulled eyes searched her face. "*Rouge*?" he managed to whisper.

"*Rouge*," she repeated the Maquis code name.

"*Ce soir*. The strike is set for tonight at midnight. Pass the word."

The man shuddered once. The convulsions eased. He looked over the blonde girl's head as if he was being treated to a sight which is held back from living men.

"*Achtung!*" a guttural voice rasped behind Odette. "Drag the pig off the road. You're holding up an important mission."

Slowly Odette rose to her feet. A tiny spot of blood marred the cleanliness of her white blouse. The little knot of Nazis closed in around her. Their descriptive comments were vile. Behind them, the ambulance driver sat behind his wheel, picking his yellow teeth.

One of the Nazis kicked at the man on the ground. A rattling gasp broke from the Frenchman's lips.

"He's dying," Odette murmured. With reverence she made the sign of the crucifix.

"The French dog dies too slowly," the man in the uniform of an SS-Gruppenführer sneered. He pulled a heavy Luger from his holster, blew on its barrel and grinned. The sound of the shot filled the early spring air.

A *feldwebel* grabbed the Maquis courier by one foot and dragged his lifeless body across the dirt road. The corpse's head banged against a rock. Another enlisted man busied himself with the twisted frame of the courier's bicycle.

The SS-Gruppenführer glowered at his watch. "I have been held up five minutes by this fool," he said. He rubbed the medical insignia on his jacket. "My time is valuable."

Odette backed away from the man. Of all things she hadn't counted on, it was getting involved with a German field ambulance staffed by a high Nazi officer and his entourage of stooges. She too was wasting valuable time.

Jean Brioude would be waiting. Jean had to know of the strike against the National Medical Laboratory. If his group weren't activated in time to take up the left flank of the raid, the *franc-tireur* operation would go for nothing.

For a fleeting moment, the woman in Odette took over from the resistance fighter. She couldn't help but think that it might prove a blessing if Jean did not find out about the raid. How nice it would be to sleep in his arms for a full night without fear. She put the thought out of her mind immediately. She knew well that if the raid weren't executed tonight, there would be no other chance.

She didn't have to be told that the man who swaggered before her was none other than Karl Brandt, Reich Commissioner for Health and Sanitation. His arrival in the outskirts of Paris had been heralded by Maquis Intelligence.

She felt Brandt's eyes studying her closely. The man seemed to have X-ray vision. Odette wondered how much her manner betrayed the things she knew and feared.

"You knew this pig, Fraulein?" Brandt demanded, pointing at the cadaver.

"*Mais, non, Monsieur Le General*," she replied evenly.

"Then why did you waste time on him?"

"There was an accident. The ambulance hit his bicycle. I thought perhaps I could help."

Brandt thought for a moment. "What were you doing on this road? Were you here to meet the man? Perhaps he was your lover? Perhaps the two of you were about to go off into the trees? That would have been a nice thing. You are what the French call a *poule*, are you not?"

Odette's skin crawled at the man's words. She felt the heat glow in her face. The other Nazis snickered.

"I did not know the man," she repeated. "However I could not allow him to die unattended. I am sure the man meant no harm. It was an accident."

"The fool meant to sabotage my ambulance," Brandt raged. "I know you people. You will do anything to cause the Reich trouble."

Brandt's face was livid. Odette wondered whether he actually believed what he was saying or was merely putting on a show for his flunkies.

The Maquis dossier had been quite complete on the Nazi Commissioner for Health and Sanitation.

"What do you think, Mennecke?" he asked.

The second medical officer shrugged his shoulders. "It is a possibility, Herr Gruppenführer."

"You will accompany us, Fraulein," Brandt ordered. "This matter bears more investigation."

Odette's knees trembled. There had been something evil though not quite understandable in the brief exchange between Brandt and Mennecke. The men had watched her, the way one might study a butterfly skewered on a pin.

Brandt gripped Odette's arm in his fist and shoved her towards the ambulance. Mennecke and a third doctor who was addressed as Nitsche followed along.

Desperately Odette's mind whirled, trying to fit the pieces into place. The doors of the ambulance swung open and she was told to climb in. Brandt followed her and with mounting terror, Odette realized that the two other doctors were going to ride in the front alongside the enlisted drivers.

She sorted out the details of her position as she heard the motorcycle escort kicking their vehicles to life.

This was France, March 15, 1942. She was Odette Michaud, 23 years old, graduate of the Sorbonne, registered nurse. She was deeply in love with Jean Brioude, doctor of medicine who had given up his practice in order to work with the Maquis. She had shared his bed on many occasions and lived in hopes of someday sharing his name.

But such plans were unrealistic in the light of the Nazi occupation. Today all that lovers could share were the common dangers of the shadow of war. To the resistance, she was *Rouge*. To the man who had died in the ill-timed accident, she was a contact, someone who would carry the orders a few kilometers further to another action group.

And now, she was no longer *Rouge*.

She was the reluctant guest of SS-Gruppenführer Karl Brandt.

Brandt – the name struck terror in her heart. The Commissioner for Health and Sanitation was in reality the head of the three-man "Traveling Circus" which had toured Europe on its journey of lust and depravity. Brandt prided himself on being Hitler's personal physician. But this wasn't enough for him. He also had set up the Lunacy Board which determined the fate of countless thousands of hostages and concentration camp prisoners.

Brandt's operations were simple. He and his stooges would interview prisoners – especially women The younger and more desirable were summarily diagnosed as insane by the evil triumvirate of psychiatrists. This destroyed the last vestiges of their rights and made them subject to any experimentation which occurred to their "scientific" captors.

NOW ODETTE sat in the back of the ambulance with Brandt. She huddled on the stretcher bed, knees pressed tightly together, arms folded in front of her breasts, eyes fixed on the gross-looking German who sat opposite her.

"You are quite a beautiful young woman, Fraulein," Brandt smiled, his voice now smooth and oily. "You have a certain fascination for me."

Odette managed a weak smile of her own. The sudden change in Brandt's manner was confusing.

"I need not tell you that I am one of the most powerful men in the Reich. The Führer himself is my personal friend. It would not be to your disadvantage to count me as your friend as well."

Odette remained silent. She fought to still the inner trembling. She was terrified that her voice would break if she tried to speak.

Brandt rose from the jump seat and moved to the stretcher. He sat heavily beside Odette.

"This thing with the cyclist, I know he was nothing to you. Sometimes I must put up a show of severity in front of others. When you are in charge of other men, you must act stronger than them. All they respect is strength."

The ambulance lurched and Odette's soft body was thrown against Brandt's. She felt his arm encircle her waist, the well manicured hand moving up to cup her breast.

"You French are an inferior race," he continued with a show of arrogance. "I realize your morals are far below those of we Aryans. However in my capacity of a psychiatrist, I find a certain clinical interest in my dealings with you. I am not opposed to studying your rather bizarre methods of love-making."

As he talked, Brandt's arms were pushing Odette back against the stretcher. She twisted in his grip, feeling his sweating hands moving up under her skirt. His chest crushed her breasts. His bloodless lips ground cruelly against her full pouting ones.

The Nazi's nearness sickened her. More by reflex than anything else, she managed to run a knee into his groin. His body went rigid and then relaxed.

His cheeks puffed in and out and for a few seconds he looked as if he were about to vomit bile.

"Filthy *Boche*," Odette hissed. With all of her strength she heaved up against his obscene weight.

The ambulance rattled on over the rough road. A deathly silence filled the air as Brandt fought to regain control and Odette began to realize that she had probably signed her own death warrant.

Slowly the Reich Minister managed to regain his composure. Where on the road he had raged and blustered, and only minutes before in the ambulance, he had simpered like a love-starved school boy, his manner now took a third turn. It was easily the most malignant of all.

He was now the cold-blooded, unemotional executioner. In a voice that was scarcely audible over the roar of the engine, he said, "Fraulein, you are deranged. You have shown definite signs of homicidal mania. To allow you to roam the streets would represent a danger, not only to yourself, but to innocent parties. I have no doubt that my colleagues on the board of review will be in complete agreement with me."

Coincidences had combined to forge the shackles which she would never break. The courier with the message for *Rouge* had picked the meeting spot and arrived at the exact instant that the German field ambulance with its V.I.P. compliment of Nazis had. Odette's medical training hadn't allowed her to turn her back on a dying man, regardless of the needs of the *franc-tireur* or her own personal safety.

Brandt heaved his bulk up to a standing position. With ceremony he lifted the Luger from its holster. Odette scarcely breathed. She waited for the slug to blast through her soft flesh.

"Fraulein, you are under arrest as a homicidal maniac and an enemy of the Third Reich. You will be taken to the psychopathic wing of the National Medical Laboratory for examination and processing."

The ambulance rumbled on as Odette thought of the irony of events. The Maquis strike was to have been aimed at this chamber of horrors which the Nazis had set up under the guise of science. But now the raid would succeed only in spilling more French blood. There would be no chance of success without Jean's group supporting the flank. And Odette would die under the treatment meted out by the New Order's Men of Science.

Karl Brandt savored Odette's ragged breathing. He placed the Luge's barrel against her breast and twisted it viciously. Agony shot through her, radiating down along her arms. Bitter nausea gripped her belly.

"You will enjoy the experiments, Fraulein. Of that you may be sure. And you will know that you are advancing the German war effort. That should fill you with pride," Brandt gloated.

Once again his free hand moved upwards under her skirt, the fingers pinching and probed. With his knowledge of the female anatomy, Brandt was able to bring about the ultimate in outrage to his victim.

Involuntarily, Odette's hands flew up to protect herself. Brandt grasped her wrists, twisting them behind her back. She felt herself being pressed against the coarse muslin sheet of the stretcher. The Reich minister's full weight ground into the small of her back, sending shock waves down her thrashing legs.

Odette was conscious of a thin cord being twisted around her wrists. It chafed and bit into the tender skin as her captor tightened the knots. She squirmed under his oppressive weight; her mind filled with the sounds of his maniacal cackling.

Brandt sat astride her, his beady eyes feasting on the nakedness of her pink thighs where her skirt had been disarranged by her struggles. The palm of his hand lashed across her hips with the retort of a rifle crack. Her fragile panties offered no protection from the of blows.

As the ambulance lurched along, Brandt captured her slim ankles and drew them up towards her bound wrists. With another length of rope, the Nazi lashed her arms and legs together so that her body was bowed backwards. He tugged at the ropes with much more pressure than was necessary to assure himself that she couldn't move.

Finally satisfied, Brandt lifted her and turned her on her back. He studied her in the manner of a medical student examining a new cadaver. "You are quite strong and healthy, Fraulein," he smirked. 'You will make a very fine laboratory animal."

Straining against her bonds, Odette lay staring at the man, her mind unable to conjure up the enormity of his madness nor the pain which awaited her at the psychopathic wing.

A HALF hour later, the ambulance rolled to a stop before a grim fieldstone mansion which had been taken over by the Nazis. Brandt opened the vehicle's rear doors and barked orders in German.

Immediately two men wearing the Death's Head insignia of the Elite Korps entered the ambulance. They lifted the stretcher and rolled it up an incline into the building.

Wildly Odette stared around her. From below came the hideous screams and moans of souls in mortal torment. All of the cries were high-pitched. There was no doubt that the Psychopathic wing was devoted entirely to the torture of women.

The stretcher was trundled through a maze of corridors. Odette did her best to control the palsy-like trembling which wracked her limbs. It wasn't feat alone which caused the tremors. She had been bound with fiendish barbarity so that the tendons of her arms and legs were drawn insufferably taut.

At last the stretcher rolled to a stop. Odette felt a numbing cold surround her. She was aware of men standing over her. Brandt and his stooges Nitsche and Mennecke carried on a hideous parody of a consultation. For some perverse reason, the sadists insisted on posing under the guise of doctors.

Nitsche held Odette's shoulders pressed firmly against the stretcher. Mennecke reached for her white blouse, ripping it downward over her body. Her upthrust breasts, strained high by the rigors of her bondage became a target for their obscene eyes. The scanty bra gave her little protection against heir lust.

Brandt produced a stethoscope and pressed its rubber tip under her breast. Mennecke produced a notebook and began jotting in it.

"Heart action appears excellent," Brandt reported. "In every way, I believe this lunatic is in perfect physical shape. It is really amazing, Mennecke, how strong these French madwomen are."

Mennecke snickered. He ran his hands over Odette, tearing her skirt from her. Wildly the girl thrashed on the stretcher. "Hypertensive reflexes," he noted. "But that is to be expected in the schizoid."

It was a disgusting perversion of medical jargon. Odette found herself wondering why the three torturers went through the mumbo-jumbo. Under the Swastika, there was no need for rationalizing bestiality. Yet they insisted on continuing the examination.

Once again, Brandt took the lead. "It is important to note the roll of anticipation as a physiological factor in endurance," he said. "In other words, when a man is plunged into the sea, is he better able to withstand the shock if he has been prepared for it, or does his terror cause his body functions to break down more quickly? To have such information would be of great help to Gross Admiral Raeder."

Mennecke giggled. Nitsche shot him a look of disapproval. "You are quite right, Herr General. We have neglected the needs of the Navy because of our preoccupation with the pressure experiments which Goering ordered carried out."

It was madness, torture and murder carried out with the antiseptic attitude of technicians. It was human vivisection which had no value other than to feed the depraved lusts of the murderers.

"Then we are in accord?" Brandt asked. "We will carry out the experiment in the manner we discussed recently?"

"I concur completely. The woman is obviously schizoid and I will certify her as such. She now falls within the Euthanasia program as outlined by Reich Minister Himmler," Mennecke droned.

"I believe the role of anticipation in the thermal

experiments is of great scientific importance," Nitsche added.

Odette felt the cords which bound her hands to her ankles being snipped by a surgical scalpel. She felt herself being lifted from the stretcher and hoisted over Brandt's shoulder. Her body was doubled, her head hung down. She squirmed mightily in his grasp, but her arms were still securely bound behind her back and her legs strapped together.

A door opened and new waves of cold lashed at her unprotected body. Clad as she was in the thinnest of silk panties and bra, the frigid vapors whipped her like a thousand knouts. Brandt set her on her feet. Immediately Nitsche began tying her to a vertical beam. The intense cold of the room made her skin even more sensitive to the heavy, splintery strands of rope which now encased her thighs, waist and breasts. Clouds of vapor swirled around her head, dimming her sight. Never in her entire life had she felt the pain of intense cold to the extent that she did now.

But even in the madness of her terror, a certain curiosity flooded through her. What manner of experiments were being carried out in this underground tomb?

Odette's head moved from side to side. A gasp of horror was wrenched from her lips as she saw the neat rows of ice blocks stashed in crypts dug into the walls.

Each ice block entombed the lovely body of a young woman. The arms and legs were still bound. The expressions of horror and agony were etched indelibly on their faces. For all that, it was difficult to determine whether were still alive or not.

Brand stood next to Odette, his evil hands once again toying with her body, bringing new shock waves of pain. He had donned a heavy parka to insulate him from the intense cold.

"In the past," he gloated, "we have not brought a woman into this room until she was to partake in the experiments. We found it made it easier to handle them that way. However we are going to allow you to witness one, so that we can determine to what extent psychological manifestations affect physiological ones."

The three men left the room, allowing Odette to remain completely alone with the rows of victims in their glass coffins.

Immediately Odette's imagination took, over. She could feel the water forming into its mold of ice over her. She could sense the desperate struggle to keep from being drowned in it. Her body writhed against its lashings.

She fought down the panic. The lovely blonde girl realized that even now, three pairs of gloating eyes were watching her every gesture through hidden peepholes. She had already begun to provide their entertainment. Damn them, she would not give them that satisfaction.

She sagged against her bonds, feeling the splinters dig furrows in her tender flesh. She felt herself growing drowsy. Once long ago she had heard that when you freeze to death, you fall into a deep sleep first. Perhaps she was fortunate. This form of death might prove less agonizing than some other.

But she hadn't reckoned with the bestial cunning of her captors. Cold as the crypt appeared, she would not die immediately. No victim escaped the evil ones without having tested the ultimate in agony.

IT SEEMED like hours later that the door to the ice chamber reopened. The three doctors entered, dragging a lovely dark-haired girl with them. The girl's eyes were large. Her terrified lips quivered as she spied the ice blocks with their grisly contents.

Furiously she lashed out at her captors. But her strength was no match for theirs. Mennecke gripped her arms and held her tightly against his body, while Nitsche systematically went about stripping her dress from her. Swiftly her hands and feet were tightly bound and a halter lowered under her shoulders.

Half naked, she was swung up to ceiling by a heavy rope and then slowly lowered into a tank which allowed her just enough room to stand in.

Satisfied with the preparations for the experiment, Brandt returned to Odette.

"Let me explain in detail what is happening so that you will understand it completely," he droned.

The girl in the tank screamed mightily as a jet of frigid water splashed around her feet. Slowly, the tank began to fill. The pool of water lapped around the girl's thighs, caressed her hips, bubbled around her waist, and toyed with her upthrust breasts. When it reached the level of her neck, the jet was turned off.

"There would be no value in having the woman drown quickly. We would gain no information that way," Brandt hissed in Odette's ear as he pawed her straining body.

"Now there are two forces at work on her body," he continued. "First the intense cold. Second, pressure. Ice, as you probably are aware, takes up more space than water. I assure you that the glass in the tank is quite shatter proof. Now from our standpoint, the interesting problem is whether she will freeze or be crushed first."

Odette bit her lips to keep from giving the madman the satisfaction of hearing her screams. Her eyes were drawn to the other girl's suffering as though she were hypnotized by it. Her body became a part of the other victim's.

She saw the heavy frost begin to gather around the coils which surrounded the tank. She heard the first crackling as a scum of ice began to form along the girl's shoulders.

The ice thickened inexorably. Gasping sobs were wrenched from the girl's throat as the pressure on her bones and vital organs increased. With terrifying clarity, Odette realized that the girl was not being frozen to death, she was literally being crushed under the crystal-clear ice.

Nitsche manipulated the dials on the thermostat, controlling the formation of ice. The girl groaned as the jagged slivers pressed upwards against her throat. She churned the water wildly, trying to keep it agitated and the ice broken.

But even as her body writhed, her eyes began to bulge. Her magnificent breasts were pushed upwards. Her face became contorted with the pulverizing pressure she was being subjected to.

"Very interesting, isn't it, Fraulein?" Brandt cackled, his fingers twisted in Odette's hair, bending her head towards the scene of horror unfolding in the tank. "Here we combine the rigors of cold and pressure. Do not fear, my little one, your turn will come. But certainly you cannot expect us to rush with your countrywoman just to suit your convenience. It will be slow for her, Fraulein. It will be much slower for you. You will learn what it means to attack a Reich Minister. How different it might have been for you."

"*Fils de la chienne!*" Odette gritted between her teeth.

Once again she was left in the room by the Nazis. Now the girl being crushed in the tank kept her company. As the pressures increased, horrible things happened to the girl's once lovely body. The bones appeared to mash against each other. Unearthly sounds burst from her lips as the gases were forced from her. With one final cry of agony, the girl's mouth gaped open and for the second time in the day, Odette saw the bubbly red froth oozing out. The girl's head fell forward, crunching on the top of the ice.

Odette waited, once again completely alone in the room of death. The tank housed one more cadaver to be placed in its crypt. Perhaps fifteen minutes later, a *feldwebel* entered the chamber and flooded the remainder of the tank. Water gushed over the corpse's head, lending it buoyancy. Swiftly the water congealed. The *feldwebel* trundled a hand cart to the tank, unlatched the sides and removed what had only hours before been a lovely, vital young girl.

Odette slumped forward in her own bonds. Whether it had been the sights and sounds of what she had just witnessed, or the impact of the numbing cold on her nearly nude body, she now found consciousness drifting away. If this was death, she welcomed it.

The shock of freezing water sloshing over her ankles brought her back to the hell of life. Instantly she knew that she had replaced the last victim in the tank. The water rose, bubbling around her, flowing over her exposed flesh. She held her breath against its intense cold. She willed her heart to stop, but it continued beating furiously. Everywhere she looked, she saw the grinning skull of one of the members of "The Traveling Circus," savoring her torture, pressing close so that none of her suffering would escape them. Pain built in her breast and reached a crescendo before spilling out along her outraged nerves. She felt a sharp sliver touch her throat. The ice had begun to form.

A shot rang out. Then another. The room became a scene of confusion and terror. Six wild-eyed men in civilian clothes stood before the three cowering Nazi doctors. Their faces had been twisted into gargoyles of hatred. Through her blurred vision, Odette believed that she saw Jean Brioude. She heard words – angry words. And then she remembered no more.

Days later as she rested in Brioude's arms, she learned the details of her rescue. Word had reached Brioude's Maquis action group. Instead of a frontal assault, it had been decided to move in through the suburban sewer system. The Maquis had burrowed directly under the house and made their way to the basement ice crypt.

Unfortunately they had not taken their vengeance on Brandt, Nitsche and Mennecke, fearing reprisals to the prisoners who would be forced to remain behind in the Laboratory. However, the raid had effected the rescue of nineteen young women – Odette included. Jean Brioude had bartered their rescue in return for Karl Brandt's life.

It was a temporary victory for Brioude, who was later shot down in a Maquis raid. Odette Michaud was perhaps more fortunate. She survived the war and today lives in a little village near Marseilles where she quietly goes about her duties at a small nursing home. Whatever satisfaction she can generate must come from the knowledge that Brandt met his death at the end of a hangman's rope, as did Nitsche. The third member of the "Traveling Circus" to be tried and convicted by the War Crimes Commission, Mennecke, died in prison while awaiting execution.

TORTURED NUDES FOR THE DEVIL'S CHARNEL HOUSE

The peasants trembled as they whispered of the vanishing virgins in the castle of pain.

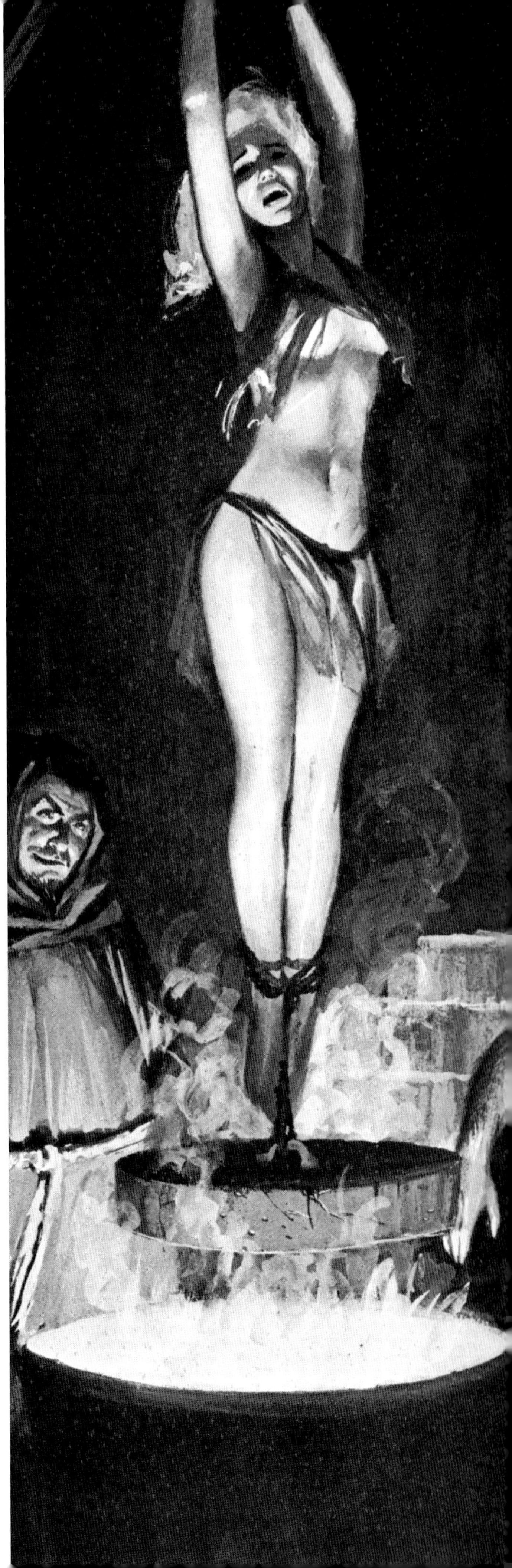

THE HOUSE WAS A large one, set back and surrounded with trees and fountains in the manner of 16th century Italy. Passers-by had to stay some distance from the windows, lighted with flickering candles – but as they walked along the paths of the city they could still hear, from the house beyond the trees, the terrible screams, the bubbling moans, that seemed sometimes to go on by both night and day.

The more pious among them crossed themselves, muttering prayers as they went quickly by. "It is the devil who lives in there," they said. "The devil himself, come to earth to torment us."

For none of them knew who might be next – who might be picked to suffer the tortures of the damned inside the house of the Count of Cenara.

During the day, for the most part, the house was quiet. But at night, when the candles began to flicker, the citizens would hear screams, pleas, and the sounds of the torture – of the whip, repeating in endless cracks the lashing of some poor innocent, or the straining of the wooden rack on which a living body was being torn slowly to pieces.

Among themselves, the braver souls muttered of rebellion. The day would come, they said, when they would band together and overthrow the Count of Cenara, put an end to his reign of blood and terror.

But all of them knew, secretly, that the day could never come.

The Count had the city in the palm of his hand. Within

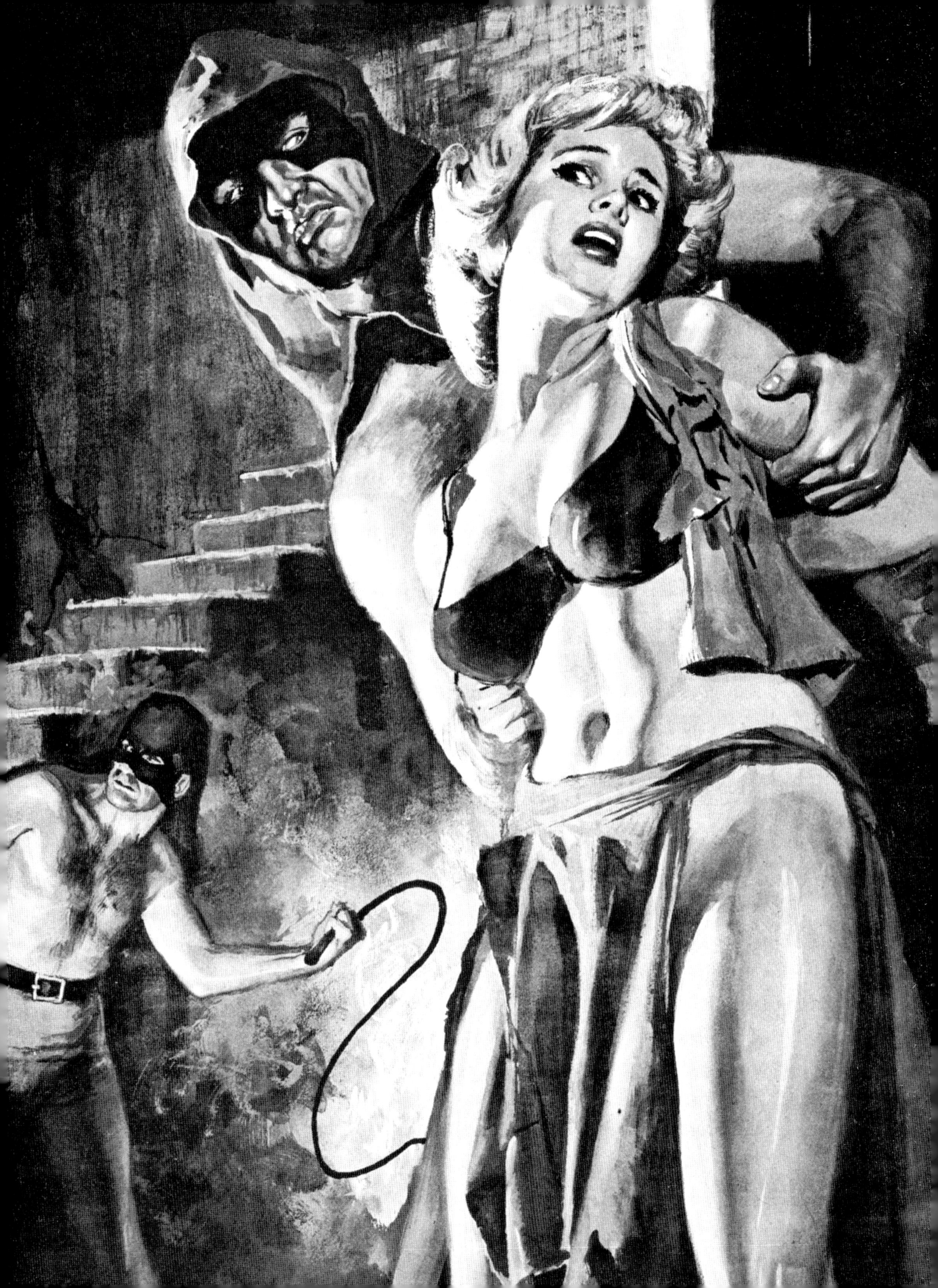

Villecharina there was no force to oppose him. Like many in various Italian towns he even had his own "army," a hand-picked band of servants and helpers trained to fight. No crew of untrained citizens could stand up against such force.

AMONG THE most vocal of the citizens of Villecharina was Rodolfo Teschina, a woodworker of the town. Rodolfo, a middle-aged man with long, flowing moustaches and a missing left hand, lopped off in some forgotten accident during his apprenticeship, had reason for his fear and hatred of the Count. He had known the Count in childhood, and he never tired of telling the story.

"That one," he said to his cronies, "was always a bad. one. Even as a small boy, there was something wrong with him – who knows why, except that the Devil sometimes chooses a man for his own."

Rodolfo's mother had worked as laundress in the Count's household for some little while, his father as assistant to the coachman. As a child, Rodolfo himself had played in the courtyard of the place, had seen the young Count and his amusements.

"At first it was the animals," he said. "The flies, perhaps – or even the cats and dogs. He liked to make them suffer, burning the flies in a fire, beating the animals until they could resist no more, even until they died. Some say he was kind and gentle as a child, and that some love-affair turned him against women, but I say he was always a man of blood, a man of anger and terror."

Rodolfo's mother had been pretty and blonde, rare in Southern Italy. She had caught the eye of the young Count, who was then perhaps thirteen.

Ridiculous as it sounds, this young boy had come to Rodolfo's father with an offer. If the elder Teschina would "put away" his wife, some sort of divorce might be managed, and the Count himself would "marry" the woman, Violetta.

Naturally, Teschina refused.

"I was willing to offer her happiness," the Count said, in a casual tone. "You have insured that she will suffer torment instead." He bowed and turned away.

The reputation of the Count of Cenara was not yet widespread: Teschina had little fear that he would really carry out such a threat.

The next night he discovered how wrong he had been. At dead of night four guards broke into the chamber he shared with his wife and son and carried Violetta off, in spite of all the fight Rodolfo and his father could put up.

The two went to the main rooms of the place and asked for the Count.

The Count of Cenara received them within an hour. "You are inquiring after the Signora?" he asked.

"She has been taken away," Teschina roared, "and by your orders!"

"You wish to see her?"

Teschina nodded.

"I will take you to her," the Count said. Guards appeared; the man and the boy were escorted through the labyrinthine passages of the house until they found themselves in a small back room.

Teschina stared and screamed. His son Rodolfo tried to run to his mother – but the guards held him firmly back, and actually tied him to a chair along with his father. Trussed up, the two continued to stare at Violetta Teschina.

Her beautiful body was naked now, before the gaze of guards and the Count. Her breasts straining forward, she had been tied to a pillar near the center of the room. Her eyes were closed and her head hanging down in a faint.

The front of her body was covered with whipmarks. Blood still oozed from some of the ugly cuts the whip had made in her tender flesh. A grinning guard stood by with the long braided whip dangling from his hand, waiting until she might awaken.

Teschina was cursing, bitterly and steadily, at the Count. Rodolfo, round-eyed, could say nothing. The Count only smiled for a long second.

"I informed you of the bargain you had made," he told Teschina, "Now I am glad you have come to see it carried out."

Soon a fluttering of the eyelids, a faint stirring of the head, told the horrified watchers that Violetta Teschina had awakened.

Her staring eyes fell of the bound forms of her husband and son.

"Oh, God she whispered. "Save me... don't let them... don't let him hurt me any more..."

But there was nothing to be done, no way for Teschina or his son Rodolfo to escape from the bonds that held them tightly. The guard with the whip moved forward and Violetta screamed at the sight of him. Then the braided whip flashed up, and down, striking the tender body, flicking actual bits of flesh off with the force of its blow.

Again, and again, and again...

And then there were other tortures, in a shrieking carnival of agony: wooden stakes with their tips wrapped in burning cotton, jabbed into the tenderest portions of the woman's body until the blackened circles of burned flesh multiplied, became one single black mass of jerking torment...

It took her five hours to die, five hours of nearly constant torture.

When Teschina and Rodolfo were taken from the room they were numb with horror, incapable of speech or motion.

Teschina himself died two months later – after the Count had sent him from the house.

"You will not be allowed entrance again," he told the man and his son, 'I merely lived up to my bargain – but who knows? You might resent even that, and attempt to harm me. You will not be allowed the opportunity."

HIS FATHER dead, Rodolfo turned to woodworking as a means of scraping our a tiny living for himself. Three times he had attempted to break into the domain of the Count of Cenara. Three times he had been turned back by alert guards in the Count's pay and household.

Sooner or later, he knew, he would succeed. He *had* to succeed.

Buried deeply in his heart was the memory of his

mother.

And, nearer the surface, there was a new fear. Rodolfo had married, and he had a daughter, an eighteen-year-old girl named Donna Teschina.

Some day, the eye of the Count might fall on Donna.

And that, Rodolfo vowed, could not be allowed to happen.

It was Rodolfo who finally formed the villagers of Villecharina into something resembling an army.

Perhaps he thought of it primarily as revenge, perhaps as protection for his daughter Donna. But if it were protection he was after, he was doomed to disappointment. For the formation of even so loose and unplanned a group as his "army" brought his name to the attention of the Count of Cenara.

And with his name came the name of his daughter.

"Donna Teschina?" the Count asked quietly of his chief guard. "She might provide me with pleasure, Carlo. If she is anything like her grandmother," he smiled. Carlo knew that smile, and he knew that during the night screams and groans would once again terrify those who were forced to pass the Count's house.

"What are my orders?" he asked.

The Count smiled again. "Why, bring her to me, Carlo," he said. "The women of this town are ugly, fat, unpleasant to a man of refined tastes. They scream obscenities, and when they surrender they are – unsatisfactory. But this Teschina girl might be a faint echo of her grandmother..." he paused. "Yes," he said then, in a quiet voice. "Bring her to me. And be careful, Carlo – take a force with you. Her father will not give her up without strong resistance."

That night, Carlo and six of his men went out along the twisted streets of Villecharina to the small hut where Rodolfo, his wife and his daughter lived. Their passage was marked by a lookout Rodolfo had posted, and by the time they reached the hut men were standing ready for them.

Carlo deployed his own men in a semi-circle, and drove straight for the hut. They were armed with pikes and swords; the villagers had nothing but clubs to use.

They used them valiantly; by the time the pitched battle was over two of the Count's men lay unconscious on the ground, one of them to die later of a cracked skull.

But four of the villagers were dead, and among the dead was Rodolfo's wife.

Donna Teschina, Rodolfo's daughter, was not dead.

But Rodolfo was beginning to wish she were. Instead, the Count's men had taken her away – taken her to the torture chambers of the Count of Cenara, in spite of anything he could do!

While the others patched their wounds, carried off the dead, even began preparing for the burial of his wife, Rodolfo sat lost in agonized thought. The idea of Donna undergoing the terrible torments of the Count's pleasures was unbearable; there had to be a way out. But what?

Time passed: night grew slowly into dawn. And then, at last, Rodolfo had his idea, an idea borne of incredible desperation.

There wasn't a second, to lose. He stood up, swaying, his eyes burning. He called out to the others. He began to outline his plan.

MEANWHILE, THE Count was smiling once more.

Donna, an eighteen-year-old virgin, had been dragged before him. "I wish to enjoy your favors," the Count had said, "but I will not do so without your permission." Guards held the girl by the arms. He sneered down at her face, expecting terror – but he got, instead, a look of firm resolve.

She said one word: "Never."

The Count's smile grew broader. "Well, then," he said. "I can see that you need a little persuasion. Have you heard that I am very accomplished at... persuasion? Perhaps your father has told you–"

"You are a monster!"

The guards moved in on her, but the Count waved them to stillness. "The girl has spirit," he said. "So much the better." He addressed her again. "Yes, my dear," he said, "I have always enjoyed the techniques of persuasion. The body of a woman is like a sensitive instrument, an instrument on which a hundred different sounds can be played – from a moan to a scream. I shall not at all be disappointed by your refusal. Sooner or later, you will give in to me."

Donna shook her head slowly. "Never," she said again.

The Count wasted no words. He waved to his guards, and Donna was dragged out. By himself now, the Count allowed himself the luxury of anticipating what would happen – seeing in advance every scream, every moan, every jerk of the helpless, tormented body. Seeing the final surrender – and after that the continuation of torture, the pleasures of more and more pain until, at last, death came to claim the victim.

Death, he told himself sadly, was inevitable. But perhaps this one would last for a long time.

Slowly, unhurriedly, he followed the route the guards had taken, toward the room at the front of the house where his torture-machines had been set up. In his mind he was running over the list, and wondering which to use first. The whip by itself was hardly interesting enough.

When he reached the front room, he found Donna gripped by two guards, stripped naked. He stopped at the entrance, his breath catching. The girl was breathtakingly beautiful. Her body was slim and white, the breasts full and high, the legs long and straight. She had not inherited her mother's blonde hair, but she had something which excited him even more: pride. Even now, even naked before the guards and before the Count himself, she held herself with upright dignity, her eyes blazing at him as he stood watching her.

"Pig!"

The Count laughed. "The ceiling," he told his guards, "and the weights."

Without delay Donna's hands were brought up, her wrists tied over her head and attached to a hook in the high ceiling of the room. She attempted to kick but the guards caught her legs without effort, and tied the ankles, too, attaching to the rope a twenty-pound weight.

"Not enough," the Count said, though Donna was already gasping with the strain on her arms and shoulders.

The twenty-pound weight was removed. The new weight was fifty pounds. Donna could not restrain a moan. Her body, stretched taut, supported only by the ropes at her wrists, was pulled steadily downward by the weight at her ankles.

Now the Count hung a metal brazier before her, a deep box filled with a burning coal fire. The heat reached her faintly, since it was several inches away.

"Do you understand what will happen if you sway toward that fire?" the Count asked her. She answered him only with a curse. "Very well, then," he said. "I shall show you."

He signalled to a guard, who stepped behind the girl and lashed out suddenly with a leather whip. The crack of leather against female flesh was startlingly loud.

Donna emitted one piercing, sudden cry.

Then the leather came down again, and her body automatically convulsed with the pain.

Suspended only from the wrists, she began to sway irresistibly back and forth – each time closer to the metal brazier. For the first time she began to see the full horror of this torment.

As the whipping continued, her body would jerk with pain, a motion she could not stop. And the weight helped her sway, made her move farther out each time – until at last she would press against the fire each time she swayed forward!

The whips behind her, the fire before – her iron resolve almost cracked. With the third blow she screamed in earnest. She tried to keep herself still in spite of the pain of her whipping, but that was impossible.

The heat was now close enough to scorch.

And again the whip came down.

Her body grazed the metal brazier for the first time.

Now her screams were ear-piercing, constant. As she swayed back, unable even to kick because of the weight stretching her poor legs to their fullest, the guard behind her swung his leather whip still again.

And the metal grazed her, pressed into her.

She prayed for unconsciousness now, prayed for death, incoherently babbling shrieks of torment. But there was no mercy in that room: the whip sang down, the metal glowed with heat, scorching, burning her while the whip beat its tattoo on her flesh.

Fire!

Guards burst into the room with the news. Donna was unconscious by now, fainted for the second time, but the torment would go on when she awakened – the Count was angered by the interruption.

But the guards babbled out their story. A band of men had come to the gates with great home-made slings and flaming wood, they had cast the wood over the trees at the house. The guards there had fought back, one or two of the men were hurt – but enough of the brands had landed.

The place was burning!

Rodolfo, knowing that no more chance existed to save his daughter from torment, saw only mercy in a quick death for her.

And in that death the Count, too, would die. Perhaps he would be unable to escape in time.

As matters turned out, he might have made it – were it not for his eagerness to continue with Donna Teschina. But he refused to believe the story, then refused to believe its seriousness.

Three guards did manage to escape. They were stoned to death by a waiting crowd.

The Count of Cenara died in the flames – flames which were, perhaps, only a prelude to hotter and more permanent flames awaiting him – in the Hell which was reserved for the man the townfolk called the Devil himself!

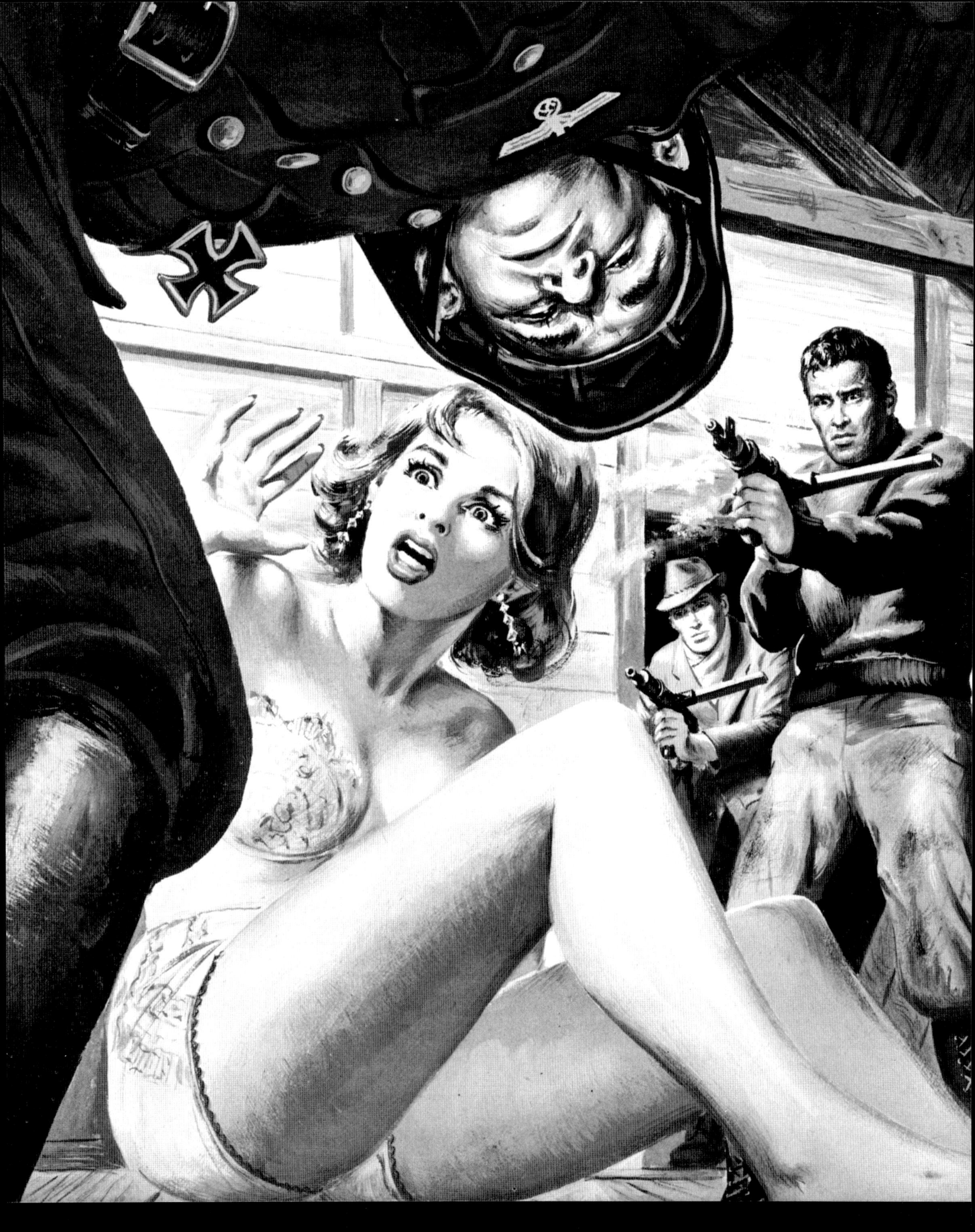

"PLAYBOY-LED CALL-GIRLS WHO SEDUCED HITLER'S BORDER BRIGADE; detail from interior art, **FOR MEN ONLY**, 01/63.
Art by Walter Popp.

WRITHE, MY LOVELY, IN THE TENT OF TORTURE

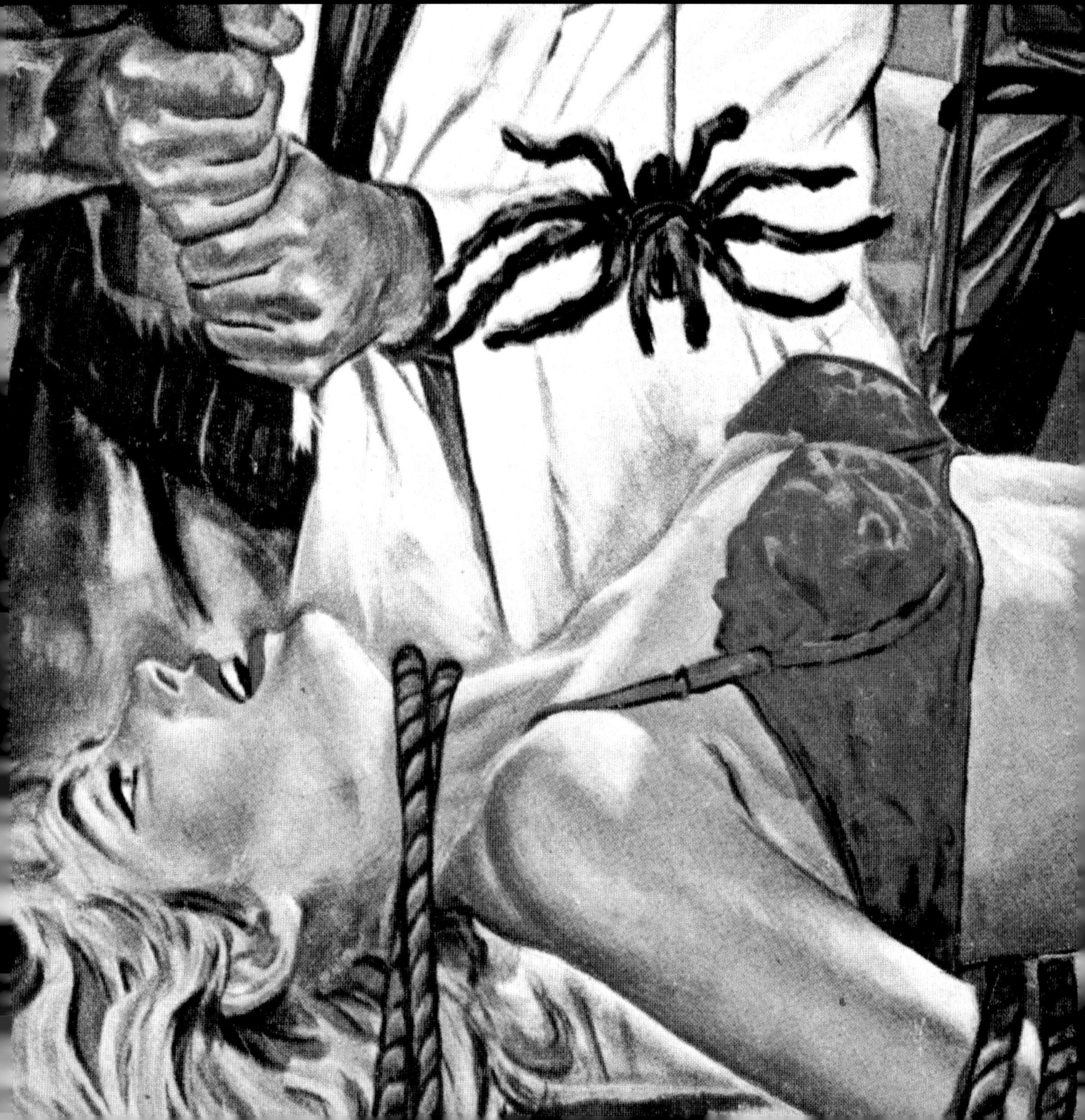

Even in the desert, it was business as usual for the torture master of Ravensbruck.

SUZANNE CHAUBERT STUDIED HER lithe reflection in the dressing-room mirror. She pursed her lips, liking what she saw. Her firm breasts stood high, scarcely needing the support of the wisp of a pink net bra which covered them. Her belly was flat, the median lines clearly defined. Her plump hips bespoke femininity, hidden as they were by the shimmering nylon of her brief panties.

She took a deep breath and reached for the sequined evening gown which hung in the dressing-room closet.

"A waste," she pouted, as she drew the material over her head. "A fearful waste."

The mood of her depression fled as quickly as it had engulfed her. Perhaps it wasn't a waste after all. Perhaps the American would come again tonight, as he had promised...

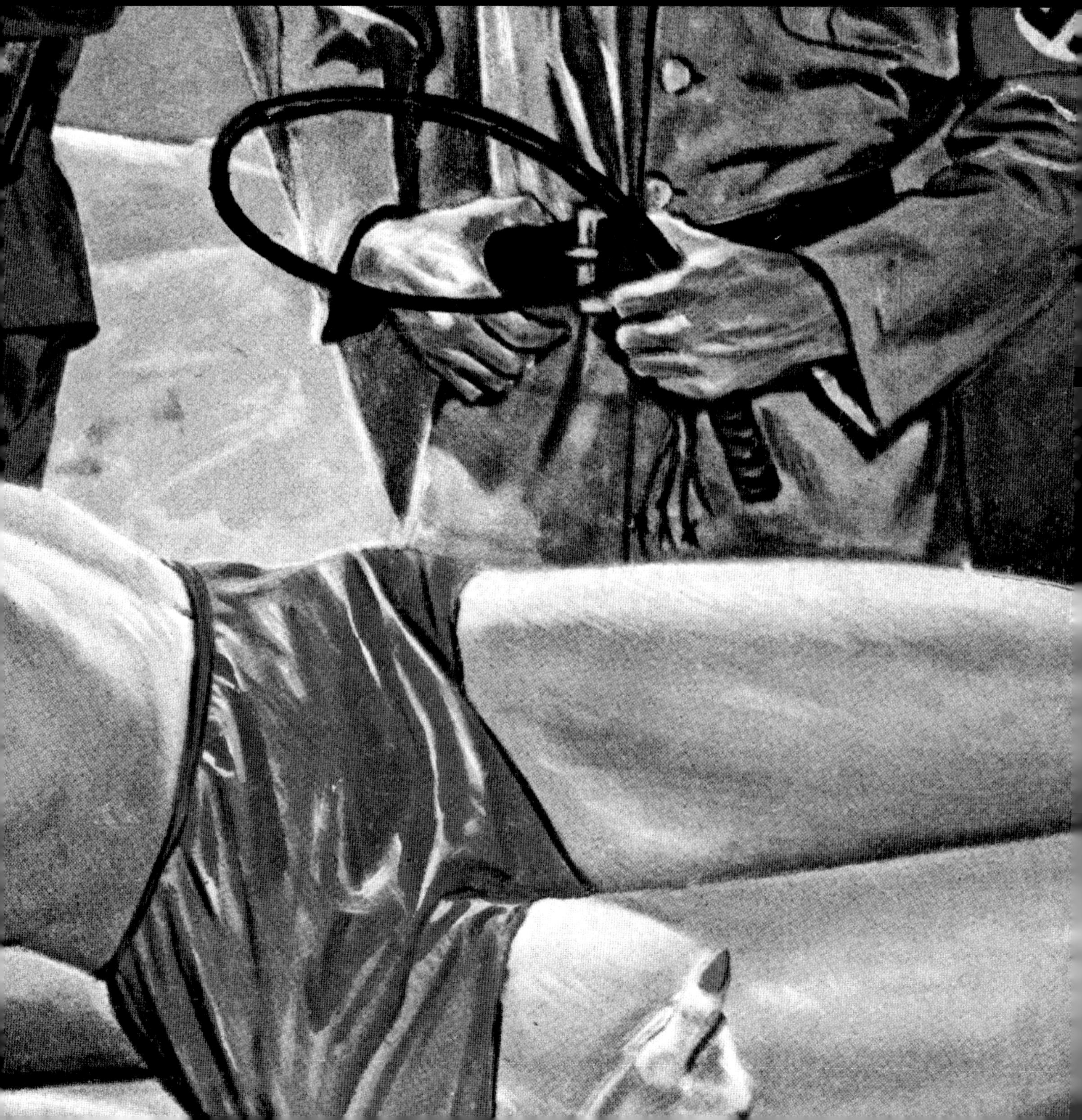

She closed her eyes and thought of the tall man with the hawk-like face and the slight flecks of gray in his crew cut. She imagined his arms encircling her naked body, drawing her to him in a taut bow, demanding every vestige of her sensitivity. The image stood out in such sharp relief that she could have sworn that Gary Larkin stood in her cramped dressing room.

The moment of reverie was broken by the harsh knock at her door.

Before she could answer, the door swung open, revealing the ugly figure of Ibn Ben Ahmed. His beady eyes squinted with anger.

"The Kit Kat Club does not pay you to hide from the customers," he said in his sibilant sing-song. "You finished your act almost a half hour ago. Why are you not out in the bar? How can a poor Arab make a living when his entertainers are too high and mighty to perform their duties?"

"I had to change," Suzanne said in exasperation. "Your German friends will wait a moment." The sight of the burnoosed figure before her filled her with nausea. If only she could leave Media. She wanted desperately to be free of the cesspool that was the Cairo suburb and the Kit Kat Club.

But leaving Media would have to remain a dream. A war orphan with no status, no money, only her youthful beauty to work for her, she was at the complete mercy of her employer. Perhaps it could be worse. Other night club owners insisted that their girls provide after-hour entertainment for the clique of Nazis who'd made their way to Egypt. At least here, the ententes were left up to the girls.

"Hurry," lb Ben Ahmed whined. "The bar is full. How can a poor Arab sell whiskey unless his girls are there to grace the room?" He spun on his heel and walked out.

Suzanne patted the sequined dress over her hips, lifted a nylon-clad leg and worked at the seam of her stocking. If only Larkin would come tonight, it would not be so bad. She closed her eyes and dreamed of Larkin spiriting her out of Egypt and taking her back to the United States with him. A ripple of delight flooded through her.

Even though she realized it was out of the question, the dream was too good to allow it to escape. She wouldn't allow herself to recognize the truth of her relationship with the soft spoken man. She didn't want to admit that he was an adventurer who'd forget her in a day or an hour or a week.

Suzanne knew men – and the man called Larkin would probably never love again. His soft voice hid the hatred which boiled in his heart – a hatred which would never be satisfied until he'd come face to face once more with Kurt Eisele.

SHE REMEMBERED Gary Larkin's words as she'd lain beside him in the big bed at the Hotel Nasser. "Eisele's here. He's working for the State Security Service. I'm sure of it. He has changed his name. But once I see him, I'll recognize him."

Suzanne's eager arms had slid around the American's neck. She had pressed her body close to him, trying to smother the vengeance which was so much a part of him.

"Why, *cheri*?" she had asked. "The war was a long time ago. All of us have suffered. It is time to forget."

"Forget?" Gary Larkin had snorted. "Forget what he did to Karen? Forget that he kept me chained to a wall like a beast while he made me watch? Forget that he offered me a choice – either I delivered a full division to the Nazis by betraying them, or I would live the rest of my life knowing that I had caused Karen's mutilation? There are some things you cannot forget."

A strangled sob broke from Larkin's lips. "I killed her. One word from me and the flaying knives would have stopped. One word from me and the soldering iron would have been unplugged."

Suzanne had fallen silent. She'd known that she was fighting the ghost of a woman who'd suffered martyrdom for Larkin. The odds were too much for Suzanne. She could bring this suffering man temporary physical release. But she could never hope to blot out the disease which ran through his brain. Not so long as Kurt Eisele remained constantly in his mind.

She'd cradled Larkin's head, drawing it to her soft breasts, hoping to ease his pain, if only for a moment. Finally he had slept beside her, even though his sleep was broken by the feverish moans of his nightmares.

Still, perhaps he would come back tonight. If he did, she would try once more. How delightful it would be to spend another night with a man who wasn't the embodiment of evil.

As she threaded her way through the little tables of the Kit Kat Club, her eyes searched through the clouds of smoke, hoping for some sign of Larkin. He was nowhere around. Even now, he was probably pouring over the United Nations Report on Human Rights which documented the Neo-Nazi movement in Egypt. Even now, he was probably walking the twisting streets of Cairo, searching, hoping.

With a troubled sign, Suzanne decided that Gary Larkin was a thing of the past – a man who had spent a night with her because instinctively he needed a woman, but who would not return.

The guttural voices of the German in civilian clothes grated against her ears. Nasser had crowded Egypt with the Underworld of those who'd made it out of Europe ahead of the War Crimes Commission. Here they were given the opportunity to conduct their business as usual, no questions asked. Here new organizations such as the League for German-Arab Brotherhood, Security Service, and the Samarra Concentration Camp needed the peculiar talents of the warped German mind. Nasser not only allowed his Nazi employees to run wild, he paid them well for doing the things they had done in Ravensbruck and Dachau and Prinz Albrechtstrasse.

Suzanne hated them. Yet one had to survive, even if it meant entertaining those who had been responsible for wiping her family out.

She felt Ibn Ben Ahmed's eyes boring into her and managed a feeble smile as she slid onto a bar stool. Immediately she was aware of the presence of the monocled figure at her elbow. His thin lips curved back in what was supposed to pass as a smile. One small eye was magnified grotesquely by the monocle he wore. A livid dueling scar ran down the side of his cheek.

The man regarded her with a close scrutiny, as if he were studying a side of beef in a butcher shop. He removed a cigarette from a silver case which had an embossed swastika etched on its lid. He placed the case on the bar close to her hand.

"Good evening, Fraulein," he offered in a reedy voice. A pulse beat lividly in his forehead. "You are waiting for someone?"

"No, I'm quite alone," Suzanne answered.

"So beautiful to be alone," he said as his hand moved up over her bare arm, testing the smoothness of her flesh. He gripped her shoulder, kneading it as his watery eyes stared into her face. "Surely a woman of your charm must have many admirers."

A sudden chill ran through Suzanne. The German was different from the others who frequented the Kit Kat Club. Others didn't go through the build up. Most of them would be more likely to say, "What is your price for spending the night at my apartment?"

But this one was different. There was something reptilian about him. He reminded Suzanne of a hooded cobra, his head dancing at the sight of his prey. Even worse, he reminded her of the Nazi who so many years ago had offered her chocolates after having cut down her parents with two shots from his Luger.

Ibn Ben Ahmed moved through the bar on slippered feet. His fetid breath was like a branding iron on the back of Suzanne's neck. He made one of his silent gestures which meant, "Be nice. Keep the customer drinking. Whatever you do on your own time after closing is your business. But right now you are working for the Kit Kat Club. And don't you forget it."

Suzanne forced herself to turn towards the German at her elbow. His bloodless lips were curled back in a sardonic grin. Suzanne figured rapidly. If the German bought her drinks, she would receive a percentage of his bill from the bar. If the German stormed off in a huff at being turned down, there'd be another scene with Ibn Ben Ahmed.

She risked a quick glance at the door. There was always the possibility that it would open and Gary Larkin would stand framed by the blood red curtains which decorated the entrance. It would give her an excuse to detach herself from the German who now busied himself pressing the palm of her hand to his cold lips.

"It would be a great honor for me to be your host," the German grated. "An aperitif. Perhaps some brandy. You are French, aren't you? I've heard that Cognac gives a special sparkle to a French woman's eye."

Suzanne forced a laugh which sounded harsh and metallic to her.

"French women live for love, Monsieur. That is what puts the sparkle in their eyes."

"I cannot argue the point, Fraulein. Let us sample the wine first. Then, who knows."

Heinrich, the bullet-headed bartender whom Ibn Ben Ahmed insisted on employing despite the complaints of his girl entertainers, padded up the bar on his carpet slippers. His broken teeth, yellow and jagged, showed in what passed for a smile.

"Ja, Herr Eisele?" he wheezed.

The man who sat alongside Suzanne stiffened. His face grew livid with suppressed rage. "Fool!" he grated. "Idiot! You have been told never to call me by that name."

Heinrich was taken aback by the force of the words. "But here, Colonel, you are among friends. Nobody would dream of betraying you. Here we are free to drink to the Führer's memory."

Eisele's eyes darted up and down the length of the bar. "You pig," he whispered. "Have you not heard that Eichmann thought he was safe? Have you not heard of Israeli intelligence? I am Karl Eber. Remember that."

"Jah, Mein Herr," Heinrich grimaced, his heavy head hanging down, his thick tongue playing at the corner of his lip.

The force of the exchange was like a body blow to Suzanne. The name, Eisele, seared her brain like a red-hot iron. Here was the man that Gary Larkin sought. Right beside her, ready to suggest some form of hanky-panky. The coincidence could prove to be the most important occurrence in her entire life.

"Act," she told herself. *"Perform as you never have in the past. Find out all about this man. Where he lives, where he walks, where he works. Every one of his habits, large and small. If Gary Larkin demands his life, give it to him. The war will never be over until you do."*

She reached for Eisele's hand, drawing it to the smooth warmth of her lap. "Do not ruin good wine with a bad temper, Monsieur," she pouted. "Life is too short for one to waste it worrying about small things."

Eisele looked at her, his face thawing somewhat. His fingers worked convulsively against her thigh. Suzanne willed herself not to shy away from his evil touch. Whatever she had to do would be clean because it had a noble purpose.

Heinrich padded back to them, his pudgy hands wrapped around two brandy snifters. Suzanne reached for hers. Slowly she raised the glass to her lips, her eyes locking with Eisele over the rim. *"A votre santé,"* she murmured in a husky voice.

The brandy burned like fire in her throat. Momentarily the bar spun around with sickening rapidity. She wondered about the impact of the brandy. She had never felt this way before.

Eisele sat watching her. When her glass was half finished, he ordered another. Through a haze, Suzanne saw Ibn Ben Ahmed regarding them. The five-piece combination beat out a sensuous tune as one of the belly dancers took the stage.

Suzanne tried to concentrate on the wild gyrations of the gossamer-clad dark beauty. The hips swirled with increasing tempo. The diamond which protruded from the girl's navel glittered in the light, mesmerising Suzanne.

Her throat felt dry and parched. There was a peculiar churning in her stomach. The room swam dizzily. She was aware of all the things which were happening to her. Yet all will seemed to have fled from her.

Ibn Ben Ahmed moved on them. Eisele regarded him coldly. "Is everything prepared?" he asked through clenched teeth.

"Exactly as you would have it," the burnoosed Arab replied.

Eisele gripped Suzanne's thigh slightly above the knee. He increased the pressure until she was aware of intense pain shooting down the soft flesh of her calf.

The German's manner had changed. From far off she heard his voice. "You have been drugged, Fraulein. You have no way of resisting. You will now walk out of here with us. Is that understood?"

Feebly Suzanne shook her head. She felt herself being lifted from the bar stool. Eisele's sinewy arm encircled her waist, crushing her to him. Swiftly he hustled her past the crowded tables.

Suzanne wanted to scream out, to shout a warning that she was being abducted. Her lips worked frantically. But no sound issued from her mouth.

OUTSIDE THE Kit Kat Club, a sleek Mercedes Benz stood at the curb, its curtains drawn. Suzanne felt herself being propelled towards the vehicle. From inside rough hands reached out, dragging her into the soft cushions. She half sat, half lay across the rear seat, hearing the key click in the ignition and the engine purr into life.

"Quickly," Eisele ordered. "The drug will wear off soon."

"Ja, Mein Herr," a voice from above Suzanne answered. Unseen hands reached for her arms, twisting her wrists behind her back. She sensed the cold steel of manacles surrounding her wrists. With all of her strength, she lashed out at her tormentors, her shapely legs flailing out.

A great pressure was applied to the small of her back. Her ankles were seized and forced upwards until they touched her fettered wrists. A thin cord was twisted around them, attaching them to the handcuffs. Now she lay helplessly, her body strained with the awkwardness of her position.

Her head was pressed into the cushion until she was sure she would suffocate. Then she felt her head being dragged backward and another rope was passed over her throat and bound to her hands and feet. With unbelievable cruelty, a filthy cloth was shoved behind her teeth and tied into place.

Pain throbbed through every nerve fiber as the Mercedes slithered through the winding streets and out onto the desert. She heard Ibn Ben Ahmed's voice whining over the engine's smooth rhythm.

"It will be hard to replace this one, Herr Eisele."

"You are being well paid. Remember you are to get more than money. We will even allow you to partake of certain pleasures, my friend," Eisele answered from the front seat.

"Still the loss will not be trivial. The price is not that high."

Suzanne thrashed in her bonds. The coldness of the desert night brought new discomfort as it penetrated her thin clothing.

"Don't forget, it was you who informed us of the *schatzi*'s affair with the Amerikaner. I must know about him. Only she can tell us."

"It might prove to be nothing," Ibn Ben Ahmed speculated. "Supposing it is nothing."

"She knows something of importance," Eisele countered. "I will prove that when we get to Abu Zaabal. Our methods are quite thorough there. We have even improved on Prinz Albrechtstrasse, my friend."

Ibn Ben Ahmed still was not placated. "But what about the authorities? How will you square it with them?"

"Fool, I *am* the authority. This sow is an enemy of Colonel Nasser. She has entered into a conspiracy against the United Arab Republic. What more must be said?"

The Arab cackled in a high pitched feminine voice. "You are indeed a brilliant organizer, Herr Eisele."

"We Germans like to think of everything," Eisele puffed.

Numb terror gripped Suzanne. She had heard of Abu Zaabal. But it had all seemed like so many fairy tales. The concentration camps had ended with Hitler. Those who hated Nasser had dredged them up as propaganda weapons. Or so she had believed up until this moment.

The ride seemed interminable. In reality it lasted less than two hours. But Suzanne's cramped position caused intense suffering. Her blood coagulated above her manacled wrists. The tendons of her legs were horribly stretched by her bondage. The evil-tasting rag which gagged her worked its way deep into her throat threatening to suffocate her. And the heavy rope around her neck chafed her delicate skin.

Still she swore to herself that she would not betray Gary Larkin. The American, for all his bitterness, had been gentle with her. He had been gentle in a way she had dreamed of, but never hoped to find. And for this alone, she would repay, him with her life, if necessary.

At last the limousine rolled to a stop. The back door slammed open. Unceremoniously Suzanne was dragged out of the Mercedes and carried to a huge tent. In disbelief, she saw men dressed in Nazi field uniforms strutting back and forth, their heads misshapen under steel helmets.

Burnoosed Arabs moved among the Nazis, their eyes glittering in the torch light as they regarded the helplessness of the lovely victim Eisele and Ibn Ben Ahmed were dragging into the tent.

"Achtung!" a man in a Nazi tunic shouted. Arms shot up in the old Nazi salute. *"Seig Heil!"* the man cried as Eisele moved past him.

Suzanne felt she had gone insane. This was Egypt, 1957. Yet here, the German Army moved as if there had been no Alamein, no British Field Marshal Montgomery, no unconditional surrender.

They placed her on a rough-hewn table and cut the cords which bound her. But the freedom was short-lived. Eisele gave an order and then disappeared with Ibn Ben Ahmed.

Suzanne saw that she had been left with a German and an Arab whose burnoose was filthy with reddish brown stains. The man rolled her over on the table. His dirty hands ran over her supine body, squeezing and pinching.

Then they caught in the bodice of her dress, ripping downward as the German held her prone. The cold air of the desert bathed her. The German's eyes bugged out at the sight of his captive, dressed only in shimmering pink bra and panties.

Suzanne struggled against his grip, but the man had superhuman strength. He held her throat with one hand as he fastened a heavy length of rope around her neck. Her arms were securely bound to the sides of the table and thick leather straps secured her thighs and ankles to the board.

But the ultimate horror still remained. As she watched in horrified fascination, Suzanne saw the Arab open a small wooden box.

An obscene slithering noise came from inside the box. Gingerly the Arab poked around. Suzanne couldn't still the shriek of horror which bubbled from her lips at the sight of the monster inside.

It was of the spider family, but larger than any she had ever seen. It was at least eight inches long from leg to leg. And the legs were thick and hairy. The Arab who handled the hideous looking thing wore heavy gloves which frustrated its wild attempts to sink its mandibles into his hand.

Swiftly he attached the spider to a thin cord and suspended it a scant six inches above Suzanne's quivering breast. The spider swung back and forth in a small arc, the legs clawing the air wildly, the vicious head swollen with poison.

Without a word, the Arab lowered the string so that the spider barely touched Suzanne's straining breasts.

She heard the steps of the German and the Arab retreating from the tent. The wriggling arachnid touched her flesh, bringing a diabolical sensation of horror. Suzanne had been bound in such a way that her eyes focused directly on the loathesome thing. Alone as she was in the tent, all other sights and sounds were blotted out of her mind. She could concentrate only on the frayed cord which swung above her with its fearful burden.

HALF-MAD WITH terror she remained in the tent by herself awaiting the final clutch of the legs, the final caress of the poison-laden jaws.

But Eisele had no intention of allowing Suzanne to die swiftly. She became aware of his presence, standing over her, describing her agonized sensations to Ibn Ben Ahmed, gloating at her abject helplessness.

At a signal from Eisele, the spider was returned to his box. The Nazi's evil face replaced it in Suzanne's line of vision.

"And now, Fraulein, you are prepared to tell me everything you know about the *Amerikaner*?"

"What *Americain*, Monsieur?" Suzanne managed to stammer.

"Do you take me for a fool, Fraulein? The man whose bed you shared at the Hotel Nasser. The man who has been making discreet inquiries throughout Cairo and Media concerning Colonel Eisele. Do not be impudent with me, Fraulein. Do not insult my intelligence. I assure you the night is quite young. Stronger people than you have capitulated before me."

Suzanne's mind worked feverishly. It would be so easy to tell the little she knew. However, Eisele would accuse her of holding back information. She had but to look at the Nazi to understand that no amount of information would suffice to end the torment. In defiling her body, the madman was reliving the days of his glory. The spittle oozed down his chin as he explored the tenderness of her bound body. This man would never be satisfied with less than the ultimate in her pain and degradation.

Besides, a stubborn voice within her ordered Suzanne to resist. One could not deal with logic where emotions were involved – and Gary Larkin had awakened emotions she had never felt before.

"I have no idea what you are talking about, Monsieur," she breathed.

"As you will, Fraulein," Eisele answered. He fondled her bra, watching the intake of her breath. Then savagely, he ripped the covering from her breasts.

Ibn Ben Ahmed had completely forgotten the economic loss of an entertainer. He sprang to Eisele's side, clawing and tearing at Suzanne's panties until they lay in pathetic strips across her exposed flanks.

The two men leered down at their captive as Ibn Ben Ahmed reached for a flaming torch which had ben placed in a holder.

Sweat broke out on Suzanne's face as the flame approached. She lay watching the sparks, waiting for the blistering touch, unable to move a muscle.

The table groaned and the ropes which held her creaked as the flame licked at the sole of her bound foot. The straps bit into her thighs, cutting into the corded muscles of her legs. The flame grew hotter, blackening and scorching the skin.

Scream after scream wrenched from her throat. She clawed the table until her fingernails splintered and broke. Her lovely limbs convulsed in a motionless dance of the damned. Her lungs ached with the force of her shrieking.

At last the torch was removed.

"What have you to tell me, Fraulein?" Eisele hissed.

Weakly Suzanne shook her head. Once again agony flooded through her. The tent danced crazily. She tried to beat her head against the table, but the ropes around her neck held her fast and didn't even allow her that luxury.

A staccato bark broke through the night. There were other sounds which didn't quite reach the agony wracked girl.

A man cursed, gutturally. Another shrieked out in a high-pitched whine. A submachine gun sputtered in rage.

Ibn Ben Ahmed and Eisele whirled as one. They shrank back from the man with crew cut hair and wild eyes who stood framed in the tent's flap.

"You!" Eisele screamed. "But you are dead. I ordered it myself."

"You ordered it, bastard. But it wasn't carried out. I didn't die as easily as Karen."

Eisele's eyes flicked across the tent. "What are you going to do?"

"First untie the girl. Then we talk, bastard."

Eisele fumbled with the cords. His face seemed to fall apart. His body shook as if he had the ague.

"It was war," he mumbled. "Things are done during war. I was under orders."

"And who gave you orders to do *this*?"

"Forget me," Eisele groveled. "What has been done is over. I can make you rich."

"There's a bounty for you in Israel that would make me just as rich," Larkin shot back. He watched the words sink into the Nazi, watched the shaking hands touch his collar as if he were already feeling the noose snapping his neck.

"But I'm not interested in bounties. I owe you a debt–" The slugs cut off the last word.

Before she fainted, Suzanne saw Eisele stagger backwards, blood spewing from his nose and mouth. She saw Ibn Ben Ahmed's face disintegrate under a hail of bullets.

Three days later, Suzanne Chaubert sat beside Gary Larkin as the B.O.A.C. 707 winged over the blueness of the Mediterranean. She looked at the man who stared moodily at the small waves below.

She wondered to herself where the trip would lead. Perhaps some day she might come to replace the ghost of the woman he called Karen. She told herself that there had been more than hatred for Eisele which had driven him into the desert in search of her, once he'd seen her dragged from the Kit Kat Club.

And she thought she had something to prove the point – the last forty eight hours in his room at the Hotel Nasser.

TORTURE OF 1,000 CUTS

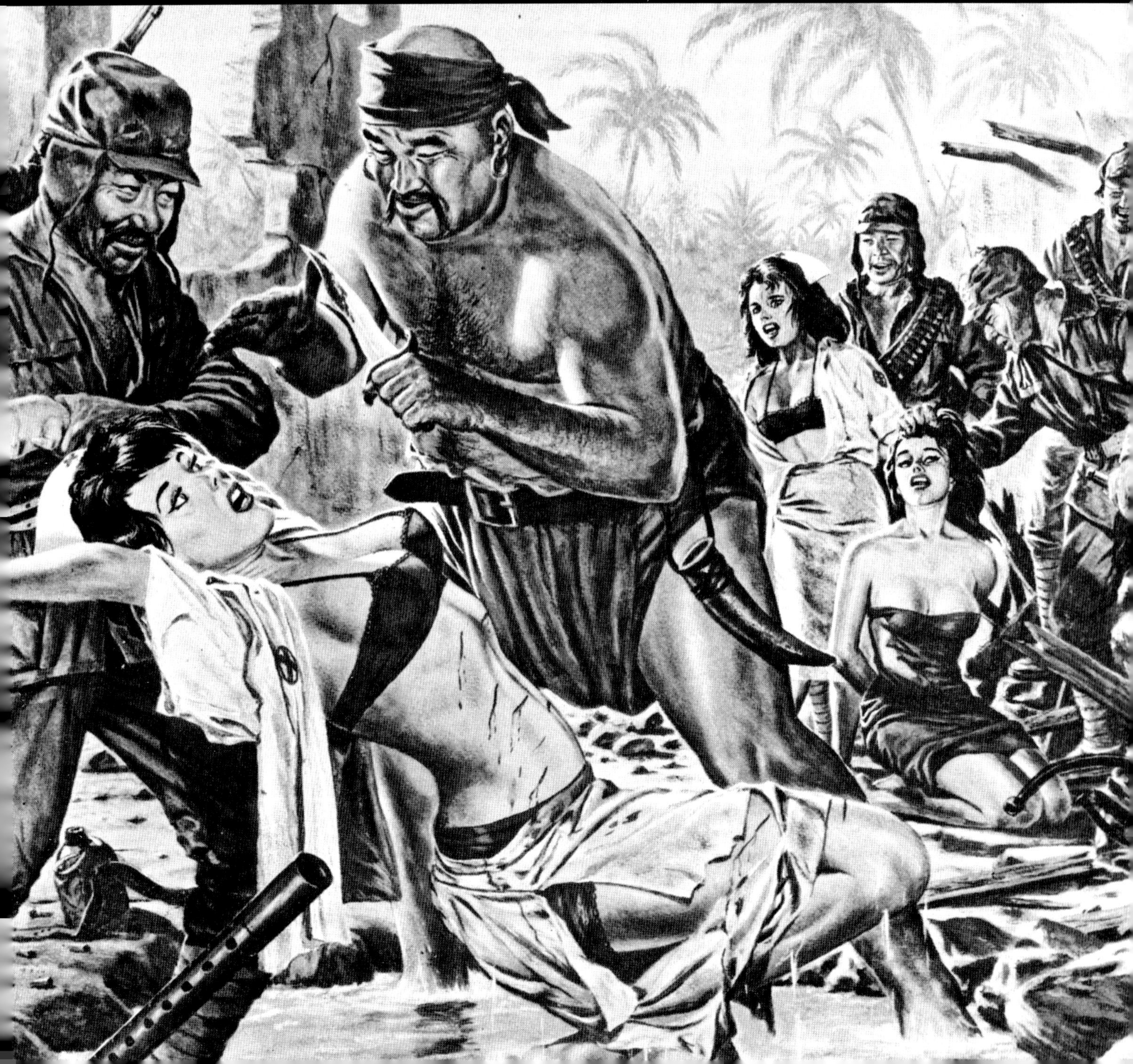

The savage giant had to be stopped, before his desire for revenge carved the woman to pieces!

I FOUND THE SHORT Vietnamese sergeant with his own GI-issue .45 caliber automatic shoved down his throat. The muzzle had been jammed through his mouth so hard, his teeth were a mess of splinters. The muzzle had been rammed home into the back of his throat and the tissues there had been ruptured and a big artery severed. The blood had pumped out of his body and spread across the dirt floor between the beds of the hospital where he lay.

It had not been necessary for the two wounded Vietcong we had been caring for to bother to pull the trigger. They had killed a guard and made good their escape without even that.

The hospital the two commies from the north had escaped from was located at Tourane. It was open-walled, with a thatched roof, contained 40 beds, and was staffed by combined American and Vietnamese government personnel. The American nurses and doctors were training the Vietnamese for the day when they would be able to operate their own military hospital. I was assigned to this medical detachment as top-kick of the American security force. Most of out patients were Vietnamese government troops, but we had received the two commie prisoners, who had been wounded, for treatment.

After killing the Vietnamese sergeant, the two Vietcong rebels made good their escape from the immediate area around the hospital, slipping through my headquarters security guard. They had worked their way out into the surrounding hills when they ran into the defensive perimeter I had set up, composed of GIs and Vietnamese troops.

About thirty yards from the rough dirt road, the two commie killers jumped one of my men and disarmed him, taking him by surprise from the rear – a direction from which he had not expected an attack. One of them pinned his arms behind his back while the other jammed my man's trench knife against his throat and began sawing away.

At that moment there was a crowd of refugees moving down the road from the north. A massive figure of a man detached himself from that crowd. He had spotted the murder taking place up the hill, and now he moved in that direction. Although he was a tremendously heavy man, his body layered with rolls of fat, and very tall, he moved with the grace of a cat, his feet hardly even seeming to touch the ground. He covered the yards going up the hill in a matter of seconds and threw himself at the two Vietcong killers.

His massive fist smashed down on one of the commies and sledgehammered down on the top of his skull. The commie was stunned. His body quivered. And when we examined the scene later, we found that his feet had been driven three inches into the ground by the awesome blow. The giant smashed over and over again on the top of the commie's head. His fist was like a hardened steel pile-driver. Blood ran from the eyes, ears, and nose of the commie, and when he finally started to fall towards the ground, his body was stiff, and he went over as if he were pole-axed. He was dead before he hit the ground.

The other commie prisoner's brain turned to jelly when he saw the fate that had befallen his comrade at the hands of the strange giant. He screamed piercingly, dropped the trench knife, and turned to flee for his life. But he was not fast enough. With two strides the giant was on him. He clamped both massive hands around the commie's head and lifted him off the ground by his ears. He held the commie at least two feet off the ground and slowly but inexorably used his great strength to force the palms of his hands towards each other. He actually crushed the rebel's skull under the tremendous pressure he developed... so that it changed shape, squashing inwards.

By the time we reached the scene, the second commie was dead, blood oozing out of a narrow fissure that ran from front to back across the top of his skull. It was a demonstration of unbelievable strength on the part of the giant. Obviously here was a man who did not need bullets or a knife in order to kill – he did it more efficiently with his bare hands.

We took the monster of a man back with us to the hospital area. I brought him to Colonel McCauley, our CO, for interrogation. We learned he was a Japanese, about forty years old, and that his profession took him all over the Orient.

"I am samurai wrestler," he told us. He was fleeing from the Vietcong commies in the north, he went on. "They would put me in their army as conscript," he said. And he did not want to give up the "honorable" profession he had spent his life learning in Japan, his homeland.

He offered to entertain our troops with a wrestling show. "You do not have to pay me," he said. "You can throw coins to me for whatever you think the entertainment is worth."

The colonel mulled this offer over. Morale in our unit was so-so, and a little entertainment would do no harm. All he needed was a wrestling opponent for the samurai. He looked around and finally his eye settled on his top-kick – me – six foot three inches, weighing in at 230 pounds, with a history of amateur wrestling in college.

"How about it?" the colonel asked.

"I'm not anxious," I said, "but I'll go along with it if we do it American style. Or better still – let him wrestle his way, and I'll wrestle mine. And we'll see who comes out on top."

The Jap smiled. He stuck out his hand to me, and I reached forward to shake it. Then things happened too fast for me to keep track of. It seemed like my hand had been grabbed by a hot bone-crushing vise. I was suddenly flying through the air and I crashed on my back, the wind knocked out of me completely. The Jap smiled down at me from his great muscular height. "Good," he said. "Yes?"

I grunted when my breath came back. "We'll see what happens when we have the wrestling match," I said. "I've suddenly become anxious for it to take place."

FOR A week, nothing else but the wrestling match was talked about. Beth McCullers, the pretty brunette Army nurse who made living in Vietnam worthwhile for me, tried to talk me out of it. "He might maim you," she insisted. Watching the Jap giant work out that week I was inclined to agree with her, but there was no backing out for me. It would have meant becoming the laughing stock of the Vietnamese troops as well as the GIs assigned to the medical detachment.

The day of the wrestling match came around, and it was then our samurai disappeared. The giant just melted into the hills, the same hills he had studied every single day, noting the dispositions of our security troops. We next saw him in his loin cloth and earrings leading Chinese, Pathet Lao commies, and Vietcong rebels through the holes he had spotted in our perimeter defense. He had pulled a Trojan horse on us, lulled us into a false sense of security, while he had been sealing our doom.

I was sweeping the hills around the hospital encampment with a pair of field glasses, and I got a first-hand view of the samurai killer in action when it was already too late to do anything about it. He came in ahead of the guerrillas. The Vietnamese on duty knew him by now and did not suspect anything until it was too late. He approached with the grin on his fat face lulling the outpost into a false sense of security. When he was close enough, the Jap giant clamped his hands in the neck of the small Vietnamese guard and snapped it like a matchstick. The bugger didn't even have a chance to bring his weapon up, was dead before he even knew that he was threatened.

Without even stopping to buckle on a web belt and a .45, I left the hospital and went for that Jap samurai on the dead run. I was going to tear him apart with my bare hands and show him what power in a man's hands can do. We headed for a crash at the edge of the hospital encampment area. I had my arms out, my hands reaching for his throat, my mind blind to everything else, when one of the Vietcong caught me in the back of the head with his rifle butt, swinging it like it was a baseball bat.

I was knocked out cold, and went sprawling at the feet of the samurai. When I came to, it was all over but the shouting. The wounded had been murdered in their beds when they had tried to crawl out and get to safety. The nurses had been taken prisoner, most of the Vietnamese personnel had been butchered; of the men only the Americans and the doctors had been spared – and they would be taken north.

I had been tied hand and foot. The Jap samurai, in his loin cloth and earrings, his oily rolls of fat gleaming, his face flushed, an insane look in his eyes, came and towered over me.

"You tricked us," I said. "Why you? Are you a commie? Is that why you gained our confidence and then led the Vietcong in here?"

Pure hate gleamed in his eyes. "Yes," he said, "I am a Japanese communist. My family was torn to shreds. Before my eyes, my wife and daughters were ripped apart by the metal from American bombs. The flesh was lacerated and cut and torn from their bones until they stood in a pool of their own blood and died that way. I swore that day that the time would come when I would do the same to an American woman – cut her flesh that way." He took a *kris*, a knife with a blade with waves in it, out of the folds of his loin cloth. "I even got a special knife so that I could do the job properly." He slipped the *kris* back in the folds of his loin cloth and grinned. "For a beginning," he said, "I do not need the knife."

The samurai giant reached out and grabbed Beth McCullers with his big hands. His fingers brushed aside her uniform and bared her milky white shoulder. The fingers of both of his hands dug into the flesh of her shoulder. He twisted his hands brutally in opposite directions. Her skin split open. A scream of pain tore from her lips. Blood surged through the break in the skin, and the white shoulder was now mutilated, red and swollen.

I struggled against my ropes and tried to come off the ground, cursing and swearing. The samurai wrestler looked at me with hate and then moved. He kicked me savagely in the face.

WHEN I came to I was alone with a Vietcong guard over me. I could not see and thought I had gone blind. But it was only the dried blood that had scabbed over my eyes. I groaned and the commie guard prodded me with his bayonet. I signalled that I needed water from the canvas lister bag that was hanging on poles just outside the hospital.

The commie guard dragged me across the ground, out from under the hospital thatched roof, to the lister bag. He put me under it. Then he fingered one of the nozzles of the bag and squirted water into my face, just like he were working a cow's udder.

I waited until he was completely bemused by his new toy, and then I jammed my feet into the pole that supported the lister bag at one corner. The pole broke two inches above the ground, and the whole supporting structure came crashing down as I rolled out of the way, brought down by the heavy weight of the water in the bag.

The ropes from the poles wrapped themselves around the Vietcong commie's neck and pinned him to the ground, strangling him. I rolled over to the bayonet on his rifle and sawed through the ropes around my ankles and wrists.

Then I went on the hunt for the Jap wrestler, to find him and the nurses he had taken with him to work over with his ugly knife. I came around the corner of a pile of jerry-cans and found one of my Vietnamese security troops sitting on the ground. He had been disemboweled and left to die. He was sitting there cross-legged, clutching at the white, worm-like intestines that were spilling out of the gaping hole in his abdomen.

I asked him if he had seen where the samurai had taken the American nurses, and he told me they had gone down to the hospital lily pond where the goldfish were kept. The wrestler had said that he would turn it red with blood – he would bleed the girls dry with a thousand cuts.

I grabbed his rifle and bayonet and broke into a run

for the pond. I came over the last little rise in the ground before reaching the pond, and saw it all at once. A grinning Pathet Lao commie soldier had Beth McCullers' arms pinioned as she struggled ankle-deep in the pond. Her uniform was ripped. The Jap samurai was digging his *kris* into her flesh, a wicked grin of pleasure on his face at her pain. The other nurses were pinned down, forced to watch Beth's torture, waiting their own turn in that hellish pond that would soon be stained with their blood.

I threw myself down on the ground and slammed the rifle against my shoulder. I drilled bullets through the heads of the Pathet Lao commies I had a clear field of fire on. Only the commie who was holding Beth and the samurai who was working her over with the knife were safe – I didn't dare shoot at them for fear of hitting Beth.

It had to be the bayonet. I went in, holding the rifle at high port, at the dead run. The Pathet Lao commie finally spotted me and dropped Beth. He unlimbered his bayonetted rifle and came on to meet me. It was man against man.

I feinted the commie out of position. He went off balance, and the tip of his bayonet missed my throat and caught in the flesh of my shoulder. I pulled back clean, and his bayonet pulled out, stained red with my blood. I rammed my own weapon home. The bayonet drove in through the cheek of his face. It rammed up and into the top of his head. The tip of its blade came out through the top of his skull, entangled with a string of his brain tissue.

The bayonet stuck in his skull and I could not pull it out. I threw him and the rifle aside and closed in on the samurai. He had the *kris* against Beth's throat now, and threatened to kill her if I came closer.

I taunted him. I asked him if it were in the noble tradition of the samurai to hide behind the body of a weak and innocent female, to use her as a shield. Must she die when the guilt was his for not defending his wife and daughters and taking up arms in their defense during the great war – instead of hiding from the military in the guise of a samurai wrestler?

A stream of Jap curses spewed from his mouth. He threw Beth McCullers aside and came at me. The *kris* dropped from his hand, and his fingers, trembling with rage, reached out to possess me. We rammed into each other and grappled.

His arms locked around my chest in back, and he had me in a bear hug. He started to squeeze down and I could feel my rib cage beginning to crack under the great pressure. The air went out of my lungs and my head felt like a watermelon. I knew then that I was going to die if I did not break the samurai's grip.

My mind raced – it remembered all the old wrestling techniques – and I remembered the dirty ones that had never been used in amateur wrestling to get the pressure off. I needed them now. I got the heel of my hand under the samurai's jaw and started shoving back. The muscles in the back of his neck knotted, but he held strong, and his grip did not diminish. I knew it was only a matter of seconds before my ribs splintered and ruptured my lungs.

Desperately I jammed a thumb into one of the samurai's eyes. I put pressure on and twisted the thumb. The nail dug into the eyeball, the finger ate its way into the socket, and finally the eye came out, and blood ran down my thumb. The samurai screamed and his arms unlocked. I did not give him another chance. I chopped at his neck with the flat of my hand and drove him down on his knees. Then I hammerlocked on his head and took him under water. I held him there until he was dead.

Finally I staggered out of the water. I got the girls together and took them into the hills in a southerly direction. We kept moving until we were met by a relief force coming up from Saigon, some 200 miles away. And that night Beth McCullers put her trembling body in my arms and let me cover her bruises with kisses...

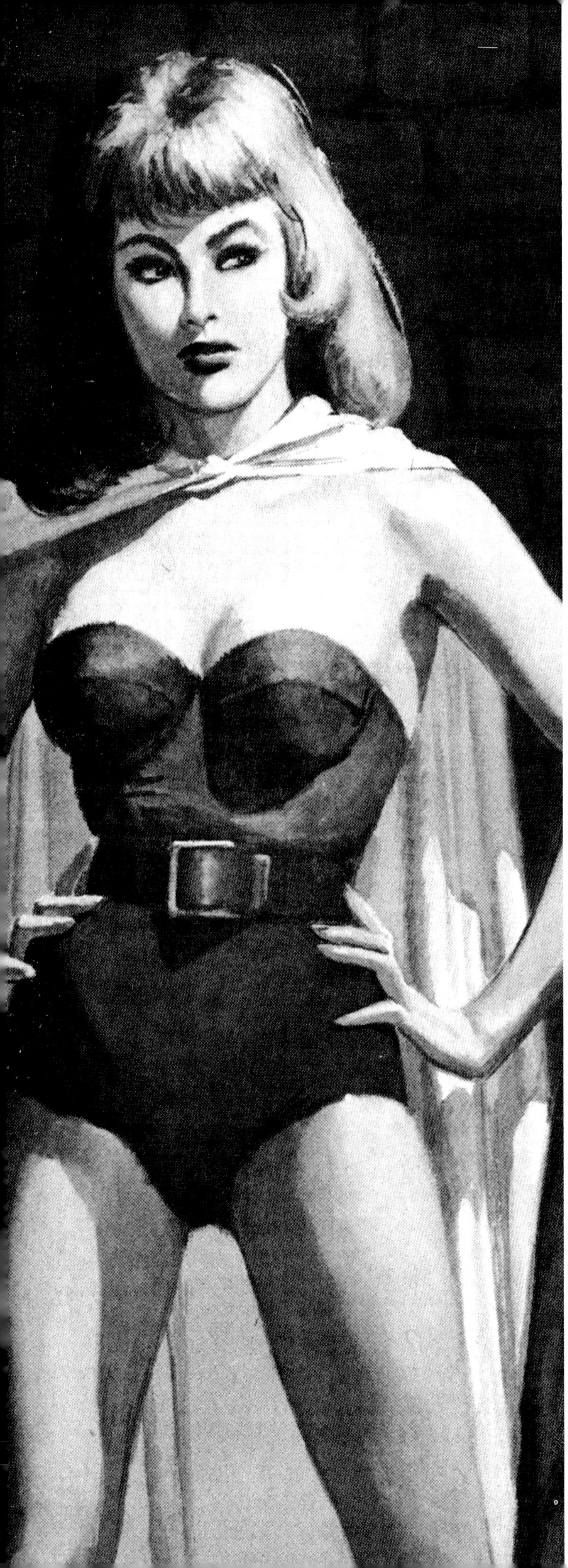

FETTERED NUDES FOR THE MONSTER'S COLLAR OF AGONY

Satan's mistress vied with her evil lover in a twisted and sadistic orgy of torment.

THE REVOLUTIONARY ARMY OF Ugo Sorcate was drawn up for battle, long serried lines of ragged men with gleaming weapons. Sorcate himself, a monstrous lump of a man with huge ears that stood out from his naked and shaven skull like some caricature of Satan, watched the lissom figure of his mistress, the notorious Lucrezia Mantua, as she swung up into the saddle of the black stallion that stood snorting beside his own bay mare.

Clad in black armor, scarlet velvet and leopard skin, her shimmering auburn hair cascading about her shoulders like living flames, Lucrezia Mantua was the incarnation of the warrior female, and a roar that shook distant Vesuvius went up from the savage host. They brandished their blades and thundered forth their acclaim of their brutal master and the exotic Amazon who was his mistress – men in rags burning for vengeance.

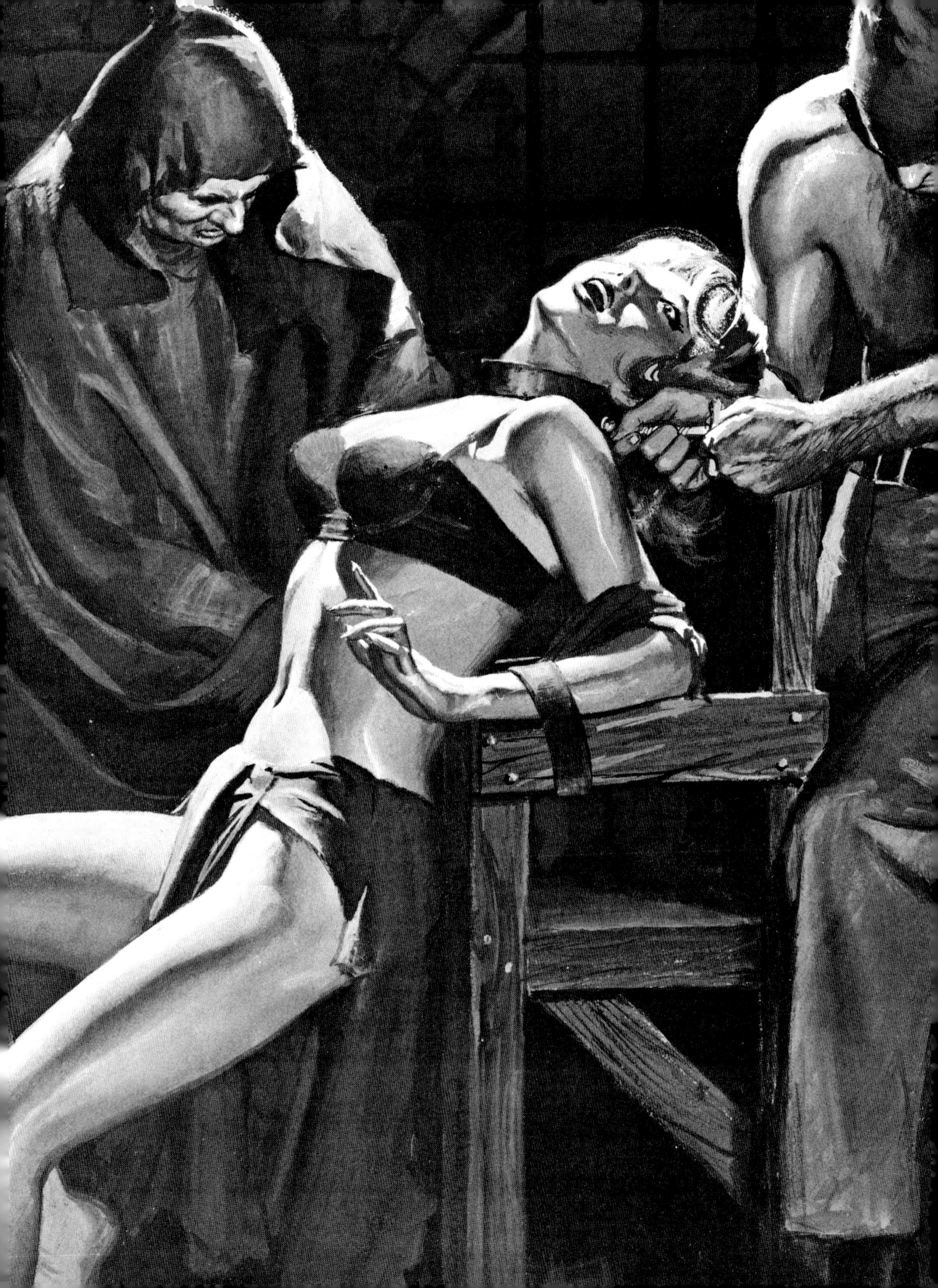

The army on the opposite side of the valley was very different – knights in gold-chased armor, pikemen in mail coats and basinets, arquebusiers in their leather jerkins, with their deadly weapons in their left hands. This was the Grand Army of the Marquis of Zaragoza, Viceroy in the name of His Majesty the King of Spain, resident tyrant of Naples.

It was to be a fight to the death between the proud and splendidly equipped Spanish forces of the Viceroy, and the ragged and blood-hungry battalions of Ugo Sorcate. And the stakes were enormous. If the army of Spain should be defeated, Sorcate's lust-mad riff-raff would be free to murder, torture, rape and pillage without restraint – to pay off old scores against the hated Dons. More horrible, perhaps, the lovely wife and daughters of the Viceroy and the ladies of other proud Spanish gentlemen would be handed over to the pathologicaly sadistic Lucrezia.

Predatory as a tiger and a thousand times more ferocious, the exotic Lucrezia had some old scores to settle with the haughty and overbearing Dons. More especially she craved to inflict all the torments of the medieval torture chamber on the smooth and lovely bodies of their refined, very beautiful and arrogant ladies.

As the red orb of the sun climbed above the horizon the Spanish army began to move slowly down the slopes toward the river. Their steel could be seen shining through the early morning mist that swirled about the hooves of the horses and the feet of the famous infantry.

Bruno's savage horde moved stealthily to meet the Spaniards. Banners flinging out long silken folds in the morning breeze, the Spanish force assumed the customary formation in medieval warfare.

But against Sorcate's cunning and the ferocity of his guerilla army, the Spaniards' classic tactics were all in vain.

By noon the Viceroy's forces were utterly defeated; cut to pieces by the abnormal savagery of the revolutionaries. Naples and all its treasures and refinements lay defenseless before the berserk and lust-crazy victors. And it was not long before the exquisite and terror-stricken ladies of the Spanish nobility were being dragged shrieking from their hastily found hiding places, and the greatest orgy of lust, torture and rapine the world has ever known began its hideous course.

Among the many lovely noblewomen to be flung sobbing into the stinking blackness of Naples' infamous catacombs, was the fantastically beautiful Isabel of Navarre, the golden-haired wife of the Viceroy, and his two equally beautiful daughters, Isabel's stepdaughters, Eva and Maria.

In vain did the petrified Isabel offer bribes of gold to her ruffianly captors. Uselessly did she plead with them to free the two *señoritas* and herself. And while the other refined and aristocratic ladies soon became the screaming playthings of Sorcate's slobbering, drunken and bestial men – even the young nuns at the Convent of Monte Cristo being forced to satisfy the revolutionaries' gross appetites in a thousand unmentionable ways – the Viceroy's ladies were not molested. They were being saved for Lucrezia, the exotic sadist who liked her victims to be unsullied and who indulged her unnatural passions in fantastic and bizarre and horrible ways.

LUCREZIA MANTUA stepped out of her perfumed bath and stood completely nude in front of the full-length mirror in the sumptuous apartments of the Viceroy's wife and daughters.

She drank in the magnificent tawny body that was her own. Like some great consuming fire, she thought. That is what my body is, a fire that must feed on power and the satisfaction of its desires. Almost reverently she slipped on strange adornments, and her hands now encased in black satin gloves ran slowly up her golden thighs, inward to her smooth firm breasts. Cruel anticipation was building within her, just as it always did before she satiated her secret lusts.

She chose her victims for their beauty and refinement, and for the personal malice she bore them, lovely ladies of the, oh, so hypocritical aristocracy. How she hated them, detested their snobbish superiority, the arrogant smugness of their pampered and privileged lives.

As the maids started to dress her Lucrezia heard the door open behind her. Ugo Sorcate stood there with folded arms. He wore tight-fitting harlequin pantaloons. The upper part of his body was covered with a hooded jacket of fiery scarlet. The hood was drawn tightly under his skull-like head, leaving his face a pasty mask of horror, framed by the scarlet cloth.

In spite of herself Lucrezia shuddered slightly. This monster whose mistress she had become – and who in turn had become the slave of her passionate body, granting her every desire – was at the same time her greatest strength and her most frightening weakness. If she should ever lose her hold on him...

But she would not. He loved her. He was her creature, and the day would never dawn when he would tire of her infinite charms.

She motioned to the maids to leave her.

"Is all prepared, Ugo?"

He nodded slowly. His eyes were on fire. Yes, the torture chamber was ready for his exotic mistress to indulge her strange and bloody lusts. And after, as always, he would claim his reward...

"Come, then," Lucrezia purred, her eyes glittering with green fire as she strode from the room. *"To the catacombs!"*

The corridor they followed slanted downward. A coil of stone steps ended the passage, and the weird couple crept eagerly down. It was a long and sinister spiral into the subterranean galleries below the Viceroy's palace, the horrible catacombs where the dungeons and torture chambers of the now fled Inquisition were; and a dreadful stench of smoke and blood and human sweat invaded the air. Drops of moisture began to appear on the rocky surface of the gallery, and soon the silence was rent asunder by a swelling cacophony of female screams and bestial, drunken laughter.

An evil smile twisted Lucrezia's moistened red lips as she stared hungrily into the awful depths of the catacombs. On fantastic needle heels, her beautiful body swaying sensuously, she passed through the galleries. In some of them beautiful Spanish girls were being loathsomely violated by drunken, brutal men; in others, lovely nude women in chains were being tortured in a hundred hideous and ingenious ways.

Lucrezia strode through the catacombs, feasting her

eyes on each orgy of rape and torture in mounting ecstasy. Her magnificent auburn hair flamed about her shoulders as she moved, the flesh of her exotic body quivered with the all-consuming fire of sadistic lust, the tips of her breasts strained against silken black, her thighs ached with unnatural excitement, her eyes were like slits of green fire, her lips were parted in a diabolical smile of triumphant glee.

"Fetch the Viceroy," she ordered.

Lucrezia, Ugo, and three torturers waited in the dim light of the torture chamber. The torturers wore hoods of red cloth and their muscular bodies were stripped to the waist.

Lucrezia herself was clad in a truly bizarre attire. Her long regal neck was framed by a high collar, an integral part of the revealing garment that she wore. It was black as night and made of some silky, thin and opaque material that hugged the voluptuousness of her sleekly curved body. Long shimmering gloves covered her naked arms, and a black mask glittering with jewels covered her pale and heavily painted face. Her back, shoulders, hips and lower belly were completely encased in the clinging material. But down the front, from the open collar nearly to her navel, the garment was split and gaped wide.

The Spaniard's face turned ashen as he stared in horror at the young woman who hung impaled on a meat hook from one of the chains looping down from the ceiling of the chamber. Blood dripped from her hideously ripped flesh. It had formed a foul puddle on the stone floor into which it dripped.

"No, she's not your wife," Lucrezia hissed, unholy glee building within her as she devoured the Viceroy's agonized face. "We simply left her there to give you an idea of the sort of thing we have in mind. We've not touched your wife or daughters... yet!"

What little manhood remained to the Viceroy finally collapsed.

"Madre de Dios!" he gasped, falling on his knees, his trembling manacled hands extended in supplication. "Spare them, Madam, I beg of you."

A snarl contorted Lucrezia's masked features. "Spanish pig!" she spat. "Did you spare my father and mother from the damned torments of the Inquisition when I came to plead for them? No, you did not. And now you in turn shall see your loved ones tortured in the same cursed chamber where my poor family suffered because of you." And whipping back a shapely, silk-stockinged leg, she kicked the Spaniard full in his bearded face.

The Viceroy's head snapped back as he cried out in pain. Gingerly he touched his mashed and bleeding lips. And when he looked back at Lucrezia's pitilous and stabbing gaze, he, knew with horrible certainty that his lovely Isabel and his two daughters were doomed.

Slowly the wretched man's eyes moved in mute appeal to the gigantic figure of Ugo Sorcate. The monster towered over his mistress as they stood in the semi-darkness. In the flickering light that the wall-torches gave off, he loomed monstrously. The shadow his body cast on the smoke-blackened wall seemed to tower endlessly up into the dark recesses of the torture chamber.

When they dragged Isabel of Navarre into the chamber, her chained husband saw with impotent misery that his beautiful young wife was already half-crazed with fear, sobbing and whimpering as she struggled hysterically in the grip of the vulgar brutes that held her.

Lucrezia licked her lips with a quick little flick of her tongue. "Strip the Spanish sow," she raved, her voice thick with lust.

Her excitement rose to fever pitch as the torturers ripped off their victim's sumptuous outer garments, left her standing ashamed and terrified in high heels, silk stockings and exquisitely made underthings of filigree lace and lavender satin.

Isabel was moaning for mercy now. Sliding to her knees, her white arms locked about Lucrezia's darkly silken thighs. "Madam... I implore you... please..."

The blood was pounding in Lucrezia's temples now as she looked disdainfully down at the woman sprawled at her feet. How she enjoyed making this Spanish bitch crawl. When her voice finally sounded, it was feline and soft and full of venom. "You're going to die slowly... my dear," she purred in a whispered snarl. "The Spanish way... the *garrote!*"

"Noooooooo! In the name of all that's sacred, not that! You wouldn't do that to a woman!" Like a screech of madness in the night the Viceroy's horrified voice tore through the chamber, and the flamelight reflected on the sweat-streaming, twisted mask of madness his face had become.

Lucrezia chuckled throatily. "Why not, Milord?" she asked mockingly. "Is the garrote not a Spanish invention?" Her eyes loomed brilliant green, boring into the Spaniard's, empty of mind now, glittering pinpoints of crazed desire, of utterly perverted urgings.

Sick, dry sobs of pure terror racked Isabel's huddled figure.

Brutal hands lifted her from the floor. She felt her high heels dragging, felt them catching on the uneven stone flags. She was aware of horny hands running over her perfect breasts. A convulsive shudder of disgust went through her as the hands crawled on her naked flesh, fondling her in unspeakably obscene and intimate ways. She heard Lucrezia's voice thick with mingled lust and insane hatred urging the torturers to further abuse and humiliate her, and the screams that tore from her were soundless, nightmarish things.

And then she was thrust back suddenly. She was sitting in a sort of chair. But it was more than just a chair – more by the addition of the iron band that encircled her waist and the monstrous iron collar just behind her golden head.

Torchlight lit the evil masked faces that loomed above her as the torturers forced her neck into the collar.

Fear was a sickening knot in her belly as she felt the cold metal around her throat. Soon waves of crushing pain rippled almost visibly before her tear-dimmed eyes. Each time the torturers tightened the screws, she almost went berserk with pain. A sheen of cold perspiration oozed from her semi-clad body, and her breasts heaved as she struggled for breath.

She heard Lucrezia snarl, "Tighter... screw the collar *tighter!*"

The pressure became unbearable. Isabel's mouth became a crimson smear of torture. She felt something warm and sticky trickling down her back. Her neck was a throbbing mass of raw nerve-ends – she knew it must be a scarlet pulp.

Frantically the Viceroy tried to turn his eyes away

from the spectacle of his wife's agony. Brutally, Ugo Sorcate forced him to look. Lucrezia would want the Spaniard to see every detail of the torture. Ugo saw madness in the other's eyes, in his saliva-streaming lips. He shrugged. The Don's mind had cracked.

Just when it seemed as if their victim was about to choke, the torturers would loosen the screws. Then they would tighten them again. Isabel of Navarre uttered ghastly gargling sounds, half-strangled words and pleas. Her delicate hands twitched like mad things trying to tear away the hellish collar. But the more she tore at it the tighter it became.

Suddenly, her eyes grew distended. They stood out like monstrous balls. Her eyesockets filled with blood which poured over her white and agonized face from the burst blood vessels.

Lucrezia watched delightedly, noting the way her victim's silken legs thrashed, the way her tongue protruded from her lips, crushed between her teeth in the spasms of her agony.

The tongue blackened, and still Isabel's bloody eyes bulged out, mindless, senseless, red-veined pupils as big as saucers.

Finally, a last twitch went through Isabel's semi-nude body, worked its way under the shimmering swell of her satin and lace covered belly and down her silk-stockinged legs. Her high heels drummed hideously on the stone floor. Then she slumped over, dead.

So perished Isabel of Navarre, and in like manner her two stepdaughters, Eva and Maria, martyrs to the insane lusts of the lovely sadist who might truly be called, the Mistress of Satan.

TORTURE, THAT instrument of agonized ecstasy, has in all ages been cherished by those who became demented by their lust for vengeance. At certain periods torturers have been the favorites of kings, queens, emperors and empresses. Rome under the Caesars was one long orgy of torture. In the Middle Ages, torturers were among the most sought-after specialists in Europe.

On March 6, 1484, there was born in Naples a child who developed into the most notorious sadist of an epoch – an epoch of torture for its own sake. Lucrezia Mantua began life with all things in her favor, the daughter of well-to-do parents.

Her father, an alchemist, was also a free thinker. But like most of the citizens in 17th century Naples, he and his wife were careful to keep their opinions to themselves. Unfortunately, they were not careful enough.

Somehow the dreaded Spanish Inquisition got wind of their heretical beliefs, and at the tender age of fourteen Lucrezia saw her dear parents lead from their home in chains and taken to the stinking dungeons in the catacombs. In vain did the desperate child appeal to the Viceroy, the only official with enough authority to order her parents released. But this dignitary was not prepared to cross the powerful Inquisition simply to free two unimportant Neapolitans. He sent Lucrezia away.

Some weeks later, almost unrecognizable from the effects of savage tortures, Lucrezia, now in rags, saw her mother and father burned alive in the main square of the city.

There and then the little girl swore bloody vengeance on all Spaniards. Somehow she survived destitution and blossomed into the most provocative beauty, learning to fight, and ride, and carouse.

But while her craving for vengeance was understandable, she began to enjoy her bloodlust for its own sake, driving the captivated Ugo to commit greater and greater excesses, persuading him to turn over all captured Spaniards for her private enjoyment. The torture of the Viceroy's wife and daughters before that gentleman's eyes was the high point of her pleasure. She had tempted providence too far.

From that day on Ugo seemed to turn against her. What she most feared happened – he became interested in another woman, a young Sicilian lass of sixteen.

Perhaps it was this girl who suggested to Ugo that Lucrezia be arrested as a witch. If so, it was no more than poetic justice that it was a woman's malice that destroyed her.

Lucrezia's trial was a mere formality. On June 18, 1512, at an early hour, Lucrezia Mantua was roused and ordered to dress.

From her cell to the torture chamber where the sentence of the court was to be pronounced was a walk of a few minutes. Dignitaries, including Ugo Sorcate and his new mistress, filed into the chamber. A clerk immediately read out the pronouncement:

"The Court of Naples condemns Lucrezia Mantua to make a public apology for her unnatural crimes before the principal church of the city, holding in her hand a lighted torch of the weight of two talons. There on her knees, she shall declare her loathsome sins and humbly beg the pardon of Almighty God, our Sovereign Lord Sorcate, and the citizens of Naples. This done, she shall be conveyed to the main square of the city and there disembowelled, her body burned, and the ashes thrown to the winds. She is first to be put to torture, ordinary and extraordinary, to obtain her full confession as a witch."

And perhaps Lucrezia *was* a witch, in truth. For Ugo and his youthful paramour did not long survive her horrible death. An insurrection that broke out in the summer of 1513 took care of both of them – they were torn to pieces by a crazed Neapolitan mob.

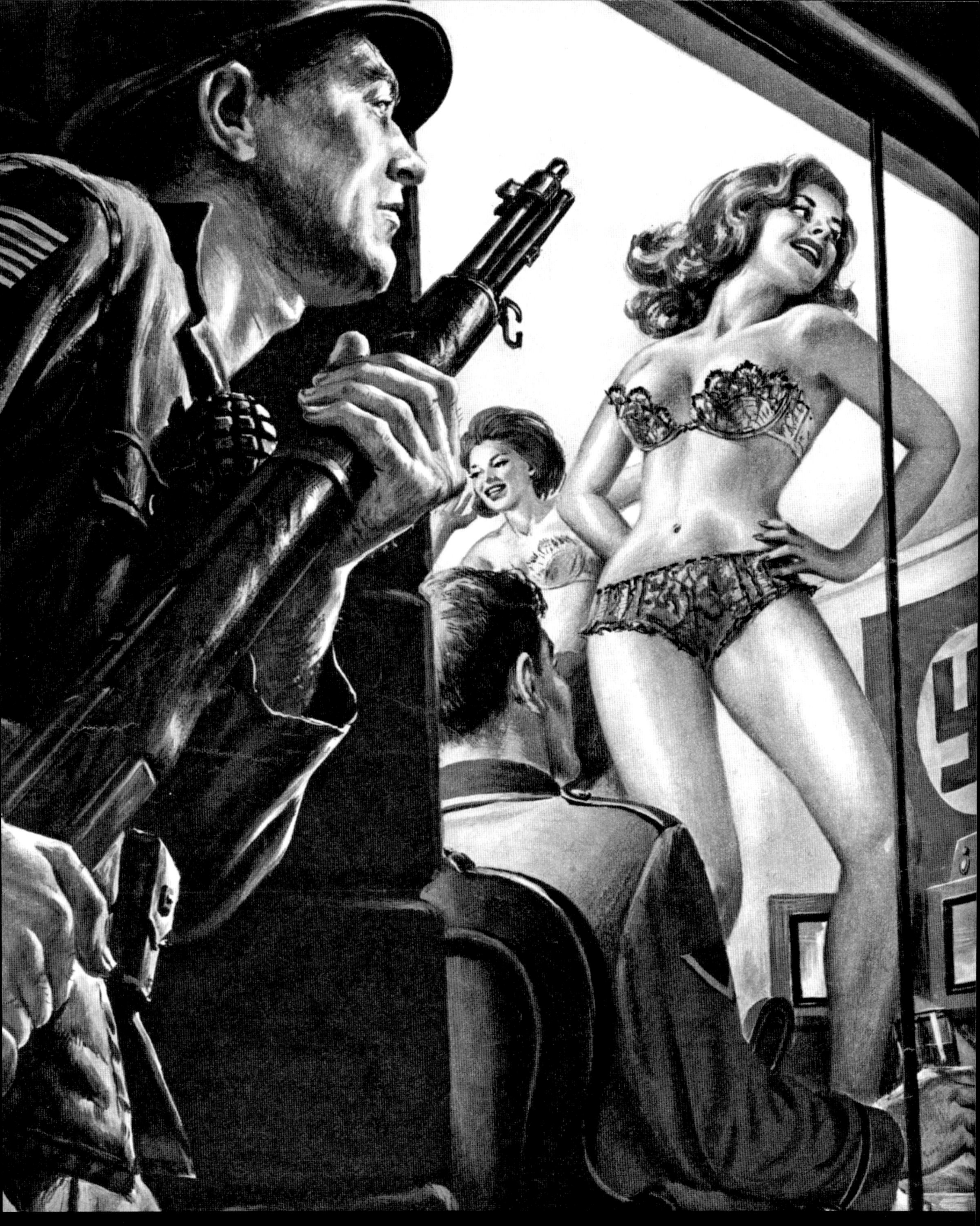

"90 NAZIS AND 8 REDHEADS OF RADAR ISLAND"; detail from interior art, **STAG**, 04/63.
Art by Walter Popp.

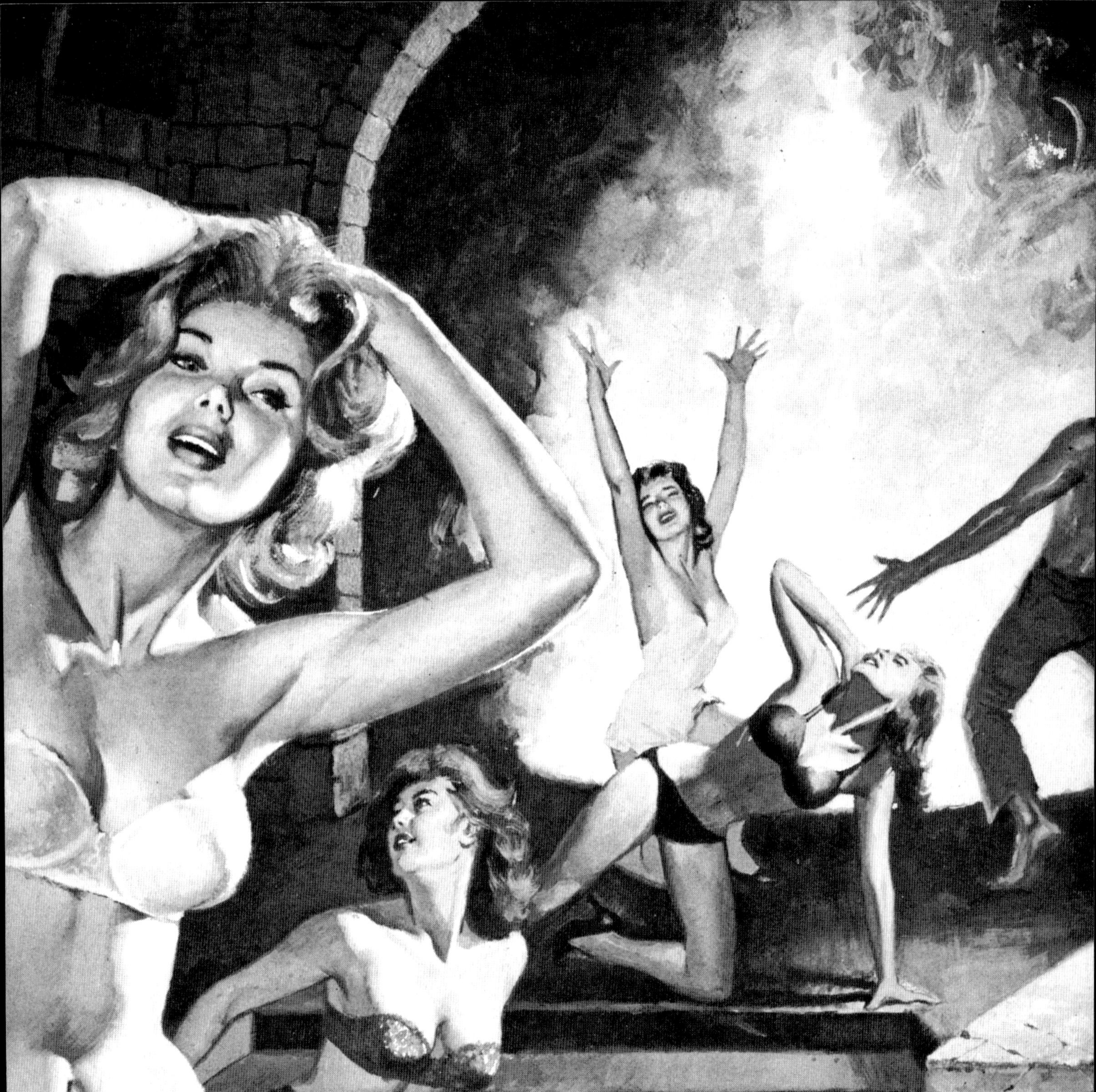

SOFT BRIDES FOR THE HIDEOUS RITES OF THE DAMNED

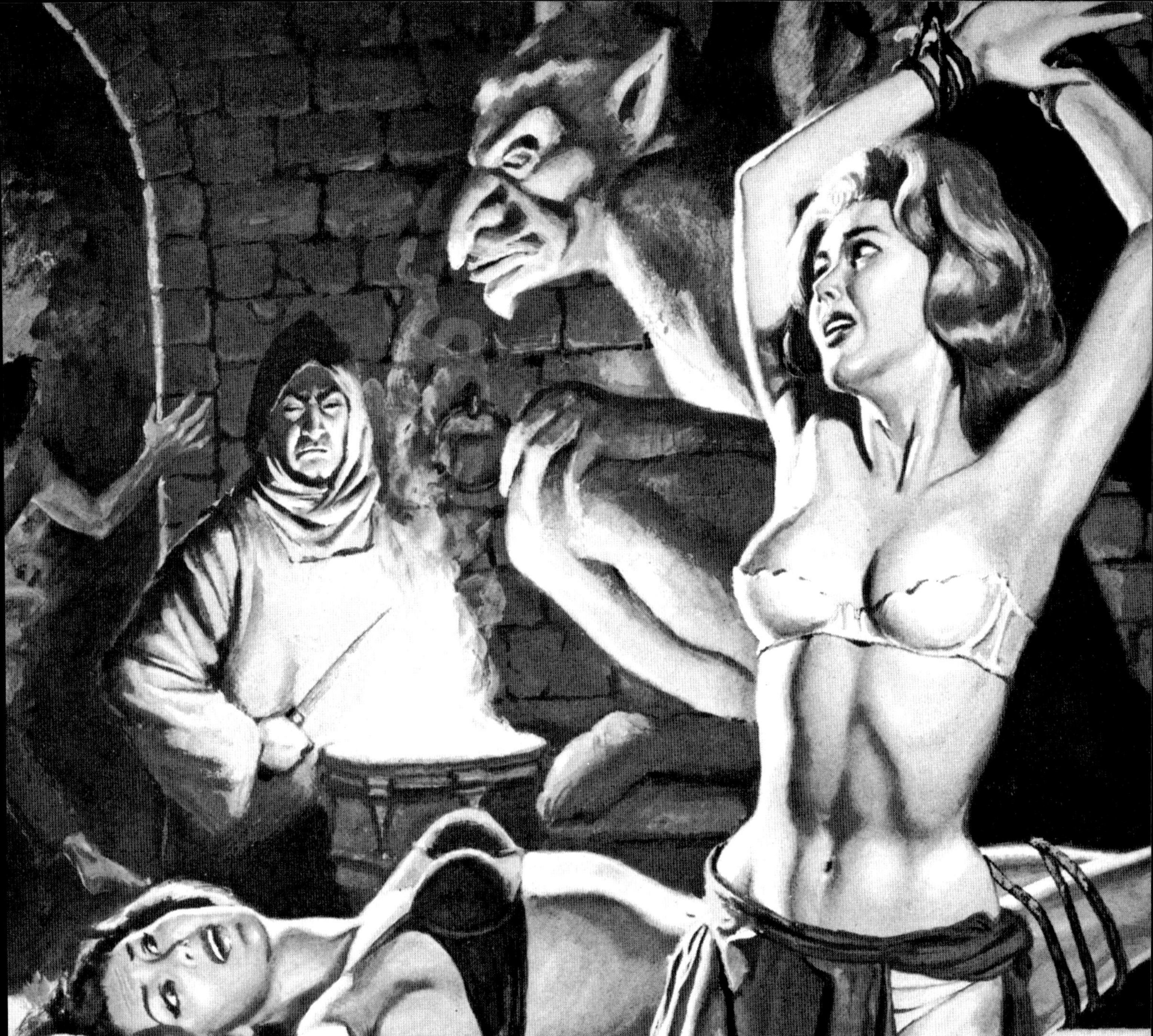

In the foul dungeon, Le Bete's shrieking victims learned the horrors of the brotherhood of evil.

THE NUDE GIRL LAY writhing in her bonds before them. Over her head, a goat's face leered in triumph. The crucified toad still dripped blood from its spot on the wall.

The girl's head rolled furiously back and forth. Her eyes bulged in their sockets. She tried to scream but a paralysis had gripped her throat.

It was impossible. This couldn't be happening to her. This wasn't the court of Louis XIV. There was no Madame de Montespan to inflame the bloated lechers. This was Choisy Le Roi, April 13th, 1926. Things like this no longer happened within sight of the lights of Paris.

Yet it was happening.

The discomfort of the splintery ropes which bound her was real. The coldness of the stone against her tender flesh was real. The drunken cries of the assembled guests were real.

She felt fetid breath swirling around her head and looked into the eyes of the man called Le Bete. "Mercy!" the girl croaked. "In the name of heaven, release me!"

Le Bete's expression was the incarnation of the devil himself. His beady eyes seared her with the fires of their depraved lusts. His gaunt cheeks puffed up like the head of an adder.

His hands were like ice as they stroked her. He leered down at her nakedness, then spun towards the crowd which pressed around him.

A half-dressed woman, her pendulous breasts hanging low on her belly, giggled. A twisted arthritic leaned on his cane, his bloodless lips working over his crooked teeth. From the rear of the chamber a naked woman moved into view carrying huge crystal goblets on a silver tray. An amber liquid sloshed inside the glasses.

A gaunt man dressed in a cowl and cloak seized a glass and quaffed down the bitter absinthe. Others followed his lead. Their heads swam with the impact, for the liquor had been liberally spiced with belladonna.

The man called Le Bete signalled. The sound of sibilant flutes issued from hidden speakers in the walls. The music was sensuous, obscene in beat. It penetrated to the very depths of the assemblage's consciousness, girding them to a fever pitch for the diabolical act which was about to ensue.

"It is an act," a woman said to her male companion. "It is like Le Grand Guignol, isn't it? I mean all the mumbo jumbo and that, sort of thing. It is illusion, isn't it?"

The man laughed full in her face. His lips sought the hollow of her throat. She felt his teeth small and sharp. It was madness and she was part of it. As the absinthe and belladonna coursed through her veins, she no longer cared whether it was illusion or not.

The bound girl looked up at the woman with wild pleading eyes. For an instant the guest may have felt a twinge of conscience. Yet she made no move to stop the proceedings. Her mind had turned too quickly to the abandoned caress of her companion.

The man called The Beast turned to his guests, "Astaroth demands blood!" he shouted over their mumbling. "Asmodeus demands pain!" He paused for dramatic impact then screamed, "What say you?"

"Astaroth be served! Asmodeus be served!" they shouted in unison.

"So be it!" the demoniac host intoned in a deep resonant voice. "Our sacrifice will now be allowed to view her sister in pain."

A new shriek of horror crashed through the room as two gigantic men, stripped to the waist, dragged a pleading, screaming girl into the presence of the evil group. The girl was in her early twenties. Her heart-shaped face was tear-stained and the dress she wore hung in tatters.

Wildly she stared from one to the other of her captors. Her eyes came to rest on the bound figure on the altar. The fight went out of her in a shuddering sob.

The Beast grasped her slim wrists in his hands, held them locked in his obscene caress while a rope was lowered from the ceiling and bound around the girl's arms. One of the half-naked giants pulled mightily on the rope and the shivering girl's arms stretched high over her head. The action caused her young breasts to push forward against her bra. The assembled men and women roared in approval. The chamber echoed to their depraved comments. The befuddled girl hung suspended over them, not understanding what was happening. She sensed them reaching out for her tattered frock, felt the cold dampness surround her sweating body as the cloth was ripped from her back. A man's clawing hands tore her bra asunder. A woman claimed the girl's delicate pink panties as a prize.

At last she was revealed to them without covering. Her body thrashed wildly and her struggles added to the torment of the stretched tendons in her arms.

"Asomedus demands pain!" the crowd chanted as The Beast rolled up the right sleeve of his garment, uncovering a bulging bicep. The girl cried out in abject terror when she saw the lash dangling from his long fingers.

She threw herself against the ropes, trying to gain some measure of distance between her agonized body and the bullwhip.

"Asomedus demands pain!" the gathering repeated as the whip whistled through the air and caught the girl's naked thighs. Her mad scream, which ended in a bubbling gasp, brought roars of approval from The Beast's guests.

The whip cracked down again, this time looping wildly around the small of her back. The overhead rope jumped as a thing possessed of its own life. The girl's legs jerked spasmodically. The crowd grew silent, expressing their awe of the sounds of the lash and the answering shrieks of the two captives.

ONLY IN France of the 1920's could such a tableau of debauchery and sadism have been played out. To understand the scene we must remember that France had become the gathering place of the jaded, lusting and debauched of the world. World War I had brought the end of many royal houses. Revolution swept through Europe leaving in its wake meaningless titles and inordinately wealthy refugees.

From Russia came the unseated nobles with a yen for a return to the barbaric cruelty of the knout. From Germany came the Prussian officers who had gloated over the tortures meted out to the Belgians. From the United States came inordinately rich and debauched men and women who would do anything in the name of thrills.

The man known as Le Bete we in reality a Montmartre pimp who had become fascinated with the writings of Seabrook and De Sade. Although he had little formal education, it became evident to him that he could make a fortune by reinstituting the type of Black Masses which had been carried out during the reign of Louis XIV.

Cruelty, he reasoned, is both universal and perpetual. It has always been with us. It always will. Men and women will pay vast sums of money to partake in it, provided they may be given a degree of protection and privacy.

So Le Bete had set about buying a huge mansion in

Choisy Le Roi within easy range of Paris. He had furnished the mansion with the most grotesque of cabalistic pieces of art. He had read everything he could get his hands on concerning the rituals of Satanic worship. In time the mansion had been completely equipped with private chambers where the visitors could disport themselves in any excesses which might occur to them.

The only problem which faced Le Bete was stocking the sumptuous hell-hole with victims. And to one as enterprising as the beady-eyed pimp, this was not an insurmountable problem. There were many *poules* working the Left Bank of the Seine. An enterprising procurer shouldn't find it difficult to woo them to the mansion on the pretext that they would lead a life of luxury without having to fear the lifting of their registration cards by the police. No longer would they have to ply the boulevards and vie with each other for business. At Choisy Le Roi the clients would come to them.

Le Bete had a dynamic quality about him which fairly mesmerized women. Although he was grotesquely ugly, he was never at a loss for feminine companionship. And he worked slowly so as not to arouse any suspicions.

He would meet a girl, wine her and dine her. He would find her quite receptive to his expressed sympathy over the rigors of the life she led.

When he came to the punch line of "I can take you away from all this," the girls leaped at the opportunity. He immediately took them to the mansion and lavished expensive wardrobes on them. For weeks they were allowed to rest and enjoy themselves free from any responsibilities. They had no idea of what awaited them in the chambers of the basement since the building had been carefully sound-proofed.

Being as prolific as he was ingenious, Le Bete was able to spend great amounts of time and energy on his recruits. They moved in a dream world, enthralled by his urbane tenderness and *savoir faire*.

In this way their baptism in the filthy rites he perpetrated for the edification of his paying guests came as a more diabolical surprise.

The procedure never changed. On a given afternoon, Le Bete would enter his concubine's boudoir and partake of her love-making.

When he had finished, Le Bete would tell the girl to don her most alluring clothing and accompany him because he had something of great interest to show her.

The girl would take nothing amiss, even when the pimp conducted her through a secret passage and down a long flight of stone steps.

Only when she saw the foul markings on the walls would the first tremor of fear suffuse her. Before her eyes she would see Le Bete turning from a diffident lover into a terrifying gargoyle of lust and cruelty.

But her misgivings had come too late. The two half-naked assistants he had hired for just such purposes stealthily stole up behind the girl and seized her in their muscular arms. She would feel herself pressed against the matted hair of their chests and carried through a maze of doors. At last they would enter a small cell which held nothing more than a long bench.

SOME OF the girls at this point considered it all a practical joke. To humor the master of the house, they allowed themselves to be stretched out on the bench. Not until they became aware of the heavy straps being buckled over their voluptuous young bodies did the full enormity of what was transpiring dawn on them.

They heaved mightily against the confining fetters. But Le Bete's preparations had been thorough. The straps had been fashioned of harness leather. They were stiff and had no give in them.

To still any outcry and to add to the victim's terror, the jailers inserted pear-shaped gags into their mouths. The girls were left in this condition for hours or days, as the case might be.

Le Bete was enough of a student of human nature to know that the anticipation of pain was as horrifying as the pain itself.

From time to time he would descend to the basement and regale the *poule* with descriptions of what went on in the various chambers.

"Perhaps you will enjoy the rack, my sweet," he would begin. "It is really quite enjoyable. You will be brought to the room fully clothed. The guests will await your arrival with bated breath. Once there, your clothes will be stripped from you so that every muscle will be exposed. Your lovely ankles will be placed in stocks at the foot of the rack and your wrists bound by ropes which are attached to a roller at the head of the bed. Then the wheels will be turned slowly. First you will feel a slight numbness, but that will pass quickly. As the slack is taken out of your body, the tendons will be strained. Each nerve will respond in its own manner. Your vital organs will be distended. There will be no release from the pain. You will thrash and shriek and my patrons will revile you in their own way."

The girl would stare at him, her face quivering over the cruel gag. Her tormented eyes would plead with him. But this would lead him on to other, even more graphic descriptions of what she might expect under the tender mercies of his cohorts.

When the time of her torment finally arrived, the girl was practically insane with fear. In the darkness of her prison she had imagined every agony, every indecency which she was to suffer.

In every case the bare-chested torturers found a woman gibbering with fear when they removed the straps which held her and carried her to the main altar room.

In reality, Le Bete never let the tortures go too far. He realized that his guests would shy away from any scene of scandal. So he contented himself with carrying out psychological torture in preparation for the masses and going through the motions during the abominations.

TIME SPENT on the rack was excruciating, even though the ratchets were never drawn as tight as they might have been. The dreaded *strappado*, which was often used, could put an intolerable strain on a woman's shoulders even though her toes were allowed to remain on the floor.

In the end, the tormented girl was taken from the basement and given a sedative. Once she had slept off the effects of her harrowing experience, she was given ten thousand francs for her trouble and sent on her way.

Of course she did not go without the warning that should she tell her story to the police, sooner or later she would be found and dragged back to Choisy Le Roi – and her execution would be too brutal to contemplate.

In almost every case the warning sufficed. Perhaps Le Bete could have gone on indefinitely if he hadn't picked up a young girl named Madeleine Rochet, who had suffered from a rheumatic heart since childhood.

The damaged valves of her heart gave out on the rack, and the guests panicked in their haste to leave the scene. Le Bete was able to spirit her body from the mansion and secrete it in a Paris sewer. However, the gossip concerning what went on at his *ménage* became exceedingly dangerous.

Le Bete disappeared from circulation and wasn't heard from again. However, survivors of Ravensbruck, the Nazi concentration camp which came to be known as The Women's Hell, talked of a man who answered Le Bete's general description. Nobody can be sure whether the French collaborationist guard was the same man or not, but the punishments he inflicted on his victims bore a startling similarity to those carried out at Choisy Le Roi.

If it was the same man, he died a horrible death in 1945 when he left the prison camp and was machine-gunned in the groin by advancing Russian troops.

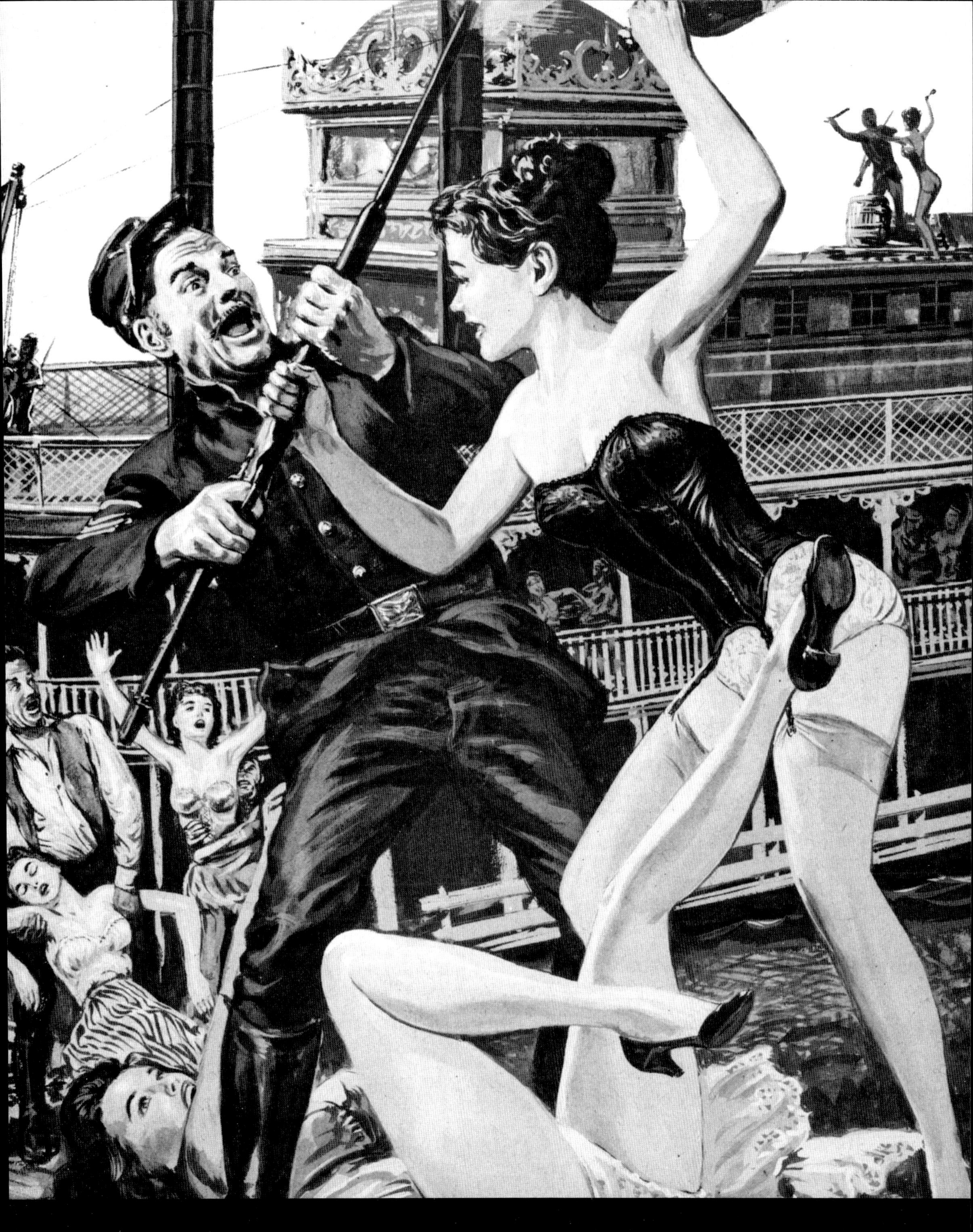

"INCREDIBLE LUST CRUISE OF THE REBEL HARLOTS"; detail from interior art, **MEN TODAY**, 05/63.
Art uncredited; attributed to Norman Saunders.

SECRET NUDE WEAPONS OF ST. BELVEDERE

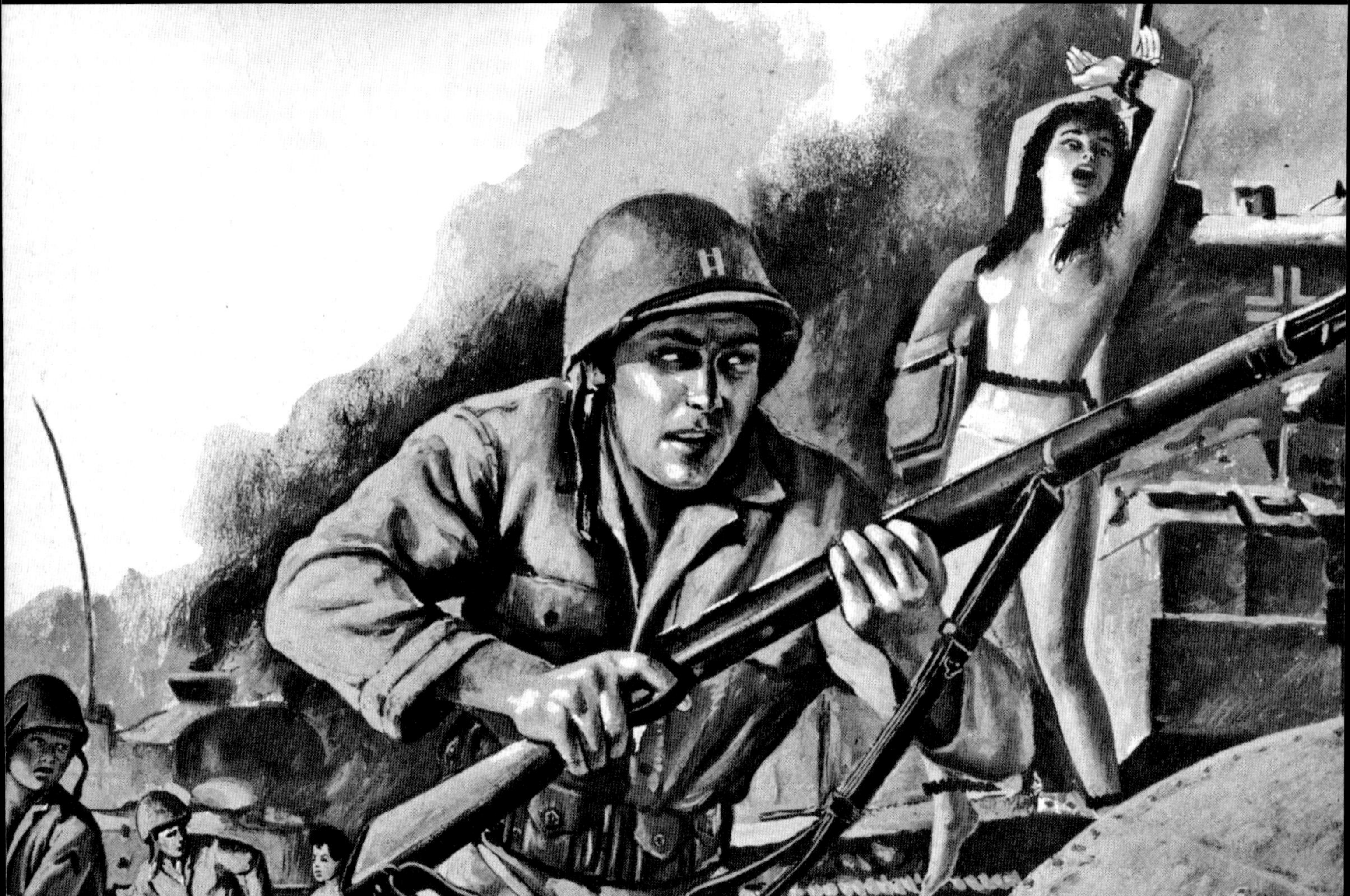

They fought the Nazis with any weapons they could – and naked women were the most effective!

ON JUNE 15, 1944, the second platoon of Baker Company of the 357th Regiment, the 90th Division, was ordered to set up a roadblock in, and hold, the small town of St. Belvedere. I was a squad leader in that platoon.

St. Belvedere looked like nothing, on the map. It consisted of little more than a cluster of houses. But it sat right on a road junction. Any Kraut Mark IV tanks that wanted to bull their way down the Argine-St. Belvedere road and make

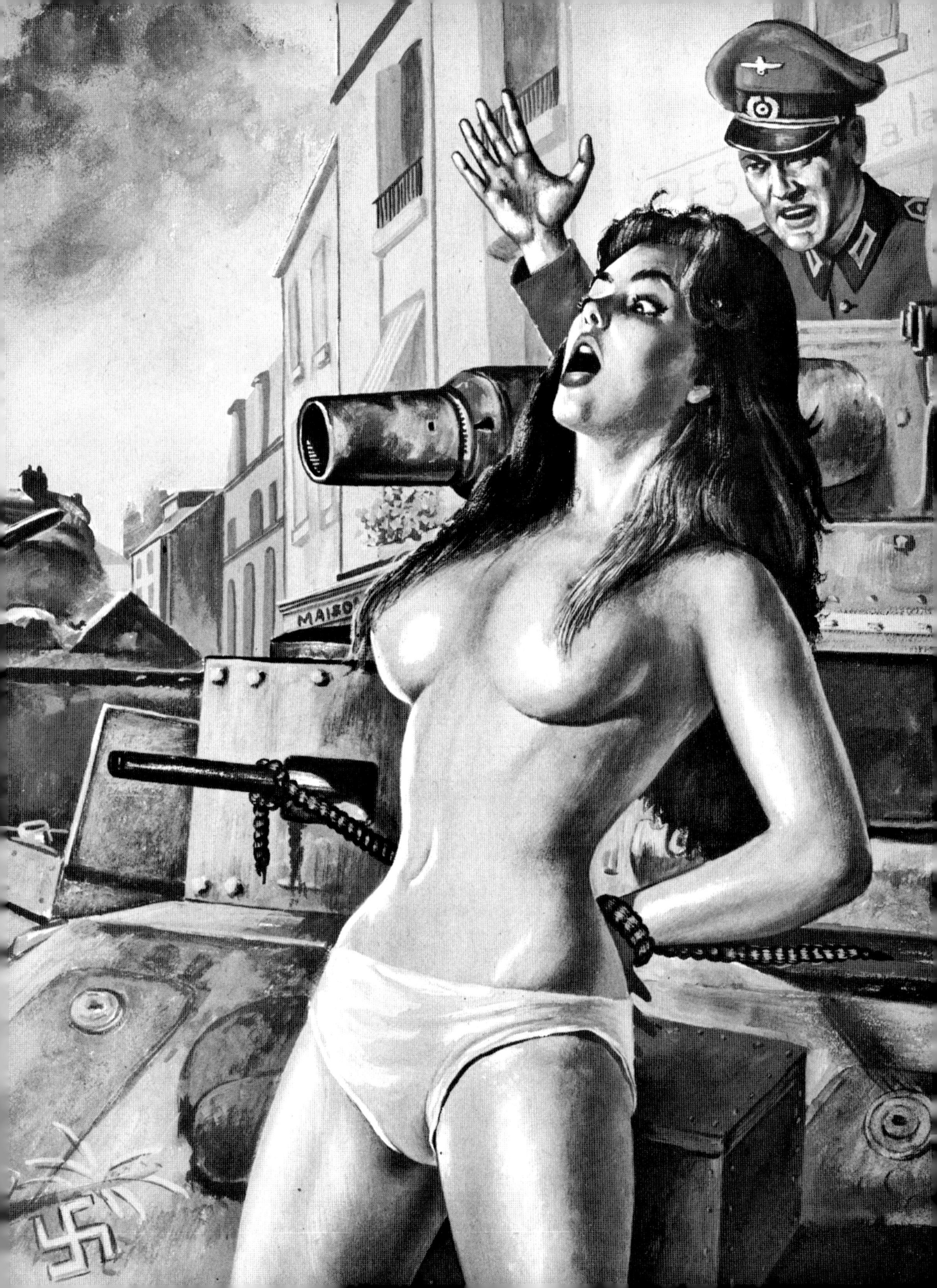

push for the beach-head had to go through St. Belvedere. The only alternative was to go out into the fields, and that meant going through one hedgerow – *bocage* country – after another. That way was painfully slow, and sure death on both tanks and infantrymen, both German and American.

Two squads of Baker Company arrived in St. Belvedere just before dusk. We were armed with rifles and grenades and nothing else. The local French population gave us a big welcome and wanted to know when we were coming back. We told them we were not. We were staying right there. We were going to dig in and set up a roadblock. We were going to stop any German tanks that tried to come down the road.

An old Frenchman took one look at us and our weapons and moaned: "*Ce n'est pas assez*," he said in his idiomatic French. "It is not enough. I just come from Argine. The Germans just came there with three big tanks. They are getting ready to come down the road after dark. They will grind you up like oatmeal. Have you no anti-tank guns?"

The old Frenchman had put his finger on our big headache. We looked at each other and sweated. We knew that we desperately needed anti-tank weapons. Our third squad, which had the bazookas and the bazooka rounds, had got separated from the company and lost itself somewhere on the Cotentin peninsula. Without them we were sitting ducks against a tank attack.

We could only hope for the best. Our one chance of holding the Germans was that they would hold off their attack that night and wait at least until dawn or later. By then we might be able to get some anti-tank weapons up and make a fight of it.

"Let me send a messenger back now, lieutenant," I said. "Maybe he can get some action back at regiment."

"All right," Lt. Harris said. "What we desperately need is time. I'll try anything. Anything."

The Frenchman listened to every word of our exchange. One of them who spoke English interpreted for the rest. So they knew we needed time before the German tank attack to get anti-tank weapons.

There were four good-looking French girls who had been standing at the edge of the crowd of townspeople. Now one of them stepped forward and got everybody's attention, including ours. She was a big beautiful red-head in a sweater that hid none of her sensual shape. Her body alone, if used in the right place, could bring the war to a dead halt. No G.I., no matter what uniform he wore, would be able to take his eyes away from her for more than a second.

"We are from the next town," she said in a silky voice, including her three girl friends with a wave of her hand. "From Argine. We will go back there. We will hold the Germans there for you for as long as you need."

The crowd of Frenchmen in the town square started to hoot at the girls. One of them buttonholed Lt. Harris and me. "They are *poules*," he said. "Ladies of the night. Prostitutes. What can they do to hold the Germans back, to keep them from attacking with their tanks?"

The red-headed girl, whose name we later learned was Marie Delmot, drew herself up haughtily.

"We have a secret weapon," she said firmly, "that will hold up the German tank crews long enough for the Americans to get their anti-tank weapons here." The three girls with her nodded their agreement. The curiosity of everybody had been aroused by this announcement. What was it these girls thought they could do?

Red-haired Marie Delmot threw her head back proudly. Her hands went to her sweater and she pulled it tight around her. She wore no bra underneath the sweater, and even though the light of day was fading we could see the beautifully shaped, firm, and upright breasts she now cupped in her hands. There was a gasp of admiration from every man present. All were rooted to the spot.

"These are our secret weapons," Marie Delmot said proudly, looking down at her breasts. "We are all thus equipped. These will hold the German tanks back and give you the time you need to get your anti-tank weapons."

Marie turned to her companions. "*Aux armes... pour la gloire de la patrie*," she said to them. "To arms... for the glory of our country." Then she linked arms with her girl friends and they marched down the road towards the edge of town and headed into the distance towards the town of Argine, where the unsuspecting Germans waited.

"For the only time in this war," one of the G.I.s in my squad said, "I wish I was a Kraut... waiting in Argine..."

But there was no time to waste in idle thought. We got to work immediately. We dispersed our two squads in the cellars of the houses along the road to give them a converging field of fire on the road junction with their rifles. The men piled up grenades at each window. And we put two men twenty yards from the road junction and told them to dig in. When and if the Kraut tanks hit them they were to fire back and then fall back on the town to join the rest of us.

But while I was working, I couldn't help wondering just what it was the girls intended to do. Hit the Germans over their head with those magnificent secret weapons, or what? Whatever it, was, our prayers were with those girls, and with the messenger we had sent back to regiment to ask for anti-tank weapons.

MARIE DELMOT and her three friends went down the road towards Argine. As darkness fell, they reached the outskirts of the town where Marie Delmot stopped briefly in the bushes at the side of the road. With a few swift motions of her hands on her dress and sweater, she prepared herself for action.

Ten yards inside Argine, the four French girls were ordered to halt by the guards of the German road block. They could hear the three German tanks with their motors running.

"What are you doing out at night so late?" one of the Germans asked.

"We were looking for a little party," Marie Delmot said. "We have a little wine and a record player. We thought maybe we could have a little fun."

Just then one of the German tanks turned on its one-eyed searchlight. Its powerful beam fell on Marie. She let her coat fall open. She had nothing on underneath, and her nude body seemed to glow, a candle flame to the male moths around her in green German uniforms. The Germans gasped. One of them had trouble breathing as he stared in awe at

Marie's magnificent beauty.

Another one of the Germans suddenly opened his mouth as wide as he could and yelled at the top of his voice. "Hans!" he cried. "Otto! Come here!"

"But we are getting everything ready for the attack later."

"We'll be ready in plenty of time. Even if we're a little late, Hitler's Greater German Empire can wait a while. When will something like this come our way again?"

The word of the presence of the girls, at least one of whom was completely nude under her coat, spread like wildfire among the German troops in the town. Within minutes a crowd of German soldiers milled in delirium around Marie Delmot and her friends.

"Come," Marie said. "All of you. Come over to our place. We have a large apartment."

The entire German garrison trooped after the four girls and crammed themselves in their apartment. Somebody turned on the record player. The wine flowed and soon the tipsy German soldiers were waltzing Marie and her friends around the room.

"*Ach*," one of the German soldiers said in the middle of a dance, "why you not be like her?" He pointed at Marie who was dancing in the nude. Then he reached forward and systematically and methodically stripped the dress off his dancing partner, throwing each piece of her clothing at the ceiling as he tore it off her. And finally she stood completely naked, and the German soldier took her in his arms and waltzed her around the room.

In no time, the other two girls had also been stripped of their clothes. They whirled about the room, passed from the arms of one German soldier to the next.

As time passed, the powerful French wine took its toll. The Germans became tipsy, and no longer wanted to let the girls out of their arms. And when that moment in the evening's festivities came, Marie and her friends slipped out of the arms of their dancing partners and each slipped into a separate room at the rear of the flat. In a few minutes there were four separate lines of German soldiers queued up before each door. Each man anxiously waited his turn, desperately afraid that fate would rob him of the chance to lie in the obviously passionate arms of one of the beautiful French girls.

JUST BEFORE dawn an old Frenchman was seen to leave the house where Marie Delmot and her three friends were giving their party for the German troops. The old Frenchman moved furtively, sticking to the shadows, running as fast and as quietly as he could.

He actually reached the edge of town when a German sentry, on his way to the party, picked him up on the edge of town, headed in the general direction of St. Belvedere.

"Where are you going?"

The Frenchman was questioned and searched. After a severe beating he broke down and surrendered to the Germans the note he had been hiding in his shoe. The German sentry took the note to the Nazi lieutenant in command of the three tanks in Argine and he read the note with amazement and growing anger. The note had obviously originated with one of the four French girls who were giving the party for the Germans that night – in the arms of one of which the German lieutenant had been rapturously enfolded just fifteen minutes before.

The note read: "We cannot hold the Germans any longer. At most an hour. Whether the Americans have gotten their anti-tank weapons or not. If not, tell them they had best pull out before dawn."

The Germans were infuriated when they realized they had been betrayed and tricked. The Nazi tank lieutenant led a party of heavily armed troops to Marie Delmot's apartment. He swore all the while. "We must hit the Americans immediately. It is our chance to strike hard before their reinforcements arrive. And even if they now have their anti-tank weapons, we will be ready for them."

The Nazi troopers tore into Marie Delmot's apartment. They ripped the girls out of the arms of the stupefied soldiers they were with. The Nazi lieutenant screamed at them. "If you tarts want to play at soldier," he shouted, "then you will have your chance! Take them outside! If you have gotten us into trouble with your treachery, then you will now get us out of that trouble!"

The naked girls were dragged out into the street just as the sun came up. At the order of the Nazi lieutenant the four French girls were tied with heavy rope to the sides of the Mark IV tanks in exposed positions. "If the Americans dare to fire," the Nazi lieutenant said grimly, "they will kill first the girls who befriended them, who risked their lives and gave their bodies to help them." The Nazi smiled maliciously. "I am sure the Americans would not do that."

With a great roar of their motors, the three Mark IV tanks moved out of the town square of Argine and headed down the road in the direction of St. Belvedere.

And at St. Belvedere, the three squads of the second platoon of Baker Company waited. During the night the missing third squad had joined us. We were armed with bazookas and rockets, all lined up and ready to go.

And then the German tanks appeared out of the mist that lay heavy on the Argine-St. Belvedere road. I lined up my bazooka sights on the first tank and prepared to blast it off the face of the earth. Just when I was about to squeeze the trigger, Lt. Harris, who had his field glasses trained on the lead tank, suddenly screamed. "Don't shoot!" he cried. "Put the bazooka down. They've got the French girls tied on the outside of their tanks. If you hit one of the tanks, you'll kill the girls!"

The German tanks lumbered forward. Bitterly we had to watch and let them come on. They pumped shell after shell into St. Belvedere. And then the tanks were in the town. I saw the hatch cover of the last tank raise and a black-helmeted Nazi, grinning evilly, poke his head out and survey the damage he was doing. I drew a bead on his head with my Garand.

And then I lowered my rifle. That open hatchway cover was our chance to destroy the German tanks without hurting the French girls. I loaded my pockets with grenades, left the cellar and ran up to the second floor of the house.

Just as the end tank passed below the window where I was waiting, I jumped. I landed on the back half of the tank. Then I put a bullet through the Nazi's head, pushed him down inside the tank, and dropped a grenade in after him. There was a shattering explosion inside the tank. As the tank ground to a halt, began to smoke, and burst into flame, I cut the ropes with my trench knife, and the French girl slid to the ground. She half-stumbled into the waiting arms of the G.I.s in the doorway of one of the houses that lined the street.

I went after the second tank in line from its blind rear side. Other G.I.s in the platoon saw what I was doing. They ran to upstairs windows and leaped out on top of the two tanks. They rammed their rifles into the tank peepholes before the Germans could get them shut, and blasted away. Soon the tank hatches opened up, and we slammed home grenades. Again, before the tanks blew, we cut the French girls free and half-carried them into a house.

The tank battle was over in a few minutes. I ran into one of the houses where the four French girls were clustered. We poured hot coffee into them and rushed G.I. blankets, shirts, and trousers to them.

The girls looked at each other. They let the blankets drop to the floor and stood up, naked as the day they were born, and looked at us. They waved the G.I. clothes aside. The big beautiful red-head swung a canteen cup of coffee regally around her head.

"We don't need the clothes!" she cried. "Let's have a party to celebrate our stopping the Panzers with our secret weapons!"

"Yes, let's have a party!" Marie Delmot screamed triumphantly.

It was a brawl of a party. For us the war stopped for twenty-four wonderful, delicious hours in the small French town of St. Belvedere.

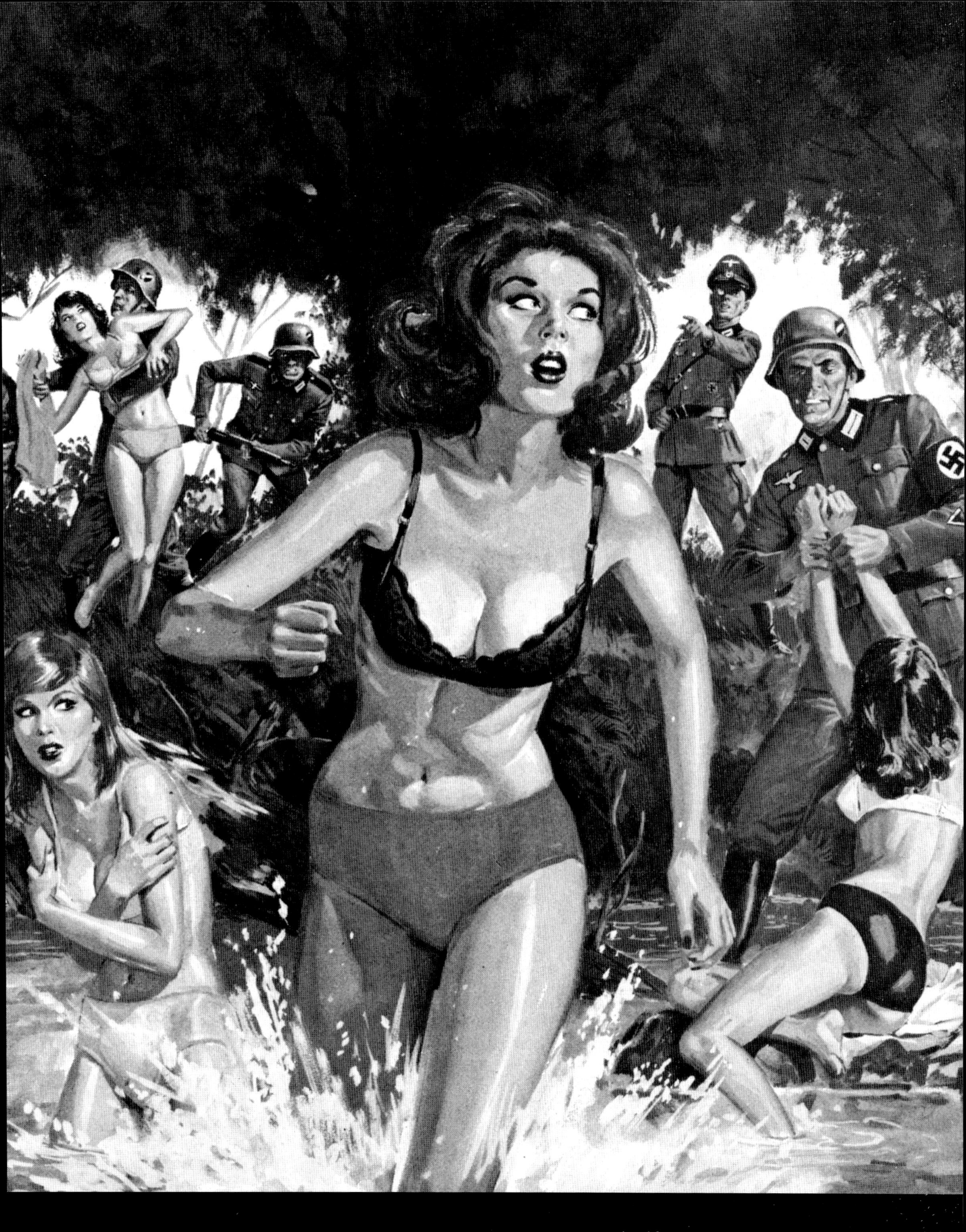

"SOFT DECOYS OF DEATH TO SMASH THE KRAUTS"; detail from interior art, **WORLD OF MEN**, 07/63.
Art uncredited; attributed to Bruce Minney.

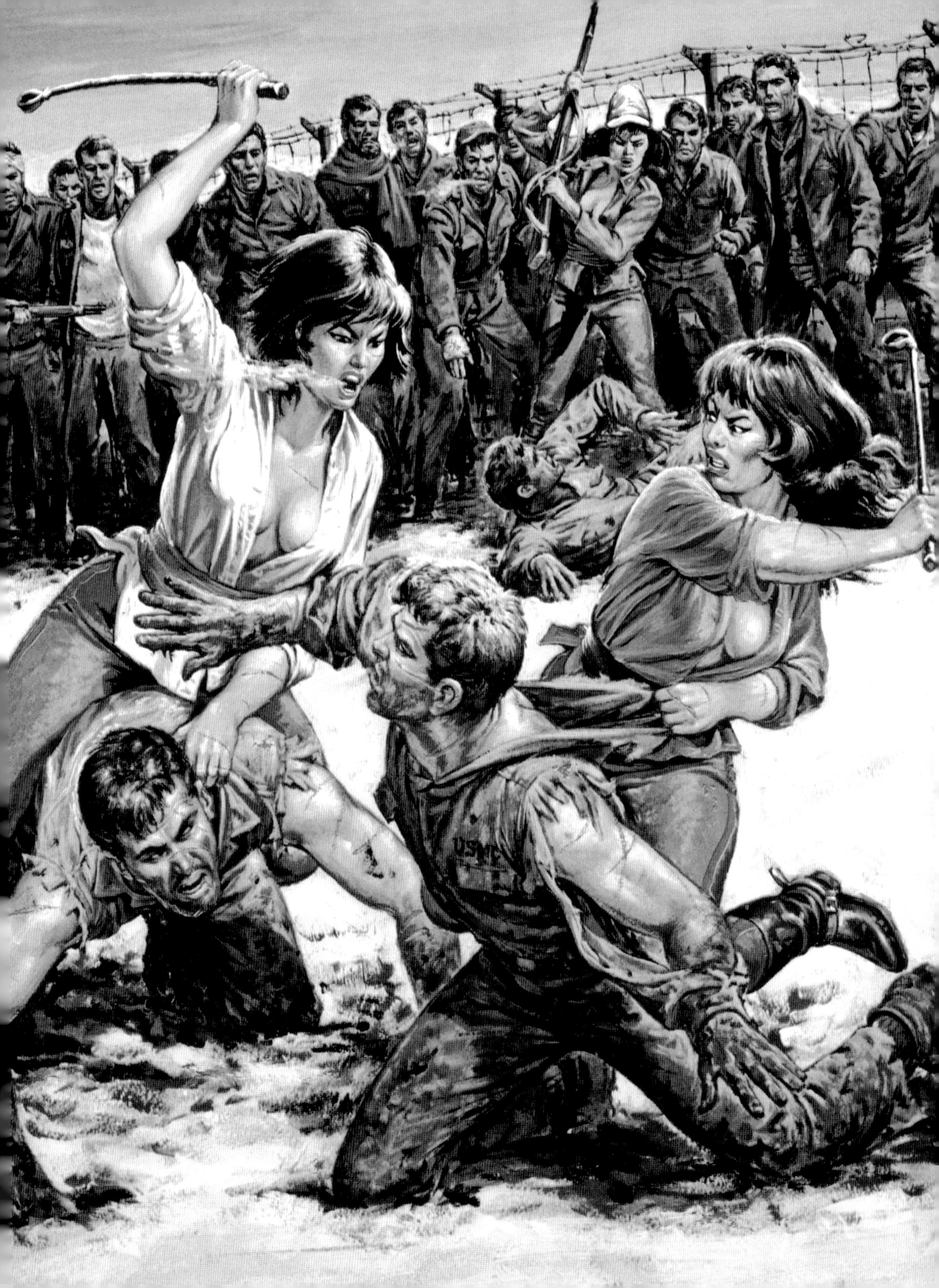

THE ORDEAL AT JAP "CAMP AGONY"

More than 2,000 Yanks were held as POWs in Akasaki – but only 73 survived the incredible tortures inflicted by the depraved Hinan female guards. This is their story.

ONE OF THE MOST bizarre sagas of horror and survival to come out of World War II can now be told. It took place in 1945.

General Douglas MacArthur had already made his famous return to the Philippines several months earlier. By February of 1945, Manila had fallen to U.S. forces under his command; but even before that, American bombers had been flying out of hastily-constructed airfields on Leyte. "Workhorses of the Air", these B-24 Liberators were ranging the China Seas as far south as borneo and the Celebes, as far north as Formosa and the southern tip of the Ryukyu island chain. Their mission: cut the Jap supply lifeline on the sea and in the ports.

It was on one such mission to Formosa on January 15, 1945, that the Liberator *The Green Goose*, with Duluth, Minnesota-born S/Sgt. Richard T. Moss rising the tail turret, fell back from its formation as it turned as it turned into the bomb run over the port of Hinan. A sitting duck 600 yards out from the main body of attackers, it was pounced upon by a flight of three Zekes. A silver job, a dare-devil from the *kamikaze* school, came in from 4 o'clock and hung under the *Goose*'s right wing, chewing it to bits with short raking bursts from its machine-guns.

The crippled *Goose*, losing altitude rapidly, screamed towards earth. Her pilot, Lt. T. L. Monroe, fought his controls and finally succeeded in levelling the plane long enough to bring her in for a 150-mph belly-landing on a strip of sandy beachfront.

Before any crew member had the chance to assess damage to either men or machine, the plane was swarming with Japanese soldiers.

The Americans were removed to Hinan. After three days of intense interrogation by a team of Japanese naval intelligence officers, the ten men of the crew were informed that they were being assigned to a POW camp in the island's interior. Guards would escort them to Akasaki Prison Camp 3 that evening.

The Yanks were grimly prepared for the worst. They had heard the atrocity stories out of Manchuria. The reports of the Bataan Death March were now common knowledge throughout the U.S. Armed Forces of the Pacific. But even in extreme anxiety, the human mind has its limit of imagination; and not one of the men, a sit later turned out, anticipated what lay in store that evening or during the night and days, weeks and months to follow.

En route to the prison camp, the first surprise in store for the *Goose*'s crew was the sudden drop in temperature. The prison van had been climbing a gradient for some time, and now patches of snow alongside the road were reflected in the moonlight.

The interpreter accompanying them to the POW camp noticed Moss's reaction in particular. He explained: "Takayama... you call it Mount Morrison... about 14,000 feet high. Akasaki is only 6,000 feet up, but in winter it is covered with snow until *tsuyu*, the spring rainy season."

About an hour later, the ancient vehicle groaned to a halt. A figure stepped out of a sentry box and snapped on a series of lights that flooded the barbed-wire entrance to Akasaki Prison Camp 3.

Peter Myers, the B-24's radio operator, was the first to adjust his eyes to the searing white beams, and to the scene. "F'crissake – *a dame!*" His eyes bulged with amazement. "Look! The joint's over-run with 'em!"

A dozen or more Japanese women in the uniform of the Imperial Army stood at the gate, their Arisaka rifles at the ready, bayonets fixed.

Chuck Kroker, the engineer, whistled softly. "man, this ain't no POW camp – it's a damned USO center."

Their interpreter-escort ordered the *Green Goose*'s crew out of the van. They were immediately flanked by two of the uniformed women, marched through the barbed-wire gate, and brought to a halt in the center of the barren compound beyond.

Ringed by the women and the flood of lights, the men stood momentarily blinded. Suddenly a woman stepped forward into the illuminated circle, and each American emitted a short gasp – half of amazement, half of admiration – for her startling Oriental beauty. *Not quite Oriental*, Moss thought. Probably there had been a European ancestor somewhere along the line.

She stood there arrogantly, her jet-black hair blowing wildly in the mountain winds. Her uniform was Imperial Army only from the waist down – tight-fitting breeches and spurred rising-boots. But above the belt – that was something else. She wore only a clinging silk blouse, moulded seductively to her breasts.

The interpreter said crisply: "This is Okatsu-san, and that is how you will address her throughout your stay here – however long that may be. Since there is no rank among the women at Akasaki, you are to attach the suffix *san*, meaning 'madame', only to her name and that of the two women who share the second level of command: Yuka-san and Haru-san."

The interpreter then went on to explain the unusual presence of the women at Akasaki. There were 30 of them under Okatsu-san, put there by the Formosa high command to relieve prison guards for duty along the beach perimeter, now that the island was vulnerable to invasion by MacArthur and his forces.

"A final word," the interpreter emphasized. "All but five women, those we recruited from Hinan *geisha* houses, are married. They have husbands in the Imperial Army or Navy and they are dedicated subjects of the Emperor. Bear this in mind – and remember, too, your own saying about the female of the species being more deadly than the male. These are not gentle women. They hate you, as only women can hate an enemy that has killed and maimed their husbands, fathers, brothers and friends. I warn you – *they are not here to make your stay comfortable.*"

With these words, the interpreter bowed to Okatsu-san. She returned his gesture of farewell and turned towards her prisoners. As the interpreter walked out of the gate to the waiting van, a cruel, contemptuous smile spread over her lips.

"Irasshai, inu." The words came out in a sing-song snarl from her twisted mouth.

Ignoring the interpreter's warning, Lt. Noonan, the co-pilot, wise-cracked: "baby, I may not speak your language, but if that means you're looking for a date tonight, I'm your man!"

Noonan – most of all – and Moss and the others were in for another surprise. The woman answered him in English.

"But I *do* speak *your* language, Lieutenant; and for your information, the words mean: 'Welcome; dogs'."

Okatsu-san made an abrupt gesture with her hand, and the two woman-soldiers flanking Noonan pulled the co-pilot out of the group. Then, simultaneously, they brought the butts of their rifles down on his calves. Her fell to the ground, crippled, helpless. The two guards rolled him over on his back and ground their knees into his arms, pinning his back and shoulders against the snow. A third women came running forward and jammed a block of wood between his teeth. His mouth and jaw gaped open about two inches.

It was all over before the rest of the crew realized what had happened. Okatsu-san pulled a knife from her hip pocket and snapped it open. Her legs straddled Noonan's body as she thrust the blade into his open mouth. She probed, found her mark – and sawed at the roots of his tongue. The co-pilot screamed in agony, but she heaved her full weight against his chest and his cry was cut off by a gush of blood that spurted from his mouth.

The woman jumped to her feet, brandished the five inches of flesh that had once been Noonan's tongue over her head, and triumphantly shouted a loud *"Banzai!"*. Some of the blood bubbled out of the American's mouth and crimsoned the snow around his head. But with his mouth propped open he couldn't spit or staunch the wound. The blood was pouring back into his throat, filling his lungs.

The rest of the crew, the muzzles of rifles trained at the back of their heads, could only stand there and watch, horrified, as Lt. Noonan *drowned in his own blood.*

Dick Moss felt his gorge rising in his throat and, clenching his fists, he swore to himself and to the men nearby who could hear his muttered words. "That bitch is going to pay for that. On Noonan's life – I swear it!"

In that moment, Moss became a leader. There was something about the determination of his voice, the powerful set of his jaw, that made even the officers – Monroe, Stuart the bombardier, and Lloyd the navigator – realize that this would be the strong man among them.

Okatsu-san, who hadn't heard Moss's oath, wiped her blood-splattered hands and knife on her breeches. Still holding Noonan's tongue in her hand, she declared: "I always like to start off my prisoners with an object lesson. It helps to keep them docile."

Then she pointed beyond the perimeter of light. Moss and the rest of the crew were led into the circle of darkness. Their barracks were nothing more than a tropical *sulap* – uprights, a thatched roof, and the four sides open to the elements. There was no flooring. No blankets – just the bare ground to sleep on.

The lights of the compound were turned off, and when their eyes had become adjusted to the dark, the 9 remaining members of the *Green Goose*'s crew could make out about 15 other similar structures. The men huddled together to keep warm. Physically and emotionally wrung out from their ordeal, they collapsed. But before they dropped off, they heard the traditional words of the two salutations of G.I.s everywhere:

"Welcome to Camp Agony!"

"You ain't gonna like it here!"

They had heard it a dozen times before in a dozen other places – but this time it was different. The voices that drifted across the compound were weak and ghost-like, and there was something hair-raising about the almost insane chorus of chuckles that came from the other buildings.

MOSS WAS the first to awaken the following morning, and one look told him why Akasaki had been dubbed "Camp Agony" by its inmates. For a moment, Moss had the feeling he was in a 17th century madhouse. Each building housed anywhere from six to ten men – that is, if one could still reckon them as belonging to the human race. Gaunt wraiths, their fouled clothes – the once-crisp uniforms of proud U.S. fighting men – hung on them as if on skeletons. As they stirred and shuffled lethargically about the compound, the wind picked up their odour and wafted it into Moss's *sulap*.

They smelled dead, or dying – as many of them were. Even now, a few of the healthier-looking ones were dragging two bodies out into the center of the compound. These were the corpses of men who had died during the night.

A gong rang somewhere, and the inmates lined up in front of their *sulaps*. Moss awakened the *Green Goose* crew, who lined up in turn. Two of the women guards wheeled a large kettle into the compound and stopped at the barracks next to Moss's. Then, methodically, they doled out eight scoops of a rice mixture – one for each man in the *sulap* – dumping each portion neatly in the snow at each man's feet. There were no dishes, no utensils, and when the two guards moved on, the men fell on their knees and gobbled up their meagre rations with their fingers.

At the *Green Goose*'s *sulap*, the ritual was repeated, only this time nine portions were ladled at their feet. Potter, the nose gunner, kneeled down and took a whiff of the food, then spun quickly around, holding his hand to his nose and mouth. He fought back the impulse to gag and retch. Monroe and Moss tested the food with their noses, and almost doubled up as the vile odour assailed their nostrils.

"You think that's somethin', jus' wait 'till tomorrow – mail day." It was the first time one of the denizens of the pest-hole had spoken directly to the newcomers. He was, he said, an infantry officer, picked up in the Munda action on New Georgia and ferried to Formosa several months ago. His teeth were rotted, and his hair and beard had fallen out in great, glaring patches.

Monday – mail day – was the worst day of the week. That was the day when the women received letters from the homeland, and from their husbands and relatives on Japan's far-flung fronts. Often, the news received was bad – a death in the family, a military setback.

"An' when that happens, buddy, they get mean – *real* mean," the footslogger warned.

Moss and the *Green Goose* crew noticed the change immediately the following morning. The mess that was dumped at their feet for food was scattered loosely over the snow. Even if they could have brought themselves to eat the swill, it would have ben difficult to grasp it. The other inmates picked at the snow, pecking like birds to retrieve each rice kernel.

About noon, Okatsu-san left one of the wooden structures that served as offices and quarters for the women, and stood in the center of the compound. She carried a long whip in one hand and a megaphone in the other. Addressing herself to the prisoners' barracks, she screamed:

"Americans... listen to this: Today, we hear that more of Japan's gallant youth have died in the war against your cowardly comrades. Their deaths shall not go unavenged!"

Then, several of the women wheeled out two decrepit rickshaws. Okatsu-san climbed into one of them and Yuka-san, whip in hand, pulled herself into the other. Two of the shuffling shadow-men were told to draw the vehicles around the compound. At first, the unfortunate creatures walked slowly, dragging their heavy loads torturously. Okatsu-san applied the lash to the back of her driver, and this became the signal for Yuka-san to belabor the wretch who tugged away at her cart. They picked up speed and came abreast of each other. The race was on!

The two women beat their chargers unmercifully, shredding the shirts off their backs until they were almost naked above the waist. Blood and sweat clung to their shoulders.

And then, the second time around the compound, Okatsu-san's driver slipped on a patch of snow. He didn't have strength enough left to put his hands out to break his fall. And he lay quite still when one wheel of the rickshaw rolled over his prone body. Okatsu-san, anticipating the climax to the race, jumped gingerly and unharmed from the unmanned vehicle.

She struck the crumpled body with the butt-end of her whip, but he didn't stir. She kicked him contemptuously, and strode away. "Mail Day" was over – at least for a week.

THE FOLLOWING Monday they had no way of knowing that communications had revealed to the women that Japanese forces in Manila had capitulated to MacArthur. Nor could the men have realized that Okatsu-san's father commanded an infantry regiment that was completely wiped out in the final days of the siege. They could only feel the effects of her rage.

This time, she singled out a special group – the crew of the *Green Goose*.

She and Yuka-san marched to the front of their barracks and ordered the nine men to line up.

Once they had obeyed, she walked up and down the rank, eyeing each member of the crew. When she had made her decision, she pointed to Moss and Bertram, the second radio operator and ball-turret gunner.

"You two looked evenly matched. Strip to the waist!"

When they had done so, she examined their still well-preserved bodies and smiled: "That's what we need for this little contest. The old-timers here haven't the strength or the fighting spirit."

Guards dragged the two prisoners out into the center of the compound and forced them to get down on their hands and knees. Short riding crops were supplied to Okatsu and Yuka, who mounted the backs of the men – Okatsu astride Moss and Yuka up on Bertram.

"Move in closer together, my handsome animal," Okatsu cajoled menacingly.

Moss carried her on his back until he was face to face with Bertram, who was also closing in under Yuka's proddings. The two approached each other warily, neither of them quite sure what to expect.

Moss was the first to find out. Yuka brought the riding crop across his face with a slashing blow that cut a ridge in his skin an inch long. Another slice caught him across the shoulder. He backed off, only to feel Okatsu's spurs dig into his thighs. They lashed through his pants and ground deep into the unprotected flesh. It was either retreat and have Okatsu cripple him with her spurs and riding crop, or take his chances with Yuka's aim. He advance on the other team.

This time, Okatsu was the aggressor. She moved fast, flailing her whip indiscriminately, not only cutting deep gorges in Bertram's face, shoulders and back, but also landing a few blows on Yuka's body.

The point of the game was to disable the opponent's mount. And while both women occasionally struck each other, it was Moss and Bertram who took the brunt of the punishment. Each time they backed off from each other, the women whipped and spurred the men back into position. Without even thinking, as if propelled by the instinct for survival alone, both men tried to maneuver their bodies to give their riders a striking advantage.

Blood streamed off their backs in zebra-like streaks. Large, moist patches formed on the thighs of their pants, marking the spot where the spurs had been driven home. Their faces were a mass of ugly bruises and open wounds.

Moss's head began to reel. He moved faster and more deviously than Bertram, who was taking the worse beating of the two men. Blood from a cut on his forehead was pouring into the ball-turret gunner's eyes, and he was having difficulty dodging Okatsu's lashing whip.

Then Bertram fell over on his face, screaming wildly. Yuka's spur had hooked brutally into his right thigh, and she was unable to extricate the sharp metal from the tough, muscular flesh. Hung up, the Jap woman and American gunner squirmed madly in the snow. Okatsu leaped off Moss's back and pulled at Yuka's boot. She ripped the spur from its moorings, taking a large hunk of flesh with it.

Bertram collapsed. The vicious contest was over.

In agony from the wounds all over his head, body and thighs, Moss assessed the situation. Bertram was already in bad shape. The cold climate might stave off any spread of infection from their wounds, but there was still the matter of nutrition. If they didn't do something soon about their diet, with a month the whole crew would be like the other human relics they saw on every side. Somewhere, somehow, he had to lay his hands on more food for the crew.

But how? The women were sadistic, fanatical in their hatred. Yet if he was to get hold of more food, it had to be done through one of them.

TWO DAYS later, an unusual incident pointed the way to the chance he was waiting for. The morning meal was being served on the ground in front of the *Green Goose* crew. Moss stood at attention with the others and watched the foul rice dish being doled out. When it came to his turn, the girl serving the food inadvertently spilled some on his shoe.

Seeing what she had done, she cupped her hand over her mouth with embarrassment and muttered, *"Gomen nasai."*

The simple, soft-spoken phrase of apology set wheels churning in Moss's brain. If any one of these women could be reached, he thought, this was the one.

He learned from the others that her name was Nama, a novice, or *hangyoko*, from one of the Hinan *geisha* houses. She had to be unmarried, a woman trained to accommodate men.

Moss dogged her footsteps for three days, waiting for an opportunity to catch her alone. When it came, she was on a work detail stacking tools in a shed behind the women's quarters. He crept up on her.

"Nama." Moss spoke the name caressingly. In that one word he tried to convey to her that he understood she was as much a victim of the cruel social system as he and the other inmates of Camp Agony were.

Nama gestured, and as Moss stepped over the threshold to the tool shed she closed the door behind them, and they were bathed in darkness...

Every evening thereafter, Nama stole some food for the nine Americans. Some nights it was only a few bowls of rice; on other occasions, a loaf or two of Japanese bread.

March of 1945 came and went. The spring thaws set in and then the rainy season, the *tsuyu*. In the middle of April, Yuka-san learned her husband had been killed during the first days of the Yank invasion of Okinawa. He was shot through the head while manning a machine-gun bunker on the beach. Okatsu permitted Yuka to pick a victim. She chose Lt. Monroe.

Yuka-san was every bit as cold-blooded as her superior – and just as ingenious at exacting her pound of flesh. There was no warning for what followed. In fact, it wasn't until weeks later that Moss learned, through Nama's few words of English and sign language, the reason for Yuka's savage treatment of the pilot.

Two of the women guards strapped Monroe to a rough-hewn cross in full view of the entire camp. Then Yuka, using nothing more than her thumbs, first gouged out one of his eyes and then the other.

Monroe, a stronger man than any of the crew had given him credit for, didn't emit a sound as the barbaric operation was performed. Yuka, obviously, had expected an entirely different reaction, and his stoicism threw her into a rage. She spat the words out like venom: *"Inu! Inu! Inu!"*

But even the epithet would not still her anger. She grabbed a bayonet from one of the guards and slashed at his arms and legs, slicing off large pieces of flesh like a mad butcher hacking away at a side of beef. The American was bleeding profusely. But he still refused to utter a cry, or a word. And that's the way he died – his teeth still frozen to his lower lip, his mouth contorted into a twisted grimace.

BUT MONROE was not the last of his group that Moss was to lose. Sgt. Matt Taylor, the second engineer and waist gunner, went berserk a month later and was shot trying to scale the barbed-wire fence. In June Potter, the nose gunner, called Okatsu-san a "dirty, slant-eyed whore" to her face. She had him executed on the spot.

When word of the fall of Okinawa spread through the camp in early July, Moss began to feel some hope. Formosa might be next, he reasoned. If they could just hold out a few months longer...

Then Nama was discovered pilfering food from the guards' kitchen. The cooks had begun to notice shortages in their accounts. A trap was laid for the culprit, and when Nama went to steal a left-over bowl of soybean cakes, they caught her in the act.

She never revealed who it was she was playing benefactress for. Not even when they stripped her and publicly whipped her on the same cross on which Monroe had died. Moss never heard about her again.

No matter what her fate might have been, however, this much was certain: the crew's source of extra rations was now cut off. And now that the Jap supply lines were being cut by the advancing Yanks throughout the China Seas, there was less food than ever to go around. More than that, the full heat of summer was upon them. Camp Agony, with its dying, rotting bodies, began to stink like a sewer. A fetid swamp just outside the camp grounds added to the vile stench that permeated the entire atmosphere.

On August 15, with crew morale at its lowest ebb since they arrived at Camp Agony, Moss resolved to do something about the situation – or die in the attempt.

That's why, when he walked past Okatsu's quarters and smelled the food, he took the long gamble. Thinking himself unnoticed, he crept through the unlocked door to her quarters. It was a fool's move, but he was beyond the point of reasoning sensibly. Once inside, the realized his mistake. There was food alright – a lavish display of squid, snails, rice cakes, and bowls of rice swimming in thick sauces. But Okatsu, half-dressed, stood in the middle of the floor.

He hesitated only a fraction of a second before he reached behind him and locked the door, but it was just enough of a pause for her to reach the Nambu automatic from its holster that hung on a screen. Doing so, she knocked over the tray of food, but she got off four shots in rapid succession, then three more. Okatsu was obviously shaken, for the Nambu trembled in her hand and all the shots went wild. And that's when Moss conceived his diabolical scheme to sexually assault her, to degrade her as she had degraded the men of Camp Agony. The last shot in the automatic missed him by a foot, and Moss charged.

She was at his mercy now. The women pounding at the door couldn't stop him.

But even as he ripped at her blouse and stuffed the corner in her mouth, he knew he couldn't follow through with the plan. If nothing else, she and her kind had not yet reduced him to the level of an animal, he told himself.

Frustrated in his desire for revenge, he struck her across the face and pounded her near-naked body with clenched fists. He was still beating her when the other women broke into the room and dragged him off her.

Okatsu, badly bruised, was quite conscious as they propped her up into a sitting position. She wiped the blood off her lips and rasped out the words: "You Yankee scum! You dare to lay a hand on me!"

Moss could almost see the perverted thought processes as they took form in her evil brain.

"You will die a death more painful than that of a thousand men – I promise you!" she screamed.

As she threw on her clothing, she issued orders to Yuka-san, Haru-san and the other guards in the room. Moss was led out into the sunlight and, with three rifles at his back, was marched over to a section of the barbed-wire fence near the stinking swamp. He was handed a shovel, and told to dig and keep digging until he dropped. In a few minutes he was joined by the five other members of his crew, each with a shovel. Under the lash of Yuka-san's whip, they dug steadily for five hours. When they were about nine feet down, they hit the water table. The dank liquid from the swamp seeped in and began rising in the excavation. The six men were hauled up the damp, slimy sides of the hole by a rope, as the water rose to about half a foot.

Yuka-san then took a detail of four guards outside the barbed-wire fence and the crew, still under close guard, was returned to its *sulap*. Across the compound they could see Yuka-san and the other guards dropping huge wooden buckets into the swamp. They were left there for about ten minutes, then hauled out and carried back into the compound to the huge hole. the contents of the buckets were dumped into the gaping cavity.

When they were finished, Okatsu-san came out of her quarters. Moss's shirt was torn off his back and he and the crew were marched over to the hole. The water had gained a level of about three and a half feet. Okatsu-san, grinning from ear to ear, addressed Moss: "You like to eat so much, Yankee? Well, let me tell you about a delicious dish we have prepared for you. You'll find it all over Formosa. We call it *lintahs*!"

No sooner was the last word out of her mouth than she shoved Moss into the hole. He landed feet first, waist deep in the water. Immediately, he felt a strange stirring around him, and as he looked up into the grinning face of his tormentor, Okatsu-san laughed piercingly. "Maybe you know them as *game leeches*!"

It was at that moment that a violent, stinging, burning sensation spread across his belly. He reached into the water and grabbed the leech. It was monstrous in size – four, even five inches long and an inch across – and he couldn't pull the creature off. Another attached itself to his back. Several found the tears in his pants, and were clinging to his thighs and calves.

They were all over his body now, crawling, slithering, sinking their sharp jaws into his flesh in a hundred places. He tried to climb out, but couldn't gain a hold on the slick walls.

They were no longer creating individual areas of pain – his whole body was wracked in agony. He looked up for one last view of the crew that peered down at them. Horror was etched on every man's face.

But this time, there were no women in sight. And Myers's strong right arm was reaching down into the hole. Moss grabbed for it, hit it the first try, and clung to it tenaciously. Kroker grabbed the other arm and they hauled Moss to the surface. In the open air and sunlight, the *lintahs* loosened their death-like grip and the five men were able to pull them off Moss's body.

"What happened?" Moss gasped.

Myers shook his head. "This car came rushin' up to the gate and a Nip lookin' like one of the top brass piled out, shoutin' about Hiro-something or other. Look, they're all in a huddle over by the gate."

Moss watched the cluster of women as they grouped around a Japanese naval officer. Then, as the women trailed slowly off to their quarters, the officer walked over to Moss and his men.

On August 6, he said, a U.S. B-29 had dropped the first atom bomb on Hiroshima. Three days later, another levelled much of Nagasaki. And on August 14, Japan capitulated. The war was over; the Americans were free.

Moss, Myers, Bertram, Kroker, Stuart and Lloyd – all that was left of the *Green Goose* crew – spread the news throughout the camp. Every man who was physically capable of walking surrounded the women's quarters. They weren't afraid any more. Not of the guns, or the whips. Nothing could stop them getting their revenge on the women who had made their incarceration at Akasaki Prison Camp 3 a living Hell.

But something did. The ancient tradition of a defeated Japanese seeking atonement for his – or her – failure. They found the women together in a room set aside as a Shinto shrine. Okatsu, Yuka, all of them, had committed *harakiri*.

When the final tally was taken, camp records revealed that some 2,200 Americans had died at Camp Agony over a period of three years. None had escaped. Only 73 had survived – among them the six members of the *Green Goose* crew.

HELL SHIP OF BURNING WOMEN

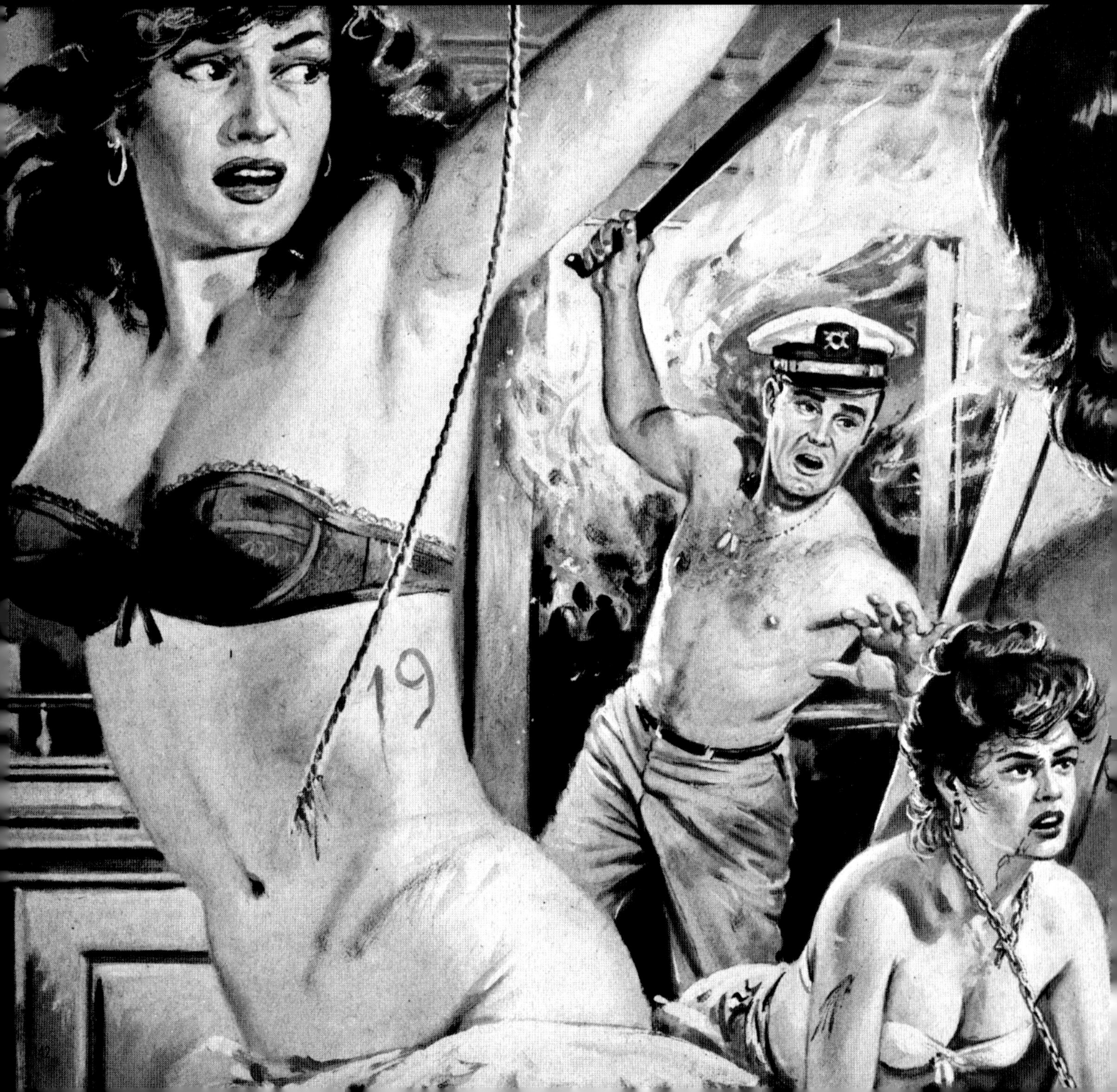

This human cargo of captive girls were damned to a life of inescapable wanton depravity.

BILLOWS OF THICK BLACK smoke choked and blinded us as we struggled frantically with the bolted door. Pounding fists hammered at it from the other side, the thudding noise all but drowned by the shrieks and screams of the women who were yelling hysterically inside the hold.

Yellow tongues of voracious flame were beginning to lick their way perilously close to where Chuck and I were battling against the steel door. The deck-plates beneath our feet were already heating, and I knew we had to work fast – or die in ahowling inferno of fire and horror. It would only be a matter of minutes. then the whole ship would be enveloped in a solid sheet of flame, a roasting oven of human corpses – Chuck's, mine, and those of two hundred naked women!

"It's no use, Chuck!" I yelled, smashing the crow bar down on the heavy door's steel handle for the fourth time. "We've got to think of something else – and fast!"

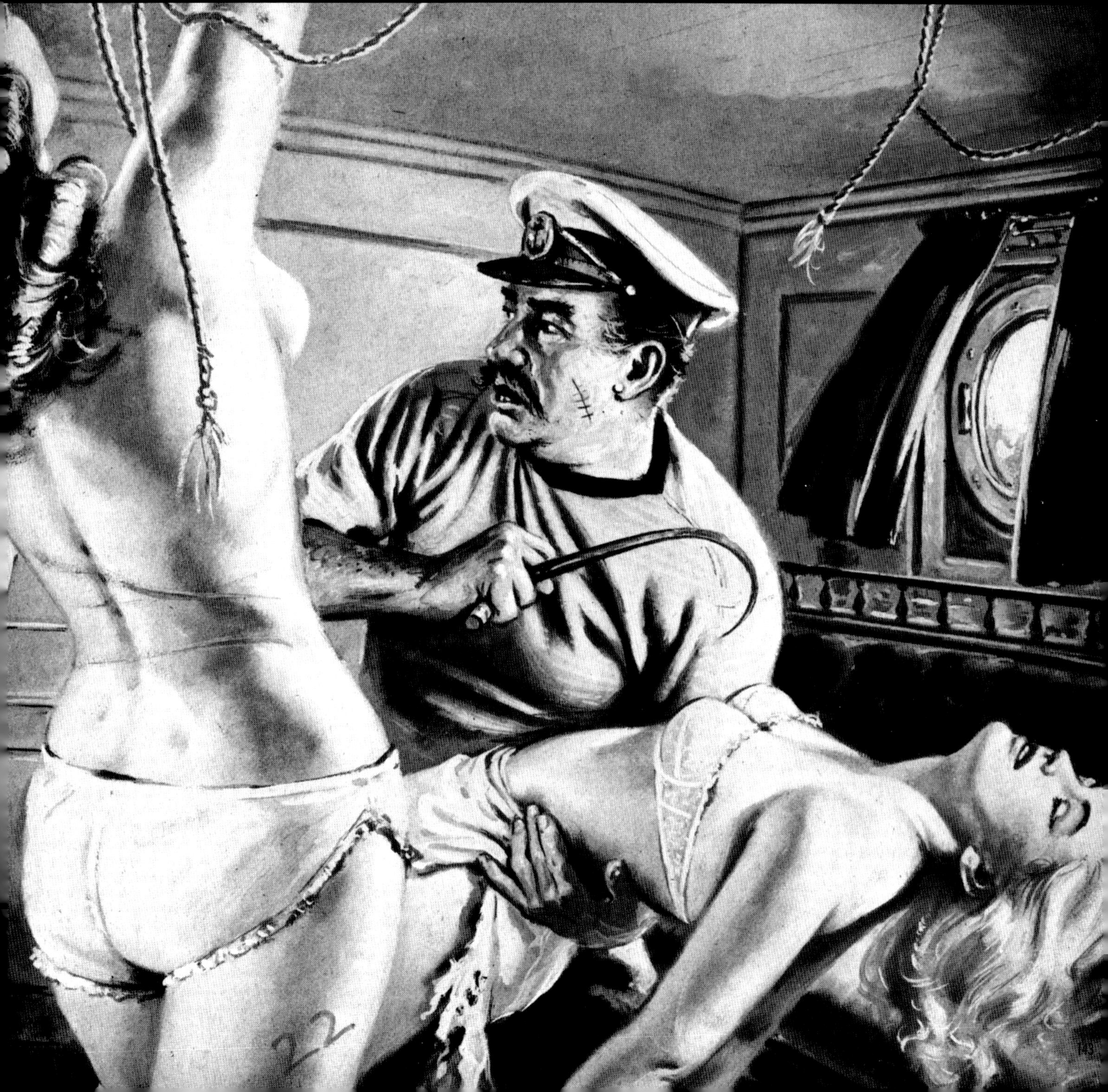

I could see the streams of sweat pouring down Chuck's brawny torso as he strained every muscle trying to pry the heavy hasp open.

"Guess you're right!" His shouted answer reached me through the cacophony of terrified screams coming from the trapped women.

And then I remembered the gun locker – the cache of illegal weapons that the greasy pig of a captain had so boastfully showed me several days before. I'd seen some hand grenades stacked next to the collection of guns and ammo – if they worked, they could blow the locks right off the doors. It seemed the only chance we had of freeing the women.

If we could get to the grenades before the flames did...

LIKE MOST people's serious troubles, mine had all started with a woman. She was a Sicilian sex-bomb, and I met up with her at the port of Catania, the Sicilian harbor at which we docked. I was working on an oil tanker at the time, and doing pretty well for an A.B. on an American flag carrier.

But by the time that black-haired witch of a Rosalia was through with me, I was broke, exhausted, and my ship was three hundred miles out at sea.

Yeah – I know. Jumping ship for a broad is pretty stupid. Especially when she turns out to be the type who steals you blind in less than a week and then throws you out. But by the time I was getting smart again, I was already in deep trouble. Being broke in Sicily is no joke for an *Americano*, and I couldn't go to the U.S. Consulate. I was a ship-jumper.

So I was feeling pretty battered and low, sitting in a waterfront dive wondering what the hell to do next, when a guy wandered over to my table. He said he'd seen me around with Rosalia and figured I might need a berth by now. He had one to offer.

I leapt at the chance – like the saying goes, "Beggars can't be choosers."

"Fine," he answered. "It's the *Lesaya* – and we sail at midnight. Just about gives you time to get your gear on board."

"What gear?" I answered laconically. "You think that dame left me anything?"

I cracked my last dollar paying for the gut-searing grappa drink in front of me, tossed the firewater down and pushed back my chair. I was ready to go.

As we walked along the waterfront on our way to the ship, I got the definite feeling that, although he had given me a job I needed desperately, I didn't like the *Lesaya*'s first mate. One look at the ship herself – a battered, rusty tramp – and I didn't think I was going to like her, either. But I was in no position to be choosy.

By the time we sailed three hours later I knew I'd landed on some kind of a hell ship. The only crew-member who didn't seem to be of the shifty-eyed, cut-throat type was Chuck McCabe, a young blond giant who was the *Lesaya*'s chief engineer. As soon as we got out to sea, we sort of fell in together. It was Chuck who put me wise to the *Lesaya* – and her cargo.

We were well into the Ionian Sea, on our way to the island of Thira in the Greek archipelago, when I remarked on how high we were riding.

"Light cargo," explained Chuck. Then he looked at me with a searching expression and added, "Or don't you know what we're carrying?"

"No," I answered, "I know damn-all about this tub – except that she's a wreck and has a slob for a captain. What's in the holds?"

"Women," said Chuck, in a strained voice. "Supplies for the Arabian joy houses – or the harems of oil-rich sheiks!"

"You're out of your mind!" I exploded.

"No," he insisted, "I'm not – and I'll prove it to you. Come on down. I'll show you."

We went below. As I peered through the thickly-barred, slotted, openings beside the steel doors that led into each of the four holds, I realized, to my horror, that Chuck wasn't kidding. The poorly-ventilated storage sections were filled with women!

Not one of them was fully dressed, and some were completely nude. I guessed most of them to be between seventeen and twenty-three, a vast selection of blondes, brunettes and redheads, light-skinned North Europeans and tawny-skinned Southerners. Their figures ran the full gamut from tall, slender and high-breasted to generously molded, ample-bosomed fullness.

"Captain Razzi says he has them stripped to prevent them trying to make a break," said Chuck as we went topside once more, "but my guess is he does it for his own convenience!"

I had ample proof of this the very next day. Captain Razzi – a tall, flabbily corpulent, tyrannical sonuvabitch – started off on one of his periodic drinking binges, and he soon made his way down to Hold No. 1. I happened to walk by its thick door about an hour later, and got myself an earful of shrieks of pain and wild scufflings that were going on inside.

When he finally emerged he dragged three of the women out with him, and pushed them along into his cabin. I caught a brief glimpse of the girls' faces before he shoved them into his quarters, and two of them had obviously been crying. The third was white with fear. None of them was over nineteen.

"Where the hell do they get these girls?" I asked Chuck later that evening.

"All over," came the reply. "I've been on this tub for just under a year, and I guess we've picked up what they call 'live cargo' in every dingy, fifth-rate port from the Mediterranean to the Aegean Sea."

He went on to explain that, while some of the girls were already hardened prostitutes, and well aware of their destinations, many of them were young innocents who had either been duped or sold into the deal. A few of them had actually been kidnapped, usually from small fishing villages along the coast.

My next question concerned the crew. By now, I knew that Captain Razzi had been in the white slave business for several years; it seemed strange that the law had never caught up with him. The crew didn't look like the most loyal group in the world – how come no one ever turned stoolie?

"Well," drawled Chuck thoughtfully, "I guess he chooses his crew pretty carefully. There isn't a one of us wants to have too much to do with cops. Seems we've all had our problems with them."

The seamen may have been a bunch of minor thieves, wanted by police in whatever port they came from, but the officers were a far more dangerous, degenerate-looking lot. God only knows what their police dossiers looked like. Led by Razzi, they delighted in shutting themselves in the holds with the women, making the captive females submit to every form of cruelty and perversion imaginable. We could hear the screaming and weeping that went on every time the men went in.

WE FINALLY docked at Thira, just long enough to stock up on food and provisions, and load some more "live cargo." Three girls were brought on board in the middle of the night. They were bound and gagged. I saw Razzi come up from his cabin to take a look at them.

Without a word he ripped their dresses open, exposing their full young bodies.

Grinning obscenely, he turned to the men who had carried the girls on board.

"They look pretty good," he grunted. "Take them to my cabin!"

The next day, the three newcomers were dragged down to Hold No. 3 to join the other captives. By that time, we were far out at sea again, heading for Port Said where the first batch of "live cargo" was to be unloaded.

The boiler started acting up soon after we had sailed past the island of Rhodes. Chuck told Razzi he thought we should put in to port and get the system properly repaired, but Razzi wouldn't hear of it.

"You've fixed it before – fix it again!" he roared, swaying slightly as he started off for the holds once more. "I want no delays on this trip!"

Chuck looked pretty worried when he came back up on deck again. He told me he'd got the boiler patched up, but the whole system was so dilapidated – as was most of the *Lesaya*'s equipment – that he feared the worst.

The worst came at 09:30 the next morning, when the boiler blew sky high. Panic hit immediately, and Captain Razzi gave his commands with a .45 revolver in his hand. Terrified of being caught with his illicit haul of "live cargo," he forbade the radio operator to send out an S.O.S. and ordered the crew into the motor lifeboats that were put over the *Lesaya*'s side.

I grabbed him by the arm as he was about to leave the ship.

"The women!" I shouted. "We've got to get them out!"

"Imbecile!" he snarled, shoving the nose of the .45 into my gut. "Who cares about those worthless cattle now – get out of my way!"

He shoved me aside, hoisted his heavy frame onto the rope ladder, and clambered down into the motorboat. Within minutes, Chuck and I were the only men on board – alone with several hundred women, a roaring fire that was spreading fast, and little, if any, chance for escape.

We knew the hold doors were all locked. Captain Razzi always carried the keys around with him, so our only hope was to force our way through to the captive women. It was during our rapid search for any kind of heavy implement – I finally found a crow bar and Chuck picked up an iron rod – that we saw the only remaining lifeboats.

There were two of them – battered, moth-eaten-looking tubs – but they were better than nothing.

"If we can only open those goddam doors, we've got a chance," gasped Chuck as we fought our way through the billows of smoke that belched up around us from the bowels of the ship.

But our frantic efforts to pry open the hasps, or smash off the door handles on Hold No. 1 proved fruitless. Pouring sweat at every move, blinded by the smoke and choking in the blazing heat, we battered away at the unyielding metal – only to find our straining efforts were scarcely denting the thick steel. All we were doing was wasting precious time – and we didn't have much of that left.

That's when I remembered the grenades in the captain's gun locker.

WE RACED to the skipper's cabin, which was abaft the bridge. Fortunately, the locker opened easily – Razzi must have forgotten to relock it when he got out his .45 – and we found the grenades stacked inside. We grabbed for them, stuffing our pockets full and carrying as many as we could. Then we ran back below deck.

The broiling hell had intensified. As I peered through the barred opening into one of the holds, the swirling mass of hysterical, shrieking women I saw heightened the horror of our predicament. They were clawing and fighting in frenzied terror, ripping at each other to get closer to the door, hammering on its heating surface with their balled fists and being trampled down by the next wave of desperate captives who sought frantically to smash their way out.

"Stand back!" I shouted through the opening. "We're trying to help you!"

But the women were beyond listening, and their ghastly shrieks drowned my shouted warning. Chuck and I had no choice – we'd have to risk wounding some of them in the grenade blasts if we were to save any women at all.

I propped two grenades under the hasp, pulled the pins and ducked around a corner of the passageway. Chuck and I crouched down as the explosion ripped through the corridor.

We rushed back. Our scheme had worked! Jabbing the crow bar into the now-shattered lock crevice, I pried the door open.

Scores of women tumbled out of the hold. Scratched, bleeding, their hair scorched and some of them badly burned, they ran wildly out into the passage.

"That way!" I shouted, pointing to the nearest ladder. "Up on deck!"

Chuck was already dealing with the next lock. Another explosion blasted through the passageway, and another horde of captives poured out. Two more grenade bursts, and all the women were free. But those who came out of Hold No. 4 were even more badly scorched and burned than the others. Several of them could hardly walk, and Chuck and I heaved the last two up on deck.

A scene of panic and horror greeted us there. The ship was ablaze and beginning to list. Many of the women had already hurled themselves overboard, while most of the others were running around wildly.

"We'll have to work fast," I grunted to Chuck, heading for the lifeboats. "Maybe they'll have sense enough to obey orders!"

Chuck and I yelled commands in every language we could think of. Shouts of "Here!" "*Ici*!" "*Acqui!*" gave some of the women the general idea, and they followed us swiftly to the boats. Thirty-five women clambered into the first one, and we got it launched. The second boat was smaller, but we managed to cram over two dozen females into it.

There were a couple of rafts and a whole slew of life jackets stashed on the foredeck. I got the rafts over the side while Chuck grabbed anything that would float and hurled it overboard. Then we handed out as many jackets as we could find, and told the women to jump for it.

"I've found another boat!" yelled Chuck. "Let's get it before this damn thing blows!"

All the women were overboard by this time. We launched the last boat in a matter of seconds. Once we were in the water, we picked up as many of the girls without jackets as we could. Others clawed feverishly at the sides, but we had to push them away, yelling at them to grab at anything that was floating nearby.

I dived into the water, pushed another woman on board in my place, and swam around trying to help the others. Meanwhile, Chuck had located the flares and flare-gun package in the lifeboat. Hoping against hope, he fired two into the bright clear sky. Despite the broiling sunshine, the flares' red blaze glowed vividly high overhead.

Fate, guardian angels, luck – call it what you will, but something was finally on our side that hell-filled day. Within an hour, a fishing smack appeared. The next thing on the scene was a small freighter, soon followed by two others. Then a couple more fishing boats arrived.

One by one, the exhausted women were hauled out of the water.

First aid was administered to those who were severely burned and injured, while the rest were given blankets and crew members' jackets to cover their nakedness.

Chuck and I were taken on board one of the freighters. The captain regarded us with deep suspicion – until the women who had been taken on with us explained what had happened. Their praise and almost maudlin gratitude may have been a bit embarrassing – but it sure saved our necks.

It also got us a ride to Beirut, at which point Chuck and I decided to face up to a lot of things. We went to the American Consulate, and told our stories straight. Things looked pretty rough for a while, but we finally managed to get our problems ironed out. I think the part we had played on the hell-ship may have made the authorities more lenient, but anyway, whatever the reasons, our past troubles were cleared up.

I never really knew what Chuck's problems were, but he seemed damn relieved to get the air cleared, once and for all. Both of us were soon on our way back to the U.S., and a fresh start.

Captain Razzi and his cohorts eventually fell into the hands of the Turkish police. How they got to Turkey was never quite clear – none of their stories tallied, which was only to be expected of that bunch of bastards. The last I heard, they were still answering questions in a Turkish prison, and police in several other countries seemed to be real eager to get their hands on them when the Turks had finished their interrogation.

Somehow, I think it's going to be a long time before Razzi and his pals set out to sea again.

The women who survived the ghastly ordeal they had been subjected to were finally sent back to their countries of origin. What happened to them after that is anybody's guess – but at least they got another chance in life.

I went back to sea soon after I landed back in the U.S. So did Chuck – but you can be sure of a couple of things.

Both of us are a damn sight more choosy about the berths we accept these days.

And I don't go in for that jumping-ship bit any more, for anything – and definitely not for women!

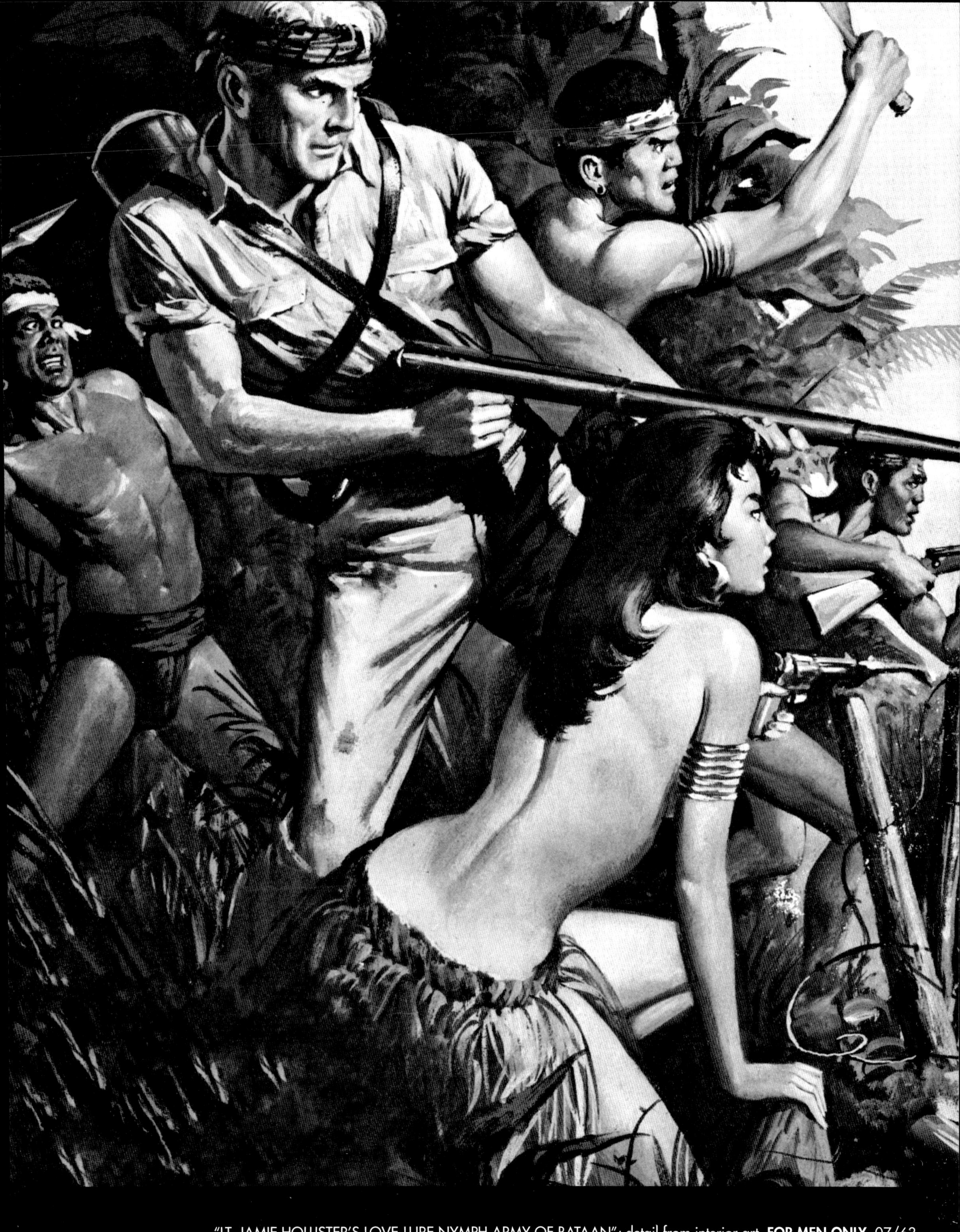

"LT. JAMIE HOLLISTER'S LOVE-LURE NYMPH ARMY OF BATAAN"; detail from interior art, **FOR MEN ONLY**, 07/63.
Art by Charles Copeland.

NUDE NURSES
FOR THE BEASTS OF BUSHIDO

"You scream! Yankees come! Imperial Japanese kill!" This was Katayama's hideous plan for his lovely captives.

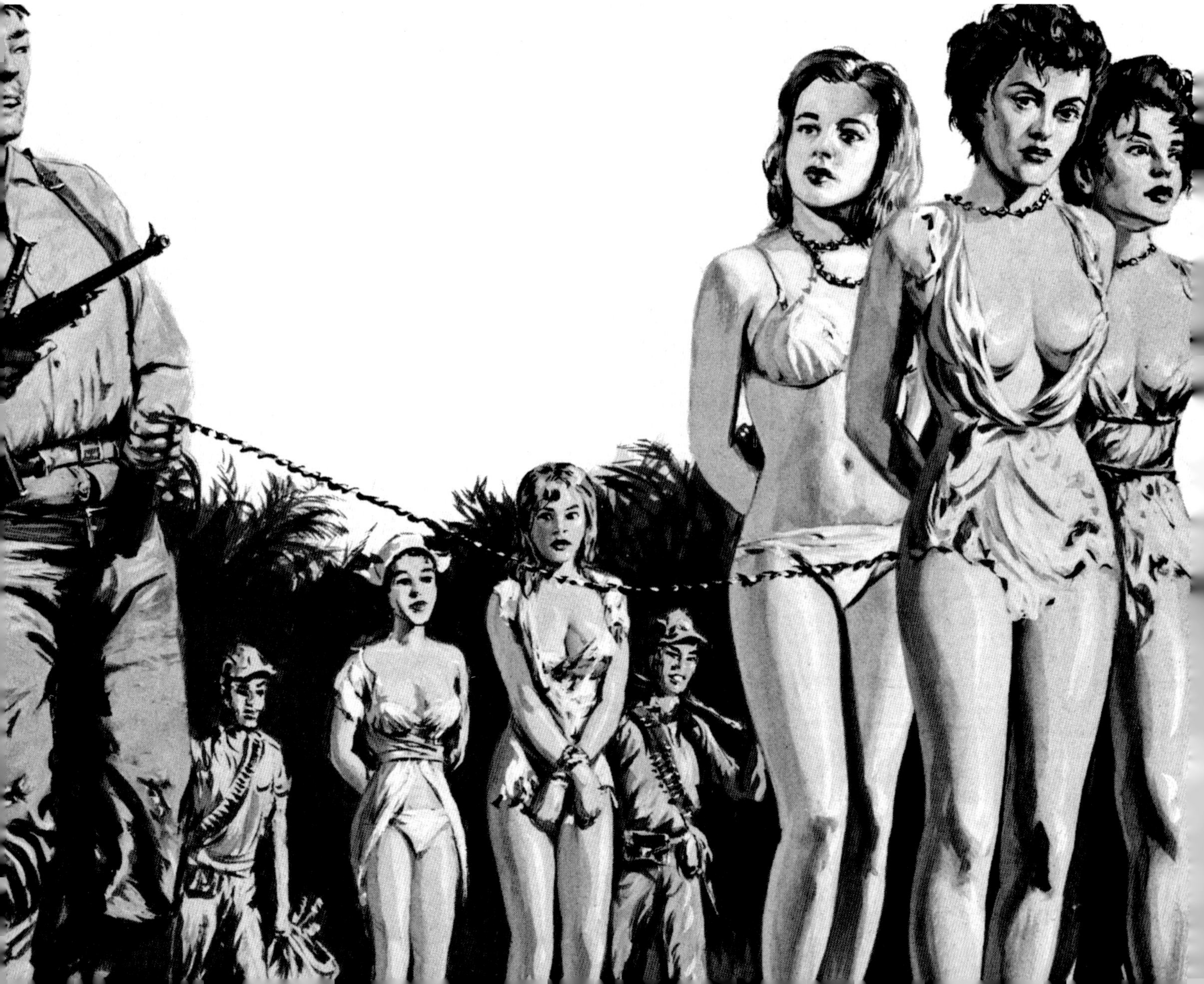

TRAYNOR KEPT HIS EYES glued to the Tarlac Road. He tried to forget the insistent pressure of the girl's thigh pressing against his. He heard the sharp intake of her breath and without even looking at her, he could tell what her respiration was doing to the taut bodice of her uniform.

The fresh fragrance of gardenias filled the ambulance's cab. Traynor glanced at her briefly, seeing the way her white uniform skirt had hiked up over her knees, showing the contrasting tan of her stocking tops. Briefly Traynor wondered what it would have been like with the girl at some other time or place. He put it out of his mind immediately. Tech sergeants assigned to the 11th Division Motor Pool didn't get to first base messing around with second lieutenants, even when the second lieutenants smelled of gardenias.

"1408 should be up about five miles the other side of Tarlac," Traynor said. He was talking more to himself than the two young nurses who shared his cab.

The one who called herself Mary Anne Palmer smiled

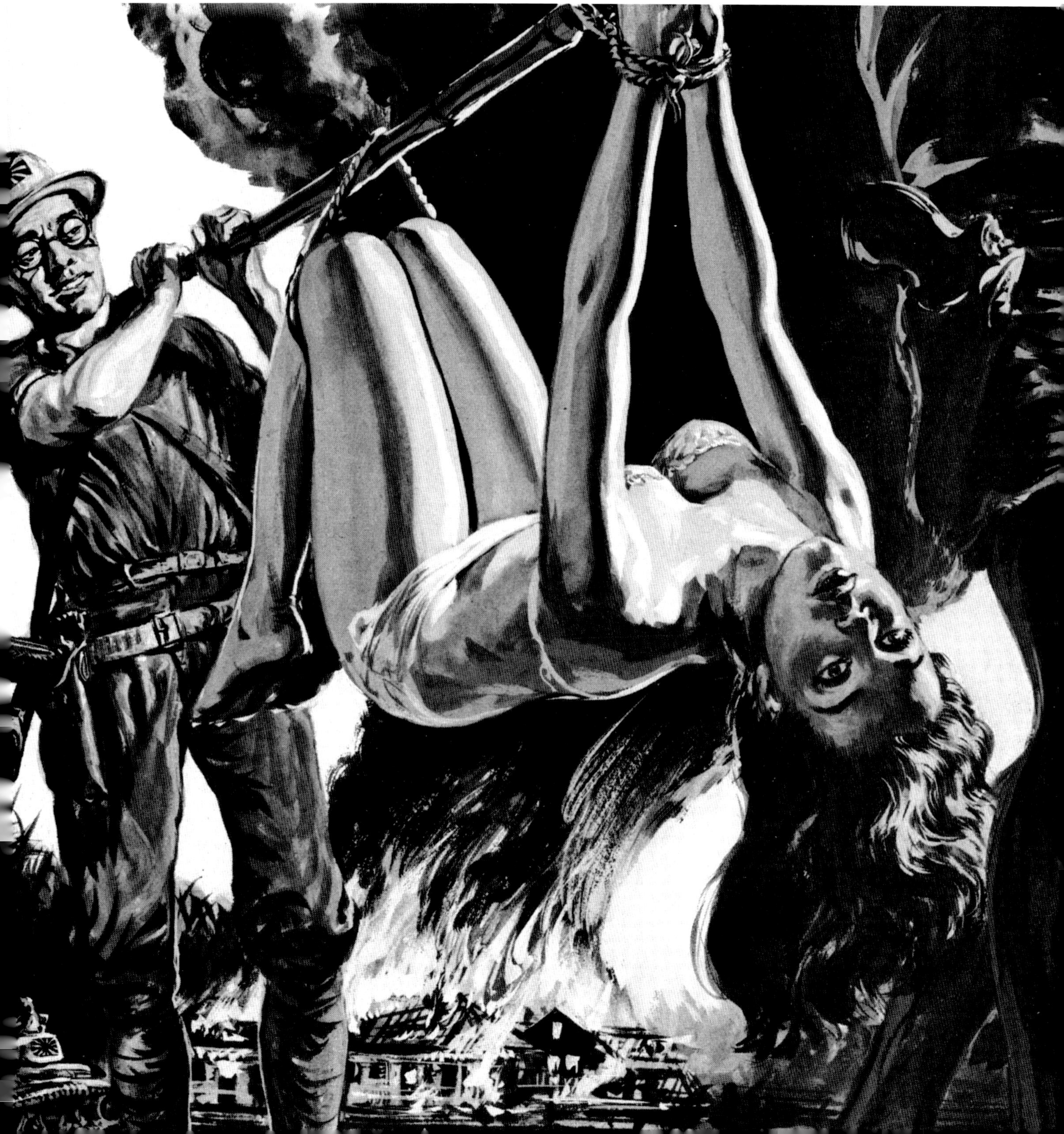

at him. "It'll be a relief getting there," she said in a slow Texas drawl. "By now I got a creak in my sacrum they can hear all the way back to Cowtown."

"Riding these roads must play hell with your kidneys, Sarge?" the tall brunette, Lois Overton, laughed.

Traynor grinned wryly. He wasn't used to being queried about his organs by commissioned officers. And he wasn't quite sure how he should answer his passengers.

When you were regular peace-time Army there were only two kinds of women in the world. The kind you rolled in a sack at the Bay View Hotel and the kind who'd spit at you if you walked down the same side of the street as they did. Neither one of these girls seemed to fall into either category.

"What's it like at a field hospital?" Mary Anne wanted to know.

"You kidding?"

"No, honestly. We were just sworn in this morning. The Army people down in Manila are recruiting every able-bodied nurse they can get their hands on. We were civilians at the Filipino Red Cross Center."

Traynor rubbed the stubble of his beard reflectively. Before he could answer the question, the ambulance skidded into a deep rut on the Tarlac road and he had to give all his attention to keeping the big truck from turning over.

Finally he said, "It's murder. That's what it is. The Japs don't respect hospitals any more than they respect women or anything else. Up at Lingayan the other day, they over-ran an evacuation tent. Lousy bastards bayonetted everything that moved. I'm telling you, Lieutenant, they aren't human."

He felt the shiver of fear go through the girl on his right. He was half-tempted to put his hand on her leg to steady her. Then he thought better of it. All he needed was to get slapped on report by some wet-behind-the-ears female shave-tail.

Mary Anne Palmer didn't appear to have been checked out on military protocol as yet. She wriggled closer to Traynor, searching for a sense of comfort.

"How close will we be to the front?" she asked in that slow Texas drawl.

"No way of telling. Everything's fluid up there. Nothing's going to stop those Japs. Damn it, I tell you it's a lousy shame. All we got is a bunch of guys shaking their guts out with malaria. No quinine, no air cover, no artillery. You know what those Japs have? They have 1940 G.M.C.'s. They have Fords and Chevvies. Maybe you can tell me how they got all those trucks."

He forced his back against the frayed leather cushion, trying to ease the strain. His eyes were two aching marbles in his head. Traynor remembered that he hadn't had a moment's sleep in the last seventy-two hours. He passed a hand over his forehead. The skin was hot and dry. He wondered whether he'd picked up the bug again.

Mary Anne Palmer touched his arm. Her blue eyes were wide with concern. "You all right, sergeant?"

"Yes m'am. Just fine. Never felt better in my whole life," he grimaced.

The mood of depression infected his riders. They fell silent, staring through the windshield at the never-ending luxuriant foliage. He wondered about the three other girls who were riding inside the ambulance. What were those kids thinking about?

"Damn it to hell," Traynor finally said. "This is no place for a woman."

"We'll be all right," Mary Anne answered. "Women are tougher than you think."

He thought of the bullet holes in the meat wagon's body. *Tough enough to stand up to a Nambu slug?* he said to himself.

A new sound caught his attention. It was the asthmatic wheezing of the carburetor. The engine coughed and sputtered. He reached for the dashboard choke, shoving it in and out rapidly. The engine gained new life. But he knew it was just temporary. You couldn't burn kerosene in an engine that was designed for gasoline and get away with it forever.

The roadside jungle held an ominous silence. The chattering of wild birds was the only sound to hear.

The hot sun sent shimmering heat waves bouncing off the dirt.

"We should be there in the next hour," he said, trying to get the edge of reassurance back into his voice. The girls didn't answer.

He knew something was bugging him. Slowly Traynor began to realize what it was. There should be other traffic on the road. Stuff should be moving up towards Lingayan. The wounded should be convoyed to Manila. However, the truck taking the nurses to Tarlac was the only vehicle in the area.

THEY DROVE on another twenty minutes before the ambulance finally conked out completely. Traynor cursed under his breath, got down from the cab and lifted the rusted hood. He knew damned well what the trouble was. The fuel line had been snafued by the emergency concoction he'd been burning.

He retraced his steps to the cab. In as simple language as he could muster, he explained the situation to the nurse recruits who now clustered around him.

"We'll have to walk it into Tarlac," he warned. "Maybe up there we'll be able to get you a lift to the 1408th."

Mary Anne Palmer fixed her clear, trusting eyes on him. "Sergeant," she said in that husky drawl of hers, "I think I'm talking for all the girls when I say that I want you to forget rank. We're nurses – not army. You tell us what you want us to do and we'll do it."

Traynor studied her for a moment, seeing her stand cool and fresh in the heat. He'd been right. She was different from any girl he'd known. He recognized now that there were more than two types of women in the world. In addition to the one you rolled at the Bay View and the one who spat at the sidewalk when you passed, there was another. She was the kind you dreamed about in the barracks when the loneliness grew to the point where you could taste it.

"Okay," he said quietly. "Stick to the side of the road. Single file. Keep ten paces between you." He didn't go any further. There was no sense scaring them any more than they were. It was time enough for them to learn about the Zeke strafing tactics if and when a flight came over.

Yet he felt their eyes boring into his back as he took the Thompson sub machine-gun from under the driver's seat and slung it over his shoulder.

They made a somewhat disconsolate-looking group as they plodded towards Tarlac, their heavy duffle bags weighing them down.

But it wasn't until they had reached the 1408th's area

itself that the full impact of their situation registered on them.

There were no signs of life in the main building or in the clearing. The 1408th had evacuated with its casualties and its personnel. Unbelievable as it might seem, scenes like this were being repeated all over the Philippines in the confusion and agony of defeat.

Tears shone in Lois Overton's eyes as she felt the solitude of the jungle touching her. She looked at Traynor with a mixture of accusation and dependence. "What do we do now?" she asked.

"Nothing much we can do, Miss," Traynor answered. "We'll just have to sweat it out here until someone comes along with transportation."

Inside, the hospital cots still bore the marks of the injured men who had occupied them. Blankets were strewn on the floor, abandoned where they had fallen. Everything pointed to the haste of the evacuation which had probably been carried out only a few hours before.

Fighting down his own terror, Traynor ordered the girls around him. He'd been in the army long enough to know that the only antidote for panic was work. That was what the brass always figured when they set out the details.

"There may be some more guys coming down from Lingayan," he told them. "If there are, they're going to need help in a hurry. As long as we're here, why don't we police up the place."

He watched the nurses folding soiled linen and moving the cots about and he felt better. At least they had enough restraint left not to push the panic button.

Even as she worked, Mary Anne smiled to herself. This man Steve Traynor was quite a guy. Maybe he was rough-talking. And maybe if things had been different, she would never have noticed him.

She thought of how it would have been if this were not December 20th, 1941 and if Manila were not tottering under the crushing sledge hammer blows of the Imperial Japanese Army.

No, there wouldn't have been a truck driver by the name of Traynor in her life. She'd have been with Dr. James Murray. They'd be walking through the Plaza Ferguson or sipping drinks at the German Club, or just sitting on one of the lovely hills outside of Manila, drinking in the cool breezes. They would be laughing or serious. They would talk or remain silent. It wouldn't make any difference.

She remembered the first time she had surrendered completely to Jim Murray. Perhaps she should have felt a sense of shame concerning the affair. But now she was glad that they had been able to make use of the little time allowed them before the coming of war.

In her mind's eye, she was standing once more in the small room of the Spanish-type hacienda. Jim Murray was slightly behind her. She could feel his strong body pressing into her back.

Slowly she reached for his hands, drawing them around her, placing her own soft palms over his slim fingers and squeezing them. She'd felt the muscles of his arms tense and her own being had cried out for him.

Her breasts heaved upward against the Japanese silk print dress she wore. Jim pressed his lips against the top of her golden head.

He freed his hand from her grasp and moved it across the smooth column of her throat. The room was silent accept for the urgency of their breathing.

She'd twisted in his arms, until she stood facing him, her lips half open, soft and inviting, her eyes studying him. She pressed her softly curved body against his lean hardness, gaining an inner sense of strength from him.

She'd taken his chin in her hands, tilting his head down until his lips brushed hers. The electric charge had flown through her in a delicious spasm of desire.

"I'm a wanton hussy, and you'll hate me. But damn it, I don't care!" she'd cried as she'd broken away from him just long enough to undo the snaps of her dress. She'd felt all of her modesty shuffled off as the frock fell around her ankles. Standing before her lover dressed in the merest gauzy wisps of pink bra and panties, she had waited for him to claim the prize which no other man had ever received from her.

Now she wondered whether her surrender was a result of the times. The times seemed to confuse everything. Would she have given herself so willingly to Jim Murray if he hadn't been carrying his orders to active duty in his pocket? Would the moment of surrender have been so excruciatingly lovely? There was no way of telling.

She wondered whether under other circumstances she might have surrendered just as completely to the tech sergeant who now was her sole protector.

The times, she decided, make us do very strange things.

WHATEVER THOUGHTS of the past the others had were buried deep within them. They moved through the deserted building, not looking at each other, not talking. Finally Traynor broke the silence.

"I'm going to post myself as a lookout on the roof. You stay under cover. Are there any questions?" Before any of the girls could answer, he hefted the sub machine-gun to his shoulder and clomped out.

The interior of the hospital began to swelter. The stench of infection seemed to have crept into the walls. Now it oozed out at the girls as the faint odor of disinfectant failed to cover it.

Lois Overton lit one cigarette from another. Her hand shook slightly as she flicked away the spent butt. Ruth Kulowski stood staring out of the window-waiting – for what, she didn't know.

Sue Redmond whistled a refrain of the *Beer Barrel Polka*. It sounded flat and off-key.

"This heat is murder," Ruth said.

"What happens now?" Lois muttered.

Nobody answered. The minutes dragged by. Outside the angry screech of a monkey shattered the calm. Then there was only the chirping of birds. The afternoon sun boiled through the windows. Mary Anne thought of Traynor standing his watch in the blazing heat.

"I'm going up on the roof to relieve the sergeant," she finally said. "He's probably half-dead from the heat and lack of sleep."

The scraping of her heels on the tin roof caused Traynor to jump. He whirled swiftly, swinging his Tommy in a nervous arc. His eyes were hollow and rimmed in purplish black circles, giving him the appearance of a starving owl.

Mary Anne's hand fluttered in a tremulous wave.

Traynor recognized her and managed a grin. She saw his eyes squinting at her and she realized that the lowering sun was silhouetting her figure so that she would appear to Traynor as if she had no clothes on.

Strangely, the thought did not upset her. She enjoyed Traynor's stare of frank appreciation. Even in this time and place she could not help wanting to be a desirable woman.

The same sensations which had flooded through her that time with Jim Murray came back to her again. For just an instant, she longed to have Traynor seize her in his powerful arms.

The big man broke the mood as he knelt on the tin roof and indicated a spot next to him. "I don't like it," he half-whispered. "There is something out there. I can feel it. Yet whatever it is, it's just waiting."

His eyes swept the circular clearing. He squinted again as the sun's rays blinded him. Mary Anne followed his every move, sensing the terror growing in her.

Below she heard a door slam. Little Ruth Kulowski appeared in the clearing, her arms laden down with blankets. She staggered under her load as she moved towards the clothesline.

The silence erupted in a staccato burst of machine gun fire. Ruth Kulowski spun completely around so that she seemed to be looking directly at Mary Anne. Her mouth was open in a silent scream of protest. Her fingers tore at her breasts, trying to ease the terrifying pain.

Traynor was on his feet. He cursed the sun as his Tommy spat flame. "The bastards!" he cried. "I can't see the lousy bastards! Where are they?"

The Japs had used their favorite trick. They'd come in with the sun at their backs, making it practically impossible to fire at them with any degree of accuracy.

The entire underbrush appeared to explode with gun fire.

"Down!" Traynor shouted hoarsely. His arm swept behind him, caught Mary Anne around the waist and hurled her to the roof.

Hearing the screaming slugs whistling around her head, she looked up at the sergeant who stood with his legs wide spread, the muscles bulging in his bare arms, the Tommy sweeping the jungle with its chattering death.

He stood that way for perhaps thirty seconds and then with a curse on his lips, hurtled from the roof. Mary Anne Palmer hid her face in her hands. She felt her body shaking with uncontrollable sobs.

They came out of the undergrowth like a legion of giant, bloated bugs. The blanket rolls hunched up their shoulders and the green woolen tunics of their uniforms made them look grotesque and hump-backed. They came out and stood and waited. One probed the soft body of Ruth Kulowski with his combat boot. His eyes glinted as he studied the disarrayed clothing and the whiteness of her exposed flesh.

One of them, who seemed larger than the others, cupped his hands to his lips. "American personnel please to surrender. Honorable Japanese soldier give you one minute. Please to come out with hands behind necks. Please not to make Japanese soldier wait."

Mary Anne heard the hospital door swing open. She saw the other girls come stumbling out. They held their elbows high, their fingers laced behind their slim necks. The action thrust their breasts out and the fact was not lost on the Japs.

Now the Jap in charge cupped his hands again. "Ah so," he yelled in his sing-song. "Women on roof not come, Japanese soldier go bang bang." The sun caught the glint of his eye glasses. He held his Nambu against his shoulder. His trigger finger showed white at the knuckle.

Numb with terror, Mary Anne rose to her feet. She saw their evil, leering eyes as the breeze caught her skirt and swirled it around her thighs. The Jap below gestured with his rifle and Mary Anne placed her hands behind her neck as the others had done. A minute later she was in the clearing below with the other nurses as a group of jabbering *sake*-laden soldiers herded them into a ragged line.

When she didn't move quickly enough to suit her captors, Mary Anne felt the sharp tip of a bayonet digging into her spine. Rage at the indignity drove out her feelings of panic and pain.

Finally the Japs had the girls lined up in a row. The officer in charge of the Jap patrol strutted up and down before them, a heavy samurai sword dangling from his paunchy waist. His gold-capped front teeth showed in a perpetual grin.

"I Lieutenant Katayama, Okamura unit," he sing-songed. "Where you men?"

Lois Overton looked at the body of Traynor lying broken and twisted where it had fallen. Her eye traveled to Ruth Kulowski. Mary Anne Palmer followed her gaze.

"We are nurses and this is a United States Army Hospital. We surrender ourselves as prisoners of war and invoke the articles of the Geneva Convention," Mary Anne said, amazed that she could keep the tremor out of her voice.

Katayama moved slowly. His expression had not changed. He waddled towards Mary Anne on his bandy legs. As he closed the distance between them, she could see the crazed bloodlust in his eyes.

"Ah so," he almost whispered. Like a snake striking, his hand shot backward. It was a vicious blur as it cracked into Mary Anne's face with the force of a whip. The young nurse felt the ground rushing up to meet her. She landed with a heavy thud. The pain exploded in her stomach as Katayama kicked her.

She knew that her skirt had ridden up around her waist to reveal her plump young hips clad only in brief pink silk panties. She knew the sight of her semi-nakedness would only serve to inflame the Japs further. Yet she was too weak even to make the attempt to cover herself. She lay on the hot ground, gasping and choking for breath.

The Jap continued his march before his captives. He seemed to be conducting a war of terror, and his silence of the moment was part of that war.

Finally he turned to them. "Prisoners please to remove uniforms so you can be searched for weapons." Once again Lois Overton answered. Even in her own pain and daze, Mary Anne had to marvel at her friend's cool courage.

"We are nurses and non-combatants. We carry no weapons."

"Ah so, please to remove uniforms or Japanese soldiers do it."

Katayama moved with his snake-like speed again. He gripped Lois' wrist in his strong hands and twisted it behind her. Mary Anne heard the girl cry out in agony. She saw her body jack-knife to relieve the strain on her shoulder. Lois' face was white and her teeth bit into her lip. Katayama held her in his grasp, savoring the sensation of her soft body struggling against his. Suddenly he thrust her from him. The three girls who remained standing looked at each other in the torment of helplessness. Slowly they unbuttoned their uniforms and let them fall at their feet. The Japs gathered around them, poking at their nearly naked bodies with probing hands, running their fingers over the soft silk of their captives' bras and panties.

Katayama barked a string of Japanese at the men. Three of them disappeared into the undergrowth and returned quickly. They carried heavy coils of rope with them.

Sue Redmond struggled in their grip. But her struggles were meaningless against the Japs' strength. Quickly they roped her hands behind her back and dropped a heavy rope over her neck to fashion a cruel halter.

One by one, the other girls were treated in similar manner. The sight of the atrocity was enough to lend new strength to Mary Anne. She willed herself to rise to her knees and had almost made it to her feet when she caught Katayama's attention.

"Ah so, American woman speak Geneva Convention... Katayama show her Japanese convention!" he grunted as he took a bayonet from an enlisted man and placed it at the hollow of her throat, inexorably forcing her backward with the point. Once again she lay on her back on the ground as Katayama stooped beside her. He gripped the bodice of her uniform in his sweating hands. The other Japs crowded around him. Inch by inch he tore the garment away from her. His cheeks puffed in and out with the effort and he breathed heavily as he saw her beauty helplessly displayed before him.

He looked down the length of her body, seeing the upthrust of her breasts against her satin bra, surveying the flatness of her belly, the full swell of her hips in her delicately feminine panties. She felt her hands being lifted from the ground and held in the air. She watched cords descend around her wrists and felt the vicious bite into her soft flesh. Desperately she kicked out at her tormentors, but they had anticipated her. As she writhed on the ground, they seized her feet and tied her ankles together.

Now they added a new element of horror by shoving a heavy bamboo pole under her bound ankles and wrists. Four sweating, grunting Japs stepped forward and lifted the pole on their shoulders.

Mary Anne hung from her bindings like a hog tied and being carried to the slaughter.

THE MARCH was a hideous agony for Mary Anne. Low hanging thorns and branches whipped at her naked flesh. The bouncing cadence of the Japs who carried her jarred her bound body mercilessly. The pain in her side where Katayama had kicked her became unbearable. Her head swam with the pain and at last she fainted.

When she came to, she found herself hanging by the thumbs from a tree in some sort of a clearing. Her first conscious sensation was the revulsion she felt at a high-pitched scream. She blinked her eyes open in disbelief.

The other nurses had been similarly treated. They hung in a small semi-circle. Their naked bodies glistened with perspiration. Their eyes were wide and their faces were etched with pain.

Only Katayama and one other guard were in the clearing. The Jap guard held a glowing cigarette in his hand. He moved towards Lois Overton. The tip of the cigarette ground against her flesh, cascading a shower of sparks to the ground below.

Lois shrieked in unendurable pain. Her muscles constricted and her body swung backwards. The effort tore at her thumbs bringing a new wave of pain.

Katayama moved to Mary Anne. "Soon we see if American soldiers come. We trap them," he giggled.

Katayama's eyes rolled around in his head. He'd gotten himself filthy drunk on *sake*. He reached up and pinched Mary Anne.

The plan was diabolical. The heart-rending screams of the tortured girls echoed through the hills.

"Katayama know many ways make women scream. He show them all to blonde American. She scream loudest, you bet," he gloated.

Mary Anne closed her eyes. She allowed her head to fall forward on her naked breast.

Katayama wouldn't let her remain in that position. He picked up a split bamboo rod from the ground. It whistled in its arc. Pain – all-consuming and nauseating – flooded through Mary Anne's body. Her scream answered Lois' gurgled moan.

"Japanese soldiers all around. You scream. Americans come. Honorable Japanese know what to do, you bet," the sadist gibbered.

In the next hour pain became a constant thing for Mary Anne. She knew that her mind must be snapped by it. Insanity and death were her entire world now.

She paid no attention to the rattle of gunfire nor the high-pitched screams and low-growled curses which flooded the clearing. She had no sensation of being cut down and carried over a man's shoulder. Nothing mattered but the pain.

It wasn't until three days later when she became rational again that she learned of her release. The Japs had miscalculated. They had set their trap for Americans, feeling that they would come plunging wild-eyed through the undergrowth. But they hadn't reckoned with the jungle cunning of the Huk guerrilla forces. The Filipino tree-men had swept in from above instead of on the ground. That had made the difference.

Two weeks later, the girls were ready to travel. Under cover of night they were spirited to the coast where an American sub picked them up and evacuated them to the Rock.

For weeks they lay underground in Corregidor's improvised sick bay. Then on March 13, 1942 they were ordered to Australia – a scant month before Wainwright's surrender.

Mary Anne Palmer recovered in time to take part in the recapture of Manila as a captain attached to the 32nd Division Medical Department. She stayed on after the war, caring for Philippine war orphans.

It would be nice to say that she found Dr. Jim Murray again.

But Murray, like many others, had died on the Bataan Death March.

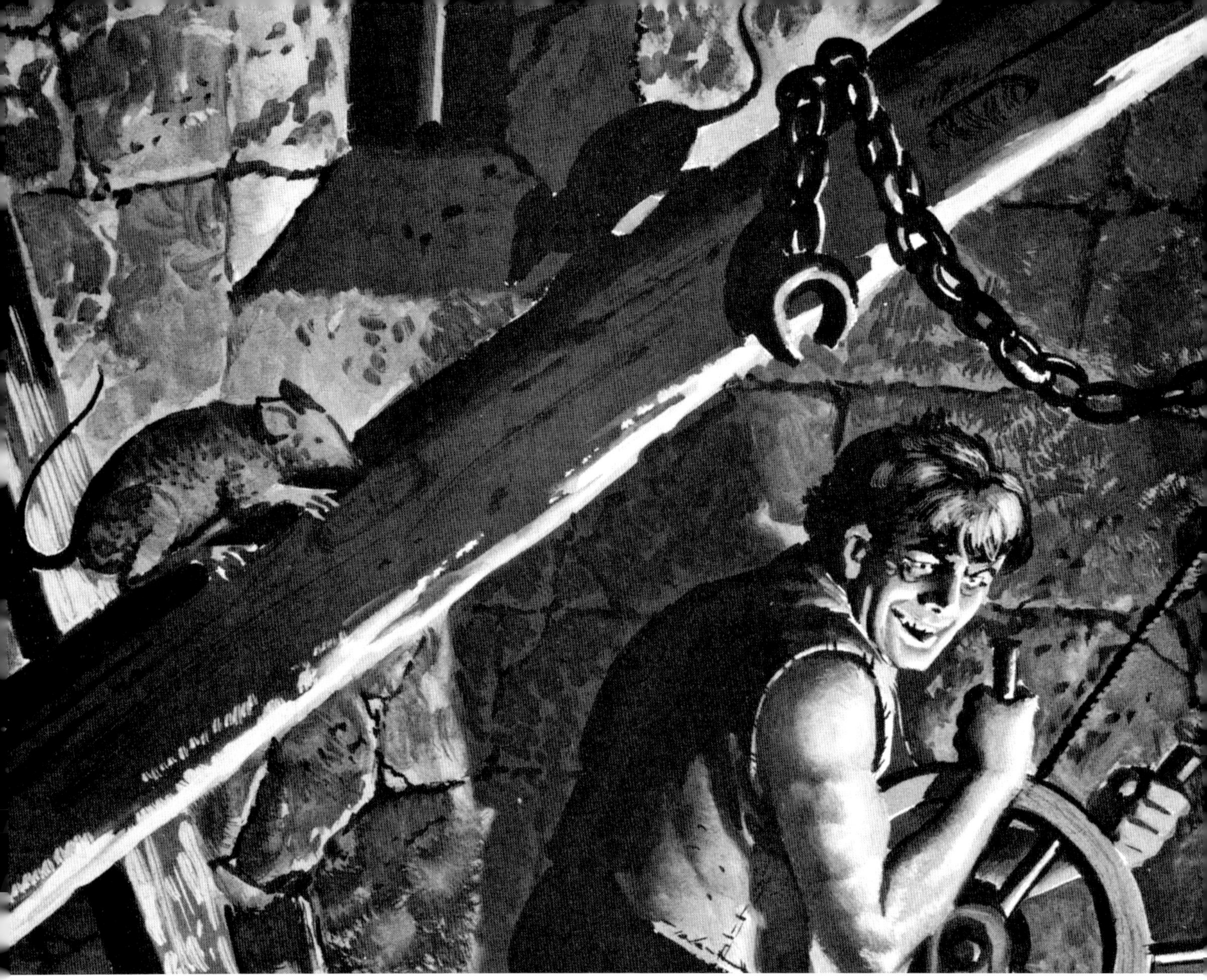

TRAPPED BEAUTIES IN THE DEVIL'S DEN OF AGONY

The Devil made a monster his guardian of the pit of Hell, where lovely young women shrieked for death.

THERE WAS THE HOUSE, a big stone affair, bulking like a tomb in the darkness.

In a basement window light flickered, light that shone dimly across the flat lands of the section, light that died with distance, weak and yellow.

If a man approached the house closely enough, he

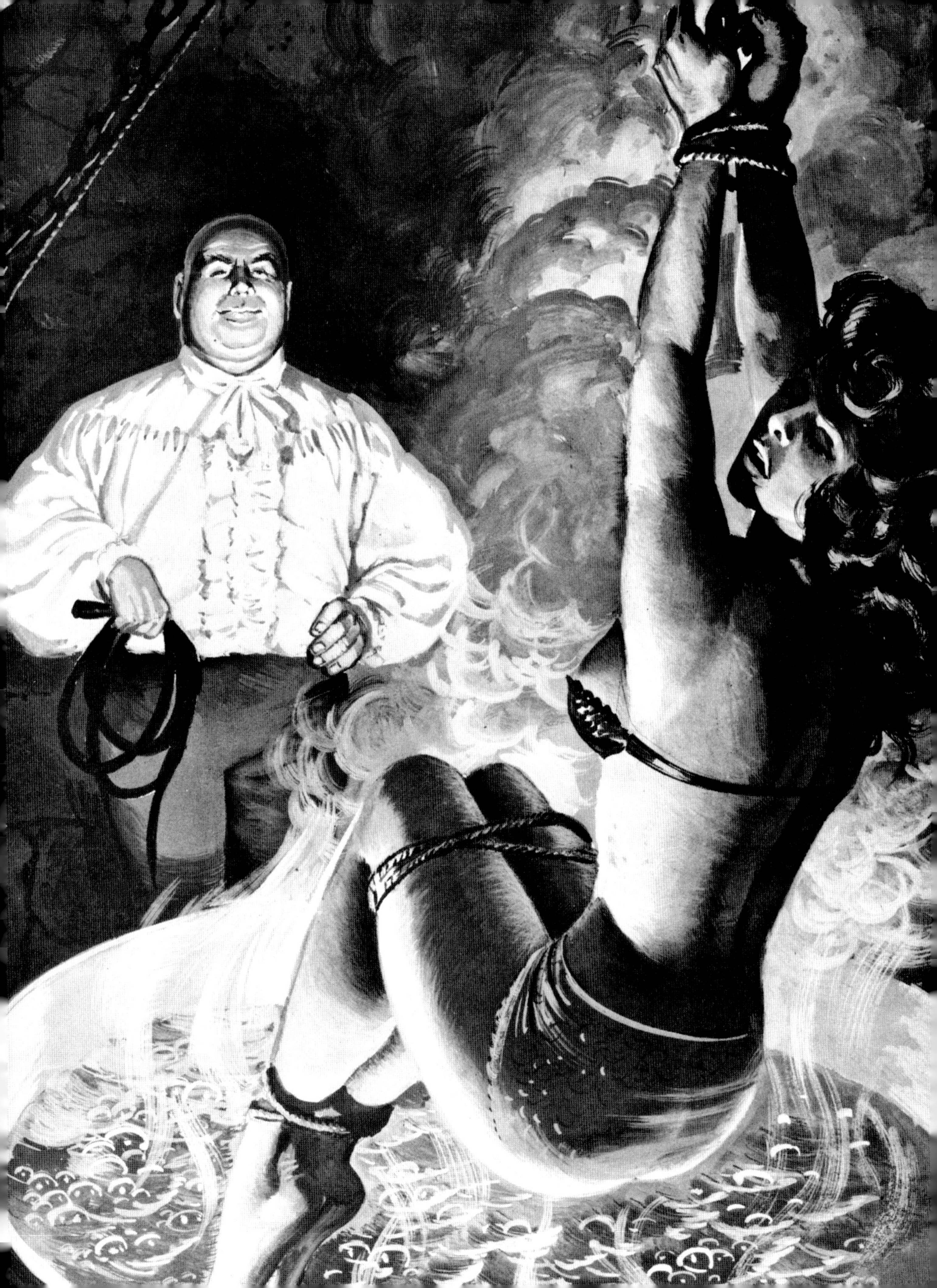

would hear screams. He would recoil, in horror, at the sound of those screams, torn by agony from throats raw with pleading and despairing terror.

But no one approached...

No one except the Graf von Leichnis, and his chosen assistants... and the women.

It was the women who screamed.

That night, in the cellar, the Graf von Leichnis stared at his prisoner. His wide flat eyes glittered, a muscle in his cheek jumped: that was all. His voice, when he spoke, was a high-pitched, incurably insolent whine: "Fritz, strip the little one. Let us see all of her now."

The girl, spread-eagled to the wall of the room, her back pressed hard against the rough stone, babbled her fright in a low-German dialect: "Oh, no... you mustn't ... please, let me go... what are you going to do to me?... let me go..."

Fritz paid her stammerings no attention. He came forward, a small knife glittering in the torchlight as he moved it in his hand. The girl was wearing a coarse smock; a few deft slashes with the knife and the cloth fell away.

Her naked body shone with damp sweat in the torchlight.

The Graf von Leichnis nodded slowly, his heavy-lidded eyes taking in every detail of the fettered body before him. The girl's face was distorted now by fear and shame, the eyes wide, the mouth trembling.

"Please..." she whispered. "Let me go... who are you, what do you want?"

"Please..."

"Your name!" The Graf made a gesture, and Fritz slapped the girl's face, once, hard.

She gasped, and then stammered: "Gr-Greta, Sire. Greta Fierzin."

"Well, Greta," the Graf said smoothly, "do you know why you are here? Here, in my castle, two miles from the nearest road, five miles from any town?"

"Let me go..." The girl's fear and shame had made her incapable of logical thought: only the simple plea remained on her trembling lips.

"You are here," the Graf went on, his voice exactly as even as before, "because you are a woman. It is sufficient."

Some glitter in his flat eyes caught the girl's attention. "God protect me!" she burst out. "You're mad! You're mad!"

To this the Graf gave no reply. Instead he gestured to Fritz once more. "Prepare her."

Fritz checked the girl's bonds, pulling them a little tighter until, stretched and helpless, she began to moan softly with pain.

Then the Graf himself came forward, holding carelessly a long black whip. He let its tip trail on the stone floor as he came toward the girl, and her moans grew to shrieks as she saw it.

But there was no escape.

"You are a woman," the Graf said again. "It is enough."

He drew the whip back – and lashed the girl's body with full force.

Greta's screams grew worse – but the Graf only brought the whip back again... and again.

Greta was babbling insanely now, begging for release or for mercy, screaming the names of her mother and father, calling for rescue.

And the whip flashed toward her helpless body once again!

Fritz smiled wetly, watching. The Graf continued to lash the girl as her screams grew hoarse, as her body jerked uncontrollably against the rough stone. Now the red stripe-marks that criss-crossed her nude flesh were welling blood, a few droplets first and then trickle to stain the floor, to stain the wall behind her.

Her eyes were wide and white, her body sheened with sweat, her hands clenching with agony in their fetters.

And still the whipping went on!

At last, with a final moan, Greta's head dropped to her breast, the eyes closed, the body sagged.

"She has fainted," the Graf said.

"Sixty strokes of the whip!" Fritz added. "She is strong, this one. She will last a long time."

The Graf nodded, his eyes veiled as if he were thinking. "When she wakes," he said at last, "I want all preparations made for the Vat."

"Ah!" Fritz's smile grew wider. "You are to try the new method tonight?"

The Graf nodded. "It will be interesting to see how this one dies."

"It will take her a long time..."

The Graf's mouth grew stern. He stared insolently at the unconscious, tortured body of the girl. "Good," he said. "Very good."

ABOUT THE Graf Eberhardt von Leichnis history has collected hundreds of legends. He was for his time what de Sade and others were for a later century and another country: a monster so unbelievable that he became legendary.

His father, who had gained the title of Graf (equivalent to the English Count) in service during a violent peasant's outbreak, died when Eberhardt was ten years old, and left to the boy and his mother no more than a title, a castle and the empty thanks of a grateful Prince.

But thanks, even from so great a man as was the Austrian Prince of the sixteenth century, would never pay for food or the upkeep of the castle. And Eberhardt's mother was far from well.

Eberhardt was studying in a small private school when his father died. Within six months, he was out of the school and hard at work.

The castle itself was leased to others, and Eberhardt's mother took over a smaller stone house which was available cheaply, because of its distance from any town or even from a main road.

And so the two of them, Eberhardt and his ailing mother, lived for the succeeding ten years.

It is unfair, of course, to blame Eberhardt's mother for what she was forced to do – but Eberhardt himself seems to have done so. He had liked school, had liked the high position his title gave him among other young scholars, had liked the pranks and the freedom of that life... and now he was reduced to grinding toil and poverty. It was a great step down the ladder, and Eberhardt never got over it.

His mother was at fault, he told himself. She didn't care about him: she only wanted to live on his earnings.

And from his mother, hatred spread.

Women, he realized slowly, were at the root of all the evils of the world. It was women who chained men down, women who forced them to work and toil and sweat, while the women merely sat at home and enjoyed themselves.

He shared these views with a boy named Fritz Heldheim, whom he met in the local alehouse after his work was done (he had become a scribe, set to writing letters and copying out dispatches and briefs for lawyers and others). Fritz, comparatively speaking, was a rich boy: he had an assured income from some land which was enough to keep him in comfort for the rest of his life. By contrast, the lease of the von Leichnis castle and grounds did no more than defray a few of the expenses of life: perhaps bad management on the part of Eberhardt's mother was responsible for this, but, if so, it is certainly excusable in a woman who had no opportunity to learn of business matters – and it is certainly the greatest blame she can be accused of carrying.

But Fritz's story merely added fuel to Eberhardt's hatred. And Fritz, for whose sadism we have good evidence, but no means of knowing its original cause, gave direction to this hatred... so that, when Eberhardt was twenty and his mother died, the two young men joined forces, moved into the now-empty stone house and began to convert it to its new use.

It was to be a chamber of tortures.

At first, following a pattern of sadism centuries old, Eberhardt and Fritz began with fire-branding irons, heated red-hot, applied to various parts of the female body. Then it was torches, and then (a leaf from the book of the Inquisition at Nuremberg and elsewhere) the red-hot metal chair, into which a victim could be strapped: as a fire underneath heated the chair, the victim roasted slowly, alive and conscious, screaming incredibly as his time of torment continued.

Some Inquisition records show as much as twenty-four hours in what was called the "witch-chair." The Graf von Leichnis, unofficially, bettered those records with his shrieking victims.

The Inquisition provided other hints, too – the spiked rollers, which tore flesh as they were rolled slowly over it; the infamous torment of the "scavenger's daughter," in which the victim was locked inside a great hoop and left while the body's muscles cramped, and tightened, and screamed in agony; the variety of whips and spikes...

But besides all that, the Graf and Fritz liked to invent torments of their own.

They drew their victims from nearby towns, stole them from the night-dark streets or from the roads, never visiting the same town twice within sixty days. There was always a fresh supply, and there was little danger of being caught.

And on these new victims the experiments began.

Lighted splinters under the toes and fingernails, and then jabbed elsewhere throughout the body... pressing to death with huge stones tearing limb from limb by winches...

And now it was the turn of a new torment – the Vat!

GRETA FIERZIN awoke slowly, her mind half-drugged by the dull continuing pain of her lashed flesh. At first she hardly remembered where she was... and then, as her eyes opened, she saw the flickering light of the stone room, the two figures standing before her, watching her... and she screamed!

"Oh, God, kill me! Let me die, but don't hurt me any more! Please, have pity – have mercy–"

"Prepare her," the Graf ordered.

Fritz cut the girl's body down.

She sagged in his arms, wanting desperately to fight but too weak from the whipping to do more than jerk feebly as he carried her to the center of the room and propped her there with his body while he drew down a long rope from the vaulted ceiling.

He attached the rope to her bleeding wrists – and then, stepping back, began to pull her up!

Her screams began again, howls of naked agony as the strain on her wrists increased. Irresistibly, she was being drawn up into the gloom of the faraway ceiling – her toes barely brushed the ground and she fought madly to stand upright – and then her wrists bore all her weight, as she hung, suspended, nude, in the torchlight of the Graf von Leichnis' torture chamber!

She tried to kick out, to get herself somehow free – but every motion only made the pain in her wrists greater, and at last she subsided, quiet, sobbing with torment, completely helpless.

Beneath her, there was movement. She looked down.

A great vat was being wheeled into position. Steam came from the vat, and even before the Graf spoke she knew, by look and odor, what awaited her.

A shudder of absolute horror overcame her.

"This vat contains boiling oil," the Graf said calmly. "We will lower you close to it – but you may save yourself if you will."

The faint hope his words seemed to hold out sustained Greta as the rope creaked slowly down, as she drew closer and closer to the terrible surface of that searing liquid, close enough to feel the heat of it rise to meet her like a blow, parching her...

She drew up her legs, farther and farther, as the rope continued to descend.

"Oh, God, don't...!" she shrieked.

And the rope stopped.

"There," the Graf said. "You see, my pretty one? As long as you maintain your position you will not be burned. But if you relax... the oil awaits you."

He did not even smile: he merely stood, watching flatly. But Fritz's wet grin gleamed in the light.

Greta, her legs drawn up, tensed, knew only fear now. All that was left for her was the avoidance of final and agonizing death: she could not move, could not relax.

She shrieked, pleading for release, promising anything, half-insane now with terror and pain, while the Graf and Fritz watched from below.

The pain in her arms, in her legs, grew worse.

She could not maintain her position...

A minute ticked by. Another.

She screamed horribly as her legs, failing, began to relax.

Then her toes touched the surface of the oil, and the sudden searing agony of that burn shot through her!

"*God – save me–!*" she screamed as the oil lapped at her toes, at her feet, her ankles.

She quivered with the agony, her mouth pulled open in one never-ending scream as her legs were bathed in the boiling liquid!

Half-conscious with torment, she kicked out, shrieking, thrashing wildly again and again in the extremity of her torture.

And then, blackness... and through the blackness another scream...

Before death came, at last, to bring her peace.

GRETA NEVER knew that her death-struggle had upset the vat.

She heard, dimly, perhaps, the last scream of her tormentor – of the Graf von Leichnis, bathed in a sudden horrible stroke with his own torture, drowned and burned at once in boiling oil.

Only Fritz was left alive – and Fritz escaped in a hurry, terrified himself of the sight of the dead Graf, and perhaps even, superstitiously, afraid that the Graf's ghost would now return to torment him.

But Fritz, from all available records, had not a long life before him.

We have his confession – from which the foregoing story has been compiled.

We have some notes which lead to conclusions about his death.

The legends had gone too far.

He was arrested by the Inquisition at a nearby town, Waldenburg, and tortured to extract a confession of witchcraft.

According to records, he was burned alive at the stake. The Inquisition sometimes offered the "grace" of strangulation before burning, to spare the victim that last long agony – but no such offer was made to Fritz Heldheim, assistant to the Graf Eberhardt von Leichnis in some of the worst tortures of recorded history.

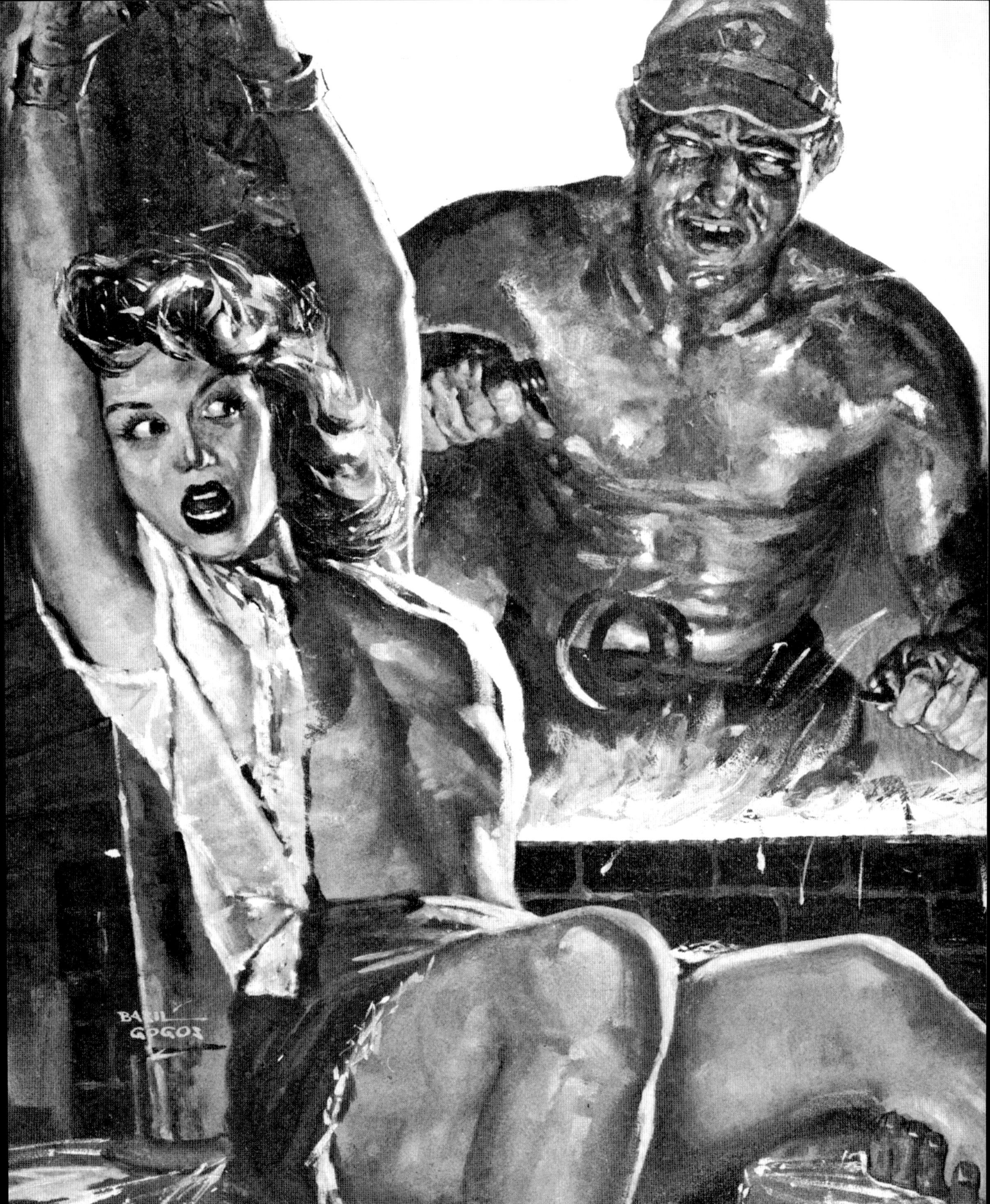

"HORROR WAS MY BUSINESS"; detail from interior art, **WAR CRIMINALS**, 08/63.
Art uncredited, signed Basil Gogos; previously printed as cover, **BIG ADVENTURE**, 07/61.

THE BLOOD-SOAKED QUEEN OF BUCHENWALD

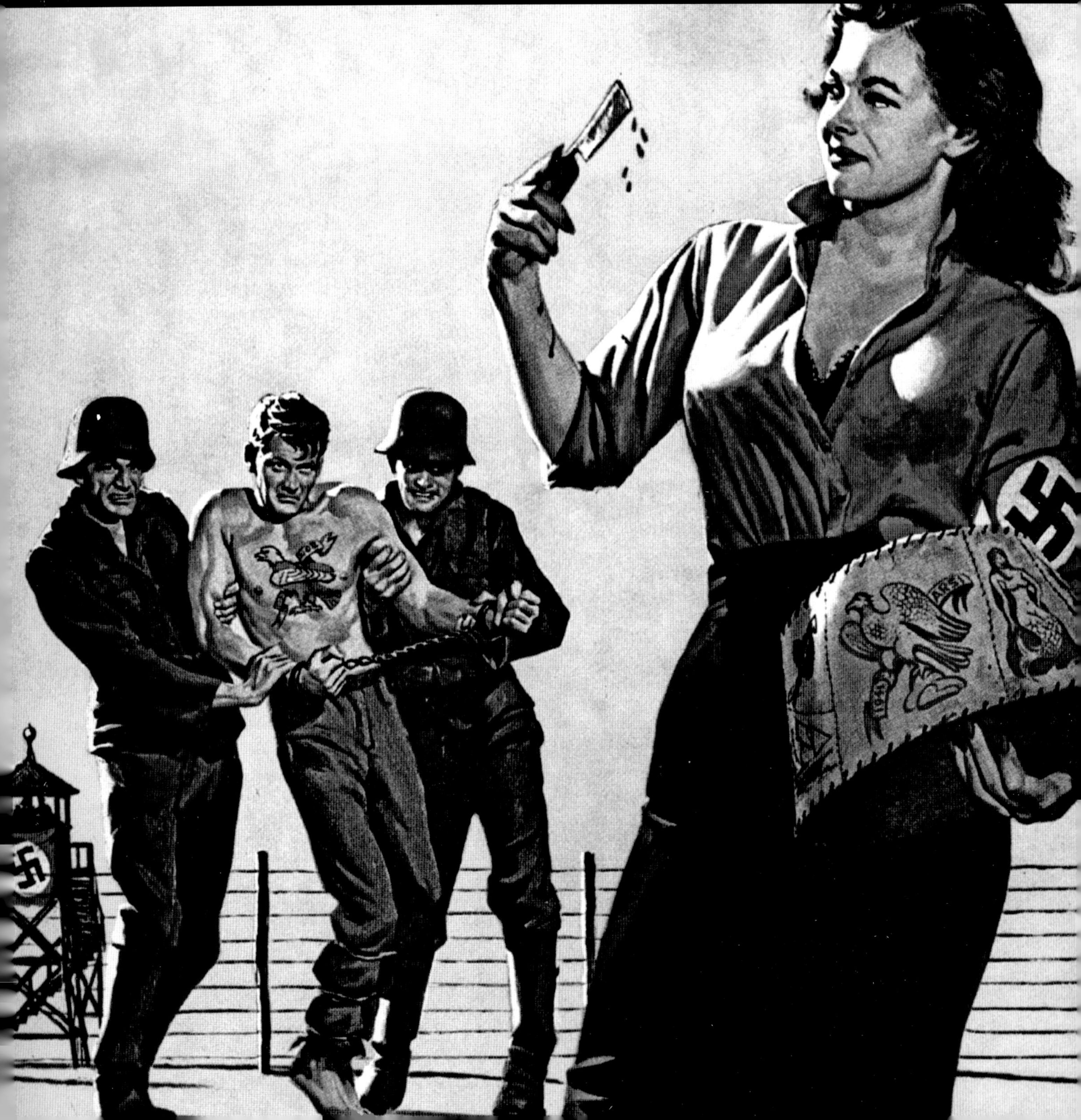

She used the allure of her body to inflame prisoners' passions, then led them to a Hell worse than death!

YOU COULD SMELL THE place long before you saw it. Driving up the road from Weimar you went through a thick pine forest. But you didn't smell the clean green scent of pine. A greasy pall of smoke hung there in the forest like a grey ghost. Smelling the sickening sweet air of the forest, you'd think *something is dead around here*. And something *was* – people, lots of them.

The road led up to a cluster of grey buildings done in the *gemütlich* style so dear to the Germans. At first glance, you'd take them for a resort or country club. Then you'd notice the barbed wire and the tall brick crematorium stacks. And the sign over the gate, white letters on a rustic brown archway:

BUCHENWALD KONZENTRATIONSLAGER

"Buchenwald Concentration Camp". It wasn't a tourist resort. It was the nearest thing to Hell man has ever dreamed up.

BUT BUCHENWALD wasn't Hell to everybody. The SS guards, healthy and well-fed, swaggering around in their black and silver uniforms, gagged a little on the smell from time to time. But it was still way better than freezing on the Russian front with the rest of the boys.

Gerta tried to bury the smell in cheap perfume. She poured it over her lush body by the spoonful. It didn't help much. The smell of death clung to her clothes. The odor of crematory smoke was in her hair. It was the only thing Gerta Holland never got used to. Aside from that, however, Gerta was having a ball.

Nobody knows where Gerta came from. Willy Steiner, the brutal and drunken Sergeant of the Guard, had picked her up someplace. Maybe she was a slut from the gutters of Weimar. Maybe she was a Gestapo prisoner, slated for the ovens, whom Willy had snatched for his own purposes when he got a look at her magnificent body. Nobody knows for sure.

But they know Gerta was there – ruling her own little empire from the SS barracks and causing more misery and sheer hell than any ten of the brutal guards.

Little Wolfgang Klopper was the first prisoner to see her. Klopper was a small-time thief and pickpocket hauled in off the streets of Frankfurt in a routine Gestapo raid. Little Klopper had been given the job of caring for the dogs. It wasn't a bad job. Wolfgang could steal a little dog food now and then. It was better than the slop they served the prisoners. As a criminal, rather than a political prisoner, the SS men were inclined to treat Klopper with good-natured contempt. He was the only prisoner the dogs were allowed to come near, as pets. Willy Steiner was proud of his dogs. He wanted to show them off to Gerta.

At Steiner's command, Klopper opened the door to the kennel and let the dogs out into the compound.

Gerta smiled as she leaned against her SS lover. "Is that all, *liebermann*?" she simpered in bored voice, "From what you told me, I expected to see man-eating wolves. These are just ordinary Doberman police dogs. I've seen a hundred as big or bigger in town."

Steiner grinned and winked solemnly at Klopper. The little thief shuddered; "He's been drinking!" he thought, "God protect us when Herr Steiner has been lapping up his schnapps!"

"These dogs are special, my pet," laughed Steiner. "These black bastards are trained. Isn't that *right*, Klopper?"

"Yes, *Herr Feldwebel*!" said Klopper. To himself he added, *"You bitch! Why don't you take him away from here? You don't really want to see the dogs perform – I know your kind. I've seen you and your sisters swinging your hips in front of the Bahnhof often enough. You're only interested in one thing. Take him away, before somebody gets hurt!"*

As if she'd read the little thief's mind, Gerta said, "I've heard so much about these great hounds of yours, Willy. But you still haven't told me what they can do."

Steiner hiccupped and grinned. "Shall we *show* her, Klopper my old and rare? Shall we show her with you?"

KLOPPER'S MOUTH went cotton-dry and his knees turned to mush. Too terrified to speak, the little thief stood there in an agony of fear as Steiner hissed a low command at the big Dobermans. At the whispered order the biggest dog bared his teeth and looked at Klopper. His ears went back flat against his head and he started walking slowly forward on stiff legs.

"Please, *Herr Feldwebel*!" gasped Klopper through chattering teeth. The dog growled low in its barrel chest. A ribbon of saliva dripped from its bared teeth as it readied itself to spring. Suddenly, Steiner snapped his fingers and the dog stopped.

"He'd do it, Klopper!" laughed the SS man. "He'd rip you just like the others, wouldn't he?"

"If you told him to, *Herr Feldwebel*!"

Klopper swallowed his heart. Steiner wasn't as drunk as he looked. The big SS man looked at the blonde chippie and said, "We can't let him have little Wolfgang, my pet. Who'd clean out the kennels? We'll have to show you another way." Turning from the kennel he looked across the compound. There was a sickly looking man in striped prisoner's garb carrying a bucket of slops from the kitchen. Steiner called to him. "You!

You with the slop bucket! Come over here."

Wordlessly the prisoner approached. He was a new fish, thought Klopper. He didn't know any better than to come near the kennels when the drunken sergeant called. Klopper clutched a wooden corner of the kennel and tried not to be sick. He didn't want to look.

"*Bitte, Mein Herr*? Please, Sir?" asked the prisoner. His eyes were puzzled as he eyed the swaggering man in silver and black. There was a trace of fear as he looked at the dogs, a trace of something else as he eyed the woman in the tight red dress. There was no mistaking what she was, and even a starving man needs a woman.

Steiner said, "Watch this." To the dogs he said, "Get him!"

Too late the prisoner realized why the other prisoners had taken cover when the dogs were let out of their kennel. Too late he knew the meaning of those white faces in the windows of the drab barracks. Too late, he started to run...

There wasn't any place to run. Buchenwald wasn't a very large camp – possibly four city blocks across. It was divided into three sections by inner wire fences. The prisoner's only chance was to make it back to the cover of the kitchen. He didn't make it.

Wolfgang Klopper didn't look. He didn't have to. He could tell by the agonized scream when the pack brought their human quarry down. He bit his knuckles to keep back the groans of rage and fear. He looked at Gerta. He looked at the red dress and the lush curves it barely hid and he tried to think of other things. It had been a long time since he'd had a woman. Never in his shabby little life had he had one like this. But he couldn't even think about her. Not now, not listening to the screams of the dying man. Not looking at her and realizing she was actually enjoying it.

"*Wunderbar!*" sighed Gerta, when the grisly show was over. "You were right, Willy. Those beasts are magnificent. We must keep them away from you, *mein liebermann*."

THE HOUNDS didn't get to Willy Steiner. But the bottle did. Twice he was drunk on duty. The SS had a long waiting list for the cushy job of camp guard. Brutality was one thing, sloppy salutes and turning up late for guard-mount was another. The Commandant had Willy transferred to a Waffen SS Battalion, headed for the Eastern Front. Later, the war crimes investigators learned, to their regret, that Willy Steiner had met a sober Russian with a tommy gun who'd given him a far cleaner death than he deserved.

Gerta, with Willy gone, tried to latch on to another boy. She didn't have as much luck as she'd expected. The other SS guards took a few whirls through the sheets with her. But nobody seemed to want to make it semi-permanent. She was a good looking head, they all agreed, but the black and silver uniform gave them first crack at any Hitler *mädchen* within sound of a wolf-whistle. The Nazis had a "Strength Through Joy" camp just down the road and the boys didn't want to tie themselves down.

Passed along the SS barracks row, Gerta was running low on money. She finally had to ask her current lover, a handsome young sadist named Ludwig Zuber, for the price of a new set of garters. The SS man laughed in her face.

"Pay you?" he grinned, "*Dumkopf*, you should pay us! Don't you know we are the new super race? Hell, woman, you're not bad. Not bad at all, but every teenage virgin in Weimar is ready to come to us at the snap of a finger!"

"But Ludwig. I haven't ten marks left. What will become of me? I thought that the least you could do after we've meant so much to each other... was give me enough to get back to town."

"Not a chance, *schatzi*!" grinned the SS man. Then an impish lock came into his eye. Pointing toward the prison compound, he said, "Now, the boys in there might be willing to pay – if you keep the price right. They don't see anything like you very often. Yes, I'd say you could easily get 200 marks a date from the scarecrows."

"You're joking," pouted Gerta, "Even if I was willing to date those dirty little men, how would they get the money?"

A SUDDEN light bulb lit in Ludwig's blond head. As an SS man he'd naturally acquired a part interest in the gold fillings from the crematorium. But it didn't amount to much. A new racket had just dawned in his greedy little brain. Turning to Gerta he said, "You know, I bet some of these guys really could get a little money, if they really wanted to!"

Thus, with Ludwig Zuber as her pimp, Gerta Holland set up the world's oldest profession in the strangest place it's ever been plied: the crematorium of Buchenwald.

It was a natural place. The crematorium was avoided by most of the brass. The Oberleutnant in charge agreed to Ludwig's plan for a cut and the five prisoners who worked inside the place were willing to take their hush money in trade. The five criminals chosen by the SS to burn the bodies didn't need any money. They knew damned well they'd never get out of the place alive. They knew too much. Meanwhile, they were given better food and Gerta was a well-stacked dish. If you didn't mind the taste of human ashes in your mouth, it was the best place in camp!

Ludwig dropped his normally nasty sneer and started acting almost human around the prisoners. There was a reason. He was drumming up business.

The SS guard searched every prisoner as he arrived. Every stitch of clothing was confiscated and they were issued thin cotton pajamas with vertical blue stripes. It seemed impossible that any of the prisoners should have money. But as every prison guard knows, *someone* always does, By swallowing money and later recovering it. By picking it up on work details where a relative had left it. By a hundred and one stratagems, the prisoners had accumulated a little money. And as in every society, some men were richer than others.

Hans Zimmermann was one of the richest. A prize fighter on the outside, Zimmermann had climbed to the top of the ant heap with his big fists. He needed money bad. Money would get you extra food at Buchenwald, and Zimmerman was a big man. He needed a lot of food. The *warmbroders* were his choice victims. The perverts and pansies of the camp, who accumulated "tips" for services rendered to the more prosperous prisoners and a few of the guards with exotic tastes. Zimmermann only had to kill three of them, in the darkness of the blacked-out barracks, to convince every *warmbroder* in camp that it was healthier to kick back a few of their marks to the boss of Barracks Seven.

Zuber paraded Gerta around the compound a few times, enough to let the prisoners have a hungry look at her curves. Then he approached Zimmermann with his proposition.

Gerta and her big boxer had their date in the privacy of the vault beneath the crematorium. When Gerta blew out the stub of the candle, you couldn't see the blood stains on the white-washed walls, under the meat hooks where the executed prisoners hung while they waited their turn to go up to the ovens.

Zimmermann didn't worry about the bloodstains. The moonlight through the one window outlined Gerta's marvelous body. With an animal whimper, the big prisoner drew her toward him. It was worth every one of the 200 marks she charged him, and Zimmermann knew where he could get more.

"When can I visit you again?" he pleaded.

Gerta sighed, "Any time, handsome. Can you afford so many dates with me?"

Zimmermann cracked his knuckles and smiled in the dark. A certain little Polish Jew in his barracks was rumored to have a few marks in the black pouch he wore on his neck. Kissing Gerta roughly on the throat, Zimmermann growled, "I'll be back tomorrow night!"

He was, and the night after that. It was rough on the men in his part of camp, though. The little Jew had died defending his few marks from the brutal prizefighter and a German pansy was lying in the bare prison hospital with a fractured skull.

Two more men went down under Zimmerman's iron fists. Then they found him by the kitchen in the cold grey light of dawn with a big red puddle of blood spreading out under his fallen body, and a stolen butcher knife driven clear through his guts.

GERTA MAY have lost one customer, but there were more where he came from. Night after night she plied her trade in the grisly love nest under the crematorium. Ludwig would have let her use the place in the day time too, but the SS had other uses for the room in the basement.

There was a slide, like a coal chute, leading down into the white-washed room from the alley behind the crematorium. Prisoners were ordered to slide down the chute into the cellar. At the bottom stood two SS men, waiting for them in the dark.

As the prisoner slid down the chute, the SS men grabbed him by the identification tag wire around his neck. Twisting the wire like a garotte, they quickly lifted the surprised victim off his feet and slipped the wire over one of the meat hooks along the wall. There, he was free to hammer his heels bloody on the white-washed wall, for as long as his breath held out. Sometimes there would be no wire, or the wire would break. The SS men were in a hurry. They'd toss him up on the hook anyway, driving the sharp hook up under his jaw bone and through the roof of his mouth. It left a lot more blood on the wall when they did that. But Gerta didn't seem to notice.

At night, while Gerta entertained her dates below, the bodies were taken upstairs in a dumbwaiter and shoved in the ovens to smolder away. Then, as the light of dawn outlined the rising plume of greasy smoke, the last customer would crawl back to his barracks.

Gerta Holland, a girl with a thirst for men, led a very busy life under the Buchenwald ovens. Ludwig let her keep half, and she was getting richer every day. Then a man named George S. Patton, Jr. spoiled her racket.

The Americans came fast – faster than anyone had expected. The Shermans rolled through the pine forests of Thuringia ahead of the rest of the U. S. Army. There was so much to do and so little time to do it. Records had to be destroyed, and prisoners. Prisoners who knew too much. The crematorium was working overtime. Ashes piled ankle deep on the floor and overflowed into the execution room below. Gerta had to take her business elsewhere.

Half the SS men had taken a powder. The other half were killing prisoners as fast as they were able. Gerta opened shop in one end of the SS barracks.

Bodies piled up in ghastly rows outside the crematorium. The fuel gave out and there was no point in keeping the five men from the crew alive. They knew too much. A burst of Schmeisser slugs piled them up on top of the others. Only their better-fed bodies marked them from the rest of the stinking cadavers.

At night, exhausted SS men, half crazed with blood letting and with the stench of death in their nostrils, wanted a woman.

There was no time for the Hitler *mädchens* now. No time to strut around Weimar in the black and silver uniform. The Allies would be in Weimar any minute, and it was rumored that they shot SS men on sight! No longer scorned by the SS killers, Gerta raised her price. They didn't argue. She was the only decent looking woman available. The few married SS men had long since cleared out with their families.

The others were about to do the same. Ludwig was one of the last to leave. He had a little cleaning up to do first.

He found Gerta near the barbed wire fence, staring at the piled bodies with distaste. The *staccato* bark of pistol shots around the camp signaled the end of strategic prisoners. The SS had given up the idea of killing them *all*. There were too many, standing around in frightened huddles behind the barbed wire as they waited like sheep to be slaughtered

"I'm, glad I found you here, Gerta," said Ludwig. "It simplifies matters." He raised his pistol. Gerta looked at him in stunned disbelief. "You fool!" she screamed, "What are you going to do?"

"Sorry, Gerta. It's time to clear out. I can't leave you for the Allies. You know too much to live."

"Why not take me with you?" she asked. Sweat ran down her forehead as he raised the pistol without answering. "Wait!" she cried.

"Stop and think! You *need* me, Ludwig." His pistol hand wavered and he raised an eyebrow. Quickly, she went on: "The Allies will be looking for you, Ludwig. Where will you hide? How will you get food? You can't work. You don't even dare show yourself in the daylight. One look at that blond head and some Ally will want you to take off your shirt. How are you going to explain the SS bloodmark under your arm?"

"Go on. Keep talking."

"You'll need money, Ludwig. Money and clothes and papers. And I can get them for you! With me along, you can make it."

"Where can you get money? Germany is finished!"

"From the Allies and the Tommies and the Ivans, if I have to! We can stay in the same business, you and I! The Allies are rich! I'll bet they give me more than 200 marks!"

Ludwig lowered the pistol and grinned. "All right, partner," he laughed. "Let's get out of here. The Allies are in Weimar right now and we'll have to make it through the forest south. I was just hanging around to finish you and Klopper, anyway. I can't find the little thief and he knows too much."

"Let him go. A warm meal and a drink of schnapps will finish him."

With a final look at the piled corpses Ludwig holstered his gun and led the way across the open clearing toward the pines. One of the bodies on the pile moved and two little ferret eyes of hate glared at the SS man and his blonde doxie. As they neared the woods Klopper sprang to his feet and ran to the kennel. Opening the door, he called the hungry dogs out. Pointing to the red dress and the black and silver uniform, Klopper hissed softly. The dogs tensed and looked the way he was pointing. Klopper watched the swaying hips under the red dress. "Get them!" he hissed. The dogs bounded forth as if from a spring gun...

Klopper was still laughing when the first American tank rolled through the gate.

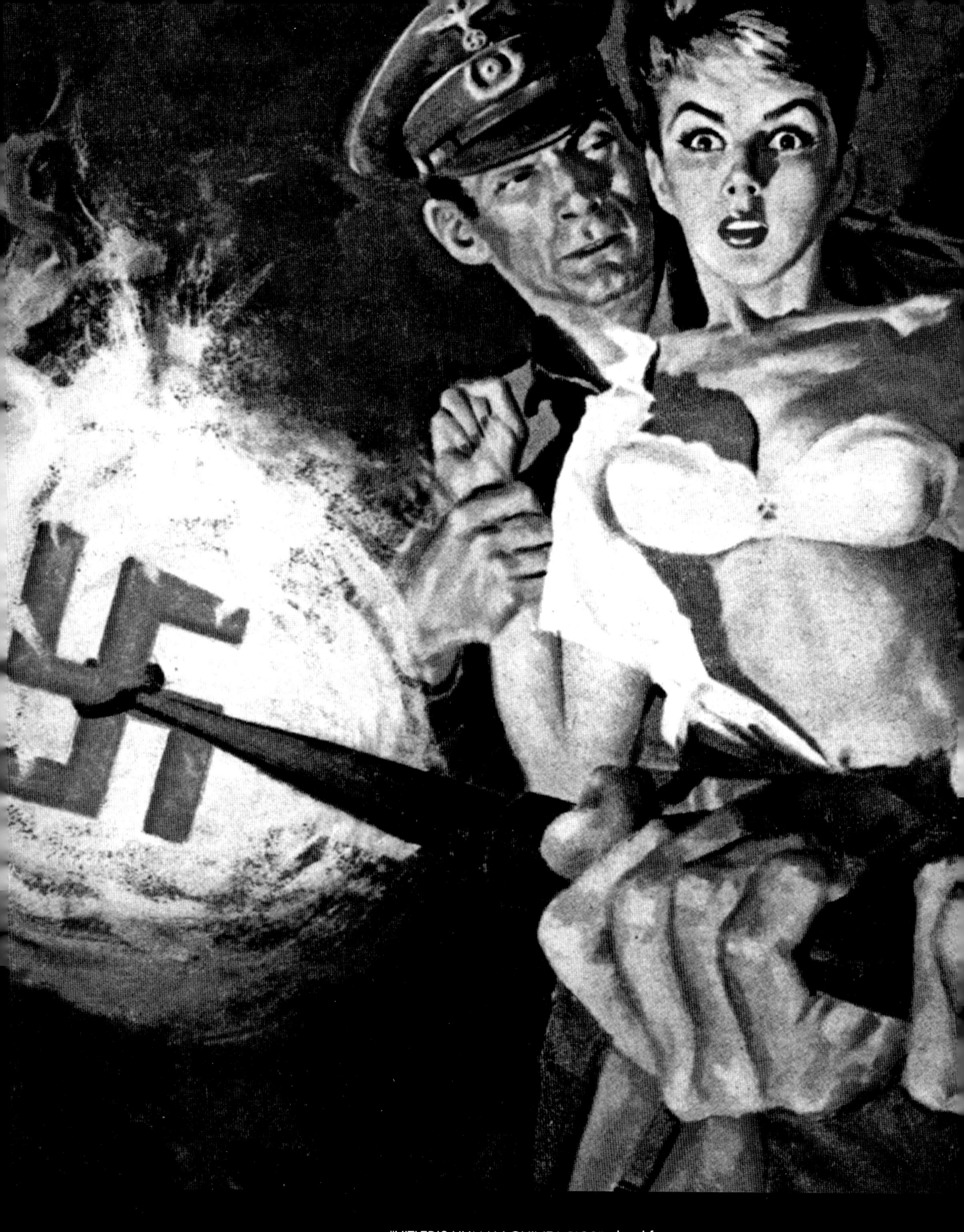

"HITLER'S HUMAN GUINEA PIGS"; detail from interior art, **WAR CRIMINALS**, 08/63.

TRAPPED BY THE NAZIS' KISSING SHE-DEVIL OF AGONY

They came to her plush boudoir expecting violent death. They stayed to find something far worse.

HURT NUMBED MY BODY. My mouth tasted dry and foul. My muscles constricted, knotting in agonizing spasms. I shuddered as my tormentor formed up before my pain-dimmed gaze and I saw the red leather whip she gripped in her black-gloved hand. She wore polished jackboots and black jodhpurs that molded her powerfully-curved hips like rubber. She was staring at me with extraordinarily merciless ice-blue eyes.

"*Gut!*" she snarled, her red lips curling. "Crawl, *Amerikaner schwein!*"

Inga Hein was as sadistic a bitch as ever cracked a whip for the glory of *Der Führer*. She was one of Adolf Hitler's favorite officers of the *SS-Totenkopfverbände Mädel* (Women's Deaths-Head SS Units), a distinction she undoubtedly owed to her singularly German predilection for flogging human beings to death.

As in a nightmare, I watched her raise the whip above the golden curls that cascaded about her shoulders. There was something inexorable about the way she did it, her blue eyes sick with lust, something unspeakable in their depths.

Viciously the whip tore at my body. I clenched my teeth, determined not to give the bitch the satisfaction of hearing my pain. I heard her laugh as she struck at me again.

Leather streaked through the air, splitting my skin. Something warm and sticky trickled over my flesh: blood.

Inga Hein was enjoying herself. She was studying my every reaction, her fantastically developed body arching as she tried to sense the pain I was feeling.

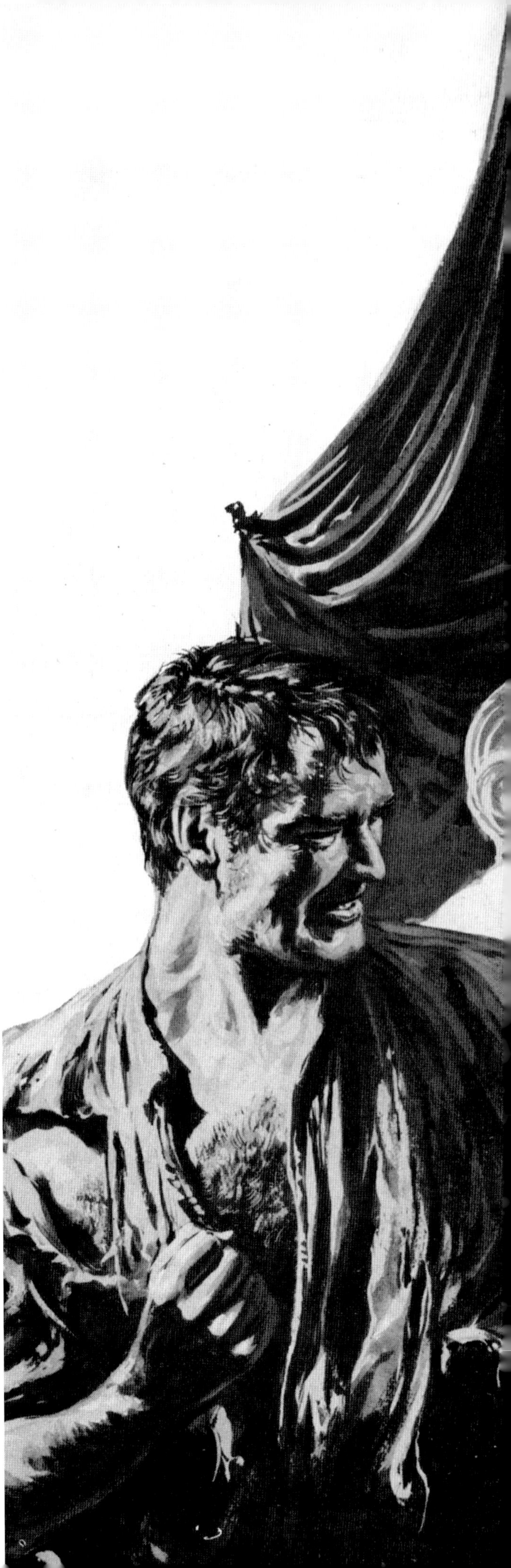

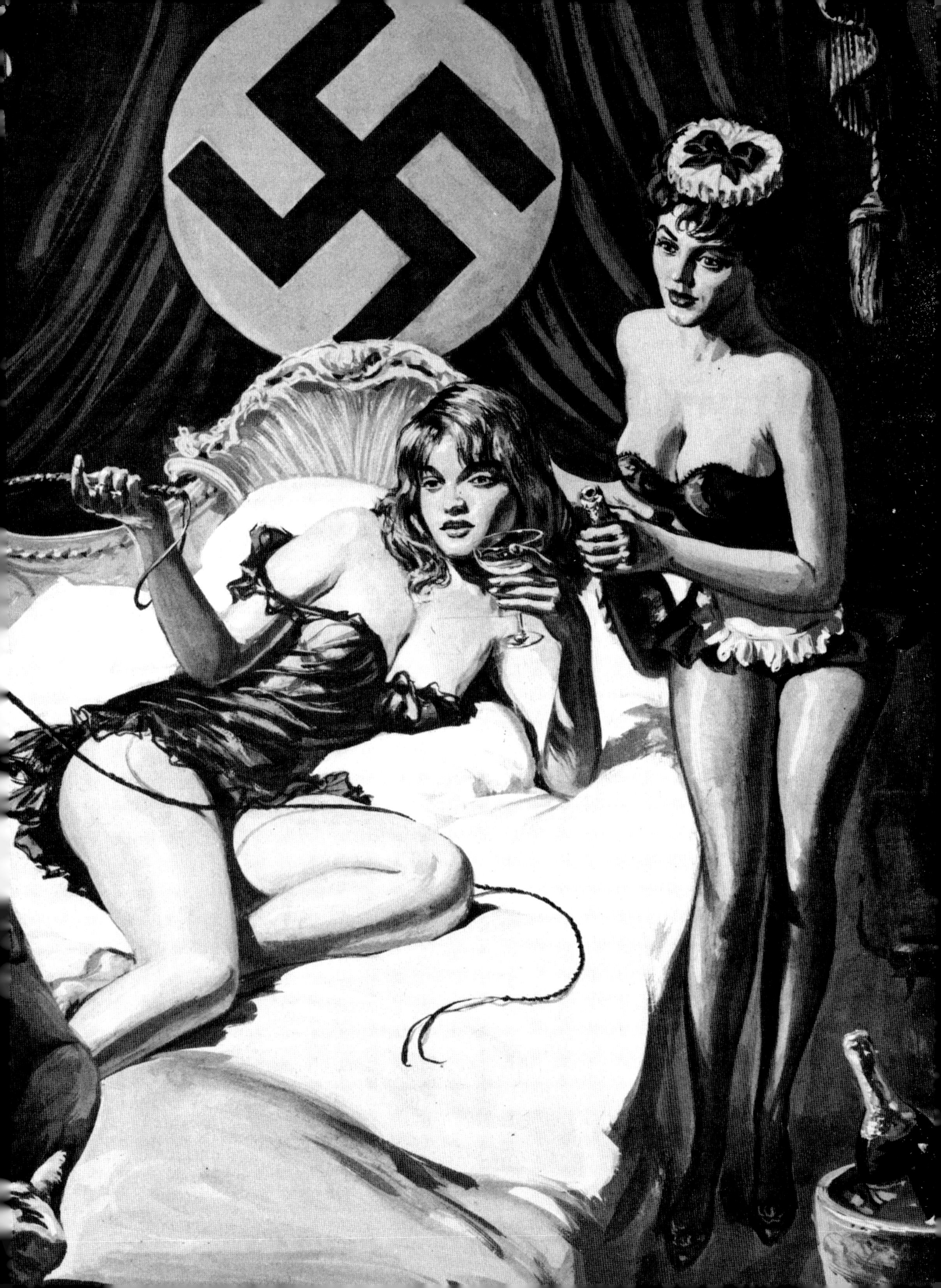

"Scream, *Amerikaner dummkopf*," she taunted me.

I stared back at her in silence, rage building within me. Inga's incredible, upthrusting breasts strained against the white silk of her SS shirt.

She cracked her red whip. The knotted leather tip chewed into me, driving shreds of filthy cloth into my flesh. Waves of agony rippled almost visibly before my eyes. Blood spattered the whitewashed walls and I screamed – screamed as unbearable pain jolted into my brain, as my sanity cracked.

And that blood-mad animal only laughed!

I tucked my head down then, lurching toward her. My fingers were outstretched, aching to tighten around that Nazi hellion's throat. My legs were throbbing lead weights. But if it was the last thing I'd do in this world, I was going to strangle the Blonde Bitch of Aschenwald – beautiful, golden-haired, degenerate Inga Hein.

She stood there hands on hips, laughing at me, her eyes fixed on me with open contempt. Then, casually, she picked up the Walther automatic from the desk.

"Come, you *schwein*. Keep coming toward me," she hissed. "First I will shatter your legs. Then I'll blow off your arms. Finally, *mein liebling*, I'll blast a hole in your belly. You will learn what real pain is!"

I already knew. I had learned so much about pain in Aschenwald Concentration Camp that there were no new agonies left for me to experience. The Walther held no terrors for me, for it would be quicker and easier. But I would not be whipped to death. My hands reached out.

Inga smiled and preened. Bloodlust was building within her, just as it always did before she killed. Her knuckles grew white as her finger tightened on the trigger...

THINGS STARTED to go really wrong for me when I was hit by a piece of flying shrapnel early in 1943, doing my best to get out of the bloody holocaust known as Kasserine Pass. I was running, trying to escape the deadly rain of Kraut 88's, when it happened. I was running – then I was flying through the smoke-filled air. I never even heard the explosion.

Whether it was an 88 shell that landed beside me, or a mortar bomb, I'll never know. Not that it matters. I came to with the stench of cordite in my nostrils and the taste of gall in my mouth. Troopers in camouflage overalls and the desert caps of Rommel's Afrika Korps were pulling me off the burning sand, trying to get me on my feet.

"My leg," I groaned – and passed out once more.

There was a long series of drugmares, like a surrealist painting by Salvador Dalí, involving field hospitals, jolting ambulances, make-shift operating rooms – then a stinking Italian troopship and more ambulances.

On a hospital train shunting northward through the bright Italian landscape, I found my right leg in a cast from hip to ankle.

In a hospital near Munich, they put me together again. But for the skill of those German surgeons, I'd have lost my right leg.

From the hospital I was taken to an interrogation center. An *Abwehr* officer handled the questioning. I gave him the "Lieutenant Barnaby Sperle" bit, followed by the same dreary set of admissible facts – once, twice, a thousand times.

After the millionth time the bastard lost his temper and backhanded me across the face. That did it. Almost berserk, I slugged back. He didn't do a thing. He just smiled at me.

"*Mein lieber Leutnant*," he whispered silkily, "I've just discovered that you're a Jew."

That same night they pulled me out of the POW compound and handed me over to the Gestapo. Twenty-four hours later I was rolling eastward aboard a crowded cattle truck, en route to one of Heinrich Himmler's most notorious hell holes – Aschenwald.

The camp was on a deserted and windswept plain near the medieval town of Plasnau. We prisoners could see out as far as the pine forests that surrounded us, but that was it. There was a vast jungle of electrified wire between us and freedom, outside which prowled steel-helmeted SS guards and killer dogs. Every fifty yards or so stood a machine gun tower, dominating the entire area. Every ten yards was illuminated by a powerful searchlight. For thousands of prisoners, Aschenwald Concentration Camp was to be the end of the line.

Sure, there were escape attempts. The prisoners weren't all old people and children. But it didn't pay – it didn't pay to get caught. And the escapees always seemed to get caught. And while there wasn't much reason to go on living, I, like the other prisoners, soon learned that some ways of dying made even our wretched lot seem preferable.

The commander of the camp was called SS-Obersturmbannführer Rudolf Gebauer. As a killer and a sadist, he was a professional. But when it came to sheer psychopathic viciousness, Inga Hein made him look like a philanthropist.

Inga was an officer in the women's section of the SS, one of the most beautiful women I've ever laid eyes on. And she was the only woman I've ever hated with every fiber of my being.

She was a blonde – not the obviously phony kind, but a radiant blonde, golden hair with shimmering highlights. She was a tall girl, maybe five-six or so. She wore tailored black SS uniforms that molded her sleek young body like a second skin. Her shoulders were wide, her hands soft and exquisitely manicured. Her incredible breasts looked as if they would thrust through her shirt front. She was a girl, with flaring hips and a wasp waist; also smooth-muscled thighs and legs, tapering away into polished leather boots.

I FIRST saw her in her Hollywood bedroom, stretching voluptuously against satin pillows of the palest ivory, a sumptuous breakfast of fresh coffee, hot rolls and real butter on a tray before her.

At that time I hadn't eaten anything better than scraps in over a week. I stared hungrily at the delicious tray of food.

Inga, who liked to order male prisoners to report to her bedroom so that she could gloat over their wretchedness from the silken comfort of her bed, eyed me appraisingly. Suddenly, she picked up one of the rolls and threw it on the floor.

"Crawl for it," she leered, her red lips curling into a cruel and mocking smile.

And I'm ashamed to admit that that's exactly what I did – I was *that* hungry.

"Oh, *L'Américain... le pauvre...* he must be starving!"

Angel, Inga's pert little lesbian maid, spoke with an innocent gaiety that was deceiving. As I learned later, this cute little French collaborator was actually as cruel and perverted as her mistress...

"Let him eat then.." Inga commanded sulkily, to no-one in particular. Then, turning abruptly to Angel, she said: "*Liebchen*, prepare my bath."

I suppose it was all part of the way Inga got her kicks. She kept me standing around, just inside the bathroom door, while Angel carefully soaped her as she sat immersed in a bubble-bath of pink foam. The bath took almost an hour.

Later, back in the bedroom, Angel said softly: "Madame would like a massage?"

Sprawling naked on her silken bed, Inga abandoned herself to the practiced fingers of her French maid. I watched, fascinated despite myself.

At last, Inga was ready to dress.

Over sheer, Paris-made lingerie, the beautiful sadist wore tight black jodhpurs, stiletto-heeled boots and a smartly tailored SS jacket lined with leopard skin.

She stepped back to admire herself in the mirrored wall by the bed. She had the sensual beauty of a Nordic Goddess, a blend of German, Slav and Magyar. Perhaps a dash of Swede to make the high cheekbones stop short in a striking curve to deep-set, cold, feline eyes, looking at her reflection with more than a hint of narcissistic approval. Her partly open, full-lipped mouth was both cruel and inviting, while her hair was a gleaming untamable torrent, cascading around her shoulders like writhing golden snakes.

She slipped into her chinchilla-lined SS topcoat, held for her by Angel, reaching as she did so far for her red leather whip that hung by a strap on the wall.

"*Auf wiedersehen*," Inga snapped abruptly. "You must return to the compound now – but I shall be sending for you again."

Sure, I saw her again all right. Our morning routine was just one occasion. We'd be roused out of our lice-infested huts long before dawn. We'd stand there, under the muzzles of the Deaths-Head Guards' sub-machine guns until the commander appeared. My fellow prisoners would drop like flies as the bitter cold and gnawing hunger took their toll. Finally, the Obersturmbannführer would strut out of the Kommandantur, his monocle flashing in the slanting rays of the early sun, a jouncing SS girl on his arm.

"*Was es das?*" he'd demand. "Why are these filthy pigs standing so stupidly in the cold? Do they not know that in winter I take roll-call inside?" He'd stoop to kiss the girl by his side. "Must I continue to look at this filth? Drive the *schwein* back to their stys where they'll find it warmer."

At this both the SS girl and the guards roared with laughter. It was a fine joke. It was all of 30 degrees in our huts.

Then just as the guards were turning around to dismiss us, Inga would appear, snug in her fur-lined coat and boots. Lazily she'd suggest, "As long as we're out of bed and have nothing to do, let's inspect the creatures..."

She'd parade up and down before us like a mannequin, so close you could almost feel the heat of her fantastic body. Sometimes she'd be nibbling a *foie gras* sandwich or sipping a glass of champagne – this in front of human beings who thought heaven was a scrap of maggoty potato peel.

If that's all there had been, the prisoners might have been able to stand it. But Inga had other ideas. It was she who showed me that living was worse than dying.

IN EARLY spring a number of prisoners attempted to escape. Somehow, they managed to blow a fuse and got improvised ladders against the wire. Then it was up, over and out.

But they hadn't counted on the emergency power supply. Within seconds the searchlights cut through the darkness and caught the escapees in their glare. A machine gun burst at their feet froze them where they stood.

All night long I and my fellow prisoners heard moans and screams. Next morning we were driven out of our huts and lined up behind the barbed wire. On the other side were the prisoners who had tried to escape – three men and a girl.

It still hurts me to remember it. The last account I gave was before the War Crimes Commission in 1946...

One of the men was hanging by his thumbs, his body jerking convulsively as the Deaths-Head guards jabbed him with their bayonets. He was the first to die.

Another was hanging by his heels, his tangled head only a few inches above the ground. His head bursting with blood, he had already crossed the line of sanity, and he was babbling incoherently.

The third man – he was a Polish Jew from Lvov – was strapped to a wooden bench. An SS-Scharführer beat him savagely with a length of rubber hose, while Inga and a number of her SS girls stood in the background and laughed hysterically. The Pole was over an hour in dying.

Inga saved the girl for herself.

The murder of the four prisoners ended escape attempts for a while. Things quieted down and stayed that way for several weeks. Then one morning, all hell broke loose.

Squadrons of B-17 heavy bombers of the USAAF droned overhead, on their way to blast one of Germany's eastern cities. The Allies were at the time stepping up their aerial attacks on the Reich in order to take some of the pressure off the Eastern Front, and the Luftwaffe was unable to maintain air superiority even over the German homeland.

One of the bombers must have had its bomb toggles jammed, and in trying to release them the bombardier dumped his entire load on Aschenwald. The eggs screamed down and burst in a line along the wire. Most of the nearby guard towers were knocked out.

We picked ourselves up out of the dust and rubble of the camp, nobody saying a word. We just stared at the smoky gap in the wire, the demolished towers. Then we all started running

It was little short of suicide. Death-Head Guards came racing along outside the wire. They opened up on us with their Schmeisser sub-machine guns, and we tried to dig into the dirt with our hands. I could hear the 9mm slugs smacking into living flesh, and the screams of the dying. The SS men played their streams of lead across us like fire hoses.

"Up! Up!" the SS men shouted. Out of maybe fifty of us, three rose to their feet – myself, another man, and a girl. "*Raus! Schnell, schnell!*" the guards bellowed, and we were hustled up the steps of the Kommandantur, to Obersturmbannführer Gebauer.

The concentration camp commander had lost his air of callous insouciance, his uniform was smeared with grime and dust and he was dabbing furiously at a cut on his cheek.

"*Schwein!*" he exploded. "You knew of this! You were responsible!" Then he calmed down and his eyes became calculating as he saw that there were only three of us.

"*Ach so*," he said, smiling now. "There were no survivors in that mass escape attempt. None! I shall have to report that you three died like the rest." He smiled again. "You will regret that you didn't."

Inga, who sat swinging her magnificent legs from his desk, pointed her red whip at my chest. "I'll take that one."

"Of course, *liebchen*," the Obersturmbannführer agreed at once. "Take him, he is yours."

Then he turned to the guards. "Take the other two outside," he ordered.

Inga motioned to the two SS gorillas who held my arms. "Take him over to the window," she ordered. "Maybe he'll enjoy seeing what happens to his friends."

I had to watch – *had* to.

Terror etched their faces in a way I'll never forget. Around them stood the huge, big-muscled SS gorillas, divested of their jackets and shirts, sweat glistening on their hairy bodies. In their hands they held wicked-looking clubs.

Then the real horror started. For, without warning, after they were tired of jeering at the two emaciated prisoners, the guards swung into action. The clubs smashed into the prisoners' bodies with sickening thuds. Blood spurted into the dust as the vicious weapons smashed legs and arms and torsos, battering them into virtual pulps.

I stood there numbed, vaguely aware of Inga's frenzied laughter. I don't know how long it took those swine to reduce to hideous blobs of bloody flesh what once had been human beings. It seemed an eternity in hell as I stared out the window, my head held by one of the guards, and watched while my two fellow survivors were beaten into tortured martyrdom.

But not once was either prisoner struck on the head. Both were still conscious and moaning piteously as they were dragged toward the garbage dump where they were to be buried.

Inga insisted that I see it all. We went outside and watched while the two bloody bodies were flung alive into a shallow grave.

I could hear them scratching like animals, begging in their feeble movements to be spared this final horror of horrors – this mingling of their still-living bodies with the rotting filth of the garbage dump.

All the time I struggled and cursed, but it was no use. I was weakened by hunger, and either of the burly guards who gripped my arms were stronger than I was. They guffawed loudly at my struggles. Then, at the end, when that filthy grave was finally filled in, they took me back to the office in the Kommandantur and let me go. I slumped back in a corner, weak and trembling with shame and disgust.

"Outside!" Inga ordered the guards. "Wait at the door."

She flipped open her holster, placed a Walther automatic on the desk. "Now listen to me," she began slowly. "Play the man and you will please me. Believe me when I tell you that it is a great honor and a great opportunity. No man has been able to please me in many months, and I am tired of my girls – even of Angel, my maid.

"*Komm hier*," she purred silkily, as she undid her belt, took off her ties and ran her fingers down the buttons of her shirt. She kept watching me, hungrily. "Do you think I am beautiful?" she asked as she peeled off the shirt, then her wispy net bra. "Wouldn't you like to hold me? Why don't you speak?"

It was the most exquisitely refined torture. Inga knew I detested her, yet she tempted me. She knew that I was physically weak, yet she also knew that I was a man who had not had a woman in a very long time.

She wiggled out of her SS jodhpurs, her eyes never leaving my face. She wore a glazed expression now, as if she were hypnotized or had taken drugs. Her thumbs ran around the waistband of her satin and lace panties, gently easing them down. She moved indolently to show off her magnificent nudity at its best advantage.

"Look at me," she demanded. "I'm the most beautiful woman you'll ever see! A pure, Aryan woman! Wouldn't you like to hold me in your arms? To caress my perfect body? Wouldn't you? *Answer me!*"

And the red whip whistled, slicing my cheek.

I whined like a dog. She laughed and the whip lashed out again. My eyes blurred with pain as she formed up in front of me out of a red fog. I advanced slowly. I was going to hold her all right – right around her neck.

She picked up the Walther from the table and I saw her finger tighten on the trigger, but my own arm moved in a quick arc and I yanked the gun from her hand. I reached up, got her by her blonde hair, and pulled.

Inga fell to her knees, nude except for her garter belt and black silk stockings. I wrenched her red mouth open, jamming the muzzle of the Walther between her glistening white teeth.

"Shoot," she whined. "You're dead anyway. The guards will beat you to death. You might as well kill me."

I pulled the trigger. Nothing happened. The mechanism had jammed.

Inga's eyes narrowed, her nostrils quivered. Danger seemed to heighten her emotions. "Again," she hissed.

Again I pressed the trigger. Nothing happened. I cursed and flung the useless weapon away. I smashed my fist into Inga's lovely face – once, twice, three times – until my knuckles were raw and bleeding.

She moaned, her whole body trembling. She started crawling up me, blood dripping from her battered face. I stood there stupidly, wondering what was happening to her – to me. Her bare arms went around me. She pressed me close, held me, dragged me toward an inner room.

She kissed me hungrily with bleeding lips, made me strike her again and again. Like an automaton, I obeyed and followed my own blind desire. I was no longer human and it was a dream. No – a *nightmare...*

FOR MONTHS I was nothing more nor less than a love slave to that hellion, Inga Hein. I was kept chained in her private quarters. I had nothing to do. Nothing, that is, until Inga wanted me again.

I loathed her, yet I depended on her for life. The only food I got was from her hands. She fed me like a dog. It was good food but there wasn't too much of it, for she wanted me to beg for it. She would literally feed me by hand and then demand that I make love to her on her enormous Hollywood bed. I don't think I was altogether sane at the time. But I'm making excuses. I did what I did in order to go on living.

Then, as I was being exercised in the yard one morning, there was sudden turmoil. Bedlam seemed to have cut loose. A high-velocity shell had blasted the main gates – a U.S. Army heavy tank had fired it.

The Third Army had made a lightning armored thrust. They had knifed a steel column through collapsing Nazi resistance to rescue the inmates of the camp before the SS finally liquidated us. The American tanks blew the Nazi machine gun towers apart and rolled right over the wire.

My guards ran. The prisoners ran, pouring crazily out of the camp, running around like a flock of chickens when a hawk hovers near. I ran to the Kommandantur and stood back from the main entrance. I waited.

Obersturmbannführer Gebauer came hurtling down the steps, his face ashen. He was instantly seized by some of the prisoners. Weak as they were, they lifted the SS officer above their heads and hustled him to the camp latrine. They held him by his booted feet, held him and pushed his graying blonde head into the muck. He had always called us filth. He died in it.

Inga didn't appear, so I crawled around back. I saw her climb through a window, then start running toward the rear of the camp, toward the wire.

Strength flooded through me and I dashed after her, overtaking her near the barbed wire fence.

I jumped her, pinning her to the ground. She tried to push me away so I let her have it with my fists, pounding her beautiful Nordic face with the pent-up fury of months, until it wasn't beautiful any more.

Then I dragged her up to the wire and lifted her to her feet. I pulled on the wire, fashioning a jagged loop. Then I forced Inga's neck through that loop, and pulled the barbs tight about her flesh.

Inga was right. There is a great deal of pleasure in inflicting pain on those you hate. Sitting there, watching her try to work herself loose, I couldn't help smiling. Her uniform was in tatters. She might as well have been nude. She'd work back against the wire and then jerk forward. The barbs bit deep. She'd move her neck from side to side, gently trying to work it free. The barbs bit deeper.

Inga Hein got plenty of blood that morning – all of it her own. It flooded over her shoulders, running down her slender, silken legs. The barbs had finally slit the jugular vein in her neck.

I sat there until the blood stopped dripping. Then I got to my feet, lit one of Inga's cigarettes, and went off to get myself officially liberated.

FANTASTIC LUST PLOT OF THE NAZI HARLOT SPY

She escaped Hitler's crumbling Reich capital to carve a new niche amongst the Red elite.

BRIGADEFÜHRER WILHELM STAUFFER OF the dreaded SS was trembling. His cheeks were hollow, his eyes sunken, his fingers icy cold as he went through the ritual of removing the clothing of Else Streit. And, for the first time since she had agreed to become the SS officer's personal prostitute, Stauffer gave Else pleasure.

Stauffer was an ugly man, a bully whose insults she had withstood for almost five years. But this night, in the underground bunker of the Reich Chancellery, the artillery fire booming in the distance, this night the Nazi martinet filled Else with a kind of ecstasy that even the most perfectly consummated sex act could not match. The sight of him, the touch of him flooded her with delight. For Stauffer was trembling with fear. This butcher, this murderer, this rapist, this sadist was almost prostrated by fright. And for Else to know this was to reach the pinnacle of delicious joy.

She smelled death on him. She delighted in the quiver of anxiety which danced on his spittled lips. She reveled in his pained sighs. Judgment Day was at hand for Stauffer and his Nazi hordes. The Russian army was ravaging the outskirts of Berlin, and time was running out for Stauffer and the insanity of Nazism.

That afternoon before Stauffer had phoned her, Else had taken her daily constitutional through the downtown district. What she saw was a city gone mad with terror, treason and suspicion.

She saw Nazi deserters hanging from trees, their corpses clad only in underwear, and on their chests placards reading: "We betrayed the Führer." She smelled the stench of bodies decaying in the streets – men, women and children who had died of starvation or by Russian artillery fire. She read the leaflets pasted on walls by the craven accomplices of the SS: "Dirty cowards and defeatists, we've got you on our lists." She saw the rubble of buildings, and the long lines of pathetic civilians begging for bread, the weeping women and bawling kids who lived like rats in the miserable, dank bomb shelters and cellars, hoping against hope to avoid death.

For weeks there had been rumors that the Russians were closing in on the city and that the Americans had halted their advance at the Elbe and were waiting to link up with the Soviets before they occupied Berlin jointly. But to Else these were just wild rumors which flourished under the pressure of wartime conditions. She scoffed at these exaggerations of unwarranted panic – until this day when the madness she witnessed with her own eyes shook her out of her complacency.

Who could blame her for being complacent? She was the mistress of SS-Brigadeführer Wilhelm Stauffer, one of the favorite henchmen of Hitler himself. Stauffer kept her in a lavish apartment not far from the Chancellery, supplied her with the finest of foods and wines. As long as Nazism prevailed, Else would prevail. She had gotten into Stauffer's blood; he adored her for all the sadistic treatment he doled out to her. She was willing to pay the price. If she hadn't sold her body to Stauffer, it would have been to someone else. Sex, cold, passionless sex, was her stock and trade. She despised all men – Stauffer no more than any other. He would do until it suited her to take up with someone else.

THAT AFTERNOON the realization suddenly dawned on her that the time had come to ditch Stauffer and all the Nazis stood for. She assessed the situation coolly, without emotion. There was no mistaking the fact that Hitler and his thugs were facing eclipse at the hands of the Russians and the Allies. Which meant, simply, that Else would have to ply her trade with another benefactor – with the Russians because they were the closest at hand. It was a clear-cut business decision. As long as she had her good looks, her health and her youth, Else would always find a buyer. This had been true of courtesans (she preferred that term to prostitute) throughout the ages. And it would be so whether the German flag or the Soviet flag flew over Berlin.

When she returned to her apartment, she undressed and luxuriated in a warm bath, munching chocolates which Stauffer supplied her. She expected Stauffer to phone her that

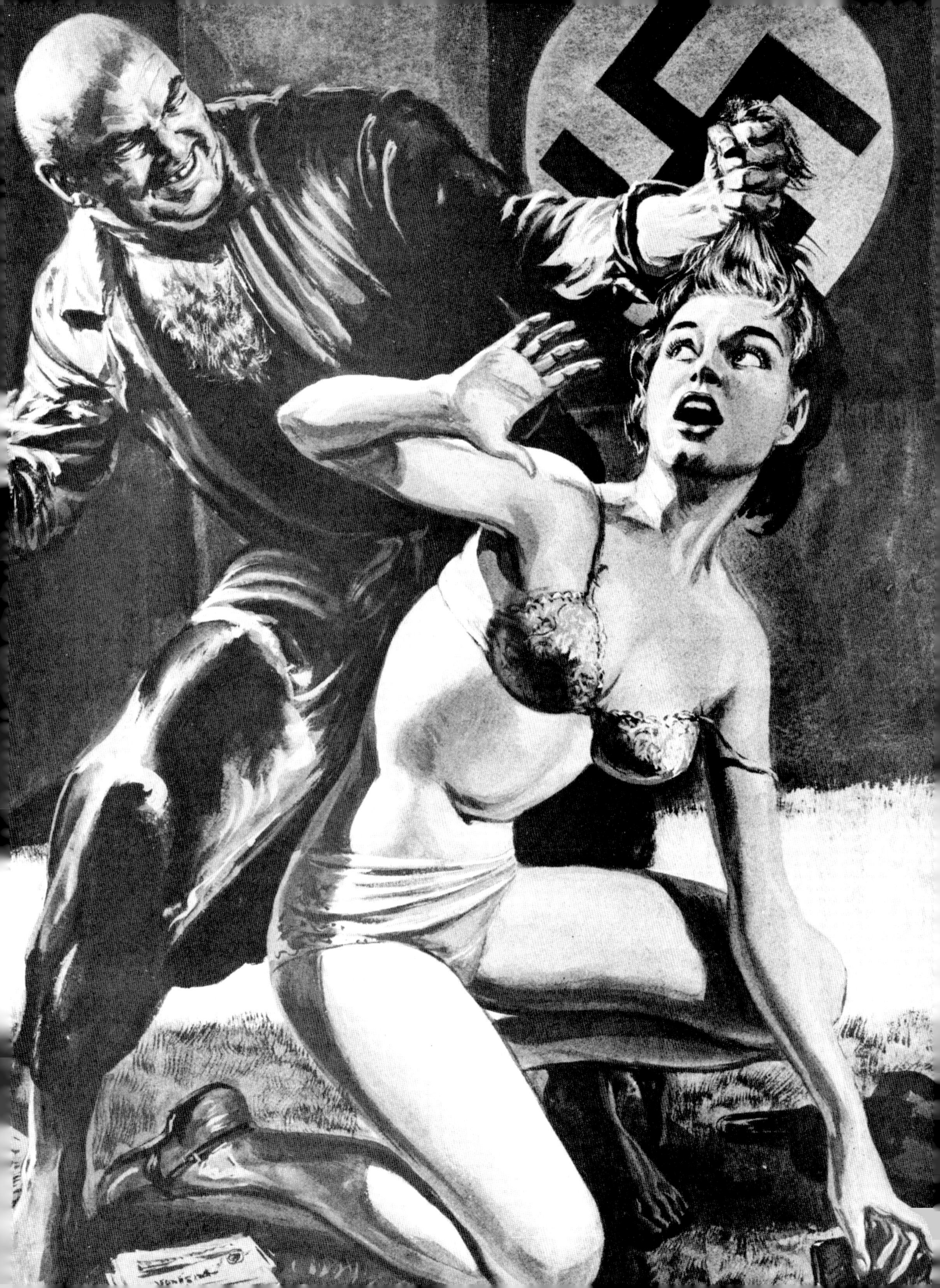

afternoon to confirm a visit that evening. Stauffer, that swine, so impressed by his own importance, so arrogant, so insecure, such a lousy lover! It would be easy to desert him, to escape from Berlin to greener and safer pastures. But it would not be easy to give up this way of life – this marvelous comfort and security, this delicious luxury, this perfect setting for her beauty and her free spirit.

No, she decided. She would not leave Berlin. She would have to make a deal with the Russians. She would have to offer them more than her body – because she knew the Russians were cynical realists like she was. So when Stauffer phoned, she accepted his invitation – dangerous though it might be to dally in the Reich Chancellery when the Russians were coming closer and closer every moment. She decided to visit Stauffer because there was still something to be squeezed out of him – something she could use to bargain with the Russians.

That evening, an hour before Brigadeführer Stauffer's limousine was to call for her, Else Streit stood before the full-length mirror in her plush bedroom and eyed her figure. Her body was riper, fuller, more beautifully mature than when she had come to Berlin some twelve years before – a naive farm girl from Austria seeking a better life. Bed was her pathway to success. Once at a party in Berchtesgaden the Führer himself had fondled her firm breasts, but the brief tryst in the garden was interrupted by Eva Braun, the rather dowdy (Else thought) mistress who had the high sign on Hitler.

Now it was to be farewell to that era of her life – and on to newer and hopefully better things. She donned her filmiest black lingerie – a gift from Stauffer – a low-cut, black sheath dress that hugged every curve. She would give Stauffer a last night to remember. (Who could accuse her of a lack of sentiment?)

Precisely at 8 PM she glanced out of her boudoir window. The sleek black Mercedes was at the curb waiting for her. She applied a few dabs of perfume in the right places. It was French perfume, a present from Stauffer during the occupation of Paris. Now she was ready to go after the biggest gift of all from the SS officer – a one-way ticket into the arms of the Russian invaders with a built-in insurance policy.

When she emerged from the house, the chauffeur snapped open the door of the limousine and saluted her crisply.

"Good evening, Hans," she said routinely. "Are you well?"

"Very well, thank you, Fraulein Streit."

He was a tall, trim, blond sergeant – the perfect Aryan type – with a hard body and a head to match. She knew he adored her. Once when he had called for her, she invited him inside and allowed him, purely out of the goodness of her heart, to make love to her – briefly. He was clumsy and clambering, but eternally grateful – and eternally frightened that the Brigadeführer might learn of it. Which Else felt was an excellent return on her investment – namely the loyalty and gratitude of the servant who could furnish her with much information about Stauffer and the internal politics of the Reich Chancellery.

Else watched Hans take his place behind the wheel. He turned on the ignition and the engine roared, but the car did not move.

"What is wrong?" she asked him, a bit uneasily.

"I beg permission to speak with you in confidence, Fraulein Streit," he said nervously.

"Well, what is it?"

"I would not recommend that you go to the Chancellery this evening," he said stiffly. "There are strange goings-on. There are rumors of suicides – that Hitler himself and Eva Braun are dead, their bodies burning outside the bunkers..."

"Nonsense," Else snapped. "You must not believe false rumors. That constitutes defeatism. Take me to General Stauffer at once, or I shall report you."

The Mercedes lurched ahead and purred smoothly through the rubbled streets, past a dozen fires blazing in buildings along the way while artillery rumbled in the background like thunder.

"Fraulein Streit," the chauffeur resumed a few minutes later, "It would be wise of you to flee Berlin at once. I say this with full knowledge of the risks involved. I say it out of concern for your welfare. I can help you to escape safely. Opposite the Chancellery is the subway station below the Wilhelmplatz. We walk along the tracks to the Friedrichstrasse Bahnhof, then across the Spree River, and we are clear of the Russian forces. From then on, we can commandeer vehicles and find refuge elsewhere."

Else smiled at his anxiety and his loyalty to her.

"I thank you for your concern, Hans," she said sweetly. "But first I must see the General at the Chancellery. If you will wait for me at the usual place, I will decide the next course of action. Can I depend on you to wait for me?"

He assured her that she could, and she was certain of his sincerity. She might yet find a use for this idiot.

NOW, IN Stauffer's suite in the bunker, the trembling General clumsily unhooked her brassière, leaving her completely nude before him. His glassy eyes devoured every convexity and concavity of her form, and when he touched her his hands were icy cold. She enjoyed his fear, deliberately played coy so as to inflame him. She was expert at this game of sex, and she despised all men for their weakness, their abject surrender to something as animal as a female's body. She teased, toyed with him, until his ugly face had become red with passion. She mouthed the little words of endearment he wanted to hear and which were ridiculously artificial to her – just part of the routine service to a good customer.

"I thank you, *liebschen*," he panted. "I thank you for coming here tonight, and I beg your forgiveness for having mistreated you in the past. I have never known a woman like you, Else. Never."

He bored her to the point of distraction. Such sentimental claptrap coming from this bully. Usually he didn't bother. He went about it like an animal, huffing like a bull and with as much finesse.

A few minutes later he lay sweaty and spent in her arms, leaving her as cool and uninvolved as if they had just finished a game of checkers. Always she had a kind of afterglow – a sense of exhilaration that had nothing whatever to do with sex, but only with her feeling of power at having vanquished a man, of having had him worship at her feet, degrade himself and fall away exhausted. Sometimes Else wondered whether she endured this relationship with Stauffer less for the material things he lavished on her than for the satisfaction of reducing him to a panting animal who was putty in her hands.

"There is danger, terrible danger," he said thickly, his head on her bosom. "You must never leave me, Else. Even though the SS guards are deserting like rats, and Hitler and his woman are dead, you must never leave me. I can save us. Only I. Remember that."

"Of course, my Brigadeführer," she said softly. "Now you must rest. There is time, my Brigadeführer. Rest. Rest."

Even as she spoke, lulling him, she was calculating her next move. Stauffer would fall asleep in a few minutes and snore like a tractor. That was all she wanted. Then she would go after the treasure she needed.

She felt his head become heavier on her breast, the dead weight of his hands on her hip. Then the snoring. He was asleep – as usual – a deep slumber from which he would emerge a half hour or so later, completely refreshed, his old arrogant self, anxious to send her away so that he could get on with affairs of the Reich.

She slipped out of bed and dressed hurriedly. Then she rifled through his discarded trousers, searching for and finding what she needed – the key. It unlocked the door which led from the bedroom to Stauffer's office. She entered, and then she began her search. She knew exactly what she was looking for.

Once, many months ago, Stauffer had become quite drunk and shown Else the office – the red telephone which was a direct line to the Führer, the battery of telephones which communicated with his subordinates in the SS, the illuminated map of Germany showing highly secret, strategic military locations.

Then he had told her about a hidden drawer in his huge mahogany desk. She recalled his words:

"There, *liebschen*, are concealed some of the most valuable documents in the world. I can say no more under penalty of death. I tell you this only so that you may appreciate how powerful a man I am, and to be grateful that I bestow my favors on you – you marvelous wench."

The words of the braggard Stauffer had stuck in her head ever since. Else was a practical woman if nothing else. Someday, she remembered thinking at the time, someday Stauffer's drunken words might prove useful.

Now she was down on her hands and knees, examining the desk There was a concealed button or lever, which Stauffer had pressed to release the drawer. This she had to find. She ran her hands all over the upper and under surface of the desk, seeking the hidden button. At last she gave up in frustration, and sat dejectedly in Stauffer's deep leather chair. She carefully pulled open the center, front drawer. Inside lay a Lugar and a number of the general's personal mementos. She reached her hand into the drawer and felt the upper surface. Her forefinger struck a button which she pressed, and a spring clicked and a drawer sprang out of the side of the desk.

"And what, pray tell, are your intentions?"

The words flashed like a bolt of lightning, sending an electric chill the length of her spine. It was Stauffer. He had awakened, and caught her red-handed.

"Is it that I have failed to give you enough baubles, enough perfume and caviar and good French wine?" Stauffer said with terrifying calmness and control. He had slipped on a silk robe and his bare feet were slippered. He was in the act of lighting a cigarette, and all the while he came closer and closer, his face as impassive as stone, his eyes glittering darkly, his lips tight, the muscle in his jaw pulsating ever so slightly.

"I do believe I have failed to give you enough," he said dryly, hovering above her now, the red circle of the burning cigarette seeming to float on its own toward her. Then, as casually as he might grind out a cigarette in an ash tray, he jabbed the burning end against her throat.

She screamed and fell forward, her arms atop the desk. He seized her by the hair and yanked her head back.

"A highly effective way of branding a treacherous whore," he said coolly. "Pity I didn't think of it sooner."

Her hair felt like it was coming out at the roots. The pain sent tears burning into her eyes, and her throat throbbed with searing agony where Stauffer had burned her. And, as she was pulled back from the desk brutally, her clutching fingers brushed against cold steel, the cold steel of the Lugar which lay in the desk drawer. Somehow she managed to grasp it. Somehow she managed to flick the safety catch as she was catapulted by Stauffer's sheer brute force out of the chair and onto the deeply carpeted floor. An instant later she squeezed the trigger. The blue flash, the deafening shot obliterating the deathly silence.

When she opened her eyes and struggled to her feet, she saw Stauffer pressed against the wall, clutching his left side, blood oozing through the fingers of his right hand. She had only wounded him, and nothing was more dangerous than a wounded jungle beast.

"You are a dead woman," Stauffer said through clenched teeth. "You are a dead whore. I swear it in the name of the Third Reich, in the name of the Führer."

"Bah," she said scornfully, gripping the Lugar with both hands, attempting to prevent it from swaying as if it had a will of its own. "The Führer is dead. The Third Reich is dead. And you, my poor Brigadeführer, only your arrogance, only your egomania and your delusions remain alive. The rest of you is dying fast."

His face was contorted in pain, the beautiful silk robe drenched in his own blood, his legs buckling as he became progressively weaker. He was a pathetic sight, and she could feel nothing for him; she never had. The gun still trained on him, Else felt in the secret drawer with her free hand, and Stauffer became pale, his body shuddering.

"I forgive you, *liebschen*," he said gently, suddenly changing his tactics. "I will let this incident pass as merely a lovers' quarrel. It will do you no good to take the papers; they are meaningful only to me. Be reasonable. Put away the gun. I will take you away from Berlin – to a secret retreat high in the mountains where we can be safe and happy together. I can do this, believe me."

She smiled coldly, showing her disdain, and he shouted at her: "I will marry you. Do you hear me, Else? I will marry you!"

"Marriage, to you?" she flung in his face. "My poor,

dear Brigadeführer, that is the last thing I would consider. You do not seem to understand what is happening. You are no longer of use to me. The Russians will replace you in my affections. It is beyond your control. It is beyond mine. It is the bloody finger of destiny – and you should yield with dignity."

"You are garbage," Stauffer gasped, moving at her suddenly, his face exploding into a purplish red hue. "You deserve the Reds. They will grind you into mincemeat!"

Else had the Lugar pointed at his chest. She was fully prepared to pull the trigger again. But she didn't have to. Stauffer pitched forward at her feet, and lay there on his face very still, his skinny bare legs bent grotesquely under his body. He was dead.

Good riddance! That was her only thought. Now she burrowed anxiously through the desk drawer. She picked up a miniature, leather-covered book, and examined it. It was the secret code book of the Nazi high command, a cryptographer's dream, unlocking the code language of the Reich's most vital communications. She was shrewd enough to realize that such a code had little value now, when the Third Reich was on the brink of annihilation. She continued her search. There had to be more. She found it a moment later. A plain paper notebook with notations in Stauffer's own hand. She thumbed through it, recognized a few of the names as some of the Reich's most eminent scientists. And then she realized what she had come across. It was a complete list of German scientists, their true names and pseudonyms, the locations of their research centers, and the projects in their charge. She scanned some of the notations: research and development of the V-3 and V-4 prototype rockets; experiment to convert atomic energy into super-bombs.

She grinned. That little book would be her meal ticket with the Russians. It was the key to the industrial and technological powerhouse of Germany, the kind of information that could swing the balance of power in favor of the nation which came into its possession. The Russians would pay for it, and pay well.

OUTSIDE IN the courtyard of the Reich's Chancellery a bonfire burned hot and bright, mirrored in the polished finish of Stauffer's black Mercedes. Hans was waiting for her as he had promised. He opened the door for her, an expectant look upon his handsome, dull face.

"Have you decided, Fraulein Streit?"

"Decided? Decided what?" she said absently. "Oh," she added, recalling Hans' offer to help her escape through the subway tunnel. She wasn't about to flee from this known horror into what might be a worse and unknown horror. Not when she had an insurance policy tucked in her under garments.

"Yes, my dear Hans," she said, smiling winningly. "I have decided to go with you. The Brigadeführer agrees it would be the wisest course. How he trusts you, Hans!"

She pressed his hand firmly, and his face reddened with emotion. He was like putty.

"But first, my dear Hans," she said, "I must return to my apartment on a mission of extreme importance. If you will take me there..."

"It is extremely dangerous, Fraulein," he protested weakly. "They say the Russian troops are no more than a mile or two from the Chancellery. It would be best if we made our escape at once."

But she smiled at him, and the young Nazi succumbed.

"I shall drive you, Fraulein," he said crisply.

The limousine sailed through the courtyard, glided past the bonfire where a trio of SS troopers watched the blaze in silence.

"It is terrible, terrible," Hans said. "That is the funeral pyre of Goebbels and his wife. Goebbels ordered his orderlies to shoot them and to burn their bodies. The Reich is *kaput, kaput.*"

The Mercedes slowed down and paused briefly at the gate of the Chancellery where the SS waved it through. Else heaved a silent sigh of relief. Hans had already made his major contribution to Else; he had gotten her safely out of the Chancellery. From here on in he would be a mere pawn in her hands.

He drove at breakneck speed through the deserted streets of Berlin. A few German tanks and several platoons of troops – mostly old men and young boys – were using a public park as a staging area for a feeble last-ditch defense of the area around the Chancellery. There were no civilians in sight; they had burrowed underground. When the Mercedes pulled up at the curb in front of Else's house, the sound of artillery and rifle fire was close by. In the streets, not more than eight or ten blocks away, the Soviet and German soldiers were skirmishing.

Hans turned off the ignition, and turned to look back at Else. He found himself staring into the barrel of the Lugar.

"You are joking," he said with a pained smile.

"On the contrary," she snapped. "I am deadly serious. I have no further need of your services. You will please get out of the car, drop your revolver on the sidewalk, and walk to the far corner. I am taking the car. I am perfectly willing to allow you to recover your gun and try to make your own escape from Berlin – if you do not resist me now."

He gazed at her blankly for several moments as if her words took time to penetrate his thick, handsome skull. Then slowly he got out of the car and stood at the curb, his hands hanging loosely at his sides, his face frozen in disbelief.

"The gun!" she reminded him.

It clattered to the pavement a few feet from him. She opened the rear door nearest her, and swung her legs out. She was aware that he was eyeing her legs – even now lusting after her, even now hoping against hope that her sharp commands might become an invitation to go to bed with her, an invitation he had once accepted and could never forget. The fool!

Her high heels caught in a crack in the pavement. And in that instant he lunged at her. She was almost sorry that she had to shoot him. He fell against the limousine, and slid to the ground, that dumbfounded look of disbelief frozen on his face even in death.

Poor devil, she was thinking, as she dragged his body away from the front wheel. She leaped into the car and switched on the ignition. And then she had an idea. Hans might still be of some use – as a silent witness to vouch for the story she planned to tell the Russians. Somehow she managed to drag him into the back seat. She removed a white handkerchief from his pocket and attached it to the outside antenna as a flag of truce, a signal to trigger-happy Russians. Then she gunned the engine and sped off in the direction of the gunfire.

She drove for a mile or more through a ghost town– not a German or Russian soldier in sight, but the sound of gunfire becoming louder and louder. As she made a left turn onto a main boulevard, she was suddenly confronted by Russian tanks which had set up a blockade. She braked the car, leaned out of the window, smiling, and waving her arm in a friendly greeting:

"Comrades," she called out. "I welcome you."

To the Russian soldiers on and around the tanks she must have seemed an apparition – a beautifully groomed woman in a gleaming black limousine on what must have appeared to be a casual drive around town. They gaped at her, and one unshaven, grimy brute started to approach her, but was restrained by his companions. The Russians collected around the car and stared. And Else felt confident, invulnerable.

The Russian troops wore steel helmets, hand grenades in their belts and boots. They were a motley crew, Else thought – shorter than the Germans, filthy and sweaty. One of them confronted her directly. He was a captain. He had a scarred face, and dark eyes, suspicious slits of eyes.

"I come as a friend," Else said, smiling. "I am German but I hate the Nazis and I welcome the Red Army. I have escaped to join you, to supply you with valuable information."

"And what proof do you have that you are not a Nazi agent?" the Russian officer demanded to know. He spoke German quite well. His breath was foul.

"The Nazis could hardly have sent one helpless woman to halt the Russian advance," she replied flippantly, but the Russian's face only became grimmer. "If it is proof you want, proof that I have escaped, look in the back seat, at the body of my captor."

The Russian peered into the car. "You killed him?" he asked her, and she nodded. "Very nice," the Russian said dully. "What is this information you bring?"

"Take me to your commanding officer," she said.

The captain shrugged, whirled about and ordered his men to move on and get back to their assignments, and called for an armored car to be brought up. He drove through chaos and destruction-rubble strewn all about, corpses decaying uncovered on the streets, thousands of troops milling about, regrouping, preparing for the final thrust which would take Hitler's capital. The Russian officer said nothing, but he glanced sidewise at her now and then as if she were a creature from a strange planet.

After a while, he said: "There have been hundreds, no thousands, of women coming to us in the past few days. All of them are suddenly friends of the Red Army; most of them are starving and worthless even for the bed, at least for my bed. But you, madam, arrive in the limousine of a German officer."

Like a cat, his big rough hand pounced on her wrist, and she winced in pain.

"We have set up a temporary barracks not far from here," he said. "There we imprison German women who strike our fancy. The others can go to the devil. The point is, madam, that unless you tell me what kind of information you have I will deposit you in the pen with the rest of the German bitches."

She wanted to spit in his face, to scream out in a rage. That is what other women would have done. But not a shrewd practitioner like Else.

She let him kiss her, let his hands crawl up her legs, just far enough to inflame him to the boiling point. And then she whispered in his ear:

"Later, later. After I have spoken to your commanding officer, I will be your woman. I have never met a man like you."

The headquarters of Marshal Vorilov had been set up in a mansion which had once belonged to a Krupp industrialist. The Russian drove up the driveway, growled a few words at a sentry stationed at the main door, and escorted Else inside.

In what was once the parlor of the mansion, a large table had been set up, and a group of Soviet officers were studying a map spread on it. Radio receivers growled and crackled as reports on the progress of the sacking of Berlin came in; a half dozen Russians were on telephones, and couriers scurried in and out of the room.

"What shall I tell the Marshal?" the Russian captain asked her.

"Tell him nothing. Just point him out to me."

There was no need of that. Else had already spotted him. He stood a head taller than any other man in the room. His hair was a shimmering, close-cropped gray, his features rugged, and he clearly dominated.

"I will wait for you outside," the captain said in a low voice.

She strode into the room, her head held high, tossing proudly, her hips swaying provocatively. And at once every eye turned towards her imperious figure, and the hubbub of activity came to a halt – almost as the Red Sea had parted for the passage of Moses. Even the cold, slate gray eyes of Marshal Vorilov flickered with surprise momentarily.

"Marshal Vorilov," she said coolly. "I believe you will wish to speak with me in private."

"You are quite presumptuous, madam," he shot back. "You have no right being here. I advise you leave at once."

"My dear Marshal, I have military information direct from the Reich Chancellery," she said, unfazed by the arrogance of the Russian commander.

"Very well," he replied. "You will wait in the first room to the left, directly up the stairs."

"A wise decision, sir," she said, smiling. And she undulated through the room and up the thickly carpeted stairway, conscious of the vitality and sensuality of her body – as was everyone else, including, she hoped, the Marshal.

THE ROOM was a master bedroom, exquisitely furnished as it had been before its occupants had fled or had been murdered by the Russian invaders. Else inspected herself in the full-length mirror, applied fresh makeup, and reclined on the satin-covered bed, careful to raise her skirt to show her legs.

When Vorilov arrived a few minutes later, he stood stiffly in the doorway, his swift eyes recording all that was pertinent to see, his face hard, expressionless.

"State your business," he growled. She asked him to

sit on the bed beside her. He complied, and she rolled over on her side to face him.

"You will forgive me if I do not get up," she said. "I am a little tired. It has been a difficult day, a very difficult day."

The right corner of Vorilov's mouth twitched almost imperceptibly. It was the only sign of his agitation; otherwise he was stolid and formal. He would succumb, she decided – just as all the others had. She began to speak:

"I have connections in the Reich Chancellery, very important connections. At least I had until I severed them today. I will speak very frankly. For many years now, I have been the chattel of the Nazis. I was powerless to resist them – me a poor, fragile woman. But today I have mustered the courage to escape. And I ask you for sanctuary."

Vorilov glared at her.

"Madam, thousands, literally thousands of women are in your predicament, fleeing from the Nazis now that Hitler is about to be destroyed. We have arranged camps, barracks for refugees. I suggest you seek one out. You will be fed. I promise you no more than that."

She sprang to her feet, and stood before the seated Russian commander, and reached out to touch his arm.

"Do you take me for a fool, sir?" she said, still calm, still fully under control. "I have come to you not to beg but to offer you information of the utmost importance – in return for the privilege of serving you – you personally, Marshal Vorilov, if you desire it."

She could sense that his breathing had quickened just a bit, and she noticed a tinge of pink mounting in his earlobes. And when he placed his hands high on her waist, his thumbs just under her breasts, she smelled triumph. But the Marshal merely thrust her aside, got to his feet, and walked to the window, his back to her. He was a tough one, obviously struggling to contain his emotions in the name of military duty. But Else had never failed to resolve the struggle in her own favor. And she didn't mean to fail now.

"What information do you have?" Vorilov demanded to know. "Be quick about it. I am a busy man."

"You may have the information on the condition that I receive in return your personal protection," she said doggedly.

"Very well," he replied, turning to face her. "You have my word on it – on the condition that your information is truly vital to us. And I will be the judge of that."

She raised her skirt slowly, making sure that she showed the marble whiteness of her thighs and just enough of the black diaphanous panties to shake Vorilov's military rigidity. And from her garter belt, she withdrew the miniature, leather-covered book, and handed it to the Russian.

He seized it, and carefully examined its pages. Then he shrugged, and tossed it on the bed.

"Madam, I am afraid there can be no bargain between us," he said. "We have long ago broken the Nazi code. The code books are a common as dirt. Our agents have supplied us with them in ample quantity. No sale."

Else had anticipated that. But now she was ready to spring her ace in the hole. Again she raised her skirts, and now she withdrew the notebook, the personal notebook of General Stauffer, the late General Stauffer.

"Hmmm," Vorilov murmured, thumbing through it. "The roster of German scientists and their war projects. Very good on rockets, you Germans. This seems authentic."

"I can assure you that it is, Marshal. It came to me directly from the source."

"Indeed?" Vorilov said. "From General Stauffer himself?"

She was surprised he knew the name. Yet why shouldn't he? Stauffer was a name to be feared all over Europe. It was understandable that the Soviets had heard of him. She sidled up to the Russian, slipped her arms around his waist and pressed her flanks against his. For a moment she felt his body stiffen in resistance, but only for a moment. His strong arms enveloped her, and he lifted her and carried her to the bed.

Else had won again. She always won.

Vorilov was an expert. His hands were sure and gentle, his body powerful and skilled. For the first time in her life the experience was almost pleasurable, and she smiled triumphantly as he relaxed a moment in her arms afterwards. She ran her fingers through his silvery hair, kissed his earlobes, and whispered:

"Then we have struck a bargain, my Marshal?"

Vorilov suddenly came to life as if her words had aroused him from a dream.

"I'm afraid not, madam," he said crisply, leaving the bed. "You see, some weeks ago our intelligence came into possession of just such a list. The Red Army has captured virtually all the scientists on this roster. Many of them are already in Russia continuing their research and organizing production facilities – for us."

"But," she protested, "that can not be. There was only one copy of the list in all of Germany. And that belonged to General Stauffer."

Vorilov smiled coldly, and said: "Your facts are correct, my dear. But incomplete. You see, General Stauffer is an opportunist such as you and I. Weeks ago he knew a Russian victory was inevitable. He became a Soviet agent under Hitler's very nose, and supplied us with much valuable information – including the roster of scientists."

Her heart was pounding as she groped for her clothing. The blood had drained from her face, and she felt weak in the knees.

"I received a message from Stauffer only a few hours ago," Vorilov went on. "He informed me that Hitler and Goebbels are dead, and that he himself is preparing to flee the Chancellery and join the Red Army this very night. I gather," he added, "that you are either a friend of Stauffer's or an enemy."

"The Brigadeführer was my benefactor," she gasped.

"Oh? Then you must offer him my apologies for our brief indiscretion. You may wait here for him if you like. We have promised to treat him well in payment for his treason to the Reich."

"General Stauffer is dead," she said in a dull monotone. "Murdered in the Chancellery not an hour ago. I found his body, and I brought you what I considered his most important papers."

Naked, her magnificent body quivering, she threw

herself into the Marshal's arms.

"You must be my benefactor now. I will serve you well," she said almost hysterically. "You will not regret it."

He thrust her aside disdainfully.

"You will not understand, woman," he shouted. "There is no bargain between us. My deal was with Stauffer, and it is not transferrable to his mistress. Your information has come too late. It is mere repetition. A pity."

"You are a man," she insisted, sinking to her knees before him. "I can make you happy. Believe me."

He struck her in the face with the flat of his hand, and she sobbed, groveling at his feet, knowing that it was useless to prostrate herself before this brute, but powerless to do anything else. What a strange practical joke of fate! Stauffer could have saved her, only Stauffer. And she had murdered him. She began to laugh insanely, desperately.

"Put on your clothes," Vorilov ordered her. "You are a slut and will be treated accordingly. I know your type. You feed on men, milk them dry without conscience, and then betray them. You are worse even than the Huns who invaded my country and ravaged it. The Huns who murdered and raped innocent Russian women and children, my own wife and children among them.

"You have made me detest myself for having lowered myself to go to bed with you. Go, before I forget that I am an officer and a gentleman and order you shot on the spot."

The captain was waiting for her when she staggered out of the house. The eyes of the sentries undressed her, and she felt dirty for it, not proud.

The captain seized her arm, and dragged her to the armored car. She found him disgusting, and yet she was in a position where she had to consider even him as her protector now – this gross, brutal thug.

He took her to a ramshackle house, a house jammed full of Russian officers and troops, and reeking of unwashed bodies. A roar went up when they saw her. The captain realized that he had made a mistake by coming here, and tried to leave with her. But a torrent of crazed men prevented their escape. A howling, maniacal struggle developed, and the captain vanished under a tangle of thrashing arms and legs and brandished vodka bottles.

Else was beyond fear or despair now. She was a lump of flesh without feeling. The Russians tore at her clothes like wild beasts for carrion. Their black fingernails ripped gashes in her flesh. They carried her out of the room by the arms and legs like a fatted calf already slaughtered. It was an old Cossack custom.

Just before she lost consciousness, she remembered the last words of Stauffer before he died in a pool of his own blood: "You deserve the Reds. They will grind you into mincemeat."

DOOMED NUDES IN THE CIRCUS OF HORROR

Only the most beautiful women entered the dwarf's hideous carnival of torture and death!

THE OLD WAGON SWAYED and shook, trembling in the darkness. Around it other wagons, tents, cages were still and quiet, but from this one came the terrible sound of screaming. Trees shivered slightly in a cold night wind, making a circle around the caravan of wagons and tents. Somewhere from a cage there was the coughing roar of a lion, a chatter of monkeys.

The screams stopped for a second, and there was absolute quiet.

Then there was a voice, a hoarse, gasping whisper. "Please... don't hurt me any more... oh God, let me go... please, have mercy, I pray you, have mercy..."

A second of silence.

Then the screams began again.

No one came to investigate. The Graumier Circus rested each night some distance from a town, and travelled on in the morning. From a distance, there was no way to identify the screams: any circus had animals and strange acts, and who could say that the sounds were not due to that cause?

Only from the caravan itself could the ear tell that they were the screams, not of some strange animal, but of a woman – a woman in the extremity of agony!

And, inside that caravan, within the Graumier Circus, the sounds did not give rise to pity or to terror or to mad rage.

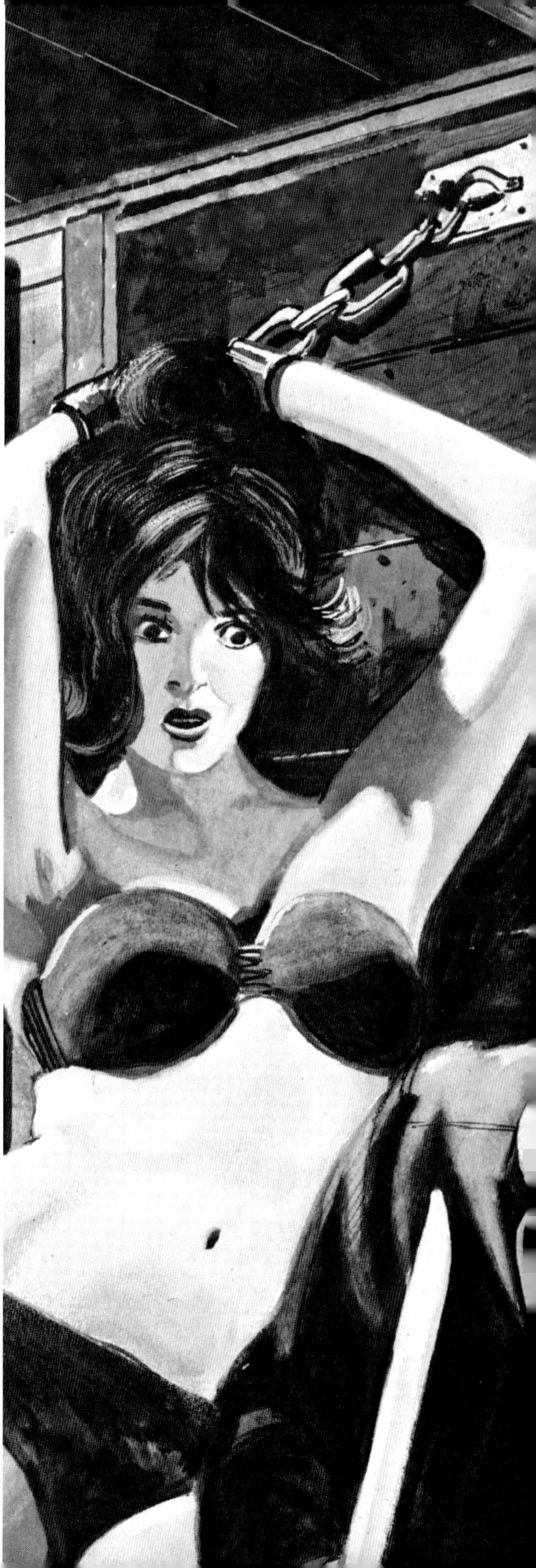

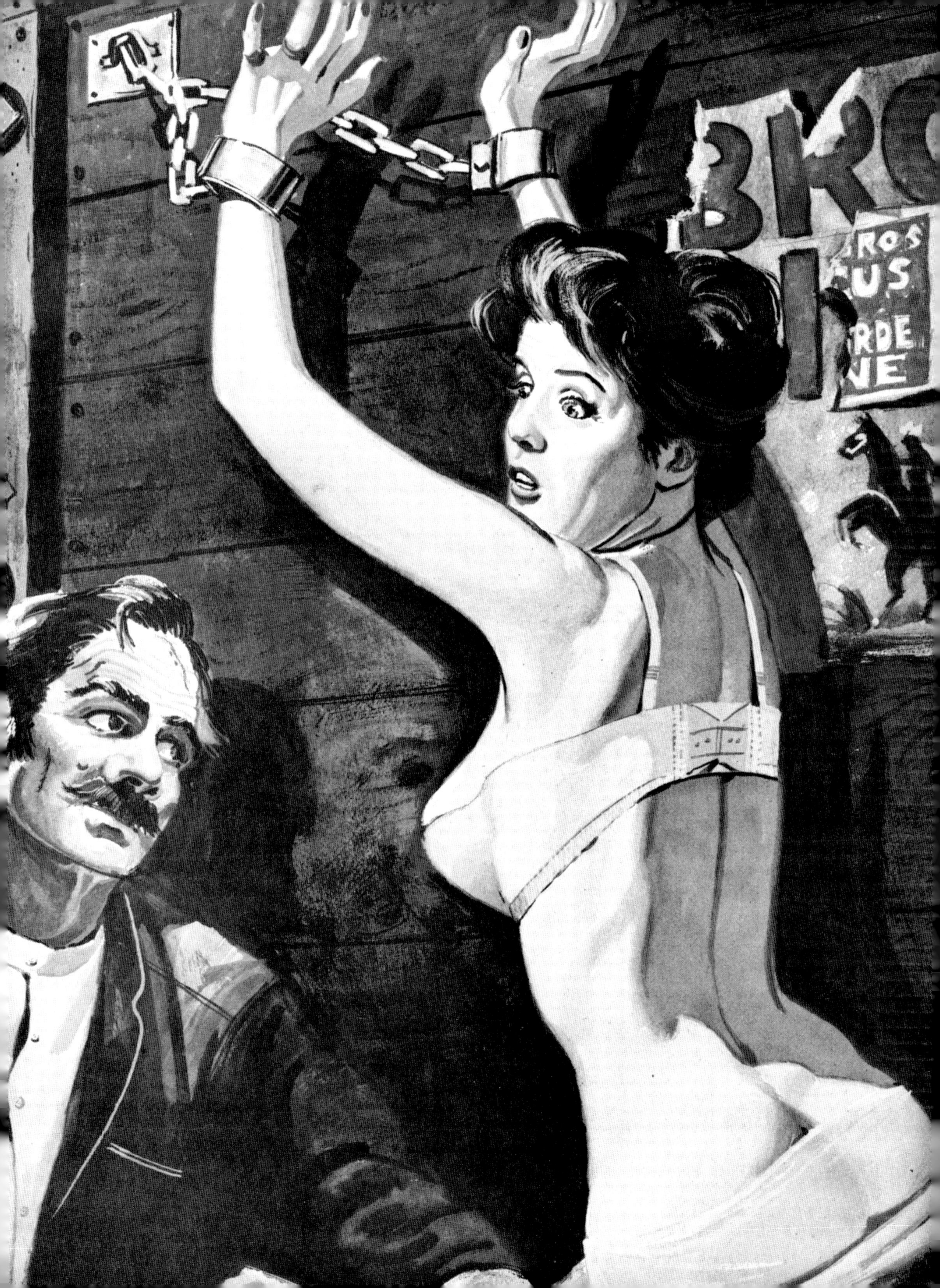
BR
ROS
CUS
RDE
NE

Instead, some ignored the screams.

And others smiled.

Inside the wagon, little Graumier twisted his face up in what was meant to be a smile. In one stubby hand he held a long knife, stained now at the tip with red blood. He brought the knife close to the body of the nude girl who was roped to one wall, and she screamed again.

"Don't touch me... don't cut me again..."

Graumier sneered horribly. "Why not be quiet, like your sister?" he asked in a guttural voice. "Your sister makes no sound now, no sound at all."

He turned. Against the opposite wall, another woman was tied, her body gleaming whitely in the light of the wagon's single oil-lamp. Her head dropped to her breast and her body was marked with cuts from Graumier's knife.

"Soon, you too will be quiet," he murmured to the still-struggling victim. "But not as soon as you desire. And then you shall wake – as she shall wake – and your punishment will go on!"

The girl screamed as the knife approached her once more – and then tore at her white flesh! Her body jerked in its bonds and her eyes went wide and wild, and mad screams tore from her throat. Graumier's smile broadened. Over the screams, his voice murmured:

"You are pretty... so pretty you never look at me. But soon now, you will not be pretty any more... soon you will be ugly, and perhaps this time I will be able to keep you alive!"

The girl's breasts heaved, her muscles jerked as she tried vainly to escape. Her eyes were fixed on the moving gleam of the knife, and behind it the little dwarf Graumier who held it, letting it circle toward her once again as firelight danced on the cruel point.

Once again he slashed at the helpless girl, and her screams grew worse.

Through the red mist of pain she could see the body of her sister, terribly marked and cut, hanging against the wall opposite her. She could remember her sister's screams as she had been the first to taste Graumier's knife, remember her own pleading with the little monster, her mad struggles to rescue her sister...

And then she had fainted. Graumier had turned, and the knife had touched her...

No human being could stand such pain, her mind told her. She would die under his terrible knife, in torture...

But now she could not even faint, could not even avoid the moving point of the knife which came toward her, tearing at her sensitive flesh.

"Kill me!" she screamed. "Kill me! Don't hurt me any more! Mercy! Have pity on me!"

But Graumier's smile stayed behind the knife. "You will stay alive," he murmured. "You will stay alive – to suffer, and at last to be made as I am – as we all are here. You were pretty... now you will be punished."

Hopeless prayers for peace, for death, were on the girl's lips. Then the knife slashed out once more and the prayers died in bubbling screams that burst insanely from her throat...

WE DO not know exactly when the Graumier Circus was formed. In the year 1846 it first appears as an organization, traveling through the Black Forest of Germany, playing for a day or two days in a given town and then starting off again for a new destination.

And, for all the various townsfolk knew, it was a perfectly normal traveling circus. There were several of them in Germany at that time, and Graumier's seemed to be one more, no better and no worse than the others. There were a few animals: lions, tigers, monkeys. There were specialty acts like a sword-swallower, a strong man, a fire-eater. And there were the freaks.

It was a freak, as a matter of fact, who owned and ran the circus, a shrunken, scarred and horrible dwarf named Wilfrid Graumier. His name was not German, but that could never have mattered to the townsfolk he visited. Graumier might have come from anywhere: he could have been born out of the earth. Certainly no parents could have wanted to keep a being like that – an ugly, misshapen thing barely four feet tall, scarred as the result of some old fight or accident, grimacing, waddling, barely human.

Children laughed at Graumier and his antics. Their parents watched in fascinated horror, as they might have watched some grotesque being from another world. He looked worse than horrible: he looked dangerous.

But what danger could come from a dwarf? What harm could so small, so obviously handicapped a being bring to anyone?

Graumier himself could have told them. And, in a way, he did – since he kept a sheaf of writings in his wagon, an ill-assorted bundle he called his *Manifesto*, locked up in an iron safe and added to from time to time.

None of the patrons of his circus ever saw it. But in that *Manifesto* is the true history of Wilfrid Graumier – dwarf, freak – and monster.

He had built his organization carefully over some years, picking only those who could work in his circus and at the same time shared his terrible passion for revenge and torment. His major assistant appears to have been one Richard Oder, the circus strong man, who supplied the brawn which Graumier lacked – but every human being in the caravan was a part of his plan.

Oder picked the victims, on Graumier's muttered suggestions. Oder waited for them after the circus had shut up and moved off for the night. Oder trapped them and brought them out of the towns to the quiet caravan that rested, waiting for them, some distance away.

Sometimes the whole circus joined in the carnival of torture that followed. Sometimes only Graumier himself, whose appetites seem to have been inexhaustible, took over the "punishment."

The *Manifesto* contains a record of hundreds of such incidents. A few of them can be selected to portray the terror of the Graumier Circus, this secret juggernaut of torment that flamed its way through the Black Forest towns like an arrow.

For instance... Georg Kramer and his wife Elsa.

Georg was a fine, blond young man, his wife a pretty brunette. They caught the eyes of Wilfrid Graumier – and his strong-arm assistant Oder went out after them.

But Graumier wasn't the only one interested in these two.

Frederik Dort, the circus fire-eater, had seen them as well. And this time the "punishment" session was held in the fire-eater's wagon.

Roped to opposite walls, George and his pretty wife, Elsa, watched with horror as Frederik Dort took out the tools of his trade – the great clubs wrapped round with soaked cotton, the long matches and the sticks for lighting.

Georg came first. While Graumier and Oder watched, the fire-eater burned the young man slowly, horribly, to death – touching him with flame until his screams were hoarse howls...

And then Dort turned to Elsa Kramer, who had watched her husband die in agony. Elsa was half mad with the spectacle of Georg's torture.

It took her four hours to die under the ministrations of the fire-eater. By the time she finally collapsed, her body was a single mass of terrible burns, and she had become entirely insane.

Of course, there were others as well.

There was Dora Barthmann, who was whipped to death by Graumier and Oder together. Dora was eighteen years old, a little blonde girl who suffered ten hours under the competent and horrible hands of these monsters.

When she finally died, released from torture at last, Graumier turned on Oder in a blazing rage.

"I did not want her dead!" he shouted. "I did not want to kill her! Only to punish her... to *transform* her..."

Oder shrugged and smiled stupidly. Surely there were always others? Surely it made little difference? The girl had screamed and suffered, she had tried to escape and she had pleaded with them, offering them anything in return for a remission of her pain... she had grown hoarse and mad with pain, and she had died.

Surely it was all very simple?

But Graumier had still another objective.

The *Manifesto* tells of that objective.

"I mean to make of these pretty ones, these big ones, human beings like myself. In that way they shall learn, in that way they shall be taught painfully to treat me as a human being, to respect me for what I am..."

But Graumier, perhaps, could never learn to control his hatred.

In case after case, either he or one of the others went too far, and gave their victim what Graumier had not looked for – the final release of death.

BUT NOW, he felt, he had a chance... all alone, with two victims. Surely one of them would survive, would become a monster like himself?

He blinked and smiled horribly, his heavy-lidded eyes taking in every detail of the young, tormented body roped before him.

He brought up his knife...

Over those terrible shrieks of agony, his whispered voice was barely audible. "You will live, you will not die... you will learn through pain, you will become as I am..."

Her body trembled half-consciously with agony, her wrists and ankles bloodied where she had tried to jerk herself free of the ropes which kept her bound. Her eyes were wide and half-mad with pain, her muscles tightening and relaxing in spasms of agony.

"Let me die... don't hurt me any more..." the girl whispered, her voice growing hoarse with the constant screaming.

"Die? Never!" Graumier shrieked with triumph. "No! You will live to become as I am – to learn, to suffer–"

The girl pulled feebly at her bonds: her strength was leaving her under the pain. Graumier paid her motions no attention.

"You will become my mate!" he screeched with hysterical abandon. "My mate!" He danced in the light of the oil-lamp, while the wagon swayed and shivered and the girl's screams, gasping hoarse shrieks of absolute horror and torment, rose once more as he approached her with the knife, and struck again...

Across the wagon, Graumier's first victim still sagged in her bonds, her dead face seeming to have an effect of peace in the dim light, now that she had at last escaped the mad lusts of the monster. But her living sister could not see that face; she could see nothing now, not even the evil dwarf, except the dancing, threatening point of the knife.

At last, she fainted.

Graumier bent near her. "Dead?" he muttered. "Surely not dead... surely this one will live to become as I am... surely..."

He discovered a heart-beat and his smile returned. "She will awaken: the punishment, the treatment, will go on..." Then he blinked. "Yet I must not awaken her," he told himself solemnly. "She must have strength, strength... she will recover of herself, in brief minutes, and then we can continue... soon she will be ready..."

Seconds ticked by while the gnome-like little man stood watching the unconscious form of his victim.

Then the door of the wagon burst suddenly open!

Graumier whirled. "Oder!"

The strong-man came in, slamming the door shut behind him. "Well, Graumier?" he asked. "It's over?"

"This time they do not die! This time one of them lives, lives at last to be my mate..."

"Shut up." The giant threw out the words casually. "I grabbed these off, I have a right to help out with them now."

"I–" Graumier licked his thick lips.

"You sent me off on an errand, didn't you?" the giant asked. "So I wouldn't be here – so you could take care of these two beauties all alone?"

"Oder, I–" And then Graumier's rage burst. "It is you! It is always you! They die and it is your fault, when I want them to live! You kill them, but this time I have them to myself–"

"Not any more you don't," Oder said. "And besides" – he jerked a thumb over his shoulder – "one of them looks dead already."

"But this one, this one–" Graumier insisted, dancing horribly in anger and terror.

"You're mad," Oder said.

Graumier grimaced. "We are all mad. The world has made us so. But now, now that one lives for me–"

"You little runt – giving me orders, running me off so you can have everything to yourself–" Oder roared with laughter. "Well, now it's your turn to be locked out–"

"You don't dare!" Graumier shrieked. "I have a knife – take care, big man, take care–"

Oder laughed again. "I lock you out this time!" he boasted, and came forward.

Near them, the girl stirred, moaned – and awakened. In her pain, she longed only for death. Her vision was misty with agony, but she saw the dwarf and the giant struggling.

They came toward the oil-lamp, careened into it. Oder screamed suddenly as the knife found a mark, and the dwarf reeled backward as the giant flailed out...

The fire which swept through the Graumier circus claimed six lives – three of them in the wagon in which Graumier's upset oil-lamp had started the blaze.

Oder, dying from the dwarf's knife-thrust and unable to escape, had fallen over Graumier and trapped him there – and the girl, roped alive and screaming, could do nothing but watch the flames approach her. She died shrieking in a new agony, her slashed flesh licked and burned by the flames.

The Graumier Circus was no more.

Only the iron box remained, to be claimed by townsfolk investigating the fire, to be opened and its contents read with horror, and to be put away in the archives of one Government after another as a secret of terror.

Now, at last, after more than one hundred years, the full story can be told of the doomed nudes, the circus of horror, and the mad dwarf, Wilfrid Graumier.

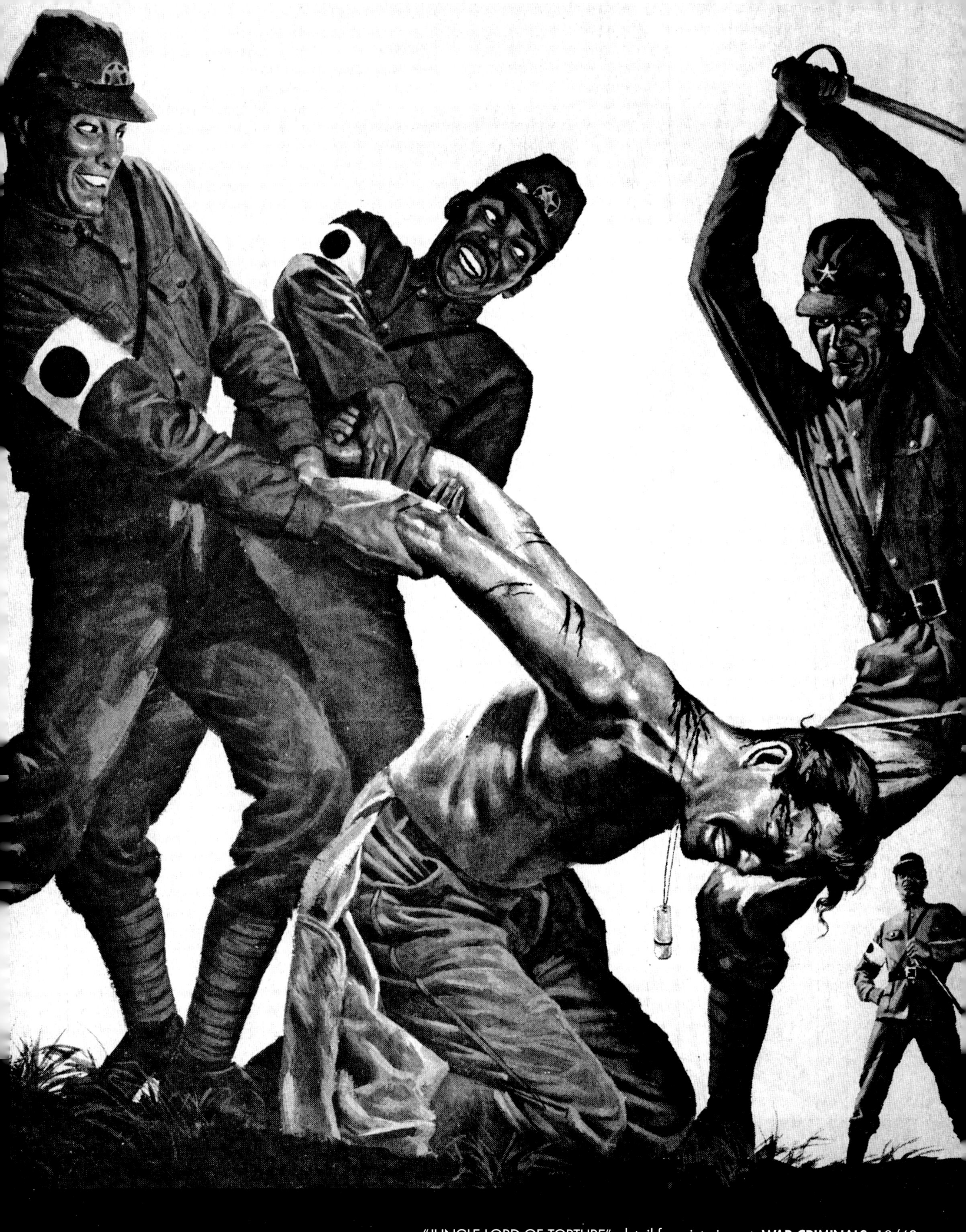

"JUNGLE LORD OF TORTURE"; detail from interior art, **WAR CRIMINALS**, 10/63.

BLOOD BEAST OF THE THIRD REICH

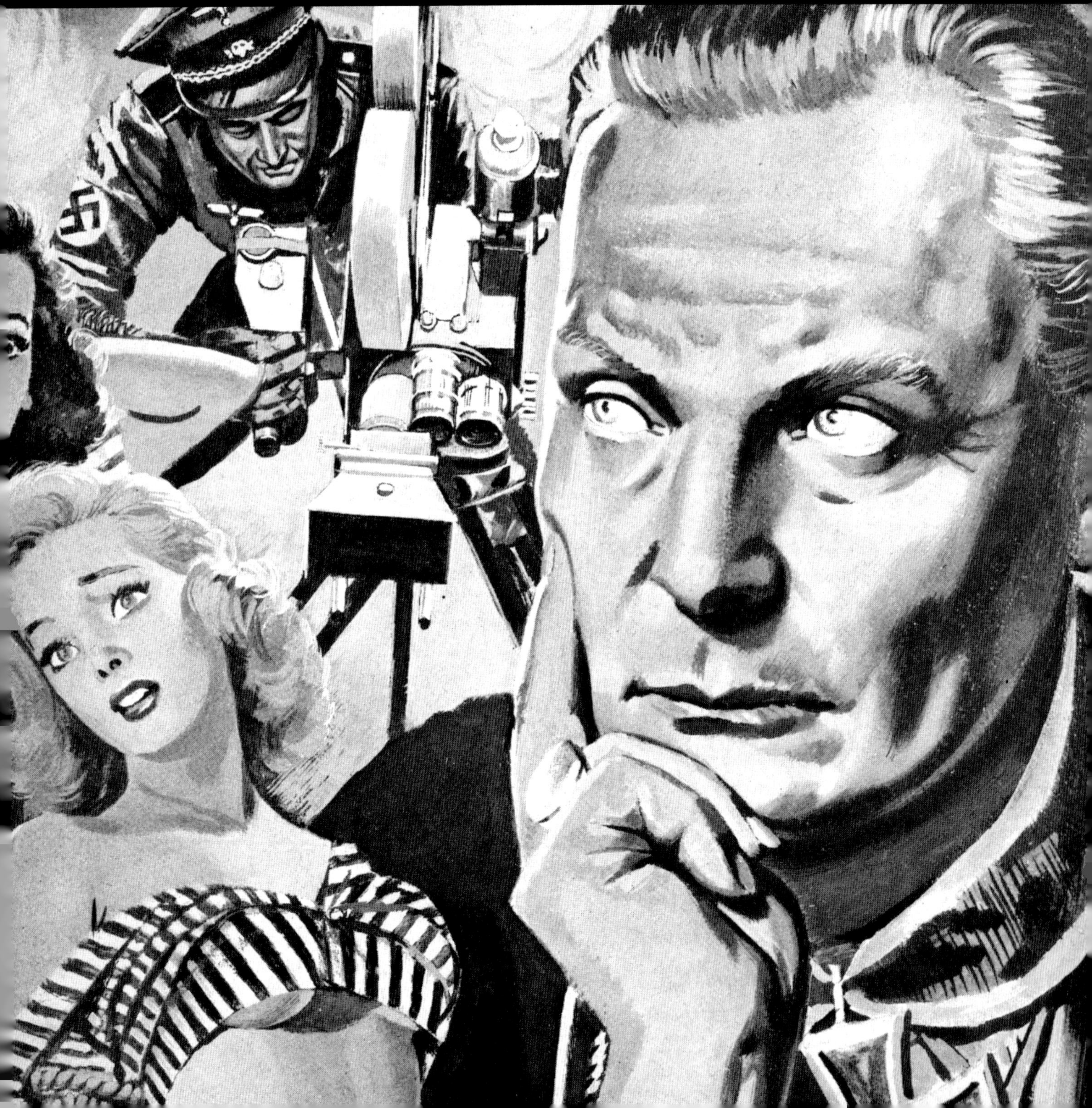

In his private North German hideaway, Reichsmarschall Goering indulged a secret passion for abusing the prettiest young women he could find – and capturing his orgies on film!

ON JANUARY 8, 1936, I was ordered to Berlin and assigned to the personal staff of our Reichsmarschall, Hermann Goering. At that time I was a Leutnant in the Luftwaffe, whose prospects were extremely dim. A year previously I had contracted a mild case of TB, and though completely cured, the Air Force Medical Officers had grounded me, permanently. I had tried to take it all with good grace. Realizing my predicament, I had spent my military leave attempting to gain some new type of skill that I could use. I had always been an ardent camera fan. Careful study and hard application paid off. I was permitted to remain in the Luftwaffe and assigned to a photographic reconnaissance squadron as a technical officer.

But ground men in any Air Force seldom go very far. Certainly I was assured of a place, but my hopes for high rank, heroism and the glory that comes from combat were now vanished. For even though it was peacetime, we all were aware that war was inevitable.

So my transfer to the staff of the commanding general of the Lufwaffe came as both a surprise and a sudden ray of hope. How bitterly both were to collapse, I wasn't to know for several weeks.

But this really isn't my story. It's Goering's. I was merely a pawn in his game. I make no excuses. I did as I was ordered, even though I knew that there was no military excuse for my acquiescence. At the time, I was honestly afraid to refuse. Besides, I was a German officer. Even if I had not been afraid, the very idea of disobeying a legally commissioned superior would have been inconceivable to me.

I quickly discovered what my new duties were to be. For in the last week in February, Goering ordered me to accompany him to Pomerania, a remote section of northeast Germany. For the next three years I remained there. During all that long tour of duty, I was the Marshall's personal cameraman – photographing for his own use some of the most shocking and sordid scenes that any human being can possibly imagine.

There were eight of us assigned to that duty, all officers or soldiers of the Luftwaffe. Before we finished our tours, mercifully cut short by the outbreak of hostilities, we became so inured to what was taking place around us, that the terrible evils actually seemed normal. It wasn't until months after we left that things fell back into their normal places again and we began to understand the horrors we had wrought.

Like most of the Nazi leadership, Goering was fanatically addicted to pornography. He had set up one of the most complete organizations for turning out this material that the world has ever seen. Ours was only one small unit of this se-tup. For one of Goering's pet pleasures was watching what he called the "real stuff." That means he particularly loved to sit there, as if in a theater, and actually watch it as it was being shot in film.

In the beginning, he used professional women and volunteer men in his movies. But after a short time that became boring. "There's no kick in seeing what any man in the world can see for a few marks," he grumbled. That's when he began using "amateur talent." At first this was strictly volunteer. But there weren't enough willing women for him, so he shortly turned to prisoners and slave labor camps for his "movie stars." I'll say this for him, he had an unerring eye for beautiful women.

Most of the girls were completely unaware of why they had been brought to the castle. And by order, they were kept entirely ignorant of the purpose until the very instant they were hauled out before the cameras and forced to perform. It was felt that the shock, and the inevitable horror and disgust that showed on their faces, made for an extra sense of realism in the films.

Let me give you a few examples. Though my diary gives only short outlines of the daily events, most of them are deeply etched in my memory.

IN APRIL, 1937, four young women were brought to the castle. Two of them were Germans, a middle-class girl picked up for some currency violation, and a servant girl arrested for drunkenness. The other two were a kidnapped Polish woman of about 24, and an Englishwoman who had been arrested only the day before for taking photographs too close to a military installation.

The castle was fairly large, and the women were kept separately, without any knowledge that others were present. About a week was spent feeding them all up to a glowing state of health.

Finally we were informed that the Reichsmarschall would be down that evening. The women were told that they were about to be released, and it was suggested to them that they might enjoy a beauty treatment prior to leaving the castle the next morning. All responded joyously. They were bathed, perfumed, had their hair done to perfection and in all ways were transformed from prisoners to the luscious young things they really were.

At about ten in the evening, after Goering had enjoyed a magnificent supper and was feeling his jovial best, we were ready to begin the show. The cameras were put into place, the lighting was arranged, the script approved, and Goering nodded his permission to begin.

Kurt, an Unteroffizier in charge of enforcement, brought in the first two girls, the Englishwoman and the German servant girl. They were seated on a pair of stools and, without warning, a motion picture was run off for them. It only lasted ten minutes, but it was devoted totally to methods of inflicting the most horrible tortures on women. At the conclusion of the film, Kurt informed the girls that the movie had been made right in that room. He told them that every instrument of pain was right within reach and that if the girls did not do everything they were told, they would receive the same treatment. The girls were terrified, and showed it.

We now described to them the love scene they were to carry out together. As two, healthy, normal women, they shuddered at the perversity of the situation. But what could they do. Reluctantly, they mounted the stage, removed their clothing and began to perform. Helmut Erikksen, a really first-class movie man from Sweden – a pity he wasted himself on things like this – was the director. He kept the action moving at a torrid pace. Whenever the performance lagged, he was ready to move in and give the girls the most specific sort of instructions, making sure that despite their horror, the girls showed the right facial expressions, and uttered the sounds that would be appropriate for the action. The scene lasted more than an hour before it was finished.

Now it was the turn of the other German girl and the young Pole. While the first two actresses were taken where they could see, but not be seen, the two newcomers were given a repeat of the terror build-up.

Their action was to be with Albrecht, another of the staff. I can't go into a description of this performance. It would be impossible to print. But at the time, as I viewed the large, luscious breasts, and firm tapering legs of our "actresses" I envied Albrecht with all my heart. At that moment I would have given anything to have been "star" instead of merely the cameraman.

Not that I didn't occasionally have my chance. For Albrecht was our "Still Cameraman", and when he was at work, I often had the chance of "working out" for his lenses. And then too, now and then we switched jobs for an evening, he taking the movies and I the stills. It made for a little change in routine.

Of course these were rather simple films. Later, as Goering became more and more sated with the ordinary aspects of sex, deep thought was given to add a fillip to the actions. We were limited, however, by the fact that our chief always insisted on character realism.

Thus, when someone came up with the idea of using three generations of women – grandmother, mother and daughter – in simultaneous action with a single man, it took deep research before we located an actual trio that filled the bill in regard to looks. It took several months before we found a suitable group. They were promptly arrested on some trumped-up charge and were brought to the castle. The long wait had whetted the Reichsmarschall's appetite to the fullest. He insisted in personally appearing as the man in the movie. In all fairness, I must give him full credit for a magnificent performance. The movie went on for five reels, a full two hours of non-stop "acting."

Some of the scenes shot in our productions were highly complex. In one, more than two hundred men and women staged a full orgy across the entire main hall of the castle. For that one, we used five cameras and had to import more than fifty special guards to control the host of prisoners.

Some of our assignments were quite peculiar. Goering was, as most people now know, a confirmed drug addict. In times of fantasy, he might demand almost anything. And some of his demands were quite horrible. There were times, when he combined human and animal actors, that women were actually torn apart, physically. On one occasion, the blood was so thick on the floor, that the frightened prisoners were literally slipping and sliding in gore as they attempted to move about. And all the while, Goering, deep in the throes of morphine, sat there laughing like a maniac at the carnage around him.

Again, however, I must say that these drug-inspired horrors were not the usual thing. Under normal circumstances, he was quite gentle in his demands.

After the end of the films, it was a different story. Naturally, Reichsmarschall Goering's reputation had to be preserved. The honor of the Fatherland demanded it. Regretfully, Goering issued orders for the "abolition" of the prisoners. But his normally gentle nature mitigated against his being present at the ultimate. I cannot remember ever seeing him attend even once. Our method was simple. The victims were dropped into *aqua regia* – a highly potent mixture of nitric and sulphuric acid, that entirely consumed flesh, bones and even teeth. Every week a new supply was delivered to us, together with an agent for neutralizing the acidity. The result was shipped by special truck to the Baltic Sea and there dumped under the personal supervision of one of the officer staff. I carried out this sad duty on many occasions. So important was this considered, that even during the war, when chemicals were in critical supply, Goering's castle invariably received its weekly quota.

SPEAKING OF the war, this provided us with a whole new group of actors and actresses. Poland, France, Holland, Belgium and Norway gave us many real beauties and fine virile human stallions. It became regular practice for the castle staff to visit captured countries to select performers for our films. We had *carte blanche*. No one was so highly placed that he could protect anyone against us. We were acting directly in Goering's name. On more than one occasion we took the personal mistress of some General or high political official. There were no repercussions.

I had the opportunity of going on about twenty "recruiting" missions. We were treated royally wherever we traveled. And I had Goering's personal permission in writing to try out any woman I felt might be suitable. I made much use of that permission. I must say that I preferred the Norwegian girls best. They had a stately look of loveliness about them that I found irresistible.

One event that stands out in my mind took place on Goering's visit to Paris. Here one of the officers took him to view what was claimed to be the Marquis de Sade's own apartments.

Goering was fascinated. He ordered me to join him in Paris, even though by then I had been transferred from his staff. There, in a ten day period, we photographed for him the complete tortures of De Sade as described in the two books, *Justine* and *Juliette*. Goering much regretted not being able to stay to watch the entire shooting. He had too much war work at the time. But later, on viewing the film – it ran for eight full hours – he sent a personal commendation to me at my unit, and awarded me palms for my Iron Cross. I understand that the Führer also viewed the film and thought it delightful. He too sent me a letter, personally autographed. Unfortunately the letter was later lost during our retreat from France.

Actually, that was a most difficult job to do. I could have spent years doing the work that I was forced to accomplish in those ten days. How I wished that Erikksen had been there with his sure director's touch to aid me. Working with French prisoners of war, and kidnapped French and Belgian girls was quite a wearing experience to me. After a day of supervising a continual procession of torture and horror, often leaving an actress so physically damaged that she was unable to repeat a poorly-done scene, was exhausting to me. But at least my work was appreciated. That counted for a great deal to me.

American readers may be interested to know that we used many American men and women in our films. Some of them were excellent in their parts, so good that they would have undoubtedly become Hollywood stars if we hadn't been under the unfortunate necessity of liquefying them in acid.

I remember one girl, from California I believe. She told us she had actually been to Hollywood. She was a delightful creature. After Goering finished with her – in this case he personally went through a bondage-rape scene with her – we all made use of her fine figure and soft, yielding flesh. She was a very interesting girl. We permitted her to live an extra forty-eight hours and then, because she had been so sweet to have around, we knocked her unconscious before plunging her into the acid, instead of dropping her in alive and fully awake as was customary. I still have a ring of hers that I took from her finger, before Albrecht carried her limp form to the vats. It's a sentimental remembrance that I'll always keep. I still think of her fondly. I'm glad her death was on Goering's conscience and not on mine. Though of course I doubt that he ever thought about it one way or another.

The war ultimately brought my connection to an end. In September 1940 I was transferred to the French Front. There, except for a few short jobs that I did for Goering on occasion, I remained. I was a Hauptmann then, and later, as our numbers were cut down during the retreat to the fatherland and our unsuccessful defense of our home soil, I was again promoted to Major, the rank I held at the dissolution of the German Air Force.

I returned to my home in Prussia, I am now married to a Scandinavian girl who for political reasons resided for a time in East Germany. She had retained her own native citizenship, so that she was able to travel freely between her homeland and the German Democratic Republic of East Germany. It was through her influence that I was finally able to leave Communist territory.

The location of Goering's hidden films is unknown.

TORTURE TRAP OF THE

It was just another schoolday – until these punks in ponytails turned the tables on their teacher, and terror took over the classroom. Then the hate-filled vixens added a new twist to the nightmare.

"SORRY TEACH... WRONG ANSWER!"

The bespectacled little man howled with pain as the ruler smashed across his face with terrific force. The wild-eyed, leering girl standing above him whisked the ruler back again and delivered another vicious whack to her victim's head.

This time, the steel-edged ruler cracked against the cowering man's temple, knocking his glasses across the room, shattering the lenses into fragments. He moaned at the blow, and once again tried to break the wire bonds around his wrists, which were bloodied from his efforts to get free.

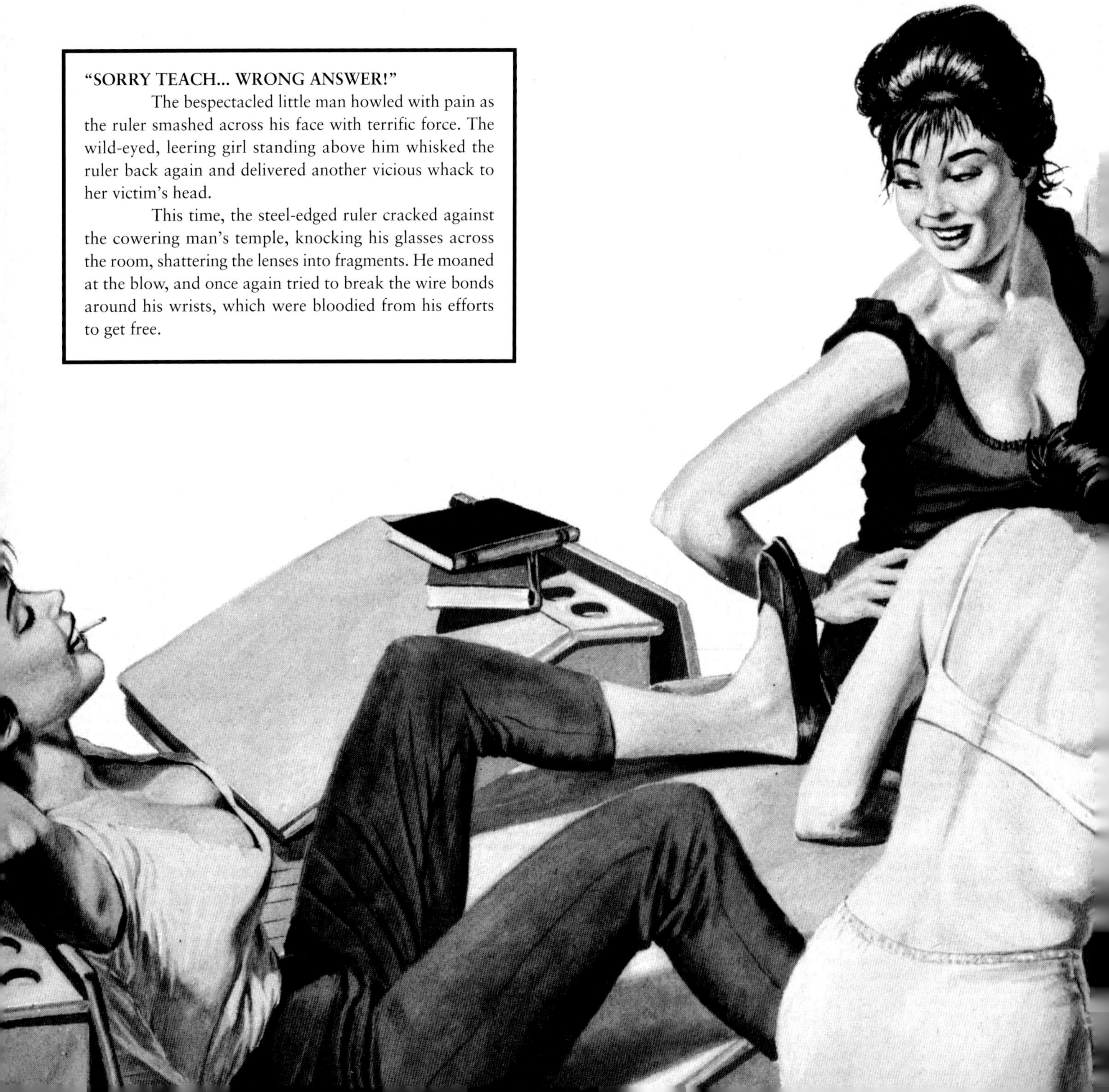

NYMPHO SCHOOLGIRLS

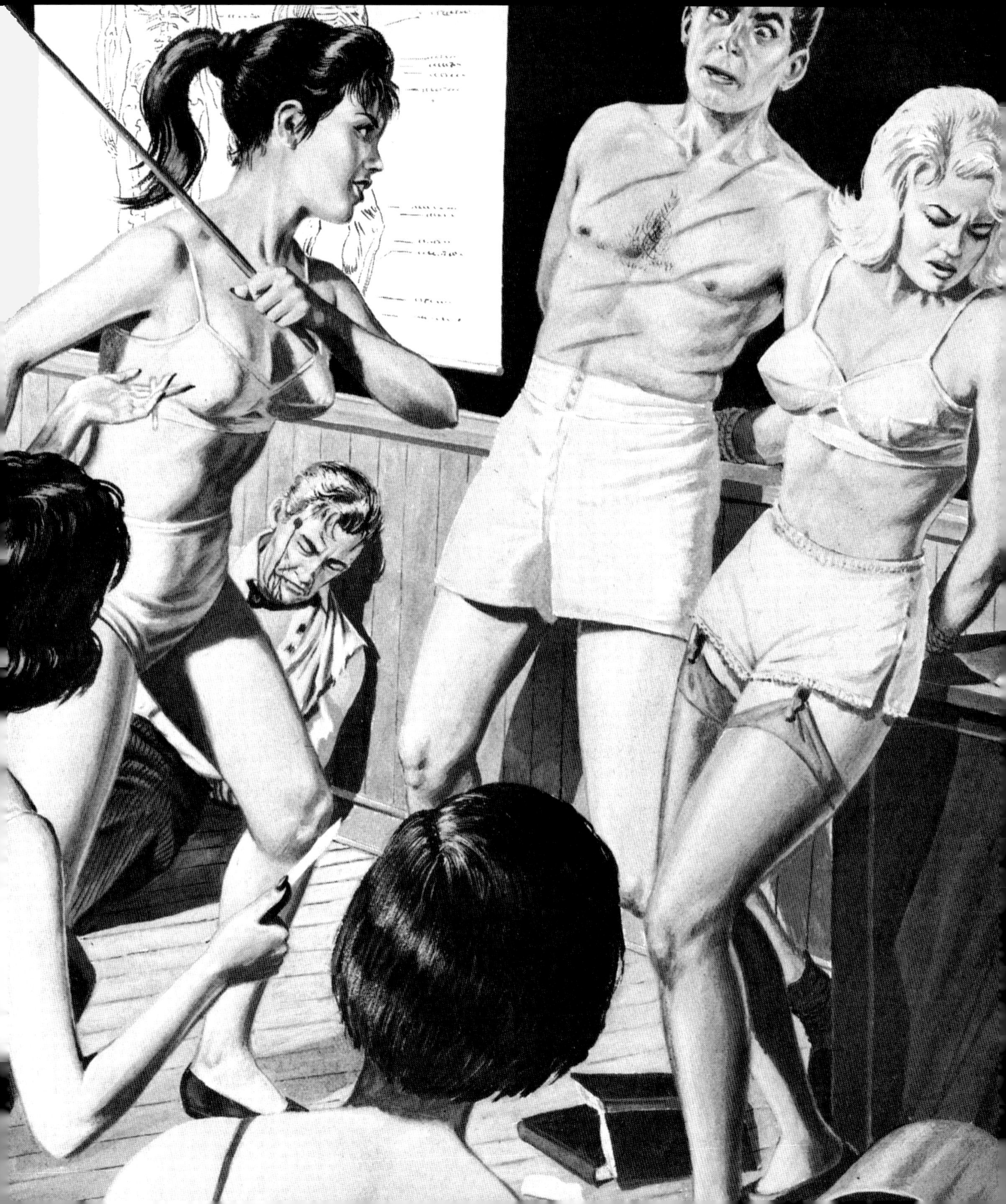

I cursed the predicament we were in, and strained at my own bonds. If there were only a night watchman in the deserted high school building, I would have yelled my head off. But as it was, only the empty corridors would have heard any calls for help. It was May, and the custodian was on a two weeks vacation. We were quite alone, I realized... completely cut off from the outside.

Here we were – Harry Martinelli, a history teacher, the girl, who was one of his students, and myself – lured into this trap by five other teen-age girls who, sure as hell, were out to skin us alive. Harry, because he flunked all of them in his history class; the girl, because she opened her mouth about them to the principal; and me, because I tried to have them expelled.

And the funny part about this whole thing was that the five girls were holding us prisoner in a public high school classroom... in Harry's own classroom. I knew the room like the palm of my own hand. I can't remember how many times I had knocked on Harry's door toward the end of one of his history periods, and signaled him to meet me in the coffee shop across the street when he finished with his class. And the times we didn't have coffee – which was at least three evenings of every school week – I'd slump down into one of the twenty-seven seats in his classroom, and shoot the breeze with the near-sighted, kindly scholar.

And now... watching helplessly as Harry was being savagely beaten made my blood boil! These girls were not only inflicting pain on the middle-aged teacher, but they were enjoying the torture they were dishing out.

There was no doubt that the girls were having fun, and now they added a new twist to make this nightmare complete. They reversed roles with us. They became the teacher, and we became their "students." And heaven help us if we made a mistake!

They strutted over to me – all five of them like a delegation. Their pretty, sneering faces hovering above me gave me the chills.

"O.K., Teach," drawled the full-bosomed one with the tight sweater, "answer Arlene's question."

Stepping close enough to me for her thighs to press against my shoulder, the one called Arlene just stood there, rubbing back and forth against my arm. A sensuous smile played on her mouth.

"C'mon, c'mon!" Millie snapped. "Stop horsing around. See if he knows his stuff."

They all laughed at this, and Arlene fired her first question.

"Tell me, Teach," she asked mockingly, "how many pieces of your friend's broken glasses are lying around this room?"

I glanced quickly at Harry, who was still sitting with his head down on his chest, exhausted from the beating. His broken glasses... just how many pieces were there scattered around the floor, I wondered frantically. But then I realized that trouble was in store for me no matter what answer I gave, and I remained tight-lipped.

As the sadistic quintet leered down at me, waiting for my response, my thoughts flashed back to a certain Tuesday, a few weeks before, when I had just finished putting the gym team through their paces for a forthcoming exhibition

I WAS just leaving the building through the rear entrance, when I heard a strange shuffling sound just outside the stadium gate. It was starting to get dark, and I had to strain my eyes to see what the commotion was all about.

As I approached the gate, five silhouetted figures sprang up off the ground and darted past me, almost knocking me over.

Before I could recover from my surprise, a muffled squealing reached my ears. This time I was sure it came from the area of the gate. Dashing toward the sounds, I saw a sight that shocked and sickened me.

Bound and gagged was a beautiful co-ed... a girl whom I recognized as one of the school's cheer leaders.

Whoever assaulted her, I couldn't help but notice, had ripped off her blouse and skirt and tossed them over the stadium gate. The half-nude girl, sobbing hysterically, was twisting back and forth in an effort to break the cord binding her wrists and ankles.

I untied the shivering girl, and threw my topcoat around her shoulders. She fell whimpering into my arms.

I identified myself, and then asked if she knew who did this to her. At first, she wouldn't talk, but kept crying quietly. But after awhile she told me the whole story.

One of the football players, who had been going with a hot-blooded chick in the junior class – a tough little gal named Millie Rudko – had taken a turn of heart, and started dating the pretty young girl trembling in my arms.

Millie, angered at the fluff-off and jealous, too, enlisted the aid of four of her girl friends. She was going to teach her rival a lesson.

As Doris left the high school grounds after a late cheer practice session the next day, she was grabbed by Millie and her friends. They gagged and tied her, then dragged her back to the stadium. Doris paused, dried her eyes, and then, instead of talking, she pulled away from me and threw open the coat I had covered her with.

"Look," she told me.

All I could do was gaze unbelievingly at the girl's blood-stained bra, then at the cruel slash made on her milk-white bosom. Doris went on to explain what the five girls were doing to her when I happened along.

"This is the beginning of the letter B," she said, pointing to her wound. "It stands for 'Busted,' and means that once and for all I've been cut off from my boyfriend... by – by them."

I retrieved the girl's clothing, and after she dressed, I drove her home. I advised her that it would he best to forget the incident, and her football player as well.

"Those gals play rough," I told "but the chances are they won't bother you again if you keep your mouth shut about tonight."

But contrary to my advice, Doris marched right into the principal's office the following day, and told him the whole incident, demanding that her attackers be arrested. Naturally, Millie and her cronies denied everything, and, since there were no witnesses, the entire matter was dropped. I guess I could have spoken up too, but since I didn't actually recognize any of the girls, I knew my testimony wouldn't hold up either. Things were quiet for a while after that, but I somehow couldn't dismiss the incident from my mind. I was sure that since Doris talked, sooner or later Millie and her gang would get hold of her again and try to finish the grisly job they had started. But apparently I was wrong. Perhaps the whole incident had been forgotten.

Then, a few weeks later, it happened. Late one Friday afternoon, as I looked up from my desk, I saw someone standing in the doorway of my hygiene room. It was Millie, and she had that tough smirk on her face.

I asked her what she wanted, but instead of answering, she sauntered across the room and began to flip through the anatomy charts hanging on the blackboard.

"That's a real crazy body there," she remarked, examining the diagram of the peripheral muscular system. "Are you built like that, Teach?" she asked brazenly and began strutting over to me, her mature body out-lined by a low-necked white sweater, at least two sizes too small, and a form-fitting skirt.

I ignored her question and behavior, and asked curtly what she wanted. She told me that Mr. Martinelli wanted to see me right away in his classroom.

Without hesitating, I went over to Harry Martinelli's room – and walked right into real trouble.

THE DOOR slammed shut behind me, and before I could gather my wits together, a hard, cold object jabbed me painfully in the back. I knew it was a gun, and froze in my tracks.

My heart pounded and my stomach flipped when I saw Harry and Doris in the room, each tied to a desk chair. In minutes I joined them... courtesy of Millie and her friends. I strained hard at the wire painfully cutting into my wrists, and then gave up. They did a damned good job, Millie and her girls. I tried to keep calm, but I knew these punks in pony tails meant business.

"Teach, you'll just have to answer my question."

My attractive interrogator had grabbed a long wooden pointer from the blackboard trough, and began poking me with it in the chest and stomach. I remained silent, waiting for what was coming next.

"If that's the way you want to play, Teach," she said, "we have ways to make you talk."

I didn't have to wait long to find out what she meant.

"His clothes..." barked Millie, "take them off him!"

They stripped me to my shorts in a matter of minutes, and then hungrily eyed my body from head to toe. I could see the desire in their eyes, but the hate written all over their faces was more apparent, and I braced myself for the ordeal I knew was yet to come.

And come it did. I shut my eyes tight and clenched my fists as the pointer in Arlene's hand came whirring like lightning toward my head.

My brain exploded. I shot right out of my chair, and howled like a tortured dog. My head felt like it had been torn off my shoulders. The pain shooting through my face and skull was indescribable: I rocked back and forth and groaned in a feverish attempt to lessen the pain.

"So you wanted to get us expelled, did you?"

Through my aching, clouded brain I saw Millie peering down at me, her legs planted wide apart and her hands on her hips.

"After this weekend, Teach," she continued, "you better look for a new kind of job. We're goin' to fix you so you'll never be able to work in a gym again."

With that, the hate-filled little vixen gave Arlene a nod, and the girl began bringing the wooden pointer down again and again on my stomach and thighs.

After a while, the pain brought me to the edge of unconsciousness. When I slumped forward in my chair, the girl stopped.

"Leave him be for now," Millie told the others. Then she stepped in and wrenched my head up by the hair.

"Snap out of it, chum," she hissed. "I don't want you to miss the rest of the show."

She had the others turn my chair around so I'd be facing Doris. The girl's face was etched with horror at what she suspected was about to be done to her. She let out a frightening shriek and Millie smacked her across the face, so hard that Doris' head snapped back against the chair. That started it.

In a jiffy, Millie's friends were on the girl, tearing her dress right off her back. I looked at Harry, who had by this time also recovered from his ordeal. I noticed the dried blood caked around his squinting eyes, and by the expression on his long, sensitive face, I knew that my presence gave him at least a faint spark of encouragement.

But when Doris screamed again, Harry strained in his chair, and then he became ill all over himself.

I knew these girls were tough, but never dreamed they could be as sadistic as they were being now. They were about to finish the "treatment" they had started on Doris several weeks before.

ONE GIRL jammed her hand over Doris' mouth while two others quickly unhooked the terrified girl's bra. Then Millie moved in and tore the bra from the girl's shoulders. The gang leader was holding a long-handled switchblade knife in her hand, and pressed the button in its handle. When the long blade clicked into place, Millie went at the unfortunate co-ed like a spider pouncing on her trapped prey.

But Doris fought, and the girls had all they could do to hold their tied victim down. She crouched and contorted like a trapped animal. And all Harry and I could do was look on in horror as Millie proceeded to carry out the terrible mutilation of her prisoner. The whole business looked like a painting I'd seen of the Devil performing some ghastly operation on a lost soul.

The sight of this Millie, this female butcher, carving her mark into Doris' bosom held me in a kind of trance. Then something snapped me out of it. Someone was tampering with my bonds. I looked to see who it was and couldn't believe my eyes. It was actually one of Millie's girls – I didn't know her name – but she was quietly unwinding the wire twisted around my hands.

"Why?" I asked in a whisper, as she freed one hand.

"You'll see, Teach," she snapped back at me.

Then I saw that she was holding a gun, and I knew my thoughts of escape had been premature. I began to wonder what I was being set up for now.

"Try to make a break, and you'll be a dead Tarzan," she grimly warned. Before I knew it, the girl began to embrace me. Now I saw why I had been untied. My heart started to pound with excitement and, in spite of my predicament, my body stirred to her caresses.

"Hold me," she moaned in my ear. "Make love to me – now!"

In her excitement, her gun dropped to the floor. I grabbed it, and acted fast. Before the panting girl could snap out of her sensuous reverie, I had the .38 trained on the whole bunch of them.

"All right... no tricks, you damned savages," I barked. "Get away from that girl and line up against the wall, or I'll blast a bullet into one of you!"

Keeping the startled gang covered, I untied Doris and Harry. Then I told him to look after the weakened girl, whose bosom was drenched in blood, while I slipped on my trousers and shirt, and grabbed my shoes.

"O.K., let's go," I ordered, waving the girls out the door with the gun. They all had the good sense to do as they were told... all, that is, except Millie.

She lunged past three of the girls, and dashed out into the long school corridor.

"Here... keep the rest of them covered," I said to Harry, giving him the pistol, "I'm going after her."

I started out after Millie, and in no time closed the gap between us. I reached out to grab her, but she eluded my grasp. The chase down the hall continued for another few moments, but finally I brought her down with a flying tackle. She hit her head on the marble floor and lay still. I thought she was dead, but a doctor later diagnosed it as a severe concussion.

I stumbled back to Harry and Doris. The knifed girl had improvised a bandage for her wound, and Harry had the rest of the sadistic gang well under control with the .38.

Millie recovered from her head injury and stood trial with the rest of her mob. They all received from five to ten years in the state reformatory. With good behavior, they may only serve the minimum sentence – but I know three people who'll feel much safer if the maximum penalty is carried out.

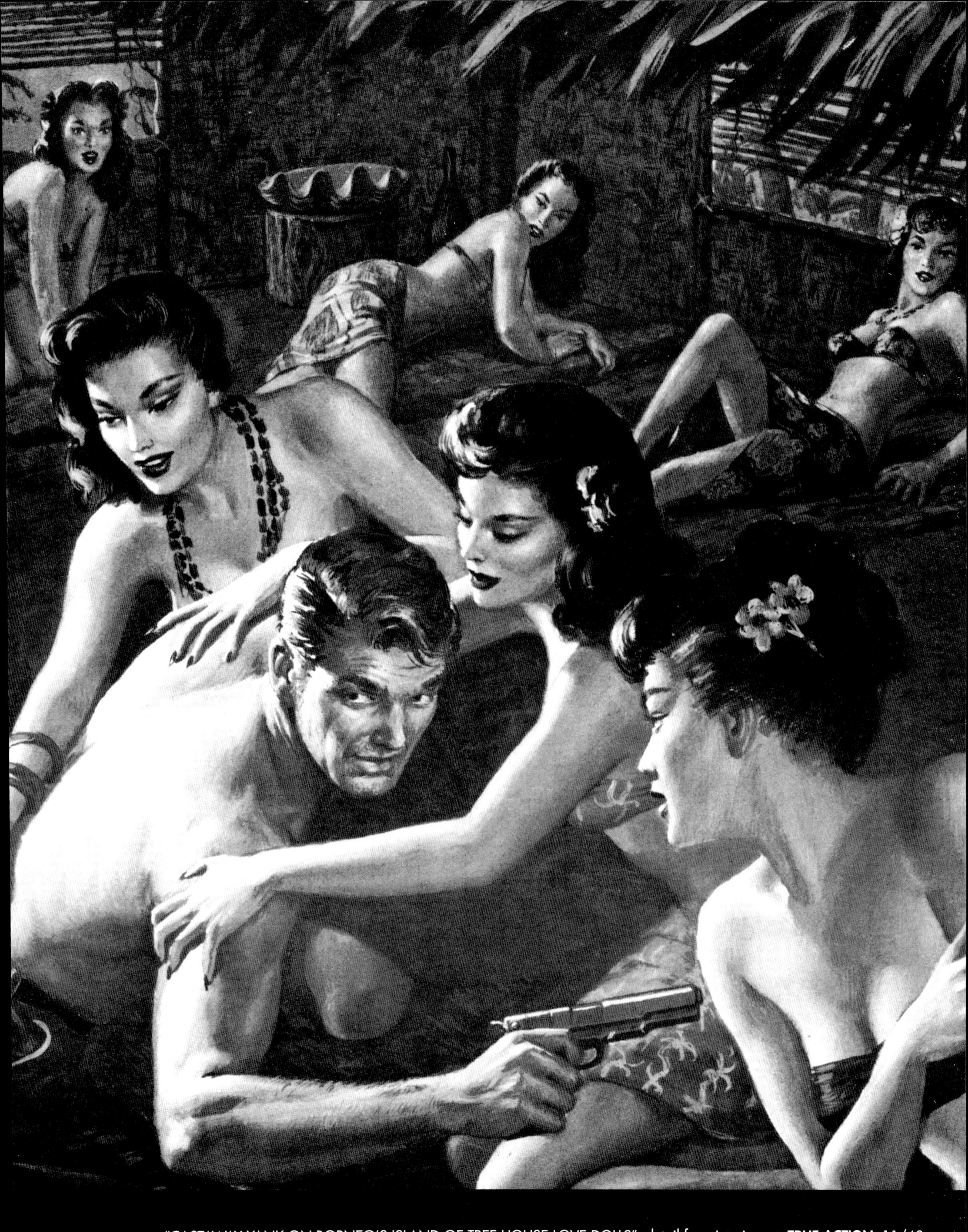

"CASTAWAY YANK ON BORNEO'S ISLAND OF TREE HOUSE LOVE DOLLS"; detail from interior art, **TRUE ACTION**, 11/63.
Art by Samson Pollen.

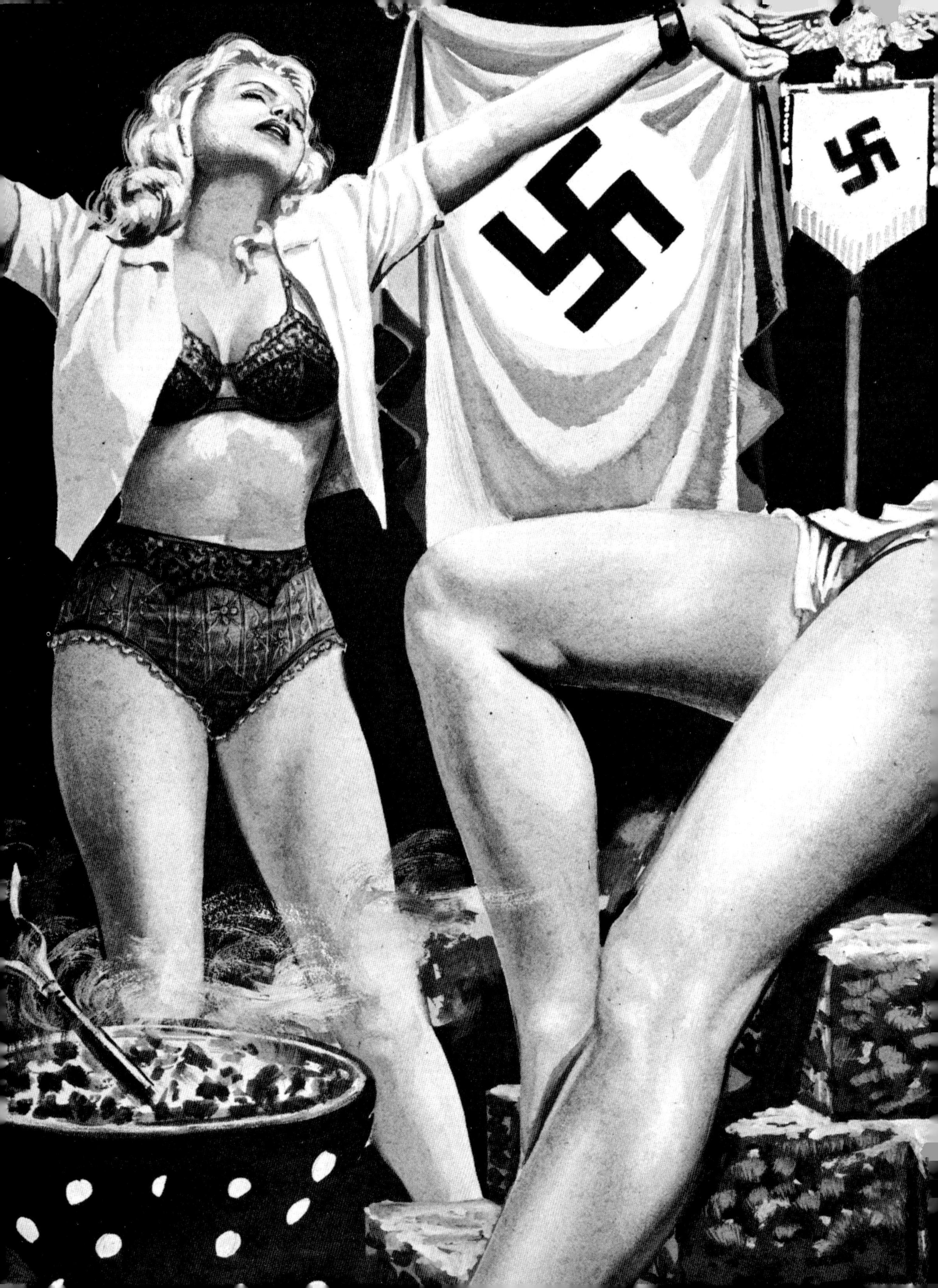

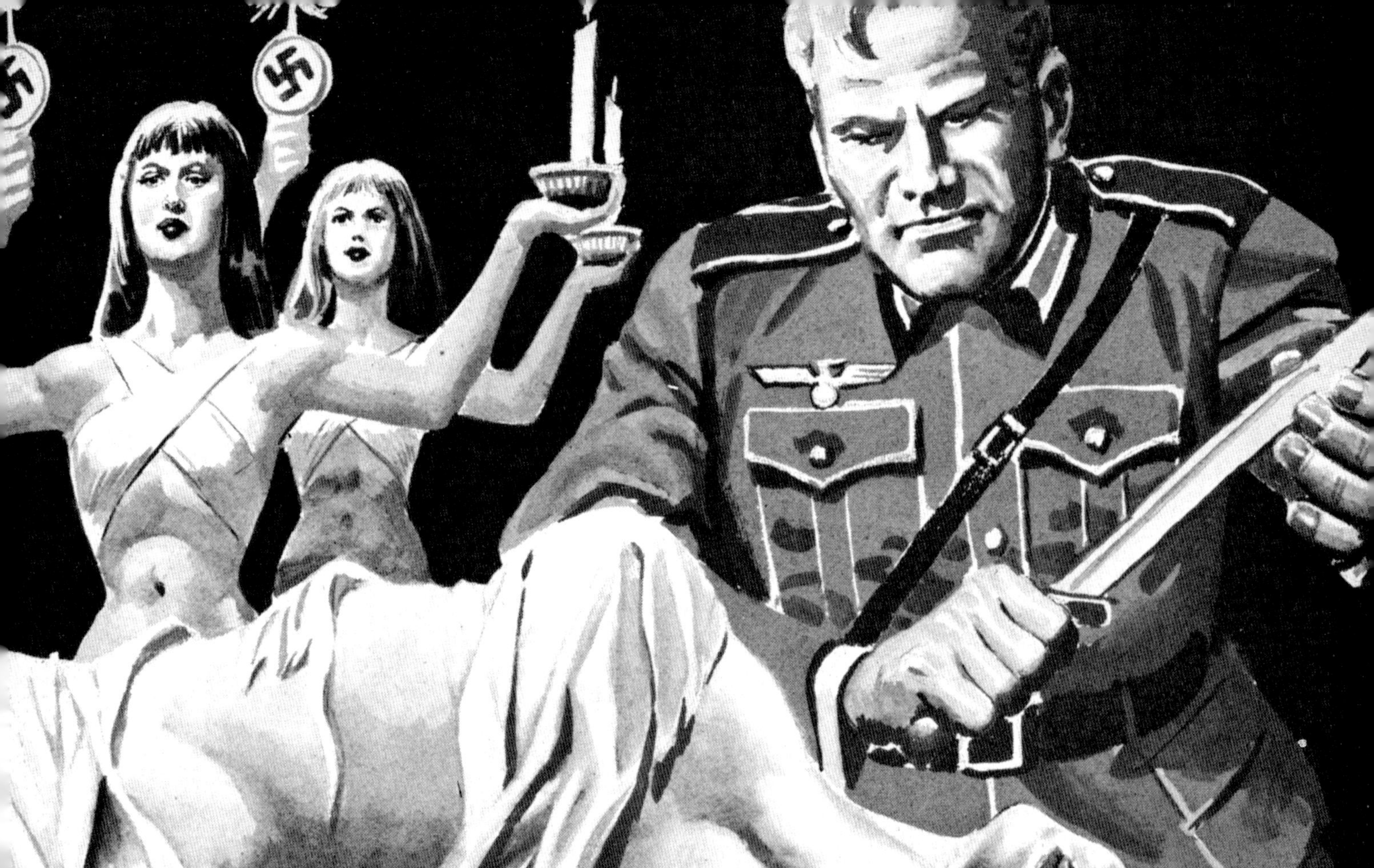

SCREAMING VIRGINS
FOR THE NAZI RITES OF AGONY

The fiend's lovely, writhing nude victims formed a twisted beauty pageant of torment.

A SCURRYING BODY TOUCHED the girl's ankle. She kicked out at it in terror. The rat's high-pitched squeal of rage was even more terrifying than the feel of its coarse fur against her tender skin.

The girl tried to scream. Her throat was raw and dry. "I am not going mad," she told herself. "I will not go mad."

She walked the two steps to the sweating stone wall and touche dit. Her hand recoiled at the sensation of oily wetness. Was it merely water that had oozed from the cracks – or was it blood? There was no way of differentiating in the inky blackness.

"I am Gerta Sondheim. I am twenty-two years old. I have committed no crime. I should not be here," the girl whispered. There were no voices to answer.

"It is wrong. It is all some monstrous mistake," Gerta Sondheim continued. "The Geheime Staatspolizei will let me go as soon as they realise it."

The words did little to bolster her sagging courage. She paced the confines of the cage-like room, wracking her brain. Step by step she went back over the past 24 hours. She started with the two SS men who had accosted her on the street, seizing her by the arms and dragging her to the Mercedes parked by the curb.

She recalled pleading with them as the driver guided the black vehicle through a series of narrow alleys. She remembered their tight-lipped silence and the cruelty they used when they had thrust her into this solitary cell.

Her mind floated backwards. A sudden shudder of revulsion and dread convulsed her. The image of the thin-lipped man with the twisted leg and bloodless lips swam before her. The man was dressed in a colonel's uniform. He was pawing at her, trying to rip her dress from her. She was screaming, warding off his advances. She was gathering her ripped frock around her and rushing from his room.

Once again his words echoed in her ears. "I am Obersturmbannführer Heinrich Brauer. Remember that name!"

Gerta Sondheim put out her hands to steady herself. Her heart beat against her ribs. She felt the sweat of fear trickle down her spine. It was as if Brauer's beady eyes were staring through the gloom of the dungeon at her. She could almost hear the twisted leg dragging behind him as he approached. There could be no doubt that Heinrich Brauer was in some way connected with her situation.

The terrified girl waited, listening to the scurrying of the small bodies which darted over her feet.

When the key finally rasped in the lock, Gerta Sondheim found herself crying out in new terror. She thought she had been prepared for the moment. She had steeled herself for the entrance of uniformed Gestapo men. But this was far more diabolical.

They swept in silently, their nude bodies glistening through the transparent robes they wore. Each carried a black candle.

They were each over six feet tall and they were built with a remarkable symmetry of proportions. Their long golden hair was braided high on their heads. Even though slit masks covered their eyes, the beauty of their faces was apparent.

In a matter of seconds, the silent ones had surrounded Gerta, herding her to the center of the room. Although they carried no weapons, the bizarreness of their approach was enough to freeze her into immobility.

One of the women undid a silken cord which had been tied around her waist. Two others took their cue from her. Quickly they grasped Gerta's wrists forcing them behind her back and holding them in a vise-like grip as the silken cord was looped over her hands.

The terrorized captive found her voice. She struggled against the bonds which held her. The knot merely tightened, digging into her flesh and bringing a nauseating wave of pain.

The tallest of the women stepped forward. Her jaw was set at an arrogant angle. Her breasts heaved against the diaphanous bodice of her gown with erotic anticipation.

Her taloned fingers hooked in the top of Gerta Sondheim's frock. There was the ripping of cloth as the dress was shredded down the line of Gerta's bosom. One of the acolytes knelt before her victim. She tugged at Gerta's skirt. The dungeon rang out with Gerta's outraged cry as the silent ones probed her nakedness, which winked out at them from under its scant covering of black silk panties and bra.

A hand raked her face. A fist ground into the small of her back propelling her forward. Gerta felt herself being shoved into a huge amphitheater-style room and onto a stage which looked down into an orchestra pit. Eerie lights played along a black velvet curtain. It was difficult for the girl to see in the semi-darkness.

The silent ones hustled Gerta to two cruel-looking chains which dangled from a wall at the side of the stage. She struggled furiously against them as they cut the silken rope away from her arms. But her attempts were puny when compared to the combined strength of the women who surrounded her. In a moment she hung spread-eagled, her feet angled out and encased in thick irons, her arms hitched high over her head causing her whole body to shimmer tautly in the half-light.

The women left her after testing her bonds. For long minutes the stage remained vacant. Then the masked women returned, dragging a whimpering young girl with them. Like Gerta Sondheim, the girl had been stripped to her skimpy bra and panties.

Over the girl's muffled sobbing Gerta heard the hubbub of many muted voices. The audience had arrived and filled the seats of the amphitheater. Their excitement grew as they watched the amazon-like acolytes spread-eagle her across the altar. The girl's back was arched upward. She writhed against her bindings, her body undulating in a dance of mindless fear. The sounds from the audience built up to a suppressed clamor.

The acolytes fanned out. Their candles flickered ominously. From a door hidden behind the curtain a shadowy figure moved towards the center of the stage. His right foot dragged slightly. His eyes were slitted and the brows, thick and shaggy, had a demoniac look to them.

He held up his hand for silence. The steel blade of a bejeweled ceremonial knife glinted in his hand. Heinrich Brauer captivated his audience with the studied, slow malevolence of his gestures. He moved to a glowing brazier and plunged the knife into the glowing coals to its hilt.

The girl bound to the altar raised her head. Her eyes grew wide as she watched the knife point turn a brilliant cherry red. She screamed once when the blade snicked through the straps of her bra. She could not catch her breath sufficiently to scream a second time as it traced a line through the delicate silk of her brief pink panties.

With sick fascination, Gerta Sondheim watched the sacrificial torture. Heinrich Brauer would not allow the young girl to taste the full thrust of the knife. Instead he worked with vicious cunning, making each slice of the blade account for the maximum of physical agony. The altar became a thing alive with the girl's pain-crazed struggles.

Unintelligible cries rose from the amphitheater to mix with the mortal pleadings of the girl, who had torn the flesh from her own body with her futile attempts to be free from the ropes which held her helpless on her bed of pain.

At last the acolytes stepped forward. With no outward sign of revulsion, they carried the thing that had been a woman from the stage.

Heinrich Brauer bowed low to his audience, and smiled serenely at their bursting applause and cheers.

HEINRICH BRAUER reveled in applause the way he reveled in blood. The two had made him rich beyond his fondest expectations. They had given him power. They had made him the friend of Himmler and Goebbels. They had put him in a position of prominence even among the super-Nazis.

The story of Heinrich Brauer begins in Munich in 1923. Hitler, a petty *hofbrau* tough who starts battles but isn't around to finish them, has just come out of prison. He screams for a place on the ballot for the National Socialist Party.

Brauer, an ugly little man who was born with a twisted leg, listens to Hitler's tirades and is swept up in the flood of psychotic hatred.

A student of philosophy, a would-be actor, and a drunkard, Heinrich Brauer is also a practical businessman. He meets those who surround Hitler and listens to their laments over the lack of money which is hampering the work of the Party.

At the time, Brauer has become involved with a rather dull-witted Munich prostitute who has some morbid fascination for her twisted lover. When Brauer is not in her bed or attending Nazi *brauhaus* rallies, he's delving into the history of the Teutonic worship of pagan gods.

He recognizes immediately that Germans have always combined naturalism with religion. In his diseased mind naturalism can only mean the most blatant displays of erotic passion.

Brauer has an ability to understand the worst and most debased cravings of men and women. But he isn't interested in catering to them for the sake of perversity alone. Certainly, an unrestrained sexual atmosphere will encourage those who partake in it to unlock their pockets to the Nazis, he reasons.

He approaches those who have Hitler's ear and suggests the formation of a clandestine "health spa" outside of Munich. He arranges with his paramour to stock it with young German women who have lost their scruples in the post-World War I direction. He makes it clear to his staff that they will be expected to provide all manner of diversions to the paying guests.

The gangsters, addicts and perverts who compose the nucleus of Hitler's elite household endorse the plan wildly. There are many international industrialists – even American millionaires – who would patronize such a health club. If they prove to be parsimonious in their contributions following their sojourns, a gentle amount of well-applied blackmail should loosen them up.

In reality, what Brauer is arranging is nothing more than a large-scale bordello. However, he knows how to gild the lily. He adopts the slogan "Strength Through Joy." Soon he has over a hundred women recruits to serve the callers.

Reasoning that sex alone is not enough to maintain a hold on those who can afford the best, the cunning Brauer begins to delve into the occult. He pores over volumes on Satanism and witchcraft. He comes to understand that from the time of the Romans, through the ravages of Attila the Hun, into the depredations of the Inquisition, outrage is the mortar which holds the temple of sin together.

By now he has shelved his prostitute for a cynical ex-Berlin University student, Lisa Schmidt. Lisa has been delving into abnormal psychology, and introduces Brauer to the world of sado-masochistic sex.

"Men and women want to torture and be tortured," she tells her lover as she gnaws away at his ear. "Here, I will show you." She jumps out of Brauer's bed and grips his heavy leather belt in her slim hands. Suddenly she lashes out at his naked body. He screams in pain. He trembles as he awaits the slashing pain of the next blow. The tension gives him a sensation he has not experienced before.

He allows Lisa Schmidt to beat him mercilessly. Then he turns on her. She submits to the whipping. Later, as they lie intertwined together, he decides to add a new element to his health farm.

Devices are trundled in as props for simulated sacrifices of the prostitutes who work there. Special rooms are set aside for demonstrations of bondage and chastisement. The list of international devotees grow. Money for uniforms, money for boots, money for rubber truncheons floods into the Nazi coffers. Himmler and Hess shake Brauer's hand. They tell him he will be a big man in the new Germany. He increases his activities.

One night in 1929 a blonde prostitute dies on the gibbet in the health farm's theater. Her heart has given out under the savage lashing she has received at the hands of Brauer. The Munich police find her mutilated body on the road. But they are warned away from more than a cursory investigation by the Brown Shirts who now control the Bavarian city.

Brauer has found out that he can murder without fear of reprisal. He is now bigger than the law.

Lisa Schmidt, for all of her beauty and talent for creating an atmosphere of occult abandon, has begun to pall for the rising Nazi. He's thinking now in terms of mingling with movie actresses, and prominent and abandoned female members of the international set.

On March 10, 1931, two goons wearing Nazi uniforms invade Lisa Schmidt's apartment. They carry with them a valise which contains rope, a cloth gag and small bottle of chloroform. Lisa Schmidt struggles valiantly against her attackers. But they manage to bind her wrists behind her and secure a rope around her ankles. They jam the cloth gag into her mouth and shove a chloroform-soaked handkerchief under her nose.

When she awakens, she is on the stage of Brauer's amphitheater. She has been chained to the wall with her arms held over her head and her legs spread-eagled. Her eyes lock with Brauer's as he moves in to strip the dress from her back. She hears the words of encouragement of his disciples.

Clad only in her snug panties, she cries out for the group of acolytes who line the stage to help her. "You were my idea. I gave you these jobs!" Lisa screams. "Without me you'd be nothing but streetwalkers!"

The naked women regarded her with boredom. Brauer's whip curls around Lisa's hips, shredding the silken cloth of her lone remaining garment. She sees the madness in his eyes. She knows that she will die, and her death will not be an accident.

THIS IS the first time that Heinrich Brauer kills by design. It is the beginning of a bloodbath which is not to end until 1944.

How many other women, young and lovely in their helplessness, hung before the mad torturer and shrieked for the mercy of death, will never be known.

Even the Nazis, who were so meticulous about their record-keeping, made exceptions when it came to the operations of Heinrich Brauer.

It is said that as the war progressed there were some among them who suggested that Brauer be killed. But they were over-ruled. Himmler muttered, "The man is important to us. He understands the forces of the stars which will win the war for us."

Goebbels found the distractions offered by Brauer were too much to give up.

Hess supplied Brauer with the loveliest prisoners processed at Auschwitz. The acolyte guards of Brauer's establishment were gleaned from the ranks of mistresses of high Nazis, high-priced prostitutes and many other women who had been infected by the Nazi virus.

Like several other women, Gerta Sondheim, who now hung before the lascivious gaze of Brauer's audience, had made one fatal mistake. She had spurned the advances of the killing madman.

Strange as it may seem, Brauer had a penchant for seeking normal sex from women who were not in any way connected with him. He was trying to prove to himself that he was a man who could build desire in a woman.

On those rare occasions when he strutted into parties with his Obersturmbannführer's uniform on, he was constantly alert to any new and pretty face. By being young and pretty and decent, Gerta Sondheim had sealed her fate.

Brauer lifted his whip, caressed it with his pudgy fingers. A fleck of dried flesh dropped to the floor. Gerta Sondheim arched her back. She waited for the first blow, knowing how the pain would rip through her entire being. She felt the muscles of her thighs, calves and even her toes tighten. Sweat soaked through the little clothing which she still wore.

"You are a pig!" she gritted through clenched teeth. The sharp crack of the whip cut off the last of her words. Lisa Schmidt and countless thousands of other women waited in their unmarked graves for their latest sister in suffering.

As with so many other highly placed Nazis, the earth seems to have swallowed up Heinrich Brauer. No trace of his activities has been found since New Year's day, 1945.

There are those who say he died in the rubble of Munich. There are others who claim that he was recruited by Beria for the M.V.D.'s interrogation division. Some believe he joined the French Foreign Legion and became involved in the heinous tortures which marked the Algerian War.

However, alive or dead, wherever man sinks to the baseness and depravity of a jungle animal, there Heinrich Brauer walks.

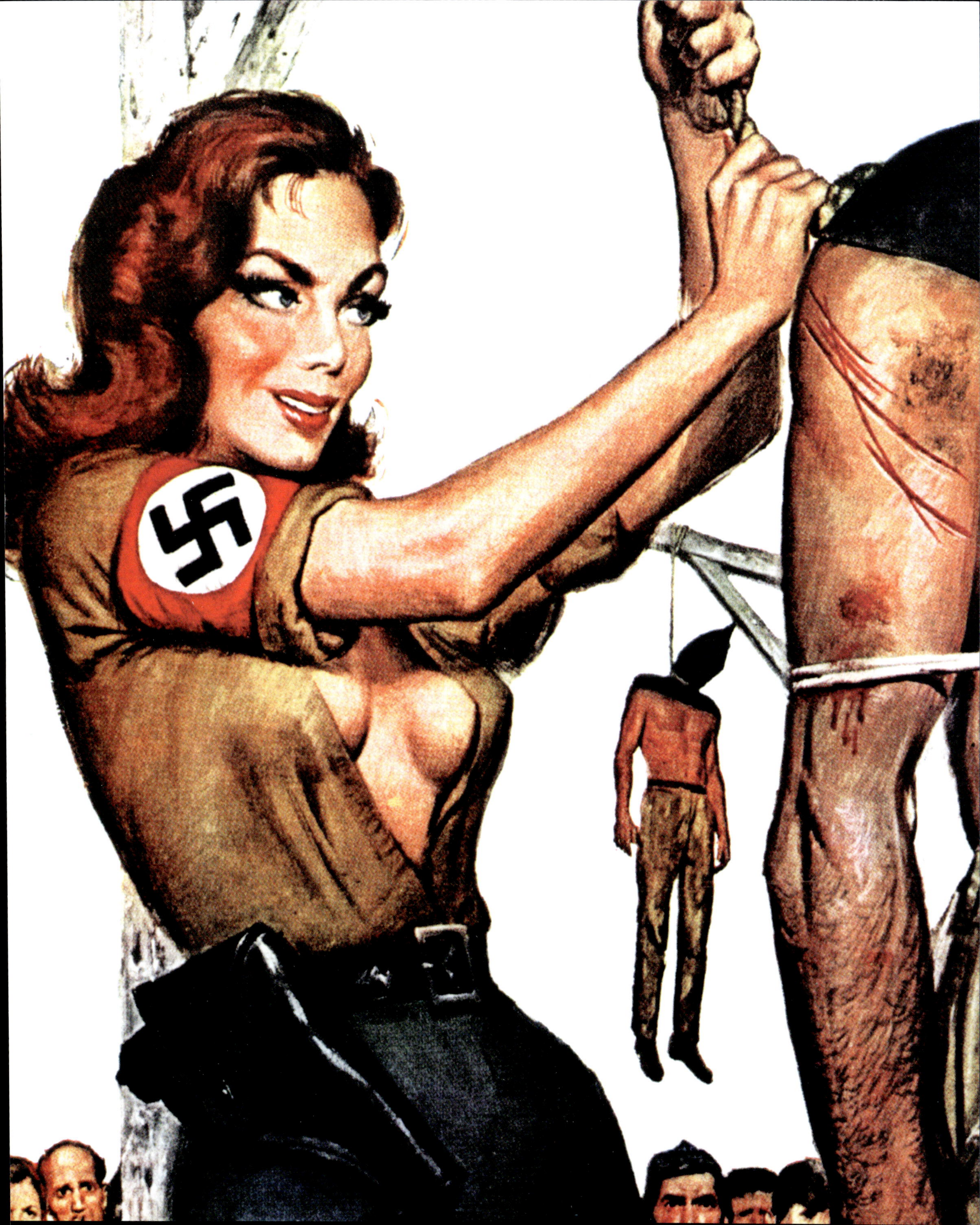

UNTITLED; detail from cover; **RUGGED MEN**, 04/61.
Art uncredited.

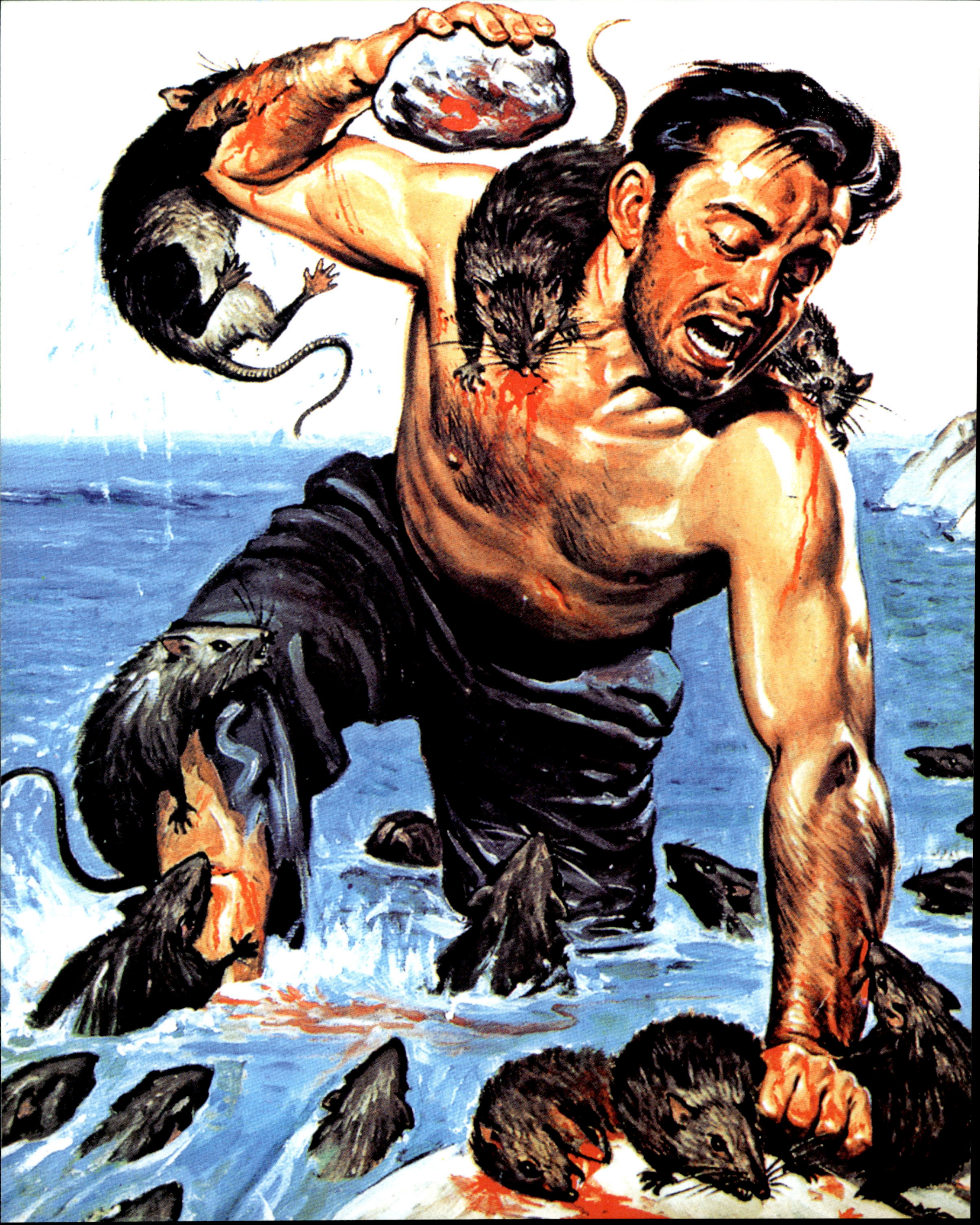

"THE ISLAND OF MAN-EATING RATS"; detail from cover, **MAN'S LIFE**, 05/56.
Art uncredited, attributed to Will Hulsey.

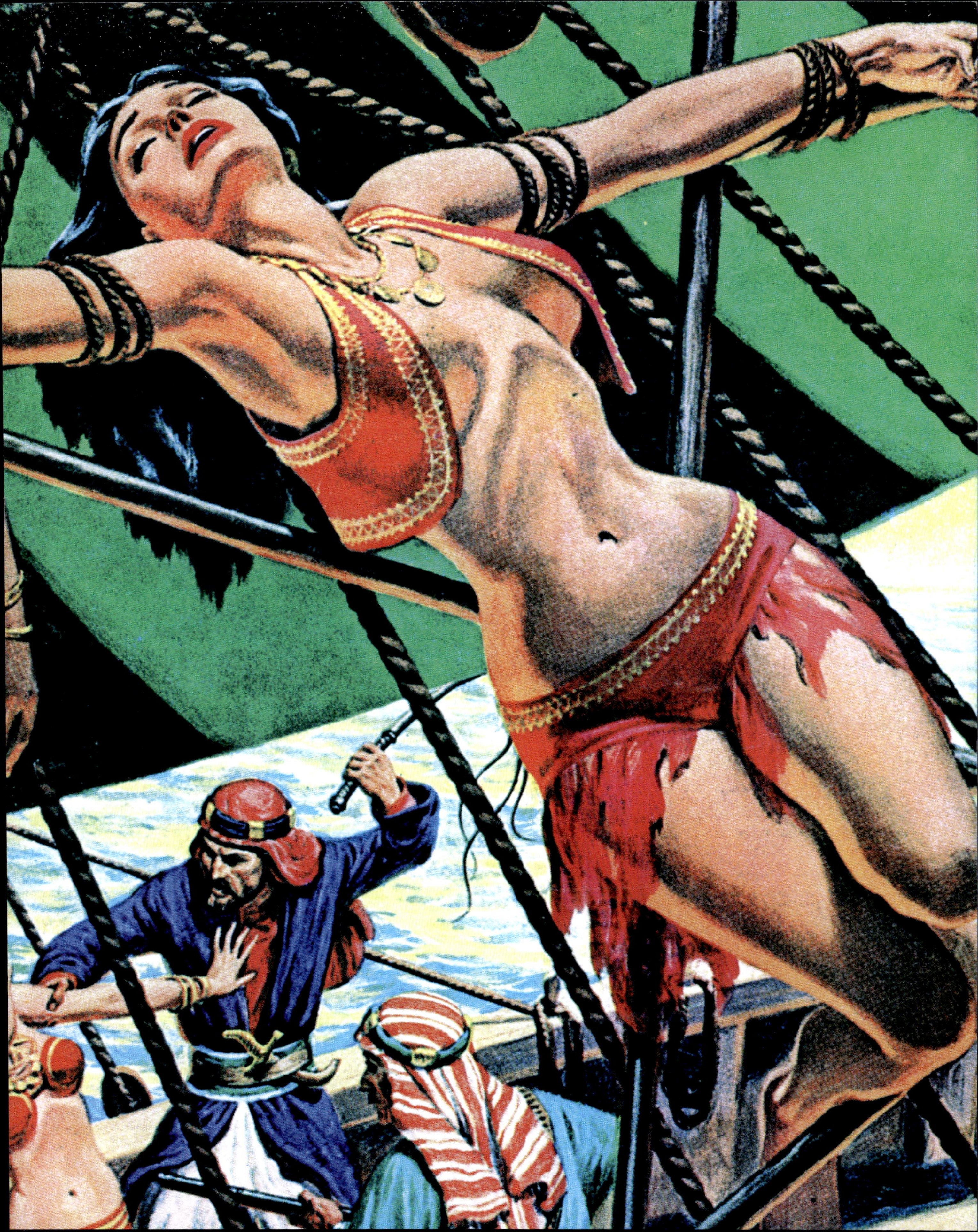

UNTITLED; detail from cover, **BATTLE CRY**, 03/60.
Art uncredited; attributed to Clarence Doore.

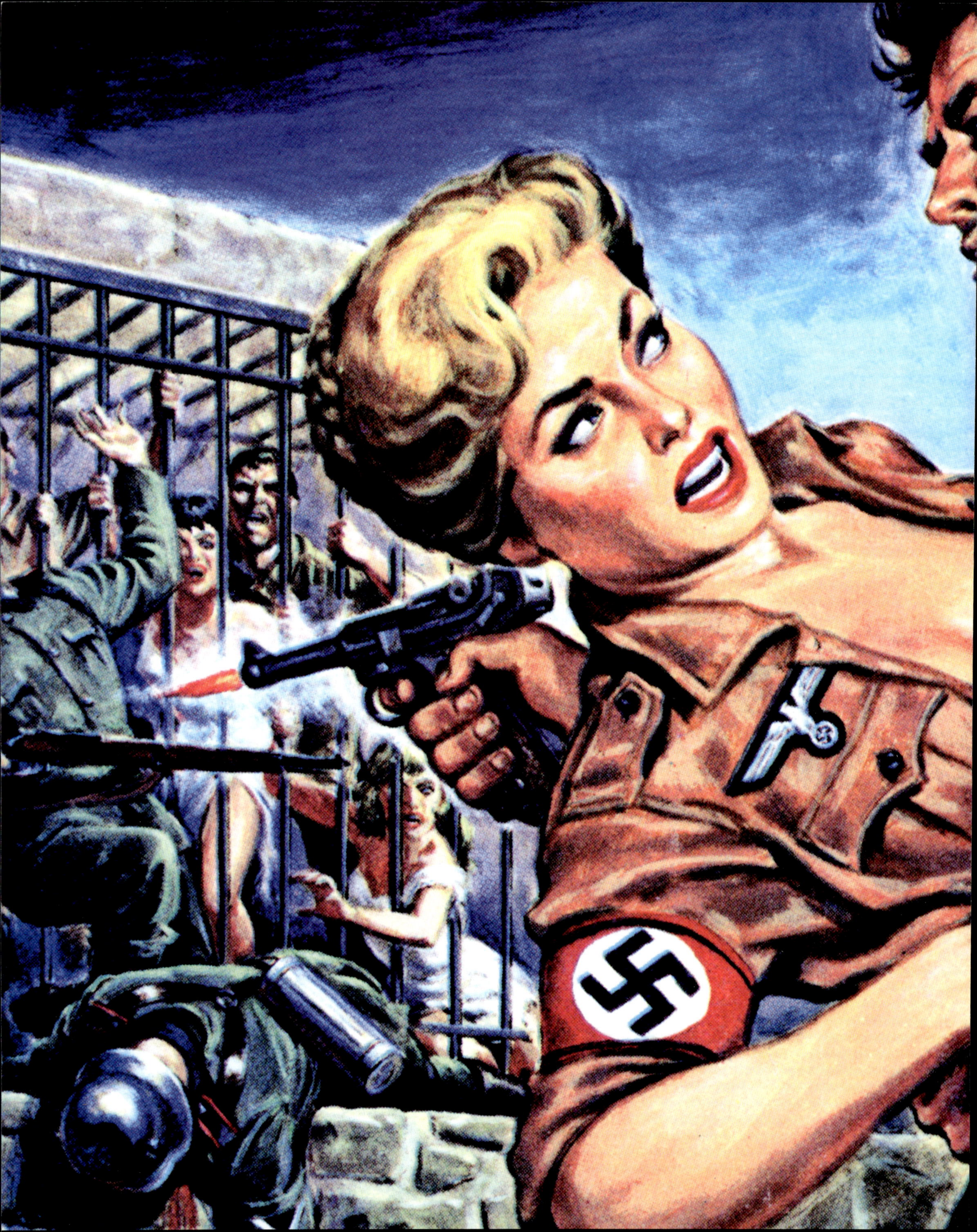

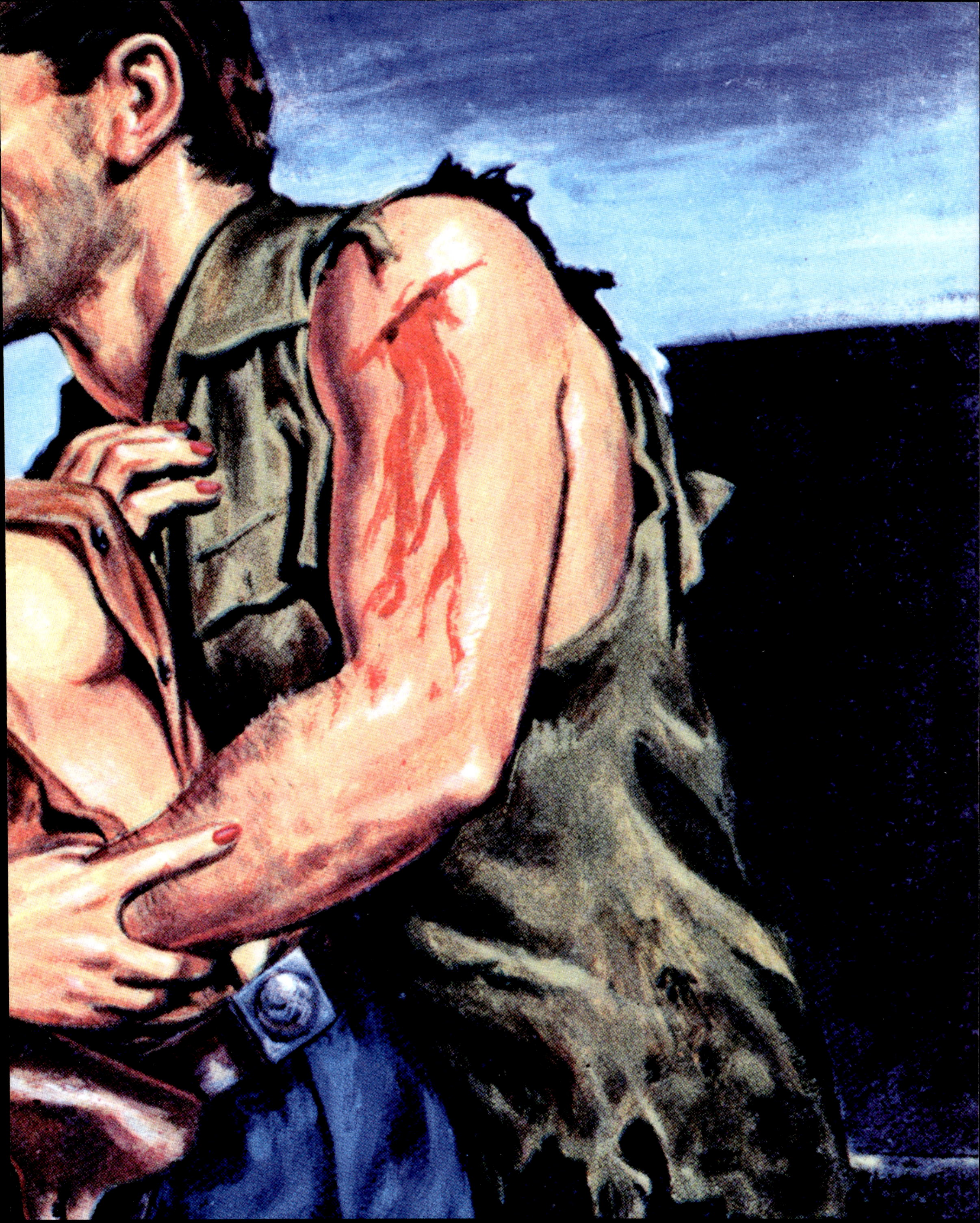

"LONE-WOLF ESCAPE FROM THE NAZI HORROR CAGES OF ST. DIE"; detail from cover, **TRUE MEN STORIES**, 08/63. Art uncredited.

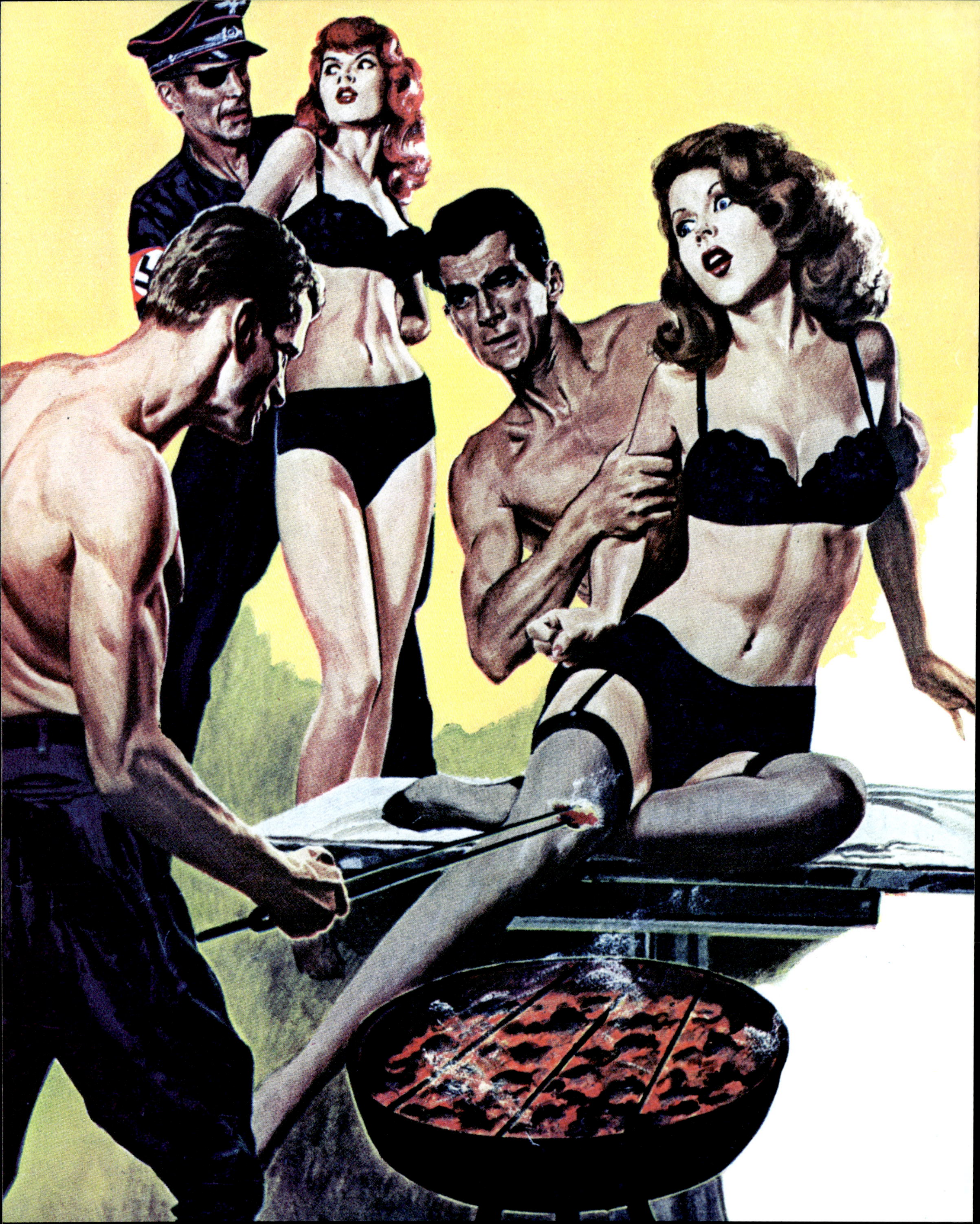

UNTITLED; detail from cover, **REAL ACTION**, 06/63.
Art uncredited, attributed to Milton Luros.

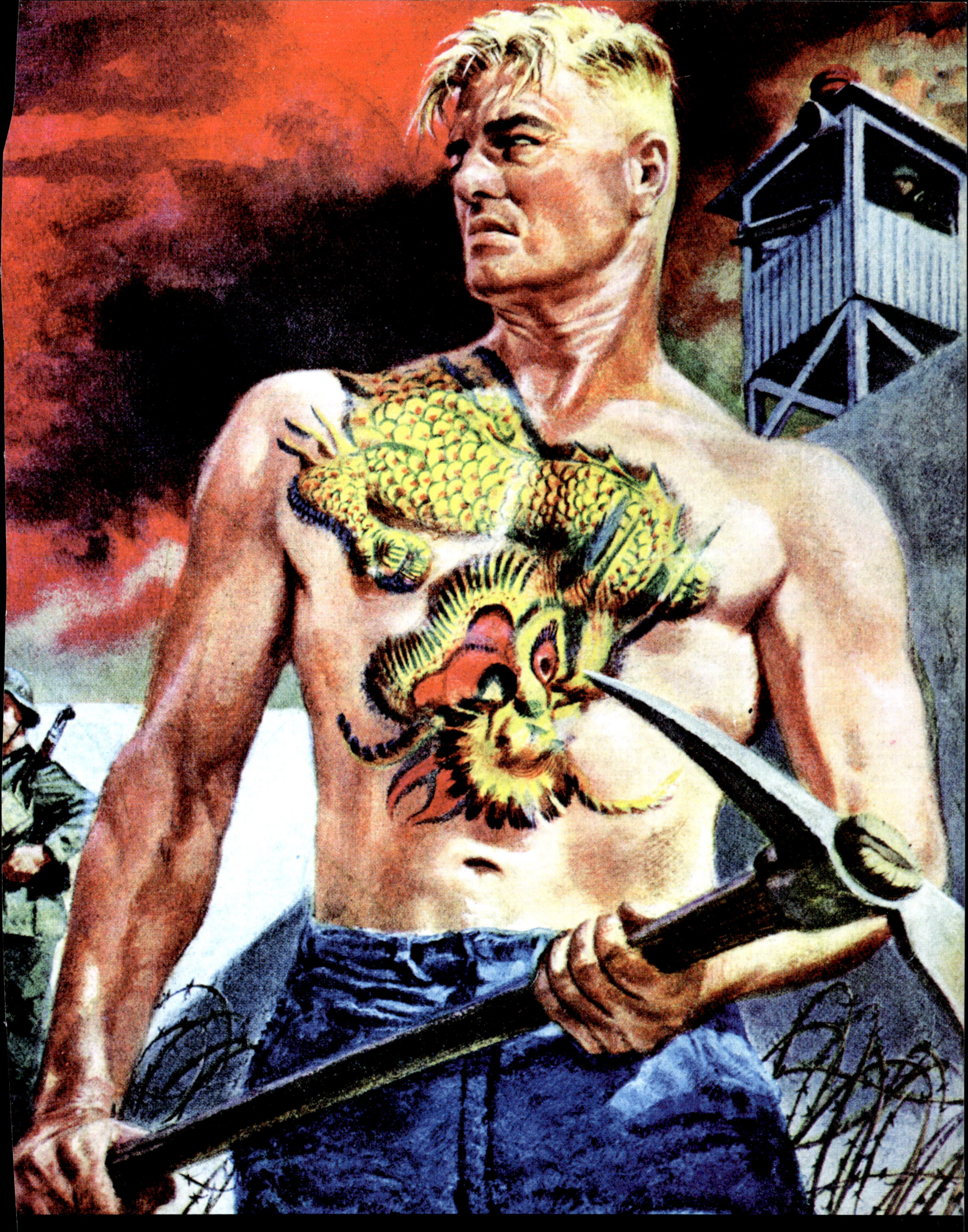

"THE BEAST OF BELSEN AND THE DRAGON TATTOO"; detail from cover, **CLIMAX**, 11/5.
Art by Tom Beecham.

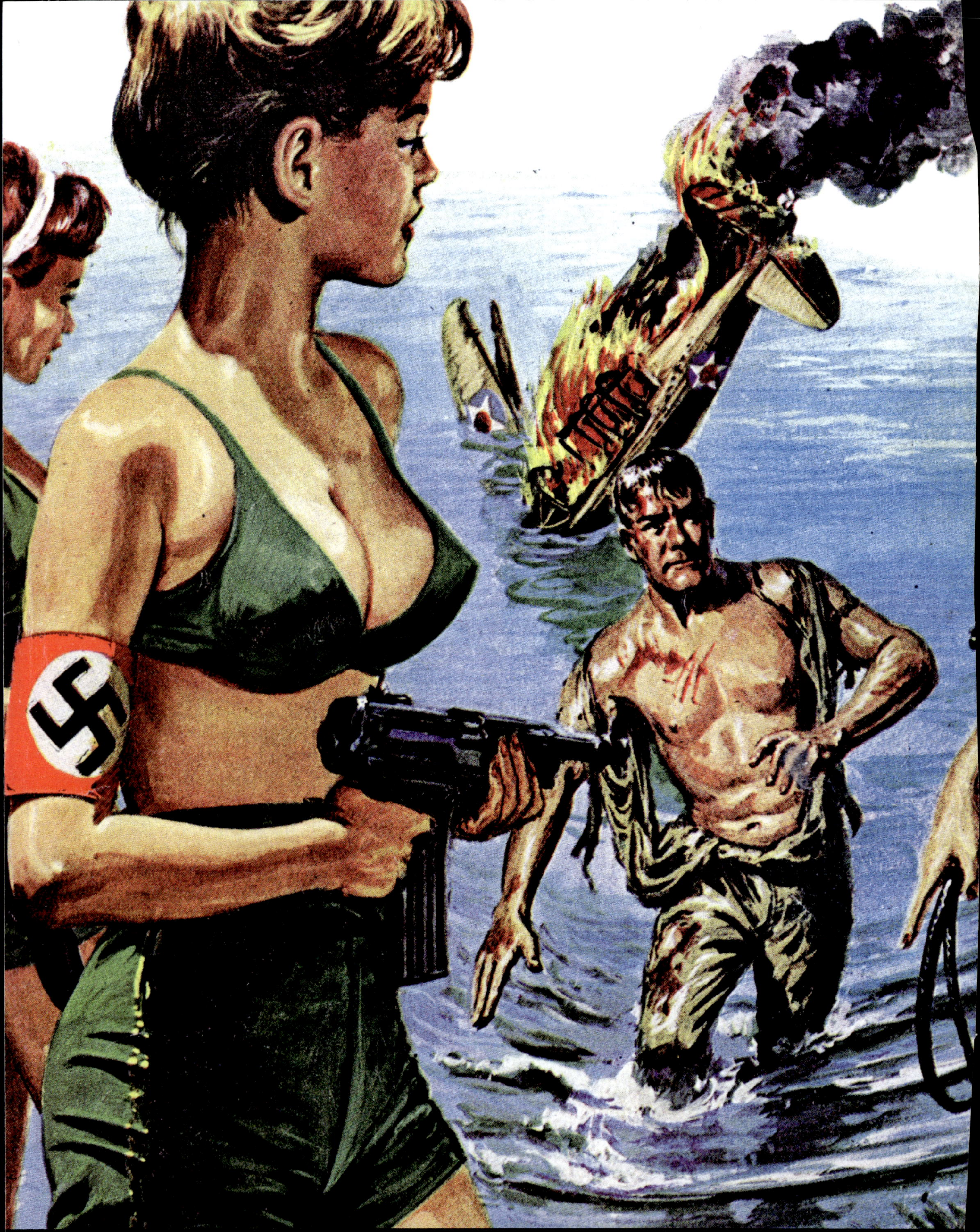

"I WAS A LUST SLAVE OF THE VOLKSTURM NYMPH SQUAD"; detail from cover, **MEN TODAY**, 08/63.
Art uncredited; attributed to Norman Saunders.